The Sapphire Rose

David Eddings was born in Washington State and grew up near Seattle. He graduated from the University of Washington and went on to serve in the US Army. Subsequently, he worked as a buyer for the Boeing Company and taught college-level English. *High Hunt*, his first novel, was a contemporary adventure, but he soon began a spectacular career as a fantasy writer with his best-selling series *The Belgariad*. He consolidated his immediate success with three further enormously popular series, *The Malloreon, The Elenium* and *The Tamuli*. Writing with his wife Leigh, three final volumes rounded off the Belgariad: *Belgarath the Sorcerer, Polgara the Sorceress* and *The Rivan Codex*. These were followed by the epic standalone fantasy *The Redemption of Althalus*, and his latest series of books, *The Dreamers*.

Voyager

DAVID EDDINGS

The Sapphire Rose

The Elenium
BOOK THREE

HarperCollins*Publishers*

Voyager
An Imprint of HarperCollins*Publishers*
77–85 Fulham Palace Road,
Hammersmith, London W6 8JB

www.voyager-books.co.uk

This paperback edition 1995

23

Previously published in paperback by Grafton 1992,
reprinted once, and by HarperCollins Science Fiction &
Fantasy 1993, reprinted twice

First published in Great Britain by
Grafton 1991

Copyright © David Eddings 1991

The Author asserts the moral right to
be identified as the author of this work

ISBN 0 586 20374 5

Set in Times

Printed and bound in Great Britain by
Clays Ltd, St Ives plc

Prologue

Otha and Azash – Excerpted from *A Cursory History of Zemoch*. Compiled by the History Department of the University of Borrata.

Following the invasion of the Elenic-speaking peoples from the steppes of central Daresia lying to the east, the Elenes gradually migrated westward to displace the thinly scattered Styrics who inhabited the Eosian continent. The tribes which settled in Zemoch were latecomers, and they were far less advanced than their cousins to the west. Their economy and social organization were simplistic, and their towns rude by comparison with the cities which were springing up in the emerging western kingdoms. The climate of Zemoch, moreover, was at best inhospitable, and life there existed at the subsistence level. The Church found little to attract her attention to so poor and unpleasant a region; and as a result, the rough chapels of Zemoch became largely unpastored and their simple congregations untended. Thus the Zemochs were obliged to take their religious impulses elsewhere. Since there were few Elene priests in the region to enforce the Church ban on consorting with the heathen Styrics, fraternization became common. As the simple Elene peasantry perceived that their Styric neighbours were able to reap significant benefits from the use of the arcane arts, it is perhaps only natural that apostasy became rampant. Whole Elenic villages in Zemoch were converted to Styric pantheism. Temples were openly erected in honour of this or that topical God, and the darker Styric cults flourished.

Intermarriage between Elene and Styric became common, and by the end of the first millennium, Zemoch could no longer have been considered in any light to be a true Elenic nation. The centuries and the close contact with the Styrics had even so far corrupted the Elenic language in Zemoch that it was scarcely intelligible to western Elenes.

It was in the eleventh century that a youthful goatherd in the mountain village of Ganda in central Zemoch had a strange and ultimately earth-shaking experience. While searching in the hills for a straying goat, the lad, Otha by name, came across a hidden, vine-covered shrine which had been erected in antiquity by one of the numerous Styric cults. The shrine had been raised to a weathered idol which was at once grotesquely distorted and at the same time oddly compelling. As Otha rested from the rigours of his climb, he heard a hollow voice address him in the Styric tongue. 'Who art thou, boy?' the voice inquired.

'My name is Otha,' the lad replied haltingly, trying to remember his Styric.

'And hast thou come to this place to pay obeisance to me, to fall down and worship me?'

'No,' Otha answered with uncharacteristic truthfulness. 'What I'm really doing is trying to find one of my goats.'

There was a long pause. Then the hollow, chilling voice continued. 'And what must I give thee to wring from thee thine obeisance and thy worship? None of thy kind hath attended my shrine for five thousand years, and I hunger for worship – and for souls.'

Otha was certain at this point that the voice was that of one of his fellow herders playing a prank on him, and he determined to turn the joke around. 'Oh,' he said in an offhand manner, 'I'd like to be the king of the world, to live forever, to have a thousand ripe young girls willing to do whatever I wanted them to do, and a mountain of gold – and, oh yes, I want my goat back.'

'And wilt thou give me thy soul in exchange for these things?'

Otha considered it. He had been scarcely aware of the fact that he had a soul, and so its loss would hardly inconvenience him. He reasoned, moreover, that if this were not, in fact, some juvenile goatherd prank, and if the offer were serious, failure to deliver even one of his impossible demands would invalidate the contract. 'Oh, all right,' he agreed with an indifferent shrug, '– but first I'd like to see my goat – just as an indication of good faith.'

'Turn thee around then, Otha,' the voice commanded, 'and behold that which was lost.'

Otha turned, and sure enough, there stood the missing goat, idly chewing on a bush and looking curiously at him. Quickly he tethered her to the bush. At heart, Otha was a moderately vicious lad. He enjoyed inflicting pain on helpless creatures. He was given to cruel practical jokes, to petty theft, and, whenever it was safe, to a form of seduction of lonely shepherdesses that had only directness to commend it. He was avaricious and slovenly, and he had a grossly overestimated opinion of his own cleverness. His mind worked very fast as he tied his goat to the bush. If this obscure Styric divinity could deliver a lost goat upon demand, what else might He be capable of? Otha decided that this might very well be the opportunity of a lifetime. 'All right,' he said, feigning simple-mindedness, 'one prayer – for now – in exchange for the goat. We can talk about souls and empires and wealth and immortality and women later. Show yourself. I'm not going to bow down to empty air. What's your name, by the way? I'll need to know that in order to frame a proper prayer.'

'I am Azash, most powerful of the Elder Gods, and if thou wilt be my servant and lead others to worship me,

11

I will grant thee far more than thou hast asked. I will exalt thee and give thee wealth beyond thine imagining. The fairest of maidens shall be thine. Thou shalt have life unending, and, moreover, power over the spirit world such as no man hath ever had. All I ask in return, Otha, is thy soul and the souls of those others thou wilt bring to me. My need and my loneliness are great, and my rewards unto thee shall be equally great. Look upon my face now, and tremble before me.'

There was a shimmering in the air surrounding the crude idol, and Otha saw the reality of Azash hovering about the roughly-carved image. He shrank in horror before the awful presence which had so suddenly appeared before him and fell to the ground, abasing himself before it. This was going much too far. At heart, Otha was a coward, however, and he was afraid that the most rational response to the materialized Azash – instant flight – might provoke the hideous God into doing nasty things to him, and Otha was extremely solicitous of his own skin.

'Pray, Otha,' the idol gloated. 'Mine ears hunger for thine adoration.'

'Oh, mighty – um – Azash, wasn't it? God of Gods and Lord of the World, hear my prayer and receive my humble worship. I am as the dust before thee, and thou towerest above me like the mountain. I worship thee and praise thee and thank thee from the depths of my heart for the return of this miserable goat – which I will beat senseless for straying just as soon as I get her home.' Trembling, Otha hoped that the prayer might satisfy Azash – or at least distract Him enough to provide him an opportunity for escape.

'Thy prayer is adequate, Otha,' the idol acknowledged, '– barely. In time thou wilt become more proficient in thine adoration. Go now thy way, and I will savour this rude prayer of thine. Return again on the morrow, and I will disclose my mind further unto thee.'

As he trudged home with his goat, Otha vowed never to return, but that night he tossed on his rude pallet in the filthy hut where he lived, and his mind was afire with visions of wealth and subservient young women upon whom he could vent his lust. 'Let's see where this goes,' he muttered to himself as the dawn marked the end of the troubled night. 'If I have to, I can always run away later.'

And that began the discipleship of a simple Zemoch goatherd to the Elder God, Azash, a God whose name Otha's Styric neighbours would not even utter, so great was their fear of Him. In the centuries which followed, Otha realized how profound was his enslavement. Azash patiently led him through simple worship into the practice of perverted rites and beyond into the realms of spiritual abomination. The formerly ingenuous and only moderately disgusting goatherd became morose and sombre as the dreaded idol fed gluttonously upon his mind and soul. Though he lived a half-dozen lifetimes, his limbs withered, while his paunch and head grew bloated and hairless and pallid-white as a result of his abhorrence of the sun. He grew vastly wealthy, but took no pleasure in his wealth. He had eager concubines by the score, but he was indifferent to their charms. A thousand, thousand wraiths and imps and creatures of ultimate darkness responded to his slightest whim, but he could not even summon sufficient interest to command them. His only joy became the contemplation of pain and death as his minions cruelly wrenched and tore the lives of the weak and helpless from their quivering bodies for his entertainment. In that respect, Otha had not changed.

During the early years of the third millennium, after the slug-like Otha had passed his nine hundredth year, he commanded his infernal underlings to carry the rude shrine of Azash to the city of Zemoch in the northeast highlands. An enormous semblance of the hideous God was constructed to enclose the shrine, and a vast temple erected about it. Beside that temple and connected to it by a labyrinthine series of passageways stood his own palace, gilt with fine, hammered gold and inlaid with pearl and onyx and chalcedony and with its columns surmounted with intricately-carved capitals of ruby and emerald. There he indifferently proclaimed himself Emperor of all Zemoch, a proclamation seconded by the thunderous but somehow mocking voice of Azash booming hollowly from the temple and cheered by multitudes of howling fiends.

There began then a ghastly reign of terror in Zemoch. All opposing cults were ruthlessly extirpated. Sacrifices of the newborn and virgins numbered in the thousands, and Elene and Styric alike were converted by the sword to the worship of Azash. It took perhaps a century for Otha and his henchmen to totally eradicate all traces of decency from his enslaved subjects. Blood-lust and rampant cruelty became common, and the rites performed before the altars and shrines erected to Azash became increasingly degenerate and obscene.

In the twenty-fifth century, Otha deemed that all was in readiness to pursue the ultimate goal of his perverted God, and he massed his human armies and their dark allies upon the western borders of Zemoch. After a brief pause, while he and Azash gathered their strength, Otha struck, sending his forces down onto the plains of Pelosia, Lamorkand and Cammoria. The horror of that invasion cannot be fully described. Simple atrocity was not sufficient to slake the savagery of the Zemoch horde, and the gross cruelties of the inhumans who accompanied the invading army are too hideous to be mentioned. Mountains of human heads were erected, captives were roasted alive and then eaten, and

14

the roads and highways were lined with occupied crosses, gibbets and stakes. The skies grew black with flocks of vultures and ravens and the air reeked with the stench of burned and rotting flesh.

Otha's armies moved with confidence towards the battlefield, fully believing that their hellish allies could easily overcome any resistance, but they had reckoned without the power of the Knights of the Church. The great battle was joined on the plains of Lamorkand just to the south of Lake Randera. The purely physical struggle was titanic enough, but the supernatural battle on that plain was even more stupendous. Every conceivable form of spirit joined in the fray. Waves of total darkness and sheets of multicoloured light swept the field. Fire and lightning rained from the sky. Whole battalions were swallowed up by the earth or burned to ashes in sudden flame. The shattering crash of thunder rolled perpetually from horizon to horizon, and the ground itself was torn by earthquake and the eruption of searing liquid rock which poured down slopes to engulf advancing legions. For days the armies were locked in dreadful battle upon that bloody field before, step by step, the Zemochs were pushed back. The horrors which Otha hurled into the fray were overmatched one by one by the concerted power of the Church Knights, and for the first time the Zemochs tasted defeat. Their slow, grudging retreat became more rapid, eventually turning into a rout as the demoralized horde broke and ran towards the dubious safety of the border.

The victory of the Elenes was complete, but not without dreadful cost. Fully half of the Militant Knights lay slain upon the battlefield, and the armies of the Elene Kings numbered their dead by the scores of thousands. The victory was theirs, but they were too exhausted and too few to pursue the fleeing Zemochs past the border.

The bloated Otha, his withered limbs no longer even able to bear his weight, was borne on a litter through the labyrinth at Zemoch to the temple, there to face the wrath of Azash. He grovelled before the idol of his God, blubbering and begging for mercy.

And at long last Azash spoke. 'One last time, Otha,' the God said in a horribly quiet voice. 'Once only will I relent. I *will* possess Bhelliom, and thou wilt obtain it for me and deliver it up to me here, for if thou dost not do this thing, my generosity unto thee shall vanish. If gifts do not encourage thee to bend to my will, perhaps torment will. Go Otha. Find Bhelliom for me and return with it here that I may be unchained and my maleness restored. Shouldst thou fail me, surely wilt thou die, and thy dying shall consume a million, million years.'

Otha fled, and thus, even in the ruins and tatters of his defeat was born his last assault upon the Elene kingdoms of the west, an assault which was to bring the world to the brink of universal disaster.

PART ONE

The Basilica

CHYRELLOS

POINTS OF INTEREST IN THE OUTER CITY

1 The Grain Exchange
2 Genidian Chapterhouse
3 Patriarch Cholda's House
4 Theological Seminary
5 Goldsmiths' Guildhall
6 Cyrinic Chapterhouse
7 Patriarch of Motera's House

8 Monastery
9 Cattle Exchange
10 Stockyards
11 Cloister
12 Patriarch of Ucera's House
13 Weavers' Guildhall
14 City Hall
15 Alcione Chapterhouse

River Kydu

THE NORTH GATE

The BASILICA

THE EAST GATE

MAROVA'S HOUSE

PANDION CHAPTERHOUSE

DOLMANT'S HOUSE

EMBAN'S HOUSE

MONASTERY

NUNNERY

THE WEST GATE

THE BARRACKS OF THE CHURCH SOLDIERS

LIBRARY

THE SOUTH GATE

THE INNER CITY

Chapter 1

The waterfall dropped endlessly into the chasm that had claimed Ghwerig, and the echo of its plunge filled the cavern with a deep-toned sound like the after-shimmer of some great bell. Sparhawk knelt at the edge of the abyss with the Bhelliom held tightly in his fist. Thought had been erased, and he could only kneel at the brink of the chasm, his eyes dazzled by the light of the sun-touched column of water falling into the depths from the surface above and his ears full of its sound.

The cave smelled damp. The mist-like spray from the waterfall bedewed the rocks, and the wet stones shimmered in the shifting light of the torrent to mingle with the last fading glimmerings of Aphrael's incandescent ascension.

Sparhawk slowly lowered his eyes to look at the jewel he held in his fist. Though it appeared delicate, even fragile, he sensed that the Sapphire Rose was all but indestructible. From deep within its azure heart there came a kind of pulsating glow, deep blue at the tips of the petals and darkening down at the gem's centre to a lambent midnight. Its power made his hand ache, and something deep in his mind shrieked warnings at him as he gazed into its depths. He shuddered and tore his eyes from its seductive glow.

The hard-bitten Pandion Knight looked around, irrationally trying to cling to the fading bits of light lingering in the stones of the Troll-Dwarf's cave as if the Child-Goddess Aphrael could somehow protect him from the jewel he had laboured so long to gain and which he now strangely feared. There was more to it than that, though. At some level below thought Sparhawk wanted to hold that faint light forever, to keep the spirit if not the person of the tiny, whimsical divinity in his heart.

Sephrenia sighed and slowly rose to her feet. Her face was weary and at the same time exalted. She had struggled hard to reach this damp cave in the mountains of Thalesia, but she had been rewarded with that joyful moment of epiphany when she had looked full into the face of her Goddess. 'We must leave this place now, dear ones,' she said sadly.

'Can't we stay a few minutes longer?' Kurik asked her with an uncharacteristic longing in his voice. Of all the men in the world, Kurik was the most prosaic – most of the time.

'It's better that we don't. If we stay too long, we'll start finding excuses to stay longer. In time, we may not want to leave at all.' The small, white-robed Styric looked at Bhelliom with revulsion. 'Please get it out of sight, Sparhawk, and command it to be still. Its presence contaminates us all.' She shifted the sword the ghost of Sir Gared had delivered to her aboard Captain Sorgi's ship. She muttered in Styric for a moment and then released the spell that ignited the tip of the sword with a brilliant glow to light their way back to the surface.

Sparhawk tucked the flower gem inside his tunic and bent to pick up the spear of King Aldreas. His chain-mail shirt smelled very foul to him just now, and his skin cringed away from its touch. He wished that he could rid himself of it.

Kurik stooped and lifted the iron-bound stone club the hideously malformed Troll-Dwarf had wielded against them before his fatal plunge into the chasm. He hefted the brutal weapon a couple of times and then indifferently tossed it into the abyss after its owner.

Sephrenia lifted the glowing sword over her head, and the three of them crossed the gem-littered floor of Ghwerig's treasure cave towards the entrance of the spiralling gallery that led to the surface.

'Do you think we'll ever see her again?' Kurik asked wistfully as they entered the gallery.

'Aphrael? It's hard to say. She's always been a little unpredictable.' Sephrenia's voice was subdued.

They climbed in silence for a time, following the spiral of the gallery steadily to the left. Sparhawk felt a strange emptiness as they climbed. They had been four when they had descended; now they were only three. The Child-Goddess, however, had not been left behind, for they all carried her in their hearts. There was something else bothering him, though. 'Is there any way we can seal up this cave once we get outside?' he asked his tutor.

Sephrenia looked at him, her eyes intent. 'We can if you wish, dear one, but why do you want to?'

'It's a little hard to put into words.'

'We've got what we came for, Sparhawk. Why should you care if some swineherd stumbles across the cave now?'

'I'm not entirely sure.' He frowned, trying to pinpoint it. 'If some Thalesian peasant comes in here, he'll eventually find Ghwerig's treasure-hoard, won't he?'

'If he looks long enough, yes.'

'And after that it won't be long before the cave's swarming with other Thalesians.'

'Why should that bother you? Do you want Ghwerig's treasure for yourself?'

'Hardly. Martel's the greedy one, not me.'

'Then why are you so concerned? What does it matter if the Thalesians start wandering around in here?'

'This is a very special place, Sephrenia.'

'In what way?'

21

'It's holy,' he replied shortly. Her probing had begun to irritate him. 'A Goddess revealed herself to us here. I don't want the cave profaned by a crowd of drunken, greedy treasure-hunters. I'd feel the same way if someone profaned an Elene Church.'

'Dear Sparhawk,' she said, impulsively embracing him. 'Did it really cost you all that much to admit Aphrael's divinity?'

'Your Goddess was very convincing, Sephrenia,' he replied wryly. 'She'd have shaken the certainty of the Hierocracy of the Elene Church itself. Can we do it? Seal the cave, I mean?'

She started to say something, then stopped, frowning. 'Wait here,' she told them. She leaned Sir Gared's sword point up against the wall of the gallery and walked back down the passage a little way, and then stopped again at the very edge of the light from the glowing sword-tip where she stood deep in thought. After a time, she returned.

'I'm going to ask you to do something dangerous, Sparhawk,' she said gravely. 'I think you'll be safe though. The memory of Aphrael is still strong in your mind, and that should protect you.'

'What do you want me to do?'

'We're going to use Bhelliom to seal the cave. There are other ways we could do it, but we have to be sure that the jewel will accept your authority. I *think* it will, but let's make certain. You're going to have to be strong, Sparhawk. Bhelliom won't want to do what you ask, so you'll have to compel it.'

'I've dealt with stubborn things before,' he shrugged.

'Don't make light of this, Sparhawk. It's something far more elemental than anything I've ever done before. Let's move on.'

They continued upward along the spiralling passage-way with the muted roar of the waterfall in Ghwerig's treasure-cave growing fainter and fainter. Then, just as they moved beyond the range of hearing, the sound seemed to change, fragmenting its one endless note into many, becoming a complex chord rather than a single tone – some trick perhaps of the shifting echoes in the cave. With the change of that sound, Sparhawk's mood also changed. Before, there had been a kind of weary satisfaction at having finally achieved a long-sought goal coupled with the sense of awe at the revelation of the Child-Goddess. Now, however, the dark, musty cave seemed somehow ominous, threatening. Sparhawk felt something he had not felt since early childhood. He was suddenly afraid of the dark. Things seemed to lurk in the shadows beyond the circle of light from the glowing sword-tip, faceless things filled with a cruel malevolence. He nervously looked back over his shoulder. Far back, beyond the light, something seemed to move. It was brief, no more than a flicker of a deeper, more intense darkness. He discovered that when he tried to look directly at it, he could no longer see it, but when he looked off to one side, it was there – vague, unformed and hovering on the very edge of his vision. It filled him with an unnamed dread. 'Foolishness,' he muttered, and moved on, eager to reach the light above them.

It was mid-afternoon when they reached the surface, and the sun seemed very bright after the dark cave. Sparhawk drew in a deep breath and reached inside his tunic.

'Not yet, Sparhawk,' Sephrenia advised. 'We want to collapse the ceiling of the cave, but we don't want to bring that overhanging cliff down on our heads at the same time. We'll go back down to where the horses are and do it from there.'

'You'll have to teach me the spell,' he said as the three

23

of them crossed the bramble-choked basin in front of the cave mouth.

'There isn't any spell. You have the jewel and the rings. All you have to do is give the command. I'll show you how when we get down.'

They clambered down the rocky ravine to the grassy plateau and their previous night's encampment. It was nearly sunset when they reached the pair of tents and the picketed horses. Faran laid his ears back and bared his teeth as Sparhawk approached him.

'What's your problem?' Sparhawk asked his evil-tempered warhorse.

'He senses Bhelliom,' Sephrenia explained. 'He doesn't like it. Stay away from him for a while.' She looked critically up the gap from which they had just emerged. 'It's safe enough here,' she decided. 'Take out Bhelliom and hold it in both hands so that the rings are touching it.'

'Do I have to face the cave?'

'No. Bhelliom will know what you're telling it to do. Now, remember the inside of the cave – the look of it, the feel, and even the smell. Then imagine the roof collapsing. The rocks will tumble down and bounce and roll and pile up on top of each other. There'll be a lot of noise. A great cloud of dust and a strong wind will come rushing out of the cave mouth. The ridge-line above the cave will sag as the roof of the cavern collapses, and there'll probably be avalanches. Don't let any of that distract you. Keep the images firmly in your mind.'

'It's a bit more complicated than an ordinary spell, isn't it?'

'Yes. This is not, strictly speaking, a spell, though. You'll be unleashing elemental magic. Concentrate, Sparhawk. The more detailed you make the image, the more power-fully Bhelliom will respond. When you've got it firmly in your mind, tell the jewel to make it happen.'

'Do I have to speak to it in Ghwerig's language?'

'I'm not sure. Try Elene first. If that doesn't work, we'll fall back on Troll.'

Sparhawk remembered the mouth of the cave, the antechamber just inside, and the long, spiralling gallery leading down to Ghwerig's treasure-cave. 'Should I bring down the roof on that waterfall as well?' he asked.

'I don't think so. That river might come to the surface again somewhere downstream. If you dam it up, someone might notice that it's not running any more and start investigating. Besides, that particular cavern is very special, isn't it?'

'Yes, it is.'

'Let's enclose it then and protect it forever.'

Sparhawk pictured the ceiling of the cave collapsing with a huge, grinding roar and a billowing cloud of rock dust. 'What do I say?' he asked.

'Call it "Blue-Rose". That's what Ghwerig called it. It might recognize the name.'

'Blue-Rose,' Sparhawk said in a tone of command, 'make the cave fall in.'

The Sapphire Rose went very dark, and angry red flashes appeared deep in its centre.

'It's fighting you,' Sephrenia said. 'This is the part I warned you about. The cave is the place where it was born, and it doesn't want to destroy it. Force it, Sparhawk.'

'Do it, Blue-Rose!' Sparhawk barked, bending every ounce of his will on the jewel in his hands. Then he felt a surge of incredible power, and the sapphire seemed to throb in his hands. He felt a sudden wild exaltation as he unloosed the might of the stone. It was far beyond mere satisfaction. It verged almost on physical ecstasy.

There was a low, sullen rumbling from deep in the ground, and the earth shuddered. Rocks deep beneath them began to pop and crack as the earthquake shattered layer upon layer of subterranean rock. Far up the ravine, the rock face looming over the mouth of Ghwerig's cave began to topple outward, then dropped straight down into the weedy basin as its base crumbled out from under it. The sound of the collapsing cliff was very loud even at this distance, and a vast cloud of dust boiled up from the rubble and then drifted off to the northeast as the prevailing wind that raked these mountains swept it away. Then, even as it had in the cave, something flickered at the edge of Sparhawk's vision – something dark and filled with malevolent curiosity.

'How do you feel?' Sephrenia asked, her eyes intent.

'A little strange,' he admitted, 'very strong for some reason.'

'Keep your mind away from that. Concentrate on Aphrael instead. Don't even think about Bhelliom until that feeling wears off. Get it out of sight again. Don't look at it.'

Sparhawk tucked the sapphire back inside his tunic.

Kurik looked up the ravine towards the huge pile of rubble now filling the basin which had lain before the mouth of Ghwerig's cave. 'That all seems so final,' he said regretfully.

'It is,' Sephrenia told him. 'The cavern's safe now. Let's keep our minds on other things, gentlemen. Don't dwell on what we've just done, or we might be tempted to undo it.'

Kurik squared his heavy shoulders and looked around. 'I'll get a fire going,' he said. He walked back towards the mouth of the ravine to gather firewood while Sparhawk rummaged through the packs for cooking utensils and something suitable for supper. After they had eaten, they sat around the fire, their faces subdued.

'What was it like, Sparhawk?' Kurik asked, 'using Bhelliom, I mean?' He glanced at Sephrenia. 'Is it all right to talk about it now?'

26

'We'll see. Go ahead, Sparhawk. Tell him.'

'It was like nothing else I've ever experienced,' the big knight replied. 'I suddenly felt as if I were a hundred feet tall and that there was nothing in the world I couldn't do. I even caught myself looking around for something else to use it for – a mountain to tear down, maybe.'

'Sparhawk! Stop!' Sephrenia told him sharply. 'Bhelliom's tampering with your thoughts. It's trying to lure you into using it. Each time you do, its hold on you grows stronger. Think about something else.'

'Like Aphrael?' Kurik suggested, 'or is she dangerous too?'

Sephrenia smiled. 'Oh yes, very dangerous. She'll capture your soul even faster than Bhelliom will.'

'Your warning's a little late, Sephrenia. I think she already has. I miss her, you know.'

'You needn't. She's still with us.'

He looked around. 'Where?'

'In spirit, Kurik.'

'That's not exactly the same.'

'Let's do something about Bhelliom now,' she said thoughtfully. 'Its grip is even more powerful than I'd imagined.' She rose and went to the small pack that contained her personal belongings. She rummaged around in it and took out a canvas pouch, a large needle and a hank of red yarn. She took up the pouch and began to stitch a crimson design on it, a peculiarly asymmetrical design. Her face was intent in the ruddy firelight, and her lips moved constantly as she worked.

'It doesn't match, little mother,' Sparhawk pointed out. 'That side's different from the other.'

'It's supposed to be. Please don't talk to me just now, Sparhawk. I'm trying to concentrate.' She continued her sewing for a time, then pinned her needle into her sleeve and held the pouch out to the fire. She spoke intently in

27

Styric, and the fire rose and fell, dancing rhythmically to her words. Then the flame suddenly billowed out as if trying to fill the pouch. 'Now, Sparhawk,' she said, holding the pouch open. 'Put Bhelliom in here. Be very firm. It's probably going to try to fight you again.'

He was puzzled, but he reached inside his tunic, took the stone and tried to put it into the pouch. A screech of protest seemed to fill his ears, and the jewel actually grew hot in his hand. He felt as if he were trying to push the thing through solid rock, and his mind reeled, shrieking to him that what he was trying to do was impossible. He set his teeth together and shoved harder. With an almost audible wail, the Sapphire Rose slipped into the pouch, and Sephrenia pulled the drawstring tight. She tied the ends into an intricate knot then took her needle and wove red yarn through that knot. 'There,' she said, biting off the yarn, 'that should help.'

'What did you do?' Kurik asked her.

'It's a form of a prayer. Aphrael can't diminish Bhelliom's power, but she can confine it so that it can't influence us or reach out to others. It's not perfect, but it's the best we can do on short notice. We'll do something a little more permanent later on. Put it away, Sparhawk. Try to keep your chain-mail between the pouch and your skin. I think that may help. Aphrael once told me that Bhelliom can't bear the touch of steel.'

'Aren't you being a little overcautious, Sephrenia?' Sparhawk asked her.

'I don't know, Sparhawk. I've never dealt with anything like Bhelliom before, and I can't even begin to imagine the limits of its power. I know enough, though, to know that it can corrupt anything – even the Elene God or the Younger Gods of Styricum.'

'All except Aphrael,' Kurik corrected.

She shook her head. 'Even Aphrael was tempted by

Bhelliom when she was carrying it up out of that abyss to bring it to us.'

'Why didn't she just keep it for herself then?'

'Love. My Goddess loves us all, and she gave up Bhelliom willingly out of that love. Bhelliom can't begin to understand love. In the end, that may be our only defence against it.'

Sparhawk's sleep was troubled that night, and he tossed restlessly on his blankets. Kurik was on watch near the edge of the circle of firelight, and so Sparhawk was left to wrestle with his nightmares alone. He seemed to see the Sapphire Rose hanging in mid-air before his eyes, its deep blue glow seductive. Out of the centre of that glow there came a sound – a song that pulled at his very being. Hovering around him, so close as to almost touch his shoulders, were shadows – more than one, certainly, but less than ten, or so it seemed. The shadows were *not* seductive. They seemed to be filled with a hatred born from some towering frustration. Beyond the glowing Bhelliom stood the obscenely grotesque mud idol of Azash, the idol he had smashed at Ghasek, the idol which had claimed Bellina's soul. The idol's face was moving, twisting hideously into expressions of the most elemental passions – lust and greed and hatred and a towering contempt that seemed born of its certainty of its own absolute power.

Sparhawk struggled in his dream, dragged first this way and then that. Bhelliom pulled at him; Azash pulled at him; and the hateful shadows pulled as well. The power of each was irresistible, and his mind and body seemed almost torn apart by those titanic conflicting forces.

He tried to scream. And then he awoke. He sat up and realized that he was sweating profusely. He swore. He was exhausted, but a sleep filled with nightmares was no cure for that bone-deep weariness. Grimly he lay back down, hoping for an oblivion without dreams.

29

It began again, however. Once again he wrestled in his sleep with Bhelliom and with Azash and with the hateful shadows lurking behind him.

'Sparhawk,' a small, familiar voice said in his ear, 'don't let them frighten you. They can't hurt you, you know. All they can do is try to frighten you.'

'Why are they doing it?'

'Because they're afraid of you.'

'That doesn't make sense, Aphrael. I'm only a man.'

Her laughter was like the peal of a small, silver bell. 'You're so innocent sometimes, father. You're not like any other man who's ever lived. In a rather peculiar way, you're more powerful than the Gods themselves. Go to sleep now. I won't let them hurt you.'

He felt a soft kiss on his cheek, and a pair of small arms seemed to embrace his head with a peculiarly maternal tenderness. The terrible images of his nightmare wavered. And then they vanished.

It must have been hours later when Kurik entered the tent and shook him into wakefulness. 'What time is it?' Sparhawk asked his squire.

'About midnight,' Kurik replied. 'Take your cloak. It's chilly out there.'

Sparhawk arose, put on his mail-shirt and tunic and then buckled his sword-belt around his waist. Then he tucked the pouch under the tunic. He picked up his traveller's cloak. 'Sleep well,' he told his friend and left the tent.

The stars were very bright, and a crescent moon had just risen above the jagged line of peaks to the east. Sparhawk walked away from the embers of their fire to allow his eyes to adjust to the darkness. He stood with his breath steaming slightly in the chill mountain air.

The dream still troubled him, though it was fading now. About the only sharp memory he really had of it was the lingering feel of the soft touch of Aphrael's lips on his cheek. He firmly closed the door of the chamber where he stored his nightmares and thought of other things.

Without the little Goddess and her ability to tamper with time, it was probably going to take them a week to reach the coast, and they were going to have to find a ship to carry them to the Deiran side of the straits of Thalesia. By now King Wargun had undoubtedly alerted every nation in the Elene kingdoms to their escape. They'd have to move carefully to avoid capture, but they nonetheless needed to go into Emsat. They had to retrieve Talen for one thing, and ships are hard to come by on deserted shores.

The night air in these mountains was chill even in summer, and Sparhawk pulled his cloak tighter about his shoulders. His mood was sombre, troubled. The events of this day were the kind that led to long thoughts. Sparhawk's religious convictions were not really all that profound. His commitment had always been to the Pandion Order rather than to the Elene faith. The Church Knights were largely engaged in making the world safe for other, gentler Elenes to perform those ceremonies the clergy felt were pleasing to God. Sparhawk seldom concerned himself with God. Today, however, he had gone through some rather profoundly spiritual events. Ruefully he admitted to himself that a man with a pragmatic turn of mind is never really prepared for religious experiences of the kind which had been thrust upon him today. Then, almost as if his hand were acting of its own volition, it strayed towards the neck of his tunic. Sparhawk resolutely drew his sword, stabbed its point into the turf and wrapped both hands firmly about its hilt. He pushed his mind away from religion and the supernatural.

It was almost over now. The time his queen would be compelled to remain confined in the crystal that sustained her life could be measured in days rather than weeks or months. Sparhawk and his friends had trekked all over the Eosian continent to discover the one thing which would cure her, and now that cure lay in the canvas pouch under his tunic. Nothing could stop him now that he had Bhelliom. He could destroy whole armies with the Sapphire Rose if need be. He sternly pulled his mind back from that thought.

His broken face grew bleak. Once his queen was safe, he was going to do some more or less permanent things to Martel, the Primate Annias and anyone who had aided them in their treason. He began to mentally draw up a list of people who had things to answer for. It was a pleasant way to pass the night-time hours, and it kept his mind occupied and out of mischief.

At dusk six days later, they crested a hill and looked down at the smoky torches and candlelit windows of the capital of Thalesia. 'You'd better wait here,' Kurik said to Sparhawk and Sephrenia. 'Wargun's probably spread descriptions of you through every city in Eosia by now. I'll go into town and locate Talen. We'll see what we can find in the way of a ship.'

'Will you be all right?' Sephrenia asked. 'Wargun could have sent out your description as well, you know.'

'King Wargun's a nobleman,' Kurik growled. 'Nobles pay very little attention to servants.'

'You're not a servant,' Sparhawk objected.

'That's how I'm defined, Sparhawk, and that's how Wargun saw me – when he was sober enough to see anything. I'll waylay some traveller and steal his clothes. That should get me by in Emsat. Give me some money in case I have to bribe some people.'

'Elenes,' Sephrenia sighed as Sparhawk led her back some distance from the road and Kurik rode at a walk on down towards the city. 'How did I ever get involved with such unscrupulous people?'

The dusk faded slowly, and the tall, resinous fir trees

around them turned into looming shadows. Sparhawk tethered Faran, their packhorse and Ch'iel, Sephrenia's white palfrey. Then he spread his cloak on a mossy bank for her to sit on.

'What's troubling you, Sparhawk?' she asked him.

'Tired maybe,' he tried to shrug it off, 'and there's always a kind of let-down after you've finished something.'

'There's more to it than that though, isn't there?'

He nodded. 'I wasn't really prepared for what happened in that cave. It all seemed very immediate and personal somehow.'

She nodded. 'I'm not trying to be offensive, Sparhawk, but the Elene religion has become institutionalized, and it's very hard to love an institution. The Gods of Styricum have a much more personal relationship with their devotees.'

'I think I prefer being an Elene. It's easier. Personal relationships with Gods are very upsetting.'

'But don't you love Aphrael – just a little?'

'Of course I do. I was a lot more comfortable with her when she was just Flute, but I still love her.' He made a face. 'You're leading me in the direction of heresy, little mother,' he accused.

'Not really. For the time being, all Aphrael wants is your love. She hasn't asked you for your worship – yet.'

'It's that "yet" that concerns me. Isn't this a rather peculiar time and place for a theological discussion, though?'

There was the sound of horses on the road, and the unseen riders reined in not far from where Sparhawk and Sephrenia were concealed. Sparhawk rose quickly, his hand going to his sword-hilt.

'They have to be around here somewhere,' a rough voice declared. 'That was his man who just rode into the city.'

33

'I don't know about you two,' another voice said, 'but I'm not really all that eager to find him, myself.'

'There are three of us,' the first voice declared pugnaciously.

'Do you think that would really make any difference to him? He's a Church Knight. He could probably cut all three of us down without even working up a sweat. We're not going to be able to spend the money if we're all dead.'

'He's got a point there,' a third voice agreed. 'I think the best idea is just to locate him for now. Once we know where he is and which way he's going, we'll be able to set up an ambush for him. Church Knight or not, an arrow in his back ought to make him docile. Let's keep looking. The woman's riding a white horse. That should make it easier to locate them.'

The horses moved on, and Sparhawk slid his half-drawn sword back into its scabbard.

'Are they Wargun's men?' Sephrenia whispered to Sparhawk.

'I wouldn't think so,' Sparhawk murmured. 'Wargun's a little erratic, but he's not the sort of man who sends out paid assassins. He wants to yell at me and maybe throw me in his dungeon for a while. I don't think he's angry enough with me to want to murder me – at least I hope not.'

'Someone else, then?'

'Probably.' Sparhawk frowned. 'I don't seem to recall having offended anyone in Thalesia lately, though.'

'Annias has a long arm, dear one,' she reminded him.

'That might be it, little mother. Let's lie low and keep our ears open until Kurik comes back.'

After about an hour they heard the slow plodding of another horse coming up the rutted road from Emsat. The horse stopped at the top of the hill. 'Sparhawk?' The quiet voice was vaguely familiar.

Sparhawk quickly put his hand to his sword hilt, and he and Sephrenia exchanged a quick glance.

'I know you're in there somewhere, Sparhawk. It's me, Tel, so don't get excited. Your man said you wanted to go into Emsat. Stragen sent me to fetch you.'

'We're over here,' Sparhawk replied. 'Wait. We'll be right out.' He and Sephrenia led their horses to the road to meet the flaxen-haired brigand who had escorted them to the town of Heid on their journey to Ghwerig's cave. 'Can you get us into the city?' Sparhawk asked.

'Nothing easier,' Tel shrugged.

'How do we get past the guards at the gate?'

'We just ride on through. The gate guards work for Stragen. It makes things a lot simpler. Shall we go?'

Emsat was a northern city, and the steep-pitched roofs of the houses bespoke the heavy snows of winter. The streets were narrow and crooked, and there were only a few people abroad. Sparhawk, however, looked about warily, remembering the three cut-throats on the road outside town.

'Be kind of careful with Stragen, Sparhawk,' Tel cautioned as they rode into a seedy district near the waterfront. 'He's the bastard son of an earl, and he's a little touchy about his origins. He likes to have us address him as "Milord". It's foolish, but he's a good leader, so we play his games.' He pointed down a garbage-littered street. 'We go this way.'

'How's Talen getting along?'

'He's settled in now, but he was seriously put out with you when he first got here. He called you some names I'd never even heard before.'

'I can imagine.' Sparhawk decided to confide in the brigand. He knew Tel, and he was at least partially sure he could trust him. 'Some people rode by the place where we were hiding before you came,' he said.

'They were looking for us. Were those some of your men?'

'No,' Tel replied. 'I came alone.'

'I sort of thought you might have. These fellows were talking about shooting me full of arrows. Would Stragen be involved in that sort of thing in any way?'

'Out of the question, Sparhawk,' Tel said quite firmly. 'You and your friends have thieves' sanctuary. Stragen would never violate that. I'll talk to Stragen about it. He'll see to it that these itinerant bowmen stay out of your hair.' Tel laughed a chilling little laugh. 'He'll probably be more upset with them because they've gone into business for themselves than because they threaten you, though. Nobody cuts a throat or steals a penny in Emsat without Stragen's permission. He's very keen about that.' The blond brigand led them to a boarded-up warehouse at the far end of the street. They rode around to the back, dismounted and were admitted by a pair of burly cut-throats standing guard at the door.

The interior of the warehouse belied the shabby exterior. It appeared only slightly less opulent than a palace. There were crimson drapes covering the boarded-up windows, deep blue carpets on the creaky floors and tapestries concealing the rough plank walls. A semicircular staircase of polished wood curved up to a second floor, and a crystal chandelier threw soft, glowing candlelight over the entryway.

'Excuse me for a minute,' Tel said. He went into a side-chamber and emerged a bit later wearing a cream-coloured doublet and blue hose. He also had a slim rapier at his side.

'Elegant,' Sparhawk observed.

'Another one of Stragen's foolish ideas,' Tel snorted. 'I'm a working man, not a clothes-rack. Let's go up, and I'll introduce you to Milord.'

The upper floor was, if anything, even more extravagantly furnished than the one below. It was expensively floored with intricate parquet, and the walls were panelled with highly polished wood. Broad corridors led off towards the back of the house, and chandeliers and standing candelabra filled the spacious hall with golden light. It appeared that some kind of ball was in progress. A quartet of indifferently talented musicians sawed at their instruments in one corner, and gaily-dressed thieves and whores circled the floor in the mincing steps of the latest dance. Although their clothing was elegant, the men were unshaven, and the women had tangled hair and smudged faces. The contrast gave the entire scene an almost nightmarish quality heightened by voices and laughter which were coarse and raucous.

The focus of the entire room was a thin man with elaborate curls cascading over his ruffed collar. He was dressed in white satin and the chair upon which he sat near the far end of the room was not quite a throne – but very nearly. His expression was sardonic, and his deep-sunk eyes had about them a look of obscure pain.

Tel stopped at the head of the staircase and talked for a moment with an ancient cutpurse holding a long staff and wearing elegant scarlet livery. The white-haired knave turned, rapped the butt of his staff on the floor and spoke in a booming voice. 'Milord,' he declaimed, 'the Marquis Tel begs leave to present Sir Sparhawk, Knight of the Church and champion of the Queen of Elenia.'

The thin man rose and clapped his hands together sharply. The musicians broke off their sawing. 'We have important guests, dear friends,' he said to the dancers. His voice was very deep and quite consciously well modulated. 'Let us pay our proper respects to the invincible Sir Sparhawk, who, with the might of his hands, defends our holy mother Church. I pray you, Sir

37

Sparhawk, approach that we may greet you and make you welcome.'

'A pretty speech,' Sephrenia murmured.

'It should be,' Tel muttered back sourly. 'He probably spent the last hour composing it.' The flaxen-haired brigand led them through the throng of dancers, who all bowed or curtsied jerkily to them as they passed.

When they reached the man in white satin, Tel bowed. 'Milord,' he said, 'I have the honour to present Sir Sparhawk the Pandion. Sir Sparhawk, Milord Stragen.'

'The thief,' Stragen added sardonically. Then he bowed elegantly. 'You honour my inadequate house, Sir Knight,' he said.

Sparhawk bowed in reply. 'It is I who am honoured, Milord.' He rigorously avoided smiling at the airs of this apparently puffed-up popinjay.

'And so we meet at last, Sir Knight,' Stragen said. 'Your young friend Talen has given us a glowing account of your exploits.'

'Talen sometimes tends to exaggerate things, Milord.'

'And the lady is –?'

'Sephrenia, my tutor in the secrets.'

'Dear sister,' Stragen said in a flawless Styric, 'will you permit me to greet you?'

If Sephrenia were startled by this strange man's knowledge of her language, she gave no indication of it. She extended her hands, and Stragen kissed her palms. 'It is surprising, Milord, to meet a civilized man in the midst of a world filled with all these Elene savages,' she said.

He laughed. 'Isn't it amusing, Sparhawk, to discover that even our unblemished Styrics have their little prejudices?' The blond pseudo-aristocrat looked around the hall. 'But we're interrupting the grand ball. My associates do so enjoy these frivolities. Let's withdraw so that their joy may be unconfined.' He raised his resonant voice

38

slightly, speaking to the throng of elegant criminals. 'Dear friends,' he said to them, 'pray excuse us. We will go apart for our discussions. We would not for all the world interrupt your enjoyment of this evening.' He paused, then looked rather pointedly at one ravishing dark-haired girl. 'I trust that you'll recall our discussion following the last ball, Countess,' he said firmly. 'Although I stand in awe of your ferocious business instincts, the culmination of certain negotiations should take place in private rather than in the centre of the dance-floor. It was very entertaining – even educational – but it did somewhat disrupt the dance.'

'It's just a different way of dancing, Stragen,' she replied in a coarse, nasal voice that sounded much like the squeal of a pig.

'Ah yes, Countess, but *vertical* dancing is in vogue just now. The horizontal form hasn't yet caught on in the more fashionable circles, and we *do* want to be stylish, don't we?' He turned to Tel. 'Your services this evening have been stupendous, my dear Marquis,' he said to the blond man. 'I doubt that I shall ever be able to adequately repay you.' He languidly lifted a perfumed handkerchief to his nostrils.

'That I have been able to serve is payment enough, Milord,' Tel replied with a low bow.

'Very good, Tel,' Stragen approved. 'I may yet bestow an earldom upon you.' He turned and led Sparhawk and Sephrenia from the ballroom. Once they were in the corridor outside, his manner changed abruptly. The veneer of affectedly bored gentility dropped away, and his eyes became alert, hard. They were the eyes of a very dangerous man. 'Does our little charade puzzle you, Sparhawk?' he asked. 'Maybe you feel that those in our profession should be housed in places like Platime's cellar in Cimmura or Meland's loft in Acie?'

'It's more commonplace, Milord,' Sparhawk replied cautiously.

'We can drop the "Milord", Sparhawk. It's an affectation – at least partially. All of this has a more serious purpose than satisfying some obscure personal quirk of mine, though. The gentry has access to far more wealth than the commons, so I train my associates to prey upon the rich and idle rather than the poor and industrious. It's more profitable in the long run. This current group has a long way to go, though, I'm afraid. Tel's coming along rather well, but I despair of ever making a lady of the countess. She has the soul of a whore, and that voice –,' he shuddered.

'Anyway, I train my people to assume spurious titles and to mouth little civilities to each other in preparation for more serious business. We're all still thieves, whores and cut-throats, of course, but we deal with a better class of customers.'

They entered a large, well-lit room to find Kurik and Talen sitting together on a large divan. 'Did you have a pleasant journey, My Lord?' Talen asked Sparhawk in a voice that had just a slight edge of resentment to it. The boy was dressed in a formal doublet and hose, and for the first time since Sparhawk had met him, his hair was combed. He rose and bowed gracefully to Sephrenia. 'Little mother,' he greeted her.

'I see you've been tampering with our wayward boy, Stragen,' she observed.

'His Grace had a few rough edges when he first came to us, dear lady,' the elegant ruffian told her. 'I took the liberty of polishing him a bit.'

'His Grace?' Sparhawk asked curiously.

'I have certain advantages, Sparhawk,' Stragen laughed. 'When nature – or blind chance – bestows a title, she has no way to consider the character of the recipient and to match

the eminence to the man. I, on the other hand, can observe
the true nature of the person involved and can select the
proper adornment of rank. I saw at once that young Talen
here is an extraordinary youth, so I bestowed a duchy upon
him. Give me three more months, and I could present him
at a court.' He sat down in a large, comfortable chair.
'Please, friends, find places to sit, and then you can tell
me how I can be of further service to you.'

Sparhawk held a chair for Sephrenia and then took a
seat not far from their host. 'What we really need at the
moment, neighbour, is a ship to carry us to the north coast
of Deira.'

'That's what I wanted to discuss with you, Sparhawk.
Our excellent young thief here tells me that your ultimate
goal is Cimmura, and he also tells me that there may
be some unpleasantness awaiting you in the northern
kingdoms. Our tipsy monarch is a man much in need of
friends, and he bitterly resents defections. As I understand
it, he's presently displeased with you. All manner of
unflattering descriptions are being circulated in western
Eosia. Wouldn't it be faster – and safer – to sail directly
to Cardos and go on to Cimmura from there?'

Sparhawk considered that. 'I was thinking of landing on
some lonely beach in Deira and going south through the
mountains.'

'That's a tedious way to travel, Sparhawk, and a very
dangerous one for a man on the run. There are lonely
beaches on every coast, and I'm sure we can find a suitable
one for you near Cardos.'

'We?'

'I think I'll go along. I like you, Sparhawk, even though
we've only just met. Besides, I need to talk some business
with Platime anyway.' He rose to his feet then. 'I'll have a
ship waiting in the harbour by dawn. Now I'll leave you.
I'm sure you're tired and hungry after your journey, and

I'd better return to the ball before our over-enthusiastic countess sets up shop in the middle of the ballroom floor again.' He bowed to Sephrenia. 'I bid you good night, dear sister,' he said to her in Styric. 'Sleep well.' He nodded to Sparhawk and quietly left the room.

Kurik rose, went to the door and listened. 'I don't think that man's entirely sane, Sparhawk,' he said in a low voice.

'Oh, he's sane enough,' Talen disagreed. 'He's got some strange ideas, but some of them might even work.' The boy came over to Sparhawk. 'All right,' he said, 'let me see it.'

'See what?'

'The Bhelliom. I risked my life several times to help steal it, and then I got disinvited to go along at the last minute. I think I'm at least entitled to take a look at it.'

'Is it safe?' Sparhawk asked Sephrenia.

'I don't really know, Sparhawk. The rings will control it, though – at least partially. Just a brief look, Talen. It's very dangerous.'

'A jewel is a jewel,' Talen shrugged. 'They're all dangerous. Anything one man wants, another is likely to try to steal, and that's the sort of thing that leads to killing. Give me gold every time. It all looks the same, and you can spend it anywhere. Jewels are hard to convert into money, and people usually spend all their time trying to protect them, and that's really inconvenient. Let's see it, Sparhawk.'

Sparhawk took out the pouch and picked open the knot. Then he shook the glowing blue rose into the palm of his right hand. Once again a brief flicker darkened the edge of his vision, and a chill passed over him. For some reason the flicker of the shadow brought the memory of the nightmare sharply back, and he could almost feel the hovering presence of those obscurely

42

menacing shapes which had haunted his sleep that night a week ago.

'God!' Talen exclaimed. 'That's incredible.' He stared at the jewel for a moment, and then he shuddered. 'Put it away, Sparhawk. I don't want to look at it any more.'

Sparhawk slipped Bhelliom back into its pouch.

'It really ought to be blood-red, though,' Talen said moodily. 'Look at all the people who've died over it.' He looked at Sephrenia. 'Was Flute really a Goddess?'

'Kurik told you about that, I see. Yes, she was – and is – one of the Younger Gods of Styricum.'

'I liked her,' the boy admitted, '– when she wasn't teasing me. But if she's a God – or Goddess – she could be any age she wanted to be, couldn't she?'

'Of course.'

'Why a child then?'

'People are more truthful with children.'

'I've never particularly noticed that.'

'Aphrael's more lovable than you are, Talen,' she smiled, 'and that may be the real reason behind her choice of form. She needs love – all Gods do, even Azash. People tend to pick little girls up and kiss them. Aphrael enjoys being kissed.'

'Nobody ever kissed *me* all that much.'

'That may come in time, Talen – if you behave yourself.'

Chapter 2

The weather on the Thalesian Peninsula, like that in every northern kingdom, was never really settled, and it was drizzling rain the following morning as bank after bank of thick, dirty clouds rolled into the straits of Thalesia off the Deiran Sea.

'A splendid day for a voyage,' Stragen observed dryly as he and Sparhawk looked through a partially boarded-up window at the rain-wet streets below. 'I hate rain. I wonder if I could find any career opportunities in Rendor.'

'I don't recommend it,' Sparhawk told him, remembering a sun-blasted street in Jiroch.

'Our horses are already on board the ship,' Stragen said. 'We can leave as soon as Sephrenia and the others are ready.' He paused. 'Is that roan horse of yours always so restive in the morning?' he asked curiously. 'My men report that he bit three of them on the way to the docks.'

'I should have warned them. Faran's not the best-tempered horse in the world.'

'Why do you keep him?'

'Because he's the most dependable horse I've ever owned. I'll put up with a few of his crotchets in exchange for that. Besides, I like him.'

Stragen looked at Sparhawk's chain-mail shirt. 'You really don't have to wear that, you know.'

'Habit,' Sparhawk shrugged, 'and there are a fair number of unfriendly people looking for me at the moment.'

'It smells awful, you know.'

'You get used to it.'

'You seem moody this morning, Sparhawk. Is something wrong?'

'I've been on the road for a long time, and I've run into some things I wasn't really prepared to accept. I'm trying to sort things out in my mind.'

'Maybe someday when we get to know each other better, you can tell me about it.' Stragen seemed to think of something. 'Oh, incidentally, Tel mentioned those three ruffians who were looking for you last night. They aren't looking any more.'

'Thank you.'

'It was a sort of internal matter really, Sparhawk. They violated one of the primary rules when they didn't check with me before they went looking for you. I can't really afford to have people setting that kind of precedent. We couldn't get much out of them, I'm afraid. They were acting on the orders of someone outside Thalesia, though. We were able to get that much from the one who was still breathing. Why don't we go and see if Sephrenia's ready?'

There was an elegant coach awaiting them outside the rear door of the warehouse about fifteen minutes later. They entered it, and the driver manoeuvred his matched team around in the narrow alley and out into the street.

When they reached the harbour, the coach rolled out onto a wharf and stopped beside a ship that appeared to be one of the kind normally used for coastal trade. Her half-furled sails were patched and her heavy railings showed signs of having been broken and repaired many times. Her sides were tarred, and she bore no name on her bow.

'She's a pirate, isn't she?' Kurik asked Stragen as they stepped down from the coach.

'Yes, as a matter of fact, she is,' Stragen replied. 'I own

45

a fair number of vessels in that business, but how did you recognize her?'

'She's built for speed, Milord,' Kurik said. 'She's too narrow in the beam for cargo capacity, and the reinforcing around her masts says that she was built to carry a lot of sail. She was designed to run other ships down.'

'Or to run away from them, Kurik. Pirates live nervous lives. There are all sorts of people in the world who yearn to hang pirates just on general principles.' Stragen looked around at the drizzly harbour. 'Let's go on board,' he suggested. 'There's not much point in standing out here in the rain discussing the finer points of life at sea.'

They went up the gangway, and Stragen led them to their cabins below deck. The sailors slipped their hawsers, and the ship moved out of the rainy harbour at a stately pace. Once they were past the headland and in deep water, however, the crew crowded on more sail, and the questionable vessel heeled over and raced across the straits of Thalesia towards the Deiran coast.

Sparhawk went up on deck about noon and found Stragen leaning on the rail near the bow looking moodily out over the grey, rain-dappled sea. He wore a heavy brown cloak, and his hat-brim dripped water down his back.

'I thought you didn't like rain,' Sparhawk said.

'It's humid down in that cabin,' the brigand replied. 'I needed some air. I'm glad you came up though, Sparhawk. Pirates aren't very interesting conversationalists.'

They stood for a time listening to the creaking of rigging and ship's timbers and to the melancholy sound of rain hissing into the sea.

'How is it that Kurik knows so much about ships?' Stragen asked finally.

'He went to sea for a while when he was young.'

46

'That explains it, I guess. I don't suppose you'd care to talk about what you were doing in Thalesia?'

'Not really. Church business, you understand.'

Stragen smiled. 'Ah, yes. Our taciturn holy mother Church,' he said. 'Sometimes I think she keeps secrets just for the fun of it.'

'We sort of have to take it on faith that she knows what she's doing.'

'*You* have to, Sparhawk, because you're a Church Knight. I haven't taken any of those vows, so I'm perfectly free to view her with a certain scepticism. I did give some thought to entering the Priesthood when I was younger, though.'

'You might have done very well. The Priesthood or the army are always interested in the talented younger sons of noblemen.'

'I rather like that,' Stragen smiled. '"Younger son" has a much nicer sound to it than "bastard", doesn't it? It doesn't really matter to me, though. I don't need rank or legitimacy to make my way in the world. The Church and I wouldn't have got along too well, I'm afraid. I don't have the humility she seems to require, and a congregation reeking of unwashed armpits would have driven me to renounce my vows fairly early on.' He looked back out at the rainy sea. 'When you get right down to it, life didn't leave me too many options. I'm not humble enough for the Church, I'm not obedient enough for the army and I don't have the bourgeois temperament necessary for trade. I did dabble for a time at court, though, since the government always needs good administrators, legitimate or not, but after I'd beaten out the dull-witted son of a duke for a position we both wanted, he became abusive. I challenged him, of course, and he was foolish enough to show up for our appointment wearing chain-mail and carrying a broadsword. No offence intended, Sparhawk,

47

but chain-mail has a few too many small holes in it to be a good defence against a well-sharpened rapier. My opponent discovered that fairly early on in the discussion. After I'd run him through a few times, he sort of lost interest in the whole business. I left him for dead – which proved to be a pretty good guess – and quietly removed myself from government service. The dullard I'd just skewered turned out to be distantly related to King Wargun, and our drunken monarch has very little in the way of a sense of humour.'

'I've noticed.'

'How did you manage to get on the wrong side of him?'

Sparhawk shrugged. 'He wanted me to participate in that war going on down in Arcium, but I had pressing business in Thalesia. How's that war going, by the way? I've been a little out of touch.'

'About all we've had in the way of information are rumours. Some say that the Rendors have been exterminated; others say that Wargun has, and that the Rendors are marching north burning everything that's the least bit flammable. Whichever rumour you choose to believe depends on your view of the world, I suppose.' Stragen looked sharply aft.

'Something wrong?' Sparhawk asked him.

'That ship back there.' Stragen pointed. 'She *looks* like a merchantman, but she's moving a little too fast.'

'Another pirate?'

'I don't recognize her – and believe me, I'd recognize her if she were in my line of business.' He peered aft, his face tight. Then he relaxed. 'She's veering off now.' He laughed briefly. 'Sorry if I seem a little over-suspicious, Sparhawk, but unsuspicious pirates usually end up decorating some wharf-side gallows. Where were we?'

Stragen was asking a few too many questions. It was

probably a good time to divert him. 'You were about to tell me about how you left Wargun's court and set up one of your own,' Sparhawk suggested.

'It took a little while,' Stragen admitted, 'but I'm rather uniquely suited for a life of crime. I haven't been the least bit squeamish since the day I killed my father and my two half-brothers.'

Sparhawk was a bit surprised at that.

'Killing my father might have been a mistake,' Stragen admitted. 'He wasn't really a bad sort, and he *did* pay for my education, but I took offence at the way he treated my mother. She was an amiable young woman from a well-placed family who'd been put in my father's household as the companion of his ailing wife. The usual sort of thing happened, and I was the result. After my disgrace at court, my father decided to distance himself from me, so he sent my mother home to her family. She died not long afterwards. I suppose I could justify my patricide by claiming that she died of a broken heart, but as a matter of fact, she choked to death on a fish bone. Anyway, I paid a short visit to my father's house, and his title is now vacant. My two half-brothers were stupid enough to join in, and now all three of them share the same tomb. I rather imagine that my father regretted all the money he'd spent on my fencing lessons. The expression on his face while he was dying seemed to indicate that he was regretting *something*.' The blond man shrugged. 'I was younger then. I'd probably do it differently now. There's not much profit involved in randomly rendering relatives down to dog-meat, is there?'

'That depends on how you define profit.'

Stragen gave him a quick grin. 'Anyway, I realized almost as soon as I took to the streets that there's not that much difference between a baron and a cutpurse or a duchess and a whore. I tried to explain that to my predecessor, but the fool wouldn't listen to me. He drew his sword on me, and I removed him from office. Then I began training the thieves and whores of Emsat. I've adorned them with imaginary titles, purloined finery and a thin crust of good manners to give them a semblance of gentility. Then I turned them loose on the aristocracy. Business is very, very good, and I'm able to repay my former class for a thousand slights and insults.' He paused. 'Have you had about enough of this malcontented diatribe yet, Sparhawk? I must say that your courtesy and forbearance are virtually superhuman. I'm tired of being rained on anyway. Why don't we go below? I've got a dozen flagons of Arcian red in my cabin. We can both get a little tipsy and engage in some civilized conversation.'

Sparhawk considered this complex man as he followed him below. Stragen's motives were clear, of course. His resentment and that towering hunger for revenge were completely understandable. What was unusual was his total lack of self-pity. Sparhawk found that he liked the man. He didn't trust him, of course. That would have been foolish, but he liked him nonetheless.

'So do I,' Talen agreed that evening in their cabin when Sparhawk briefly recounted Stragen's story and confessed his liking for the man. 'That's probably natural, though. Stragen and I have a lot in common.'

'Are you going to throw that in my teeth again?' Kurik asked him.

'I'm not lobbing stones in your direction, father,' Talen said. 'Things like that happen, and I'm a lot less sensitive about it than Stragen is.' He grinned then. 'I was able to use our similar backgrounds to some advantage while I was in Emsat, though. I think he took a liking to me, and he made me some very interesting offers. He wants me to come to work for him.'

'You've got a promising future ahead of you, Talen,'

Kurik said sourly. 'You could inherit either Platime's position or Stragen's – assuming you don't get yourself caught and hanged first.'

'I'm starting to think on a larger scale,' Talen said grandly. 'Stragen and I did some speculating about it while I was in Emsat. The thieves' council is very close to being a government now. About all it really needs to qualify is some single leader – a king maybe, or even an emperor. Wouldn't it make you proud to be the father of the Emperor of the Thieves, Kurik?'

'Not particularly.'

'What do you think, Sparhawk?' the boy asked, his eyes filled with mischief. 'Should I go into politics?'

'I believe we can find something more suitable for you to do, Talen.'

'Maybe, but would it be as profitable – or as much fun?'

They reached the Elenian coast a league or so to the north of Cardos a week later and disembarked about midday on a lonely beach bordered on its upper end with dark fir trees.

'The Cardos road?' Kurik asked Sparhawk as they saddled Faran and Kurik's gelding.

'Might I make a suggestion?' Stragen asked from nearby.

'Certainly.'

'King Wargun's a maudlin man when he's drunk – which is most of the time. Your defection probably has him blubbering in his beer every night. He offered a sizeable reward for your capture in Thalesia and Deira, and he's probably circulated the same offer here. Your face is well-known in Elenia, and it's about seventy leagues from here to Cimmura – a good week of hard travel at least. Do you really want to spend that much time on a well-travelled road under those circumstances? – Particularly in view of the fact that *somebody* wants to shoot you full of arrows rather than just turn you over to Wargun?'

'Perhaps not. Can you think of an alternative?'

'Yes, as a matter of fact, I can. It may take us a day or so longer, but Platime once showed me a different route. It's a bit rough, but very few people know about it.'

Sparhawk looked at the thin blond man with a certain amount of suspicion. 'Can I trust you, Stragen?' he asked bluntly.

Stragen shook his head in resignation. 'Talen,' he said, 'haven't you ever explained thieves' sanctuary to him?'

'I've tried, but sometimes Sparhawk has difficulty with moral concepts. It goes like this, Sparhawk. If Stragen lets anything happen to us while we're under his protection, he'll have to answer to Platime.'

'That's more or less why I came along, actually,' Stragen admitted. 'As long as I'm with you, you're still under my protection. I like you, Sparhawk, and having a Church Knight to intercede with God for me in case I happen to be accidentally hanged couldn't hurt.' His sardonic expression returned then. 'Not only that, watching out for all of you might expiate some of my grosser sins.'

'Do you really have that many sins, Stragen?' Sephrenia asked him gently.

'More than I can remember, dear sister,' he replied in Styric, 'and many of them are too foul to be described in your presence.'

Sparhawk looked quickly at Talen, and the boy nodded gravely. 'Sorry, Stragen,' he apologized. 'I misjudged you.'

'Perfectly all right, old boy.' Stragen grinned. 'And perfectly understandable. There are days when I don't even trust myself.'

'Where's this other road to Cimmura?'

Stragen looked around. 'Why, do you know, I actually

believe it starts just up there at the head of this beach. Isn't that an amazing coincidence?'

'That was your ship we sailed on?'

'I'm a part owner, yes.'

'And you suggested to the captain that this beach might be a good place to drop us off?'

'I *do* seem to recall such a conversation, yes.'

'An amazing coincidence, all right,' Sparhawk said dryly.

Stragen stopped, looking out to sea. 'Odd,' he said, pointing at a passing ship. 'There's that same merchantman we saw up in the straits. She's sailing very light. Otherwise she couldn't have made such good time.' He shrugged. 'Oh well. Let's go to Cimmura, shall we?'

The 'alternative route' they followed was little more than a forest trail that wound up across the range of mountains that lay between the coast and the broad tract of farmland drained by the Cimmura River. Once the track came down out of the mountains, it merged imperceptibly with a series of sunken country lanes meandering through the fields.

Early one morning when they were midway across that farmland, a shabby-looking fellow on a spavined mule cautiously approached their camp. 'I need to talk with a man named Stragen,' he called from just out of bow-shot.

'Come ahead,' Stragen called back to him.

The man did not bother to dismount. 'I'm from Platime,' he identified himself to the Thalesian. 'He told me to warn you. There were some fellows looking for you on the road from Cardos to Cimmura.'

'*Were?*'

'They couldn't really identify themselves after we encountered them, and they aren't looking for anything any more.'

'Ah.'

'They were asking questions before we intercepted them, though. They described you and your companions to a number of peasants. I don't think they wanted to catch up with you just to talk about the weather, Milord.'

'Were they Elenians?' Stragen asked intently.

'A few of them were. The rest seemed to be Thalesian sailors. Someone's after you and your friends, Stragen, and I think they've got killing on their minds. If I were you, I'd get to Cimmura and Platime's cellar just as quickly as I could.'

'My thanks, friend,' Stragen said.

The ruffian shrugged. 'I'm getting paid for this. Thanks don't fatten my purse at all.' He turned his mule and rode off.

'I *knew* I should have turned and sunk that ship,' Stragen noted. 'I must be getting soft. We'd better move right along, Sparhawk. We're awfully exposed out here.'

Three days later, they reached Cimmura and reined in on the north rim of the valley to look down at the city, smoky and mist-plagued. 'A distinctly unattractive place, Sparhawk,' Stragen said critically.

'It's not much,' Sparhawk conceded, 'but we like to call it home.'

'I'll be leaving you here,' Stragen said. 'You have things to attend to and so do I. Might I suggest that we all forget we ever met each other? You're involved in politics and I in theft. I'll leave it to God to decide which occupation is the more dishonest. Good luck, Sparhawk, and keep your eyes open.' He half-bowed to Sephrenia from his saddle, turned his horse and rode down to the grimy city below.

'I could almost grow to like that man,' Sephrenia said. 'Where to, Sparhawk?'

'The chapterhouse,' the big Pandion decided. 'We've been away for quite some time, and I'd like to know how

54

things stand before I go to the palace.' He squinted up at the noonday sun, bleary and wan-looking in the pervading haze that hung over Cimmura. 'Let's stay out of sight until we find out who's controlling the city.'

They kept to the trees and rode on around Cimmura on the north side. Kurik slipped down from his gelding at one point and crept to the edge of the bushes to have a look. His expression was grave when he returned. 'There are church soldiers manning the battlements,' he reported.

Sparhawk swore. 'Are you sure?'

'The men up there are wearing red.'

'Let's move on anyway. We've got to get inside the chapterhouse.'

The dozen or so ostensible workmen outside the fortress of the Pandion Knights were still laying cobblestones.

'They've been at that for almost a year now,' Kurik muttered, 'and they still haven't finished. Do we wait for dark?'

'I don't think that would do much good. They'll still be watching, and I don't want it generally known that we're back in Cimmura.'

'Sephrenia,' Talen said, 'can you make a column of smoke come up from just inside the city walls near the gate?'

'Yes,' she replied.

'Good. We'll make those bricklayers go away then.' The boy quickly explained his plan.

'That isn't really too bad, Sparhawk,' Kurik said rather proudly. 'What do you think?'

'It's worth a try. Let's do it and see what happens.'

The red uniform Sephrenia created for Kurik did not look all that authentic, but the smudges and smoke-stains she added covered most of the discrepancies. The important things were the gold-embroidered epaulettes which identified him as an officer. The burly squire then led his horse through the bushes to a spot near the city gate.

Then Sephrenia began to murmur in Styric, gesturing with her fingers as she did so.

The column of smoke that rose from inside the walls was very convincing, thick, oily black and boiling dreadfully.

'Hold my horse,' Talen said to Sparhawk, slipping down from his saddle. He ran out to the edge of the bushes and began to shriek, 'Fire!' at the top of his lungs.

The so-called workmen gaped at him stupidly for a moment, then turned to stare in consternation at the city.

'You always have to yell "fire",' Talen explained when he returned. 'It gets people to thinking in the right direction.'

Then Kurik galloped up to the spies outside the gate of the chapterhouse. 'You men,' he barked, 'there's a house on fire in Goat Lane. Get in there and help put the fire out before the whole city starts to burn.'

'But sir,' one of the workmen objected, 'we were ordered to stay here and keep an eye on the Pandions.'

'Do you have anything you value inside the city walls?' Kurik asked him bluntly. 'If that fire gets away from us, you can stand here and keep an eye on it while it burns. Now move, all of you! I'm going up to that fortress to see if I can persuade the Pandions to lend a hand.'

The workmen looked at him, then dropped their tools and ran towards the illusory conflagration as Kurik rode on towards the drawbridge of the chapterhouse.

'Slick,' Sparhawk complimented Talen.

'Thieves do it all the time,' the boy shrugged. 'We have to use real fire, though. People run outside to gawk at fires. That provides an excellent opportunity to look around inside their houses for things of value.' He looked towards the city gate. 'Our friends seem to be out of sight. Why don't we ride on before they come back?'

Two Pandion Knights in black armour rode gravely out to meet them as they reached the drawbridge. 'Is that a fire in the city, Sparhawk?' one of them asked in some alarm.

'Not really,' Sparhawk replied. 'Sephrenia's entertaining the church soldiers.'

The other knight grinned at Sephrenia. Then he straightened. 'Who art thou who entreateth entry into the house of the Soldiers of God?' he began the ritual.

'We don't have time for that, brother,' Sparhawk told him. 'We'll go through it twice next time. Who's in charge here now?'

'Lord Vanion.'

That was surprising. Preceptor Vanion had been much involved in the campaign in Arcium when last Sparhawk had heard of him. 'Do you have any idea of where I might locate him?'

'He's in his tower, Sparhawk,' the second knight advised.

Sparhawk grunted. 'How many knights are here right now, brother?'

'About a hundred.'

'Good. I may need them.' Sparhawk nudged Faran with his heels. The big roan turned his head to look at his master with some surprise. 'We're busy now, Faran,' Sparhawk explained to his horse. 'We'll go through the ritual some other time.'

Faran's expression was disapproving as he started across the drawbridge.

'Sir Sparhawk!' a ringing voice came from the stable door. It was the novice, Berit, a rangy, raw-boned young man whose face was split with a broad grin.

'Shout a little louder, Berit,' Kurik said reprovingly. 'Maybe they'll be able to hear you in Chyrellos.'

'Sorry, Kurik,' Berit apologized, looking abashed.

'Get some other novices to look after our horses and come with us,' Sparhawk told the young man. 'We have things to do, and we have to talk with Vanion.'

'Yes, Sir Sparhawk.' Berit ran back into the stable.

'He's such a nice boy,' Sephrenia smiled.

'He might work out,' Kurik said grudgingly.

'*Sparhawk*,' a hooded Pandion said with some surprise as they entered the arched door leading into the chapterhouse. The knight pushed back his hood. It was Sir Perraine, the Pandion who had posed as a cattle-buyer in Dabour. Perraine spoke with a slight accent.

'What are you doing back in Cimmura, Perraine?' Sparhawk asked, clasping his brother knight's hand. 'We all thought you'd taken root in Dabour.'

Perraine seemed to recover from his surprise. 'Ah –' he began, 'once Arasham died, there wasn't much reason for me to remain in Dabour. We'd all heard that King Wargun was pursuing you all over western Eosia.'

'Pursuing isn't catching, Perraine,' Sparhawk grinned. 'We can talk later. But now my friends and I have to go and talk with Vanion.'

'Of course.' Perraine bowed slightly to Sephrenia and walked on out into the courtyard.

They went up the stairs to the south tower where Vanion's study was located. The Preceptor of the Pandion Order wore that white Styric robe, and his face had aged even more in the short time since Sparhawk had last seen him. The others were also there, Ulath, Tynian, Bevier and Kalten. Their presence seemed somehow to make the room shrink. These were very large men, not only in sheer physical size, but also in terms of their towering reputations. The room seemed somehow full of bulky shoulders. As was customary among Church Knights when inside their chapterhouses, they all wore monks' robes over their mail-shirts.

'Finally!' Kalten said, letting out an explosive breath. 'Sparhawk, why didn't you get word to us to let us know how you were?'

'Messengers are a little hard to find in Troll-country, Kalten.'

'Any luck?' Ulath asked eagerly. Ulath was a huge, blond-braided Thalesian, and Bhelliom had a special meaning for him.

Sparhawk looked quickly at Sephrenia, silently asking permission.

'All right,' she said, 'but only for a minute.'

Sparhawk reached down inside his tunic and drew out the canvas pouch in which he carried Bhelliom. He pulled open the drawstring, lifted out the most precious object in the world and placed it on the table Vanion used for a writing desk. Even as he did so, there came again that faint flicker of the darkness somewhere off in a dim corner. The hound of darkness his nightmare had conjured up in the mountains of Thalesia followed him still, and the shadow seemed larger and darker now as if each re-emergence of Bhelliom somehow increased its size and its brooding menace.

'Do not look too deeply into those petals, gentlemen,' Sephrenia warned. 'Bhelliom can capture your souls if you look at it too long.'

'God!' Kalten breathed. 'Look at that thing!'

Each glowing petal of the Sapphire Rose was so perfect that one could almost see dew clinging to it. From deep within the jewel emanated a blue light and an almost overpowering command to look upon it and observe its perfection.

'Oh, God,' Bevier prayed fervently, 'defend us from the

seduction of this stone.' Bevier was a Cyrinic Knight and an Arcian. Sometimes Sparhawk felt that he was excessively pious. This, however, was not one of those times. If even half of what he had already sensed was true, Sparhawk knew that Bevier's fear of Bhelliom was well placed.

Ulath, the huge Thalesian, was muttering in Troll. 'Not kill, Bhelliom-Blue-Rose,' he said. 'Church Knights not enemies to Bhelliom. Church Knights protect Bhelliom from Azash. Help make what is wrong right again, Blue-Rose. I am Ulath-from-Thalesia. If Bhelliom have anger, send anger against Ulath.'

Sparhawk straightened. 'No,' he said firmly in the hideous Troll-tongue. 'I am Sparhawk-from-Elenia. I am he who kills Ghwerig-Troll-Dwarf. I am he who brings Bhelliom-Blue-Rose to this place to heal my queen. If Bhelliom-Blue-Rose do this and still have anger, send anger against Sparhawk-from-Elenia and not against Ulath-from-Thalesia.'

'You fool!' Ulath exploded. 'Have you got any idea of what that thing can do to you?'

'Wouldn't it do the same sort of things to you?'

'Gentlemen, please,' Sephrenia said to them wearily. 'Stop this nonsense at once.' She looked at the glowing rose on the table. 'Listen to me, Bhelliom-Blue-Rose,' she said firmly, not even bothering to speak in the language of the Trolls. 'Sparhawk-from-Elenia has the rings. Bhelliom-Blue-Rose must acknowledge his authority and obey him.'

The jewel darkened briefly, and then the deep blue light returned.

'Good,' she said. 'I will guide Bhelliom-Blue-Rose in what must be done, and Sparhawk-from-Elenia will command it. Blue-Rose must obey.'

The jewel flickered, and then the light returned.

'Put it away now, Sparhawk.'

Sparhawk put the rose back into its pouch and slipped it back under his tunic.

'Where's Flute?' Berit asked, looking around.

'*That*, my young friend, is a very, very long story,' Sparhawk told him.

'Not dead?' Sir Tynian asked in a shocked tone. 'Surely not dead.'

'No,' Sparhawk told him. 'That would be impossible. Flute is immortal.'

'No human is immortal, Sparhawk,' Bevier protested in a shocked voice.

'Exactly,' Sparhawk replied. 'Flute's *not* human. She's the Styric Child-Goddess Aphrael.'

'Heresy!' Bevier gasped.

'You wouldn't think so if you'd been in Ghwerig's cave, Sir Bevier,' Kurik told him. 'I saw her rise from a bottomless abyss with my own eyes.'

'A spell, perhaps?' But Bevier did not seem quite so sure of himself now.

'No, Bevier,' Sephrenia said. 'No spell could have accomplished what she did in that cave. She was – and is – Aphrael.'

'Before we get involved in a theological dispute here, I need some information,' Sparhawk said. 'How did you all get away from Wargun, and what's happening in the city?'

'Wargun wasn't really a problem,' Vanion told him. 'We came through Cimmura on our way south, and things went more or less the way we'd planned them at Acie. We threw Lycheas into the dungeon, put the Earl of Lenda in charge and persuaded the army and the church soldiers here in Cimmura to march south with us.'

'How did you manage that?' Sparhawk asked with some surprise.

'Vanion's a very good persuader,' Kalten grinned. 'Most

of the generals were loyal to Primate Annias, but when they tried to object, Vanion invoked that Church Law the Earl of Lenda mentioned back at Acie and took command of the army. The generals still objected until he marched them all down to the courtyard. After Ulath had beheaded a few of them, most of the rest decided to change sides.'

'Oh, *Vanion*,' Sephrenia said in a tone of profound disappointment.

'I was a bit pressed for time, little mother,' he apologized. 'Wargun was in a hurry to get started. He wanted to butcher the entire Elenian officer corps, but I talked him out of that. Anyway, we joined with King Soros of Pelosia at the border and marched down into Arcium. The Rendors turned tail and ran when they saw us coming. Wargun intends to chase them down, but I think that's just for his personal entertainment. The other Preceptors and I managed to convince him that our presence in Chyrellos during the election of the new Archprelate was vital, so he let each of us take a hundred knights.'

'That was generous of him,' Sparhawk said sardonically. 'Where are the knights from the other orders?'

'They're camped outside Demos. Dolmant doesn't want us to move into Chyrellos until the situation there solidifies.'

'If Lenda's in charge at the palace, why are there church soldiers on the walls of the city?'

'Annias found out what we'd done here, of course. There are members of the Hierocracy who are loyal to him, and they all have their own troops. He borrowed some of those men and sent them here. They freed Lycheas and imprisoned the Earl of Lenda. They control the city at the moment.'

'We ought to do something about that.'

Vanion nodded. 'We were on our way to Demos with the other orders when we chanced to find out what was happening here. The other orders went on to Demos to be in position to move on Chyrellos and we came here to Cimmura. We only arrived late last night. The knights were all eager to go into the city as soon as we got here, but we've been campaigning hard, and they're all tired. I want them to be a little better rested before we correct things inside the walls.'

'Are we likely to have any problems?'

'I doubt it. Those church soldiers aren't Annias's men. They're on loan from the other Patriarchs, and their loyalties are a little vague. I think a show of force is probably about all it's going to take to make them capitulate.'

'Are the remaining six knights who were involved in the spell in the throne-room among your hundred?' Sephrenia asked him.

'Yes,' Vanion replied a little wanly. 'We're all here.' He looked at the Pandion sword she was carrying. 'Do you want to give me that?' he asked.

'No,' she said firmly. 'You're carrying enough already. It isn't going to be much longer anyway.'

'You're going to reverse the spell?' Tynian asked, '– before you use Bhelliom to cure the queen, I mean?'

'We have to,' she told him. 'Bhelliom has to touch her skin in order to cure her.'

Kalten went to the window. 'It's late afternoon now,' he said. 'If we're going to do this today, we'd better get started.'

'Let's wait until morning,' Vanion decided. 'If the soldiers try to resist, it might take a while to subdue them, and I don't want any of those people slipping away in the dark to warn Annias until we've had time to get reinforcements here.'

'How many soldiers are at the palace?' Sparhawk asked.

'My spies report a couple of hundred,' Vanion replied, 'hardly enough to cause us any problems.'

'We're going to have to come up with a way to seal the city for a few days if we don't want to see a relief column wearing red tunics coming up the river,' Ulath said.

'I can take care of that,' Talen told him. 'I'll slip into town just before dark and go and talk to Platime. He'll seal the gates for us.'

'Can he be trusted?' Vanion asked.

'Platime? Of course not, but I think he'll do that much for us. He hates Annias.'

'That's it then,' Kalten said gaily. 'We can move out at dawn and have everything tidied up by lunchtime.'

'Don't bother to set a place at the table for the bastard Lycheas,' Ulath said bleakly, testing the edge of his axe with his thumb. 'I don't think he's going to have much of an appetite.'

Chapter 3

Kurik woke Sparhawk early the following morning and helped him into his formal black armour. Then, carrying his sword-belt and plumed helmet, Sparhawk went to Vanion's study to await the dawn and the arrival of the others. This was the day. He had striven towards this day for a half a year and more. Today he would look full into the eyes of his queen, salute her and swear his oath of fealty. A terrible impatience welled up in him. He wanted to get on with it, and he swore at the sluggard sun for its leisurely rising. 'And then, Annias,' he almost purred, 'you and Martel are going to become no more than footnotes to history.'

'Did you get hit on the head when you had that fight with Ghwerig?' It was Kalten, who was also wearing his formal black armour and who entered with his helmet under his arm.

'Not really,' Sparhawk replied, 'why?'

'You're talking to yourself. Most people don't do that, you know.'

'You're wrong, Kalten. Almost everybody does it. Most of the time, though, it involves rewriting past conversations – or planning ones yet to come.'

'Which were you doing just now?'

'Neither. I was sort of warning Annias and Martel what to expect.'

'They couldn't hear you, you know.'

'Maybe not, but giving them some kind of warning is the knightly thing to do. At least *I'll* know I said it – even if they don't.'

'I don't think I'll bother with that when I go after Adus,' Kalten grinned. 'Do you have any idea of how long it would take to pound a thought into Adus? Oh, who gets to kill Krager, by the way?'

'Let's give him to somebody who does something nice for us.'

'Sounds fair.' Kalten paused, and his face grew serious. 'Is it going to work, Sparhawk? Will Bhelliom *really* cure Ehlana – or have we just been fooling ourselves?'

'I think it's going to work. We have to believe that it will. Bhelliom's very, very powerful.'

'Have you ever used it at all?'

'Once. I collapsed a ridge-line in the mountains of Thalesia with it.'

'Why?'

'It needed to be done. Don't think about Bhelliom, Kalten. It's very dangerous to do that.'

Kalten looked sceptical. 'Are you going to let Ulath shorten Lycheas a bit when we get to the palace? Ulath really enjoys doing that to people – or I could hang the bastard, if you'd prefer.'

'I don't know,' Sparhawk said. 'Maybe we should wait and let Ehlana make the decision.'

'Why bother her with it? She's probably going to be a little weak after all this, and as her champion, you really ought to try to spare her any exertion.' Kalten squinted at Sparhawk. 'Don't take this wrong,' he said, 'but Ehlana *is* a woman, after all, and women are notoriously tender-hearted. If we leave it up to her, she may not let us kill him at all. I'd rather have him safely dead before she wakes up. We'll apologize to her, of course, but it's very hard to un-kill somebody, no matter how sorry you are.'

'You're a barbarian, Kalten.'

'Me? Oh, by the way, Vanion's got our brothers putting on their armour. We should all be ready by the time the sun's up and the people in the city open the gates.' Kalten frowned. 'That might present a problem, though. There'll be church soldiers at the gates, and they may try to slam them shut in our faces when they see us coming.'

'That's what battering rams are for,' Sparhawk shrugged.

'The queen might get a little cross with you if she finds out that you've been knocking down the gates of her capital city.'

'We'll make the church soldiers repair them.'

'It's honest work right enough, and that's something church soldiers know very little about. I'd suggest you take a hard look at that stretch of cobblestones outside our gate before you make any final decisions, though. Church soldiers aren't very handy with tools.' The big blond man sank into a chair, his armour creaking. 'It's taken us a long time, Sparhawk, but it's almost over now, isn't it?'

'Very nearly,' Sparhawk agreed, 'and once Ehlana's well again, we can go looking for Martel.'

Kalten's eyes brightened. 'And Annias,' he added. 'I think we should hang him from the arch of the main gate of Chyrellos.'

'He's a Church Primate, Kalten,' Sparhawk said in a pained voice. 'You can't do that to him.'

'We can apologize to him later.'

'How exactly do you propose to do that?'

'I'll work something out,' Kalten replied in an offhand manner. 'Maybe we could call it a mistake or something.'

The sun had risen by the time they gathered in the courtyard. Vanion, looking pale and drawn, struggled down the stairs with a large case. 'The swords,' he explained tersely to Sparhawk. 'Sephrenia says we'll need them when we get to the throne-room.'

'Can't somebody else carry them for you?' Kalten asked him.

'No. They're my burden. As soon as Sephrenia comes down, we'll get started.'

The small Styric woman seemed very calm, even remote, when she emerged from the chapterhouse with Sir Gared's sword in her hands and with Talen close behind her.

'Are you all right?' Sparhawk asked her.

'I've been preparing myself for the ritual in the throne-room,' she replied.

'There might be some fighting,' Kurik said. 'Is it really a good idea for us to bring Talen along with us?'

'I can protect him,' she said, 'and his presence is necessary. There are reasons, but I don't think you'd understand them.'

'Let's mount up and go,' Vanion said.

There was a great deal of clinking as the hundred black-armoured Pandion Knights climbed into their saddles. Sparhawk took his customary place at Vanion's side with Kalten, Bevier, Tynian and Ulath close behind them and the column of Pandions strung out to the rear. They crossed the drawbridge at a trot and bore down on the startled group of church soldiers outside the gate. At a curt signal from Vanion, a score of Pandions swung out from the column and encircled the so-called workmen. 'Hold them here until the rest of us take the city gates,' Vanion instructed. 'Then bring them into the city and rejoin us.'

'Yes, My Lord,' Sir Perraine replied.

'All right, gentlemen,' Vanion said then, 'I think a gallop is in order at this point. Let's not give the soldiers in the city too much time to prepare for our arrival.'

They thundered across the rather short distance between the chapterhouse and the east gate of Cimmura. Despite Kalten's concern about the possibility of the gates being closed to them, the soldiers there were too surprised to react in time.

'Sir Knights!' an officer protested shrilly. 'You can't

68

enter the city without the Prince Regent's authorization!'

'With your permission, Lord Vanion?' Tynian asked politely.

'Of course, Sir Tynian,' Vanion consented. 'We have pressing matters to attend to, and we don't really have time for idle chit-chat here.'

Tynian moved his horse forward. The knight from Deira was deceptively moon-faced. He had the sort of countenance one would normally associate with good humour and a generally happy approach to life. His armour, however, concealed a massively-developed upper torso and powerful arms and shoulders. He drew his sword. 'My friend,' he said pleasantly to the officer, 'would you be so good as to step aside so that we may proceed? I'm sure none of us wants any unpleasantness here.' His tone was civil, almost conversational.

Many of the church soldiers, long accustomed to having things their own way in Cimmura, were not really prepared to have anyone question their authority. It was the officer's misfortune to be one of those soldiers. 'I must forbid your entry into the city without specific authorization from the Prince Regent,' he declared stubbornly.

'That's your final word then?' Tynian asked in a regretful tone.

'It is.'

'It's your decision, friend,' Tynian said. Then he raised up in his stirrups and swung a vast overhand blow with his sword.

Since the officer could not believe that anyone would actually defy him, he made no move to protect himself. His expression was one of amazement as Tynian's heavy, broad-bladed sword struck the angle between his neck and shoulder and sheared diagonally down into his body. Blood fountained up from the dreadful wound, and the suddenly limp body hung from Tynian's sword, held there by the crushed-in edges of the great rent in the officer's steel breastplate. Tynian leaned back in his saddle, removed his foot from his stirrup and kicked the body off his sword-blade. 'I *did* ask him to move out of our way, Lord Vanion,' he explained. 'Since he chose not to, what just happened is entirely his responsibility, wouldn't you say?'

'It was indeed, Sir Tynian,' Vanion agreed. 'I see no blame accruing to you in this matter. You were the very soul of courtesy.'

'Let's proceed then,' Ulath said. He slipped his war-axe from its sling at the side of his saddle. 'All right,' he said to the wide-eyed church soldiers, 'who's next?'

The soldiers fled.

The knights who had been guarding the workmen came up at a trot, herding their prisoners ahead of them. Vanion left ten of them to hold the gates, and the column moved on into the city. The citizens of Cimmura were fully aware of the situation at the palace, and when they saw a column of bleak-faced Pandion Knights in their ominous black armour riding through the cobbled streets, they knew immediately that a confrontation was imminent. Doors slammed up and down the street, and shutters were hastily closed from the inside.

The knights rode on through now-deserted streets.

There was a sudden spiteful buzz from behind them, and a heavy clang. Sparhawk half-wheeled Faran.

'You really ought to watch your back, Sparhawk,' Kalten told him. 'That was a crossbow bolt, and it would have taken you right between the shoulder-blades. You owe me what it's going to cost me to have my shield re-enamelled.'

'I owe you more than that, Kalten,' Sparhawk said gratefully.

'Strange,' Tynian said. 'The crossbow's a Lamork weapon. Not many church soldiers carry them.'

'Maybe it was something personal,' Ulath grunted. 'Have you offended any Lamorks lately, Sparhawk?'

'Not that I know of.'

'There won't be much point in extended conversation when we get to the palace,' Vanion said. 'I'll order the soldiers to throw down their arms when we arrive.'

'Do you think they'll do it?' Kalten asked.

Vanion grinned mirthlessly. 'Probably not – at least not without several object lessons. When we get there, Sparhawk, I want you to take your friends here and secure the door to the palace. I don't think we'll want to chase church soldiers up and down the halls.'

'Right,' Sparhawk agreed.

The church soldiers, warned by the men who had fled from the city gates, had formed up in the palace courtyard, and the largely ornamental palace gates were closed.

'Bring up the ram,' Vanion called.

A dozen Pandions rode forward with a heavy log carried in rope slings attached to their saddles. It took them perhaps five minutes to batter down the gates, and then the Church Knights streamed into the courtyard.

'Throw down your weapons!' Vanion shouted to the confused soldiers in the yard.

Sparhawk led his friends around the perimeter of the courtyard to the large doors that gave entry into the palace. There they dismounted and climbed the stairs to confront the dozen soldiers on guard in front of the door. The officer in charge drew his sword. 'No one may enter!' he barked.

'Get out of my way, neighbour,' Sparhawk said in his deadly quiet voice.

'I don't take orders from –' the officer began. Then his eyes glazed as there was a sudden sound like that a melon might make when dropped on a stone floor as Kurik deftly brained him with his spiked chain mace. The officer dropped, twitching.

'That's something new,' Sir Tynian said to Sir Ulath. 'I never saw a man with brains coming out of his ears before.'

'Kurik's very good with that mace,' Ulath agreed.

'Any questions?' Sparhawk asked the other soldiers ominously.

They stared at him.

'I believe you were told to drop your weapons,' Kalten told them.

They hurriedly shed their arms.

'We're relieving you here, neighbours,' Sparhawk informed them. 'You may join your friends out there in the yard.'

They quickly went down the stairs.

The mounted Pandions were slowly advancing on the church soldiers standing in the courtyard. There was some sporadic resistance from the more fanatic of the soldiers, and the Pandion Knights provided a sizeable number of those 'object lessons' their Preceptor had mentioned. The centre of the courtyard soon flowed with blood, and it was littered with unattached heads, arms and a few legs. More and more of the soldiers saw the direction the fight was going, threw away their weapons and raised their hands in surrender. There was one stubborn pocket of resistance, but the knights pushed the struggling soldiers up against one wall and slaughtered them.

Vanion looked around the yard. 'Herd the survivors into the stables,' he ordered, 'and post a few guards.' Then he dismounted and walked back to the shattered gate. 'It's all over now, little mother,' he called to Sephrenia, who had waited outside with Talen and Berit. 'It's safe to come in now.'

72

Sephrenia rode her white palfrey into the courtyard, shielding her eyes with one hand. Talen, however, looked around with bright vicious eyes.

'Let's get rid of this,' Ulath said to Kurik, bending to pick up the shoulders of the dead officer. The two of them carried the body off to one side, and Tynian thoughtfully scraped the puddle of brains off the top step with one foot.

'Do you people always chop your enemies to pieces like this?' Talen asked Sparhawk as he dismounted and went over to help Sephrenia down from her horse.

Sparhawk shrugged. 'Vanion wanted the soldiers to see what would happen to them if they offered any more resistance. Dismemberment is usually quite convincing.'

'*Must* you?' Sephrenia shuddered.

'You'd better let us go in first, little mother,' Sparhawk said as Vanion joined them with twenty knights. 'There may be soldiers hiding in there.'

As it turned out, there were a few, but Vanion's knights efficiently flushed them from their hiding places and took them to the main door and gave them pointed instructions to join their comrades in the stables.

The doors to the council chamber were unguarded, and Sparhawk opened the door and held it for Vanion.

Lycheas was cowering, slack-lipped and trembling behind the council table with the fat man in red, and Baron Harparin was desperately yanking on one of the bell-pulls. 'You can't come in here!' Harparin said shrilly to Vanion in his high-pitched, effeminate voice. 'I command you to leave at once on the authority of King Lycheas.'

Vanion looked at him coldly. Sparhawk knew that Vanion bore a towering contempt for the disgusting pederast. 'This man irritates me,' he said in a flat voice, pointing at Harparin. 'Will someone please do something about him?'

Ulath strode around the table, his war-axe in his hands.

'You wouldn't dare!' Harparin squealed, cringing back and still yanking futilely at the bell-pull. 'I'm a member of the royal council. You wouldn't dare do anything to me.'

Ulath did, in fact, dare. Harparin's head bounced once and then rolled across the carpet to come to rest near the window. His mouth was agape, and his eyes were still bulging in horror. 'Was that more or less what you had in mind, Lord Vanion?' the big Thalesian asked politely.

'Approximately, yes. Thank you, Sir Ulath.'

'How about these other two?' Ulath pointed his axe at Lycheas and the fat man.

'Ah – not just yet, Sir Ulath.' The Pandion Preceptor approached the council table carrying the case containing the swords of the knights who had fallen. 'Now, Lycheas, where is the Earl of Lenda?' he demanded.

Lycheas gaped at him.

'Sir Ulath,' Vanion said in a tone like ice.

Ulath grimly lifted his blood-stained axe.

'No!' Lycheas screamed. 'Lenda's confined down in the cellars. We didn't hurt him at all, Lord Vanion. I swear to you that he's –'

'Take Lycheas and this other one down to the dungeon,' Vanion ordered a pair of his knights. 'Release the Earl of Lenda and replace him in the cell with these. Then bring Lenda here.'

'If I may, My Lord?' Sparhawk asked.

'Of course.'

'Lycheas the bastard,' Sparhawk said formally, 'as Queen's Champion, it is my distinct pleasure to place you under arrest on the charge of high treason. The penalty is rather well known. We'll attend to that just as soon as it's convenient. Thinking about it might give

74

you something to occupy the long, tedious hours of your confinement.'

'I could save you a great deal of time and expense, Sparhawk,' Ulath offered helpfully, hefting his axe again.

Sparhawk pretended to consider it. 'No,' he said regretfully. 'Lycheas has run rough-shod over the people of Cimmura. I think they're entitled to the spectacle of a nice, messy public execution.'

Lycheas was actually blubbering in terror as Sir Perraine and another knight dragged him past the wide-eyed head of Baron Harparin and out of the room.

'You're a hard and ruthless man, Sparhawk,' Bevier noted.

'I know.' Sparhawk looked at Vanion. 'We'll have to wait for Lenda,' he said. 'He's got the key to the throne-room. I don't want Ehlana to wake up and find that we've chopped her door down.'

Vanion nodded. 'I need him for something anyway,' he said. He put the sword case on the council table and sat down in one of the chairs. 'Oh, by the way,' he said, 'cover Harparin up before Sephrenia gets here. Things like that distress her.' It was yet another clue, Sparhawk thought. Vanion's concern for Sephrenia went far beyond what was customary.

Ulath went to the window, jerked down one of the drapes and turned back, pausing only to kick Harparin's head back over beside the pederast's body, then he covered the remains with the drape.

'A whole generation of little boys will sleep more securely now that Harparin's no longer with us,' Kalten observed lightly, 'and they'll probably mention Ulath in their prayers every night.'

'I'll take all the blessings I can get,' Ulath shrugged.

Sephrenia entered with Talen and Berit in tow. She looked around. 'I'm pleasantly surprised,' she noted. 'I was more or less expecting additional carnage.' Then her eyes narrowed. She pointed at the draped body lying by the wall. 'What's that?' she demanded.

'The late Baron Harparin,' Kalten told her. 'He left us rather suddenly.'

'Did you do that, Sparhawk?' she accused.

'Me?'

'I know you all too well, Sparhawk.'

'Actually, Sephrenia, it was me,' Ulath drawled. 'I'm very sorry if it bothers you, but then, I'm Thalesian. We're widely reputed to be barbarians.' He shrugged. 'One is more or less obliged to uphold the reputation of his homeland, wouldn't you say?'

She refused to answer that. She looked around at the faces of the other Pandions in the room. 'Good,' she said. 'We're all here. Open that case, Vanion.'

Vanion opened the sword-case.

'Sir Knights,' Sephrenia addressed the Pandions in the room as she laid Sir Gared's sword on the table beside the case. 'Some months ago, twelve of you joined with me in casting the enchantment which has sustained the life of Queen Ehlana. Six of your brave companions have gone into the House of the Dead since then. Their swords, however, must be present when we undo the enchantment that we may cure the queen. Thus, each of you who were there must carry the sword of one of your fallen brothers as well as your own. I will work the spell which will make it possible for you to take up those swords. We will then proceed to the throne-room, where the swords of the fallen will be taken from you.'

Vanion looked startled. 'Taken? By whom?'

'Their original owners.'

'You're going to summon ghosts into the throne-room?' he asked in astonishment.

'They will come unsummoned. Their oaths ensure that. As before, you'll encircle the throne with your swords extended. I'll undo the spell, and the crystal will disappear. The rest is up to Sparhawk – and Bhelliom.'

'What exactly am I supposed to do?' Sparhawk asked her.

'I'll tell you at the proper time,' she replied. 'I don't want you to do anything prematurely.'

Sir Perraine escorted the aged Earl of Lenda into the council chamber.

'How was the dungeon, My Lord of Lenda?' Vanion asked lightly.

'Damp, Lord Vanion,' Lenda replied, 'Also dark and very smelly. You know how dungeons are.'

'No,' Vanion laughed. 'Not really. It's an experience I'd prefer to forgo.' He looked at the old courtier's lined face. 'Are you all right, Lenda?' he asked. 'You look very tired.'

'Old men always look very tired, Vanion.' Lenda smiled gently, 'and I'm older than most.' He straightened his thin old shoulders. 'Being thrown into the dungeon from time to time is an occupational hazard for those in public service. You get used to it. I've been in worse.'

'I'm sure Lycheas and that fat fellow will enjoy the dungeon, My Lord,' Kalten said lightly.

'I doubt that, Sir Kalten.'

'We've made them aware of the fact that the end of their confinement will mark their entrance into another world. I'm sure they'll prefer the dungeon. Rats aren't all *that* bad.'

'I didn't notice Baron Harparin,' Lenda said. 'Did he escape?'

'Only in a manner of speaking, My Lord,' Kalten

replied. 'He was being offensive. You know how Harparin was. Sir Ulath gave him a lesson in courtesy – with his axe.'

'This day is top-filled with joyful surprises then,' Lenda chortled.

'My Lord of Lenda,' Vanion said rather formally, 'we're going to the throne-room now to restore the queen. I'd like to have you witness that restoration so that you can confirm her identity in case any doubts arise later. The commons are superstitious, and there are those who might want to circulate rumours to the effect that Ehlana is not who she appears to be.'

'Very well, My Lord Vanion,' Lenda agreed, 'but how do you plan to restore her?'

'You'll see,' Sephrenia smiled. She held out her hands over the swords and spoke at some length in Styric. The swords glowed briefly as she released the spell, and the knights who had been present during the encasement of the Queen of Elenia stepped to the table. She talked to them briefly in low tones, and then each of them took up one of the swords. 'Very well,' she said, 'let us proceed to the throne-room.'

'This is all very mysterious,' Lenda said to Sparhawk as they walked down the corridor towards the throne-room.

'Have you ever seen real magic performed, My Lord?' Sparhawk asked him.

'I don't believe in magic, Sparhawk.'

'That may change shortly, Lenda,' Sparhawk smiled.

The old courtier produced the key from an inside pocket and unlocked the door to the throne-room. Then they all followed Sephrenia inside. The room was dark. During Lenda's confinement, the candles had been allowed to go out. Sparhawk, nonetheless, could still hear the measured drumbeat of his queen's heart echoing in the darkness.

78

Kurik stepped back outside and brought in a torch. 'Fresh candles?' he asked Sephrenia.

'Definitely,' she replied. 'Let's not awaken Ehlana to a dark room.'

Kurik and Berit replaced the burned-out candle-stubs with fresh tapers. Then Berit looked curiously at the young queen he had served so faithfully without ever having seen her. His eyes grew suddenly wide as he stared at her, and he seemed to catch his breath. His look was one of totally appropriate veneration, but there was, Sparhawk thought, perhaps a bit more to it than simple respect. Berit was about the same age as Ehlana, and she *was* very beautiful, after all.

'That's much better,' Sephrenia said, looking around at the candlelit throne-room. 'Sparhawk, come with me.' She led him to the dais upon which the throne stood.

Ehlana sat as she had for all these months. She wore the crown of Elenia on her pale, blonde head, and she was enfolded in her state robes. Her eyes were closed, and her face serene.

'Just a few more moments, my queen,' Sparhawk murmured. Strangely, his eyes were filled with tears, and his heart was in his throat.

'Remove your gauntlets, Sparhawk,' Sephrenia told him. 'You'll want the rings to touch Bhelliom when you use it.'

He took off his mailed gauntlets, then reached inside his surcoat, removed the canvas pouch and untied the drawstring.

'All right, gentlemen,' Sephrenia said then to the surviving knights, 'take your places.'

Vanion and the other five Pandions spaced themselves out around the throne, each of them holding his own sword and that of one of his fallen brothers.

Sephrenia stood beside Sparhawk and began to form the

incantation in Styric, her fingers weaving an accompaniment. The candles dimmed and flared almost in time to the sonorous spell. At some time during her incantation, the room became gradually filled with that familiar smell of death. Sparhawk tore his eyes from Ehlana's face to risk a quick look around the circle of knights. Where there had been six before, there were now twelve. The filmy shapes of those who had fallen one by one in the preceding months had returned unbidden to take their swords one last time.

'Now, Sir Knights,' Sephrenia instructed the living and the dead alike, 'point your swords at the throne.' And she began to speak a different incantation. The tip of each sword began to glow, and those incandescent points of light grew brighter and brighter until they surrounded the throne with a ring of pure light. Sephrenia raised her arm, spoke a single word, then brought the arm sharply down. The crystal encasement surrounding the throne wavered like water, and then it was gone.

Ehlana's head sagged forward, and her body began to tremble violently. Her breathing was suddenly laboured, and the heart-beat which still echoed through the room faltered. Sparhawk leaped up onto the dais to go to her aid.

'Not yet!' Sephrenia told him sharply.

'But –'

'Do as I say!'

He stood helplessly over his stricken queen for a minute that seemed to last for an hour. Then Sephrenia stepped forward and lifted Ehlana's chin with both her hands. The queen's grey eyes were wide and vacant, and her face was twisted grotesquely.

'Now, Sparhawk,' Sephrenia said, 'take Bhelliom in your hands and touch it to her heart. Be sure the rings are touching the stone. At the same time, command it to heal her.'

He seized the Sapphire Rose in both hands, and then he gently touched the flower gem to Ehlana's breast. 'Heal my queen, Bhelliom-Blue-Rose!' he commanded in a loud voice.

The enormous surge of power coming from the jewel between his hands sent Sparhawk to his knees. The candles flickered and dimmed as if some dark shadow had passed over the room. Was it something fleeing? Or was it perhaps that shadow of dread that followed him and haunted all his dreams? Ehlana stiffened, and her slender body was slammed against the back of her throne. A hoarse gasp came from her throat. Then her wide-eyed stare was suddenly rational, and she gazed at Sparhawk in astonishment.

'It is done!' Sephrenia said in a trembling voice, and then she slumped weakly down on the dais.

Ehlana drew in a deep, shuddering breath. 'My Knight!' she cried out feebly, extending her arms to the black-armoured Pandion kneeling before her. Though her voice was weak, it nonetheless was full and rich, a woman's voice now and not the childish one Sparhawk remembered. 'Oh, my Sparhawk, you have come back to me at last.' She laid her trembling arms about his armoured shoulders, inserted her face beneath his raised visor and kissed him lingeringly.

'Enough of that for now, children,' Sephrenia told them. 'Sparhawk, carry her to her chambers.'

Sparhawk was very disturbed. Ehlana's kiss had been anything but childlike. He tucked Bhelliom away, removed his helmet and tossed it to Kalten. Then he gently picked up his queen. She put her pale arms about his shoulders and her cheek to his. 'O, I have found thee,' she breathed, 'and I love thee, and I will not let thee go.'

Sparhawk recognized the passage she was quoting, and it seemed wildly inappropriate. He grew even more troubled. There was obviously a serious mistake here somewhere.

Chapter 4

Ehlana was going to be a problem, Sparhawk decided as he removed his armour not long after he had presented himself to his queen the following morning. Though she had never been far from his thoughts during his exile, he found that he had to make a number of difficult adjustments. When he had left, their relative positions had been clearly defined. He was the adult; she was the child. That had changed now, and they were both treading the unfamiliar ground of the monarch and subject relationship. He had been told by Kurik and others that the girl he had raised almost from babyhood had shown remarkable mettle during the few months before Annias had poisoned her. Hearing about it was one thing; experiencing it was another. This is not to say that Ehlana was ever harsh or peremptory with him, for she was not. She felt, he thought – and hoped – a genuine affection for him, and she did not give him direct commands so much as give the impression that she *expected* him to accede to her wishes. They were functioning in a grey area, and there were all sorts of opportunities for serious missteps on either side.

Some recent incidents were perfect examples of that sort of thing. In the first place, her request that he sleep in a chamber adjoining hers was, he felt, highly inappropriate, even slightly scandalous. When he had tried to point that out, however, she had laughed at his fears. His armour, he reasoned, had provided some small defence against wagging tongues. Times were troubled, after all, and the Queen of Elenia needed protection. As her champion, Sparhawk had the obligation, the right even, to stand guard over her. When he had presented himself to her that morning once again in full armour, however, she had wrinkled her nose and suggested that he change clothes immediately. He knew that was a serious mistake. The Queen's Champion in armour was one thing, and no one with a reasonable regard for his own health would be likely to make an issue of Sparhawk's proximity to the royal person. If he were dressed in doublet and hose, though, that would be quite another thing. The servants were bound to talk, and the gossip of palace servants had a way of spreading throughout the city.

Sparhawk looked dubiously into the mirror. His doublet was silver-trimmed black velvet, and his hose were grey. The clothing bore some faint resemblance to a uniform, and the black half-boots he had chosen had a more military appearance than the pointed shoes currently in fashion at court. He rejected the slender rapier out of hand and belted on his heavy broadsword instead. The effect was slightly ludicrous, but the presence of the heavier weapon quite clearly stated that Sparhawk was in the queen's apartments on business.

'That's absolutely absurd, Sparhawk,' Ehlana laughed when he returned to the sitting-room where she lay prettily propped up by pillows on a divan and with a blue satin coverlet across her knees.

'My Queen?' he said coolly.

'The broadsword, Sparhawk. It's completely out of place with those clothes. Please take it off at once and wear the rapier I ordered to be provided for you.'

'If my appearance offends you, Your Majesty, I'll withdraw. The sword, however, stays where it is. I can't protect you with a knitting needle.'

Her grey eyes flashed. 'You –' she began hotly.

'*My* decision, Ehlana,' he cut across her objections.

84

'Your safety is my responsibility, and the steps I take to insure it are not open to discussion.'

They exchanged a long, hard stare. This would not be the last time their wills would clash, Sparhawk was sure.

Ehlana's eyes softened. 'So stern and unbending, my champion,' she said.

'Where Your Majesty's safety is concerned, yes.' He said it flatly. It was probably best to get that clearly understood right at the outset.

'But why are we arguing, my knight?' She smiled whimsically, fluttering her eyelashes at him.

'Don't do that, Ehlana,' he told her, automatically assuming the tutorial manner he had used when she was a little girl. 'You're the queen, not some coy chambermaid trying to get her own way. Don't ask or try to be charming. Command.'

'Would you take off the sword if I commanded you to, Sparhawk?'

'No, but the usual rules don't apply to me.'

'Who decided that?'

'I did. We can send for the Earl of Lenda if you'd like. He's well versed in the law, and he can give us his opinion on the matter.'

'But if he decides against you, you'll ignore him, won't you?'

'Yes.'

'That's not fair, Sparhawk.'

'I'm not trying to be fair, My Queen.'

'Sparhawk, when we're alone like this, do you suppose we could dispense with the "Your Majestys" and "My Queens"? I do have a name, after all, and you weren't afraid to use it when I was a child.'

'As you wish,' he shrugged.

'Say it, Sparhawk. Say Ehlana. It's not a hard name, and I'm sure you won't choke on it.'

He smiled. 'All right, Ehlana,' he gave up. After her defeat on the issue of the sword, she needed a victory of some kind to restore her dignity.

'You're so much more handsome when you smile, my champion. You should try it more often.' She leaned back on her pillows, her face thoughtful. Her pale blonde hair had been carefully combed that morning, and she wore a few modest but quite expensive pieces of jewellery. Her cheeks were prettily rosy, which was in quite some contrast to her very fair skin. 'What did you do in Rendor after the idiot Aldreas sent you into exile?'

'That's hardly the proper way to speak of your father, Ehlana.'

'He wasn't much of a father, Sparhawk, and his intellect wasn't exactly what you'd call towering. The efforts he expended entertaining his sister must have softened his brains.'

'Ehlana!'

'Don't be such a prude, Sparhawk. The whole palace knew about it – the whole city, probably.'

Sparhawk decided that it was time to find a husband for his queen. 'How did you find out so much about Princess Arissa?' he asked her. 'She was sent to that cloister near Demos before you were born.'

'Gossip lingers, Sparhawk, and Arissa was hardly what you'd call discreet.'

Sparhawk cast about for a way to change the subject. Although Ehlana *seemed* to be aware of the basic implications of what she was saying, he could not bring himself to give credence to the notion that she could be so worldly. Some part of his mind stubbornly clung to the notion that beneath her evident maturity, she was still the same innocent child he had left ten years before. 'Hold out your left hand,' he told her. 'I have something for you.' The tone of their relationship was still indistinct. They both felt that keenly, and it made them uncomfortable. Sparhawk swung back and forth between a stiffly correct formality and an abrupt, almost military manner of command. Ehlana seemed to fluctuate, at one moment the coltish, knobbly-kneed girl he had trained and moulded, and in the next a full-fledged queen. At a somewhat deeper level, they were both extremely aware of the changes a short decade had brought to Ehlana. The process known as 'filling out' had done some very significant things to the Queen of Elenia. Since Sparhawk had not been present to grow gradually accustomed to them, they were thrust upon his awareness in full flower. He tried as best he could to avoid looking at her without giving offence. For her part, Ehlana seemed quite self-conscious about her recently-acquired attributes. She seemed to waver between a desire to show them off – even to flaunt them – and an embarrassed wish to conceal them behind anything that lay at hand. It was a difficult time for them both.

At this point something should be clarified in Sparhawk's defence. Ehlana's almost overpowering femininity, coupled with her queenly manner and disconcerting candour had distracted him, and the rings looked so much alike that he should be forgiven for taking his own off by mistake. He slipped it on her finger without giving any thought to the implications.

Despite the similarity of the two rings, there were a few minuscule differences, and women are notoriously adept at recognizing such tiny variations. Ehlana gave the ruby ring he had just placed on her finger what appeared to be no more than a cursory glance, then with a squeal of delight, she threw her arms about his neck, nearly pulling him off-balance in the process, and glued her lips to his.

It is unfortunate, perhaps, that Vanion and the Earl of Lenda chose that moment to enter the room. The old earl coughed politely, and Sparhawk, flushing to the roots of his hair, gently but firmly disengaged the queen's arms from about his neck.

The Earl of Lenda was smiling knowingly, and one of Vanion's eyebrows was curiously raised. 'Sorry to interrupt, My Queen,' Lenda said diplomatically, 'but since your recovery appears to be progressing so well, Lord Vanion and I thought it might be a suitable time to bring you up to date on certain matters of state.'

'Of course, Lenda,' she replied, brushing aside the implied question of just exactly what she and Sparhawk had been doing when the pair had entered the room.

'There are some friends outside, Your Majesty,' Vanion said. 'They will be able to brief you on some events in greater detail than the earl and I would be able to.'

'Then show them in, by all means.'

Sparhawk stepped to a sideboard and poured himself a glass of water; his mouth was very dry for some reason.

Vanion went outside for a moment and returned with Sparhawk's friends. 'I believe you know Sephrenia, Kurik and Sir Kalten, Your Majesty,' he said. He then introduced the others, judiciously omitting references to Talen's professional activities.

'I'm so pleased to meet you all,' Ehlana said graciously. 'Now, before we begin, I have an announcement to make. Sir Sparhawk here has just proposed marriage to me. Wasn't that nice of him?'

Sparhawk had the glass to his lips at that point, and he went into an extended fit of choking.

'Why, whatever is the matter, dear?' Ehlana asked innocently.

He pointed at his throat, making strangling noises.

When Sparhawk had somewhat regained his breath and a few shreds of his composure, the Earl of Lenda looked at his queen. 'I gather then that Your Majesty has accepted your champion's proposal?'

'Of course I have. That's what I was doing when you came in.'

'Oh,' the old man said. 'I see.' Lenda was a consummate politician, and he was able to make statements like that without cracking a smile.

'Congratulations, My Lord,' Kurik said gruffly, seizing Sparhawk's hand in a grip of iron and shaking it vigorously.

Kalten was staring at Ehlana. '*Sparhawk?*' he demanded incredulously.

'Isn't it odd how your closest friends never fully understand your greatness, my dear?' she said to Sparhawk. 'Sir Kalten,' she said then, 'your boyhood friend is the paramount knight in the world. Any woman would be honoured to have him as her husband.' She smiled smugly. 'I'm the one who *got* him, however. All right, friends, please be seated and tell me what's been happening to my kingdom while I've been ill. I trust you'll be brief. My betrothed and I have many plans to make.'

Vanion had remained standing. He looked around at the others. 'If I leave out anything important, don't hesitate to step in and correct me,' he said. He looked up at the ceiling. 'Where to begin?' he mused.

'You might start by telling me what it was that made me so ill, Lord Vanion,' Ehlana suggested.

'You were poisoned, Your Majesty.'

'*What?*'

'A very rare poison from Rendor – the same one that killed your father.'

'Who was responsible?'

'In your father's case, it was his sister. In yours, it was the Primate Annias. You knew that he's had his eyes on the throne of the Archprelate in Chyrellos, didn't you?'

'Of course. I was doing what I could to stand in his way. If he reaches that throne, I think I'll convert to Eshandism

89

– or maybe even become Styric. Would your God accept me, Sephrenia?'

'Goddess, Your Majesty,' Sephrenia corrected. 'I serve a Goddess.'

'What an extraordinarily practical notion. Would I have to cut off my hair and sacrifice a few Elene children to her?'

'Don't be absurd, Ehlana.'

'I'm only teasing, Sephrenia,' Ehlana laughed, 'but isn't that what the Elene commons say about Styrics? How did you find out about the poisonings, Lord Vanion?'

Vanion quickly described Sparhawk's meeting with the ghost of King Aldreas and the recovery of the ring which now – mistakenly – decorated the champion's hand. He then moved on, covering the *de facto* rule of Annias and the elevation of the queen's cousin to the Prince Regency.

'Lycheas?' she exclaimed at that point. 'Ridiculous. He can't even dress himself.' She frowned. 'If I was poisoned and it was the same poison that killed my father, how is it that I'm still alive?'

'We used magic to sustain you, Queen Ehlana,' Sephrenia told her.

Vanion then spoke of Sparhawk's return from Rendor and their growing conviction that Annias had poisoned her primarily to gain access to her treasury in order to finance his campaign for the Archprelacy.

Sparhawk took up the story at that point and told the young lady who had so recently netted him of the trip of the group of Church Knights and their companions to Chyrellos, then to Borrata and finally on down into Rendor.

'Who is Flute?' Ehlana interrupted him at one point.

'A Styric foundling,' he replied. 'At least we *thought* she was. She seemed to be about six years old, but she turned out to be much, much older than that.' He continued his account, describing the trek across Rendor and the meeting with the physician in Dabour who had finally told them that only magic could save the stricken queen. He then went on to tell her of the meeting with Martel.

'I never liked him,' she declared, making a face.

'He's working for Annias now,' Sparhawk told her, 'and he was in Rendor at the same time we were. There was a crazy old religious fanatic down there – Arasham – and he was the spiritual leader of the kingdom. Martel was trying to persuade him to invade the western Elene kingdoms as a diversion to give Annias a free hand during the election of the new Archprelate. Sephrenia and I went to Arasham's tent, and Martel was there.'

'Did you kill him?' Ehlana asked fiercely.

Sparhawk blinked. This was a side of her he had never seen. 'The time wasn't exactly right, My Queen,' he apologized. 'I came up with a subterfuge instead and persuaded Arasham not to invade until he received word from me. Martel was furious, but he couldn't do anything about it. He and I had a nice chat later, and he told me that he was the one who had found the poison and passed it on to Annias.'

'Would that stand up in a court of law, My Lord?' Ehlana asked the Earl of Lenda.

'It would depend on the judge, Your Majesty,' he replied.

'We have nothing to worry about on that score, Lenda,' she said grimly, 'because *I'm* going to be the judge – also the jury.'

'Most irregular, Your Majesty,' he murmured.

'So was what they did to my father and me. Go on with the story, Sparhawk.'

'We returned here to Cimmura and went to the chapter-house. That's where I received the summons to go to the royal crypt under the cathedral to meet with your father's ghost. He told me a number of things – first that it was your aunt who had poisoned him and that it was Annias who'd poisoned you. He also told me that Lycheas was the result of certain intimacies between Annias and Arissa.'

'Thank God!' Ehlana exclaimed. 'I was half-afraid that he was my father's bastard. It's bad enough to have to admit that he's my cousin, but a brother? Unthinkable.'

'Your father's ghost also told me that the only thing that could save your life was the Bhelliom.'

'What's the Bhelliom?'

Sparhawk reached inside his doublet and drew out the canvas pouch. He opened it and drew out the Sapphire Rose. 'This is Bhelliom, Your Majesty,' he told her. Once again he felt more than saw that annoying flicker of darkness at the very edge of his vision. He shook off the feeling as he held out the jewel.

'How exquisite!' she cried, reaching out for it.

'No!' Sephrenia said sharply. 'Don't touch it, Ehlana! It could destroy you!'

Ehlana shrank back, her eyes wide. 'But Sparhawk's touching it,' she objected.

'It knows him. It may know you as well, but let's not take any chances. We've all spent too much time and effort on you to waste it at this point.'

Sparhawk tucked the jewel back into its pouch and put it away.

'There's something else you should know, Ehlana,' Sephrenia continued. 'Bhelliom is the most powerful and precious object in the world, and Azash wants it desperately. That's what was behind Otha's invasion of the west five hundred years ago. Otha has Zemochs – and others – here in the west trying to find the jewel. We must deny it to him at any cost.'

'Should we destroy it now?' Sparhawk asked her bleakly. The question cost him a great deal of effort to say for some reason.

'Destroy it?' Ehlana cried, 'but it's so beautiful!'

'It's also evil,' Sephrenia told her. She paused. 'Perhaps evil isn't the right term, though. It has no concept of the difference between good and evil. No, Sparhawk, let's keep it for a while longer until we're certain Ehlana is past any danger of a relapse. Go on with the story. Try to be brief. Your queen is still very weak.'

'I'll cut this short then,' he said. He told his queen of their search of the battlefield at Lake Randera and of how they were finally able to locate Count Ghasek. The queen listened intently, almost seeming to hold her breath as he recounted the events at Lake Venne. He quickly sketched in King Wargun's interference – though he did not use that exact word – and finally described the dreadful encounter in Ghwerig's cave and the revelation of Flute's real identity. 'And that's where things stand now, My Queen,' he concluded. 'King Wargun's battling with the Rendors down in Arcium; Annias is in Chyrellos awaiting the death of Archprelate Cluvonus; and you're back on your throne where you belong.'

'And also newly betrothed,' she reminded him. She was obviously not going to let him forget that. She thought for a moment. 'And what have you done with Lycheas?' she asked intently.

'He's back in the dungeon where he belongs, Your Majesty.'

'And Harparin and that other one?'

'The fat one's in the dungeon with Lycheas. Harparin left us rather suddenly.'

'You let him escape?'

Kalten shook his head. 'No, Your Majesty. He started screaming and trying to order us out of the council

93

chamber. Vanion got bored with all the noise and had Ulath chop off his head.'

'How very appropriate. I want to see Lycheas.'

'Shouldn't you rest?' Sparhawk asked her.

'Not until I have a few words with my cousin.'

'I'll fetch him,' Ulath said. He turned and left the room.

'My Lord of Lenda,' Ehlana said then, 'will you preside over my royal council?'

'As Your Majesty wishes,' Lenda said with a low bow.

'And Lord Vanion, would you also serve – when your other duties permit?'

'I'd be honoured, Your Majesty.'

'As my consort and champion, Sparhawk will also have a seat at the council table – and I think Sephrenia as well.'

'I am Styric, Ehlana,' Sephrenia pointed out. 'Would it be wise to put a Styric on your council, given the feelings of the Elene commons about our race?'

'I'm going to put an end to that nonsense once and for all,' Ehlana said firmly. 'Sparhawk, can you think of anyone else who might be useful on the council?'

He thought about it, and suddenly an idea came to him. 'I know a man who isn't of noble birth, Your Majesty, but he's very clever and he understands a great deal about a side of Cimmura you probably don't even know exists.'

'Who is this man?'

'His name's Platime.'

Talen burst out laughing. 'Have you lost your mind, Sparhawk?' he said. 'You're going to let Platime into the same building with the treasury and the crown jewels?'

Ehlana looked a bit puzzled. 'Is there some problem with this man?' she asked.

'Platime's the biggest thief in Cimmura,' Talen told her. 'I know that for a fact because I used to work for him.

94

He controls every thief and beggar in the city – also the swindlers, cut-throats and whores.'

'Watch your language, young man!' Kurik barked.

'I've heard the term before, Kurik,' Ehlana said calmly. 'I know what it means. Tell me, Sparhawk, what's your reasoning behind this suggestion?'

'As I said, Platime's very clever – in some ways almost brilliant, and, though it's a little odd, he's a patriot. He has a vast understanding of the society of Cimmura, and he has ways of finding information that I can't even guess at. There's nothing that happens in Cimmura – or in most of the rest of the world, for that matter – that he doesn't know about.'

'I'll interview him,' Ehlana promised.

Then Ulath and Sir Perraine dragged Lycheas into the room. Lycheas gaped at his cousin, his mouth open and his eyes bulging in astonishment. 'How –?' he began, then broke off, biting his lip.

'You didn't expect to see me alive, Lycheas?' she asked in a deadly tone.

'I believe it's customary to kneel in the presence of your queen, Lycheas,' Ulath growled, kicking the bastard's feet out from under him. Lycheas crashed to the floor and grovelled there.

The Earl of Lenda cleared his throat. 'Your Majesty,' he said, 'during the time of your illness, Prince Lycheas insisted that he be addressed as "Your Majesty". I'll have to consult the statutes, but I believe that constitutes high treason.'

'That's what I arrested him for at least,' Sparhawk added.

'That's good enough for me,' Ulath said, raising his axe. 'Say the word, Queen of Elenia, and we'll have his head on a pole at the palace gate in a matter of minutes.'

Lycheas gaped at them in horror and then began to cry,

pleading for his life while his cousin pretended to think it over. At least Sparhawk *hoped* that she was pretending. 'Not here, Sir Ulath,' she said a bit regretfully. 'The carpeting, you understand.'

'King Wargun wanted to hang him,' Kalten said. He looked up. 'You've got a nice high ceiling in here, Your Majesty, and good stout beams. It won't take me but a moment to fetch a rope. We can have him dancing in the air in no time, and hanging's not nearly as messy as beheading.'

Ehlana looked at Sparhawk. 'What do you think, dear? Should we hang my cousin?'

Sparhawk was profoundly shocked at the cold-blooded way she said it.

'Ah – he has a great deal of information that could be useful to us, My Queen,' he said.

'That might be true,' she said. 'Tell me, Lycheas, have you anything you'd like to share with us while I think this over?'

'I'll say anything you want, Ehlana,' he blubbered.

Ulath cuffed him across the back of the head. 'Your Majesty,' he prompted.

'What?'

'You call the queen "Your Majesty",' Ulath said, cuffing him again.

'Y-your Majesty,' Lycheas stammered.

'There's something else too, My Queen,' Sparhawk continued. 'Lycheas is Annias's son, you recall.'

'How did you find out about that?' Lycheas exclaimed.

Ulath cuffed him again. 'He wasn't talking to you. Speak when you're spoken to.'

'As I was saying,' Sparhawk went on. 'Lycheas is Annias's son, and he might be a useful bargaining chip in Chyrellos when we go there to try to keep Annias off the Archprelate's throne.'

'Oh,' she said petulantly, 'all right – I suppose – but as soon as you're done with him, turn him over to Sir Ulath and Sir Kalten. I'm sure they'll find a way to decide which one of them gets to send him on his way.'

'Draw straws?' Kalten asked Ulath.

'Or we could roll the dice,' Ulath countered.

'My Lord Lenda,' Ehlana said then, 'why don't you and Lord Vanion take this wretch somewhere and question him. I'm getting sick of the sight of him. Take Sir Kalten, Sir Perraine and Sir Ulath with you. Their presence might encourage him to be more forthcoming.'

'Yes, Your Majesty,' Lenda said, concealing a smile.

After Lycheas had been dragged from the room, Sephrenia looked the young queen full in the face. 'You weren't seriously considering that, were you, Ehlana?' she asked.

'Oh, of course not – well, not *too* seriously, anyway. I just want Lycheas to sweat a bit. I think I owe him that.' She sighed wearily. 'I think I'd like to rest now,' she said. 'Sparhawk, do be a dear and carry me in to bed.'

'That's hardly proper, Ehlana,' he said stiffly.

'Oh, bother proper. You may as well get used to thinking of me and beds at the same time anyway.'

'*Ehlana!*'

She laughed and held out her arms to him.

As Sparhawk bent and lifted his queen in his arms, he happened to catch a glimpse of Berit's face. The young novice was giving him a look of undisguised hatred. There was going to be a problem here, Sparhawk saw. He decided to have a long talk with Berit just as soon as the opportunity presented itself.

He carried Ehlana into the other room and tucked her into a very large bed. 'You've changed a great deal, My Queen,' he said gravely. 'You're not the same person I left ten years ago.' It was time to get that out into the open so that they could both stop tiptoeing around it.

'You've noticed,' she said archly.

'That's part of it right there,' he told her, reverting to his professorial tone. 'You're still only eighteen years old, Ehlana. It's not becoming for you to assume the worldly airs of a woman of thirty-five. I strongly recommend a more innocent public pose.'

She squirmed around in the bed until she was lying on her stomach with her head at the foot. She rested her chin in her hands, wide-eyed and ingenuous, her lashes fluttering and with one foot coyly kicking at her pillow. 'Like this?' she asked.

'Stop that.'

'I'm just trying to please you, my betrothed. Was there anything else about me you'd like to change?'

'You've grown hard, child.'

'Now it's your turn to stop something,' she said firmly. 'Don't call me "child" any more, Sparhawk. I stopped being a child the day Aldreas sent you to Rendor. I could be a child as long as you were here to protect me, but once you were gone, I couldn't afford that any more.' She sat up cross-legged on the bed. 'My father's court was a very unfriendly place for me, Sparhawk,' she told him gravely. 'I was dressed up and displayed at court functions where I could watch Aldreas and his sister covertly fondling each other and Annias smirking in the background. Any friends I had were immediately sent away – or killed – so I was forced to entertain myself by eavesdropping on the empty-headed gossip of the chambermaids. As a group, chambermaids tend to be quite wanton. I drew up a chart once – you taught me to be methodical, you'll remember. You wouldn't believe what goes on below stairs. My chart indicated that one aggressive little minx had very nearly outstripped Arissa herself in her conquests. Her

98

availability was almost legendary. If I sometimes seem "worldly" – wasn't that your term? – you can blame it on the tutors who took up my education when you left. After a few years – since any friendship I displayed for the lords and ladies of the court was an immediate cause for their exile or worse – I came to rely on the servants. Servants expect you to give them orders, so I give orders. It's a habit now. It worked out rather well for me, though. Nothing happens in the palace that the servants don't know about, and before long, they were telling me everything. I was able to use that information to protect myself from my enemies, and everybody at court except Lenda was my enemy. It wasn't much of a childhood, Sparhawk, but it prepared me far better than empty hours spent rolling hoops or wasting affection on rag dolls or puppies. If I seem hard, it's because I grew up in hostile territory. It may take you some years to soften those sharp edges, but I'm sure I'll enjoy your efforts in that direction.' She smiled winsomely, but there was still a kind of pained defensiveness in her grey eyes.

'My poor Ehlana,' he said, his heart in his throat.

'Hardly poor, dear Sparhawk. I have you now, and that makes me the richest woman in the world.'

'We've got a problem, Ehlana,' he said seriously.

'I don't see any problems. Not now.'

'I think you misunderstood when I gave you my ring by mistake.' He regretted that instantly. Her eyes opened as wide as they might have had he slapped her in the face. 'Please don't take what I just said wrong,' he rushed on. 'I'm just too old for you, that's all.'

'I don't care how old you are,' she said defiantly. 'You're mine, Sparhawk, and I'll *never* let you go.' Her voice was so filled with steel that he almost shrank from her.

'I was sort of obliged to point it out,' he backstepped.

He *had* to ease her past that dreadful moment of injury. 'Duty, you understand.'

She stuck her tongue out at that. 'All right, now that you've made your genuflection in duty's direction, we won't ever mention it again. When do you think we should have the wedding – before or after you and Vanion go to Chyrellos and kill Annias? I'm rather in favour of getting right on with it, personally. I've heard all sorts of things about what goes on between a husband and wife when they're alone, and I'm really very, very curious.'

Sparhawk turned bright red at that.

Chapter 5

'Is she asleep?' Vanion asked when Sparhawk emerged from Ehlana's bedroom.

Sparhawk nodded. 'Did Lycheas tell you anything useful?' he asked.

'A number of things – mostly verification of things we've already guessed,' Vanion replied. The Preceptor's face was troubled, and the strain of bearing the swords of the fallen knights still showed on him, although he looked more vigorous now. 'My Lord of Lenda,' he said, 'is the queen's apartment here secure? I'd rather not have some of the things Lycheas told us becoming general knowledge.'

'The rooms are quite secure, My Lord,' Lenda assured him, 'and the presence of your knights in the corridors will probably discourage anyone who's afflicted with a burning curiosity.'

Kalten and Ulath entered, and they both had vicious grins on their faces. 'Lycheas is having a very bad day,' Kalten smirked. 'Ulath and I were recalling a number of lurid executions we'd seen in the past while we were escorting him back to his cell. He found the notion of being burned at the stake particularly distressing.'

'And he almost fainted when we raised the possibility of racking him to death,' Ulath chuckled. 'Oh, by the way, we stopped by the palace gate on our way back here. The church soldiers we captured are repairing it.' The towering Genidian Knight set his axe in the corner. 'Some of your Pandions have been out in the streets, Lord Vanion. It seems that quite a number of the citizens of Cimmura have dropped out of sight.'

Vanion gave him a puzzled look.

'They seem a bit nervous for some reason,' Kalten explained. 'Annias has been in control of the city for quite a while now, and some people, nobles and commons alike, always have their eyes open for the main chance. They went out of their way to accommodate the good Primate. Their neighbours know who they are, though, and there have been a few incidents, I understand. When there's a sudden change of power, many people want to demonstrate their loyalty to the new regime in some visible way. There appear to have been several spontaneous hangings and a fair number of houses are on fire. Ulath and I suggested to the knights that they put a stop to that at least. Fires do tend to spread, you know.'

'I just love politics, don't you?' Tynian grinned.

'Mob rule should always be suppressed,' the Earl of Lenda said critically. 'The mob is the enemy of *any* government.'

'By the way,' Kalten said curiously to Sparhawk, 'did you *really* propose to the queen?'

'It's a misunderstanding.'

'I was fairly sure it was. You've never struck me as the marrying kind. She's going to hold you to it anyway, though, isn't she?'

'I'm working on that.'

'I wish you all the luck in the world, but quite frankly, I don't hold out much hope for you. I saw some of the looks she used to throw your way when she was a little girl. You're in for an interesting time, I think.' Kalten was grinning.

'It's such a comfort to have friends.'

'It's time you settled down anyway, Sparhawk. You're getting to be too old to be running around the world picking fights with people.'

'You're as old as I am, Kalten.'

'I know, but that's different.'

'Have you and Ulath decided who gets to dispose of Lycheas yet?' Tynian asked.

'We're still discussing it.' Kalten gave the big Thalesian a suspicious look. 'Ulath's been trying to foist a set of dice on me.'

'Foist?' Ulath protested mildly.

'I saw one of those dice, my friend, and it had four sixes on it.'

'That's a lot of sixes,' Tynian noted.

'It is indeed.' Kalten sighed. 'To be honest with you, though, I don't really think Ehlana's going to let us kill Lycheas. He's such a pathetic lump that I don't think she'll have the heart. Oh well,' he added, 'there's always Annias.'

'And Martel,' Sparhawk reminded him.

'Oh yes. There's *always* Martel.'

'Which way did he go after Wargun chased him away from Larium?' Sparhawk asked. 'I always like to keep track of Martel. I wouldn't want him to get himself into any trouble.'

'The last time we saw him, he was going east,' Tynian said, shifting the shoulder plates of his heavy Deiran armour.

'East?'

Tynian nodded. 'We thought he'd go south to Umanthum, but we found out later that he'd moved his fleet to Sarrinium after the burning of Coombe – probably because Wargun has ships patrolling the straits of Arcium. He's most likely back in Rendor by now.'

Sparhawk grunted. He unhooked his sword-belt, laid it

on the table and sat down. 'What did Lycheas tell you?' he asked Vanion.

'Quite a bit. It's fairly obvious that he didn't know everything Annias was doing, but surprisingly, he's managed to pick up a great deal of information. He's brighter than he looks.'

'He'd almost have to be,' Kurik said. 'Talen,' he said to his son, 'don't do that.'

'I was just looking, father,' the boy protested.

'Don't. You might be tempted.'

'Lycheas told us that his mother and Annias have been lovers for years now,' Vanion told them, 'and it was Annias who suggested to Arissa that she attempt to seduce her brother. He'd come up with a rather obscure bit of Church doctrine that appeared to permit a marriage between them.'

'The Church would never permit such an obscenity,' Sir Bevier declared flatly.

'The Church has done many things in her history that don't conform to contemporary morality, Bevier,' Vanion said. 'At one time, she was very weak in Cammoria, and there had been a tradition of incestuous marriages in the royal house of that kingdom. The Church made allowances in order to continue her work there. Anyway, Annias reasoned that Aldreas was a weak king, and Arissa would be the real ruler of Elenia if she married him. Then, since Annias more or less controlled Arissa, he'd be the one making the decisions. At first that seemed to be enough for him, but then his ambition began to run away with him. He started eyeing the Archprelate's throne in Chyrellos. That was about twenty years ago, I gather.'

'How did Lycheas find out about it then?' Sparhawk asked him.

'He used to visit his mother in that cloister at Demos,'

Vanion replied. 'Arissa's reminiscences were rather wide-ranging, I understand, and she was quite candid with her son.'

'That's revolting,' Bevier said in a sick voice.

'Princess Arissa has a peculiar kind of morality,' Kalten told the young Arcian.

'At any rate,' Vanion said, 'Sparhawk's father stepped in at that point. I knew him very well, and *his* morality was much more conventional. He was greatly offended by what Aldreas and Arissa were doing. Aldreas was afraid of him, so when he suggested a marriage to a Deiran Princess instead, Aldreas rather reluctantly agreed. The rest is fairly well known. Arissa went into an absolute fury and ran off to that brothel down by the riverside – sorry about that, Sephrenia.'

'I've heard about it before, Vanion,' she replied. 'Styrics are not nearly as unworldly as you Elenes sometimes believe.'

'Anyway, Arissa stayed in the brothel for several weeks, and when she was finally apprehended, Aldreas had no choice but to confine her in that cloister.'

'That raises a question,' Tynian said. 'Considering the amount of time she spent in that brothel and the number of customers she had, how can anyone be sure just *who* Lycheas's father was?'

'I was just coming to that,' Vanion replied. 'She assured Lycheas during one of his visits that she was pregnant *before* she went to the brothel. Aldreas married the Deiran Princess, and she died giving birth to Queen Ehlana. Lycheas was about six months old at the time, and Annias was doing his best to get Aldreas to legitimize him and make him his heir. That was too much even for Aldreas, and he flatly refused. It was about at that time that Sparhawk's father died, and Sparhawk here took his hereditary position as King's Champion. Annias began to grow alarmed at Ehlana's progress after Sparhawk took charge of her education. By the time she was eight, he decided that he had to get her champion away from her before he could make her so strong that he wouldn't be able to control her. That's when he persuaded Aldreas to send Sparhawk into exile in Rendor, and then he sent Martel to Cippria to kill him to make sure he'd never come back and complete Ehlana's education.'

'But he was too late, wasn't he?' Sparhawk smiled. 'Ehlana was already too strong for him.'

'How did you manage that, Sparhawk?' Kalten asked. 'You've never really been what you'd call a very inspiring teacher.'

'Love, Kalten,' Sephrenia said quite softly. 'Ehlana's loved Sparhawk since she was very young, and she tried to do things the way he'd have wanted her to do them.'

Tynian laughed. 'You did it to yourself then, Sparhawk,' he said.

'Did what?'

'You made a woman of steel, and now she's going to force you to marry her – and she's strong enough to get away with it.'

'Tynian,' Sparhawk said acidly, 'you talk too much.' The big Pandion was suddenly irritated – all the more so because he privately had to admit that Tynian was probably right.

'The point here, though, is that none of this is really very new or surprising,' Kurik noted. 'It's certainly not enough to keep Lycheas's head on his shoulders.'

'That came a little later,' Vanion told him. 'Ehlana frightened him so much when she seemed on the verge of having him summarily executed that he was babbling at first. Anyway, after Annias had forced Aldreas to send Sparhawk into exile, the king began to change. He actually started to develop some backbone. It's a little hard sometimes to know why people do things.'

'Not really, Vanion,' Sephrenia disagreed. 'Aldreas was under the thumb of the Primate, but in his heart he knew that what he was doing was wrong. Perhaps he felt that his champion might have been able to rescue his soul, but once Sparhawk was gone, Aldreas began to realize that he was totally alone. If his soul was going to be saved, he was going to have to do it himself.'

'She might be very close to right, you know,' Bevier marvelled. 'Perhaps I should make some study of the ethics of Styricum. A synthesis of Elene and Styric ethical thought might be very interesting.'

'Heresy,' Ulath observed flatly.

'I beg your pardon?'

'We're not supposed to consider the possibility that other ethics have any validity, Bevier. It's a little short-sighted, I'll admit, but our Church is like that sometimes.'

Bevier rose to his feet, his face flushed. 'I will not listen to insults directed at our holy mother,' he declared.

'Oh, sit down, Bevier,' Tynian told him. 'Ulath's only teasing you. Our Genidian brothers are much more deeply versed in theology than we give them credit for.'

'It's the climate,' Ulath explained. 'There's not a great deal to do in Thalesia in the winter – unless you like to watch it snow. We have a lot of time for meditation and study.'

'For whatever reason, Aldreas began to refuse some of Annias's more outrageous demands for money,' Vanion continued his account, 'and Annias started to get desperate. That's when he and Arissa decided to murder the king. Martel provided the poison, and Annias made arrangements to slip Arissa out of that cloister. He probably could have poisoned Aldreas himself, but Arissa

107

begged him to let her do it because she wanted to kill her brother herself.'

'Are you really sure you want to marry into that family, Sparhawk?' Ulath asked.

'Do I have any choice at this point?'

'You could always run away. I'm sure you could find work in the Tamul Empire on the Daresian continent.'

'Ulath,' Sephrenia said, 'hush.'

'Yes, ma'am,' he said.

'Go ahead, Vanion,' she instructed.

'Yes, ma'am,' he duplicated Ulath's intonation perfectly. 'After Arissa had killed Aldreas, Ehlana ascended the throne. She turned out to be Sparhawk's true pupil. She absolutely denied Annias access to her treasury and she was on the verge of packing him off to a monastery. That's when he poisoned her.'

'Excuse me, Lord Vanion,' Tynian interrupted. 'My Lord of Lenda, attempted regicide is a capital offence, isn't it?'

'Throughout the civilized world, Sir Tynian.'

'I thought that might be the case. Kalten, why don't you put in an order for a bale of rope? And Ulath, you'd better send to Thalesia for a couple of spare axes.'

'What's this?' Kalten asked.

'We have evidence now that Lycheas, Annias and Arissa have all committed high treason – along with a fair number of other confederates.'

'We knew that before,' Kalten said.

'Yes,' Tynian smiled, 'but now we can prove it. We have a witness.'

'I was sort of hoping to take care of suitable rewards myself,' Sparhawk objected.

'It's always better to do such things legally, Sparhawk,' Lenda told him. 'It avoids arguments later on, you understand.'

108

'I wasn't really planning to leave anyone around to argue with me, My Lord.'

'I think you'd better shorten his chain a bit, Lord Vanion,' Lenda suggested with a sly smile. 'His fangs seem to be getting longer.'

'I noticed that,' Vanion agreed. Then he went on. 'Annias was a little confounded when Sephrenia's spell kept Ehlana from dying the way her father had, but he went ahead and set Lycheas up as Prince Regent anyway, reasoning that an incapacitated queen was the same as a dead one. He took personal charge of the Elenian treasury and started buying Patriarchs right and left. That's when his campaign to gain the Archprelacy gained momentum and became more obvious. It was at about that point in Lycheas's story that My Lord of Lenda here suggested to him quite firmly that he hadn't yet said anything momentous enough to keep his neck off Ulath's chopping block.'

'Or out of my noose,' Kalten added grimly.

Vanion smiled. 'Lenda's suggestion had the desired effect on Lycheas,' he said. 'The Prince Regent became a gold mine of information at that point. He said that he can't actually prove it, but he's picked up some strong hints that Annias has been in contact with Otha, and that he's seeking his aid. The Primate has always pretended to be violently prejudiced against Styrics, but that may have been a pose to conceal his real feelings.'

'Probably not,' Sephrenia disagreed. 'There's a world of difference between western Styrics and Zemochs. The annihilation of western Styricum would have been one of Otha's first demands in exchange for any assistance.'

'That's probably true,' Vanion conceded.

'Did Lycheas have anything at all solid to base his suspicions upon?' Tynian asked.

'Not much,' Ulath told him. 'He saw a few meetings

taking place is about all. It's not quite enough to justify a declaration of war just yet.'

'War?' Bevier exclaimed.

'Naturally,' Ulath shrugged. 'If Otha's been involving himself in the internal affairs of the western Elene kingdoms, that's cause enough to go east and do war upon him.'

'I've always liked that expression,' Kalten said. '"Do war." It sounds so permanent – and so messy.'

'We don't need a justification if you really want to go and destroy Zemoch, Ulath,' Tynian said.

'We don't?'

'Nobody ever got around to drawing up a peace treaty after the Zemoch invasion five hundred years ago. Technically, we're still at war with Otha – aren't we, My Lord of Lenda?'

'Probably, but resuming hostilities after a five-hundred-year truce might be a little hard to justify.'

'We've just been resting up, My Lord,' Tynian shrugged. I don't know about these other gentlemen, but *I* feel fairly well-rested now.'

'Oh, dear,' Sephrenia sighed.

'The important thing here,' Vanion went on, 'is that on several occasions Lycheas saw one particular Styric closeted with Annias. Once, he was able to overhear a part of what they were saying. The Styric had a Zemoch accent – or so Lycheas believes.'

'That's Lycheas, all right,' Kurik observed. 'He's got the face of a sneak and an eavesdropper.'

'I'll agree to that,' Vanion said. 'Our excellent Prince Regent couldn't hear the whole conversation, but he told us that the Styric was telling Annias that Otha had to get his hands on a particular jewel or the Zemoch God would withdraw His support. I think we can all make some fairly educated guesses about which jewel he was talking about.'

110

Kalten's face grew mournful. 'You're going to be a spoil-sport about this, aren't you, Sparhawk,' he lamented.

'That one escapes me.'

'You're going to tell the queen about this, I suppose, and then she'll decide that the information's important enough to keep Lycheas's head on his neck or his feet on the floor.'

'I'm sort of obliged to keep her advised, Kalten.'

'I don't suppose we could persuade you to wait a while, could we?'

'Wait? How long?'

'Only until after the bastard's funeral.'

Sparhawk grinned at his friend. 'No, I'm afraid not, Kalten,' he said. 'I'd really like to oblige you, but I've got my own skin to consider. It might make my queen cross with me if I start hiding things from her.'

'That's about all Lycheas really knows,' Vanion told them. 'Now, we need to make a decision. Cluvonus is almost dead, and as soon as he dies, we'll have to join the other orders at Demos for the ride to Chyrellos. That's going to leave the queen totally unprotected here. We don't know when Dolmant's going to send us the command to march, and we don't know how long it's going to take the Elenian army to get back from Arcium. What are we going to do about the queen?'

'Take her with us,' Ulath shrugged.

'I think you might get quite an argument there,' Sparhawk said. 'She's only recently been restored to her throne, and she's the sort who takes her respon-sibilities very seriously. She'll definitely get her back up if you suggest that she abandon her capital at this point.'

'Get her drunk,' Kalten said.

'Do *what*?'

'You don't want to just rap her on the head, do you?

Get her tipsy, wrap her in a blanket and tie her across a saddle.'

'Have you lost your mind? This is the *queen*, Kalten, not one of your blowsy barmaids.'

'You can apologize later. The important thing is to get her to safety.'

'It may not come to any of that,' Vanion said. 'Cluvonus might hang on for a while yet. He's been on the brink of death for months now, but he's still alive. He might even outlive Annias.'

'That shouldn't be too hard for him,' Ulath said bleakly. 'Annias doesn't have much in the way of life expectancy just now.'

'If I could persuade you gentlemen to curb your blood-lust for a moment,' the Earl of Lenda interposed, 'I think the important thing for now is to get someone to King Wargun down in Arcium and to persuade him to release the Elenian army – and enough Pandion Knights to keep the general staff in line when they get here. I'll compose a letter to him advising in the strongest terms that we need the Elenian army back here in Cimmura just as quickly as they can get here.'

'You'd better ask him to release the militant orders as well, My Lord,' Vanion suggested. 'I think we're going to need them in Chyrellos.'

'You might also send a letter to King Obler,' Tynian added, 'and to Patriarch Bergsten. Between them, they can probably prevail on Wargun. The King of Thalesia drinks too much, and he enjoys a good war, but he's still a thoroughly political animal. He'll see the necessity of protecting Cimmura and taking control of Chyrellos immediately – if someone explains it to him.'

Lenda nodded his agreement.

'All this still doesn't solve our problem, gentlemen,' Bevier said. 'Our messenger to Wargun could very well

112

be no more than a day's ride away when word reaches us that the Archprelate has died. That puts us right back into the same situation. Sparhawk will have to persuade a very reluctant queen to abandon her capital with no visible danger in view.'

'Blow in her ear,' Ulath said.

'What was that?' Sparhawk asked.

'It usually works,' Ulath said. 'At least it does in Thalesia. I blew in a girl's ear in Emsat once, and she followed me around for days.'

'That's disgusting!' Sephrenia said angrily.

'Oh, I don't know,' Ulath said mildly. '*She* seemed to enjoy it.'

'Did you pat her on top of the head too, and scratch her chin – the way you'd have done if she'd been a puppy?'

'I never thought of that,' Ulath admitted. 'Do you think it might have worked?'

She began to swear at him in Styric.

'We're getting a little far afield here,' Vanion said. 'We can't compel the queen to leave Cimmura, and there's no way to be absolutely certain that a force large enough to hold the walls can reach the city before we're called away.'

'I think the force is already here, Lord Vanion,' Talen disagreed. The boy was dressed in the elegant doublet and hose Stragen had provided for him in Emsat, and he looked not unlike a youthful nobleman.

'Don't interrupt, Talen,' Kurik said. 'This is serious business. We don't have time for childish jokes.'

'Let him speak, Kurik,' the Earl of Lenda said intently. 'Good ideas can sometimes come from the most unusual places. Exactly what is this force you spoke of, young man?'

'The people,' Talen replied simply.

'That's absurd, Talen,' Kurik said. 'They aren't trained.'

'How much training do you really need in order to pour boiling pitch down on the heads of a besieging army?' Talen shrugged.

'It's a very interesting notion, young man,' Lenda said. 'There *was*, in fact, an outpouring of popular support for Queen Ehlana after her coronation. The people of Cimmura – and of the surrounding towns and villages – might very well come to her aid. The problem, though, is that they don't have any leaders. A mob of people milling around in the streets without anyone to direct them wouldn't be much of a defence.'

'There *are* leaders about, My Lord.'

'Who?' Vanion asked the boy.

'Platime for one,' Talen offered, 'and if Stragen's still here, he'd probably be fairly good at it as well.'

'This Platime's a sort of a scoundrel, isn't he?' Bevier asked dubiously.

'Sir Bevier,' Lenda said, 'I've served on the royal council of Elenia for many years now, and I can assure you that not only the capital, but the entire kingdom as well has been in the hands of scoundrels for decades now.'

'But –' Bevier started to protest.

'Is it the fact that Platime and Stragen are *official* scoundrels that upsets you, Sir Bevier?' Talen asked lightly.

'What do you think, Sparhawk?' Lenda asked. 'Do you think this Platime fellow could really direct some kind of military operation?'

Sparhawk thought it over. 'He probably could,' he said, 'particularly if Stragen's still here to help him.'

'Stragen?'

'He holds a position similar to Platime's among the thieves in Emsat. Stragen's a strange one, but he's extremely intelligent, and he's had an excellent education.'

'They can call in old debts as well,' Talen said. 'Platime

114

can draw men from Vardenais, Demos, the towns of Lenda and Cardos – not to mention the men he can get from the robber bands operating out in the countryside.'

'It's not really as if they were going to have to hold the city for an extended period of time,' Tynian mused. 'Only until the Elenian army gets here, and a great deal of what they'll be doing is going to be pure intimidation. It's unlikely that Primate Annias will be able to spare more than a thousand church soldiers from Chyrellos to cause problems here, and if the tops of the city walls are lined with a superior force, those soldiers will be very reluctant to attack. You know, Sparhawk, I think the boy's come up with a remarkably good plan.'

'I'm overcome by your confidence, Sir Tynian,' Talen said with an extravagant bow.

'There are veterans here in Cimmura as well,' Kurik added, 'former army men who can help direct the workers and peasants in the defence of the city.'

'It's all terribly unnatural, of course,' the Earl of Lenda said sardonically. 'The whole purpose of government has always been to keep the commons under control and out of politics entirely. The only purpose the common people really have for existing is to do the work and pay the taxes. We may be doing something here that we'll all live to regret.'

'Do we really have any choice, Lenda?' Vanion asked him.

'No, Vanion, I don't think we have.'

'Let's get started with it then. My Lord of Lenda, I believe you have some correspondence to catch up with, and Talen, why don't you go and see this Platime fellow?'

'May I take Berit with me, My Lord Vanion?' the boy asked, looking at the young novice.

'I suppose so, but why?'

115

'I'm sort of the official envoy from one government to another. I should have an escort of some kind to make me look more important. That sort of thing impresses Platime.'

'One government to another?' Kalten asked. 'Do you actually think of Platime as a head of state?'

'Well, isn't he?'

As Sparhawk's friends were filing out, Sparhawk briefly touched Sephrenia's sleeve. 'I need to talk with you,' he said quietly.

'Of course.'

He went to the door and closed it. 'I probably should have told you about this before, little mother,' he said, 'but it all seemed so innocuous at the beginning –' He shrugged.

'Sparhawk,' she told him, 'you know better than that. You must tell me everything. I'll decide what's innocuous and what isn't.'

'All right. I think I'm being followed.'

Her eyes narrowed.

'I had a nightmare right after we took Bhelliom away from Ghwerig. Azash was mixed up in it and so was Bhelliom. There was something else as well though – something I can't put a name to.'

'Can you describe it?'

'Sephrenia, I can't even see it. It seems to be some sort of shadow – something dark that's right on the very edge of my vision – like a flicker of movement to one side and slightly behind me. I get the feeling that it doesn't like me very much.'

'Does it only come to you when you're dreaming?'

'No. I see it now and then when I'm awake too. It seems to appear whenever I take Bhelliom out of its pouch. There are other times as well, but I can almost count on seeing it anytime I open the pouch.'

'Do that now, dear one,' she instructed. 'Let's find out if I can see it too.'

Sparhawk reached inside his doublet, took out the pouch and opened it. He removed the Sapphire Rose and held it in his hand. The flicker of darkness was immediately there. 'Can you see it?' he asked.

Sephrenia looked carefully around the room. 'No,' she admitted. 'Can you feel anything coming from the shadow?'

'I can tell that it isn't fond of me.' He put Bhelliom back into the pouch. 'Any ideas?'

'It might be something connected with Bhelliom itself,' she suggested a bit dubiously. 'To be perfectly honest with you, though, I don't really know that much about Bhelliom. Aphrael doesn't like to talk about it. I think the Gods are afraid of it. I know a little bit about how to use it, but that's about all.'

'I don't know if there's any connection,' Sparhawk mused, 'but somebody's definitely interested in doing me in. There were those men on the road outside Emsat, that ship that Stragen thought might be following us and those outlaws who were looking for us on the Cardos road.'

'Not to mention the fact that somebody tried to shoot you in the back with a crossbow when we were on our way to the palace,' she added.

'Could it be another Seeker perhaps?' he suggested.

'Something like that maybe. Once the Seeker takes control of somebody, the man becomes a mindless tool. These attempts on your life seem to be a bit more rational.'

'Could Azash have some creature who could manage that?'

'Who knows what kinds of creatures Azash can raise? I know of a dozen or so different varieties, but there are probably scores of others.'

'Would you be offended if I tried logic?'

'Oh, I *suppose* you can – if you feel you must.' She smiled at him.

'All right. First off, we know that Azash has wanted me dead for a long time now.'

'All right.'

'It's probably even more important to Him now, though, because I've got Bhelliom, and I know how to use it.'

'You're stating the obvious, Sparhawk.'

'I know. Logic's like that sometimes. It doesn't *always* happen, but these attempts to kill me *usually* come sometime not long after I've taken out the Bhelliom and caught a glimpse of that shadow.'

'Some kind of connection, you think?'

'Isn't it possible?'

'Almost anything's possible, Sparhawk.'

'All right then. If the shadow's something like the Damork or the Seeker, it's probably coming from Azash. That "probably" makes the logic a little shaky, but it's something to sort of consider, wouldn't you say?'

'Under the circumstances I'd almost have to agree.'

'What do we do about it then? It's an interim hypothesis, and it ignores the possibility of pure coincidence, but shouldn't we take some steps just in case there *is* some connection?'

'I don't think we can afford not to, Sparhawk. I think the first thing you should do is to keep Bhelliom inside that pouch. Don't take it out unless you absolutely have to.'

'That makes sense.'

'And if you *do* have to take it out, be on your guard for an attempt on your life.'

'I sort of do that automatically anyway – all the time. I'm in a nervous kind of profession.'

'*And*, I think we'd better keep this to ourselves. If that shadow comes from Azash, it can turn our friends against us. Any one of them could turn on you at any time at all.

118

If we tell them what we suspect, the shadow – or whatever it is – will probably know what's in their thoughts. Let's not warn Azash that we know what He's doing.'

Sparhawk steeled himself to say it, and when he did, it was with a vast reluctance. 'Wouldn't it solve everything if we were just to destroy Bhelliom right here and now?' he asked her.

She shook her head. 'No, dear one,' she said. 'We may still need it.'

'It's a simple answer, though.'

'Not really, Sparhawk.' Her smile was bleak. 'We don't know for sure what kind of force the destruction of Bhelliom might release. We might lose something fairly important.'

'Such as?'

'The city of Cimmura – or the entire Eosian continent, for all I know.'

It was nearly dusk when Sparhawk quietly opened the door to his queen's bedroom and looked in on her. Her face was framed by that wealth of pale blonde hair fanning out on the pillow and catching the golden light of the single candle on the stand at the side of her bed. Her eyes were closed, and her face softly composed. He had discovered in the past day or so that an adolescence spent in the corrupt court dominated by the Primate Annias had marked her face with a kind of defensive wariness and a flinty determination. When she slept, however, her expression had the same soft, luminous gentleness that had caught at his heart when she was a child. Privately, and now without reservation, he admitted that he loved this pale girl-child, although he was still adjusting his conception of her in that regard. Ehlana was much a woman now and no longer a child. With an obscure kind of twinge, Sparhawk admitted to himself that he really was wrong for her. There was a temptation to take advantage of her girlish infatuation, but he knew that to do so would not only be morally wrong, but could also cause her much suffering later in her life. He determined that under no circumstances would he inflict the infirmities of his old age upon the woman he loved.

'I know you're there, Sparhawk.' Her eyes did not open, and a soft smile touched her lips. 'I always used to love that when I was a child, you know. Sometimes, particularly when you started lecturing me on theology, I'd doze off – or pretend to. You'd talk on for a while, and then you'd just sit there, watching me. It always made me feel so warm and secure and totally safe. Those moments were probably the happiest in my life. And just think, after we're married, you'll watch me go to sleep in your arms every night, and I'll know that nothing in the world can ever hurt me, because you'll always be there watching over me.' She opened her calm grey eyes. 'Come here and kiss me, Sparhawk,' she told him, extending her arms.

'It's not proper, Ehlana. You're not fully dressed, and you're in bed.'

'We're betrothed, Sparhawk. We have a certain leeway in such matters. Besides, I'm the queen. *I'll* decide what's proper and what's not.'

Sparhawk gave up and kissed her. As he had noted before, Ehlana was most definitely no longer a child. 'I'm too old for you, Ehlana,' he reminded her gently once again. He wanted to keep that firmly in front of both of them. 'You do know that I'm right, don't you?'

'Nonsense.' She had not yet removed her arms from about his neck. 'I forbid you to get old. There, does that take care of it?'

'You're being absurd. You might as well order the tide to stop.'

'I haven't tried that yet, Sparhawk, and until I do, we won't really know that it wouldn't work, will we?'

'I give up,' he laughed.

'Oh good. I just *adore* winning. Was there something important you wanted to tell me, or did you just stop by to ogle me?'

'Do you *mind*?'

'Being ogled? Of course not. Ogle to your heart's content, beloved. Would you like to see more?'

'*Ehlana!*'

Her laughter was a silvery cascade.

'All right, let's get down to more serious matters.'

'I *was* being serious, Sparhawk – *very* serious.'

121

'The Pandion Knights, myself included, are going to have to leave Cimmura before long, I'm afraid. The revered Cluvonus is failing fast, and as soon as he dies, Annias is going to make a try for the Archprelate's throne. He's flooded the streets of Chyrellos with troops loyal to him, and unless the militant orders are there to stop him, he'll gain that throne.'

Her face took on that flinty expression again. 'Why don't you take that gigantic Thalesian, Sir Ulath, run on down to Chyrellos and chop Annias's head off? Then come right back. Don't give me time to get lonely.'

'Interesting notion, Ehlana. I'm glad you didn't suggest it in front of Ulath, though. He'd be on his way to the stables to saddle the horses by now. The point I was trying to make is that when we leave, you're going to be left defenceless here. Would you consider coming along with us?'

She thought about it. 'I'd love to, Sparhawk,' she said, 'but I don't really see how I can just now. I've been incapacitated for quite some time, and I've got to stay here in Cimmura to repair the damage Annias caused while I was asleep. I have responsibilities, love.'

'We were fairly sure you'd feel that way about it, so we've come up with an alternative plan to ensure your safety.'

'You're going to use magic and seal me up in the palace?' Her eyes were impish as she teased him.

'We hadn't considered that,' he conceded. 'It probably wouldn't work, though. As soon as Annias found out what we'd done, he'd probably send soldiers here to try to retake the city. His underlings would be able to run the kingdom from outside the palace walls, and you wouldn't be able to do much to stop them. What we *are* going to do is put together a kind of an army to protect you – and the city – until your own army has time to come back from Arcium.'

'The term "a kind of an army" sounds a little tentative, Sparhawk. Where are you going to get that many men?'

'Off the streets, and from the farms and villages.'

'Oh, that's just fine, Sparhawk. Wonderful.' Her tone was sarcastic. 'I'm to be defended by ditch-diggers and ploughboys?'

'Also by thieves and cut-throats, My Queen.'

'You're actually serious about this, aren't you?'

'Very much so. Don't close your mind just yet, though. Wait until you hear the details, and there are a pair of scoundrels on their way here to meet you. Don't make any decisions until after you've talked with them.'

'I think you're completely mad, Sparhawk. I still love you, but your mind seems to be slipping. You can't make an army out of hod-carriers and clod-hoppers.'

'Really? Where do you suppose the common soldiers in your army come from, Ehlana? Aren't they recruited from the streets and farms?'

She frowned. 'I hadn't thought of that, I suppose,' she conceded, 'but without generals, I'm not going to have much of an army, you know.'

'That's what the two men I just mentioned are coming here to discuss with you, Your Majesty.'

'Why is it that "Your Majesty" always sounds so cold and distant when you say it, Sparhawk?'

'Don't change the subject. You'll agree to withhold judgement, then?'

'If you say so, but I'm still a little dubious about this. I wish *you* could stay here.'

'So do I, but –' He spread his hands helplessly.

'When will there ever be time for just us?'

'It won't be much longer, Ehlana, but we *have* to beat Annias. You understand that, don't you?'

She sighed. 'I suppose so.'

Talen and Berit returned not long afterwards with Platime and Stragen. Sparhawk met them in the sitting-room while Ehlana attended to those minute details that are always involved in making a woman 'presentable'.

Stragen was at his elegant best, but the waddling, black-bearded Platime, chief of beggars, thieves, cut-throats and whores, looked distinctly out of place. 'Ho, Sparhawk!' the fat man bellowed. He had forgone his food-spotted orange doublet in favour of one in blue velvet that didn't fit him very well.

'Platime,' Sparhawk replied gravely. 'You're looking quite natty this evening.'

'Do you like it?' Platime plucked at the front of his doublet with a pleased expression. He turned a full circle, and Sparhawk noted several knife holes in the back of the thief's finery. 'I've had my eye on it for several months now. I finally persuaded the former owner to part with it.'

'Milord.' Sparhawk bowed to Stragen.

'Sir Knight,' Stragen responded, also bowing.

'All right, what's this all about, Sparhawk?' Platime demanded. 'Talen was babbling some nonsense about forming up a home guard of some kind.'

'Home guard. That's a good term,' Sparhawk approved. 'The Earl of Lenda will be along in a few moments, and then I'm sure Her Majesty will make her entrance from that room over there – where she's probably listening at the door right now.'

From the queen's bed-chamber came the stamp of an angry foot.

'How's business been?' Sparhawk asked the gross leader of the underside of Cimmura.

'Quite good, actually,' the fat man beamed. 'Those foreign church soldiers the Primate sent to prop up the bastard Lycheas were very innocent. We robbed them blind.'

'Good. I always like to see friends get on in the world.'

The door opened, and the ancient Earl of Lenda shuffled into the room. 'Sorry to be late, Sparhawk,' he apologized. 'I'm not very good at running any more.'

'Quite all right, My Lord of Lenda,' Sparhawk replied. 'Gentlemen,' he said to the two thieves, 'I have the honour to present the Earl of Lenda, head of Her Majesty's council of advisers. My Lord, these are the two men who will lead your home guard. This is Platime, and this, Milord Stragen from Emsat.'

They all bowed – at least Platime *tried* to bow. 'Milord?' Lenda asked Stragen curiously.

'An affectation, My Lord of Lenda,' Stragen smiled ironically. 'It's a carry-over from a misspent youth.'

'Stragen's one of the best,' Platime put in. 'He's got some strange ideas, but he does very well – better even than me some weeks.'

'You're too kind, Platime,' Stragen murmured with a bow.

Sparhawk crossed the room to the door to the queen's bed-chamber. 'We're all assembled, My Queen,' he said through the panel.

There was a pause, and then Ehlana, wearing a pale-blue satin gown and a discreet diamond tiara, entered. She stopped, looking around with a queenly bearing. 'Your Majesty,' Sparhawk said formally, 'may I present Platime and Stragen, your generals?'

'Gentlemen,' she said with a brief inclination of her head.

Platime tried to bow again, badly, but Stragen more than made up for it.

'Pretty little thing, isn't she?' Platime observed to his blond companion.

125

Stragen winced.

Ehlana looked a bit startled. To cover the moment, she looked around the room. 'But where are our other friends?' she asked.

'They've returned to the chapterhouse, My Queen,' Sparhawk informed her. 'They have preparations to make. Sephrenia promised to come back later, though.' He extended his arm and escorted her to a rather ornate chair by the window. She sat and carefully arranged the folds of her gown.

'May I?' Stragen said to Sparhawk.

Sparhawk looked puzzled.

Stragen went to the window, nodding to Ehlana as he passed, and drew the heavy drapes. She stared at him. 'It's most imprudent to sit with one's back to an open window in a world where there are crossbows, Your Majesty,' he explained with another bow. 'You have many enemies, you know.'

'The palace is totally secure, Milord Stragen,' Lenda objected.

'Do you want to tell him?' Stragen wearily asked Platime.

'My Lord of Lenda,' the fat man said politely, 'I could get thirty men inside the palace grounds in about ten minutes. Knights are all very well on a battlefield, I suppose, but it's hard to look up when you're wearing a helmet. In my youth, I studied the art of burglary. A good burglar is as much at home on a rooftop as he is on a street.' He sighed. 'Those were the days,' he reminisced. 'There's nothing like a nice neat burglary to set the pulse to racing.'

'But it might be a bit difficult for a man weighing twenty-one stone,' Stragen added. 'Even a slate roof can only hold so much weight.'

'I'm not really all *that* fat, Stragen.'

126

'Of course not.'

Ehlana looked genuinely alarmed. 'What are you doing to me, Sparhawk?' she asked.

'Protecting you, My Queen,' he replied. 'Annias wants you dead. He's already proved that. As soon as he finds out about your recovery, he'll try again. The men he sends to kill you won't be gentlemen. They won't leave their cards with the footman at the door when they come to call. Between them, Platime and Milord Stragen know just about everything there is to know about slipping into places unobserved, and they'll be able to take the proper steps.'

'We can guarantee Your Majesty that no one will get past us alive,' Stragen assured her in his beautiful deep voice. 'We'll try not to over-inconvenience you, but there'll be certain restrictions on your freedom of movement, I'm afraid.'

'Such as not sitting near an open window?'

'Precisely. We'll draw up a list of suggestions and pass them on to you through the Earl of Lenda. Platime and I are men of business, and Your Majesty might find our presence distressing. We'll remain in the background as much as possible.'

'Your delicacy is exquisite, Milord,' she told him, 'but I'm not all that much distressed by the presence of honest men.'

'Honest?' Platime laughed coarsely. 'I think we've just been insulted, Stragen.'

'Better an honest cut-throat than a dishonest courtier,' Ehlana said. 'Do you really do that? Cut throats, I mean?'

'I've slit a few in my time, Your Majesty,' he admitted with a shrug. 'It's a quiet way to find out what a man has in his purse, and I've always been curious about that sort of thing. Speaking of that, you might as well tell her, Talen.'

127

'What's this?' Sparhawk asked.

'There's a small fee involved, Sparhawk,' Talen said.

'Oh?'

'Stragen volunteered his services free of charge,' the boy explained.

'Just for the experience, Sparhawk,' the blond northerner said. 'King Wargun's court is a bit crude. The court of Elenia is reputed to be exquisitely courteous and totally depraved. A studious man always seizes these opportunities to expand his education. Platime, on the other hand, is not quite so studious. He wants something a little more tangible.'

'Such as?' Sparhawk bluntly asked the fat man.

'I'm beginning to give some thought to retirement, Sparhawk – some quiet country estate where I can entertain myself in the company of a bevy of immoral young women – begging Your Majesty's pardon. Anyway, a man can't really enjoy his declining years if there are a number of hanging offences lurking in his background. I'll protect the queen with my life if she can find it in her heart to grant me a full pardon for my past indiscretions.'

'Just what sort of indiscretions are we talking about here, Master Platime?' Ehlana asked suspiciously.

'Oh, nothing really worth mentioning, Your Majesty,' he replied deprecatingly. 'There were a few incidental murders, assorted thefts, robberies, extortions, burglaries, arson, smuggling, highway robbery, cattle-rustling, pillaging a couple of monasteries, operating unlicensed brothels – that sort of thing.'

'You *have* been busy, haven't you, Platime?' Stragen said admiringly.

'It's a way to pass the time. I think we'd better just make it a general pardon, Your Majesty. I'm bound to forget a few offences here and there.'

'Is there any crime you *haven't* committed, Master Platime?' she asked sternly.

'Barratry, I think, Your Majesty. Of course I'm not sure what it means, so I can't be entirely positive.'

'It's when a ship captain wrecks his ship in order to steal the cargo,' Stragen supplied.

'No, I've never done that. Also, I've never had carnal knowledge of an animal, I've never practised witchcraft, and I've never committed treason.'

'Those are the more really serious ones, I suppose,' Ehlana said with a perfectly straight face. 'I *do* so worry about the morals of foolish young sheep.'

Platime roared with sudden laughter. 'I do myself, Your Majesty. I've spent whole nights tossing and turning about it.'

'What kept you untainted by treason, Master Platime?' the Earl of Lenda asked curiously.

'Lack of opportunity, probably, My Lord,' Platime admitted, 'although I rather doubt I'd have gone into that sort of thing anyway. Unstable governments make the general populace nervous and wary. They start protecting their valuables, and that makes life very hard for thieves. Well, Your Majesty, do we have a bargain?'

'A general pardon in exchange for your services – for so long as I require them?' she countered.

'What's that last bit supposed to mean?' he demanded suspiciously.

'Oh, nothing at all, Master Platime,' she said innocently. 'I don't want you to get bored and abandon me just when I need you the most. I'd be desolate without your company. Well?'

'Done, by God!' he roared. He spat in his hand and held it out to her.

She looked at Sparhawk, her face confused.

129

'It's a custom, Your Majesty,' he explained. 'You also spit in your hand, and then you and Platime smack your palms together. It seals the bargain.'

She cringed slightly, then did as he instructed. 'Done,' she said uncertainly.

'And there we are,' Platime said boisterously. 'You're now the same as my very own little sister, Ehlana, and if anybody offends you, or threatens you, I'll gut him for you, and then you can pour hot coals into his gaping belly with your own two little hands.'

'You're so very kind,' she said weakly.

'You've been had, Platime,' Talen howled with laughter.

'What are you talking about?' Platime's face darkened.

'You've just volunteered for a lifetime of government service, you know.'

'That's absurd.'

'I know, but you did it all the same. You agreed to serve the queen for as long as she wants you to, and you didn't even raise the question of pay. She can keep you here in the palace until the day you die.'

Platime's face went absolutely white. 'You wouldn't do that to me, would you, Ehlana?' he pleaded in a choked voice.

She reached up and patted his bearded cheek. 'We'll see, Platime,' she said. 'We'll see.'

Stragen was doubled over with silent laughter. 'What's this home guard business, Sparhawk?' he asked when he had recovered.

'We're going to mobilize the common people to defend the city,' Sparhawk said. 'As soon as Kurik gets here, we'll work out the details. He suggested that we round up army veterans and press them into service as sergeants and corporals. Platime's men can serve as junior officers, and you and Platime, under the direction of the Earl of Lenda, will act as our generals until the regular Elenian army returns to relieve you.'

Stragen thought it over. 'It's a workable plan,' he approved. 'It doesn't take nearly as much training to defend a city as it does to attack one.' He looked at his large, crestfallen friend. 'If it's all right, Your Majesty,' he said to Ehlana, 'I'll take your protector here somewhere and pour some ale into him. He looks a trifle distraught for some reason.'

'As you wish, Milord,' she smiled. 'Can you think of any crimes *you* might have committed in my kingdom you'd like to have me pardon? On the same terms?'

'Ah, no, Your Majesty,' he replied. 'The thieves' code forbids my poaching in Platime's private preserve. If it weren't for that, I'd rush out and murder somebody – just for the sake of spending the rest of my life in your divine company.' His eyes were wicked.

'You're a very bad man, Milord Stragen.'

'Yes, Your Majesty,' he agreed, bowing. 'Come along, Platime. It won't seem nearly so bad once you get used to it.'

'That was very, very slick, Your Majesty,' Talen said after they had left. 'Nobody's *ever* swindled Platime that way before.'

'Did you really like it?' She sounded pleased.

'It was brilliant, My Queen. Now I can see why Annias poisoned you. You're a very dangerous woman.'

She beamed at Sparhawk. 'Aren't you proud of me, dear?'

'I think your kingdom's safe, Ehlana. I just hope the other monarchs are on their guard, that's all.'

'Would you excuse me for a moment?' she asked,

looking at her still-moist palm. 'I'd like to wash my hands.'

It was not long afterwards when Vanion gravely led the others into the queen's sitting-room. The Preceptor bowed perfunctorily to Ehlana. 'Have you talked with Platime yet?' he asked Sparhawk.

'It's all arranged,' Sparhawk assured him.

'Good. We're going to have to ride to Demos tomorrow morning. Dolmant sent word that Archprelate Cluvonus is on his deathbed. He won't last out the week.'

Sparhawk sighed. 'We knew it was coming,' he said. 'Thank God we had time to take care of things here before it happened. Platime and Stragen are somewhere in the palace, Kurik – drinking probably. You'd better get together with them and work out some kind of organizational plans.'

'Right,' the squire said.

'A moment, Master Kurik,' the Earl of Lenda said. 'How are you feeling, Your Majesty?' he asked Ehlana.

'I'm fine, My Lord.'

'Do you think you're strong enough to make a public appearance?'

'Of course, Lenda. I'm perfectly all right.'

'Good. Once our generals and Master Kurik have gathered up our home guard, I think a few short speeches from you might go a long way towards firing them up – appeals to their patriotism, denunciations of the church soldiers, a few veiled references to the perfidy of the Primate Annias, that sort of thing.'

'Of course, Lenda,' she agreed. 'I like to make speeches anyway.'

'You'll have to stay here until you've got things all set up,' Sparhawk said to Kurik. 'You can join us in Chyrellos when Cimmura's secure.'

Kurik nodded and quietly left.

'That's a very good man, Sparhawk,' Ehlana said.

'Yes.'

Sephrenia had been looking critically at the rosy-cheeked queen. 'Ehlana,' she said.

'Yes?'

'You really shouldn't pinch your cheeks like that to make them pink, you know. You'll bruise your skin. You're very fair, and your skin is delicate.'

Ehlana blushed. Then she laughed ruefully. 'It *is* a bit vain, isn't it?'

'You're a queen, Ehlana,' the Styric woman told her, 'not a milk-maid. Fair skin is more regal.'

'Why do I always feel like a child when I'm talking with her?' Ehlana asked no one in particular.

'We all do, Your Majesty,' Vanion assured her.

'What's happening in Chyrellos now?' Sparhawk asked his friend. 'Did Dolmant give you any details?'

'Annias controls the streets,' Vanion replied. 'He hasn't done anything overt yet, but his soldiers are letting themselves be seen. Dolmant thinks he'll try to call for the election before Cluvonus is even cold. Dolmant has friends, and they're going to try to stall things until we get there, but there's only so much they'll be able to do. Speed is vital now. When we rejoin the other orders, there'll be four hundred of us. We'll be outnumbered, but our presence should be felt. There's something else, too. Otha's crossed the border into Lamorkand. He's not advancing yet, but he's issuing ultimatums. He's demanding the return of Bhelliom.'

'Return? He never had it.'

'Typical diplomatic flim-flammery, Sparhawk,' the Earl of Lenda explained. 'The weaker your position, the bigger the lie you tell.' The old man pursed his lips thoughtfully. 'We know – or at least we can presume

– that there's an alliance between Otha and Annias, right?'

'Yes,' Vanion agreed.

'Annias knows – or should – that our tactic to counter him will be to play for time. Otha's move at this point gives the election a certain urgency. Annias will argue that the Church must be united to face the threat. Otha's presence on the border will terrify the more timid members of the Hierocracy, and they'll rush to confirm Annias. Then both he and Otha will get what they want. It's very clever, actually.'

'Did Otha go so far as to mention Bhelliom by name?' Sparhawk asked.

Vanion shook his head. 'He's accused you of stealing one of the national treasures of Zemoch, that's all. He left it rather deliberately vague. Too many people know about the significance of Bhelliom. He can't really come right out and mention it by name.'

'It's fitting together more and more tightly,' Lenda said. 'Annias will declare that only *he* knows a way to make Otha withdraw. He'll stampede the Hierocracy into electing him. Then he'll wrest Bhelliom from Sparhawk and deliver it to Otha as a part of their bargain.'

'It's going to take quite a bit of "wresting",' Kalten said bleakly. 'The militant orders will all fall into line behind Sparhawk.'

'That's probably what Annias hopes you'll do,' Lenda told him. 'Then he'll have every justification for disbanding the militant orders. Most of the Church Knights will obey the Archprelate's command to disband. The rest of you will be outlaws, and Annias will let the commons know that you're keeping the one thing that will stave off Otha. As I said, it's very clever.'

'Sparhawk,' Ehlana said in a ringing voice, 'when you get to Chyrellos, I want Annias apprehended on the charge

134

of high treason. I want him delivered to me in chains. Bring Arissa and Lycheas as well.'

'Lycheas is already here, My Queen.'

'I know that. Take him with you to Demos and imprison him with his mother. I want him to have plenty of time to describe the present circumstances to Arissa.'

'It's a useful idea, Your Majesty,' Vanion said delicately, 'but we'll hardly have enough force in Chyrellos to take Annias into custody right at first.'

'I know that, Lord Vanion, but if the arrest warrant and the specification of charges is delivered to Patriarch Dolmant, it may help him in delaying the election. He can always call for a Church investigation of the charges, and those things take time.'

Lenda rose and bowed to Sparhawk. 'My boy,' he said, 'no matter what else you may have done or may yet do, your finest work sits upon that throne. I'm proud of you, Sparhawk.'

'I think we'd better start moving,' Vanion said. 'We've got a lot of preparations to make.'

'I'll have copies of the warrant for the Primate's arrest in your hands by the third hour after midnight, Lord Vanion,' Lenda promised, 'along with a number of others. We have a splendid opportunity here to clean up the kingdom. Let's not waste it.'

'Berit,' Sparhawk said. 'My armour's in that room over there. Take it back to the chapterhouse, if you would please. I think I'm going to need it.'

'Of course, Sir Sparhawk.' Berit's eyes, however, were still flat and unfriendly.

'Stay a moment, Sparhawk,' Ehlana said as they all started towards the door. He dropped behind the others and waited until the door closed.

'Yes, My Queen,' he said.

'You must be so very, very careful, my beloved,' she

said with her heart in her eyes. 'I'd die if I lost you now.'
Mutely, she held out her arms to him.

He crossed to where she sat and embraced her. Her kiss
was fierce. 'Go quickly, Sparhawk,' she said in a voice near
to tears. 'I don't want you to see me crying.'

Chapter 7

They left for Demos shortly after sunrise the following morning, riding at a jingling trot with a forest of pennon-tipped lances strung out behind them as the hundred Pandions rode resolutely eastward.

'It's a good day to be on the road,' Vanion said, looking around at the sun-drenched fields. 'I just wish – Oh, well.'

'How are you feeling now, Vanion?' Sparhawk asked his old friend.

'Much better,' the Preceptor replied. 'I'll be honest with you, Sparhawk. Those swords were very, *very* heavy. They gave me some fairly strong hints of what it's going to be like to grow old.'

'You'll live forever, my friend,' Sparhawk smiled.

'I certainly *hope* not, not if it means feeling the way I felt when I was carrying those swords.'

They rode on in silence for a while.

'This is a long chance, Vanion,' Sparhawk said sombrely. 'We're going to be badly outnumbered in Chyrellos, and if Otha starts across Lamorkand, it's going to be a close race between him and Wargun. Whichever one gets to Chyrellos first will win.'

'I think we're getting very close to one of those articles of the faith, Sparhawk. We're going to have to trust God in this. I'm sure He doesn't want Annias to be Archprelate, and I'm *very* sure he doesn't want Otha in the streets of Chyrellos.'

'Let's hope not.'

Talen and Berit were riding not far behind. Over the

months, a certain friendship had grown up between the novice and the young thief, a friendship based in part upon the fact that they were both a bit uncomfortable in the presence of their elders.

'Exactly what's this election business all about, Berit?' Talen asked. 'What I'm getting at is how does it work exactly? I'm a little shaky on that sort of thing.'

Berit straightened in his saddle. 'All right, Talen,' he said, 'when the old Archprelate dies, the Patriarchs of the Hierocracy gather in the Basilica. Most of the other high Churchmen are there as well, and the kings of Eosia are usually also present. Each of the kings makes a short speech at the beginning, but no one else is permitted to speak during the Hierocracy's deliberations – only the Patriarchs, and they're the only ones who have votes.'

'You mean that the Preceptors can't even vote?'

'The Preceptors *are* Patriarchs, young man,' Perraine said from just behind them.

'I didn't know that. I wondered why everybody sort of stepped aside for the Church Knights. How is it that Annias is running the Church in Cimmura then? Where's the Patriarch?'

'Patriarch Udale is ninety-three years old, Talen,' Berit explained. 'He's still alive, but we're not sure he even knows his own name. He's being cared for in the Pandion Mother-house at Demos.'

'That makes it difficult for Annias, doesn't it? As a Primate, he can't talk – or vote, and there's no way he can poison this Udale if he's in the Mother-house.'

'That's why he needs money. He has to buy people to do his talking – and his voting – for him.'

'Wait a minute. Annias is only a Primate, isn't he?'

'That's right.'

Talen frowned. 'If he's only a Primate and the others

are Patriarchs, how does he think he stands a chance at election?'

'A Churchman doesn't have to be a Patriarch to ascend the throne of the Church. On several occasions, some simple village priest has become the Archprelate.'

'It's all very complicated, isn't it? Wouldn't it just be simpler for us to move in with the army and put the man we want on the throne?'

'That's been tried in the past. It never really worked out. I don't think God approves.'

'He'll approve a lot less if Annias wins, won't He?'

'There could be something to what you say, Talen.'

Tynian rode forward, and there was a grin on his broad face. 'Kalten and Ulath are amusing themselves by terrorizing Lycheas,' he said. 'Ulath's been lopping off saplings with his axe, and Kalten's coiled a noose. He's been pointing out overhanging tree-limbs to Lycheas. Lycheas keeps fainting. We had to chain his hands to his saddle-bow to keep him from falling out of his saddle.'

'Kalten and Ulath are simple fellows,' Sparhawk observed. 'It doesn't take much to keep them amused. Lycheas will have a great deal to tell his mother when we get to Demos.'

About midday, they turned southeast to ride across country. The weather held fair. They made good time and reached Demos late the following day. Just before the column swung south towards the encampment of the knights of the other three orders, Sparhawk, Kalten and Ulath took Lycheas around the northern edge of town to the cloister in which Princess Arissa was confined. The cloister had yellow sandstone walls, and it stood in a wooded glen where birds sang from the limbs in the late afternoon sunshine.

Sparhawk and his friends dismounted at the gate and rather roughly jerked the chained Lycheas from his saddle.

'We'll need to speak with your Mother Superior,' Sparhawk told the gentle little nun who opened the gate for them. 'Is Princess Arissa still spending most of her time in that garden near the south wall?'

'Yes, My Lord.'

'Please ask the Mother Superior to join us there. We're delivering Arissa's son to her.' He took Lycheas by the scruff of the neck and dragged him across the courtyard towards the walled garden where Arissa spent her long hours of confinement. Sparhawk was coldly angry for a number of reasons.

'Mother!' Lycheas cried when he saw her. He broke free from Sparhawk and stumbled towards her, his imploring hands hampered by his chains.

Princess Arissa came to her feet, her face outraged. The circles under her eyes had lessened, and her look of sullen discontent had faded to be replaced by one of smug anticipation. 'What's the meaning of this?' she demanded, embracing her cowering son.

'They threw me in the dungeon, mother,' Lycheas blubbered, 'and they've been threatening me.'

'How *dare* you treat the Prince Regent so, Sparhawk?' she burst out.

'The situation has greatly changed, Princess,' Sparhawk informed her coolly. 'Your son isn't Prince Regent any more.'

'No one has the authority to depose him. You'll pay for this with your life, Sparhawk.'

'I sort of doubt that, Arissa,' Kalten disagreed with a broad grin. 'I'm sure you'll be delighted to hear that your niece has recovered from her illness.'

'Ehlana? That's impossible!'

'As a matter of fact, it isn't. I know that as a true daughter of the Church, you'll join with us all in praising God for his miraculous intervention. The royal council

140

almost swooned with delight. The Baron Harparin was so pleased that he completely lost his head.'

'But no one ever recovers from –' she bit her lip.

'From the effects of darestim?' Sparhawk completed her sentence for her.

'How did you –?'

'It wasn't really all that hard, Arissa. It's all falling apart on you, Princess. The queen was most displeased with you and your son – and the Primate Annias as well, of course. She's commanded us to take the three of you into custody. You can consider yourself under arrest at this point.'

'On what charge?' she exclaimed.

'High treason, wasn't it, Kalten?'

'I think those were the words the queen used, yes. I'm sure it's all a misunderstanding, Your Highness,' the blond man smirked at Queen Ehlana's aunt. 'You, your son and the good Primate should have no trouble explaining things at your trial.'

'Trial?' Her face blanched.

'I think that's the normal procedure, Princess. Ordinarily, we'd have just hanged your son and then you as well, but you both have a certain eminence in the kingdom, so certain necessary formalities are in order.'

'That's absurd!' Arissa cried. 'I'm a princess. I can't be charged with such a crime.'

'You might try to explain that to Ehlana,' Kalten replied. 'I'm sure she'll be very interested in your arguments – before she passes sentence.'

'You'll also be charged with the murder of your brother, Arissa,' Sparhawk added. 'Princess or not, that alone would be enough to hang you. But we're a bit pressed for time. I'm sure your son will be able to explain it all to you in greater detail.'

An aged nun entered the garden, her expression disapproving at the presence of men within her walls.

'Ah, Mother Superior,' Sparhawk greeted her with a bow. 'By order of the crown, I'm to confine these two criminals until they can be brought to trial. Do you by chance have penitents' cells within your walls?'

'I'm sorry, Sir Knight,' the Mother Superior said very firmly, 'but the rules of our order forbid confining penitents against their will.'

'That's all right, mother,' Ulath smiled. 'We'll take care of it. We'd sooner die than offend the ladies of the Church. I can assure you that the princess and her son will be unwilling to leave their cells – both of them being so engulfed in repentance, you understand. Let's see, I'll need a couple of lengths of chain, some stout bolts, a hammer and an anvil. I'll close up those cells with no trouble whatsoever, and you and your good sisters won't need to concern yourselves with politics.' He paused and looked at Sparhawk. 'Or did you want me just to chain them to the walls?'

Sparhawk actually considered it. 'No,' he decided finally, 'probably not. They're still members of the royal family, and certain courtesies are involved.'

'I have no choice but to accede to your demands, Sir Knights,' the Mother Superior said. She paused. 'There are rumours abroad that the queen has recovered,' she said. 'Can that possibly be true?'

'Yes, Mother Superior,' Sparhawk told her. 'The queen is well, and the government of Elenia is once again in her hands.'

'Praise God!' the old nun exclaimed. 'And will you soon be removing our unwanted guests from within our walls?'

'Soon, mother. Very soon.'

'We shall cleanse the chambers the princess has contaminated then – and offer prayers for her soul, of course.'

'Of course.'

'How very, very touching,' Arissa said sardonically,

142

appearing to have slightly recovered. 'If this grows any more cloying, I think I'll vomit.'

'You're starting to irritate me, Arissa,' Sparhawk said coldly. 'I don't recommend it. If I weren't under the queen's orders, I'd strike off your head here and now. I'd advise you to make your peace with God, because I'm quite sure you'll be meeting Him face to face before long.' He looked at her with extreme distaste. 'Get her out of my sight,' he told Kalten and Ulath.

About fifteen minutes later, Kalten and Ulath came back from within the cloister.

'All secure?' Sparhawk asked them.

'It'd take a blacksmith an hour to open those cell-doors,' Kalten replied. 'Shall we go then?'

They had gone no more than a half-mile when Ulath suddenly shouted, 'Look out, Sparhawk!' and roughly shoved the big Pandion from his saddle.

The crossbow bolt whizzed through the empty air where Sparhawk had been an instant before and buried itself to the vanes in a tree at the roadside.

Kalten's sword came whistling from its sheath, and he spurred his horse in the direction from which the bolt had come.

'Are you all right?' Ulath asked, dismounting to help Sparhawk to his feet.

'A little bruised is all. You push very firmly, my friend.'

'I'm sorry, Sparhawk. I got excited.'

'Perfectly all right, Ulath. Push as hard as you like when these things happen. How did you happen to see the bolt coming?'

'Pure luck. I happened to be looking that way, and I saw the bushes move.'

Kalten was swearing when he rode back. 'He got away,' he reported.

'I'm getting *very* tired of that fellow,' Sparhawk said, pulling himself back into the saddle.

'You think it might be the same one that took a shot at you back in Cimmura?' Kalten asked him.

'This isn't Lamorkand, Kalten. There isn't a crossbow standing in the corner of every kitchen in the kingdom.' He thought about it for a moment. 'Let's not make an issue of this when we see Vanion again,' he suggested. 'I can sort of take care of myself, and he's got enough on his mind already.'

'I think it's a mistake, Sparhawk,' Kalten said dubiously, 'but it's your skin, so we'll do it your way.'

The knights of the four orders were waiting in a well-concealed encampment a league or so to the south of Demos. Sparhawk and his friends were directed to the pavilion where their friends were conversing with Preceptor Abriel of the Cyrinic Knights, Preceptor Komier of the Genidians and Preceptor Darellon of the Alciones. 'How did Princess Arissa take the news?' Vanion asked.

'She was moderately discontented about it all,' Kalten smirked. 'She wanted to make a speech, but since about all she really wanted to say was, "You can't do this," we cut her off.'

'You did *what*?' Vanion exclaimed.

'Oh, not that way, My Lord Vanion,' Kalten apologized. 'Poor choice of words there perhaps.'

'Say what you mean, Kalten,' Vanion told him. 'This is no time for misunderstandings.'

'I wouldn't actually behead the princess, Lord Vanion.'

'*I* would,' Ulath muttered.

'May we see the Bhelliom?' Komier asked Sparhawk.

Sparhawk looked at Sephrenia, and she nodded, although a bit dubiously.

Sparhawk reached inside his surcoat and removed the canvas pouch. He untied the drawstring then shook the

144

Sapphire Rose out into his hand. It had been several days since he had felt even the faintest twinge of that shadowy, unnamed dread, but it returned once again as soon as his eyes touched the Sapphire Rose, and once again that shapeless shadow, even darker and larger now, flickered just beyond his field of vision.

'Dear God,' Preceptor Abriel gasped.

'That's it, all right,' the Thalesian Komier grunted. 'Get it out of sight, Sparhawk.'

'But –' Preceptor Darellon protested.

'Did you want to keep your soul, Darellon?' Komier asked bluntly. 'If you do, don't look at that thing for more than a few seconds.'

'Put it away, Sparhawk,' Sephrenia said.

'Have we had any news about what Otha's doing?' Kalten asked as Sparhawk dropped Bhelliom back into its pouch.

'He appears to be holding firm at the border,' Abriel replied. 'Vanion told us about the confession of the bastard Lycheas. It's very likely that Annias has asked Otha to stand on the border making menacing noises. Then the Primate of Cimmura can claim that he knows a way to stop the Zemochs. That should sway a few votes his way.'

'Do we think that Otha knows Sparhawk's got Bhelliom?' Ulath asked.

'Azash does,' Sephrenia said, 'and that means Otha does as well. Whether the news reached Annias yet is anybody's guess.'

'What's happening in Chyrellos?' Sparhawk asked Vanion.

'The latest word we have is that Archprelate Cluvonus is still hanging on by a thread. There's no way we can hide the fact that we're coming, so we're just going to bull our way on through to Chyrellos. There's been a change of plans now that Otha's made his move. We want to reach Chyrellos *before* Cluvonus dies. It's obvious that Annias is going to try to force the election as soon as he can now. He can't really start giving orders until after that. Once Cluvonus dies, though, the Patriarchs Annias controls can start calling for votes. Probably the first thing they'll vote on is the sealing of the city. That won't be a matter of substance, so Annias probably has the votes to get it passed.'

'Can Dolmant make any kind of estimate about how the vote stands just now?' Sparhawk asked.

'It's close, Sir Sparhawk,' Preceptor Abriel told him. Abriel was the leader of the Cyrinic Knights in Arcium. He was a solidly-built man in his sixties with silvery hair and an ascetic expression. 'A fair number of Patriarchs aren't in Chyrellos.'

'A tribute to the efficiency of Annias's assassins,' the Thalesian Komier said dryly.

'Most probably,' Abriel agreed. 'At any rate, there are one hundred and thirty-two Patriarchs in Chyrellos now.'

'Out of how many?' Kalten asked.

'One hundred and sixty-eight.'

'Why such an odd number?' Talen asked curiously.

'It was arranged that way, young man,' Abriel explained. 'The number was selected so that it would take one hundred votes to elect a new Archprelate.'

'One hundred and sixty-seven would have been closer,' Talen said after a moment.

'To what?' Kalten asked.

'The hundred votes. You see, one hundred votes is 60 per cent of –' Talen looked at Kalten's uncomprehending expression. 'Ah – never mind, Kalten,' he said. 'I'll explain later.'

'Can you come up with those numbers in your head, boy?' Komier asked with some surprise. 'We've wasted a bale of paper grinding out computations then.'

146

'It's a trick, My Lord,' Talen said modestly. 'In my business you sometimes have to deal with numbers very rapidly. Could I ask how many votes Annias has right now?'

'Sixty-five,' Abriel replied, 'either firm or strongly leaning towards him.'

'And we have?'

'Fifty-eight.'

'Nobody wins then. He needs thirty-five more votes, and we need forty-two.'

'It's not quite that simple, I'm afraid,' Abriel sighed. 'The procedure set down by the Church Fathers says that it takes one hundred votes – or a like proportion of those present and voting – to elect a new Archprelate, or to decide all matters of substance.'

'And *that's* what used up that bale of paper,' Komier said sourly.

'All right,' Talen said after a moment's thought. 'Annias only needs eighty votes then, but he's still fifteen short.' He frowned. 'Wait a minute,' he said. 'Your numbers don't add up. You've only accounted for one hundred and twenty-three votes, and you said there were one hundred and thirty-two Patriarchs in Chyrellos.'

'Nine of the Patriarchs have still not decided,' Abriel told him. 'Dolmant suspects that they're just holding out for bigger bribes. There are votes from time to time on non-substantive matters. In those cases, it only takes a simple majority to win. Sometimes the nine will vote with Annias and sometimes they won't. They're demonstrating their power to him. They'll vote to their own advantage, I'm afraid.'

'Even if they all vote with Annias every time, they still won't make any difference,' Talen said. 'No matter how you stretch nine votes, you can't turn them into fifteen.'

'But he doesn't need fifteen,' Preceptor Darellon said

147

wearily. 'Because of all the assassinations and all the church soldiers in the streets of Chyrellos, seventeen of the Patriarchs opposed to Annias have gone into hiding somewhere in the Holy City. They aren't present and voting, and that changes the numbers.'

'This is all beginning to make my head ache,' Kalten said to Ulath.

Talen was shaking his head. 'I think we're in trouble, My Lords,' he said. 'Without those seventeen to raise the total, the number to win is sixty-nine. Annias only needs four more votes.'

'And as soon as he can come up with enough money to satisfy four of those nine hold-outs, he'll win,' Sir Bevier said. 'The boy's right, My Lords. We're in trouble.'

'We have to change the numbers then,' Sparhawk said.

'How do you change numbers?' Kalten asked. 'A number is a number. You can't change it.'

'You can if you add to it. What we have to do when we get to Chyrellos is find those seventeen Patriarchs who are hiding and get them safely back to the Basilica to participate in the vote. That would bring the number Annias needs to win back up to eighty, and he can't reach that number.'

'But neither can we,' Tynian pointed out. 'Even if we brought them back, we'd still only have fifty-eight votes.'

'Sixty-two actually, Sir Tynian,' Berit corrected respectfully. 'The Preceptors of the four orders are also Patriarchs, and I don't think any of them would vote for Annias, would you, My Lords?'

'That changes the number again,' Talen said. 'Add the seventeen and the four, and the total is one hundred and thirty-six. That raises the number needed to win to eighty-two – eighty-one and a fraction, actually.'

'An unreachable number for either side,' Komier said in a gloomy voice. 'There's still no way we can win.'

148

'We don't have to win the vote in order to come out on top, Komier,' Vanion said. 'We're not trying to elect anybody. All we're trying to do is keep Annias off the throne. We can win with a stalemate.' Sparhawk's friend rose to his feet and began to pace up and down in the pavilion. 'As soon as we reach Chyrellos, we'll get Dolmant to send a message to Wargun down in Arcium declaring that there's a religious crisis in the Holy City. That will put Wargun under *our* orders. We'll include a command signed by the four of us that he's to suspend his operations in Arcium and ride for Chyrellos with all possible speed. If Otha starts to move, we're going to need him there anyway.'

'How are we going to get enough votes for such a declaration?' Preceptor Darellon asked.

'I wasn't planning to put it to a vote, my friend,' Vanion smiled thinly. 'Dolmant's reputation will convince Patriarch Bergsten that the declaration is official, and Bergsten can order Wargun to march on Chyrellos. We can apologize for the misunderstanding later. By then though, Wargun will be in Chyrellos with the combined armies of the west.'

'Less the Elenian army,' Sparhawk insisted. 'My queen is sitting in Cimmura with only a pair of thieves to protect her.'

'I'm not trying to offend you, Sir Sparhawk,' Darellon said, 'but that's hardly crucial at this point.'

'I'm not so sure, Darellon,' Vanion disagreed. 'Annias desperately needs money now. He has to have access to the Elenian treasury – not only to bribe the remaining nine, but also to keep the votes he already has. It wouldn't take too many defections to put the throne completely out of his reach. Protecting Ehlana – and her treasury – is even more vital now than it was before.'

149

'Perhaps you're right, Vanion,' Darellon conceded. 'I hadn't thought of that, I guess.'

'All right then,' Vanion continued his analysis, 'when Wargun reaches Chyrellos with his forces, the balance of power in the Holy City shifts. Annias's grip on his adherents is fairly tenuous as it is, and I'd guess that in many cases it's based rather strongly on the fact that his soldiers control the streets. As soon as that changes, I think a goodly part of his support will begin to dissolve. As I see it, gentlemen, our job is to reach Chyrellos before Cluvonus dies, get that message off to Wargun and then start rounding up the Patriarchs who are in hiding so that we can get them back into the Basilica to participate in the voting.' He looked at Talen. 'How many do we need – what's the absolute minimum we have to have to keep Annias from winning?'

'If he can somehow get those nine, he'll have seventy-four votes, My Lord. If we can find six of the ones in hiding, the total number voting will be one hundred and twenty-five. Sixty per cent of that is seventy-five. He loses at that point.'

'Very good, Talen,' Vanion said. 'That's it then, gentlemen. All we have to do is go to Chyrellos, take the city apart and find six Patriarchs who are willing to vote against Annias. We nominate somebody – anybody – to stand for election and keep taking votes until Wargun arrives.'

'It's still not the same as winning, Vanion,' Komier grumbled.

'It's the next best thing to it,' Vanion replied.

Sparhawk's sleep was restless that night. The darkness seemed filled with vague cries and moans and a sense of unnamed terror. Finally he rose from his bed, threw on a monk's robe and went looking for Sephrenia.

As he had about half-expected, he found her sitting in the doorway of her tent with her teacup in her hands. 'Don't you ever sleep?' he asked, half in irritation.

'Your dreams are keeping me awake, dear one.'

'You know what I'm dreaming?' He was astounded.

'Not the details, but I know that something's upsetting you.'

'I saw the shadow again when I showed Bhelliom to Vanion and the other Preceptors.'

'Is that what's disturbing you?'

'In part. Someone took a shot at me with a crossbow when Ulath, Kalten and I were coming here from the cloister where Arissa's confined.'

'But that was *before* you took Bhelliom out of the pouch. Maybe the incidents aren't linked after all.'

'Maybe the shadow saves them up – or maybe it can see them coming in the future. It might be that the shadow doesn't need to have me touch Bhelliom in order to send somebody to kill me.'

'Does Elene logic usually involve so many maybe's?'

'No, it doesn't, and that bothers me a little bit. It doesn't bother me enough to make me discard the hypothesis, though. Azash has been sending things to kill me for quite some time now, little mother, and they've all had some sort of supernatural quality about them. This shadow that I keep catching a glimpse of obviously isn't natural, or you'd have been able to see it too.'

'That's true, I suppose.'

'Then I'd be sort of foolish to drop my guard just because I can't *prove* that Azash sent the shadow, wouldn't I?'

'Probably, yes.'

'Even though I can't actually prove it, I *know* that there's some kind of connection between Bhelliom and that flicker in the corner of my eye. I don't know what the connection is just yet, and maybe that's why some

151

random incidents seem to be clouding the issue. To be on the safe side, though, I'm going to assume the worst – that the shadow belongs to Azash and it's following Bhelliom itself and that it's sending humans to try to kill me.'

'That makes sense.'

'I'm glad you approve.'

'You'd already made up your mind about this, Sparhawk,' she said to him, 'so why did you come looking for me?'

'I needed to have you listen while I talked my way through it.'

'I see.'

'Besides, I like your company.'

She smiled fondly at him. 'You're such a good boy, Sparhawk. Now, why don't we talk about why you're keeping this last attempt on your life from Vanion?'

He sighed. 'You *don't* approve of that, I see.'

'No, as a matter of fact, I don't.'

'I don't want him putting me in the middle of the column with armoured knights holding their shields over me. I *have* to be able to see what's coming at me, Sephrenia. I'll start trying to claw my way out of my skin if I can't.'

'Oh, dear,' she sighed.

Faran was in a foul humour. A day and a half of nearly continual hard riding had made his disposition definitely take a turn for the worse. Some fifteen leagues from Chyrellos, the Preceptors halted the column, ordered the knights to dismount and walk their horses for a time. Faran tried to bite Sparhawk three times as the big knight was climbing out of his saddle. The bites were intended more as an indication of disapproval than arising from any serious desire to injure or maim. Faran had discovered early in life that biting his master when he was wearing full armour only led to aching teeth. When the big roan half-whirled and kicked Sparhawk solidly on

152

the hip, however, Sparhawk felt that it was time to take steps. With Kalten's help, he rose to his feet, pushed back his visor and pulled himself hand over hand up the reins to glare directly into the ugly warhorse's face. 'Stop it!' he snapped.

Faran glared back at him with hate-filled eyes.

Sparhawk moved his hand very quickly then and grasped the roan's left ear in his gauntleted fist. Grimly he began to twist.

Faran ground his teeth together, and tears actually appeared in his eyes. 'Do we understand each other?' Sparhawk grated.

Faran kicked him in the knee with one fore-hoof.

'It's up to you, Faran,' Sparhawk told him. 'You're going to look ridiculous without that ear, though.' He twisted harder until his horse grudgingly squealed in pain.

'Always nice talking with you, Faran,' Sparhawk said, releasing the ear. Then he stroked the sweat-soaked neck. 'You big old fool,' he said gently. 'Are you all right?'

Faran flicked his ears – his right one, anyway – with an ostentatious display of indifference.

'It's really necessary, Faran,' Sparhawk explained. 'I'm not riding you this hard for fun. It won't be much farther. Can I trust you now?'

Faran sighed and pawed at the ground with one fore-hoof.

'Good,' Sparhawk said. 'Let's walk for a while.'

'That is truly uncanny,' Preceptor Abriel said to Vanion. 'I've never seen horse and man so totally linked before.'

'It's a part of Sparhawk's advantage, my friend,' Vanion said. 'He's bad enough by himself, but when you put him on that horse, he turns into a natural disaster.'

They walked on for a mile or so, then remounted and rode on through the afternoon sunlight towards the Holy City.

It was nearly midnight when they crossed the wide bridge over the River Arruk and approached one of the west gates of Chyrellos. The gate, of course, was guarded by church soldiers. 'I cannot grant you entry until sunrise, My Lords,' the captain in charge of the guard detachment said firmly. 'By order of the Hierocracy, no one under arms may enter Chyrellos during the hours of darkness.'

Preceptor Komier reached for his axe.

'A moment, my friend,' Preceptor Abriel cautioned mildly. 'I believe there's a way to resolve this difficulty without unpleasantness. Captain,' he addressed the red-tunicked soldier.

'Yes, My Lord?' The captain's voice was insultingly smug.

'This order you mentioned, does it apply to members of the Hierocracy itself?'

'My Lord?' The captain seemed confused.

'It's a simple question, Captain. A yes or a no will suffice. Does the order apply to the Patriarchs of the Church?'

'No one may hinder a Church Patriarch, My Lord,' the captain floundered a bit.

'Your Grace,' Abriel corrected.

The captain blinked stupidly.

'The correct form of address when speaking to a Patriarch is "Your Grace", Captain. By Church Law, my three companions and I are, in fact, Patriarchs of the Church. Form up your men, Captain. We will inspect them.'

The captain hesitated.

'I speak for the Church, Lieutenant,' Abriel said. 'Will you defy her?'

'Uh – I'm a captain, Your Grace,' the man mumbled.

'You *were* a captain, Lieutenant, but not any more. Now, would you like to be a sergeant again? If not, you'll do as I say immediately.'

154

'At once, Your Grace,' the shaken man replied. 'You there!' he shouted. 'All of you! Fall in and prepare for inspection!'

The appearance of the detachment at the gate was, in Preceptor – ah, shall we say instead *Patriarch* – Darellon's words, disgraceful. Reprimands were freely distributed in blistering terms, and then the column entered the Holy City without any further hindrance. There was no laughter – nor even any smiles – until the armoured men were well out of earshot of the gates. The discipline of the Knights of the Church is the wonder of the known world.

Despite the lateness of the hour, the streets of Chyrellos were heavily patrolled by church soldiers. Sparhawk knew these kinds of men, and he knew that their loyalty was for sale. They served only for the pay in most cases. Because of their numbers here in the Holy City, they had become accustomed to behaving with a certain arrogant rudeness. The appearance of four hundred armoured Church Knights in the streets at the ominous hour of midnight engendered what Sparhawk felt to be a becoming humility, however – at least among the common troops. It took the officers a bit longer to grasp the truth. It always does, somehow. One obnoxious young fellow tried to block their path, demanding to examine their documents. He seemed quite puffed-up with his own importance and failed to look behind him. He was thus unaware of the fact that his troops had discreetly gone somewhere else. He continued to deliver his peremptory commands in a shrill voice, demanding this and insisting on that until Sparhawk loosened Faran's reins and rode him down at a deliberate walk. Faran made a special point of grinding his steel-shod hooves into a number of very sensitive places on the officer's body.

'Feel better now?' Sparhawk asked his horse.

Faran nickered wickedly.

'Kalten,' Vanion said, 'let's get started. Break the column up into groups of ten. Fan out through the city and let it be generally known that the Knights of the Church offer their protection to any Patriarch desiring to go to the Basilica to participate in the voting.'

'Yes, My Lord Vanion,' Kalten said. 'I'll go and wake up the Holy City. I'm sure everybody is breathlessly waiting to hear the news I bring.'

'Do you think there's ever going to be any hope that someday he'll grow up?' Sparhawk said.

'I rather hope not,' Vanion said gently. 'No matter how old the rest of us get, we'll always have an eternal boy in our midst. That's sort of comforting, really.'

The Preceptors, followed by Sparhawk, his friends and a twenty-man detachment under the command of Sir Perraine proceeded along the broad avenue.

Dolmant's modest house was guarded by a platoon of soldiers, and Sparhawk recognized their officer as one loyal to the Patriarch of Demos. 'Thank God!' the young man exclaimed as the knights reined in just outside Dolmant's gate.

'We were in the area and thought we'd stop by to pay a courtesy call,' Vanion said with a dry smile. 'His Grace has been well, I trust?'

'He'll be much better now that you and your friends are here, My Lord. It's been a bit tense here in Chyrellos.'

'I can imagine. Is His Grace still awake?'

The officer nodded. 'He's meeting with Emban, Patriarch of Ucera. Perhaps you know him, My Lord?'

'Heavy-set fellow – sort of jolly?'

'That's him, My Lord. I'll tell His Grace you've arrived.'

Dolmant, Patriarch of Demos, was as lean and severe as always, but his ascetic face actually broke into a broad smile when the Church Knights trooped into his study.

'You made good time, gentlemen,' he told them. 'You all know Emban, of course.' He indicated his stout fellow Patriarch.

Emban was definitely more than 'heavy-set'. 'Your study's starting to resemble a foundry, Dolmant,' he chuckled, looking around at the armoured knights. 'I haven't seen so much steel in one place in years.'

'Comforting, though,' Dolmant said.

'Oh my, yes.'

'How do things stand in Cimmura, Vanion?' Dolmant asked intently.

'I'm happy to report that Queen Ehlana has recovered and now has her government firmly in her own hands,' Vanion replied.

'Thank God!' Emban exclaimed. 'I think Annias just went into bankruptcy.'

'You managed to find the Bhelliom then?' Dolmant asked Sparhawk.

Sparhawk nodded. 'Would you like to see it, Your Grace?' he asked.

'I don't believe so, Sparhawk. I'm not supposed to admit its power, but I've heard some stories – folklorish superstition no doubt – but let's not take any chances.'

Sparhawk heaved an inward sigh of relief. He did not much fancy another encounter with that flickering shadow nor the prospect of walking around for several days with the uneasy feeling that someone might be aiming a crossbow at him.

'It's peculiar that the news of the queen's recovery hasn't reached Annias yet,' Dolmant observed. 'At least he's shown no signs of chagrin so far.'

'I'd be very surprised if he's heard of it yet, Your Grace,' Komier rumbled. 'Vanion sealed the city to keep the Cimmurans at home. As I understand it, people who try to leave are turned back quite firmly.'

157

'You didn't leave your Pandions there, did you, Vanion?'

'No, Your Grace. We found assistance elsewhere. How's the Archprelate?'

'Dying,' Emban replied. 'Of course, he's been dying for several years, but he's a little more serious about it this time.'

'Is Otha making any more moves, Your Grace?' Darellon asked.

Dolmant shook his head. 'He's still encamped just inside the border of Lamorkand. He's making all kinds of threats and demanding that the mysterious Zemoch treasure be returned to him.'

'It's not so mysterious, Dolmant,' Sephrenia told him. 'He wants Bhelliom, and he knows Sparhawk has it.'

'Someone's bound to suggest that Sparhawk turn it over to him in order to prevent an invasion,' Emban suggested.

'That will never happen, Your Grace,' she said firmly. 'We'll destroy it first.'

'Have any of the Patriarchs who were in hiding returned as yet?' Preceptor Abriel asked.

'Not a one,' Emban snorted. 'They're probably down the deepest ratholes they can find by now. Two of them had fatal accidents a couple of days ago, and the rest went to ground.'

'We have knights scouring the city looking for them,' Preceptor Darellon reported. 'Even the most timid of rabbits might regain some degree of courage if they're protected by Church Knights.'

'Darellon,' Dolmant said reproachfully.

'Sorry, Your Grace,' Darellon said perfunctorily.

'Will that change the numbers?' Komier asked Talen. 'The two that died, I mean?'

'No, My Lord,' Talen said. 'We weren't counting them anyway.'

Dolmant looked puzzled.

'The lad has a gift for figures,' Komier explained. 'He can compute things in his head faster than I can with a pencil.'

'Sometimes you amaze me, Talen,' Dolmant said. 'Could I perhaps interest you in a career in the Church?'

'Counting the contributions of the faithful, Your Grace?' Talen asked eagerly.

'Ah – no, I don't think so, Talen.'

'Have the votes changed at all, Your Grace?' Abriel asked.

Dolmant shook his head. 'Annias still has a simple majority. He can bull through anything that isn't a matter of substance. His toadies are calling for votes on just about anything that comes up. He wants to keep a running count for one thing, and the voting keeps us all locked in the audience chamber.'

'The numbers are about to change, Your Grace,' Komier said. 'My friends and I have decided to participate this time.'

'Now *that's* unusual,' Patriarch Emban said. 'The Preceptors of the militant orders haven't participated in a vote of the Hierocracy for two hundred years.'

'We're still welcome, aren't we, Your Grace?'

'As far as I'm concerned you are, Your Grace. Annias might not like it too much, though.'

'How very unfortunate for him. What does that do to the numbers, Talen?'

'It just went up from sixty-nine votes to seventy-one and a fraction, my Lord Komier. That's the 60 per cent Annias needs to win.'

'And a simple majority?'

'He's still got that. He only needs sixty-one.'

'I don't think any of the neutral Patriarchs will go over to him on a matter of substance until he meets their price,'

Dolmant said. 'They'll probably abstain, and then Annias needs –' he frowned, thinking hard.

'Sixty-six votes, Your Grace,' Talen supplied. 'He's one vote short.'

'Delightful boy,' Dolmant murmured. 'Our best course then is to make every vote a vote of substance – even a vote to light more candles.'

'How do we do that?' Komier asked. 'I'm a little rusty on the procedure.'

Dolmant smiled faintly. 'One of us rises to his feet and says "substance".'

'Won't we just be voted down?'

Emban chuckled. 'Oh no, my dear Komier,' he said. 'A vote on whether a question is a matter of substance or not is itself a matter of substance. I think we've got him, Dolmant. That one vote he doesn't have will keep him off the Archprelate's throne.'

'Unless he can get his hands on some money,' Dolmant said, 'or unless more Patriarchs happen to die. How many of us does he have to kill in order to win, Talen?'

'All of you might help him a bit,' Talen grinned.

'Mind your manners,' Berit barked.

'Sorry,' Talen apologized, 'I should have added "Your Grace", I suppose. Annias needs to reduce the total number voting by at least two in order to have the 60 per cent he needs, Your Grace.'

'We'll have to assign knights to protect the loyal Patriarchs then,' Abriel said, 'and that's going to reduce the number out in the city trying to locate the missing members. It's starting to hinge on taking control of the streets. We need Wargun here very badly.'

Emban looked at him, puzzled.

'It's something we came up with at Demos, Your Grace,' Abriel explained. 'Annias is intimidating Patriarchs because Chyrellos is awash with church soldiers. If a Patriarch – either you or Patriarch Dolmant – declares a religious crisis and orders Wargun to suspend operations down in Arcium and to bring his armies here to Chyrellos, the whole picture changes. The intimidation starts going the other way at that point.'

'Abriel,' Dolmant said in a pained voice, 'we do not elect an Archprelate by intimidation.'

'We live in the real world, Your Grace,' Abriel replied. 'Annias was the one who chose the rules of this game, so I think we're sort of obliged to play his way – unless you happen to have another set of dice.'

'Besides,' Talen added, 'it would give us at least one more vote.'

'Oh?' Dolmant said.

'Patriarch Bergsten's with Wargun's army. We could probably persuade him to vote right, couldn't we?'

'Why don't we put our heads together and compose a letter to the King of Thalesia, Dolmant?' Emban grinned.

'I was just about to suggest the same thing myself, Emban. And perhaps we should forget to tell anyone else about it. Conflicting orders from some other Patriarch would just confuse Wargun, and he's confused enough as it is.'

Chapter 8

Sparhawk was tired, but he slept poorly. His mind seemed filled with numbers. Sixty-nine changed into seventy-one, then eighty, then back, and the nine and seventeen – no fifteen – hovered ominously in the background. He started to lose track of what the numbers meant, and they became just numbers that arrayed themselves threateningly before him, armoured and with weapons in their hands, and, as it almost always did when he slept now, the shadowy thing haunted his dreams. It did not do anything, but merely watched – and waited.

Sparhawk did not really have the temperament for politics. Too many things reduced themselves in his mind to battlefield imagery, and superior strength and training and individual bravery counted for much on a battlefield. In politics, however, the feeblest were equal to the strongest. A palsied hand shakingly raised to vote had a power equal to that of a mailed fist. His instincts told him that the solution to the problem rested in his scabbard, but the killing of the Primate of Cimmura would tear the west apart at a time when Otha stood armed and poised on the eastern marches.

He finally gave up and slipped quietly from his bed to avoid waking the sleeping Kalten. He put on his soft monk's robe and padded through the night-dark halls of the house to Dolmant's study.

Sephrenia was there, as he had about half-expected her to be. She sat before a small fire that crackled on the hearth, her teacup in her hands and her eyes a mystery.

162

'You're troubled, aren't you, dear one?' she said to him quietly.

'Aren't you?' He sighed and sank into a chair, extending his long legs out in front of him. 'We're not suited for this, little mother,' he said moodily, 'neither one of us. I'm not arranged in such a way that I can palpitate with delight over the change of a number, and I'm not positive that you even understand what numbers mean. Since Styrics don't read, can any of you actually understand any number larger than the sum of your fingers and toes?'

'Are you trying to be insulting, Sparhawk?'

'No, little mother, I could never do that – not to you. I'm sorry. I'm a bit sour this morning. I'm fighting the kind of war I don't understand. Why don't we frame some sort of prayer and ask Aphrael to change the minds of certain members of the Hierocracy? That would be nice and simple and probably head off a great deal of bloodshed.'

'Aphrael wouldn't do that, Sparhawk.'

'I was afraid you might say that. That leaves us the unpleasant alternative of playing in somebody else's game then, doesn't it? I wouldn't mind that so much – if I understood the rules a little better. Frankly, I'd much prefer swords and oceans of blood.' He paused. 'Go ahead and say it, Sephrenia.'

'Say what?'

'Sigh and roll your eyes heavenward and say, "Elenes" in your most despairing tone.'

Her eyes went hard. 'That was uncalled for, Sparhawk.'

'I was only teasing you,' he smiled. 'We can do that with those we love without giving offence, can't we?'

Patriarch Dolmant entered quietly, his face troubled. 'Is no one sleeping tonight?' he asked.

'We have a big day ahead of us tomorrow, Your Grace,' Sparhawk replied. 'Is that why you're up as well?'

Dolmant shook his head. 'One of my servants fell ill,' he explained, '– a cook. I don't know why the other servants sent for me. I'm no physician.'

'I think it's called trust, Your Grace,' Sephrenia smiled. 'You're supposed to have certain special contacts with the Elene God. How is the poor fellow?'

'It appears to be quite serious. I sent for a physician. The fellow isn't much of a cook, but I'd rather he didn't die under my roof. What really happened in Cimmura, Sparhawk?'

Sparhawk quickly sketched in the events which had occurred in the throne-room and the substance of the confession of Lycheas.

'Otha?' Dolmant exclaimed. 'Annias actually went *that* far?'

'We can't really prove it, Your Grace,' Sparhawk told him. 'It might be useful at some point to let the information drop in Annias's presence, however. It might throw him off balance a bit. Anyway, at Ehlana's command, we've confined Lycheas and Arissa in that cloister near Demos, and I'm carrying a sizeable number of warrants for the arrest of assorted people on charges of high treason. Annias's name figures quite prominently in one of those warrants.' He paused. 'There's a thought,' he said. 'We could march the knights to the Basilica, arrest Annias and take him back to Cimmura in chains. Ehlana was talking very seriously of hangings and beheadings when we left.'

'You can't take Annias out of the Basilica, Sparhawk,' Dolmant said. 'It's a church, and a church is sanctuary for all civil crimes.'

'Pity,' Sparhawk murmured. 'Who's in charge of Annias's toadies in the Basilica?'

'Makova, Patriarch of Coombe. He's been more or less running things for the past year. Makova's an ass, and he's totally venal, but he's an expert on Church

Law, and he knows a hundred technicalities and loop-holes.'

'Is Annias attending the meetings?'

'Most of the time, yes. He likes to keep a running count of the votes. He's spending his spare time making offers to the neutral Patriarchs. Those nine men are very shrewd. They never come right out and openly accept his offers. They answer with their votes. Would you like to watch us play, little mother?' Dolmant said it with a faint irony.

'Thank you all the same, Dolmant,' she declined, 'but there are a goodly number of Elenes who are firmly convinced that if a Styric ever enters the Basilica, the dome will fall in on itself. I don't enjoy being spat on all that much, so I think I'll stay here, if I may.'

'When have the meetings usually been commencing?' Sparhawk asked the Patriarch.

'It varies,' Dolmant replied. 'Makova holds the chair – that was a simple majority vote. He's been playing with his authority. He calls the meetings on a whim, and the messengers delivering those calls somehow always seem to lose their way when they come looking for those of us who are opposed to Annias. I think Makova started out by trying to slip through a substantive vote while the rest of us were still in bed.'

'What if he calls a vote in the middle of the night, Dolmant?' Sephrenia asked.

'He can't,' Dolmant explained. 'Sometime in antiquity, some Patriarch with nothing better to do codified the rules dealing with meetings of the Hierocracy. History tells us that he was a tiresome old windbag with an obsession about meaningless detail. He was the one responsible for the absurd rule about the one hundred votes – or 60 per cent – on substantive matters. He also – probably out of pure whim – set down the rule that the Hierocracy could only deliberate during the hours of daylight. Many of his rules are stupid frivolities, but he talked for six straight weeks, and finally his brothers voted to accept his rules just to shut him up.' Dolmant touched his cheek reflectively. 'When this is all over, I may just nominate the silly ass for sainthood. Those petty, ridiculous rules of his may be all that's keeping Annias off the throne now. At any rate, we've made a practice of all being in place at dawn, just to be safe. It's a rather petty form of retaliation, actually. Makova's not customarily an early riser, but he's been greeting the sun with the rest of us for the past several weeks. If he's not there, we can vote in a new chairman and proceed without him. All sorts of inconvenient votes could take place.'

'Couldn't he just have those votes repealed?' she asked.

Dolmant actually smirked. 'A vote to repeal is a matter of substance, Sephrenia, and he doesn't have the votes.'

There was a respectful knock on the door, and Dolmant answered it. A servant spoke with him for a moment.

'That cook just died,' Dolmant said to Sparhawk and Sephrenia, sounding a bit shocked. 'Wait here a moment. The physician wants to talk with me.'

'Strange,' Sparhawk murmured.

'People *do* die of natural causes, Sparhawk,' Sephrenia told him.

'Not in *my* profession – at least not very often.'

'Maybe he was old.'

Dolmant returned, his face very pale. 'He was poisoned!' he exclaimed.

'What?' Sparhawk demanded.

'That cook of mine was poisoned, and the physician says that the poison was in the porridge the man was preparing for breakfast. That porridge could have killed everyone in the house.'

'Perhaps you'd like to reconsider your position on the

166

notion of arresting Annias, Your Grace,' Sparhawk said grimly.

'Surely you don't believe –' Dolmant broke off, his eyes suddenly very wide.

'He's already had a hand in the poisoning of Aldreas and Ehlana, Your Grace,' Sparhawk said. 'I doubt that he'd choke very much over a few Patriarchs and a score or so Church Knights.'

'The man's a monster!' Then Dolmant started to swear, using oaths more common to a barracks than a theological seminary.

'You'd better tell Emban to circulate word of this to the Patriarchs loyal to us, Dolmant,' Sephrenia advised. 'It appears that Annias may have come up with a cheaper way to win an election.'

'I'd better start rousing the others,' Sparhawk said, rising to his feet. 'I want to tell them about this, and it takes a while to get into full armour.'

It was still dark when they set out for the Basilica accompanied by fifteen armoured knights from each of the four orders. Sixty Church Knights, it had been decided, was a force with which few would care to interfere.

The sky to the east was beginning to show that first pale stain of daylight when they reached the great domed church which was at the very centre of the Holy City – its thought and spirit as well as its geography. The entrance into the city of the column of Pandions, Cyrinics, Genidians and Alciones the previous night had not gone unnoticed, and the torchlit bronze portal leading into the vast court before the Basilica was guarded by a hundred and fifty red-tunicked church soldiers under the command of that same captain who, at Makova's orders, had attempted to prevent the departure of Sparhawk and his companions from the Pandion chapterhouse on their journey to Borrata.

'Halt!' he commanded in an imperious, even insulting tone.

'Would you attempt to deny entrance to Patriarchs of the Church, Captain?' Preceptor Abriel asked in a level tone, 'knowing that you thereby imperil your soul?'

'His neck too,' Ulath muttered to Tynian.

'Patriarch Dolmant and Patriarch Emban may freely enter, My Lord,' the captain said. 'No true son of the Church could refuse them entry.'

'But what of these other Patriarchs, Captain?' Dolmant asked him.

'I see no other Patriarchs, Your Grace.' The captain's tone hovered on insult.

'You're not looking, Captain,' Emban told him. 'By Church Law, the Preceptors of the militant orders are also Patriarchs. Stand aside and let us pass.'

'I have heard of no such Church Law.'

'Are you calling me a liar, Captain?' Emban's normally good-humoured face had gone iron-hard.

'Why – certainly not, Your Grace. May I consult with my superiors on this matter?'

'You may not. Stand aside.'

The captain started to sweat. 'I thank Your Grace for correcting my error,' he floundered. 'I was not aware that the Preceptors also enjoyed ecclesiastical rank. All Patriarchs may freely enter. The rest, I'm afraid, must wait outside.'

'He'd *better* be afraid if he's going to try to enforce that,' Ulath grated.

'Captain,' Preceptor Komier said, 'all Patriarchs are entitled to a certain administrative staff, aren't they?'

'Certainly, My Lord – Uh, Your Grace.'

'These knights are *our* staff. Secretaries and the like, you understand. If you deny *them* entrance, I'll expect to see a long file of the black-robed underlings of the *other* Patriarchs filing out of the Basilica in about five minutes.'

'I can't do *that*, Your Grace,' the captain said stubbornly.

'Ulath,' Komier barked.

'If I may, Your Grace,' Bevier interposed. Bevier, Sparhawk noted, was holding his lochaber axe loosely in his right hand. 'The captain and I have met before. Perhaps I can reason with him.' The young Cyrinic Knight moved his horse forward. 'Though our relations have never been cordial, Captain,' he said, 'I beseech you not to so risk your soul by defying our holy mother, the Church. With this in mind, will you freely stand aside as the Church has commanded you to do?'

'I will not, Sir Knight.'

Bevier sighed regretfully. Then, with an almost negligent swing of his dreadful axe, he sent the captain's head flying. Bevier, Sparhawk had noted, did that on occasion. Just as soon as he was certain that he was on firm theological ground, the young Arcian habitually took sometimes shockingly direct action. Even now, his face was serene and untroubled as he watched the captain's headless body standing stock still for several seconds, and then he sighed as the body collapsed.

The church soldiers gasped and cried out in horror and alarm as they recoiled and reached for their weapons.

'That tears it,' Tynian said. 'Here we go.' He reached for his sword.

'Dear friends,' Bevier addressed the soldiers in a gentle but commanding voice, 'you have just witnessed a truly regrettable incident. A soldier of the Church has wilfully defied our mother's lawful command. Let us join together now to offer up a fervent prayer that All-Merciful God shall see fit to forgive his dreadful sin. Kneel, dear friends, and pray.' Bevier shook the blood off his axe, spattering a number of soldiers in the process.

First a few, then more, and finally all of the soldiers sank to their knees.

'Oh, God!' Bevier led them in prayer, 'we beseech Thee to receive the soul of our dear brother, but recently departed, and grant him absolution for his grievous sin.' He looked around. 'Continue to pray, dear friends,' he instructed the kneeling soldiers. 'Pray not only for your former captain, but for yourselves as well, lest sin, ever devious and cunning, creep into *your* hearts even as it crept into his. Defend your purity and humility with vigour, dear friends, lest you share your captain's fate.' Then the Cyrinic Knight all in burnished steel and pristine white surcoat and cape, moved his horse forward at a walk, threading his way through the ranks of the kneeling soldiers, bestowing blessings with one hand and holding his lochaber axe in the other.

'I *told* you he was a good boy,' Ulath said to Tynian as the party followed the beatifically smiling Bevier.

'I never doubted it for a moment, my friend,' Tynian replied.

'Lord Abriel,' Patriarch Dolmant said as he guided his horse past the kneeling soldiers, many of whom were actually weeping, 'have you questioned Sir Bevier of late on the actual substance of his beliefs? I may be wrong, but I seem to detect certain deviations from the true teachings of our holy mother.'

'I shall catechize him most penetratingly on the matter, Your Grace – just as soon as I have the opportunity.'

'There's no great rush, My Lord,' Dolmant said benignly. 'I don't feel that his soul is in any immediate danger. That is a truly *ugly* weapon he carries, however.'

'Yes, Your Grace,' Abriel agreed. 'It truly is.'

Word of the sudden demise of the offensive captain

at the gate had spread rather quickly. There was no interference from the church soldiers at the massive doors of the Basilica – indeed, there seemed to be no church soldiers around at all. The heavily armed knights dismounted, formed up into a military column and followed their Preceptors and the two Patriarchs into the vast nave. There was a noisy clatter as the party knelt briefly before the altar. Then they rose and marched off down a candlelit corridor towards the administrative offices and the Archprelate's audience chamber.

The men standing guard at the door to the chamber were not church soldiers, but rather were members of the Archprelate's personal guard. Their loyalties were to the office itself, and they were totally incorruptible. They were also, however, sticklers for the letter of Church Law, in which they were probably more well versed than many of the Patriarchs sitting in the chamber. They immediately recognized the ecclesiastical eminence of the Preceptors of the four orders. Coming up with a reason why the rest of the entourage should be admitted took a bit longer, however. It was Patriarch Emban, fat, sly and with a nearly encyclopedic knowledge of Church Law and custom, who pointed out the fact that any Churchman with proper credentials and at the invitation of a Patriarch must be freely admitted. Once the guards had agreed to that, Emban gently pointed out that the Church Knights were *de facto* Churchmen as members of technically cloistered orders. The guards mulled that over, conceded Emban's point and ceremoniously opened the huge doors. Sparhawk noticed a number of poorly-concealed smiles as he and his friends filed inside. The guards by definition were incorruptible and totally neutral. This did not, however, preclude their having private opinions.

The audience chamber was as large as any secular

throne-room. The throne itself, massive, ornate, constructed of solid gold and standing on a raised dais backed by purple drapes, was at one end of the hall, and on either side, rising in tier upon tier, stood the high-backed benches. The first four tiers were crimson-cushioned, indicating that those seats were reserved for the Patriarchs. Above those seats and separated from them by velvet ropes of deepest purple were the plain wooden seats of the galleries for the spectators. A lectern stood before the throne, and Patriarch Makova of Coombe in Arcium stood at the lectern, droning out a speech filled with ecclesiastical bombast. Makova, lean-faced, pockmarked and obviously sleepy, turned irritably as the huge doors opened and the knights followed the Patriarchs of Demos and Ucera into the vast chamber.

'What's the meaning of this?' Makova demanded in an outraged tone.

'Nothing out of the ordinary, Makova,' Emban replied. 'Dolmant and I are merely escorting some of our brother Patriarchs in to join in our deliberations.'

'I see no Patriarchs,' Makova snapped.

'Don't be tiresome, Makova. All the world knows that the Preceptors of the militant orders hold rank equal to ours and are, therefore, members of the Hierocracy.'

Makova glanced quickly at a weedy-looking monk sitting off to one side at a table piled high with massive books and ancient scrolls. 'Will the assemblage hear the words of the law clerk on this matter?' he asked.

There was a rumble of assent, though the looks of consternation on the faces of at least some of the Patriarchs clearly showed that they already knew the answer. The weedy monk consulted several large tomes, then rose, cleared his throat and spoke in a rusty-sounding voice. 'His Grace, the Patriarch of Ucera, has correctly cited the law,' he said. 'The Preceptors of the militant orders

172

are indeed members of the Hierocracy, and the names of the current holders of those offices have been duly entered in the rolls of this body. The Preceptors have not chosen to participate in deliberations for some two centuries past, but they have the rank nonetheless.'

'Authority not exercised no longer exists,' Makova snapped.

'I'm afraid that's not entirely true, Your Grace,' the monk apologized. 'There are many historical precedents for resuming participation. At one time, the Patriarchs of the kingdom of Arcium refused to participate in the deliberations of the Hierocracy for eight hundred years as a result of a dispute over proper vestments, and –'

'All right. All right,' Makova said angrily, 'but these armoured assassins have no right to be here.' He glared at the knights.

'Wrong again, Makova,' Emban said smugly. 'By definition, the Church Knights are members of religious orders. Their vows are no less binding and legitimate than ours. They are thus Churchmen and may act as observers – provided that they are invited by a sitting Patriarch.' He turned. 'Sir Knights,' he said, 'would you be so good as to accept my personal invitation to witness our proceedings?'

Makova looked quickly at the scholarly monk, and the weedy fellow nodded.

'What it boils down to, Makova,' Emban said in an unctuous tone tinged with malice, 'is that the Knights of the Church have as much right to be present as the serpent Annias, who sits in unearned splendour in the north gallery – chewing his lower lip in dismay, I note.'

'You go too far, Emban!'

'I don't really think so, old boy. Shall we take a vote on something, Makova, and find out how much your support has been eroded?' Emban looked around.

'But we're interrupting the proceedings. I pray you, my brother Patriarchs and dear guests, let us take our seats so that the Hierocracy may continue its empty deliberations.'

'Empty?' Makova gasped.

'Totally empty, old boy. Until Cluvonus dies, nothing we decide here has any meaning whatsoever. We're simply amusing ourselves – and earning our pay, of course.'

'That's a very offensive little man,' Tynian murmured to Ulath.

'Good though,' the huge Genidian Knight grinned.

Sparhawk knew exactly where he was going. 'You,' he muttered to Talen, who had probably been admitted by mistake, 'come with me.'

'Where are we going?'

'To irritate an old friend,' Sparhawk grinned mirthlessly. He led the boy up the stairs to an upper gallery where the emaciated Primate of Cimmura sat with a writing desk in front of him and a fair number of black-robed sycophants on either side. Sparhawk and Talen went to places on the bench directly behind Annias. Sparhawk saw that Ulath, Berit and Tynian were following, and he waved them off warningly even as Dolmant and Emban escorted the armoured Preceptors to places on the lower, cushioned tiers.

Sparhawk knew that Annias sometimes blurted things out when he was surprised, and he wanted to find out if his enemy had in any way been involved in the attempted mass poisoning at Dolmant's house that morning. 'Why, can that *possibly* be the Primate of Cimmura?' he said in feigned surprise. 'What on *earth* are you doing so far away from home, Annias?'

Annias turned to glare at him. 'What are you up to, Sparhawk?' he hissed.

174

'Observing, that's all,' Sparhawk replied, removing his helmet and depositing his gauntlets in it. He unbuckled his shield and removed his sword-belt. He leaned them against the back of Annias's seat. 'Will those be in your way, neighbour?' he asked mildly. 'It's a bit hard to sit down comfortably when you're so encumbered with the tools of your trade, you know.' He sat. 'How have you been, Annias? I haven't seen you for months now.' He paused. 'You're looking a bit gaunt and pasty-faced, old boy. You really ought to get more fresh air and exercise.'

'Be still, Sparhawk,' Annias snapped. 'I'm trying to listen.'

'Oh, of course. We can have a nice long talk later – catch up on each other's accomplishments and the like.' There was nothing out of the ordinary in Annias's reaction, and Sparhawk became a little less certain of the man's guilt.

'If it pleases you, my brothers,' Dolmant was saying, 'a number of events have recently occurred, and I feel obligated to report them to the Hierocracy. Though our primary tasks are ageless, we nonetheless function in the world and must keep abreast of current events.'

Makova looked questioningly up towards Annias. The Primate took up a quill and a scrap of paper. Sparhawk rested his arms on the back of his enemy's seat and looked over the man's shoulder as he scribbled the terse instruction, 'Let him talk.'

'Tiresome, isn't it, Annias,' Sparhawk said in a pleasant tone. 'It would be so much more convenient if you could do your own talking, wouldn't it?'

'I told you to shut up, Sparhawk,' Annias grated, handing his note to a young monk to carry to Makova.

'My, aren't *we* testy this morning,' Sparhawk observed. 'Didn't you sleep well last night, Annias?'

Annias turned to glare at his tormentor. 'Who's that?' he demanded, pointing at Talen.

'My page,' Sparhawk replied. 'It's one of the encumbrances of knightly rank. He sort of fills in while my squire is otherwise occupied.'

Makova had glanced at the note. 'We always welcome the words of the learned Primate of Demos,' he declaimed loftily, 'but please be brief, Your Grace. We have important business to attend to here.' He stepped away from the lectern.

'Of course, Makova,' Dolmant replied, stepping to the vacated place. 'Briefly then,' he began, 'as a result of the full recovery of Queen Ehlana, the political situation in the kingdom of Elenia has radically changed, and –'

Cries of astonishment echoed through the hall, and there was a confused babble of voices. Sparhawk, still leaning on the back of Annias's seat, was pleased to see the Primate's face grow totally white as he half-started to his feet. 'Impossible!' the Churchman gaped.

'Amazing, isn't it, Annias?' Sparhawk said, 'and so totally unexpected. I'm sure you'll be happy to know that the queen sends you her *very* best wishes.'

'Explain yourself, Dolmant!' Makova half-shouted.

'I was only trying to be brief – as you requested, Makova. No more than a week ago, Queen Ehlana recovered from her mysterious ailment. Many look upon that as miraculous. Upon her recovery, certain facts came to light, and the former Prince Regent – and his mother, I understand – are currently under arrest on the charge of high treason.'

Annias fell back in his seat in a near-faint.

'The revered and respected Earl of Lenda now presides over the royal council, and warrants for a number of co-conspirators in the foul plot against the queen have been issued over his seal. The Queen's Champion is

176

presently searching out these miscreants and will doubtless bring them all before the bar of justice – either human or divine.'

'The Baron Harparin was next in line to preside over the Elenian royal council,' Makova protested.

'The Baron Harparin is presently standing before the bar of the Highest Justice, Makova,' Dolmant said in a deadly tone. 'He faces the Ultimate Judge. There is, I fear, scant hope for his acquittal – though we may pray that it be otherwise.'

'What happened to him?' Makova gasped.

'I'm told that he was accidentally beheaded during the changeover of administrations in Cimmura. Regrettable, perhaps, but that sort of thing happens now and then.'

'Harparin?' Annias gasped in dismay.

'He made the mistake of offending Preceptor Vanion,' Sparhawk murmured in his ear, 'and you know how short-tempered Vanion can be at times. He was very sorry afterwards, of course, but by then Harparin was lying in two separate places. He absolutely *destroyed* the carpeting in the council chamber – all that blood, you know.'

'Who else are you chasing, Sparhawk?' Annias demanded.

'I don't have the list with me at the moment, Annias, but there *are* a number of prominent names on it – names I'm sure you'd recognize.'

There was a stir at the door, and two frightened-looking Patriarchs crept into the hall and then scurried to places on the red-cushioned benches. Kalten stood grinning at the door for a moment, then left again.

'Well?' Sparhawk whispered to Talen.

'Those two bring the total up to one hundred and nineteen,' Talen whispered back. 'We've got forty-five, and Annias still has sixty-five. He needs seventy-two now instead of seventy-one. We're getting closer, Sparhawk.'

It took the secretary of the Primate of Cimmura some while longer to complete *his* computations. Annias scribbled a one-word note to Makova. Sparhawk, watching over the Primate's shoulder read the single word, 'vote'.

The issue Makova put to the vote was a pure absurdity. Everyone knew that. The only question the vote was designed to answer was upon which side the nine neutral Patriarchs clustered in a now-frightened group near the door would come down. After the tally, Makova announced the results in a tone of dismay. The nine had voted in a block *against* the Primate of Cimmura.

The huge door opened again, and three black-robed monks entered. Their cowls were raised, and their pace was ritualistically slow. When they reached the dais, one of their number removed a folded black cover from beneath his robe, and the three solemnly spread it over the throne to announce that the Archprelate Cluvonus had finally died.

Chapter 9

'How long will the city be in mourning?' Tynian asked Dolmant that afternoon when they had gathered once again in the Patriarch's study.

'A week,' Dolmant replied. 'The funeral takes place then.'

'And nothing happens during that period?' the blue-cloaked Alcione Knight asked. 'No sessions of the Hierocracy or anything?'

Dolmant shook his head. 'No. We're supposed to spend the period in prayer and meditation.'

'It's a breathing-space,' Vanion said, 'and it should give Wargun time to get here.' He frowned. 'We still have a problem, though. Annias doesn't have any more money, and that means that his hold on his majority grows shakier every day. He's probably growing desperate by now, and desperate men do rash things.'

'He's right,' Komier agreed. 'I expect Annias will take to the streets at this point. He'll hold his own votes by terror, and try to reduce the number voting by eliminating Patriarchs loyal to us until he gets the number down to the point where he has a substantive majority. I think it's time to fort up, gentlemen. We'd better get our friends all together behind some good stout walls where we can protect them.'

'I'll certainly agree,' Abriel concurred. 'Our position is vulnerable at this moment.'

'Which of your chapterhouses is closest to the Basilica?' Patriarch Emban asked them. 'Our friends are going to have to file back and forth through the streets to participate in deliberations. Let's not expose them to any more danger than we have to.'

'Our house is closest,' Vanion told him, 'and it has its own well. After what happened this morning, I don't want to give Annias access to our drinking water.'

'Supplies?' Darellon asked.

'We keep enough on hand to withstand a six-month siege,' Vanion replied. 'Soldiers' rations, I'm afraid, Your Grace,' he apologized to the corpulent Emban.

Emban sighed. 'Oh, well,' he said, 'I've been meaning to lose some weight anyway.'

'It's a good plan,' the white-cloaked Preceptor Abriel said, 'but it does have a drawback. If we're all in one chapterhouse, the church soldiers can surround us. We'll be penned up inside with no way to get to the Basilica at all.'

'Then we'll fight our way through,' Komier said, cramming his ogre-horned helmet on his head irritably.

Abriel shook his head. 'People get killed in fights, Komier. The vote is very close. We can't afford to lose a single Patriarch at this point.'

'We can't win either way,' Tynian said.

'I'm not so sure,' Kalten disagreed.

'Can you see a way out of it?'

'I think so.' Kalten looked at Dolmant. 'I'll need permission for this, Your Grace,' he said.

'I'm listening. What's your plan?'

'If Annias decides to resort to naked force, that means that any semblance of civil order goes out of the window, doesn't it?'

'More or less, yes.'

'Then if he's not going to pay any attention to the rules, why should we? If we want to cut down on the number of church soldiers surrounding the Pandion chapterhouse, all we have to do is give them something more important to do.'

'Set fire to the city again?' Talen suggested.

'That might be a little extreme,' Kalten said. 'We can keep the notion in reserve, though. At this moment, however, the votes Annias has got are the most important things in his life. If we start peeling them off one by one, he'll do just about anything to protect what he's got left, won't he?'

'I will *not* allow you to start butchering Patriarchs, Kalten,' Dolmant said in a shocked voice.

'We don't have to kill anybody, Your Grace. All we have to do is imprison a few. Annias is fairly intelligent. He'll get the point after a while.'

'You'll need *some* kind of charge, Sir Kalten,' Abriel said. 'You can't just imprison Patriarchs of the Church for no reason at all – regardless of the circumstances.'

'Oh, we have charges, My Lord Abriel – all sorts of charges – but "crimes against the crown of Elenia" has the nicest ring to it, wouldn't you say?'

'I hate it when he tries to be clever,' Sparhawk muttered to Tynian.

'You'll love this one, Sparhawk,' Kalten said. He threw back his black cloak with an expression of insufferable smugness. 'How many of those arrest warrants Lenda signed for you back in Cimmura have you still got in your pocket?'

'Eight or ten, why?'

'Are there any of those people whose company you'd absolutely die without for the next several weeks?'

'I could probably live without most of them.' Sparhawk thought he saw which way his friend was going.

'All we have to do is substitute a few names then,' Kalten said. 'The documents are official, so it's going to *look* legal – sort of. After we've picked up four or five of his bought-and-paid-for Patriarchs and dragged them off to the Alcione chapterhouse – which just

181

happens to be way over on the far side of town – won't Annias do everything in his power to get them back? I'd sort of expect the number of soldiers gathered around the Pandion chapterhouse to diminish drastically at that point.'

'Amazing,' Ulath said. 'Kalten actually came up with a workable idea.'

'About the only thing I can see wrong with it is the business of substituting names,' Vanion said. 'You can't just scratch out one name and replace it with another – not on an official document.'

'I didn't say anything about scratching out names, My Lord,' Kalten said modestly. 'Once, when we were novices, you gave Sparhawk and me leave to go home for a few days. You scribbled a note to get us out through the gate. We just happened to keep the note. The scribes in the scriptorium have something that totally washes out ink. They use it when they make mistakes. The date on that note of yours kept mysteriously changing. You might almost call it miraculous, mightn't you?' He shrugged. 'But then, God's always been sort of fond of me.'

'Would it work?' Komier bluntly asked Sparhawk.

'It did when we were novices, My Lord,' Sparhawk assured him.

'You actually *knighted* these two, Vanion?' Abriel asked.

'It was a slow week.'

The grins in the room were broad now.

'Totally reprehensible, Kalten,' Dolmant said. 'I'd have to absolutely forbid it – if I thought that you were in any way serious about it. You were just speculating, weren't you, my son?'

'Oh, absolutely, Your Grace.'

'I was sure that was the case.' Dolmant smiled benignly, even piously, and then he winked.

'Oh, dear,' Sephrenia sighed. 'Isn't there *one* honest Elene in the world? You too, Dolmant?'

'I didn't agree to anything, little mother,' he protested with exaggerated innocence. 'We were only speculating, weren't we, Sir Kalten?'

'Certainly, Your Grace. Pure speculation. Neither of us would ever *seriously* consider something so reprehensible.'

'My feelings exactly,' Dolmant said. 'There, Sephrenia, does that set your mind at rest?'

'You were a much nicer boy when you were a Pandion novice, Dolmant,' she reproved him.

There was a stunned silence as they all stared at the Patriarch of Demos.

'Oh dear,' Sephrenia said mildly, her eyes dancing and a faint smile hovering at the corners of her mouth. 'I suppose I really shouldn't have said that, should I have, Dolmant?'

'Did you really have to do that, little mother?' he asked her in a pained tone.

'Yes, dear one, I believe I did. You've started to become just a little too impressed with your own cleverness. It's my responsibility as your teacher – and your friend – to curb that whenever possible.'

Dolmant tapped one finger on the table in front of him. 'I trust we'll all be discreet about this, gentlemen?'

'Wild horses couldn't drag it out of us, Dolmant,' Emban grinned. 'As far as I'm concerned, I never even heard it – and that'll probably hold true until the next time I need a favour from you.'

'Were you any good, Your Grace?' Kalten asked respectfully. 'As a Pandion, I mean?'

'He was the best, Kalten,' Sephrenia said rather proudly. 'He was even a match for Sparhawk's father. We were all saddened when the Church found other duties for him. We lost a very good Pandion when he took holy orders.'

Dolmant was still looking around at his friends, his expression suspicious. 'I thought I'd buried it completely,' he sighed. 'I never thought you'd betray me, Sephrenia.'

'It's not exactly as if it were shameful, Your Grace,' Vanion said.

'It might prove to be politically inconvenient,' Dolmant said. 'At least *you* were able to control your tongue, brother.'

'Not to worry, Dolmant,' Emban said expansively. 'I'll keep an eye on your friends here, and as soon as I suspect that one of them is starting to have difficulty controlling his tongue, I'll order him to that monastery at Zemba down in Cammoria where the brothers all take vows of silence.'

'All right then,' Vanion said, 'let's get started, gentlemen. We have a number of friendly Patriarchs to round up, and Kalten, I want you to go start practising forgery. The names you'll be substituting on those arrest warrants will have to be in the handwriting of the Earl of Lenda.' He paused thoughtfully, looking at his blond subordinate. 'You'd better take Sparhawk with you,' he added.

'I can manage, My Lord.'

Vanion shook his head. 'No, Kalten,' he disagreed, 'I don't think so. I've seen your attempts at spelling before.'

'Bad?' Darellon asked him.

'Terrible, my friend. Once he wrote down a six-letter word, and he didn't manage to get a single letter right.'

'Some words are difficult to spell, Vanion.'

'His own *name*?'

'But you can't do this!' the Patriarch of Cardos protested shrilly as Sparhawk and Kalten dragged him from his house a few days later. 'You can't arrest a Patriarch of the Church for anything while the Hierocracy's in session.'

'But the Hierocracy's not in session just now, Your Grace,' Sparhawk pointed out. 'They're in recess during the period of official mourning.'

'I still cannot be tried by a civil court. I demand that you present these specious charges before an ecclesiastical court.'

'Take him outside,' Sparhawk curtly instructed the black-armoured Sir Perraine.

The Patriarch of Cardos was dragged from the room.

'Why the delay?' Kalten asked.

'Two things. Our prisoner didn't really seem all that surprised at the charges, did he?'

'Now that you mention it, no.'

'I think maybe Lenda missed a few names when he was drawing up that list.'

'That's always possible. What was the other thing?'

'Let's send a message to Annias. He knows that we can't touch him as long as he stays inside the Basilica, doesn't he?'

'Yes.'

'All right then, let's imprison him there and curtail his freedom of movement – for its irritation value if nothing else. We still owe him for that poisoned cook.'

'How do you plan to do that?'

'Watch – and follow my lead.'

'Don't I always?'

They went out to the courtyard of the Patriarch's luxurious house, a house built, Sparhawk was sure, on the backs of the Elenian taxpayers. 'My colleague and I have considered your request for an ecclesiastical hearing, Your Grace,' the big Pandion said to the prisoner. 'We find that your argument has merit.' He began to leaf through his sheaf of warrants.

'You'll deliver me to the Basilica for a hearing there then?' the Patriarch asked.

'Hmm?' Sparhawk said absently, still reading.

'I said, are you going to take me to the Basilica and present these absurd charges there?'

'Ah, I don't think so, Your Grace. That would really be inconvenient.' Sparhawk pulled out the warrant for the arrest of the Primate of Cimmura and showed it to Kalten.

'That's the one, all right,' Kalten said. 'That's the fellow we want.'

Sparhawk rolled up the warrant and tapped it against his cheek. 'Here's what we're going to do, Your Grace,' he said. 'We're going to take you to the Alcione chapterhouse and confine you there. These charges originated in the kingdom of Elenia, and any ecclesiastical proceedings would have to be conducted by the head of the Church in that kingdom. Since Primate Annias is acting for the Patriarch of Cimmura during His Grace's incapacity, that makes him the man who would preside over this hearing. Strange how things work out, isn't it? Since Primate Annias is the one in authority in this matter, we'll freely turn you over to him. All he has to do is to come out of the Basilica, go to the Alcione chapterhouse and order us to turn you over to him.' He glanced at a red-tunicked officer being guarded by the bleak-looking Sir Perraine. 'The captain of your guard here will serve as an excellent messenger. Why don't you have a word with him and explain the situation? Then we'll send him to the Basilica to tell Annias about it. Tell him to ask the good Primate to come and visit us. We'll be overjoyed to see him on neutral ground, won't we, Kalten?'

'Oh, absolutely,' Kalten replied fervently.

The Patriarch of Cardos gave them a suspicious look, then quickly conferred with the captain of his guard detachment. He kept glancing at the rolled-up warrant in Sparhawk's hand as he spoke.

'Do you think he got the point?' Kalten murmured.

'I certainly hope so. I did everything but hit him over the head with it.'

The Patriarch of Cardos returned, his face stiff with anger.

'Oh, one other thing, Captain,' Sparhawk said to the church soldier, who was preparing to leave. 'Would you be so good as to convey a personal message to the Primate of Cimmura for us? Tell him that Sir Sparhawk of the Pandion Order invites him to come out from under the dome of Basilica to play in the streets – where certain petty little restrictions won't interfere with our fun.'

Kurik arrived that evening. He was travel-stained and looked weary. Berit escorted him into Dolmant's study, and he sank into a chair. 'I'd have been here a bit sooner,' he apologized, 'but I stopped off in Demos to see Aslade and the boys. She gets very cross when I ride through town and don't stop.'

'How is Aslade?' Patriarch Dolmant asked.

'Fatter,' Kurik smiled, 'and I think she's getting a little silly as the years creep up on her. She was feeling nostalgic, so she took me up into the hayloft.' His jaw set slightly. 'I had a long talk with the boys about letting thistles grow in the hayfield later, though.'

'Do you have any idea of what he's talking about, Sparhawk?' Dolmant asked in perplexity.

'Yes, Your Grace.'

'But you're not going to explain it to me, are you?'

'No, Your Grace, I don't think so. How's Ehlana?' he asked his squire.

'Difficult,' Kurik grunted. 'Unprincipled. Abrasive. Wilful. Overbearing. Demanding. Sneaky. Unforgiving – just your average, run-of-the-mill young queen. I

187

like her, though. She reminds me of Flute for some reason.'

'I wasn't asking for a description, Kurik,' Sparhawk said. 'I was inquiring as to her health.'

'She seems fine to me. If there was anything wrong with her, she wouldn't be able to run that fast.'

'Run?'

'She seems to feel that she missed a great deal while she was asleep, so she's trying to catch up. She's had her nose in every corner of the palace by now. Lenda's seriously contemplating suicide, I think, and the chambermaids are all in a state of despair. You can't hide a speck of dust from her. She may not have the best kingdom in the world when she's finished, but she's certainly going to have the neatest.' Kurik reached inside his leather vest. 'Here,' he said, pulling out a very thick packet of folded parchment. 'She wrote you a letter. Give yourself time to read it, My Lord. It took her two days to write it.'

'How's the home guard idea working out?' Kalten asked.

'Quite well, actually. Just before I left, a battalion of church soldiers arrived outside the city. The battalion commander made the mistake of standing too near the gate when he demanded admittance. A couple of citizens dumped something on him.'

'Burning pitch?' Tynian surmised.

'No, Sir Tynian,' Kurik grinned. 'The two fellows make their living draining and cleaning cesspools. The officer received the fruit of their day's labour – about a hogshead full. The colonel – or whatever he was under all of that – lost his head and ordered an assault on the gate. That's when the rocks and burning pitch came into play. The soldiers set up camp not too far from the east wall to think things over, and late that night a score or so of Platime's cut-throats climbed down ropes from the parapet and visited their camp. The soldiers didn't have too many officers left the following morning. They milled around out there for a while, and then they went away. I think your queen's quite safe, Sparhawk. As a group, soldiers aren't very imaginative, and unconventional tactics tend to confuse them. Platime and Stragen are having the time of their lives, and the common people are beginning to take a certain pride in their city. They're even sweeping the streets on the off chance that Ehlana might ride by on one of her morning inspections.'

'Those idiots aren't letting her out of the palace, are they?' Sparhawk exclaimed angrily.

'Who's going to stop her? She's safe, Sparhawk. Platime put the biggest woman I've ever seen to guarding her. The woman's almost as big as Ulath, and she carries more weapons than a platoon.'

'That would be Mirtai, the giantess,' Talen said. 'Queen Ehlana's perfectly safe, Sparhawk. Mirtai's an army all by herself.'

'A woman?' Kalten asked incredulously.

'I wouldn't recommend calling her that to her face, Kalten,' the boy said seriously. 'She thinks of herself as a warrior, and nobody in his right mind argues with her. She wears men's clothes most of the time, probably because she doesn't want to be pestered by fellows who like their women large. She's got knives attached to her in some of the most unexpected places. She's even got a pair built into the soles of her shoes. Not much of those two knives stick out past her toes, but it's enough. You *really* wouldn't want her to kick you in certain tender places.'

'Where did Platime ever come across a woman like that?' Kalten asked him.

'He bought her,' Talen shrugged. 'She was about fifteen at the time and hadn't reached her full growth. She didn't speak a word of Elene, I've been told. He tried to put her to work in a brothel, but after she'd crippled or killed a dozen or so potential customers, he changed his mind.'

'Everybody speaks Elene,' Kalten objected.

'Not in the Tamul Empire, I understand. Mirtai's a Tamul. That's why she has such a strange name. I'm afraid of her, and I don't say that about many people.'

'It's not only the giantess, Sparhawk,' Kurik continued. 'The common people know their neighbours, and they know everybody who has unreliable political opinions. The people are fanatically loyal to the queen now, and every one of them makes it his personal business to keep an eye on his neighbours. Platime's rounded up just about everybody in town who's the least bit suspect.'

'Annias has a lot of underlings in Cimmura,' Sparhawk fretted.

'He *used* to, My Lord,' Kurik corrected. 'There were a number of messy object lessons, and if there's anyone left in Cimmura who doesn't love the queen, he's being very careful to keep that fact to himself. Can I have something to eat? I'm famished.'

The funeral of Archprelate Cluvonus was suitably stupendous. Bells tolled for days, and the air inside the Basilica was tainted with incense and with chants and hymns solemnly delivered in archaic Elene, a language very few present could still comprehend. All clerics wore sober black in most situations, but such solemn occasions as this brought forth a rainbow of brightly-coloured vestments. The Patriarchs all wore crimson, and the Primates were robed in the colours of their kingdom of origin. Each of the nineteen cloistered orders of monks and nuns had its own special colour, and each colour had its own special significance. The nave of the Basilica was a riot of often conflicting colours, more closely resembling the site of a Cammorian country fair than a place where a solemn funeral was being conducted. Obscure little rituals and superstitious hold-overs from antiquity were religiously performed, although no one had the faintest notion of their significance. A sizeable number of priests and monks, whose sole duties in life were to perform those rituals and antiquated ceremonies, appeared briefly in public for the only times in their lives. One aged monk, whose sole purpose in life was to carry a black velvet cushion upon which rested a dented and very tarnished salt-cellar thrice around the Archprelate's bier, became so excited that his heart fluttered and stopped, and a replacement for him had to be appointed on the spot. The replacement, a pimply-faced young novice of indifferent merit and questionable piety, wept with gratitude as he realized that his position in life was completely secure now, and that he would only be required actually to do any work once every generation or so.

The interminable funeral droned on and on, punctuated by prayers and hymns. At specified points, the congregation stood; at others, they knelt; and at still others they sat back down again. It was all very solemn, and not very much of it made any real sense.

The Primate Annias sat as near as he dared to the velvet rope separating the Patriarchs from the spectators on the north side of the vast nave, and he was surrounded by flunkies and sycophants. Since Sparhawk could not get close to him, the big Pandion settled instead for sitting in the south gallery directly opposite, where, surrounded by his friends, he could look directly into the grey-faced Churchman's eyes. The gathering of the Patriarchs opposed to Annias inside the walls of the Pandion chapterhouse had proceeded according to plan, and the apprehension and imprisonment of six Patriarchs loyal to the Primate – or at least to his money – had also gone off without a hitch. Annias, his frustration clearly showing on his face, busied himself by scribbling notes to the Patriarch of Coombe, which were delivered by various members of a squad of youthful pages. For each note Annias dispatched to Makova, Sparhawk dispatched one to Dolmant. Sparhawk had a certain advantage in this. Annias actually had to write the notes. Sparhawk simply sent folded scraps of blank paper. It was a ploy to which Dolmant had rather surprisingly agreed.

Kalten slipped into a seat on the other side of Tynian, scribbled a note of his own and passed it down to Sparhawk. 'Good luk,' the note read. 'Fyve moor of are missing patriarks showd up at the bak gait of the chapterhowse a half our ago. They herd we were protekting our frends, and they maid a run for it. Forchunate, wot?' Sparhawk winced slightly. Kalten's grasp on the spelling of the Elene language was probably even looser than Vanion had feared. He showed the note to Talen. 'How does this affect things?' he whispered.

Talen squinted. 'The number voting only changes by one,' he whispered back. 'We locked away six of Annias's votes and got back five more of ours. We've got fifty-two now, he's got fifty-nine, and there are still the nine neutrals. That's a total of one hundred and twenty votes. It still takes seventy-two to win, but not even the nine votes would help him now. They'd only give him sixty-eight, which makes him four votes short.'

'Give me the note,' Sparhawk said. He scribbled the numbers under Kalten's message and then added the two sentences, 'I'd suggest that we suspend all negotiations with the neutrals at this point. We don't need them now.' He handed the note to Talen. 'Take this to Dolmant,' he instructed, 'and it's perfectly all right to grin just a bit while you're on your way down to him.'

'A vicious grin, Sparhawk? A smirk, maybe?'

'Do your best.' Sparhawk took another piece of paper,

192

wrote the information on it and passed it among his armoured friends.

The Primate Annias was suddenly confronted by a group of Church Knights beaming at him from across the nave of the Basilica. His face darkened, and he began to gnaw nervously on one fingernail.

At long last the funeral ceremony wound to its conclusion. The throng in the nave rose to its feet to file along behind the body of Cluvonus to its resting place in the crypt beneath the floor of the Basilica. Sparhawk took Talen and dropped back to have a word with Kalten. 'Where did you learn how to spell?' he asked.

'Spelling is the sort of thing with which no gentleman ought to concern himself, Sparhawk,' Kalten replied loftily. He looked around carefully to be sure he wouldn't be heard. 'Where *is* Wargun?' he whispered.

'I haven't any idea,' Sparhawk whispered back. 'Maybe they had to sober him up. Wargun's sense of direction isn't too good when he's been drinking.'

'We'd better come up with an alternative plan, Sparhawk. The Hierocracy's going back into session just as soon as Cluvonus gets laid away.'

'We've got enough votes to hold Annias off.'

'It's only going to take about two ballots to prove that to him, my friend. He'll start getting rash at that point, and we're badly outnumbered here.' Kalten looked at the heavy wooden beams lining the stairway down into the crypt. 'Maybe I should set fire to the Basilica,' he said.

'*Are you out of your mind?*'

'It would delay things, Sparhawk, and we need a delay very badly just about now.'

'I don't think we have to go *that* far. Let's keep those five Patriarchs under wraps for now. Talen, without those five votes, where do we stand?'

193

'One hundred and fifteen voting, Sparhawk. That means sixty-nine to win.'

'That makes him one vote short again – even if he can buy the neutrals. He'll probably hold off on any kind of confrontation if he thinks he's that close. Kalten, take Perraine and go back to the chapterhouse and get those five Patriarchs. Put them in bits and pieces of armour to disguise them and then form up fifty or so knights to bring them here. Take them into an antechamber. We'll let Dolmant decide when he needs them.'

'Right.' Kalten grinned wickedly. 'We've beaten Annias, though, haven't we, Sparhawk?'

'It looks that way, but let's not start celebrating until there's someone else sitting on that throne. Now get moving.'

There were speeches when the still crimson-robed Hierocracy resumed its deliberations. The speeches were for the most part eulogies delivered by Patriarchs too unimportant to have participated in the formal services in the nave. The Patriarch Ortzel of Kadach, brother of the Baron Alstrom in Lamorkand, was particularly tedious. The session broke up early and resumed again the following morning. The Patriarchs who were opposed to Annias had gathered the previous evening and had selected Ortzel to be their standard-bearer. Sparhawk still had grave reservations about Ortzel, but he kept them to himself.

Dolmant held the five Patriarchs who had so recently returned to his ranks in reserve. Disguised in mismatched armour, they sat with a platoon of Church Knights in a squadroom not far from the audience chamber.

After the Hierocracy had come to order, Patriarch Makova rose to his feet and placed the name of Primate Annias in nomination for the Archprelacy. His nominating speech went on for almost an hour, but the applause greeting it was not particularly fulsome. Then Dolmant rose and nominated Ortzel. Dolmant's speech was more to the point, but it was followed by more enthusiastic applause.

'Do they vote now?' Talen whispered to Sparhawk.

'I don't know,' Sparhawk admitted. 'That's up to Makova. He's holding the chair at the moment.'

'I'd *really* like to see a vote, Sparhawk,' Talen said urgently.

'Aren't you sure of your numbers?' Sparhawk said it with a certain apprehension.

'Of course I am, but numbers are only numbers. A lot of things can happen when you get people involved in something. Take that, for example.' Talen pointed at a page hurriedly carrying a note from the nine uncommitted Patriarchs to Dolmant. 'What are they up to now?'

'They probably want to know why Dolmant suddenly stopped offering them money,' Sparhawk replied. 'Their votes are worthless at this point, although they probably don't fully understand that as yet.'

'What do you think they'll do now?'

'Who knows?' Sparhawk shrugged, 'and who cares?'

Makova, standing at the lectern, glanced over a sheaf of notes. Then he looked up and cleared his throat. 'Before we move on to our initial vote, my brothers,' he began, 'a matter of great urgency has just come to my attention. As some of you may be aware, the Zemochs are massing on the eastern border of Lamorkand with obviously warlike intent. I believe that we may expect with some certainty that Otha will invade the west – possibly within the next few days. It is, therefore, vital that the deliberations of this body be concluded with all possible haste. Our new Archprelate will be faced almost immediately upon his elevation with the direst crisis to face our Church and her faithful sons in the past five centuries.'

'What's he doing?' Sir Bevier whispered to Sparhawk. 'Everybody in Chyrellos knows that Otha's already in eastern Lamorkand.'

'He's stalling,' Sparhawk said, frowning, 'but he doesn't have any reason to stall.'

'What's Annias up to?' Tynian asked, glaring across the audience chamber at the Primate of Cimmura, who sat smiling smugly.

'He's waiting for something to happen,' Sparhawk replied.

'What?'

'I don't have any idea, but Makova's going to keep talking until it does.'

Then Berit slipped into the audience chamber, his face pale and his eyes wild. He half-stumbled up the stairs and pushed his way along the bench to where Sparhawk sat. 'Sir Sparhawk!' he burst out.

'Keep your voice down, Berit!' Sparhawk hissed. 'Sit down and pull yourself together!'

Berit sat and drew in a deep breath.

'All right,' Sparhawk said. 'Speak quietly and tell us what's happening.'

'There are two armies approaching Chyrellos, My Lord,' the novice said tersely.

'*Two?*' Ulath said in some surprise. Then he spread his hands. 'Maybe Wargun split his forces for some reason.'

'It's not King Wargun's army, Sir Ulath,' Berit said. 'As soon as we saw them coming, some Church Knights rode out to find out just who was approaching the city. The ones coming down from the north seem to be Lamorks.'

'Lamorks?' Tynian asked, puzzled. 'What are *they* doing here? They should be on the border facing Otha.'

'I don't think these particular Lamorks are interested in Otha, My Lord,' Berit told him. 'Some of the knights who rode out were Pandions, and they

196

identified the leaders of the Lamork army as Adus and Krager.'

'*What?*' Kalten exclaimed.

'Keep it quiet, Kalten!' Sparhawk grated. 'And the other army, Berit?' he asked, although he already knew the answer.

'Mostly Rendors, My Lord, but there are a fair number of Cammorians as well.'

'And their leader?'

'Martel, My Lord.'

PART TWO

The Archprelate

The Battle of
CHYRELLOS
Stage 1

CAMMORIANS

CAMMORIANS

R. KYDU

R. SARRIN

LAMORKS

RENDORS

R. ARRUK

MERCENARIES

The Battle of
CHYRELLOS
Stage 2

LAMORKS

CAMMORIANS

CAMMORIANS

R. Kydu

R. Sarrin

RENDORS

R. Arjuk

MERCENARIES

THE INNER CITY

The Battle of
CHYRELLOS
Final Stage

FIRST ARMY

SECOND ARMY

THIRD ARMY

THE BASILICA

THE INNER CITY

Arcuk

R. Sarin

R. Kyobu

OCCUPIED
ZONE

Chapter 10

Patriarch Makova's voice droned on and on as morning sunlight streamed into the audience chamber through the foot-thick, triangular panes of leaded crystal in a large round window high up in the wall behind the shrouded throne of the Archprelate. Dust motes hovered golden in those morning streams of light, tracing the elongated outline of each perfect triangle in the still, unmoving air. Makova spoke at great length about the horrors of the Zemoch war some five centuries ago and then went into a detailed analysis of the failures of Church policy during that period of turmoil.

Sparhawk scribbled a brief note to Dolmant, Emban and the Preceptors to advise them of the armies approaching the Holy City.

'Will the church soldiers defend Chyrellos?' Bevier whispered.

'I think the best we can hope for is some token resistance,' Sparhawk replied.

'What's *keeping* Wargun?' Kalten demanded of Ulath.

'I can't even begin to guess.'

'Might this not be a good time to make our apologies and leave quietly?' Tynian suggested. 'Makova's not really telling us anything we don't already know.'

'Let's see what Dolmant says first,' Sparhawk replied. 'I don't want to give Annias any clues about what we might do at this point. We know why he was stalling now, but let's see what he does next. It's going to take Martel a while to deploy his forces anyway, so we've got time yet.'

'Not very much,' Tynian muttered.

'The usual course of action in such circumstances is to demolish the bridges,' Bevier advised. 'That would delay the approaching armies.'

Sparhawk shook his head. 'There are ten different bridges across those two rivers, Bevier, and we only have four hundred knights. I don't think we dare risk those men just for the sake of a few hours' delay.'

'Not to mention the fact that the Lamorks coming from the north won't have any bridges to cross at all,' Tynian added.

The door to the ornate audience chamber opened, and an excited monk hurried to the lectern, his sandals slapping on the polished marble floor and the breath of his passing setting the illuminated dust-motes hanging in the sunny triangles to swirling and dancing. The monk bowed deeply and handed Makova a folded sheet of paper.

Makova quickly read the message, and a thin smile of triumph crossed his pock-marked face. 'I have just received some important information, my brothers,' he announced. 'Two sizeable bodies of pilgrims are approaching Chyrellos. While I know that many of us are other-worldly and abstracted from current events, it's no secret that certain tensions exist in Eosia at this time. Mightn't it be wise of us to adjourn so that we may use such resources available to us to gather more information about these men so that we might better assess the situation?' He looked around. 'Without objection, it is so ordered. The Hierocracy stands in recess until tomorrow morning.'

'Pilgrims,' Ulath snorted contemptuously as he rose to his feet.

Sparhawk, however, sat staring hard across the chamber at the Primate of Cimmura, who looked back at him with a faint smile on his face.

Vanion had risen with the other Patriarchs and looked

204

quickly up at Sparhawk. He made a curt motion with one hand and moved towards the door.

'Let's get out of here,' Sparhawk muttered to his friends over the sound of the excited conversation in the chamber. The black-robed Patriarchs were filing slowly towards the door, their progress impeded by knots of their brothers who had stopped to discuss the matter. Sparhawk led his armoured friends out to the stairway and then down to the marble floor of the audience chamber. The big Pandion resisted his impatient impulse to shove assorted clergymen out of his way as he descended.

He encountered Annias near the door. 'Ah, there you are, Sparhawk,' the thin, grey-faced Primate of Cimmura said with a faintly malicious smile. 'Do you plan to visit the city wall to witness the approach of the throngs of the faithful?'

Sparhawk kept a very tight rein on his temper at that point. 'Interesting notion, neighbour,' he drawled in a tone hovering on insult, 'but I thought I might go and have a bite of lunch instead. Would you care to join me, Annias? Sephrenia's roasting a goat, I think. Roast goat thickens the blood, I'm told, and you've been looking just a bit watery of late, if you don't mind my saying so.'

'So kind of you to invite me, Sparhawk, but I have a pressing engagement elsewhere. Church business, you understand.'

'Of course. Oh, by the way, Annias, when you speak with Martel, give him my regards. Tell him how eager I am to continue the conversation we began back in Dabour.'

'I'll be certain to tell him, Sir Knight. Now, if you'll excuse me.' There was a faint look of annoyance on the Primate's face as he turned and went out through the wide doorway.

'What was that all about?' Tynian asked.

'You have to know Sparhawk a little better,' Kalten

205

told him. 'He'd have died before he gave Annias any satisfaction right there. He didn't even blink when I broke his nose. He just gave me a friendly smile and then kicked me in the stomach.'

'Did *you* blink?'

'No, as a matter of fact, I was too busy trying to get my breath back. What are we doing, Sparhawk?'

'Vanion wants to talk with us.'

The Preceptors of the militant orders were talking together tensely just to one side of the huge door. Patriarch Emban of Ucera was with them. 'I think our major concern at the moment is the condition of the city gates,' Preceptor Abriel was saying. Abriel's burnished armour and his gleaming white surcoat and cloak gave him a deceptively saint-like appearance, but there was not much of saintliness in his face just now.

'Do you think we can count on the church soldiers at all?' the blue-cloaked Preceptor Darellon asked. Darellon was a slender man and seemed not quite robust enough to carry his heavy Deiran armour. 'They could demolish the bridges at least.'

'I wouldn't advise it,' Emban said bluntly. 'They take their orders from Annias, and Annias isn't likely to put any impediments in the way of this Martel person. Sparhawk, exactly what are we facing out there?'

'You tell him, Berit,' Sparhawk told the raw-boned young novice. 'You're the one who actually saw them.'

'Yes, My Lord,' Berit agreed. 'We have Lamorks coming down from the north, Your Grace,' he told Emban, 'and Cammorians and Rendors coming up from the south. Neither army is actually massive, but in combination they're serious enough to threaten the Holy City.'

'This army to the south,' Emban said, 'how are they deployed?'

'The Cammorians are in the van, Your Grace, and

covering the flanks. The Rendors are in the centre and bringing up the rear.'

'Are they wearing those traditional black Rendorish robes?' Emban pressed, his eyes intent.

'It's rather difficult to say, Your Grace,' Berit replied. 'They're beyond the rivers and there's a great deal of dust out there. They seemed to be dressed differently from the Cammorians, though. That's about all I can really say.'

'I see. Vanion, is this young man any good?'

'Very good, Your Grace,' Sparhawk answered for his Preceptor. 'We have high expectations for him.'

'Good. Can I borrow him? And I think I'll want your squire Kurik as well. I need something, and I want them to go and get it for me.'

'Of course, Your Grace,' Sparhawk agreed. 'Go with him, Berit. Kurik's at the chapterhouse. You can pick him up there.'

Emban waddled away with Berit close behind him.

'We'd better split up, My Lords,' Preceptor Komier suggested. 'Let's go and have a look at those gates. Ulath, you're with me.'

'Yes, My Lord.'

'Sparhawk,' Vanion said, 'you come with me. Kalten, I want you to stay close to Patriarch Dolmant. Annias might try to take advantage of the confusion, and Dolmant's the one he has to worry about the most. Do your very best to keep His Grace inside the Basilica. It's a little safer in here.' Vanion put on his plumed black helmet and turned with a swirl of his inky cloak.

'Which way, My Lord?' Sparhawk asked when they emerged from the Basilica and started down the marble steps to the broad court below.

'We'll go to the south gate,' Vanion said grimly. 'I want to have a look at Martel.'

'Right,' Sparhawk agreed. 'I'd be the last in the world to

207

say "I told you so", Vanion, but I did, you know. I wanted to kill Martel right from the start.'

'Don't push it, Sparhawk,' Vanion snapped tersely as he hauled himself up into his saddle. His face became grimly set. 'The situation's changed, though. You have my permission now.'

'It's a little late,' Sparhawk muttered as he mounted Faran.

'What was that?'

'Nothing, My Lord.'

The south gate of the city of Chyrellos had not been closed for over two centuries, and its condition was painfully obvious. Many of its timbers showed signs of dry rot, and the massive chains that operated it were thick with rust. Vanion took one look and shuddered. 'Totally indefensible,' he growled. 'I could kick that thing down all by myself. Let's go on top of the wall, Sparhawk. I want to see these armies.'

The top of the city wall was crowded with citizens, artisans, merchants and common labourers. There was an almost holiday air in the colourfully-dressed throng as they milled about atop the wall, gaping at the approaching army.

'Watch who you're shoving,' one workman said belligerently to Sparhawk. 'We got our right to look the same as you.' He smelled strongly of cheap ale.

'Go somewhere else and look, neighbour,' Sparhawk told him.

'You can't order me around. I got my rights.'

'You want to look, is that it?'

'That's what I'm here for.'

Sparhawk seized him by the front of his canvas smock, lifted him out over the edge of the wall and dropped him. The wall was about fifteen feet high at that point, and the breath whooshed out of the drunken labourer as he hit the ground. 'The approaching army's out that way, neighbour,' Sparhawk said pleasantly, leaning out over the edge and pointing southward. 'Why don't you stroll on out there and have a closer look – just to exercise your rights?'

'You can be very abrasive when you set your mind to it, Sparhawk,' Vanion chided his friend.

'I didn't like his attitude,' Sparhawk grunted. 'Neighbours,' he said then to those crowded around them, 'would anyone else like to assert his rights?' He glanced over the wall. The drunken labourer was scrambling towards the questionable safety of the city, limping, gibbering with terror and with his eyes starting from his face.

A place on the top of the wall immediately opened for the two Pandions.

Vanion looked out at the approaching force of Cammorians and Rendors. 'That's sort of what I'd hoped,' he said to Sparhawk. 'The bulk of Martel's forces are still marching up from the rear, and they're piling up behind the bridges.' He pointed at the vast dust-cloud rising for several miles to the south. 'He won't be able to get those men here until almost dark. I doubt that his deployment will be complete before noon tomorrow. That gives us a little bit of time at least. Let's go back down.'

Sparhawk turned to follow his Preceptor, but then stopped and turned back. An ornate carriage with the emblem of the Church prominently embossed on its sides had just emerged from the south gate. The monk who was driving it had a suspiciously familiar set to his shoulders. Just before the carriage turned west, a bearded man wearing the cassock of a Patriarch peered briefly out of the carriage window. The carriage was no more than thirty yards away, so Sparhawk could easily identify the supposed clergyman inside.

It was Kurik.

Sparhawk started to swear.

'What's the matter?' Vanion asked him.

'I'm going to have a long talk with Patriarch Emban,' Sparhawk grated. 'That's Kurik and Berit in that carriage.'

'Are you sure?'

'I'd recognize Kurik a hundred yards away on a dark night. Emban had no right to endanger them like that.'

'It's too late to do anything about it now. Come along, Sparhawk. I want to go and talk with Martel.'

'Martel?'

'Maybe we can surprise an answer or two out of him. Do you think he's arrogant enough to honour a flag of truce – just to demonstrate his advantage at this point?'

Sparhawk nodded slowly. 'Probably. Martel's ego's a vast open sore. He'd go through the motions of being honourable even if it involved walking through fire.'

'That's more or less the way I see him too. Let's go and find out if we're right, but don't get so caught up in exchanging insults with him that you forget to keep your eyes open, Sparhawk. What we really want to do is to get a closer look at his army. I need to know if it's just some rabble he's scraped together from country fairs and roadside taverns or something more serious.'

A commandeered bedsheet – although Vanion *did* offer to pay the frightened innkeeper for it even as Sparhawk was stripping it from the bed of an upstairs room – provided them with a flag of truce. It popped and flapped quite satisfyingly from Sparhawk's lance as the two black-armoured knights thundered out through the south gate towards the approaching army. They rode to a hilltop and stopped there. Sparhawk turned Faran slightly so that the stiff breeze caught their improvised flag and blew it out for all to see. Though they were some distance from the van of Martel's army, Sparhawk could hear distant shouts and commands. The army gradually undulated to a stop, and not long after, Martel, accompanied by one of his soldiers, rode out from the midst of their troops. Martel also carried a lance, and a white cape that looked suspiciously like that of a Cyrinic Knight flapped from it. Sparhawk squinted at him. 'I wonder,' he mused. 'Bhelliom brought Ehlana back from the brink of death. I wonder if I could persuade it to do the same for Martel.'

'Why would you want to?'

'So I could kill him again, My Lord. I could make killing Martel over and over again my life's work with just a little encouragement.'

Vanion gave him a very hard look, but he didn't say anything.

Martel wore a very expensive suit of armour, its cuirass and shoulder-plates embossed with gold and silver and with the steel itself highly burnished. It appeared to be of Deiran forging, and it was much more elegant than the functional armour of the Church Knights. When he was within a few yards of Sparhawk and Vanion, he thrust the butt of his lance into the ground and removed his ornate, white-plumed helmet. His white hair flowed out behind him in the stiff breeze. 'My Lord,' he said with exaggerated courtesy, inclining his head to Vanion.

Vanion's face was icy. He did not speak to the knight he had expelled from the Pandion Order, but motioned Sparhawk forward instead.

'Ah,' Martel said in a tone that might even have been one of genuine regret, 'I expected better of you, Vanion,' he said. 'Oh well, I'll talk with Sparhawk instead. Feel free to listen in, if you'd like.'

Sparhawk also drove the butt of his lance into the turf, and he also removed his helmet as he nudged Faran forward.

'You're looking well, old boy,' Martel said.

211

'You look about the same – except for the fancy armour.'

'I recently had occasion to do some thinking,' Martel replied. 'I've gathered up a great deal of money in the last several years, but it occurred to me that I wasn't enjoying it very much. I decided to buy some new toys.'

'That's a new horse too, isn't it?' Sparhawk looked at Martel's bulky black mount.

'Do you like him? I could get you one from the same stable, if you'd like.'

'I'll stick with Faran.'

'Did you ever civilize that ugly brute?'

'I sort of like him the way he is. What are your intentions here, Martel?'

'Isn't it obvious, old boy? I'm going to seize the Holy City. If I were speaking for public approval, I could put a better face on it and use the word "liberate", I suppose, but since we're such old friends, I suppose I can afford to be frank. To put it in plain terms, Sparhawk, I'm going to march into the Holy City, and, as the saying goes, bend it to my will.'

'You mean you're going to *try*, Martel.'

'Who's going to stop me?'

'Your own good sense, I hope. You're a bit deranged, but you've never been stupid.'

Martel gave him a mocking half-bow.

'Where did you come up with all the troops on such short notice?'

'Short notice?' Martel laughed. 'You don't pay much attention to things, do you, Sparhawk? You spent too much time in Jiroch, I'm afraid. All that sun.' He shuddered. 'By the way, have you heard from the lovely Lillias lately?' He threw that in quickly, obviously showing off his knowledge of Sparhawk's activities for the past several years in the hope of discomfiting his former brother.

'She was well – last I heard.' Sparhawk gave no hint that he was at all surprised.

'I may just take her when this is all over. She's a significant sort of woman, I noticed. It might amuse me to dally with your former mistress.'

'Get lots of rest, Martel. I don't really think you've got enough stamina for Lillias. You still haven't answered my question, though.'

'Thought you could answer it for yourself, old boy, now that I've nudged your memory a bit. I gathered the Lamorks while I was up there fomenting discord between Baron Alstrom and Count Gerrich. The Cammorian mercenaries are always available. All I had to do was pass the word, and they came running. The Rendors weren't that difficult, once I'd disposed of Arasham. Incidentally, he kept croaking the word "Ramshorn" while he was dying. Could that possibly have been that secret word you cooked up? Very pedestrian, Sparhawk. Most unimaginative. The new spiritual leader of Rendor is a much easier man to manage.'

'I've met him,' Sparhawk said shortly. 'I wish you joy in his companionship.'

'Oh, Ulesim's not so bad – as long as you stay upwind of him. Anyway, I landed in Arcium, sacked and burned Coombe and marched on Larium. I must say that Wargun took his own sweet time getting there, though. When he arrived, I rode away and then led him around in circles down in Arcium. It was a way to amuse myself while I was awaiting word of the passing of the revered Cluvonus. Did you give him a nice funeral, by the way?'

'Fairly standard.'

'I'm sorry I missed it.'

'There's something else you should be sorry about, Martel. Annias isn't going to be able to pay you. Ehlana's recovered and cut him off from her treasury again.'

'Yes, I'd heard about that – from Princess Arissa and her son. I freed them from that cloister as a favour to the Primate of Cimmura. There was a slight misunderstanding while I was releasing them, though, and all the nuns in that cloister died quite suddenly. Regrettable, perhaps, but you religious types really shouldn't become involved in politics, you know. My soldiers also set fire to the cloister as we were riding away. I'll convey your best wishes to Arissa when I rejoin my troops. She's been staying in my pavilion since we left Demos. The horrors of her confinement quite unnerved her, and I've been sort of offering what comfort I could.'

'That's one more you owe me, Martel,' Sparhawk grated.

'One more what?'

'Those nuns are another reason for me to kill you.'

'Feel free to try at any time, old boy. How on earth did you manage to cure Ehlana, though? I was assured down in Rendor that there was no possible cure.'

'Your informants were wrong. We found out what the cure was in Dabour. Actually that's why Sephrenia and I were really there. You might call spoiling your plans there in Arasham's tent a sort of a bonus.'

'I was really put out with you about that, you know.'

'How are you going to pay your troops?'

'Sparhawk,' Martel said wearily, 'I'm about to capture the richest city in the world. Have you any idea of how much loot's available inside the walls of Chyrellos? My troops joined me eagerly – for no pay at all – just for the chance to browse around in there.'

'I hope they're ready for a protracted siege, then.'

'It's not going to take me all that long to get inside, Sparhawk. Annias will open the gates for me.'

'Annias doesn't have enough votes in the Hierocracy to do that.'

214

'I rather imagine that my presence here will alter the vote somewhat.'

'Would you like to settle this right here and now? Just you and me?' Sparhawk offered.

'Why should I do that when I've already got the advantage, old boy?'

'All right. Try to get into Chyrellos then, and maybe we can find one of those alleys you're so fond of.'

'I yearn for the day, dear brother,' Martel smiled. 'Well, Vanion, has your tame ape here wheedled enough answers out of me to suit you yet, or should I go on?'

'Let's go back,' Vanion said abruptly to Sparhawk.

'Always a pleasure talking with you, Lord Vanion,' Martel called mockingly after them.

'Do you really think Bhelliom might possibly bring him back from the grave?' Vanion asked Sparhawk as they rode back towards the city. 'I wouldn't mind killing him a time or two myself.'

'We can ask Sephrenia, I suppose.'

They gathered once again in the red-draped study of Sir Nashan, the portly Pandion who was in charge of the chapterhouse here. The chapterhouse, unlike those of the other orders, was just inside the walls of the ancient inner city, the original Chyrellos. Each of the Preceptors gave a report on one of the gates of the city. None of the reports was particularly encouraging. Abriel, as senior Preceptor, rose to his feet. 'What do we think, gentlemen?' he said. 'Is there any possible way we can hold the entire city?'

'Absolutely out of the question, Abriel,' Komier said bluntly. 'Those gates wouldn't keep out a herd of sheep, and even counting the church soldiers, we don't have enough men to hold off the kind of force gathering out there.'

'You're raising a very unpleasant notion, Komier,' Darellon said.

215

'I know, but I don't see very many options, do you?'

'Not really.'

'I'm sorry, My Lords,' Sir Nashan said deferentially, 'but I don't quite follow what you've got in mind.'

'We'll have to pull back to the walls of the inner city, Nashan,' Vanion told him.

'And abandon the rest?' Nashan exclaimed. 'My Lords, we're talking about the largest – and richest city in the world!'

'We have no choice, Sir Nashan,' Abriel explained. 'The walls of the inner city were built in antiquity. They're much higher and stronger than the largely ornamental walls that encircle the rest of Chyrellos. We can defend the inner city – for a time, at least – but we have no chance of holding the whole city.'

'We're going to have to make some hard and unpleasant choices here,' Preceptor Darellon said. 'If we pull back to the inner walls, we're going to have to close the gates to the general population. We won't have sufficient supplies in the old city to sustain that many people.'

'We won't be able to do a thing until we can take command of the church soldiers, though,' Vanion said. 'Four hundred of us couldn't possibly hold out against Martel's army.'

'I might be able to help you there,' Patriarch Emban said. Emban was sprawled in a large chair, his fat hands on his paunch. 'It's going to depend on just how arrogant Makova's feeling in the morning, however.' Emban had been evasive when Sparhawk had demanded some sort of explanation about what he had sent Kurik and Berit to do.

'We're going to have a certain tactical advantage,' Komier said thoughtfully. 'Martel's troops are mercenaries. As soon as they get inside the outer city, they're going to stop for some constructive looting. That's going to give us more time.'

Emban chuckled. 'It's also going to distract a sizeable portion of the Hierocracy,' he grinned. 'Many of my fellow Patriarchs have lavish houses out beyond the inner walls. They'll view the sacking of the outer city with a certain anguish, I'd imagine. That *might* just reduce their enthusiasm for the candidacy of the Primate of Cimmura. *My* house, however, is here inside the old walls. I'll be able to think quite clearly – and so will you, won't you, Dolmant?'

'You're a bad man, Emban,' Dolmant told him.

'But God appreciates my efforts, Dolmant, no matter how sneaky or underhanded. All of us live but to serve – each in his own special way.' He paused, frowning slightly. 'Ortzel's our candidate. I'd have probably chosen someone else, but there's a tide of conservatism in the Church just now, and Ortzel's so conservative that he doesn't even believe in fire. We may have to work on him just a bit, Dolmant. He's not exactly what you'd call lovable.'

'That's *our* problem, Emban – yours and mine,' Dolmant pointed out. 'I think we should concern ourselves with military matters at the moment.'

'I suspect that our next step will have to be charting out routes for withdrawal,' Abriel said. 'If the Patriarch of Ucera here is successful in transferring command of the church soldiers over to us, we'll have to move them back inside the inner walls rapidly before the general population realizes what we're doing. Otherwise, we'll have mobs of refugees in here with us.'

'This is brutal, My Lords,' Sephrenia chided them. 'You're abandoning innocent people to the mercy of a horde of savages. Martel's men won't be satisfied with just looting. There are certain to be atrocities out there.'

Dolmant sighed. 'War is never civilized, little mother,' he told her. 'One other thing. From now on, you *will*

217

accompany us to the Basilica every day. I want you where we can protect you.'

'As you wish, dear one,' she replied.

Talen's face was mournful. 'I don't suppose you could see your way clear to sort of let me slip outside the inner walls before you close the gates, could you?' he asked Sparhawk.

'No,' Sparhawk replied, 'but why would you want to be out there?'

'To look after my share of the loot, naturally. This is a once in a lifetime opportunity.'

'You would surely not join in the looting of houses, would you, Talen?' Bevier asked in a shocked tone.

'Of course not, Sir Bevier. I'd let Martel's soldiers do that. It's when they're back out in the street with their arms full of the things that they've stolen that the thieves of Chyrellos will move in and pick them over. Martel's going to lose a lot of men in the next few days, I'd imagine. I can almost guarantee that an epidemic of stab-wounds is going to break out in his ranks before this is all over. There are beggars out there who'll never have to beg again.' The boy sighed again. 'You're robbing my childhood of all its fun, Sparhawk,' he accused.

'There is absolutely no danger whatsoever, my brothers,' Makova scoffed the following morning when the Hierocracy reconvened. 'The commander of my own personal guard, Captain Gorta –' He paused a moment to give the Preceptors of the militant orders a hard stare. The sudden demise of the previous captain of his troops obviously still rankled. 'Captain Erden, that is – went out at great personal risk to question these approaching pilgrims most closely, and he assures me that they are no more than that – pilgrims, faithful sons of the Church – and that they are making this pilgrimage to the Holy City in order

218

to join their voices with others in thanksgiving when the new Archprelate is elevated to the holy throne.'

'Now, that's really amazing, Makova,' Patriarch Emban drawled. 'As it so happens, I sent observers of my own out of the city, and they had an entirely different kind of report. How do you imagine we can reconcile these differences?'

Makova's smile was brief, even frosty. 'The Patriarch of Ucera is well known for his jocularity,' he said. 'He is indeed a droll and jolly fellow, and his merry japes frequently relax our tensions at stressful moments, but is this really the time for hilarity, my dear Emban?'

'Do you see me smiling, Makova?' Emban's tone had quite nearly the bite of a dagger-thrust to the kidneys. He rose, grunting. 'What *my* people report, dear brothers, is that this horde of so-called pilgrims at our gates is anything but friendly.'

'Nonsense,' Makova snapped.

'Perhaps,' Emban said, 'but I've taken the liberty of having one of these "pilgrims" brought here to the Basilica so that we may examine him more closely. He may not choose to speak very much, but much can be gleaned from observing a man's demeanour, his bearing, his origins – even his clothing.' Emban clapped his hands sharply together before Makova could object or exert his authority.

The door to the chamber opened, and Kurik and Berit entered. They each held an ankle of the black-robed man they were bringing in to be interviewed, and they dragged the inert body across the marble floor, leaving a long crimson smear of blood on the white stone behind them.

'What are you *doing*?' Makova half-shrieked.

'Merely presenting evidence, Makova. No rational decision can be made without a thorough examination of the evidence, can it?' Emban pointed at a spot not too far in

219

front of the lectern. 'Put the witness there, my friends,' he instructed Kurik and Berit.

'I *forbid* this!' Makova howled.

'Forbid away, old boy,' Emban shrugged, 'but it's too late now. Everybody in the chamber has already seen this man, and we all know what he is, don't we?' Emban waddled over to the corpse lying spread-eagled on the marble floor. 'We can all tell by this man's features what his nation of origin was, and his black clothing confirms it. My brothers, what we have here was obviously a Rendor.'

'Patriarch Emban of Ucera,' Makova said desperately, 'I arrest you on the charge of murder.'

'Don't be an ass, Makova,' Emban said. 'You can't arrest me while the Hierocracy's in session. Besides, we're inside the Basilica, and I claim sanctuary.' He looked at Kurik. 'Did you really have to kill him?' he asked.

'Yes, Your Grace,' the burly squire replied. 'The situation made it necessary – but we said a brief prayer over him afterwards, though.'

'Most exemplary, my son,' Emban said. 'I will therefore grant you and your young companion here full absolution for your part in sending this miserable heretic to face the infinite mercy of God.' The fat man looked around the chamber. 'Now,' he said, 'to return to our interrogation of this "pilgrim". We have here a Rendor – armed with a sword, you'll note. Since the only Rendors currently on this part of the Eosian continent are Eshandists, we must conclude that this "pilgrim" was one as well. Given their views, would we expect Eshandist heretics to come to the Holy City to celebrate the elevation of a new Archprelate? Has our dear brother Makova somehow miraculously converted the heretics of the south to the worship of the true God and rejoined them with the body of our holy mother Church? I pause for the reply of the esteemed Patriarch of Coombe.' He stood looking expectantly at Makova.

'I'm certainly glad he's on *our* side,' Ulath murmured to Tynian.

'Truly.'

'Ah,' Emban said as Makova looked at him helplessly. 'It was too much to hope for, I suppose. We must all apologize to God for our failure to seize this opportunity to heal the wound in the body of our holy mother. Our regret, however, and our bitter tears of disappointment must not dim our eyes to the harshness of reality. The "pilgrims" at our gates are not what they seem. Our dear brother Makova has been cruelly deceived, I'm afraid. What stands at the gates of Chyrellos is not a multitude of the faithful, but a ravening army of our most hated foes bent on destroying and desecrating the very centre of the true faith. Our own personal fate, my brothers, is of no moment, but I should advise you all to make your peace with God. The horrors the Eshandist heretics inflict upon members of the higher clergy are too well known to require repeating. I myself am totally resigned to facing the flames.' He paused, then grinned. He clapped both hands to his huge paunch. 'I'll make a jolly fire, though.'

A titter of nervous laughter rippled through the chamber.

'Our own fates, my brothers, are not important,' Emban continued. 'What matters here is the fate of the Holy City and the fate of the Church. We face a cruel but simple decision. Do we surrender our mother to the heretics, or do we fight?'

'Fight!' one Patriarch shouted, springing to his feet. 'Fight!'

The cry was quickly taken up. Soon the entire Hierocracy was on its feet, roaring out the word, 'Fight!'

Emban clasped his hands behind his back somewhat theatrically and bowed his head. When he lifted his face, tears were actually streaming down his cheeks. He turned slowly, giving everyone in the audience chamber ample opportunity to see those tears. 'Alas, my brothers,' he said in a broken voice. 'Our vows forbid us to lay aside our cassocks and vestments and to take up the sword. We stand helpless in this dreadful crisis. We are doomed, my brothers, and our holy mother Church is doomed with us. Alas that I have lived so long that I must witness this terrible day. Where can we turn, brothers? Who will come to our aid? Who has the power to protect us in this darkest hour? What manner of men are there in all the world who can defend us in this dreadful, fatal conflict?'

There was a breathless pause.

'The Church Knights!' a feeble old voice wheezed from one of the red-cushioned benches. 'We must turn to the Knights of the Church! Not even the powers of Hell can prevail against them!'

'The Church Knights!' the Hierocracy roared as in one voice. 'The Church Knights!'

Chapter 11

The excited tumult in the large chamber continued for some time as Patriarch Emban of Ucera stood gravely in the centre of the long marble floor, just *happening* to have placed himself in the precise centre of that elongated circle of light streaming down through the round window behind the vacant throne. As the babble of voices began to die out, Emban raised one pudgy hand. 'Indeed, my brothers,' he continued, his voice carrying just that right note of gravity, 'the invincible Knights of the Church could easily defend Chyrellos, but the knights are committed at this time to the defence of Arcium. The Preceptors are here, of course, taking their rightful places among us, but each of them has but a token force here, certainly not enough to fight off the armies of darkness encircling us. We cannot whisk the full might of the militant orders from the rocky plains of Arcium to the Holy City in the twinkling of an eye; and even if we could, how could we convince the commanders of the army in that sorely beset kingdom that our need is greater than theirs and thus persuade them to release the knights to come to our aid?'

Patriarch Ortzel of Kadach rose to his feet, his severe face framed by his pale, greying hair. 'If I may speak, Emban,' he said. The Patriarch of Kadach was the compromise candidate of the faction opposed to Annias, and he spoke with a certain authority.

'Of course,' Emban said. 'I eagerly await the wisdom of my esteemed brother from Lamorkand.'

'The paramount duty of the Church is to survive so that she may continue her work,' Ortzel said in his harsh voice.

'All other considerations must be secondary to that. Will we all concede that point?'

There was a murmur of agreement.

'There are times when sacrifices must be made,' Ortzel continued. 'If a man's leg be caught between the rocks at the bottom of a tidal pool and the rising waters be lapping at his chin, must not the man regretfully sacrifice the limb in order to save his life? Thus it is with us. In sorrow must we sacrifice the whole of Arcium if need be to save our life – which is our holy mother Church. What we are faced with here, my brothers, is a crisis. In times past, the Hierocracy has been extremely reluctant to impose the stern and stringent requirements of this most extreme of measures, but the situation facing us is doubtless the severest trial facing our holy mother since the Zemoch invasion five centuries ago. God is watching us, my brothers, and He will surely judge us and our fitness to continue our stewardship of His beloved Church. I, therefore, as the laws which govern us require, demand that an immediate vote be taken. The question upon which we will vote can be stated most simply. "Does the current situation in Chyrellos constitute a Crisis of the Faith?" Yes or no?'

Makova's eyes were wide with shock. 'Surely,' he burst out, 'surely the situation is not *that* critical! We have not even tried negotiation with the armies at our gates as yet, and –'

'The Patriarch is not in order,' Ortzel said abruptly. 'The question of Crisis of the Faith is not open to discussion.'

'Point of Law!' Makova shouted.

Ortzel looked intimidatingly at the weedy monk who served as law clerk. 'Speak the law,' he commanded.

The monk was trembling violently, and he began to desperately paw through his books.

224

'What's happening here?' Talen asked in confusion. 'I don't understand.'

'Crisis of the Faith is almost never invoked,' Bevier told him, 'probably because the kings of western Eosia object so violently. In a Crisis of the Faith, the Church assumes control of everything – governments, armies, resources, money – everything.'

'But wouldn't a Crisis of the Faith require a substantive vote?' Kalten asked. 'Or even unanimity?'

'I don't think so,' Bevier said. 'Let's see what the law clerk has to say.'

'Isn't it sort of redundant at this point anyway?' Tynian asked. 'We've already sent for Wargun and told him that there's a Church crisis.'

'Somebody probably neglected to tell Ortzel,' Ulath replied. 'He's a stickler for legalities, and there's no real point in disturbing his sensibilities, is there?'

The weedy monk, his face absolutely white, rose and cleared his throat. His voice was squeaky with fright as he began. 'The Patriarch of Kadach has correctly cited the law,' he declared. 'The question of Crisis of the Faith must be put to an immediate secret vote.'

'*Secret?*' Makova exclaimed.

'Such is the law, Your Grace, and the vote is to be decided by a simple majority.'

'But –'

'I must remind the Patriarch of Coombe that further discussion is not in order.' Ortzel's voice cracked like a whip. 'I call for the vote.' He looked around. 'You,' he snapped at the clergyman sitting not far from the goggle-eyed Annias, 'fetch the instruments of the vote. They are, as I recall, in the chest at the right hand of the Archprelate's throne.'

The clergyman hesitated, looking fearfully at Annias.

'*Move, man!*' Ortzel roared.

225

The priest jumped to his feet and ran to the shrouded throne.

'Somebody's going to have to explain this to me a little better,' Talen said in a baffled tone.

'Later, Talen,' Sephrenia told him softly. Sephrenia, wearing a heavy black robe that looked slightly ecclesiastical and concealed her race and sex, sat amongst the Church Knights, almost totally concealed by their armoured bulk. 'Let's watch the exquisite dance being performed before us.'

'Sephrenia,' Sparhawk chided her.

'Sorry,' she apologized. 'I'm not poking fun at your Church, Sparhawk, just at all this involuted manoeuvring.'

The instruments of the vote consisted of a fairly large black box, quite dusty and totally unadorned, and two plain leather bags securely held shut with stamped leaden seals.

'Patriarch of Coombe,' Ortzel said quite concisely. 'You hold the chair at the moment. It is your duty to break the seals and cause the ballots to be distributed.'

Makova glanced quickly at the law clerk, and the little monk nodded. Then Makova took up the two bags, prised open the leaden seals and took an object from each. They were perhaps the size of a common penny. One was white and the other black. 'We will vote with these,' he declared to his fellow Patriarchs, holding the counters up. 'Is it agreed that the black means no and the white yes?'

There was a rumble of agreement.

'Distribute the counters then,' Makova instructed a pair of youthful pages. 'Each member of the Hierocracy shall receive one white counter and one black.' He cleared his throat. 'As God gives you wisdom, my brothers, vote your consciences in this matter.' Some trace of colour had returned to Makova's face.

226

'He's been counting votes,' Kalten said. 'He's got fifty-nine, and he *thinks* we've only got forty-seven. He doesn't know about the five Patriarchs hiding in that closet. I'd imagine those five votes will come as quite a surprise to him. He'll still win, though.'

'You're forgetting the neutrals, Kalten,' Bevier reminded him.

'They'll just abstain, won't they? They're still looking for bribes. They're not going to offend either side.'

'They can't abstain, Kalten,' Bevier told him, 'not on *this* vote. Church Law says that they have to come down on one side or the other of this question.'

'Where did you learn so much about this, Bevier?'

'I told you that I'd studied military history.'

'What's military history got to do with this?'

'The Church declared a Crisis of the Faith during the Zemoch invasion. I looked into it as part of my study.'

'Oh.'

As the two pages were distributing the counters, Dolmant rose and walked to the huge doors. He spoke briefly to the members of the Archprelate's guard standing outside and returned to his seat. It was when the two boys distributing the counters were nearly at the end of the fourth row of the crimson-cushioned benches that the door opened, and the five nervous Patriarchs who had been in hiding filed in.

'What's the meaning of this?' Makova was goggle-eyed.

'The Patriarch of Coombe is not in order,' Ortzel reminded him. Ortzel seemed to enjoy saying that to Makova. 'My brothers,' he began to address the five, 'we are presently voting on –'

'It is *my* responsibility to instruct our brothers,' Makova said vehemently.

'The Patriarch of Coombe is in error,' Ortzel said in a clipped voice. 'It was *I* who put the question before the

227

Hierocracy, and, therefore, the responsibility is *mine*.' He quickly explained the vote to his five fellow Patriarchs. He stressed the gravity of the situation to them, something Makova surely would not have done.

Makova regained his composure.

'He's counting votes again,' Kalten muttered. 'He's still got more than we have. It all hangs on the neutrals now.'

The black box was placed on a table in front of Makova's lectern, and the Patriarchs filed by, each depositing one of his counters in the slot on the top of the box. Some were quite obvious about which counter they were depositing. Others were not.

'I'll take care of the tallying,' Makova declared.

'No,' Ortzel said flatly, 'at least not alone. It was *I* who placed the question before the Hierocracy, and *I* will assist you.'

'I'm beginning to like Ortzel more and more,' Tynian said to Ulath.

'Yes,' Ulath agreed. 'Maybe we misjudged him.'

Makova's face grew more grey as he and Ortzel began to tally up the votes. There was a hushed, almost breathless silence as the tallying continued.

'And done,' Ortzel said curtly. 'Announce the totals, Makova.'

Makova threw a quick, apologetic glance at Annias. 'The vote stands at sixty-four yes and fifty-six no,' he muttered almost inaudibly.

'Say it again, Makova,' Ortzel prompted. 'Some of our brothers have failing hearing.'

Makova gave him a look filled with hatred and repeated the totals in a louder voice.

'We got the neutrals!' Talen exulted, '*and* we stole three of Annias's votes as well.'

'Well then,' Emban said mildly, 'I'm glad that's been settled. We have much to consider, my brothers, and very

228

little time. Am I correct in assuming that it is the will of the Hierocracy that we send immediately for the Church Knights – *and* the armies of western Eosia as well – to come to our defence with all possible haste?'

'Will you leave the kingdom of Arcium totally defenceless, Emban?' Makova demanded.

'Just what's threatening Arcium at the moment, Makova? All the Eshandists are camped outside *our* gates. Do you want another vote?'

'Substance,' Makova said flatly, insisting on a 60 per cent majority on the question.

'Point of Law,' Emban replied. His fat face had an almost saintly expression. He looked at the law clerk. 'What is the law on matters of substance under these circumstances?' he asked.

'Saving only the election of an Archprelate, a substantive vote is not required in time of Crisis of the Faith, Your Grace,' the monk replied.

'I rather thought that might be the case,' Emban smiled. 'Well, Makova, do we vote or not?'

'I'll withdraw the question of substance,' Makova conceded grudgingly, 'but exactly how do you propose to get a messenger out of a besieged city?'

Ortzel rose again. 'As my brothers may be aware, I am a Lamork,' he said. 'We are well accustomed to sieges in Lamorkand. Last night I sent twenty of my own men in disguise to the outskirts of the city and beyond. They are awaiting only that signal which even now rises as a plume of red smoke from the dome of this very Basilica. I would surmise that they are already riding hard for Arcium – at least they'd better be, if they know what's good for them.'

'I'm going to *like* him,' Kalten grinned.

'You dared to do this without the consent of the Hierocracy as a whole, Ortzel?' Makova gasped.

'Was there ever any doubt concerning the outcome of the voting, Makova?'

'I begin to catch a strong smell of collusion here,' Sephrenia said lightly.

'My brothers,' Emban continued, 'the crisis we presently face is clearly a military one, and for the most part, we are not military men. How may we avoid the errors, the confusion, the delays which untrained and unworldly Churchmen must inevitably cause as they flounder through unfamiliar complexities? The leadership of the Patriarch of Coombe has been exemplary, and I'm sure we join together in expressing our heartfelt gratitude to him, but, regrettably, the Patriarch of Coombe is no more well versed in military science than I, and I'll confess it freely, my brothers, I can't tell one end of a sword from the other.' He smiled broadly. 'Quite obviously, *my* training has been with eating implements rather than with those of war. I'd be happy to accept any challenge in that area, however. My opponent and I could happily duel to the death on a well-roasted ox.'

The Hierocracy laughed at that. The tension was somewhat relaxed by the laughter.

'We need a military man, my brothers,' Emban continued. 'We need a general now instead of a chairman. We have four such generals in our very midst. These, of course, are the Preceptors of the four orders.'

There was an excited stir, but Emban held up one hand. '*But*,' he continued, 'do we dare distract one of these towering military geniuses from the vital task of defending Chyrellos? I think not. Where then should we look?' He paused. 'I must now break a solemn promise I made to one of my brothers,' he confessed. 'I pray that both he and God will be able to find it in their hearts to forgive me. We do, in fact, have a man with military training in our midst, dear brothers. He has modestly concealed this

230

fact, but a modesty which deprives us of his talent in this time of crisis is no virtue.' His broad round face took on an expression of genuine regret. 'Forgive me, Dolmant,' he said, 'but I have no choice in this matter. My duty to the Church comes even before my duty to a friend.'

Dolmant's eyes were frosty.

Emban sighed. 'I expect that when we conclude this meeting, my dear brother from Demos will thrash me thoroughly, but I'm well padded, and the bruises won't be all that visible – I hope. In his youth, the Patriarch of Demos was an acolyte in the Pandion order, and –'

There was a sudden amazed babble in the chamber.

Emban raised his voice. 'Preceptor Vanion of that order, who was himself a novice at the self-same time, assures me that our saintly brother from Demos was a consummate warrior and might very well have risen to the rank of Preceptor himself had not our holy mother found other uses for his vast talents.' He paused again. 'Praise God, my brothers, that we were never faced with *that* decision. Choosing between Vanion and Dolmant would likely have been a task beyond our combined wisdom.' He continued for a time, heaping praise upon Dolmant. Then he looked around. 'What is our decision, my brothers? Shall we beseech our brother of Demos to guide us in this time of our gravest peril?'

Makova stared at him. His mouth opened a couple of times as if he were on the verge of speaking, but each time, he clamped it tightly shut.

Sparhawk put his hands on the bench in front of him, leaned forward and spoke quietly to the elderly monk sitting in front of him. 'Has Patriarch Makova been suddenly struck dumb, neighbour?' he asked. 'I'd have thought he'd be climbing the walls by now.'

'In a very real sense the Patriarch of Coombe *has* been struck dumb, Sir Knight,' the monk replied. 'There's a

231

long-standing custom – even a rule – in the Hierocracy that a Patriarch may not speak to his own candidacy for any post – no matter how remote that candidacy may be. It's considered immodest.'

'Sensible custom, that one,' Sparhawk said.

'I feel much the same way, Sir Knight,' the monk smiled. 'Makova tends to put me to sleep for some reason.' Sparhawk grinned at him. 'Me too,' he said. 'I suppose we should both pray for greater patience – one of these days.'

Makova looked around desperately, but none of his friends saw fit to speak – either because of a lack of anything flattering to say about him, or because they could see which way a vote would go. 'Vote,' he said somewhat sullenly.

'Good idea, Makova,' Emban smiled. 'Let's move right along. Time's fleeing even as we speak.'

The vote this time was sixty-five for Dolmant's assuming the chair and fifty-five against. Another of the supporters of the Primate of Cimmura had defected.

'My brother from Demos,' Emban said to Dolmant when the tally had been completed and announced, 'would you be so kind as to assume the chair?'

Dolmant came forward while Makova angrily gathered up his papers and stalked away from the lectern.

'You honour me beyond my ability to express my gratitude, my brothers,' Dolmant said. 'For the moment, let me merely say thank you so that we may more quickly deal with the crisis at hand. Our most immediate need is for a greater force under the command of the Knights of the Church. How may we address that need?'

Emban had not even bothered to sit down. 'The force of which our revered chairman speaks is at hand, my brothers,' he said to the assemblage. 'Each of us has a detachment of church soldiers at his disposal. In view of the current crisis, I propose that we immediately turn control of those troops over to the militant orders.'

'Will you strip us of our only protection, Emban?' Makova protested.

'The protection of the Holy City is far more important, Makova,' Emban told him. 'Will history say of us that we were so cowardly that we refused our aid to our holy mother in her time of need out of timidity and a craven concern for our own skins? Pray God that no such poltroon contaminates us by his presence in our midst. What says the Hierocracy? Shall we make this insignificant sacrifice for the sake of the Church?'

The rumble of assent this time was slightly pained in some quarters.

'Will any Patriarch call for a vote on the matter?' Dolmant asked with cool correctness. He looked around at the now-silent tiers. 'Then let the recorder set down the fact that the suggestion of the Patriarch of Ucera was accepted by general acclamation. The scribes will then draw up suitable documents which each member of the Hierocracy will sign, transferring command of his personal detachment of church soldiers over to the militant orders for the defence of the city.' He paused. 'Will someone please ask the commander of the Archprelate's personal guard to present himself before the Hierocracy?'

A priest scurried to the door, and shortly thereafter a brawny officer with red hair, a polished breastplate and armed with an embossed shield and antiquated short sword entered. His expression clearly showed that he was aware of the army at the city gates.

'One question, Colonel,' Dolmant said to him. 'My brothers have asked me to chair their deliberations. In the absence of an Archprelate, do I speak in his stead?'

The colonel considered it for a moment. 'You do, Your Grace,' he admitted, looking somewhat pleased.

233

'That's unheard of,' Makova protested, obviously a bit chagrined that he had not taken advantage of this obscure rule during his *own* tenure as chairman.

'So is this situation, Makova,' Dolmant told him. 'A Crisis of the Faith has only been declared five times in the history of the Church, and in each of the four preceding crises, a vigorous Archprelate occupied the throne which so sadly stands empty before us. When faced with unique circumstances, we must improvise. This is what we're going to do, Colonel. The Patriarchs are each going to sign documents turning command of their individual detachments of soldiers over to the Church Knights. To save time and unnecessary arguments, as soon as those documents are signed, you and your men will escort each Patriarch to the barracks of their sundry forces where the Patriarch may confirm his written command in person.' He turned then to look at the Preceptors. 'Lord Abriel,' he said, 'will you and your fellow Preceptors dispatch knights to take command of the soldiers just as soon as they are released and to assemble them in a place of your choosing? Our deployment must be quick and unfaltering.'

Abriel stood. 'We will, Your Grace,' he declared, 'and gladly.'

'Thank you, My Lord Abriel,' Dolmant said. He looked back at the ranks of the Hierocracy, rising tier upon tier above him. 'We have done what we can, my brothers,' he said to them. 'It seems most appropriate now that we proceed immediately to turn our soldiers over to the Knights of the Church, and then perhaps we might each devote ourselves to seeking counsel from God. Perhaps He, in His infinite wisdom, will suggest further steps we might take to defend His beloved Church. Therefore, without objection, the Hierocracy stands in recess until such time as this crisis has passed.'

'Brilliant,' Bevier exclaimed. 'In one series of master-strokes, they've wrested control of the Hierocracy from Annias, stripped him of all his soldiers and forestalled the taking of any votes while we're not here to stop them.'

'It's kind of a shame that they broke off so quickly,' Talen said. 'The way things stand right now, we only need one more vote to elect our *own* Archprelate.'

Sparhawk was elated as he and his companions joined the crush at the door to the audience chamber. Although Martel was still a grave threat to the Holy City, they had succeeded in wresting control of the Hierocracy from Annias and his underlings, and the weakness of the Primate of Cimmura's grasp on his votes was clearly demonstrated by the defection of four of his bought and paid-for Patriarchs. As he started to move slowly from the chamber, he felt again that now-familiar sense of overpowering dread. He half-turned. This time, he even partially saw it. The shadow was back behind the Archprelate's throne, seeming to undulate softly in the dimness. Sparhawk's hand went to the front of his surcoat to make sure that Bhelliom was still where it belonged. The jewel was secure, and he knew that the drawstring on the pouch was tightly tied. It appeared that his reasoning had been slightly faulty. The shadow *could* make an appearance independently of the Bhelliom. It was even here inside the most consecrated building of the Elene faith. He had thought that here of all places he would be free of it, but it was not so. Troubled, he continued with his friends from the room which now seemed dark and chill.

The attempt on Sparhawk's life came almost immediately after he saw the shadow. A cowled monk, one of the many in the crowd at the door, spun suddenly and drove a small dagger directly at the big Pandion's un-visored face. It was only Sparhawk's trained reflexes that saved him. Without thinking, he blocked the dagger stroke with his armoured forearm and then seized the monk. With a despairing cry, the monk drove his little dagger into his own side. He stiffened abruptly, and Sparhawk felt a violent shudder pass through the body of the man he was holding. Then the monk's face went blank, and he sagged limply.

'Kalten!' Sparhawk hissed to his friend. 'Give me a hand! Keep him on his feet.'

Kalten stepped swiftly to the other side of the monk's body and took his arm.

'Is our brother unwell?' another monk asked them as they half-carried the body out through the door.

'Fainted,' Kalten replied in an offhand manner. 'Some people can't stand crowds. My friend and I will take him into some side chamber and let him get his breath.'

'Slick,' Sparhawk muttered a quick compliment.

'You see, Sparhawk, I *can* think on my feet.' Kalten jerked his head towards the door of a nearby antechamber. 'Let's take him in there and have a look at him.'

They dragged the body into the chamber and closed the door behind them. Kalten pulled the dagger from the monk's side. 'Not much of a weapon,' he said disdainfully.

'It was enough,' Sparhawk growled. 'One little nick with it stiffened him up like a plank.'

'Poison?' Kalten guessed.

'Probably – unless the sight of his own blood overpowered him. Let's have a look.' Sparhawk bent and tore open the monk's robe.

The 'monk' was a Rendor.

'Isn't *that* interesting?' Kalten said. 'It looks as if that crossbowman who's been trying to kill you has started hiring outside help.'

'Maybe this *is* the crossbowman.'

'No way, Sparhawk. The crossbowman's been hiding in the general population. Anybody with half a brain would recognize a Rendor. He couldn't have just mingled with the crowd.'

'You're probably right. Give me the dagger. I think I'd better show it to Sephrenia.'

'Martel really doesn't want to meet you, does he?'

'What makes you think Martel's behind this?'

'What makes you think he isn't? What about this?' Kalten pointed at the body on the floor.

'Leave it. The caretakers here in the Basilica will run across it eventually and dispose of it for us.'

Many of the church soldiers submitted their resignations when they discovered that they were being placed under the command of the Church Knights – the officers did, at any rate. Resignation is not an option available to common soldiers. These resignations, however, were not accepted, but the knights were not totally insensitive to the feelings of the various colonels, captains and lieutenants who felt strong moral compunctions about commanding their forces under such circumstances. They graciously divested such officers of their rank and enrolled them as common soldiers. They then marched the red-tunicked troops to the great square in front of the Basilica for deployment on the walls and at the gates of the inner city.

'Did you have any trouble?' Ulath asked Tynian as the two of them, each leading a sizeable detachment of soldiers, met at an intersection.

'A few resignations was about all,' Tynian shrugged. 'I have a whole new group of officers in this batch.'

'So do I,' Ulath replied. 'A lot of old sergeants are in charge now.'

'I ran across Bevier a while back,' Tynian said as the two rode towards the main gate of the inner city. 'He

237

doesn't seem to be having the same problem for some reason.'

'The reason should be fairly obvious, Tynian,' Ulath grinned. 'Word of what he did to that captain who tried to keep us out of the Basilica has got around.' Ulath pulled off his ogre-horned helmet and scratched his head. 'I think it was the praying afterwards that chilled everybody's blood the most. It's one thing to lop off a man's head in the heat of a discussion, but praying for his soul afterwards has a very unsettling effect on most people for some reason.'

'That's probably it,' Tynian agreed. He looked back at the soldiers straggling disconsolately towards the site of what was very likely to be actual fighting. Church soldiers for the most part did not enlist in order to fight, and they viewed the impending unpleasantness with a vast lack of enthusiasm. 'Gentlemen, gentlemen,' Tynian chided them, 'this won't do at all. You must try to *look* like soldiers at least. Please straighten up those ranks and try to march in step. We *do* have some reputation to maintain, after all.' He paused a moment. 'How about a song, gentlemen?' he suggested. 'The people are always encouraged when soldiers sing as they march into battle. It's a demonstration of bravery, after all, and it shows a manly contempt for death and dismemberment.'

The song which rose from the ranks was feeble, and Tynian insisted that the soldiers start again – several times – until the full-throated bawling of the column satisfied his need for a display of martial enthusiasm.

'You're a cruel sort of fellow, Tynian,' Ulath noted.

'I know,' Tynian agreed.

Sephrenia's reaction to the news of the failed attack by the disguised Rendor was almost one of indifference. 'You're sure you saw the shadow behind the Archprelate's throne just before the attack?' she asked Sparhawk.

He nodded.

'Our hypothesis still seems quite valid then.' She said it almost with satisfaction. She looked at the small, poison-smeared dagger lying on the table between them. 'Hardly the sort of thing you'd want to use against an armoured man,' she observed.

'A scratch would have done the trick, little mother.'

'How could he have scratched you when you were wrapped in steel?'

'He tried to stab me in the face, Sephrenia.'

'Keep your visor closed then.'

'Won't that look a little ridiculous?'

'Which do you prefer? Ridiculous or dead? Did any of our friends see the attempt?'

'Kalten did – or at least he knew that it happened.'

She frowned. 'I was hoping that we could sort of keep this between ourselves – at least until we know what's going on.'

'Kalten knows that someone's been trying to kill me – they all do, for that matter. They all think it's just Martel and that he's up to his usual tricks.'

'Let's sort of leave it at that then, shall we?'

'There have been some desertions, My Lord,' Kalten reported to Vanion as the group gathered on the steps of the Basilica. 'There was no way we could keep word of what we were doing from reaching some of those outlying barracks.'

'It was to be expected,' Vanion said. 'Did anybody happen to look over the outer wall to see what Martel's doing?'

'Berit's been keeping an eye on things, My Lord,' Kalten replied. 'That boy's going to make an awfully good Pandion. We ought to try to keep him alive if we can. Anyway, he reports that Martel's almost completed

239

his deployment. He could probably give the order to march on the city now. I'm surprised that he hasn't, really. I'm sure some of Annias's toadies have reached him by now to report what happened in the Basilica this morning. Every moment he delays just gives us more time to get ready for him.'

'Greed, Kalten,' Sparhawk told his friend. 'Martel's very greedy, and he can't believe that his greed's not universal. He thinks we'll try to defend the whole of Chyrellos, and he wants to give us time to get spread so thin that he'll be able to walk over us. He'd never be able to bring himself to believe that we'd abandon the outer city and concentrate on defending the inner walls.'

'I suspect that many of my brother Patriarchs feel much the same way,' Emban said. 'The voting might have been much tighter if those of them with palaces in the outer city had been aware of the fact that we're going to abandon their houses to Martel.'

Komier and Ulath came up the marble steps to join them. 'We're going to have to pull down some houses just outside the walls,' Komier said. 'Those are Lamorks to the north of the city, and Lamorks use crossbows. We don't want any rooftops out there for them to shoot at us from.' The Genidian Preceptor paused. 'I'm not very experienced at sieges,' he admitted. 'What kind of engines is this Martel likely to bring against us?'

'Battering rams,' Abriel told him, 'catapults, assault towers.'

'What's an assault tower?'

'It's a sort of high structure. They roll it up until it's flush against the wall. Then the soldiers come spilling out right in the middle of us. It's a way to cut down on the sort of casualties they'll take with scaling ladders.'

'Roll?' Komier asked.

'The towers are on wheels.'

Komier grunted. 'We'll leave the rubble from the houses we pull down lying in the streets then. Wheels don't run too well across piles of building blocks.'

Berit came galloping into the broad square and along the quickly opened path through the ranks of the church soldiers massed in front of the Basilica. He leapt from his saddle and ran up the stairs. 'My Lords,' he said a little breathlessly, 'Martel's men are beginning to assemble their siege engines.'

'Will someone explain that to me?' Komier asked.

'The engines are transported in pieces, Komier,' Abriel told him. 'When you get to the place where you're going to fight, you have to put them together.'

'How long's that likely to take? You Arcians are the experts on castles and sieges.'

'Quite a few hours, Komier. The mangonels will take longer. He'll have to construct those here.'

'What's a mangonel?'

'It's a sort of oversized catapult. It's too big to transport – even if you break it down. They use whole trees when they build them.'

'How big a rock can it throw?'

'A half-ton or so.'

'The walls won't take too many of those.'

'That's sort of the idea, I think. He'll be using the standard catapults at first, though. The mangonels will probably take at least a week to build.'

'The catapults and battering rams and towers should keep us occupied until then, I suppose,' Komier said sourly. 'I *hate* sieges.' Then he shrugged. 'We'd better get at it.' He looked disdainfully at the church soldiers. 'Let's set these enthusiastic volunteers to work tearing down houses and cluttering up the streets.'

* * *

241

At some point not long after dark, some of Martel's scouts discovered that the outer walls of Chyrellos were undefended. A few of them, the stupider ones, reported back. For the most part, however, these scouts proved to be the vanguard of the looters. An hour or so before midnight Berit woke Sparhawk and Kalten to report that there were troops in the outer city. Then he turned to leave again.

'Where are you going?' Sparhawk asked bluntly.

'Back out there, Sir Sparhawk.'

'No you're not. You stay inside the inner walls now. I don't want you getting yourself killed.'

'Somebody has to keep an eye on things, Sir Sparhawk,' Berit objected.

'There's a cupola on top of the dome of the Basilica,' Sparhawk told him. 'Go and get Kurik, and then the two of you go up there to watch.'

'All right, Sir Sparhawk.' Berit's tone was slightly sullen.

'Berit,' Kalten said as he pulled on his mail-shirt.

'Yes, Sir Kalten?'

'You don't have to like it, you know. All you have to do is to do it.'

Sparhawk and the others went through the ancient narrow streets of the inner city and mounted to the wall. The streets of the outer city were filled with bobbing torches as the mercenaries under Martel's command ran from house to house, stealing what they could. The occasional screams of women clearly said that looting was not the only thing on the minds of the attacking force. A crowd of panicky and wailing citizens stood outside the now-closed gates of the inner city, pleading to be admitted, but the gates remained steadfastly closed to them.

A somewhat delicate Patriarch with sagging pouches

242

under his eyes came running up the stairs to the top of the wall. 'What are you *doing*?' he almost shrieked at Dolmant. 'Why aren't these soldiers out there defending the city?'

'It's a military decision, Cholda,' Dolmant replied calmly. 'We don't have enough men to defend the whole of Chyrellos. We've had to pull back inside the walls of the old city.'

'*Are you mad?* My house is out there!'

'I'm sorry, Cholda,' Dolmant told him, 'but there's nothing I can do.'

'But I *voted* for you!'

'I appreciate that.'

'My house! My things! My treasures!' Patriarch Cholda of Mirischum stood wringing his hands. 'My beautiful house! All my furnishings! My gold!'

'Go and take refuge in the Basilica, Cholda,' Dolmant told him coldly. 'Pray that your sacrifice may find favour in the eyes of God.'

The Patriarch of Mirischum turned and stumbled back down the stairs, weeping bitterly.

'I think you lost a vote there, Dolmant,' Emban said.

'The voting's all over, Emban, and I'm sure I could live without that particular vote anyway.'

'I'm not so sure, Dolmant,' Emban disagreed. 'There's still one ballot yet to come. It's fairly important, and we might just need Cholda before it's over.'

'They've started,' Tynian said sadly.

'What has?' Kalten asked him.

'The fires,' Tynian replied, pointing out across the city as a sudden pillar of golden orange flame and black smoke shot up through the roof of a house. 'Soldiers always seem to get careless with their torches when they're looting at night.'

'Isn't there something we can do?' Bevier asked urgently.

'Not a thing, I'm afraid,' Tynian said, 'except maybe pray for rain.'

'It's the wrong season for it,' Ulath said.

'I know,' Tynian sighed.

Chapter 12

The looting of the outer city continued throughout the day on into the night. The fires spread quickly, since no one was available to check them, and the city was soon enveloped in a thick pall of smoke. From the top of the wall, Sparhawk and his friends could see wild-eyed mercenaries running through the streets, each carrying an improvised sack over his shoulder. The crowd of citizens gathered before the gates of the inner city to plead for admittance melted away as Martel's mercenaries began to appear.

There were murders, of course – many of them in plain sight – and there were other atrocities as well. One unshaven Cammorian dragged a young woman from a house by the hair and disappeared with her up an alley. Her screams quite clearly told the watchers what was happening to her.

A red-tunicked young church soldier standing beside Sparhawk atop the city wall began to weep openly. Then, as the somewhat shame-faced Cammorian emerged from the alley, the soldier raised his bow, aimed and released all in one motion. The Cammorian doubled over, clutching at the arrow buried to the feathers in his belly.

'Good man,' Sparhawk said shortly to the young fellow.

'That could have been my sister, Sir Knight,' the soldier said, wiping at his eyes.

Neither of them was really prepared for what happened next. The woman, dishevelled and weeping, emerged from the alley and saw her attacker writhing in the rubble-littered street. She lurched to where he lay and kicked him solidly in the face several times. Then, seeing that he was unable to defend himself, she snatched his dagger from his belt. It were best, perhaps, not to describe what she did to him next. His screams, however, echoed in the streets for quite some time. When at last he fell silent, she discarded the bloody knife, opened the sack he had been carrying and looked inside. Then she wiped her eyes on her sleeve, tied the sack shut and dragged it back to her house.

The soldier who had shot the Cammorian started to retch violently.

'Nobody's very civilized in those circumstances, neighbour,' Sparhawk told him, laying a comforting hand on his shoulder, 'and the lady *did* have a certain justification for what she just did.'

'That must have hurt him terribly,' the soldier said in a shaking voice.

'I think that's what she had in mind, neighbour. Go and get a drink of water and wash your face. Try not to think about it.'

'Thank you, Sir Knight,' the young fellow said, swallowing hard.

'Perhaps not *all* church soldiers are so bad,' Sparhawk muttered to himself, revising a long-held opinion.

As the sun went down, they gathered in Sir Nashan's red-draped study in the Pandion chapterhouse, what Sir Tynian and Sir Ulath had come to call – not entirely in jest – 'the high command', the Preceptors, the three Patriarchs and Sparhawk and his friends. Kurik, Berit and Talen, however, were not present.

Sir Nashan hovered diffidently near the door. Nashan was an able administrator, but he was just a bit uncomfortable in the presence of so much authority. 'If there's nothing further you need, My Lords,' he said, 'I'll leave you to your deliberations now.'

'Stay, Nashan,' Vanion told him. The Preceptor smiled. 'We certainly don't want to dispossess you, and your knowledge of the city may prove very useful.'

'Thank you, Lord Vanion,' the stout knight said, slipping into a chair.

'I think we've stolen a march on your friend Martel, Vanion,' Preceptor Abriel said.

'Have you looked over the wall lately, Abriel?' Vanion asked dryly.

'As a matter of fact, I have,' Abriel said, 'and that's exactly what I'm talking about. As Sir Sparhawk told us yesterday, this Martel couldn't believe that we'd abandon the outer city without a fight, so he didn't take it into account when he made his plans. He made no attempt to keep his scouts out of the city, and those scouts are just the forerunners of the main body of looters. As soon as his scouts found that the city was unprotected, they rushed in to loot the houses and most of the rest of the army followed. Martel's completely lost control of his forces now, and he won't regain it until the outer city is picked clean. Not only that, as soon as his soldiers have as much as they can carry, they'll begin to desert.'

'I cannot encourage theft,' Patriarch Ortzel said rigidly, 'but under the circumstances –' A faint, almost sly smile touched his thin lips.

'Wealth needs to be redistributed from time to time, Ortzel,' Emban pontificated. 'People with too much money have too much time to think up assorted sins to commit. Perhaps this is God's way of restoring the filthy rich to a condition of wholesome poverty.'

'I wonder if you'd feel the same way if your *own* house were being looted.'

'That might influence my opinion, all right,' Emban conceded.

'God's ways are mysterious,' Bevier said devoutly. 'We

247

had no choice but to abandon the outer city, and that may be the one thing that will save us.'

'I don't think we can count on enough desertions from Martel's ranks to grow complacent, gentlemen,' Vanion said. 'The rampage of his troops will gain us some time, I'll grant you.' He looked around at the other Preceptors. 'A week, perhaps?' he asked.

'At the very most,' Komier said. 'There are a lot of men out there, and they're very busy. It's not going to take them all that long to strip the city.'

'And that's when the killing's going to start,' Kalten said. 'As you said, Lord Komier, there are a lot of men out there, and I'm fairly sure that not all of them got into the city. The ones who are still outside are just as greedy as the ones who got here first. It's going to be chaotic for a while, I think, and it's going to take Martel quite a bit longer to regain control.'

'He's probably right,' Komier grunted. 'Either way, we've got some time. There are four gates into the inner city here, and most of them aren't much better than the ones in the outer wall. One gate's easier to defend than four, so why don't we fix it that way?'

'Are you going to make the gates disappear by magic, Komier?' Emban asked. 'I know the Church Knights are trained to do many unusual things, but this *is* the Holy City, after all. Would God really approve of that sort of thing on his own doorstep?'

'I never even thought of magic,' Komier admitted. 'Actually, I wasn't going to use anything like that. It's very hard to batter down a gate if there are two or three collapsed houses piled up behind it, isn't it?'

'Almost impossible,' Abriel agreed.

Emban grinned broadly. 'Isn't Makova's house fairly close to the east gate of the inner city?' he asked.

'Now that you mention it, Your Grace, I do believe it is,' Sir Nashan replied.

'A fairly substantial house?' Komier said.

'It certainly should be,' Emban said, 'considering what he paid for it.'

'What the Elenian taxpayers paid for it, Your Grace,' Sparhawk corrected.

'Ah, yes. I'd almost forgotten that. Would the Elenian taxpayers be willing to contribute that very expensive house to the defence of the Church?'

'They'd be delighted, Your Grace.'

'We'll certainly look the house of the Patriarch of Coombe over very carefully when we're selecting the ones to tear down,' Komier promised.

'The only question now is the whereabouts of King Wargun,' Dolmant said. 'Martel's blunder has bought us some time, but it won't keep him out of the inner city forever. Could your messengers have gone astray, Ortzel?'

'They're good, solid men,' Ortzel said, 'and an army of the size of Wargun's shouldn't be hard to find. Besides, the messengers you and Emban sent earlier should have reached him quite some time ago, shouldn't they?'

'Not to mention the ones the Earl of Lenda sent from Cimmura,' Sparhawk added.

'The absence of the King of Thalesia is a mystery,' Emban said, 'and it's becoming increasingly inconvenient.'

The door opened, and Berit entered. 'Excuse me, My Lords,' he apologized, 'but you wanted to be informed if anything unusual was happening out in the city.'

'What have you seen, Berit?' Vanion asked him.

'I was up in that little house on top of the dome of the Basilica, My Lord –'

'Cupola,' Vanion corrected.

249

'I can never remember that word,' Berit confessed. 'Anyway, you can see the whole city from up there. The ordinary people are fleeing from Chyrellos. They're streaming out through all of the gates in the outer wall.'

'Martel doesn't want them underfoot,' Kalten said.

'*And* he wants the women out of town,' Sparhawk added bleakly.

'I didn't quite understand that, Sparhawk,' Bevier said.

'I'll explain it to you later,' Sparhawk told him, glancing at Sephrenia.

There was a knock on the door, and a Pandion Knight entered. He was holding Talen by the arm, and the boy from the streets of Cimmura had a disgusted expression on his face and a fair-sized sack in one hand. 'You wanted to see this young fellow, Sir Sparhawk?' the Pandion asked.

'Yes,' Sparhawk replied. 'Thank you, Sir Knight.' He looked rather sternly at Talen. 'Where have you been?' he asked directly.

Talen's expression grew evasive. 'Ah – here and there, My Lord,' he replied.

'You *know* that's not going to work, Talen,' Sparhawk said wearily. 'I'll get the answer out of you eventually anyway, so why bother trying to hide it?'

'To keep in practice, I suppose,' Talen shrugged. 'You'll twist my arm until I tell you, won't you, Sparhawk?'

'Let's hope it doesn't come to that.'

'All right,' Talen sighed. 'There are thieves in the streets of the inner city, and there are a lot of interesting things going on out beyond the walls. I managed to find a way to slip out there. I've been selling that information.'

'How's business?' Patriarch Emban asked him. Emban's eyes were bright.

'Not too bad, actually,' Talen said professionally. 'Most of the thieves here inside the walls don't have too much to bargain with. You don't make much profit sitting on the things you've stolen, but I'm easy to do business with. I just charge them a percentage of what they're able to steal from the soldiers outside the walls.'

'Open the sack, Talen,' Sparhawk ordered him.

'I'm really shocked at you, Sparhawk,' Talen said. 'There are holy men in this room. Is it really proper to expose them to – well, you know.'

'Open the sack, Talen.'

The boy sighed, laid the sack on Sir Nashan's desk and opened it. There were a number of largely decorative items inside – metal goblets, small statues, thick chains, assorted eating utensils and a rather intricately engraved tray about the size of a dinner plate. All of the items appeared to be made of solid gold.

'You got all *this* just for selling information?' Tynian asked incredulously.

'Information's the most valuable thing in the world, Sir Tynian,' Talen replied loftily, 'and I'm not doing anything immoral or illegal. My conscience is perfectly clear. Not only that, I'm making my contribution to the defence of the city.'

'I don't quite follow that reasoning,' Sir Nashan said.

'The soldiers out there aren't giving up what they've stolen willingly, Sir Knight,' Talen smirked. 'The thieves know they'll feel that way, so they don't bother to make requests. Martel's lost a fair number of his troops since the sun went down.'

'Most reprehensible, young man,' Ortzel said reprovingly.

'My hands are completely clean, Your Grace,' Talen replied innocently. 'I haven't personally stabbed a single soldier in the back. What the villains from the street do out there isn't *my* responsibility, is it?' The boy's eyes shone with innocence.

'Give it up, Ortzel,' Emban chuckled. 'None of us are

251

worldly enough to argue with this young fellow.' He paused. 'Dolmant,' he said, 'tithing is a well-established practice, isn't it?'

'Of course,' the Patriarch of Demos said.

'I was sure it was. Given the unusual circumstances here, I'd say that the young fellow should contribute a quarter of his profits to the Church, wouldn't you?'

'It sounds about right to me,' Dolmant agreed.

'A *quarter*?' Talen exclaimed. 'That's highway robbery!'

'Actually, we aren't on a highway, my son,' Emban smiled. 'Would you like to settle up after each of your excursions? Or should we wait until you've gathered all your profits and we can take care of it all at once?'

'After you've settled up with the Patriarch Emban, Talen,' Vanion said, 'I have this burning curiosity about this secret way you've found to get in and out of the city.'

'It's not really much of a secret, Lord Vanion,' Talen said deprecatingly. 'About all it really consists of are the names of a squad of enterprising church soldiers who have the night watch in one of the towers on the wall. They've got a nice long rope with knots tied in it to make climbing up and down easy. They're willing to rent out the rope, and I'm willing to rent out their names and the location of the tower they're guarding. Everybody's making a nice profit.'

'Including the Church,' Patriarch Emban reminded him.

'I was sort of hoping you'd forgotten about that, Your Grace.'

'Hope is a cardinal virtue, my son,' Emban said piously, 'even when it's misplaced.'

Kurik came in carrying a Lamork crossbow. 'I think we may be in luck, My Lords,' he said. 'I happened to look into the armoury of the Archprelate's personal guard in

252

the Basilica. They've got racks and racks of these down there, and barrels of bolts.'

'An eminently suitable weapon,' Ortzel approved. Ortzel *was* a Lamork, after all.

'They're slower than a longbow, Your Grace,' Kurik pointed out, 'but they *do* have an extraordinary range. I think they'll be very effective in breaking up charges against the inner city before they can pick up much momentum.'

'Do you know how to use this weapon, Kurik?' Vanion asked him.

'Yes, Lord Vanion.'

'Start training some church soldiers then.'

'Yes, My Lord.'

'A number of things are turning our way, my friends,' Vanion said. 'We have a defensible position, a parity of weapons and a certain delay working for us.'

'I'd still be happier if Wargun were here,' Komier said.

'So would I,' Vanion agreed, 'but we'll just have to make do with what we've got until he gets here, I'm afraid.'

'There's something else we need to concern ourselves with, gentlemen,' Emban said gravely. 'Assuming that all goes well, the Hierocracy's going to go back into session just as soon as Martel's been driven off. Abandoning the outer city is going to alienate a sizeable number of Patriarchs. If you let a man's house be looted and burned, he's not going to be very fond of you or want to vote for you. We've got to find some way to prove the connection between Annias and Martel. If we don't, we're doing all this just for the exercise. I can talk as fast as the next man, but I can't perform miracles. I need something to work with.'

It was about midnight when Sparhawk climbed the stairs to the wall of the old city not far from the south gate, the most defensible of the four and the one it had been decided to leave unblocked. Chyrellos was burning in earnest now. A looter, upon entering a house to find it already empty, feels a certain angry frustration, and he usually vents those feelings by setting fire to the place. Such behaviour is totally predictable and, in a certain sense, quite natural. The looters, their faces more desperate now as the number of unpillaged houses diminished, ran from building to building waving torches and weapons. Kurik, always practical, had stationed the church soldiers he was training with crossbows on the walls, and the looters provided those men with moving targets upon which to practise. There were not too many hits, but the soldiers appeared to be improving.

Then, from a narrow street at the edge of the zone of collapsed houses just beyond practical crossbow range, a sizeable number of well-armed men on horseback emerged. The man in the lead was astride a glossy black horse, and he wore embossed Deiran armour. He removed his helmet. It was Martel, and close behind him were the brutish Adus and the weasel-like Krager.

Kurik joined Sparhawk and his blond friend. 'I can order the soldiers to shoot at them, if you'd like,' the squire said to Sparhawk. 'Somebody might get lucky.'

Sparhawk scratched his chin. 'No, I don't think so, Kurik,' he said.

'You're passing up an awfully good opportunity, Sparhawk,' Kalten said. 'If Martel catches a stray cross-bow bolt in the eye, that whole army out there will fall apart.'

'Not just yet,' Sparhawk said. 'Let's see if I can irritate him just a bit first. Martel sometimes blurts things out when he's irritated. Let's see if I can jolt something out of him.'

'That's a fair distance for shouting,' Kalten said.

'I don't have to shout,' Sparhawk smiled.

'I wish you wouldn't do that,' Kalten complained. 'It always makes me feel so inadequate.'

'You should have paid attention to your lessons when you were a novice then.' Sparhawk focused his attention on the white-haired man and wove the intricate Styric spell. 'It sort of went to pieces on you, didn't it, Martel?' he asked in a conversational tone.

'Is that you, Sparhawk?' Martel's voice was just as conversational as he too utilized the spell they had both learned as novices. 'So awfully good to hear your voice again, old boy. I didn't quite follow your comment, though. Things seem to be going fairly well from where *I* sit.'

'Why don't you see how many of your soldiers you can interest in an assault on these walls about now? Take as long as you want, old boy, I'm not going anywhere.'

'It was really very clever to desert the city, Sparhawk. I wasn't really expecting that.'

'We sort of liked it. It must be causing you a great deal of anguish every time you think about all the loot that's getting away from you, though.'

'Who said it's getting away? I made a few speeches to my men. Most of my army's still under control – out there in the meadows on the other sides of those rivers. I pointed out to them that it's much easier to let the enterprising types do all the work of looting. Then, when they come out, we take the loot away from them and put it all into a common pile. Everybody will share equally.'

'Even you?'

'Oh, good God no, Sparhawk,' Martel laughed. 'I'm the general. I take my share first.'

'The lion's share?'

'I *am* the lion, after all. We'll all grow very, very wealthy once we break into the treasure vaults below the Basilica.'

'That's going a little far even for *you*, Martel.'

'Business is business, Sparhawk. You and Vanion stripped me of my honour, so now all I can do is solace myself with money – and satisfaction, of course. I think I'll have your head mounted when this is all over, my friend.'

'It's right here, Martel. All you have to do is come here and claim it. It's going to take your soldiers a long time to loot the city, and you don't really have much time to waste.'

'It won't take them all *that* long, Sparhawk. They're moving along at a very good clip, you know. A man who thinks he's working for himself is always more industrious.'

'That's only the first wave of looters. They're the ones who are concentrating on gold. The next wave will go looking for silver. Then the third wave will start tearing houses apart looking for the hiding places where people keep valuables. I'd guess that it's going to be a month or so before they've stolen everything in Chyrellos – down to the last brass candlestick. You don't really have a month, old boy – not with Wargun wandering around out there with half the manpower in Eosia behind him.'

'Ah yes, Wargun, the drunken King of Thalesia. I'd almost forgotten him. What *do* you suppose happened to him? It's so unlike him to be this tardy.'

Sparhawk broke the spell. 'Order your soldiers to drop some arrows on him, Kurik,' he said bleakly.

'What's the trouble, Sparhawk?' Kalten asked.

'Martel's found some way to keep Wargun away from Chyrellos. We'd better go and advise the Preceptors. I'm afraid we're all alone here.'

Chapter 13

'He didn't say it exactly, Vanion,' Sparhawk reported. 'You know how he is, but there was that sort of implied smirk in his voice that he knows is so irritating. We both know Martel well enough to know what he meant.'

'What exactly did he say again, Sir Sparhawk?' Dolmant asked.

'We were talking about Wargun, Your Grace, and he said, "What *do* you suppose has happened to him? It's so unlike him to be this tardy."' Sparhawk did his best to imitate Martel's intonation.

'It does have a knowing sort of ring to it, doesn't it?' Dolmant agreed. 'I don't know Martel as well as the two of you do, but that has the sound of a man who's terribly pleased with himself.'

'Sparhawk's right,' Sephrenia told them. 'Martel's worked out some way to keep Wargun away. The question is how.'

'How isn't important, little mother,' Vanion said. The four of them were sitting together in a small room adjacent to Sir Nashan's study. 'What's important now is keeping this information away from the soldiers. The Church Knights are trained to accept desperate circumstances. The soldiers aren't. About all they're clinging to at the moment is the expectation of seeing Wargun's armies coming across the meadows lying to the west of the River Arruk. The inner city's not really surrounded yet, and the looters aren't paying any attention to other people. We could have desertions by the score if word of this gets out. Advise the Church

Knights quietly – and in confidence. I'll tell the other Preceptors.'

'And I'll tell Emban and Ortzel,' Dolmant promised.

The week seemed to drag, although there were many, many things that had to be done. Houses were pulled down and their rubble used to block the three gates which Komier had decided were only marginally defensible. Kurik continued to train selected church soldiers in the use of their crossbows. Berit gathered a group of young monks, and they traded off keeping watch from the cupola atop the Basilica dome. Emban scurried about inside the Basilica itself, trying to maintain his hold on votes, although that grew more and more difficult. None of the defenders had the temerity to refuse the Patriarchs of the Church the right to ascend the walls to look out at the city, and the view from those walls was not very encouraging. A fair number of Patriarchs, several of them in the very forefront of the fight to keep the Primate of Cimmura off the throne, lamented bitterly as the fires approached those quarters of the city in which their houses lay, and not a few told Emban to his face that he could forget about any future support. Emban grew drawn-looking, and he began to complain of pains in his stomach as he watched his support melting before his eyes.

Annias did nothing. He simply waited.

And Chyrellos continued to burn.

Sparhawk stood atop the wall early one evening looking out over the burning city. His mood was sombre. He heard a slight clinking behind him and turned quickly.

It was Sir Bevier. 'Not too promising, is it?' the young Arcian said, also looking out at Chyrellos.

'Not really,' Sparhawk agreed. He looked directly at his young friend. 'How long do you think these walls will stand up to a mangonel, Bevier?'

258

'Not very long, I'm afraid. The walls were built in antiquity. They weren't meant to stand up to modern siege-engines. Perhaps Martel won't bother to construct them. They take a long time to build, and the workers have to know exactly what they're doing. A poorly constructed mangonel will kill more of its crew than it will the enemy. There's a great deal of stress involved when you load one.'

'We can hope, I suppose. I think these walls will stand up to ordinary catapults, but if he starts lobbing half-ton boulders at us –' Sparhawk shrugged.

'Sparhawk.' It was Talen. The boy came quickly up the stairs from below. 'Sephrenia wants to see you at the chapterhouse. She says it's urgent.'

'Go ahead, Sparhawk,' Bevier said. 'I'll keep watch here.'

Sparhawk nodded and went down the stairs to the narrow street below.

Sephrenia met him in the lower hall. Her face was even more pale than usual.

'What is it?' Sparhawk asked her.

'It's Perraine, dear one,' she replied in a hushed voice. 'He's dying.'

'*Dying?* There haven't been any attacks yet. What happened to him?'

'He's killed himself, Sparhawk.'

'*Perraine?*'

'He's taken poison of some kind, and he refuses to tell me what it is.'

'Is there any way –?'

She shook her head. 'He wants to talk with you, Sparhawk. You'd better hurry. I don't think there's much time.'

Sir Perraine lay on a narrow cot in a cell-like room. His face was deathly pale, and he was sweating profusely.

'You certainly took your time, Sparhawk,' he said in a weak-sounding voice.

'What's this all about, Perraine?'

'It's something appropriate. Let's not waste any time with this. There are some things you need to know before I leave.'

'We can talk about that after Sephrenia gives you the antidote.'

'There isn't going to be any antidote. Just be still and listen to me.' Perraine sighed deeply. 'I've betrayed you, Sparhawk.'

'You aren't capable of that, Perraine.'

'Anyone's capable of it, my friend. All he needs is some kind of reason. I had one, believe me. Hear me out. I don't have much time left.' He closed his eyes for a moment. 'You've noticed that someone's been trying to kill you lately, haven't you?'

'Yes, but what's –'

'It was me, Sparhawk – or people I'd hired.'

'*You?*'

'Thank God I failed.'

'Why, Perraine? Have I insulted you somehow?'

'Don't be foolish, Sparhawk. I was acting on orders from Martel.'

'Why would you take orders from Martel?'

'Because he was holding something over my head. He was threatening someone who was more precious to me than my life itself.'

Sparhawk was stunned. He started to speak, but Perraine held up one hand. 'Don't talk, Sparhawk,' he said. 'Listen. There isn't much time. Martel came to me in Dabour just after Arasham died. I went for my sword, of course, but he just laughed at me. He told me to put up the sword if I cared anything at all about Ydra.'

'Ydra?'

'The woman I love. She's from northern Pelosia. Her father's barony adjoins the one belonging to my father. Ydra and I have loved each other since we were children. I'd die for her without giving it a second thought. Martel knew that somehow, and he reasoned that if I were willing to die for her, I'd also be willing to kill. He told me that he'd given her soul to Azash. I didn't believe him. I didn't think he could really do that.'

Sparhawk remembered Count Ghasek's sister, Bellina. 'It can be done, Perraine,' he said bleakly.

'That's what I found out. Martel and I travelled to Pelosia, and he showed Ydra to me when she was performing some obscene rite before an image of Azash.' Tears stood openly in Perraine's eyes. 'It was horrible, Sparhawk, horrible.' He choked back a sob. 'Martel told me that if I didn't do exactly as he told me, her corruption would increase until her soul was totally lost. I wasn't sure if he could really do what he said he would, but I couldn't take the chance.'

'He could do it all right, Perraine,' Sparhawk assured him. 'I've seen it.'

'I was going to kill her,' Perraine went on, his voice growing weaker, 'but I just couldn't bring myself to do it. Martel watched me struggle with myself, and he just laughed at me. If you ever get the opportunity, I hope you kill him.'

'You have my word on that, Perraine.'

Perraine sighed again, and his face grew even more pale. 'An excellent poison, this one,' he noted. 'Anyway, Martel had his fist around my heart. He told me to go to Arcium and to join Vanion and the other Pandions there. At the first opportunity, I was to make my way back to the chapterhouse in Cimmura. Somehow he knew that you were going to Thalesia and that you'd most likely be returning through Emsat. He gave me money and

261

instructed me to start hiring murderers. I had to do everything he told me to do. Most of the time it was my assassins who made the attempts on you, but once, when we were coming through Demos on our way here, I actually shot a crossbow at you myself. I could try to pretend that I missed on purpose, but that would be a lie. I was really trying to kill you, Sparhawk.'

'And the poison at Dolmant's house?'

'That was me as well. I was getting desperate. You have uncommonly good luck, my friend. I tried everything I could think of, and I just couldn't kill you.'

'And the Rendor who tried to stick a poisoned knife in me in the Basilica?'

Perraine looked a bit startled. 'I had nothing to do with that, Sparhawk. I swear. We've both been in Rendor, and we both know how undependable they are. Someone else must have sent him – maybe even Martel himself.'

'What made you change your mind, Perraine?' Sparhawk asked sadly.

'Martel's lost his hold on me. Ydra's dead.'

'I'm sorry.'

'I'm not. Somehow she realized what was happening. She went to the chapel in her father's house and prayed all night. Then, just as the sun was coming up, she drove a dagger into her heart. She'd sent one of her footmen here with a letter explaining everything that had happened. He arrived just before Martel's army encircled the city. She's free now, and her soul is safe.'

'Why did you take poison then?'

'I'm going to follow her, Sparhawk. Martel's stolen my honour, but he can never steal my love.' Perraine stiffened on his narrow cot, and he twisted in agony for a moment. 'Yes,' he gasped, 'an excellent poison. I'd recommend it by name, but I don't altogether trust our little mother here. Given half a chance, I think she could resurrect a stone.'

262

He smiled at their teacher. 'Can you find it in your heart to forgive me, Sparhawk?'

'There's nothing to forgive, Perraine,' Sparhawk said in a thick voice, taking his friend's hand.

Perraine sighed. 'I'm sure they'll strike my name from the Pandion rolls, and I'll be remembered with contempt.'

'Not if I can help it, they won't,' Sparhawk told him. 'I'll protect your honour, my friend.' He gripped Perraine's hand tightly in an unspoken pledge.

Sephrenia reached across the bed and took the dying man's other hand.

'It's almost over,' Perraine said in a faint whisper. 'I wish –' And then he fell silent.

Sephrenia's wail of grief was almost like that of a hurt child. She pulled Perraine's limp body to her.

'There's no time for that!' Sparhawk told her sharply. 'Will you be all right here for a while? I have to go and get Kurik.'

She stared at him in astonishment.

'We have to dress Perraine in his armour,' Sparhawk explained. 'Then Kurik and I can take him to one of those streets just inside the wall. We'll shoot a crossbow bolt into his chest and lay him in the street. They'll find him later, and everyone will believe that one of Martel's mercenaries shot him off the wall.'

'But Sparhawk, why?'

'Perraine was my friend, and I promised to protect his honour.'

'But he tried to kill you, dear one.'

'No, little mother, *Martel* tried to kill me. He forced Perraine to help him. The guilt's all Martel's, and one of these days before very long, I'm going to make him answer for it.' He paused. 'You might start thinking about that hypothesis of ours,' he added. 'This seems to poke

263

quite a large hole in it.' Then he remembered the Rendor with the poisoned knife. 'Either that or there's more than just one assassin out there to worry about,' he added.

The first probing attacks came after about five days of looting. They were tentative, designed primarily to identify strong points – and weak ones. The defenders had certain advantages here. Martel had received his training from Vanion, and Vanion could, therefore, predict almost exactly what the white-haired former Pandion would do, and, moreover, he could marshal his forces so as to dissemble and deceive. The probing attacks grew stronger. They came sometimes at dawn, sometimes late in the day and sometimes in the middle of the night when darkness shrouded the smoky city. The Church Knights were always on the alert. They never removed their armour, and they slept in snatches whenever and wherever they could.

It was when the outer city lay almost entirely in ruins that Martel moved his siege engines into place to begin the steady pounding of the inner city. Large rocks rained from the sky, crushing soldiers and citizens alike. Large baskets were mounted on some of Martel's catapults, and bushels of crossbow bolts were launched high into the air to drop indiscriminately into the ancient city. Then came the fire. Balls of burning pitch and naphtha came sailing over the walls to ignite the roofs and to fill the streets with great splashes of searing fire. There were as yet no half-ton boulders, however.

The defenders endured. There was nothing else they could do.

Lord Abriel began to construct engines of his own to respond, but aside from the rubble of destroyed houses, there was very little at hand to throw back at Martel in reply.

They endured, and each stone, each fireball, each

shower of arrows dropping from the sky in a deadly rain only increased their hatred of the besiegers.

The first serious assault came not long after midnight eight days after the looting had begun. A disorganized horde of Rendorish fanatics came shrieking out of the dark, smoky streets to the southwest bent on attacking a somewhat shaky bartizan on the corner of the old wall in that quarter. The defenders rushed to that point. Sheets of arrows and crossbow bolts swept through the black-robed ranks of the Rendors, felling them in windrows like new-mown wheat. The shrieks took on that note of agony that has risen from every battlefield since the beginning of time. On and on, however, came the Rendors, men so wildly gripped by religious frenzy that they paid no heed to their dreadful casualties, some of them even ignoring mortal wounds as they dragged themselves towards the walls.

'The pitch!' Sparhawk shouted to the soldiers who were feverishly shooting arrows and bolts down into the seething mass of the attackers below. Cauldrons of boiling pitch were dragged to the edge of the walls even as the scaling ladders came angling up from below to clatter against the weather-worn battlements. The Rendors, shrieking war cries and religious slogans, came scrambling up the rude ladders only to fall howling and writhing from those ladders as great waves of scalding pitch engulfed them, burning, searing.

'Torches!' Sparhawk commanded.

Half a hundred flaming torches sailed out over the walls to ignite the pools of liquid pitch and naphtha below. A great sheet of flame shot up to bathe the walls and to burn those Rendors still clinging to their ladders as ants sizzle, shrivel and fall from a log cast into a fire. Burning men ran from the crowd below, shrieking, stumbling blindly and trailing streams of dripping flame like comets as they ran.

Still the Rendors came, and still the scaling ladders ponderously rose from their ranks, pushed from the rear by hundreds of hands to swing up and up, then to hesitate, standing vertically, and then to slowly fall against the wall. Fanatics, wild-eyed and some actually foaming at the mouth, were desperately climbing even before the ladders fell into place. From the top of the walls, the defenders pushed the ladders away with long poles, and the ladders reversed their rise, teetered back out to stand momentarily motionless and then toppled backwards, carrying the men near their tops to their deaths below. Hundreds of Rendors crowded near the base of the walls to avoid the arrows from above, and they dashed out to scramble up the ladders towards the tops of the walls.

'Lead!' Sparhawk commanded then. The lead had been Bevier's idea. Each sarcophagus in the crypt beneath the Basilica had been surmounted by a leaden effigy of its inhabitant. The sarcophagi were now unadorned, and the effigies had been melted down. Bubbling cauldrons stood at intervals along the tops of the walls, and at Sparhawk's command, they were pushed forward and overturned to pour down in great silvery sheets on the Rendors clustered at the base of the wall. The shrieks this time did not last for long, and no man ran blazing from the attack after he had been entombed in liquid lead.

Some few, then more did reach the tops of the walls. The church soldiers met them with a bravery born of desperation, and they held the fanatics long enough to permit the knights to come to their aid. Sparhawk strode forward at the head of the phalanx of black-armoured Pandions. He swung his heavy broadsword steadily, rhythmically. The broadsword is not a weapon with much finesse, and the big Pandion Knight did not so much fight his way through the shrieking Rendors as chop open a wide path. His sword was an instrument of dismemberment, and hands

266

and whole arms flew spinning from his strokes to rain down on the faces of attackers still on the scaling ladders. Heads went sailing out to fall either on the outside of the wall or on the inside, depending on the direction of Sparhawk's swing. The knights following him and disposing of the wounded were soon wading in blood. One Rendor, quite skinny and waving a rusty sabre, stood howling before the man in black armour bearing down on him. Sparhawk altered his swing slightly and sheared the man almost in two at the waist. The Rendor was hurled against the battlements by the force of the blow, and the remaining shred of flesh ripped as the upper torso toppled outwards. The man's lower half caught up on one of the battlements, the legs threshing wildly. The Rendor's upper torso did not quite reach the ground below, but hung head downwards from a long rope of purple bowel that steamed in the cool night air. The torso swung slowly back and forth, jerking slightly downwards as its intestines gradually unravelled.

'Sparhawk!' Kalten shouted as Sparhawk's arm began to grow weary. 'Get your breath! I'll take over here!'

And so it went until the top of the wall was once again secure and all the scaling ladders had been shoved away. The Rendors milled around below, still falling victim to arrows and to large rocks thrown down on them from the walls.

And then they broke and fled.

Kalten came back, panting and wiping his sword. 'Good fight,' he said, grinning.

'Tolerable,' Sparhawk agreed laconically. 'Rendors aren't very good fighters, though.'

'Those are the best kind to face,' Kalten laughed. He pulled back one foot to kick the bottom half of the skinny Rendor off the wall.

'Leave him where he is,' Sparhawk said shortly. 'Let's give the next wave of attackers something to look at while they're crossing the field to get here. You might as well tell the people cleaning up down on the inside of the wall to save any loose heads they come across as well. We'll set them on stakes along the battlements.'

'Object lessons again?'

'Why not? A man who's attacking a defended wall is entitled to know what's likely to happen to him, wouldn't you say?'

Bevier came hurrying down the bloody parapet. 'Ulath's been hurt!' he shouted to them from several yards away. He turned to lead them back to their injured friend, and the church soldiers melted out of his way. Perhaps unconsciously, Bevier was still brandishing his lochaber axe.

Ulath lay on his back. His eyes were rolled back in his head, and blood was running out of his ears.

'What happened?' Sparhawk demanded of Tynian.

'A Rendor ran up behind him and hit him on the head with an axe.'

Sparhawk's heart sank.

Tynian gently removed Ulath's horned helmet and gingerly probed through the Genidian Knight's blond hair. 'I don't think his head's broken,' he reported.

'Maybe the Rendor didn't swing hard enough,' Kalten surmised.

'I saw the blow. The Rendor swung as hard as he could. That blow should have split Ulath's head like a melon.' He frowned, tapping on the bulging knot of horn that joined the two curling points jutting from each side of their friend's conical helmet. Then he examined the helmet closely. 'Not a scratch,' he marvelled. He took out his dagger and scraped at the horn, but was unable to even mar its shiny surface. Then, finally overcome by curiosity, he picked up Ulath's fallen war-axe and hacked at the horn several times without even chipping it. 'That's amazing,' he said. 'That's the hardest stuff I've ever come across.'

'That's probably why Ulath's still got his brains inside his head,' Kalten said. 'He doesn't look too good, though. Let's carry him to Sephrenia.'

'You three go on ahead,' Sparhawk told them regretfully. 'I've got to talk with Vanion.'

The four Preceptors stood together some distance away where they had been observing the attack.

'Sir Ulath's been hurt, My Lord,' Sparhawk reported to Komier.

'Is it bad?' Vanion asked quickly.

'There's no such thing as a good injury, Vanion,' Komier said. 'What happened, Sparhawk?'

'A Rendor hit him in the head with an axe, My Lord.'

'In the head, you say? He'll be all right then.' He reached up and rapped his knuckles on his own ogre-horned helmet. 'That's why we wear these.'

'He didn't look very good,' Sparhawk said gravely. 'Tynian, Kalten and Bevier are taking him to Sephrenia.'

'He'll be all right,' Komier insisted.

Sparhawk pushed Ulath's injury to the back of his mind. 'I think I've put my finger on some of Martel's strategy, My Lords. He saddled himself with those Rendors for a specific reason. Rendors aren't really very good at modern warfare. They don't wear any kind of protective armour – not even helmets – and they're pitifully incapable of any form of swordsmanship. We swept them off the top of that wall the way you'd mow a hayfield. All they really have is a raging fanaticism, and they'll attack in the face of insurmountable odds. Martel's going to keep throwing them at us to wear us down and to reduce our numbers. Then, after he's weakened and exhausted us, he'll throw in his Cammorian and Lamork mercenaries. We've got to work out some way to keep those Rendors off the walls. I'm going to talk with Kurik. Maybe he can come up with a few ideas.'

Kurik, as a matter of fact, could. His years of experience, and the reminiscences of grizzled old veterans he had met from time to time provided him with a large number of very nasty ideas. There were objects he called caltrops: fairly simple, four-pronged steel things that could be made in such a way that no matter how far they were thrown, they would always land with one steel, sharp-pointed prong pointing upward. Rendors did not wear boots, but only soft leather sandals. A generous smearing of poison on the pointed prongs made the caltrops lethal as opposed to merely inconvenient. Ten-foot long beams with sharpened stakes attached to them to protrude like the spines of a hedgehog and once again doctored with poison provided fairly insurmountable barriers when rolled down long beams to lie in profusion out in front of the walls. Long log pendulums swinging from the battlements parallel to the walls would sweep scaling ladders away like cobwebs. 'None of these will actually hold off really serious attacks, Sparhawk,' Kurik said, 'but they'll slow people down to the point where crossbowmen and regular archers can pick them off. Not very many attackers will reach the walls.'

'That's sort of what we had in mind,' Sparhawk said. 'Let's commandeer the citizenry and put them to work on these ideas. All that the people of Chyrellos are doing right now is sitting around eating. Let's give them a chance to earn their keep.'

The construction of Kurik's obstacles took several days, and there were several more Rendorish attacks in the interim. Then Preceptor Abriel's catapults scattered the caltrops in profusion in front of the walls, and the hedgehogs rolled down long beams to lie in tangles and clusters some twenty yards or so out from the walls. After that, very few Rendors reached the walls, and the ones who did were not encumbered by scaling ladders. They would normally mill around shouting slogans and hacking at the walls with their swords until the bowmen on top of the walls had the leisure to kill them. After a few of those abortive attacks, Martel pulled back for a day or so to reconsider his strategy. It was still summer, however, and the hordes of dead Rendors lying outside the walls began to bloat in the sun. The smell of rotting flesh made the inner city distinctly unpleasant.

One evening, Sparhawk and his companions took advantage of the lull to return to the chapterhouse for much-needed baths and a hot meal. Before they did anything else, however, they stopped by to visit Sir Ulath. The big Genidian Knight lay in his bed. His eyes were still unfocused, and he had a confused look on his face. 'I'm getting tired of just lying around, brothers,' he said in a slurred voice, 'and it's hot in here. Why don't we go out and hunt down a Troll? Slogging through the snow should cool off our blood a little.'

'He thinks he's in the Genidian Mother-house at Heid,' Sephrenia told the knights quietly. 'He keeps wanting to go Troll-hunting. He thinks I'm a serving wench, and he's been making all sorts of improper suggestions to me.'

Bevier gasped.

'And then sometimes he cries,' she added.

'Ulath?' Tynian said in some amazement.

'It may be a subterfuge, though. The first time he did it, I tried to comfort him, and it turned into a sort of wrestling match. He's very strong, considering his condition.'

'Will he be all right?' Kalten asked. 'I mean, will he regain his senses?'

'It's very hard to say, Kalten. That blow bruised his brain, I think, and you never know how something like that's going to turn out. I think you'd better leave, dear ones. Don't excite him.'

Ulath began to make a long, rambling speech in the

271

language of the Trolls, and Sparhawk was surprised to discover that he still understood the language. The spell Aphrael had cast in Ghwerig's cave seemed to still have some of its potency left.

After he had bathed and shaved, Sparhawk put on a monk's robe and joined the others in the nearly-deserted refectory where their meal was laid on a long table.

'What's Martel going to do next?' Preceptor Komier was asking Abriel.

'He'll probably fall back on fairly standard siege tactics,' Abriel replied. 'Most likely he'll settle down and let his siege engines pound us for a while. Those fanatics were just about his only chance for a quick victory. This may drag out for quite some time.'

They all sat quietly, listening to the monotonous crash of large rocks falling into the city around them.

Then Talen burst into the room. His face was smudged and his clothes were dirty. 'I just saw Martel, My Lords!' he said excitedly.

'We've all seen him, Talen,' Kalten said, sprawling deeper into his chair. 'He rides up outside the walls now and then to have a look around.'

'He wasn't outside the walls, Kalten,' Talen said. 'He was in the cellar under the Basilica.'

'What are you saying, boy?' Dolmant demanded.

Talen drew in a deep breath. 'I – um – well, I wasn't entirely honest with you gentle. ¬¬ when I told you how I was getting the thieves of Chyrellos out of the inner city,' he confessed. He held up one hand. 'I *did* arrange for a meeting between the thieves and those church soldiers on the wall with their rope. That part was completely true. About the only thing I *didn't* tell you was that I found another way as well. I just didn't want to bore you with a lot of extra details. Anyway, not long after we got here, I happened to be down in the lowest cellar under the

Basilica, and I found a passageway. I don't know what it was used for originally, but it leads off to the north. It's perfectly round, and the stones of the walls and floor are very smooth. I followed it, and it took me out into the city.'

'Does it show any signs of being used as a passageway at all?' Patriarch Emban asked.

'Not when I went through it the first time, no, Your Grace. The cobwebs were as thick as ropes.'

'Oh, that thing,' Sir Nashan said. 'I've heard about it, but I never got around to investigating it. The old torture-chambers are down in that cellar. It's the sort of place most people want to avoid.'

'The passageway, Nashan,' Vanion said to him. 'What's it for?'

'It's an old aqueduct, My Lord. It was part of the original construction of the Basilica. It runs north to the River Kydu to carry water to the inner city. Everybody tells me that it collapsed centuries ago.'

'Not all of it, Sir Knight,' Talen told him. 'It runs far enough out into the main city to be useful. To make it short, I was looking around and I found this – what was it you called that passage?'

'An aqueduct,' Nashan supplied.

'That's a peculiar word. Anyway, I found it, and I followed it, and it came out in the cellar of a warehouse several streets on out in the city. It doesn't go any farther than that, though, but it doesn't really have to. There's a door leading out from the cellar into an alley. That's the information I was selling to the thieves of Chyrellos. Anyway, I was down in that cellar this afternoon, and I saw Martel come sneaking out of that passageway. I hid and he went on by. He was alone, so I followed him, and he went into a kind of store-room. Annias was waiting for him there. I couldn't hear what they were saying, but they

273

had their heads very close together like men doing some very serious plotting. They talked together for a while, and then they left the store-room. Martel told Annias to wait for the usual signal and then to meet him again down there. He said, "I'll want you somewhere safe when the fighting starts." Then Annias said that he was still worried about the possibility of Wargun showing up, but Martel laughed and said, "Don't worry about Wargun, my friend. He's blithely ignorant of everything that's happening here." Then they left. I waited a while and came right here.'

'How did Martel find out about the aqueduct?' Kalten asked him.

'Some of his men probably chased one of the thieves and found it,' Talen shrugged. 'Everybody gets civic-spirited when it comes to chasing thieves. I've been chased by absolute strangers sometimes.'

'That explains Wargun's absence,' Komier said bleakly. 'All our messengers have probably been ambushed.'

'And Ehlana's still sitting in Cimmura with only Stragen and Platime to defend her,' Sparhawk said in a worried tone. 'I think I'll go down to that cellar and wait for Martel. He'll come along eventually and I can waylay him.'

'Absolutely not!' Emban said sharply.

'Your Grace,' Sparhawk objected, 'I think you're overlooking the fact that if Martel dies, this siege dies with him.'

'And I think *you're* overlooking the fact that our real goal here is to defeat Annias in the election. I need a report of a conversation between Annias and Martel to swing the votes I need to beat the Primate of Cimmura. Our situation here is getting very tenuous, gentlemen. Every time those fires out there sweep into a new quarter, we lose a few more votes.'

'Wouldn't Talen's report of a meeting between Annias

and Martel make the Hierocracy suspicious, Your Grace?' Kalten asked.

'Most of the Hierocracy have never heard of Martel, Sir Kalten,' Emban replied, 'and this boy's not the most reliable of witnesses. *Somebody* in Chyrellos is bound to know that he's a thief. We have to have a totally incorruptible and reliable witness. One whose neutrality and objectivity can never be questioned.'

'The commander of the Archprelate's personal guard, perhaps?' Ortzel suggested.

'The very man,' Emban agreed, snapping his fingers. 'If we can get him down into the cellar where he can hear Martel and Annias talking, it might give me something to place before the Hierocracy.'

'Aren't you overlooking the fact that when Martel comes through that aqueduct, he's going to have a small army with him, Your Grace?' Vanion asked. 'He said something about wanting to get Annias to safety before the fighting starts. That sounds to me as if he plans to lead a surprise attack into the Basilica itself. Your witness won't find a very attentive audience if all the Patriarchs are running for their lives.'

'Don't trouble me with these details, Vanion,' Emban said airily. 'Just post some men down there.'

'Gladly, but where do I get the men?'

'Take some of those fellows off the walls. They're not doing anything useful anyway.'

Vanion's face turned very red, and a thick vein started to throb in his forehead.

'You'd better let me tell him, Vanion,' Komier suggested. 'We don't want you to come down with the apoplexy.' He turned casually to the fat little Patriarch. 'Your Grace,' he said mildly, 'when you're planning a surprise attack, you usually want to divert your enemy's attention. Doesn't that sort of make sense?'

'Well –' Emban said a bit dubiously.

'At least that's the way *I'd* do it, and Martel's had a great deal of training. I sort of suspect that what's going to happen is that Martel's going to wait until he gets those mangoes built –'

'Mangonels,' Preceptor Abriel corrected.

'Whatever,' Komier shrugged. 'Then he's going to start bashing down our walls. *Then* he's going to attack the walls with every man he can muster. Believe me, Your Grace, the men on the walls – or what's left of the walls – are going to be very, very busy. *That's* when Martel's going to come into the cellar, and we're *not* going to have any men to spare to meet him.'

'Why do you have to be so blasted clever, Komier?' Emban snapped.

'What do we do then?' Dolmant asked them.

'We don't have any choice, Your Grace,' Vanion replied. 'We're going to have to collapse that aqueduct so that Martel can't get through.'

'But if you do that, we won't have any report of the meeting between Annias and Martel!' Emban protested shrilly.

'Try to look at the whole picture, Emban,' Dolmant said patiently. 'Do we really want Martel voting when we elect a new Archprelate?'

Chapter 14

'They're ceremonial troops, Your Grace,' Vanion objected. 'This isn't a parade or a formal changing of the guard.' The four of them, Vanion, Dolmant, Sparhawk and Sephrenia were gathered in Sir Nashan's study.

'I've seen them training in the courtyard outside their barracks, Vanion,' Dolmant said patiently. 'I still remember enough of my own training to recognize professionals when I see them.'

'How many of them are there, Your Grace?' Sparhawk asked.

'Three hundred,' the Patriarch replied. 'As the Archprelate's personal guard, they're wholly committed to the defence of the Basilica.' Dolmant leaned back in his chair, tapping his fingertips together. 'I don't see that we have much choice, Vanion,' he said. His lean, ascetic face seemed almost to glow in the candlelight. 'Emban was right, you know. All our scrambling for votes has gone out of the window now. My brothers in the Hierocracy are very attached to their houses.' He made a sour face. 'It's one of the few forms of vanity left for members of the higher clergy. We all wear plain cassocks, so we can't show off our clothing; we don't marry, so we can't show off our wives; we're committed to peace, so we can't demonstrate our prowess on the battlefield. All that's left for us are our palaces. We lost at least twenty votes when we pulled back to the walls of the inner city and abandoned the palaces of my brothers to Martel's looters. We absolutely *must* have some evidence of the collusion between Annias and Martel. If we can do that, we turn it around. The burning of the palaces becomes Annias's fault instead of ours.' He looked at Sephrenia then. 'I'm going to have to ask you to do something, little mother,' he said.

'Of course, Dolmant.' She smiled at him fondly.

'I can't even ask you officially,' he said with a rueful smile, 'because it has to do with things I'm not supposed to believe in any more.'

'Ask me as a former Pandion, dear one,' she suggested. 'That way we can both ignore the fact that you've fallen in with evil companions.'

'Thank you,' he said dryly. 'Is there some way you can collapse that aqueduct without actually being in the cellar?'

'I can take care of that, your Grace,' Sparhawk offered. 'I can use Bhelliom.'

'No, actually you can't,' Sephrenia reminded him. 'You don't have both rings.' She looked back at Dolmant. 'I can do what you ask,' she told him, 'but Sparhawk will have to be in the cellar. I can channel the spell through him.'

'Better and better, actually,' Dolmant said. 'Vanion, see what you think of this. You and I talk with Colonel Delada, the commander of the Archprelate's guard. We put his guardsmen in the cellar under the command of somebody reliable.'

'Kurik?' Sparhawk suggested.

'The very man,' Dolmant approved. 'I suspect that I'd still obey automatically if Kurik barked an order at me.' Dolmant paused. 'Why didn't you ever knight him, Vanion?'

'Because of his class prejudices, Dolmant,' Vanion laughed. 'Kurik believes that knights are frivolous, empty-headed men. Sometimes I almost think he's right.'

'All right then,' Dolmant continued. 'We put Kurik and the guardsmen in the cellar to wait for Martel – well out of sight of course. What's likely to be the first sign that Martel's main assault on our walls is starting?'

'Boulders dropping out of the sky, I'd say, wouldn't you, Sparhawk? That'll be the sign that his mangonels are in place. He won't start his attack until he's sure that they're working properly.'

'And that would be the most probable time for him to start through the aqueduct, wouldn't it?'

Vanion nodded. 'There'd be too much chance of them being discovered if they crept into the cellar any sooner.'

'This is fitting together even more tightly.' Dolmant seemed pleased with himself on that score. 'We make Sparhawk and Colonel Delada wait on the walls for the first boulders. When they start crashing down, the two of them go down to the cellar to eavesdrop on the conversation between Martel and Annias. If the Archprelate's guard can't hold the entrance to the aqueduct, Sephrenia will collapse the tunnel. We block the secret attack, get the evidence against Annias, and we may very well capture Annias and Martel themselves. What do you think, Vanion?'

'It's an excellent plan, Your Grace,' Vanion said with a straight face. Sparhawk also saw a number of gaps. The years seem to have clouded Dolmant's strategic sense in a few areas. 'I can only see one drawback,' Vanion added.

'Oh?'

'Once those engines batter down the walls, we're likely to have hordes of mercenaries here in the inner city with us.'

'That would be a bit inconvenient, wouldn't it?' Dolmant conceded with a slight frown. 'Let's talk with Colonel Delada anyway. I'm sure something will turn up.'

Vanion sighed and followed the Patriarch of Demos from the room.

'Was he always like that?' Sparhawk asked Sephrenia.

'Who?'

'Dolmant. I think he's pushing optimism about as far as it can be pushed.'

'It's your Elene theology, dear one,' she smiled. 'Dolmant's professionally committed to the notion of Providence. Styrics look upon that as the worst form of fatalism. What's troubling you, dear one?'

'A perfectly good logical construction has fallen apart on me, Sephrenia. Now that we know about Perraine, I don't have any way at all to connect that shadow with Azash.'

'Why are you so obsessed with hard evidence, Sparhawk?'

'I beg your pardon?'

'Just because you can't logically prove a connection, you're ready to discard the whole idea. Your reasoning was fairly tenuous to begin with anyway. About all you were really doing was trying to distort things to make your logic fit your feelings – a sort of a justification for a leap of faith. You felt – you believed – that the shadow came from Azash. That's good enough for me. I'm more comfortable with the notion of trusting your feelings than your logic anyway.'

'Be nice,' he chided.

She smiled. 'I think it's time to discard logic and start relying on those leaps of faith, Sparhawk. Sir Perraine's confession erases any connection between that shadow you keep seeing and the attempts on your life, doesn't it?'

'I'm afraid so,' he admitted, 'and to make matters even worse, I haven't even *seen* the shadow lately.'

'Just because you haven't seen it doesn't mean it's not still there. Tell me exactly what you felt each time you saw it.'

'There was a chill,' he replied, 'and an overpowering sense that whatever it was hated me. I've been hated before, Sephrenia, but not like that. It was inhuman.'

'All right, we can rely on that then. It's something supernatural. Anything else?'

'I was afraid of it.' He admitted it flatly.

'You? I didn't think you knew what the word meant.'

'I know, all right.'

She thought about it, her tiny, perfect face creased with thought. 'Your original theory was really quite shaky, Sparhawk,' she told him. 'Would it *really* make much sense for Azash to have some brigand kill you and then to have to chase down the brigand in order to retrieve Bhelliom from him?'

'It's a little cumbersome and roundabout, I suppose.'

'Exactly, let's look at the possibility of pure coincidence.'

'I'm not supposed to do that, little mother. Providence, you understand.'

'Stop that.'

'Yes ma'am.'

'Suppose that Martel subverted Perraine on his own – without consulting with Annias – that's assuming that it's Annias who's the one dealing with Otha and not Martel.'

'I don't really think Martel would go so far as to have personal dealings with Otha.'

'I wouldn't be too sure, Sparhawk. But let's assume that killing you was Martel's idea and not Otha's – or some involuted scheme Azash came up with. *That* would cover the hole in your logic. The shadow could still be related to Azash and have absolutely no connection whatsoever with the attempts on your life.'

'What's it doing then?'

'Watching, most likely. Azash wants to know where you are, and He *definitely* wants to know where Bhelliom is. That might explain why you almost always see that shadow when you remove the jewel from the pouch.'

'This is starting to make my head ache, little mother.

281

But if everything goes the way Dolmant's planned it, we'll have both Martel and Annias in custody before long. We ought to be able to get a few answers out of them – enough to clear up my headache anyway.'

Colonel Delada, commander of the Archprelate's personal guard, was a stocky, solidly-built man with short-cut reddish hair and a lined face. Despite his largely ceremonial position, he carried himself like a warrior. He wore the burnished breastplate, round embossed shield and the traditional short sword of his unit. His knee-length cape was crimson, and his visorless helmet had a horse-hair crest. 'Are they really that big, Sir Sparhawk?' he asked as the two of them looked out at the smoking ruins from the flat roof of a house abutting the inner city wall.

'I really don't know, Colonel Delada,' Sparhawk replied. 'I've never seen one either. Bevier has, though, and he tells me that they're at least as big as a fair-sized house.'

'And they can really throw rocks the size of oxen?'

'That's what they tell me.'

'What's the world coming to?'

'They call it progress, my friend,' Sparhawk said wryly.

'The world would be a better place if we hanged all the scientists and engineers, Sir Sparhawk.'

'And the lawyers too.'

'Oh yes, definitely the lawyers. *Everybody* wants to hang all the lawyers.' Delada's eyes narrowed. 'Why are all of you being so secretive around me, Sparhawk?' he demanded irritably. In Delada's case all the clichés about red-haired people seemed to apply.

'We have to protect your strict neutrality, Delada. You're going to see something – and we hope hear something – that's very important. Later on, you're going to be called on to give testimony about it. There are going to be people who'll try very hard to throw doubts on your testimony.'

'They'd better not,' the colonel said hotly.

Sparhawk smiled. 'Anyway, if you don't know anything at all in advance about what you're going to see and hear, nobody will be able to raise any question at all about your impartiality.'

'I'm not stupid, Sparhawk, and I *have* got eyes. This has to do with the election hasn't it?'

'Just about everything in Chyrellos has to do with the election now, Delada – except maybe that siege out there.'

'And I wouldn't wager any significant amounts of money that the siege isn't involved too.'

'That's one of those areas we aren't supposed to talk about, Colonel.'

'Ah-ha!' Delada said triumphantly. 'Just as I thought!'

Sparhawk looked out over the wall. The important thing was to be able to prove beyond doubt the collusion between Martel and Annias. Sparhawk was a bit apprehensive about that. If the conversation between the Primate of Cimmura and the renegade Pandion did *not* reveal Martel's identity, all Delada would be able to report to the Hierocracy would be a highly suspicious conversation between Annias and an unnamed stranger. Emban, Dolmant and Ortzel, however, had been adamant. Delada was absolutely *not* to be supplied with any information which could contaminate his testimony. Sparhawk was particularly disappointed in Patriarch Emban on that score. The fat Churchman was devious and deceitful on every other count. Why should he suddenly become ethical on this one crucial point?

'It's starting, Sparhawk,' Kalten called from the torchlit wall. 'The Rendors are coming out to clear away our obstructions.'

The rooftop was slightly higher than the wall, and Sparhawk could clearly see over the fortification. The Rendors came rushing out, howling as before. Heedless of the poison smeared on the stakes of the hedgehogs, they rolled the obstructions out of the way. Many, caught up in a frenzied religious ecstasy, even went so far as to throw themselves needlessly on the poisoned stakes. Broad avenues were soon cleared away, and the assault towers began to trundle out of the still-smoking city, moving slowly towards the walls. The assault towers, Sparhawk saw, were constructed of thick planks covered by green cowhides which had been dipped in water so many times that rivulets actually ran from them. No crossbow bolt or javelin would be able to penetrate the planks, and burning pitch and naphtha would not be able to set fire to the dripping hides. One by one, Martel was countering all their defences.

'Do you actually anticipate fighting in the Basilica, Sir Sparhawk?' Delada asked.

'We can hope not, Colonel,' Sparhawk replied. 'It's best to be ready though. I really appreciate your deploying those guardsmen of yours down in that cellar – particularly since I can't tell you why we need them there. We'd have had to pull men off the walls otherwise.'

'I have to assume you know what you're doing, Sparhawk,' the colonel said ruefully. 'Putting the whole detachment under the command of your squire sort of upset my second in command, though.'

'It was a tactical decision, colonel. That cellar's full of echoes. Your men won't be able to understand shouted commands. Kurik and I have been together for a long time, and we've worked out ways to deal with situations like that one.'

Delada looked out at the assault towers lumbering across the open space in front of the walls. 'Big, aren't they?' he said. 'How many men can you crowd into one of those things?'

'That depends on how fond of the men you are,' Sparhawk told him, moving his shield in front of his body to ward off the arrows which had already begun to drop onto the roof, 'several hundred at least.'

'I'm not familiar with siege tactics,' Delada admitted. 'What happens now?'

'They roll up to the walls and try to charge the defenders. The defenders try to push the towers over. It's very confusing and very noisy and a lot of people get hurt.'

'When do those mangonels come into play?'

'Probably when several of the towers are firmly in place against the walls.'

'Won't they be dropping boulders on their own men?'

'The men in the towers aren't very important. A lot of them are Rendors – like the ones out there who got killed clearing away the obstructions. The man who's in charge of that army isn't exactly what you'd call a humanitarian.'

'Do you know him?'

'Oh, yes. Very well.'

'And you want to kill him, don't you?' Delada asked shrewdly.

'The thought's crossed my mind a few times.'

One of the towers was now quite close to the wall, and the defenders, trying to dodge the hail of arrows and crossbow bolts, threw grappling hooks on long ropes over the roof of the lumbering structure. Then they began to pull on the ropes. The tower swayed, rocked back and forth and finally toppled with a resounding crash. The men inside began to scream, some in pain and some in terror. They knew what came next. The fall of the tower had broken the planks, and the tower lay open like a shattered egg. The cauldrons of pitch and naphtha

285

poured down upon the wreckage and the struggling men, and the torches set the boiling liquid on fire.

Delada swallowed hard as the despairing screams of the burning men came shockingly up from the base of the wall. 'Does that happen very often?' he asked in a sick voice.

'We *hope* so,' Sparhawk said bleakly. 'Every one of them we kill outside the walls is one less who gets inside.' Sparhawk wove a quick spell and spoke to Sephrenia, who was waiting inside the chapterhouse. 'We're just about ready to engage out here, little mother,' he reported. 'Any hints of Martel yet?'

'Nothing, dear one.' Her voice seemed almost to whisper in his ear. 'Be very careful, Sparhawk. Aphrael will be very cross with you if you allow yourself to be killed.'

'Tell her she's welcome to lend a hand, if she'd like.'

'Sparhawk!' The tone was half-shocked and half-amused.

'To whom were you speaking, Sir Sparhawk?' Delada's voice was baffled, and he was looking around to see if anyone were near them.

'You're relatively devout, aren't you, Colonel?' Sparhawk asked him.

'I'm a son of the Church, Sparhawk.'

'It might upset you if I told you, then. The militant orders have permission to go beyond what's allowed to ordinary members of the Elene faith. Why don't we just let it go at that.'

Despite the best efforts of the defenders, several towers reached the wall, and the drawbridges at their tops swung down onto the battlements. One of the towers touched the wall just beside the gate, and Sparhawk's friends were ready for it. Tynian led their charge as they dashed across the drawbridge and into the tower itself. Sparhawk held his breath as his friends struggled inside the tower out of his sight. The sounds from within bespoke the ferocity of the fight. There was the crash of arms and screams and groans. Then Tynian and Kalten came back out, ran across the thick-planked drawbridge and seized a large bubbling cauldron of boiling pitch and naphtha in their steel-clad arms. They lurched back across the drawbridge with it and disappeared inside again. The screams from within suddenly intensified as they dumped the pitch down into the faces of the men on ladders inside the tower.

The knights emerged from the tower. When Kalten reached the wall, he took up a torch and flipped it into the structure with a negligent-appearing toss. The tower acted much like a chimney. Black smoke billowed from the gaping doorway the drawbridge had covered, and then dark orange flame boiled out through the roof. The screaming inside the tower increased, and then it died out.

The counter-attacks of the knights along the walls were sufficient to ward off the first wave of attackers, but the defence of the battlements had cost many lives. The sheets of arrows and the heavier bolts from the crossbows had raked the tops of the walls in a virtual storm, and many of the church soldiers and not a few of the knights had fallen prey to them.

'They'll come again?' Delada asked sombrely.

'Of course,' Sparhawk said shortly. 'The siege engines will pound the walls for a time now, and then more towers will come across that open area.'

'How long can we hold out?'

'Four – maybe five of those attacks. Then the mangonels will start to break down the walls. The fighting will start inside the city at that point.'

'We can't possibly win, can we, Sparhawk?'

'Probably not.'

'Chyrellos is doomed then?'

'Chyrellos was doomed the moment those two armies

287

appeared, Delada. The strategy behind the attack on the city was very thorough – you might almost say brilliant.'

'That's a peculiar attitude under these circumstances, Sparhawk.'

'It's called professionalism. One's supposed to admire the genius of one's opponent. It's a pose, of course, but it helps to build a certain abstraction. Last stands are very gloomy, and you need something to keep your spirits up.'

Then Berit clambered up through the trap-door on the roof upon which Sparhawk and Delada stood. The novice's eyes were wide, seemingly slightly unfocused, and his head was jerking. 'Sir Sparhawk!' he exclaimed, his voice unnecessarily loud.

'Yes, Berit?'

'What did you say?'

Sparhawk looked at him more closely. 'What's the matter, Berit?' he asked.

'I'm sorry, Sir Sparhawk. I can't hear you. They rang the bells in the Basilica when the attack started. All the bells are up in the cupola on top of the dome. You never heard so much noise.' Berit reached up and thumped the heel of his hand against the side of his head.

Sparhawk took him by the shoulders and looked directly into his face. 'What's happening?' he bellowed, exaggeratedly mouthing the words.

'Oh, I'm sorry, Sir Sparhawk. The bells sort of rattled me. There are thousands of torches coming across the meadows on the other side of the River Arruk. I thought you ought to know.'

'Reinforcements?' Delada said hopefully.

'I'm sure they are,' Sparhawk replied, 'but for which army?'

There was a heavy, booming crash behind them, and a

fair-sized house collapsed in on itself as a huge boulder caved in its roof.

'God!' Delada exclaimed. 'That boulder was enormous! These walls will never withstand that kind of pounding.'

'No,' Sparhawk agreed. 'It's time for us to go to the cellar, Colonel.'

They went through the trap-door and started down the ladder.

'They started throwing those big rocks earlier than you thought, Sparhawk,' the colonel noted. 'That's sort of a good sign, wouldn't you say?'

'I'm afraid I don't quite follow that.'

'Wouldn't that suggest that the army to the west is a relief column for us?'

'The troops outside our walls are mercenaries, Colonel. They *could* be in a hurry to get through our walls so that they won't have to share the loot with their friends out there on the other side of the river.'

The lowest cellars of the Basilica were constructed of gigantic stones that had been laboriously chiselled and then carefully laid in long, low barrel vaults supported here and there by massive buttresses. The weight of the entire structure towering above rested entirely upon those mighty arches. It was dim and cool and quite damp in these cellars lying even below the crypt where the bones of long-dead Churchmen mouldered in dark silence.

'Kurik!' Sparhawk hissed to his squire as he and Delada passed the barred gate of an area set off from the rest of the cellar where Sparhawk's squire and Delada's guardsmen waited.

Kurik came to the bars on quiet feet.

'The mangonels have started,' Sparhawk told him, 'and there's a big army coming in from the west.'

'You're just full of good news, aren't you, My Lord?'

Kurik paused. 'This isn't really a very nice place in here, Sparhawk. There are chains and manacles hanging from the walls, and there's a place towards the back that would have warmed Bellina's heart.'

Sparhawk looked briefly at Delada.

Delada coughed. 'It's no longer used,' he said shortly. 'There was a time when the Church would go to any lengths to stamp out heresy. Interrogations were conducted down here and confessions obtained. It wasn't one of the brighter chapters in the history of our holy mother.'

'Some stories about that have leaked out,' Sparhawk nodded. 'Wait here with the guardsmen, Kurik. The colonel and I have to go and get into place before either of our visitors arrive. When I whistle for the attack, don't wait around, because I'll really need you at that point.'

'Have I ever let you down, Sparhawk?'

'No, as a matter of fact, you haven't. Sorry I even mentioned it.' He led the colonel deeper into the labyrinthine cellar. 'We're going to go into a fairly large room, Colonel,' he explained. 'There are all sorts of nooks and crannies along the walls. The young fellow who found the place brought me down here and showed it to me. He tells me that the two men we're interested in usually meet there. You'll be able to identify at least one of them. Hopefully, their conversation will identify the other. Pay very close attention to what they say, please. As soon as the conversation's over, I want you to go directly back to your quarters and lock your door. Don't open it for anybody but me, Lord Vanion or Patriarch Emban. If it makes you feel better, for a brief period of time, you'll be the most important man in Chyrellos, and we'll set whole armies to protecting you.'

'This is all very mysterious, Sparhawk.'

'It has to be for now, my friend. I hope that when you hear the conversation, you'll understand why. Here's the

290

door.' Sparhawk carefully pushed the rotting door open, and the two of them entered a large, dark chamber festooned with cobwebs. A rough table and two chairs sat near the door, and the thick stub of a single candle sat on a cracked saucer in the centre of the table. Sparhawk led the way to the rear of the chamber and back into a deep alcove. 'Take off your helmet,' he whispered, 'and wrap your cloak around your breastplate. We don't want any chance of reflection to warn anybody that we're here.'

Delada nodded.

'I'm going to blow out our candle now,' Sparhawk told him, 'and we'll have to be absolutely quiet. If we need to talk, we'll have to whisper very softly into each other's ears.' He blew out the candle, bent and laid it on the floor.

They waited. Somewhere far off in the darkness, water was dripping slowly. No matter how tight any drain may seem, there is always seepage, and water, like smoke, will always find the place it is seeking.

It might have been five minutes – or an hour – or even a century, when a muffled clinking came from the very far end of the vast cellar. 'Soldiers,' Sparhawk breathed to Delada. 'Let's hope the man leading them doesn't bring them all inside this place.'

'Indeed,' Delada breathed back.

Then a dark-robed and hooded man slipped through the doorway, shielding a single candle with one hand. He lit the candle on the table, blew out his own and threw back his hood.

'I should have known,' Delada whispered to Sparhawk. 'It's the Primate of Cimmura.'

'It is indeed, my friend. It is indeed.'

The soldiers came nearer. They were making some effort to muffle the clinking of their equipment, but soldiers as a group have never been much good at stealth. 'This is far

291

enough,' a familiar voice commanded. 'Draw back a little way. I'll call if I need you.'

There was a pause, and then Martel entered. He was carrying his helmet, and his white hair shone in the light of the single guttering candle on the table in front of the Primate. 'Well, Annias,' he drawled, 'we made a good try, but the game's played out.'

'What are you talking about, Martel?' Annias snapped. 'Everything's going our way.'

'It changed direction on us about an hour ago.'

'Stop trying to be cryptic, Martel. Tell me what's happening.'

'There's an army marching in from the west, Annias.'

'That other wave of Cammorian mercenaries you told me about?'

'I rather suspect that those mercenaries have been ground into dog-meat by now, Annias.' Martel unbuckled his sword-belt. 'Hate to break it to you this way, old boy, but that's Wargun's army marching in from the west. They stretch out as far as the eye can reach.'

Sparhawk's heart leapt with exultation.

'Wargun?' Annias cried. 'You said you'd taken care of keeping him away from Chyrellos.'

'Thought I had, old boy, but somehow someone got through to him.'

'His army's even bigger than yours?'

Martel sank wearily into his chair. 'God, I'm tired,' he confessed. 'I haven't slept for two days. You were saying?'

'Has Wargun got more men than you have?'

'Lord yes. He could chew me up in the space of a few hours. I really don't think we ought to wait for him. All *I* have to worry about is how long it's going to take Sparhawk to kill me. In spite of that face of his, Sparhawk's a gentle person. I'm sure he'd make quick work of me. I'm really disappointed in Perraine. I thought he might be able to do something permanent about my former brother. Oh, well. Ydra pays the penalty for his failure, I suppose. As I was saying, Sparhawk should be able to do for me in well under a minute. He's a much better swordsman than I am. *You*, however, have much more to be concerned about. Lycheas tells me that Ehlana wants your head on a plate. I once caught a glimpse of her face in Cimmura just after her father died and before you poisoned her. Sparhawk's gentle, but Ehlana's made of stone, and she hates you, Annias. She might very well decide to take your head off all by herself. She's a slender girl, and it might take her half a day to hack through your neck.'

'But we're so *close*,' Annias protested in anguished frustration. 'The Archprelate's throne is almost within my grasp.'

'You'd better ungrasp it then. It might be very heavy to carry when you're running for your life. Arissa and Lycheas are in my pavilion packing a few things already, but you're not going to have that kind of time, I'm afraid. You'll be leaving from here – with me. Get one thing very clear, Annias. I won't wait for you – not ever. If you start to fall behind, I'll leave you.'

'There are things I *have* to have, Martel.'

'I'm sure there are. I can think of a few offhand myself – your head for one – and Lycheas says that the blond ape who runs with Sparhawk has developed an unwholesome passion for hanging people. I know Kalten well enough to realize how clumsy he is. He's almost certain to botch the job, and being the guest of honour at a botched hanging isn't my idea of a pleasant way to pass an afternoon.'

'How many men did you bring here into this cellar?' Annias's voice was fearful.

'About a hundred, that's all.'

'Are you mad? We're right in the middle of an encampment of Church Knights!'

'Your cowardice is starting to show, Annias.' Martel's voice was thick with contempt. 'That aqueduct isn't very wide. Would you really want to have to clamber over the top of a thousand well-armed mercenaries when the time comes to start running?'

'Run? Where can we run to? Where can we possibly go?'

'Where else? We go to Zemoch. Otha will protect us.'

Colonel Delada drew in his breath with a sharp hiss.

'Be still, man,' Sparhawk muttered.

Martel rose to his feet and began to pace up and down, his face ruddy in the candlelight. 'Try to follow me on this, Annias,' he said. 'You gave Ehlana darestim, and darestim's *always* fatal. There's no cure, and ordinary magic could not have reversed the effects. I know that because I was trained in magic by Sephrenia myself.'

'That Styric witch!' Annias said from between clenched teeth.

Martel seized him by the front of his robe and half-lifted him from his chair. 'Be very careful what you say, Annias,' Martel said from between his teeth. 'Don't insult my little mother, or you'll wish that it was Sparhawk who caught you. As I said, he's basically a gentle sort of person. I'm not. I can do things to you Sparhawk would never dream of.'

'Surely you don't still have any feeling for her.'

'That's *my* business, Annias. All right then. If only magic could have cured the queen and ordinary magic wouldn't have worked, what does that leave us?'

'Bhelliom?' Annias guessed, rubbing his hand over the wrinkles Martel's fist had gathered up in the front of his robe.

'Precisely. Sparhawk's somehow managed to get his

294

hands on it. He used it to cure Ehlana, and more than likely he's still got it with him. It's not the sort of thing you leave lying around. I'll send the Rendors out to knock down the bridges over the Arruk. That should delay Wargun for a while and give you and me more time to run. We'd better go north for a little way and get out of the main battle zone before we turn east towards Zemoch.' He grinned mirthlessly. 'Wargun's always wanted to exterminate the Rendors anyway. If I send them out to destroy the bridges, he'll get his chance, and God knows *I* won't miss them all that much. I'll order the rest of my troops to make a stand against Wargun on the east bank of the river. They'll engage him in a splendid battle – which might even last for a couple of hours before he butchers the lot of them. That's about all the time you and I and our friends are going to have to get clear of this place. We can count on Sparhawk to be right behind us, and we can be absolutely sure that he'll have Bhelliom with him.'

'How do we know that? You're guessing, Martel.'

'Do you mean to say that you've been around Sparhawk for all these years and haven't got to know him yet? I'm not trying to be insulting, old boy, but you're an absolute idiot, do you know that? Otha's massed in eastern Lamorkand, and he'll be marching into western Eosia within a matter of days. He'll slaughter everything in sight – men, women, children, cattle, dogs, wild animals and even fish. Preventing that is the primary duty of the Church Knights, and Sparhawk's what they had in mind when they founded the four orders. He's all duty and honour and implacable resolve. I'd give my soul to be a man like Sparhawk. He's got the one thing in his possession that will absolutely stop Otha cold. Do you really think there's anything in the world that would prevent him from bringing Bhelliom with him? Use your head, Annias.'

'What good's it going to do us to run if we know that Sparhawk's right behind us with Bhelliom in his hands? He'll obliterate Otha and us along with him.'

'Not very likely. Sparhawk's moderately stupendous, but he's not a God. Azash, however, is, and Azash has wanted Bhelliom since before the beginning of time. Sparhawk will chase us, and Azash will be waiting for him. Azash will destroy him in order to take Bhelliom from him. Then Otha will invade. Since we'll have done such a tremendous service for him, he'll reward us – lavishly. He'll put you on the Archprelate's throne and give *me* the crown of any Elenian kingdom I choose – perhaps even all of them. Otha's lost his hunger for power in the last thousand years or so. I'll even set Lycheas up as Regent – or even King – of Elenia, if you want – although I can't for the life of me think of any reason you'd want that. Your son's a snivelling cretin, and the sight of him turns my stomach. Why don't you have him strangled, and then you and Arissa can try again? If you both concentrate, you might even be able to produce a real human being instead of an eel.'

Sparhawk felt a sudden chill. He looked around. Though he could not see it, he knew that the shadowy watcher which had followed him from Ghwerig's cave was somewhere here in the room. Could it possibly be that merely the mention of Bhelliom's name was enough to summon it?

'But how do we know that Sparhawk will be able to follow us?' Annias was asking. 'He doesn't know about our arrangement with Otha, so he won't have the faintest idea of where we're going.'

'You *are* naive, aren't you, Annias?' Martel laughed. 'Sephrenia can listen in on a conversation from at least five miles away, and she can arrange to have everyone in the room with her hear it as well. Not only that, there are hundreds of places in this cellar that are within earshot of this room. Believe me, Annias, one way or another, Sparhawk's listening to us at this very moment.' He paused. 'Aren't you, Sparhawk?' he added.

Chapter 15

Martel's question hung in the musty dimness. 'Stay here,' Sparhawk whispered bleakly to Delada. He reached for his sword.

'Not very likely,' the colonel replied, his tone just as grim. He also drew his sword.

It was really neither the time nor the place for arguments. 'All right, but be careful. I'll take Martel. You grab Annias.'

The two of them stepped out of their place of concealment and walked towards the single candle guttering on the table.

'Why, if it isn't my dear brother Sparhawk,' Martel drawled. 'So awfully good to see you again, old boy.'

'Look quickly, Martel. You aren't going to be seeing much of anything for very long.'

'I'd love to oblige you, Sparhawk, but I'm afraid we'll have to postpone it again. Pressing business, you understand.' Martel took Annias by the shoulder and pushed him towards the door. 'Move!' he snapped. The two of them went quickly out as Sparhawk and Delada rushed forward, swords in hand.

'Stop!' Sparhawk snapped to his companion.

'They're getting away, Sparhawk!' Delada objected.

'They already have.' Sparhawk said it with a hot disappointment souring his mouth. 'Martel's got a hundred men out there in those corridors. We need you alive, Colonel.' Sparhawk whistled shrilly even as he heard the rush of many feet in the corridor outside. 'We'll have to defend the door until Kurik and the guardsmen get here.'

The two of them went quickly to the rotting door and took their places, one on either side of it. At the last moment, Sparhawk stepped out into plain view a few feet back from the arched opening in the massive stone wall. His position gave his sword full play, but the soldiers rushing through the entrance were hampered in their swings by the rocks of the sides and top of the archway.

Martel's mercenaries discovered very quickly what a bad idea it was to rush up on Sparhawk when he was angry, and Sparhawk was very angry at that point. The bodies piled up in the doorway as he savagely vented his rage on the scruffy-looking soldiers.

Then Kurik was there with Delada's guardsmen, and Martel's men fell back, defending the passageway leading towards the opening of the aqueduct into which Martel and Annias had already fled. 'Are you all right?' the squire asked quickly, looking in through the doorway.

'Yes,' Sparhawk replied. Then he reached out and caught Delada's arm as the colonel started to push past him.

'Let me go, Sparhawk,' Delada said from between tight lips.

'No, Colonel. Do you remember what I told you a while ago about your being the most important man in Chyrellos for a while?'

'Yes.' Delada's tone was sullen.

'That particular eminence started just a few minutes ago, and I'm *not* going to let you get yourself killed just because you're feeling pugnacious at the moment. I'll take you to your quarters now and post a guard outside your door.'

Delada rammed his sword back into its sheath. 'You're right, of course,' he said. 'It's just that –'

'I know, Delada. I feel the same way myself.'

After he had seen to the colonel's safety, Sparhawk returned to the cellar. The guardsmen under Kurik's command were in the process of mopping up and flushing out any mercenaries who were trying to hide. Kurik came back through the torchlit darkness. 'I'm afraid Martel and Annias got completely away, Sparhawk,' he reported.

'He was ready for us, Kurik,' Sparhawk said glumly. 'Somehow he knew we'd either be down here or that Sephrenia could work a spell so that we could hear him. He was saying a lot of things for my benefit.'

'Oh?'

'The army coming in from the west is Wargun's.'

'It's about time he got here.' Kurik suddenly grinned.

'Martel also announced which way he's going. He *wants* us to follow him.'

'I'll be overjoyed to oblige him. Did we get what *we* want, though?'

Sparhawk nodded. 'When Delada's done with his report, Annias won't get a single vote.'

'That's something anyway.'

'Put some captain in charge of these guardsmen, and let's go and find Vanion.'

The Preceptors of the four orders were standing atop the walls near the gates looking with some puzzlement out at the now-retreating mercenaries. 'They just broke off the attack for no reason,' Vanion said as Sparhawk and Kurik joined them.

'They had a reason, right enough,' Sparhawk replied. 'That's Wargun over there across the river.'

'Thank God!' Vanion exclaimed. 'Word must have reached him after all. How did things go in the cellar?'

'Colonel Delada heard a *very* interesting conversation. Martel and Annias got away, though. They're going to make a run for Zemoch to seek Otha's protection. Martel's going to send his Rendors out to destroy the bridges to give the rest of his mercenaries time to deploy. He doesn't have much hope that they'll be able to do much more than inconvenience Wargun. All he's really hoping for is enough delay to give him time to get away.'

'I think we'd better go and talk with Dolmant,' Preceptor Darellon said. 'The situation has changed a bit. Why don't you round up your friends, Sir Sparhawk, and we'll go back to the chapterhouse.'

'Pass the word, Kurik,' Sparhawk told his squire. 'Let all our friends know that King Wargun's come to our rescue.'

Kurik nodded.

The Patriarchs were enormously relieved to hear of King Wargun's approach and even more relieved to hear that Annias had incriminated himself. 'The colonel can even testify about the arrangement Annias and Martel have with Otha,' Sparhawk told them. 'The only unfortunate part of the whole business was that Annias and Martel escaped.'

'How long will it take for word of this turn of events to reach Otha?' Patriarch Emban asked.

'I think we'll almost have to assume that Otha will know about the change in the situation here almost as soon as it happens, Your Grace,' Preceptor Abriel told him.

Emban nodded with a look of distaste. 'More of that magic business, I suppose.'

'It's going to take Wargun quite some time to regroup and start to march into Lamorkand to meet the Zemochs, isn't it?' Dolmant said.

'A week or ten days, Your Grace,' Vanion agreed, 'and even that's cutting it a little fine. Advance elements from both armies will be able to move out more rapidly, but neither main force will be able to start in less than a week.'

'How far can an army move in a day?' Emban asked.

'Ten miles maximum, Your Grace,' Vanion replied.

'That's absurd, Vanion. Even *I* can walk ten miles in four hours, and I don't move very fast.'

301

'That's when you're walking alone, Your Grace.' Vanion smiled. 'A man out for a stroll doesn't have to worry about keeping the rear of a column from straggling, and when the time comes to sleep for the night, he can roll himself in his cloak under a bush. It takes quite a bit longer to set up an encampment for an army.'

Emban grunted, laboriously hauled himself to his feet and waddled to the map of Eosia hanging on the wall of Sir Nashan's study. He measured off some distances. 'They'll meet about here then,' he said, stabbing one finger at a spot on the map, '– on that plain to the north of Lake Cammoria. Ortzel, what's the country like around there?'

'Relatively flat,' the Lamork Patriarch replied. 'It's mostly farmland with a few patches of woods here and there.'

'Emban,' Dolmant said gently, 'why don't we let King Wargun work out the strategy? We have our own business to attend to, you know.'

Emban laughed a bit sheepishly. 'I guess I'm a born busybody,' he said. 'I can't stand letting anything go by without sticking my nose into it.' He clasped his hands reflectively behind his back. 'We'll have everything under control in Chyrellos just as soon as Wargun gets here. I think it's safe to say that Colonel Delada's testimony will eliminate the candidacy of the Primate of Cimmura once and for all, so why don't we clear away this election business right away – before the Hierocracy has time to gather its collective breath. Patriarchs are political animals, and as soon as they've had the time to collect their wits, they're going to start to see all sorts of opportunities in the present situation. We don't really need a number of unanticipated candidacies clouding things over right now. Let's keep it simple if we can. Not only that, we alienated a fair number of Patriarchs when we decided to let the outer city burn.

302

Let's catch the Hierocracy while it's still overwhelmed with thanksgiving and gratitude and fill that empty chair in the Basilica before they start brooding about lost houses and the like. We've got the upper hand for the moment. Let's use it before our support starts to crumble.'

'That's all you ever really think about, isn't it, Emban?' Dolmant said.

'Somebody has to, my friend.'

'We'd better get Wargun into the city first, though,' Vanion told them. 'Is there anything we can do to help him?'

'We can move out of the inner city just as soon as Martel's generals start turning around to face his army,' Komier suggested. 'We can hit them from behind and sting them enough to force them to chase us back inside the walls. Then they'll have to divert enough troops to keep us penned up in here. That should reduce the force facing Wargun a little bit.'

'What I'd *really* like to do is figure out some way to defend those bridges across the Arruk,' Abriel said. 'Replacing them is what's going to cost Wargun time – and lives.'

'I don't see that there's very much we can do about that,' Darellon said. 'We don't have enough men to keep the Rendors away from the river-bank.'

'We *have* got enough to disrupt things inside the city though,' Komier asserted. 'Why don't we go back to the wall and size things up a bit? I need something to do to take the taste of that siege out of my mouth anyway.'

There was fog as dawn approached, for the summer was drawing to a close and the two rivers which joined at Chyrellos fumed grey, wispy tendrils of mist from their dark surfaces in the cool of the night, and the tendrils joined together to form first a haze that softened the orange torchlight, then a mist which enshrouded distant

303

houses and finally that thick, clinging fog so common in cities which are built along rivers.

There was enthusiasm in the ranks for the action. There were tactical reasons for the plan, of course, but tactics are for generals, and the common soldiery was more interested in revenge. They had endured the pounding of siege engines; they had beaten off fanatics climbing scaling ladders; and they had faced the assault towers. Until now they had been forced to bear whatever the besiegers had hurled at them. This was their chance to even some scores, to chastise their chastisers, and they marched forth from the inner city with looks of grim anticipation on their faces.

Many of Martel's mercenaries had joined him with enthusiasm when there had been the prospect of loot and rapine and easy assaults on meagrely defended walls. Their enthusiasm waned, however, at the notion of meeting a vastly superior force in open country. They became peace-loving men at that point and crept through the foggy streets in search of places where their newly-found pacifist sentiments would not be offended. The sortie in force from the inner city came as a great surprise and an even greater disappointment to men bent merely upon leading simple lives untainted by strife.

The fog, of course, helped enormously. The defenders of the inner city had only to fall upon men who were not wearing the armour of Church Knights or the red tunics of church soldiers. The torches these sudden pacifists carried made them easy targets for Kurik's now-proficient crossbowmen.

Since men on horseback make too much noise, the Church Knights moved through the streets on foot. After a time, Sparhawk joined Vanion. 'All we're doing here is picking off deserters,' he advised his Preceptor.

'Not entirely, Sparhawk,' Vanion disagreed. 'The church

soldiers have been under siege, and that sort of thing wears down men's spirits. Let's give our questionable allies the chance for a little revenge before we turn them back over to the Patriarchs.'

Sparhawk nodded his agreement and then he, Kalten and Kurik moved out to take the lead.

A shadowy figure carrying an axe appeared at a torchlit intersection. The outline showed that whoever it was wore neither armour nor the tunic of a church soldier. Kurik raised his crossbow and took aim. At the last instant, he jerked his weapon upward, and the bolt whizzed up towards the pre-dawn sky. Kurik started to swear sulphurously.

'What's the matter?' Kalten hissed.

'That's Berit,' Kurik said from between clenched teeth. 'He always rolls his shoulders that way when he walks.'

'Sir Sparhawk?' the novice called into the darkness, 'are you down there?'

'Yes.'

'Thank God. I think I've walked down every burned-out alley in Chyrellos looking for you.'

Kurik banged one fist against a wall.

'Talk to him about it later,' Sparhawk said. 'All right, Berit,' he called, 'you've found me. What's important enough for you to go around risking your skin to try to share it?'

Berit came down the street to join them. 'The Rendors appear to be gathering near the west gate, Sir Sparhawk. There are thousands of them.'

'What are they doing?'

'I think they're praying. They're having some kind of ceremony at any rate. There's a skinny, bearded fellow standing on a pile of rubble haranguing them.'

'Could you hear any of what he was saying?'

'Not very much, Sir Sparhawk, but he did say one word

305

fairly often, and all the rest bellowed out the word each time he said it.'

'What was the word?' Kurik demanded.

'Ramshorn, I think it was, Kurik.'

'That's got a familiar ring to it, Sparhawk,' Kurik said.

Sparhawk nodded. 'It appears that Martel brought Ulesim along to keep the Rendors in line.'

Berit gave him a puzzled look. 'Who's Ulesim, Sir Sparhawk?'

'The current spiritual leader of the Rendors. There's a twisted piece of a sheep's horn that's a kind of badge of office.' He thought of something. 'The Rendors are just sitting around listening to sermons?' he asked the novice.

'If that's what you want to call all that babbling, yes.'

'Why don't we go back and talk with Vanion?' Sparhawk suggested. 'This might be very useful.'

The Preceptors and Sparhawk's friends were not far behind. 'I think we've just had a bit of luck, My Lords,' Sparhawk reported. 'Berit's been out wandering around in the streets. He says that the Rendors are all gathered near the west gate and that their leader's whipping them into a frenzy.'

'You actually let a novice go out there alone, Sir Sparhawk?' Abriel asked disapprovingly.

'Kurik's going to talk to him about that later, My Lord.'

'What was this leader's name again?' Vanion asked thoughtfully.

'Ulesim, my Lord. I've met him. He's a total idiot.'

'What would the Rendors do if something happened to him?'

'They'd disintegrate, My Lord. Martel said that he was going to order them to tear down the bridges. Apparently

306

they haven't started yet. Rendors need a lot of encouragement and some rather careful directions before they start on anything. Anyway, they look upon their religious leader as a semi-divinity. They won't do anything without his express command.'

'That might just be the way to save your bridges, Abriel,' Vanion said. 'If something happens to this Ulesim, the Rendors may just forget what they're supposed to do. Why don't we gather up our forces and pay them a call?'

'Bad idea,' Kurik said shortly. 'Sorry Lord Vanion, but it really is. If we march on the Rendors in force, they'll fight to the death to defend their holy man. All we'll do is get a lot of men needlessly killed.'

'Do you have an alternative?'

Kurik patted his crossbow. 'Yes, My Lord,' he said confidently. 'Berit says that Ulesim's making a speech to his people. A man who's talking to a crowd usually stands up on something. If I can get to within two hundred paces of him –' Kurik left it hanging.

'Sparhawk,' Vanion decided, 'take your friends and protect Kurik. Try to slip through the city until you can get him and that crossbow close enough to this Ulesim to remove him. If those Rendorish fanatics fly all to pieces and don't destroy the bridges, Wargun will be able to cross the river before the other mercenaries are ready for them. Mercenaries are the most practical soldiers in the world. They're not very enthusiastic about hopeless battles.'

'You think they'll capitulate?' Darellon asked.

'It's worth a try,' Vanion said. 'A peaceful solution of some kind here could save us a lot of men on both sides, and I think we're going to need every man we can lay our hands on – even the Rendors – when we come up against Otha.'

Abriel suddenly laughed. 'I wonder how God's going

to feel about having His Church defended by Eshandist heretics?'

'God's tolerant,' Komier grinned. 'He might even forgive them – a little.'

The four knights, Berit and Kurik crept through the streets of Chyrellos towards the west gate. A faint breeze had come up, and the fog was rapidly dissipating. They reached a large burned-out area near the west gate to find thousands of tightly-packed and heavily armed Rendors gathered in the thinning mist about a heaped-up pile of rubble. Atop the rubble stood a familiar figure.

'That's him, all right,' Sparhawk whispered to his companions as they took refuge in the gutted remains of a house. 'There he stands in all his glory – Ulesim, most-favoured-disciple-of-holy-Arasham.'

'What was that?' Kalten asked.

'That's what he called himself down in Rendor. It was a self-bestowed title. I guess he wanted to spare Arasham the effort of selecting somebody.'

Ulesim was in a state bordering on hysteria, and his speech had little in the way of coherence to recommend it. He held one bony arm aloft, and he was tightly clutching something. After about every fifteen words, he would shake the object in his hand vigorously and bellow, 'RAMSHORN!' His followers then would roar back, 'RAMSHORN!'

'What do you think, Kurik?' Sparhawk whispered as they all looked over a half-collapsed wall.

'I think he's crazy.'

'Of course he's crazy, but is he in range?'

Kurik squinted across the top of the crowd at the ranting fanatic. 'It's a goodly way,' he said dubiously.

'Give it a try anyway,' Kalten said. 'If your bolt falls short – or even goes over – somebody of Rendorish persuasion's bound to catch it for you.'

Kurik laid his crossbow across the top of the broken wall to steady it and took careful aim.

'God has revealed it to me!' Ulesim was shrieking to his followers. 'We must destroy the bridges which are the work of the Evil One! The forces of darkness beyond the river will assault you, but Ramshorn will protect you! The power of the Blessed Eshand has joined with that of Holy Arasham to fill the Talisman with unearthly might! Ramshorn will give you victory!'

Kurik squeezed the lever of his crossbow slowly. The thick bow made a deep-toned 'twang' as it sped the bolt towards its mark.

'You are invincible!' Ulesim was shrieking. 'You are –'

Whatever else it was that they were was never revealed. The vanes of a crossbow bolt were suddenly protruding from Ulesim's forehead just above his eyebrows. He stiffened, his eyes wide and his mouth suddenly gaping. Then he crumpled into a heap atop the rubble.

'Good shot,' Tynian congratulated Kurik.

'Actually, I was trying to hit him in the belly,' Kurik confessed.

'That's all right, Kurik,' the Deiran laughed. 'It was more spectacular this way anyhow.'

A vast groan of shock and dismay ran through the crowd of Rendors.

Then the word 'crossbow' raced through the mob. A number of unfortunates had obtained such weapons from the Lamorks in one way or another. They were torn to pieces on the spot by their frenzied compatriots. A fair number of the black-robed men from the south ran off through the streets, howling and tearing at their garments. Others slumped to the ground, weeping in despair. Still others stood staring in stunned disbelief at the place where Ulesim had only recently stood haranguing them. There was also, Sparhawk noticed, a fair amount of on-the-spot politics going on. There were those in the crowd who felt that they had a claim on the recently-vacated position, and they began to take steps to ensure their elevation to eminence, reasoning that power rests more securely in the hands of sole survivors. Adherents of this or that candidate joined in, and the huge crowd was soon embroiled in what could only be called a general riot.

'Political discussion is quite spirited among the Rendors, isn't it?' Tynian observed mildly.

'I noticed that,' Sparhawk agreed. 'Let's go and tell the Preceptors about Ulesim's accident.'

Since the Rendors were now militantly indifferent to bridges, ramshorns or the impending battle, the commanders of Martel's army saw that they had no chance whatsoever against the human sea on the far side of the river. Mercenaries are the most realistic of all soldiers, and soon a sizeable detachment of officers rode across one of the bridges under a flag of truce. They returned just before daybreak. The mercenary commanders conferred for a few moments, and then they formed up and, pushing the rioting Rendors ahead of them, they marched out of Chyrellos and laid down their arms in surrender.

Sparhawk and the others gathered atop the wall of the outer city right beside the open west gate as the kings of western Eosia rode quite formally across the bridge to enter the Holy City. King Wargun, flanked by the mail-shirted Patriarch Bergsten, King Dregos of Arcium, King Soros of Pelosia and the ancient King Obler of Deira rode at the head of the column. Directly behind them came an ornate open carriage. Four people sat in the carriage. They were all robed and hooded, but the sheer bulk of one of them sent a chill through Sparhawk. Surely they wouldn't have – And then, apparently at some command from the slightest of them, the four pushed back their hoods. The fat one was Platime. Stragen was the second. The third was a woman whom Sparhawk did not recognize and the fourth, slender and blonde and looking altogether lovely, was Ehlana, Queen of Elenia.

Chapter 16

Wargun's entry into Chyrellos was hardly triumphant. The commoners of the Holy City had not been in a position to stay abreast of current affairs, and one army looks very much like another to ordinary people. For the most part, they stayed under cover as the kings of Eosia passed on their way to the Basilica.

Sparhawk had little chance to speak with his queen when they all arrived at the Basilica. He had things to say to her, of course, but they were not the sort of things he wanted to say in public. King Wargun gave his generals a few abrupt commands, and then they followed the Patriarch of Demos inside for one of the get-togethers which normally mark such occasions.

'I'll have to admit that this Martel of yours is very clever,' the King of Thalesia conceded a bit later, leaning back in a chair with an ale tankard in his hand. They had gathered in a large, ornate meeting-room in the Basilica. The room had a long, polished table, a marble floor and thick burgundy drapes at the windows. The kings were present as were the Preceptors of the four orders, Patriarchs Dolmant, Emban, Ortzel and Bergsten and Sparhawk and the others, including Ulath, who still exhibited moments of vagueness but appeared to be on the mend. Sparhawk's face was stony as he looked across the table at his bride-to-be. He had many things he wanted to say to Ehlana, and a few he was saving up for Platime and Stragen as well. He was controlling his temper with some difficulty.

'After the burning of Coombe,' Wargun went on,

'Martel took a weakly defended castle perched on top of a crag. He strengthened the defences, left a sizeable garrison there and then moved on to lay siege to Larium. When we came up behind him, he fled east. Then he swung south, and finally he went west again towards Coombe. I spent weeks chasing him. It *seemed* that he'd led his whole army into that castle, and I settled down to starve him out. What I *didn't* know was that he'd been detaching whole regiments from his army to hide in the countryside as he marched, and so he reached that castle with no more than a very small force. He sent that force inside the walls and closed the gates, and then he rode away, leaving *me* to besiege an impregnable castle, and leaving *him* free to regather his forces and march on Chyrellos.'

'We sent a great many messages to you, Your Majesty,' Patriarch Dolmant said.

'I'm sure you did, Your Grace,' Wargun said sourly, 'but only one of them reached me. Martel cluttered most of Arcium with small bands of ambushers. I expect that most of your messengers are lying in ditches down there in God's own rock-garden. Sorry, Dregos,' he apologized to the Arcian King.

'That's all right, Wargun,' King Dregos forgave him. 'God had a reason for putting so much rock in Arcium. Paving roads and building walls and castles gives my people something to do other than starting wars with each other.'

'If there were ambushers out, how did *anybody* manage to reach you, Your Majesty?' Dolmant asked.

'That was the strange part of it, Dolmant,' Wargun replied, scratching at his tousled head. 'I never really *did* get the straight of it. The fellow who got through is from Lamorkand, and it appears that he just rode openly all the way across Arcium and no one paid any attention to him. Either he's the luckiest man alive or God loves

313

him more than most – and he doesn't look all that lovable to me.'

'Is he nearby, Your Majesty?' Sephrenia asked the King of Thalesia, her eyes strangely intent.

'I think so, little lady,' Wargun belched. 'He said something about wanting to make a report to the Patriarch of Kadach. He's probably out there in the hall somewhere.'

'Do you suppose we might ask him a few questions?'

'Is it really important, Sephrenia?' Dolmant asked her.

'Yes, Your Grace,' she replied, 'I think it might be. There's something I'd like to verify.'

'You,' Wargun said sharply to one of the soldiers standing at the door, 'see if you can find that seedy-looking Lamork who's been trailing after us. Tell him to come in here.'

'At once, Your Majesty.'

'Naturally "at once". I gave an order, didn't I? *All* my orders are obeyed at once.' King Wargun was already on his fourth tankard of ale, and his grip on civility was beginning to slip. 'Anyway,' he went on, 'the fellow arrived at that castle I was besieging no more than two weeks ago. After I read his message, I gathered up the army and we all came here.'

The Lamork who was escorted into the room was, as Wargun had said, a bit on the seedy-looking side. He was obviously neither a warrior nor Churchman. He had thin, lank, dun-coloured hair and a big nose.

'Ah, Eck,' Patriarch Ortzel said, recognizing one of his servants. 'I should have guessed that you'd have been the one to make it through. My friends, this is one of my servants – Eck by name – a very sneaky fellow, I've found. He's most useful when stealth is required.'

'I don't think stealth had much to do with it this time, Your Grace,' Eck admitted. He had a nasal sort of voice that seemed to go with his face. 'As soon as we saw your

314

signal, we all rode off to the west as fast as our horses could run. We started to run into ambushes before we even reached the Arcian border, though. That's when we decided to split up. We thought that one of us at least might get through. Personally, I didn't have much hope of that. There seemed to be a man with a longbow behind every tree. Anyway, I hid out in a ruined castle near Darra to think things over. I couldn't see any way to get your message through at all. I didn't know where King Wargun was, and I didn't dare ask any travellers for fear that they were some of the men who'd been killing my friends.'

'Perilous situation,' Darellon said.

'I thought so myself, My Lord,' Eck agreed. 'I hid in that ruin for two days, and then one morning, I heard the strangest sound. It seemed to be music of some kind. I thought it might be a shepherd, but it turned out to be a little girl with a few goats. She was making the music on those pipes that herders carry. The little girl seemed to be about six or so, and I knew as soon as I saw her that she was Styric. Everyone knows that it's bad luck to have anything at all to do with Styrics, so I stayed hidden in the ruins. I certainly didn't want her to give me away to any of the people who were looking for me. She came right up to me as if she knew exactly where I was, though, and she told me to follow her.' He paused, his face troubled. 'Now, I'm a grown man, Your Grace, and I don't take orders from children – and particularly not from Styric ones – but there was something very strange about this little girl. When she told me to do something, I went right ahead and started to do it before I even stopped to think about it. Isn't that odd? To make it short, she led me out of those ruins. The men who were looking for me were all around, but they just acted as if they couldn't even see us. The little girl led me all the way across Arcium. Now, that's a long,

315

long way, but for some reason it only took us three days
– four actually when you count the day when we stopped
so that one of her nanny-goats could give birth to a pair of
kids – cute little beasts they were, too. The little girl even
insisted that I carry them on my horse when we moved
on. Well sir, we reached the castle where King Wargun's
army was laying siege to some Rendors inside, and that's
when the little girl left me. It's the oddest thing. I don't
like Styrics, but I actually cried when she went away. She
gave me a little kiss before she left, and I can still feel it
on my cheek. I've thought about it a lot since then, and
I've decided that maybe Styrics aren't so bad after all.'

'Thank you,' Sephrenia murmured.

'Well, sir,' Eck went on, 'I went to the army and told
them that I had a message for King Wargun from the
Hierocracy. The soldiers took me to His Majesty, and
I gave him the document. After he read it through, he
gathered up his army, and we made a forced march to get
here. That's about all there was, My Lords.'

Kurik was smiling gently. 'Well, well,' he said to
Sephrenia, 'it looks as if Flute's still around – and in
more than just spirit – doesn't it?'

'So it would seem,' she agreed, also smiling.

'Document?' Patriarch Emban said to Patriarch Ortzel.

'I took the liberty of speaking for the Hierocracy,'
Ortzel confessed. 'I gave each of my messengers a copy
for King Wargun. I thought it might be all right, under the
circumstances.'

'It's quite all right with *me*,' Emban said. 'Makova might
not have liked it very much, though.'

'I'll apologize to him someday – if I happen to think
about it. I wasn't really sure whether any of the other
messages had reached King Wargun, so I more or less
briefed him on everything that's been happening.'

It had taken a few moments for what they were saying

to seep through King Wargun's awareness. 'Are you saying that I moved my army on the orders of one single Patriarch – who isn't even a Thalesian?' he roared.

'No, Wargun,' the huge Patriarch Bergsten said firmly. 'I fully approve of the actions of the Patriarch of Kadach, so you moved your army on *my* orders. Would you like to argue with *me* about it?'

'Oh,' Wargun said contritely, 'that's different then.' Patriarch Bergsten was not really the sort one argued with. Wargun moved on quickly. 'I read over the document a couple of times and decided that a side trip to Cimmura might be in order. I sent Dregos and Obler with the main body of the army on ahead and took the Elenian army back up there so that they could defend their capital city. When we got there, we found the place defended by the common citizens, if you can imagine that, and when I demanded entry, they wouldn't open the gates for me until that fat one over there gave his approval. To be honest with you, I couldn't really see where Cimmura was in all that much danger. Those shopkeepers and common workmen were handling themselves in a very professional manner up on those walls, I'll tell the world. Anyway, I went to the palace to meet with the Earl of Lenda and this pretty young lady who wears the crown. That's when I saw that rascal over there.' He pointed at Stragen. 'He'd hemstitched a fourth cousin of mine with that rapier of his up in Emsat, and I'd put a price on his head – more out of family feeling than for any particular affection for the cousin, since the man made me sick just to look at him. He had a habit of picking his nose in public, and I find that disgusting. He won't do it any more, though. Stragen skewered him thoroughly. Anyway, I was going to have this rogue hanged, but Ehlana there talked me out of it.' He took a long drink. 'Actually,' he belched, 'she threatened to declare war on me if I didn't drop the idea. She's a very

317

feisty young lady, I discovered.' He suddenly grinned at Sparhawk. 'I understand that congratulations are in order, my friend, but I don't know that I'd take off my armour until you get to know her better.'

'We know each other very well, Wargun,' Ehlana said primly. 'Sparhawk virtually raised me from a baby, so if I sometimes have a few rough edges, you have him to thank for it.'

'I probably should have suspected something like that,' Wargun laughed to the others, 'because when I told Ehlana about what was happening here in Chyrellos, she insisted on bringing her army along to help with the fighting. I absolutely forbade it, and all she did was reach out, tweak my whiskers and say, "That's all right, Wargun. I'll race you to Chyrellos then." Now, I don't let *anyone* pull my whiskers, so I was going to spank her right there on the spot, queen or no queen, but then that enormous woman over there stepped in.' He looked at the woman Sparhawk surmised was Mirtai, the Tamul giantess, and shuddered. 'I couldn't believe that she could move that fast. She had a knife to my throat before I could even blink. I tried to explain to Ehlana that I had more than enough men to capture Chyrellos, but she said something about having an investment to protect. I never really got the straight of that. Anyway, we all marched out of Cimmura and joined with Dregos and Obler and came on down here to the Holy City. Now, could somebody explain to me what's really been happening here?'

'The usual Church politics,' Patriarch Emban told him dryly. 'You know how much our mother adores intrigue. We were fighting a delaying action in the meetings of Hierocracy, manipulating votes, kidnapping Patriarchs – that sort of thing. We were barely able to keep the Primate of Cimmura off the throne, and then Martel showed up and laid siege to the Holy City. We pulled back inside the

318

walls of the inner city for one of those tedious last stands. Things were starting to get serious by the time you arrived last night.'

'Has Annias been seized as yet?' King Obler asked.

'I'm afraid not, Your Majesty,' Dolmant replied. 'Martel managed to spirit him out of the city just before dawn.'

'That's truly unfortunate,' Obler sighed. 'He could still come back and make a serious bid for the Archprelacy then, couldn't he?'

'We'd be overjoyed to see him, Your Majesty,' Dolmant said with a mirthless smile. 'I'm sure you've heard of the connection between Annias and Martel and the suspicions we have about some sort of arrangements between them and Otha. As luck had it, we were able to take the commander of the Archprelate's personal guard to a place where he could overhear Annias and Martel talking. The colonel's completely neutral, and everybody knows it. Once he reports what he heard to the Hierocracy, Annias will be expelled from the Church – at the very least.' He paused. 'Now then,' he went on, 'the Zemochs are massed in eastern Lamorkand as a part of the arrangement between Otha and Annias. As soon as Otha finds out that their plans have gone awry here in Chyrellos, he'll start to march west. I'd suggest that we do something about that.'

'Have we any idea of which way Annias went?' Ehlana asked, her eyes glittering.

'He and Martel took Princess Arissa and your cousin Lycheas, and they're all running to Otha for protection, My Queen,' Sparhawk told her.

'Is there any way you could intercept them?' she demanded fiercely.

'We can try, Your Majesty,' he shrugged. 'I wouldn't hold out much hope, though.'

'I *want* him, Sparhawk,' she said fiercely.

'I'm very sorry, Your Majesty,' Patriarch Dolmant interposed, 'but Annias has committed crimes against the Church. *We* get him first.'

'So that you can lock him away in some monastery to pray and sing hymns the rest of his life?' she asked with disdain. 'I have much more interesting plans for him, Your Grace. Believe me, if I get my hands on him first, I will *not* surrender him to the Church – at least not until I've finished with him. After that, you can have what's left.'

'That will do, Ehlana,' Dolmant told her sharply. 'You're right on the verge of open disobedience to the Church. Don't make the mistake of pushing this too far. In point of fact, though, it's not a monastery that's waiting for Annias. The nature of the crimes he's committed against the Church merits burning at the stake.'

Their eyes locked, and Sparhawk groaned inwardly.

Then Ehlana laughed, a bit shamefaced. 'Forgive me, Your Grace,' she apologized to Dolmant. 'I spoke in haste. Burning, did you say?'

'At the very least, Ehlana,' he replied.

'I will, of course, defer to our holy mother. I would sooner die than appear undutiful.'

'The Church appreciates your obedience, my daughter,' Dolmant said blandly.

Ehlana clasped her hands piously and gave him a wholly spurious little smile of contrition.

Dolmant laughed in spite of himself. 'You're a naughty girl, Ehlana,' he chided.

'Yes, Your Grace,' she admitted. 'I suppose I am at that.'

'This is a very dangerous woman, my friends,' Wargun told his fellow monarchs. 'I think we should all make a special point of not getting in her way. All right, what's next?'

Emban slid lower in his chair and sat tapping his fat

fingertips together. 'We'd more or less decided that we should settle the question of the Archprelacy once and for all, Your Majesty. That was before you even entered the city. It's going to take some time for you to prepare your forces to march towards central Lamorkand, isn't it?' he asked.

'At least a week,' Wargun replied glumly, 'possibly two. I've got units strung out half-way back to Arcium – mostly stragglers and supply wagons. It's going to take a while to get them organized, and troops really get jammed up when they have to cross bridges.'

'We can give you ten days at most,' Dolmant told him. 'Do your staging and organizing as you march.'

'It's not done that way, Your Grace,' Wargun objected.

'It will be this time, Your Majesty. Soldiers on a march spend more time sitting around waiting than they do walking. Let's put that time to good use.'

'You'll also want to keep your soldiers out of Chyrellos,' Patriarch Ortzel added. 'Most of the citizens have fled, so the city's deserted. If your men become distracted with looking through unoccupied houses, they'll be a little difficult to round up when the time comes to march.'

'Dolmant,' Emban said, 'you're holding the chair in the Hierocracy. I think we should go into session first thing tomorrow morning. Let's keep our brothers away from the outer city today – for their own safety, of course, since there still might be a few of Martel's mercenaries hiding in the ruins. Primarily, though, we don't want them to get a chance to examine the damage to their houses too closely before we go into formal session. We've seriously alienated a fair number of Patriarchs, and even with Annias discredited, we don't want some spur-of-the-moment coalition confusing the issues here. I think we should hold some sort of service in the nave before we go into session. Probably something solemn

321

and having to do with thanksgiving. Ortzel, would you officiate? You're going to be our candidate, so let's give everybody the chance to get used to looking at you. And, Ortzel, try to smile now and then. Honestly, your face won't break.'

'Am I so very, very stern, Emban?' Ortzel replied with a faint half-smile.

'Perfect,' Emban said. 'Practise that exact smile in a mirror. Remember that you're going to be a kindly, loving father – at least that's what we want them to think. What you do after you get to the throne is between you and God. All right then. The services will remind our brothers that they're Churchmen first and property-owners second. We'll march directly to the audience chamber from the nave. I'll talk to the choirmaster and have a lot of singing echoing through the Basilica – something exalted to put our brothers in the proper mood. Dolmant will call us to order, and we'll begin with an update – let everybody know the details of what's been happening. That's for the benefit of the Patriarchs who've been hiding in cellars since the siege began. It's perfectly proper to call in witnesses under those circumstances. I'll select them to make sure they're eloquent. We want a lot of lurid descriptions of rape, arson and pillage to stir up a certain disapproval of the behaviour of the recent visitors to our city. Our parade of witnesses will culminate with Colonel Delada, and he'll report the conversation between Annias and Martel. Let them mull that over for a little bit. I'll talk to some of our brothers and have them prepare speeches full of outraged indignation and denunciations of the Primate of Cimmura. Then Dolmant will appoint a committee to investigate the matter. We don't want the Hierocracy to get sidetracked.' The fat little Patriarch thought it over. 'Let's adjourn for a noon meal at that point. Give them a couple of hours to work themselves up about the perfidy of Annias. Then, when we go back into session, Bergsten will make a speech about the need for all considered speed. Don't give the appearance of rushing things, Bergsten, but remind them that we're in a Crisis of the Faith. Then urge that we proceed directly with the voting. Wear your armour and carry that axe. Let's set the tone of being on a wartime footing. Then we'll have the traditional speeches by the kings of Eosia. Make them stirring, Your Majesties. Lots of references to cruel war and Otha and the foul designs of Azash. We want to frighten our brothers enough so that they'll vote their consciences instead of politicking in back hallways and trying to make deals with each other. Keep your eyes on me, Dolmant. I'll nose out any Patriarchs with the uncontrollable urge towards political chicanery and identify them to you. As chairman, you can recognize whomever you choose. And under *no* circumstances whatsoever accept a move to adjourn. Don't let anybody break the momentum. Go immediately into the nominations at that point. Let's get into the voting before our brothers have time to start thinking up mischief. Speed the vote right along. We want Ortzel on that throne before the sun goes down. And Ortzel, you keep your mouth shut during the deliberations. Some of your opinions are controversial. Don't air them in public – at least not tomorrow.'

'I feel like an infant,' King Dregos said wryly to King Obler. 'I thought I knew a *little* bit about politics, but I've never seen the art practised so ruthlessly before.'

'You're in the big city now, Your Majesty,' Emban grinned at him, 'and *this* is the way we play here.'

King Soros of Pelosia, a man of extreme piety and an almost child-like reverence had nearly fainted a number of times during Patriarch Emban's cold-blooded scheme to manipulate the Hierocracy. He finally bolted, muttering something about wanting to pray for guidance.

'Keep an eye on Soros tomorrow, Your Grace,' Wargun

advised Emban. 'He's a religious hysteric. When he makes his speech, he might just decide to expose us. Soros spends all his time talking to God, and sometimes that unsettles a man's wits. Is there any possible way we can skip over him during the speeches?'

'Not legitimately,' Emban said.

'We'll talk with him, Wargun,' King Obler said. 'Maybe we can persuade him to be too ill to attend tomorrow's session.'

'I'll make him sick, all right,' Wargun muttered.

Emban rose to his feet. 'We all have things to attend to, ladies and gentlemen,' he said, 'so as they say, let's get cracking.'

Sparhawk stood up. 'The Elenian embassy was damaged during the siege, My Queen,' he said to Ehlana in a neutral tone. 'May I offer you the somewhat Spartan comfort of the Pandion chapterhouse instead?'

'You're cross with me, aren't you, Sparhawk?' she asked him.

'It might be more appropriate if we discussed that in private, My Queen.'

'Ah,' she sighed. 'Well, let's go ahead and go to your chapterhouse so you can scold me for a while. Then we can move right on into the kissing and making up. That's the part *I'm* really interested in. At least you won't be able to spank me – not with Mirtai standing guard over me. Have you ever met Mirtai, by the way?'

'No, My Queen.' Sparhawk looked at the silent Tamul woman who stood behind Ehlana's chair. Mirtai's skin had a peculiarly exotic bronze tinge to it, and her braided hair was a glossy black. In a woman of normal size, her features would have been considered beautiful, and her dark eyes, slightly upturned at the corners, ravishing. Mirtai, however, was not of normal size. She towered a good hand's-breadth above Sparhawk. She wore a white satin blouse with full sleeves and a garment that was more like a knee-length kilt than a skirt, belted at her waist. She wore black leather boots and had a sword at her side. Her shoulders were broad and her hips lithely slender. Despite her size, she seemed perfectly proportioned. There was, however, something ominous about her expressionless gaze. She did not look at Sparhawk the way a woman would normally look at a man. She was an unsettling sort of person.

Sparhawk, stiffly correct, offered his steel-clad arm to his queen and escorted her out through the nave and to the marble steps outside the Basilica. There was a ringing tap on his armoured back as they stepped out onto the broad landing at the top of the stairs. He looked around. Mirtai had rapped on his armour with one knuckle. She took a folded cloak from off her arm, shook it out and held it for Ehlana.

'Oh, it's not really *that* cool, Mirtai,' Ehlana objected.

Mirtai's face went flinty, and she shook the cloak once commandingly.

Ehlana sighed and permitted the giantess to settle the cloak about her shoulders. Sparhawk was looking directly at the bronze woman's face, so there could be no question about what happened next. Without changing expression, Mirtai gave him a slow wink. For some reason, that made him feel a great deal better. He and Mirtai were going to get along very well, he decided.

Since Vanion was busy, Sparhawk escorted Ehlana, Sephrenia, Stragen, Platime and Mirtai to Sir Nashan's study for their discussions. He had spent the morning preparing and sharpening a number of scathing remarks that verged just on the edge of being treasonous.

Ehlana, however, had studied politics since childhood, and she knew that one needs to be quick – even abrupt – when one's position is none too strong. 'You're unhappy

325

with us,' she began before Sparhawk even had the door closed. 'You feel that I have no business being here and that my friends here are at fault for allowing me to place myself in danger. Is that more or less it, Sparhawk?'

'Approximately, yes.' *His* tone was frosty.

'Let's simplify things then,' she went on quickly. 'Platime, Stragen and Mirtai *did*, in fact, protest most violently, but I'm the queen, so I overruled them. Do we agree that I have that authority?' *Her* tone had an edge to it, a note of challenge.

'She really did, Sparhawk,' Platime said in a conciliatory tone. 'Stragen and I yelled at her for an hour about it, and then she threatened to have us thrown into the dungeon. She even threatened to revoke my pardon.'

'Her Majesty is a very effective bully, Sparhawk,' Stragen concurred. 'Don't ever trust her when she smiles at you. That's when she's the most dangerous, and when the time comes, she uses her authority like a bludgeon. We even went so far as to try to lock her in her apartment, but she just told Mirtai to kick the door down.'

Sparhawk was startled. 'That's a very thick door,' he said.

'It *used* to be. Mirtai kicked it twice, and it split right down the middle.'

Sparhawk looked at the bronze woman with some surprise.

'It wasn't difficult,' she said. Her voice was soft and musical, and it was touched with just the faintest tinge of an exotic accent. 'Doors inside of houses dry out, and they split quite easily if you kick them just right. Ehlana can use the pieces for firewood when winter comes.' She spoke with quiet dignity.

'Mirtai is very protective of me, Sparhawk,' Ehlana said. 'I feel completely secure when she's around, and she's teaching me to speak the language of the Tamuls.'

326

'Elene is a coarse and ugly language,' Mirtai observed.

'I've noticed that,' Sephrenia smiled.

'I'm teaching Ehlana the Tamul tongue so that I will not be ashamed to have my owner clucking at me like a chicken.'

'I'm *not* your owner any longer, Mirtai,' Ehlana insisted. 'I gave you your freedom right after I bought you.'

Sephrenia's eyes were outraged. '*Owner!*' she exclaimed.

'It's a custom of Mirtai's people, little sister,' Stragen explained. 'She's an Atan. They're a warrior race, and it's generally believed that they need guidance. The Tamuls feel that they aren't emotionally equipped to handle freedom. It seems to cause too many casualties.'

'Ehlana was ignorant to even make the suggestion,' Mirtai said calmly.

'*Mirtai!*' Ehlana exclaimed.

'Dozens of your people have insulted me since you became my owner, Ehlana,' the Tamul woman said sternly. 'They would all be dead now if I were free. That old one – Lenda – even let his shadow touch me once. I know that you're fond of him, so I'd have regretted killing him.' She sighed philosophically. 'Freedom is very dangerous for one of my kind. I prefer not to be burdened with it.'

'We can talk about it some other time, Mirtai,' Ehlana said. 'Now we have to pacify my champion.' She looked Sparhawk full in the face. 'You have no reason to be angry with Platime, Stragen or Mirtai, my beloved,' she told him. 'They did everything they could to keep me in Cimmura. Your quarrel is with me and with me alone. Why don't we excuse them so that we can scream at each other privately?'

'I'll go along with them,' Sephrenia said. 'I'm sure you'll both be able to speak more freely if you're alone.' She followed the two thieves and the bronze giantess from the room. She paused at the door. 'One last thing, children,' she added. 'Scream all you want, but no hitting – and I don't want either of you to come out of here until you've resolved this.' She went out and closed the door behind her.

'Well?' Ehlana said.

'You're stubborn,' Sparhawk said flatly.

'It's called being strong-willed, Sparhawk. That's considered to be a virtue in kings and queens.'

'What on earth possessed you to come to a city under siege?'

'You forget something, Sparhawk,' she said. 'I'm not really a woman.'

He looked her slowly up and down until she blushed furiously – he owed her that, he felt. 'Oh?' He knew he was going to lose this fight anyway.

'Stop that,' she said. 'I'm a queen – a reigning monarch. That means that I sometimes have to do things that an ordinary woman wouldn't be allowed to do. I'm already at a disadvantage because I'm a woman. If I hide behind my own skirts, none of the other kings will take me seriously, and if they don't take *me* seriously, they won't take Elenia seriously either. I *had* to come here, Sparhawk. You understand that, don't you?'

He sighed. 'I don't like it, Ehlana, but I can't argue with your reasoning.'

'Besides,' she added softly, 'I was lonesome for you.'

'You win,' he laughed.

'Oh good,' she exclaimed, clapping her hands together delightedly. 'I just *adore* winning. Now, why don't we move right on into the kissing and making up?'

They did that for a while. 'I've missed you, my stern-faced champion,' she sighed. Then she banged her knuckles on his cuirass. 'I didn't miss *this* though,' she added. She gave him an odd look. 'Why did you have such a strange expression on your face when that Ick fellow –'

'Eck,' he corrected.

'Sorry – when he was talking about the little girl who guided him through Arcium to King Wargun?'

'Because the little girl was Aphrael.'

'A Goddess? She actually appears before ordinary people? Are you absolutely sure?'

He nodded. 'Absolutely,' he told her. 'She made him more or less invisible, and she compressed a ten-day journey into three. She did the same things for us on a number of occasions.'

'How remarkable.' She stood, idly drumming her finger-tips on his armour.

'Please don't do that, Ehlana,' he said. 'It makes me feel like a bell with legs.'

'Sorry. Sparhawk, are we *really* sure we want Patriarch Ortzel on the Archprelate's throne? Isn't he awfully cold and stern?'

'Ortzel's rigid, right enough, and his Archprelacy's going to cause the militant orders some difficulty. He's violently opposed to our using magic, for one thing.'

'What earthly good is a Church Knight if he can't use magic?'

'We *do have* other resources as well, Ehlana. Ortzel wouldn't have been my first choice, I'll admit, but he holds strictly to the teachings of the Church. No one like Annias will ever get into a position of any kind of authority if Ortzel's in charge. He's rigid, but he follows Church doctrine to the letter.'

'Couldn't we find somebody else – somebody we like a little more?'

'We don't select Archprelates because we're fond of them, Ehlana,' he chided. 'The Hierocracy tries to select the man who'll be best for the Church.'

'Well, of *course* it does, Sparhawk. Everybody knows that.' She turned sharply. 'There it is again,' she said with exasperation.

'There what is?' he asked her.

'You wouldn't be able to see it, love,' she told him. 'Nobody can see it but me. At first I thought that everyone around me was going blind. It's a sort of shadow or something. I can't really see it – not clearly, anyway – but it sort of hovers around behind my back where I can only catch very brief glimpses of it. It always makes me very cold for some reason.'

Sparhawk half-turned, being careful to make it look casual. The shadow appeared to have grown larger and darker, and its malevolence was more pronounced. Why should it have been following Ehlana, though? She had not even touched the Bhelliom. 'It should go away in time,' he said carefully, not wanting to alarm her. 'Don't forget that Annias gave you a very rare and powerful poison. There are bound to be some lingering after-effects.'

'I suppose that's it.'

Then he understood. It was her ring, of course. Sparhawk silently berated himself for not having thought of that possibility earlier. Whatever it was that was behind the shadow would certainly want to keep an eye on both rings.

'I thought we were making up,' Ehlana said.

'We are.'

'Why aren't you kissing me then?'

He was attending to that when Kalten came in.

'Didn't you ever learn how to knock?' Sparhawk asked him sourly.

'Sorry,' Kalten said. 'I thought Vanion was in here. I'll see if I can find him somewhere else. Oh, by the way, here's something to brighten your day a little more, though – if it really needs it – Tynian and I were out with Wargun's soldiers flushing deserters out of the houses. We found an old friend hiding in the cellar of a wine shop.'

'Oh?'

'For some reason, Martel left Krager behind. We'll all get together with him for a nice chat – just as soon as he sobers up – and after you two have finished whatever it is you're doing here.' He paused. 'Would you like me to lock the door for you?' he asked. 'Or maybe stand guard outside?'

'Get out of here, Kalten.' It wasn't Sparhawk who gave the command, however.

Chapter 17

Krager was not in very good shape when Kalten and Tynian half-carried him into Sir Nashan's study early that evening. His thin hair was dishevelled, he was unshaven, and his near-sighted eyes were bloodshot. His hands were shaking violently, and his expression was one of misery, a misery that had nothing to do with his capture. The two knights dragged Martel's underling to a plain chair in the centre of the room and sat him in it. Krager buried his face in his shaking hands.

'I don't think we're going to get much out of him when he's in this condition,' King Wargun growled. 'I've been through that sort of thing myself, and I know. Give him some wine. He'll be more or less coherent when his hands stop shaking.'

Kalten looked at Sir Nashan, and the plump Pandion pointed at an ornate cabinet in the corner. 'It's only for medicinal purposes, Lord Vanion,' Nashan explained quickly.

'Of course,' Vanion said.

Kalten opened the cabinet and took out a crystal decanter of Arcian red wine. He poured a large goblet full and handed it to Krager. The suffering man spilled half of it, but he did manage to get the rest down. Kalten poured him another. And then another. Krager's hands began to grow more steady. He looked around, blinking. 'I see that I've fallen into the hands of mine enemies,' he said in a voice made rusty by years of hard drinking. 'Ah well,' he shrugged, 'fortunes of war, I suppose.'

'Your situation here is not enviable,' Lord Abriel told him ominously.

Ulath took out a whetstone and began sharpening his axe. It made a very unpleasant sound.

'Please,' Krager said wearily, 'I'm not feeling well. Spare me the melodramatic threats. I'm a survivor, gentlemen. I fully understand the situation here. I'll co-operate with you in exchange for my life.'

'Isn't that just a bit contemptible?' Bevier sneered.

'Of course it is, Sir Knight,' Krager drawled, 'but I'm a contemptible sort of person – or hadn't you noticed? Actually, I deliberately placed myself in a position so that you could capture me. Martel's plan was very good – as far as it went – but when it started to fall apart, I decided that I didn't really want to share his fortunes when they were on the decline. Let's save time, gentlemen. We all know that I'm too valuable to kill. I know too much. I'll tell you everything I know in exchange for my life, my freedom and ten thousand gold crowns.'

'What about your loyalties?' Patriarch Ortzel asked sternly.

'Loyalty, Your Grace?' Krager laughed. 'To Martel? Don't be absurd. I worked for Martel because he paid me well. We both knew that. But now you're in a position to offer me something of much greater value. Do we have a bargain?'

'Some time on the rack might lower your asking price a bit,' Wargun told him.

'I'm not a robust man, King Wargun,' Krager pointed out, 'and my health's never been what you'd call very good. Do you really want to gamble on my expiring under the ministrations of your torturers?'

'Let it lie,' Dolmant said. 'Give him what he wants.'

'Your Grace is a wise and gracious man.' Krager laughed

suddenly. 'Awfully sorry about the pun there, Patriarch Dolmant. It was accidental, I assure you.'

'There's one restriction, however,' Dolmant went on. 'Under the circumstances, we could hardly set you free until such time as your former master is apprehended. By your own admission, you're not very dependable. Besides, we'll need a little confirmation of what you tell us.'

'Perfectly understandable, Your Grace,' Krager agreed. 'But no dungeons. My lungs aren't very strong, and I really should avoid damp places.'

'A monastery then?' Dolmant countered.

'Totally acceptable, Your Grace – on the condition that Sparhawk is not permitted to come within ten miles of the place. Sparhawk's irrational sometimes, and he's wanted to kill me for years now – haven't you, Sparhawk?'

'Oh, yes,' Sparhawk admitted freely. 'I'll tell you what, Krager. I'll pledge myself to keep my hands off you until after Martel is dead.'

'Fair enough, Sparhawk,' Krager replied – 'if you'll also vow to give me a week's head start before you come after me. Do we have a bargain, gentlemen?'

'Tynian,' Preceptor Darellon said, 'take him out into the hallway while we discuss this.'

Krager rose shakily to his feet. 'Come along then, Sir Knight,' he said to Tynian. 'You too, Kalten, and don't forget to bring the wine.'

'Well?' King Wargun asked after the closely-guarded prisoner had left the room.

'Krager himself is unimportant, Your Majesty,' Vanion said, 'but he's absolutely right about the importance of the information he has. I'd advise accepting his terms.'

'I hate to give him all that gold, though,' Wargun growled moodily.

'In Krager's case, it's not really a gift,' Sephrenia said

334

quietly. 'If you give Krager that much money, he'll drink himself to death within six months.'

'That doesn't sound like much of a punishment to me.'

'Have you ever seen a man die of the after-effects of drink, Wargun?' she asked.

'I can't say that I have.'

'You might stop by an asylum sometime and watch the process. You may find it very educational.'

'Are we agreed then?' Dolmant asked, looking around. 'We give this sewer-rat what he asks and confine him to the monastery until such time as we know that he can't report anything significant to Martel?'

'All right,' Wargun gave in grudgingly. 'Bring him back in and let's get on with this.'

Sparhawk went to the door and opened it. A scarred man with a shaved head was speaking urgently with Tynian.

'Kring?' Sparhawk asked with some surprise, recognizing the Domi of the band of marauding horsemen from the eastern marches of Pelosia. 'Is that you?'

'Well, Sparhawk,' Kring said. 'It's good to see you again. I was just bringing friend Tynian here some news. Did you know that the Zemochs are massed in eastern Lamorkand?'

'We'd heard about it, yes. We were more or less planning to take steps.'

'Good. I've been off with the army of the King of the Thalesians, and one of my men from back home caught up with me here. When you ride out to take those steps you were talking about, don't concentrate too much on Lamorkand. The Zemochs are marauding into eastern Pelosia as well. My tribesmen have been gathering ears by the bale. I thought the Knights of the Church ought to know about that.'

'We're in your debt, Domi,' Sparhawk said. 'Why don't

335

you show friend Tynian here where you're camped? We're a bit involved with the Kings of Eosia at the moment, but just as soon as we can break free, we'll pay you a call.'

'I'll make preparations then, Sir Knight,' Kring promised. 'We'll take salt together and talk of affairs.'

'Indeed we will, my friend,' Sparhawk promised.

Tynian followed Kring back down the corridor and Sparhawk and Kalten took Krager back into Nashan's study.

'Very well, Krager,' Patriarch Dolmant said quite firmly. 'We'll agree to your terms – provided that you'll agree to confinement in a monastery until it's safe to release you.'

'Of course, Your Grace,' Krager agreed quickly. 'I need some rest anyway. Martel's had me running back and forth across the continent for over a year now. What would you like to hear first?'

'How did this connection between Otha and the Primate of Cimmura begin?'

Krager leaned back in his chair, crossing his legs and swirling his wine glass thoughtfully. 'As I understand it, it all started shortly after the old Patriarch of Cimmura fell ill and Annias took over his responsibilities in the cathedral there. Up until then, the Primate's goal appeared to have been largely political. He wanted to marry his doxy off to her brother so that he'd be able to run the kingdom of Elenia. After he got a taste of the kind of power the Church could put into a man's hands, however, his horizons began to expand. Annias is a realist, and he's fully aware of the fact that he's not universally loved.'

'That may be the understatement of the century,' Komier muttered.

'You've noticed that, My Lord,' Krager said dryly. 'Even Martel despises him, and I can't for the life of me understand how Arissa can bring herself to crawl into the same bed with him. Anyway, Annias knew that he was going to need help in reaching the Archprelate's throne. Martel got wind of what he had in mind, and he disguised himself and slipped into Cimmura to talk with him. I'm not sure exactly how, but at some time in the past, Martel had made contact with Otha. He wouldn't ever really talk about it, but I sort of gather that it was in some way connected with his being expelled from the Pandion order.'

Sparhawk and Vanion exchanged a look. 'It was,' Vanion said. 'Go on.'

'Annias rejected the notion at first, but Martel can be very convincing when he wants to be, and finally the Primate agreed to at least open negotiations. They found a disreputable Styric who was outcast from his band, and they had a long talk with him. He agreed to act as their emissary to Otha, and in due time, a bargain was struck.'

'And what was this bargain?' King Dregos of Arcium asked.

'I'll get to that in a bit, Your Majesty,' Krager promised. 'If I jump around in this, I might forget details.' He paused and looked around. 'I hope you're all taking note of how co-operative I'm being here. Otha sent some of his people to Elenia to provide assistance to Annias. A great deal of that assistance was in the form of gold. Otha's got tons of it.'

'What?' Ehlana exclaimed. 'I thought Annias had poisoned my father and me primarily to get his hands on the Elenian treasury in order to finance his drive for the Archprelacy.'

'I'm not trying to be offensive, Your Majesty,' Krager said, 'but the Elenian treasury couldn't have begun to cover the kind of expenses Annias was incurring. His control of it, however, concealed the *real* source of his funding. Embezzlement is one thing, but consorting with

337

Otha is quite something else. You and your father were actually poisoned for no other reason than to hide the fact that Annias had an unlimited supply of Otha's gold. Things went on more or less according to plan. Otha provided money and some occasional Styric magic to help Annias obtain his interim goals. Everything was going along fairly well until Sparhawk came back from Rendor. You're a very disruptive sort of fellow, Sparhawk.'

'Thank you,' Sparhawk replied.

'I'm sure you know most of the rest of the details, My Lords,' Krager continued. 'Ultimately, we all wound up here in Chyrellos, and the rest, as they say, is history. Now, getting back to your question, King Dregos. Otha bargains very hard and he asked a great price from Annias for his aid.'

'What did Annias have to give him?' Patriarch Bergsten, the huge Thalesian Churchman, asked.

'His soul, Your Grace,' Krager replied with a shudder. 'Otha insisted that Annias convert to the worship of Azash before he'd provide any magic or any money. Martel witnessed the ceremony, and he told me about it. That was one of my duties, incidentally. Martel gets lonesome from time to time, and he needs somebody to talk to. Martel's not particularly squeamish, but even *he* was sickened by the rites that celebrated Annias's conversion.'

'Did Martel convert too?' Sparhawk asked intently.

'I sort of doubt it, Sparhawk. Martel doesn't really have *any* religious convictions. He believes in politics, power and money, not Gods.'

'Which one of them is really in charge?' Sephrenia asked. 'Which one is the leader and which the follower?'

'Annias *thinks* he's the one who's giving the orders, but frankly, I rather doubt it. All of his contacts with Otha are through Martel, but Martel makes contacts of his own that Annias doesn't know about. I can't swear to it, but I think there's a separate arrangement between Martel and Otha. It's the sort of thing Martel would do.'

'There's something more behind all of this, isn't there?' Patriarch Emban asked shrewdly. 'Otha – and Azash – weren't really very likely to expend all that money and energy just for the sake of the badly tarnished soul of the Primate of Cimmura, were they?'

'Of course not, Your Grace,' Krager agreed. 'The plan, of course, was to attempt to get what they wanted by following the plan Annias and Martel had already laid out. If the Primate of Cimmura had managed to bribe his way into the Archprelacy, he'd have been able to achieve everything they all wanted without resorting to war, and wars are sometimes chancy.'

'And what are the things they wanted?' King Obler asked.

'Annias is obsessed with becoming Archprelate. Martel's willing to let him have that. It's not going to mean anything anyway, if this all goes according to plan. What Martel wants is power, wealth and legitimacy. Otha wants domination of the entire Eosian continent, and, of course, Azash wants the Bhelliom – and the souls of everyone in the whole world. Annias will live forever – or very close to it – and he was going to spend the next several centuries using his power as Archprelate to gradually bring the Elenes over to the worship of Azash.'

'That's monstrous!' Ortzel exclaimed.

'Moderately so, yes, Your Grace,' Krager agreed. 'Martel will get an imperial crown with only slightly less power than Otha's. He'll rule all of western Eosia. Then you'll have the four of them – Otha and Martel as emperors, Annias as high priest of the Church and Azash as God. Then they'll be able to turn their attention to the Rendors and to the Tamul empire in Daresia.'

'How did they propose to get Bhelliom for Azash?' Sparhawk asked bleakly.

'Subterfuge, deceit, outright purchase or main force, if necessary. Listen to me, Sparhawk.' Krager's face was suddenly deadly serious. 'Martel's led you to believe that he'll go north a little way and then turn towards eastern Lamorkand to join with Otha. He's going to Otha, all right, but Otha's *not* in Lamorkand. His generals are much better at fighting wars than he is. He's still in his capital in the city of Zemoch itself. *That's* where Martel and Annias are going, and they want you to follow them.' He paused. 'I was told to tell you that, of course,' he admitted. 'Martel wants you to follow him to Zemoch and to bring Bhelliom with you. They're all afraid of you for some reason, and I don't think it's just because you've managed to find Bhelliom. Martel doesn't want to face you directly, and that's not really like him. They want you to go to Zemoch so that *Azash* can deal with you.' Krager's face twisted in sudden anguish and horror. 'Don't go, Sparhawk,' he pleaded. 'For God's sake, don't go! If Azash takes Bhelliom away from you, the world is doomed.'

The vast nave of the Basilica was filled to overflowing very early the following morning. The citizens of Chyrellos had begun timidly returning to what was left of their homes almost as soon as King Wargun's army had rounded up the last of Martel's mercenaries. The people of the Holy City were probably no more pious than other Elenes, but Patriarch Emban made a gesture of pure humanitarianism. He let word be spread through the city that the Church storehouses would be opened to the populace immediately after the thanksgiving services were concluded. Since there was no food to be had anywhere else in Chyrellos, the citizens responded. Emban reasoned that a congregation

340

numbering in the thousands would impress upon his fellow Patriarchs the gravity of the situation and encourage them to take their duties seriously. Besides, Emban *did* feel a certain compassion for the truly hungry. His own bulk made him peculiarly sensitive to the pangs of hunger.

Patriarch Ortzel celebrated the rites of thanksgiving. Sparhawk noticed that the lean, harsh Churchman spoke in an altogether different tone when addressing a congregation. His voice was almost gentle, and he sometimes verged on actual compassion.

'Six times,' Talen whispered to Sparhawk as the Patriarch of Kadach led the throng in the final prayer.

'What?'

'He smiled six times during his sermon. I counted. A smile doesn't look all that natural on his face, though. What did we decide to do about what Krager told us yesterday? I fell asleep.'

'We noticed that. We're going to have Krager repeat what he told us to the entire Hierocracy right after Colonel Delada reports the conversation between Martel and Annias.'

'Will they believe him?'

'I think so. Delada's the unimpeachable witness. Krager's merely providing confirmation and filling in details. Once they've been forced to accept Delada's testimony, they won't have much difficulty choking down what Krager has to say.'

'Clever,' Talen said admiringly. 'Do you know something, Sparhawk? I've almost decided to give up the idea of becoming the emperor of thieves. I think I'll enter the Church instead.'

'God defend the faith,' Sparhawk prayed.

'I'm sure He will, my son,' Talen smiled benignly.

As the celebration concluded and the choir broke into exalted song, pages moved through the ranks of the Patriarchs delivering the announcement that the Hierocracy would resume deliberations immediately. Six more of the missing ecclesiasts had been discovered in various places in the outer city, and two emerged from hiding places within the Basilica itself. The rest were still unaccounted for. As the Patriarchs of the Church solemnly filed out of the nave and into the corridor leading towards the audience chamber, Emban, who had stayed behind to speak with a number of people, scurried past Sparhawk and Talen, puffing and sweating. 'Almost forgot something,' he said as he passed them. 'Dolmant's got to order the Church storehouses opened. Otherwise, we're liable to have a riot on our hands.'

'Would I have to get as fat as he is if I want to run things in the Church?' Talen whispered. 'Fat men don't run very well when things go wrong, and something's bound to go wrong for Emban eventually.'

Colonel Delada stood near the door to the audience chamber. His breastplate and helmet gleamed, and his crimson cloak was immaculate. Sparhawk stepped out of the line of Church Knights and clergymen entering the chamber and spoke briefly to him. 'Nervous?' he asked.

'Not really, Sir Sparhawk. I'll admit that I'm not looking forward to this, though. Do you think they'll ask me any questions?'

'They might. Don't let them rattle you. Just take your time and report exactly what you heard in that cellar. Your reputation will be speaking with you, so nobody can doubt your word.'

'I just hope I don't start a riot in there,' Delada said wryly.

'Don't worry about that. The riot's going to start when they hear the witness who's going to come *after* you.'

'What's he going to say, Sparhawk?'

'I'm not at liberty to tell you – at least not until after you've delivered your report. I'm not permitted to do anything at all to tamper with your neutrality at this point. Good luck in there.'

The Patriarchs of the Church were gathered in little clusters in the chamber talking in subdued tones. Emban's carefully staged thanksgiving service had lent a solemn tone to the morning, and no one really wanted to break it. Sparhawk and Talen mounted to the gallery where they customarily sat with their friends. Bevier was hovering protectively over Sephrenia, his face showing his concern. Sephrenia sat serenely in her gleaming white robe. 'There's no reasoning with her,' Bevier said as Sparhawk joined them. 'We managed to slip Platime, Stragen and the Tamul woman in here disguised as clergymen, but Sephrenia absolutely insisted upon wearing her Styric robe. I've tried time and again to explain to her that no one is permitted to witness the deliberations of the Hierocracy but the kings and members of the clergy, but she won't listen to me.'

'I *am* a member of the clergy, dear Bevier,' she told him simply. 'I'm a priestess of Aphrael – the high priestess, actually. Let's just say that I'm here to observe as a sort of tentative gesture in the direction of ecumenicism.'

'I wouldn't mention that until after the election's over, little mother,' Stragen advised. 'You'll start a theological debate that might just go on for several centuries, and we're a little pressed for time just now.'

'I sort of miss our friend from across the way,' Kalten said, pointing at the place in the gallery where Annias had customarily sat. 'I'd give a great deal to watch his face crumble as this morning's proceedings unfold.'

Dolmant had entered, and after a brief conference with Emban, Ortzel and Bergsten, he took his place at the lectern. His presence there brought order to the room.

343

'My brothers and my dear friends,' he began, 'we have seen momentous events since last we gathered here. I've taken the liberty of asking a number of witnesses to testify so that we may all be fully familiar with the situation here before we begin our deliberations. First, however, I must speak of the present condition of the citizens of Chyrellos. The besieging army has stripped the city of food, and the people are in desperate need. I ask the permission of the Hierocracy to open the Church storehouses so that we may alleviate their suffering. As representatives of the Church, charity is one of our primary duties.' He looked around. 'Do I hear any objections?' he asked.

There was total silence.

'Then it is so ordered. Let us then without further delay, welcome the reigning monarchs of western Eosia as our most honoured observers.'

The people in the chamber rose to their feet respectfully.

There was a brazen trumpet fanfare from the front of the chamber, and a large bronze door swung ponderously open to admit the royalty of the continent. All were garbed in their state robes and wore their crowns. Sparhawk scarcely glanced at Wargun and the other kings, but fixed his eyes on the perfect face of his betrothed. Ehlana was radiant. Sparhawk sensed that during the ten years of his exile in Rendor, very few people had paid much attention to his queen and that it was only at court functions and ceremonies that she had been granted any significance whatsoever. Thus, she enjoyed ceremonial occasions more than is common among the various members of other royal families. She moved with the other monarchs at a stately pace, her hand resting lightly on the arm of her distant kinsman, the ancient King Obler of Deira, towards the thrones sitting in a semicircle extending from the sides of the dais and the golden throne of the Archprelate.

As chance had it – or perhaps not entirely chance – the circle of prismed light from the large round window behind the thrones fell full upon the throne of Elenia, and Ehlana took her place surrounded by a blazing halo of golden sunshine. That seemed altogether appropriate to Sparhawk.

After the monarchs had seated themselves, the others in the chamber resumed their places. Dolmant greeted the monarchs each in turn and even made passing reference to the absent King of Lamorkand, who, with Otha camped just inside his border, had other things on his mind. Then the Patriarch of Demos moved smoothly into the business of providing a quick summary of recent events, a summary which seemed to many to be directed to people who had spent the past several weeks on the moon. Emban's witnesses dwelt fulsomely upon the destruction of the outer city and the atrocities committed by Martel's mercenaries. Everyone knew of these horrors, of course, but describing them in lurid detail aroused a certain mood of outrage and a thirst for revenge which Emban had felt might be helpful in moving the Hierocracy in the direction of militancy and impressing upon them the need for expeditious action. Probably the most important fact to be revealed by this half-dozen or so witnesses was the name of the man who had commanded the attacking army. Martel's name figured prominently in the accounts of three of the witnesses, and, before he called Colonel Delada, Dolmant provided a brief history of the renegade Pandion, describing him as primarily a mercenary but omitting any reference to his connection to the Primate of Cimmura. He then called for the testimony of the commander of the Archprelate's personal guard, noting in passing the legendary neutrality of these dedicated men.

Delada's memory proved to be remarkable. He glossed over the source of his knowledge of the location of the

345

meeting, ascribing it to the 'excellent military intelligence activities of the Church Knights'. He described the cellar and the long-forgotten aqueduct which had provided such dangerous access to the Basilica itself. He then repeated the conversation between Martel and Annias almost verbatim. The fact that he delivered his account in a completely unemotional tone lent a great deal of weight to his report. Despite his personal feelings in the matter, Delada adhered strictly to his code of neutrality. His report was punctuated frequently by cries of shock and stunned amazement from the Hierocracy and the assembled spectators.

Patriarch Makova, his pockmarked face pale and his speech faltering, rose to question the colonel. 'Is it at all possible that the voices you heard in that dark cellar were *not*, in fact, the voices of the two men who were supposedly speaking – that this was some elaborate subterfuge designed to discredit the Primate of Cimmura?'

'No, Your Grace,' Delada replied firmly, 'that is not in any way possible. The one man was most definitely the Primate Annias, and he addressed the other man as Martel.'

Makova began to perspire. He tried another tack. 'Who was it that escorted you to that cellar, Colonel?'

'Sir Sparhawk of the Pandion Order, Your Grace.'

'Well now,' Makova said triumphantly, smirking around at the other members of the Hierocracy, 'there we have it, then. Sir Sparhawk has long held a personal enmity for Primate Annias. He has quite obviously swayed this witness.'

Delada came to his feet, his face a fiery red. 'Are you calling me a liar?' he demanded, his hand reaching for his sword-hilt.

Makova recoiled, his eyes suddenly very wide.

'Sir Sparhawk told me absolutely nothing in advance,

Patriarch Makova,' Delada said from between clenched teeth. 'He wouldn't even tell me who either of the men in that cellar were. I identified Annias all on my own and Martel from Annias's own mouth. And I'll tell you something else as well. Sparhawk is the champion of the Queen of Elenia. If *I* held that position, the head of the Primate of Cimmura would be decorating a pole in front of the Basilica right now.'

'How *dare* you?' Makova gasped.

'The man you're so eager to put on the Archprelate's throne poisoned Sparhawk's queen and he's running to Zemoch right now to beg Otha to protect him from Sparhawk's anger. You'd better find somebody else to vote for, Your Grace, because even if the Hierocracy makes the mistake of electing Annias of Cimmura to the Archprelacy, he'll never live to assume that throne, since if Sparhawk doesn't kill him – *I will!*' Delada's eyes were ablaze and his sword was half-drawn.

Makova shrank back.

'Ah –' Dolmant said mildly, 'would you like a moment to compose yourself, Colonel?' he suggested.

'I *am* composed, Your Grace,' Delada retorted, ramming his sword back into its scabbard. 'I'm not nearly as angry now as I was a few hours ago. I haven't once questioned the honour of the Patriarch of Coombe.'

'Spirited, isn't he?' Tynian whispered to Ulath.

'Red-haired people are like that sometimes,' Ulath replied sagely.

'Did you want to ask the colonel any more questions, Makova?' Emban inquired with an innocent expression.

Makova stalked back to his seat, refusing to answer.

'Wise decision,' Emban murmured just loud enough to be heard.

A nervous laugh ran through the Hierocracy.

It was not so much the information that Annias had been

behind the attack on the city that so shocked and outraged the Hierocracy – they were all ranking churchmen, and they fully understood the lengths to which ambition could drive a man. Although Annias's methods were extreme and totally reprehensible, the Hierocracy could understand his motives and perhaps even secretly admire a man willing to go to such lengths to achieve his goal. It was his alliance with Otha, however, that went completely beyond the pale. Many of the Patriarchs who had quite willingly sold their votes to Annias squirmed uncomfortably as they began to realize the full extent of the depravity of the man to whom they had allied themselves.

Lastly, Dolmant called Krager, and the Patriarch of Demos made no attempt whatsoever to conceal Krager's character and fundamental unreliability.

Krager had been tidied up a bit, he was wearing chains on his wrists and ankles as an indication of his status, and he turned out to be a brilliant witness. He made no effort to offer excuses for himself, but was bluntly, even brutally, honest about his many flaws. He even went so far as to provide the details of the arrangement that was protecting his head. The implication that he had very solid reasons for absolute truthfulness was not lost on the Hierocracy. Faces blanched. Many Patriarchs prayed audibly. There were cries of outrage and horror as Krager in a matter-of-fact tone described in detail the monstrous conspiracy which had come so very close to success. He did *not*, however, make any reference to Bhelliom. That omission had been decided upon fairly early on in the planning. 'It might have all worked, too,' Krager concluded in a tone of regret. 'If only we'd had one more day before the armies of the western kingdoms arrived in Chyrellos, the Primate of Cimmura would be sitting on that very throne. His first act would have been to order the militant orders disbanded, and his second to order the Elene monarchs to return to

348

their own kingdoms and demobilize their armies. Then Otha would have marched in without any resistance, and within a generation, we'd all be bowing to Azash. It was such a very good plan,' Krager sighed, 'and it would have made me one of the richest men in the world.' He sighed again. 'Ah, well,' he concluded.

Patriarch Emban had been sprawled in his seat, carefully assessing the mood of the Hierocracy. He hauled himself to his feet. 'Do we have any questions for this witness?' he asked, looking pointedly at Makova.

Makova would not answer him. Makova would not even look at him.

'Perhaps, my brothers,' Emban continued, 'this might be the proper time to adjourn for lunch.' He smiled rather broadly and clapped his hands to his paunch. 'That suggestion coming from me didn't really surprise anyone very much, did it?' he asked then.

They laughed, and that seemed to relax the tension. 'This morning has given us many things to consider, my brothers,' the little fat man continued seriously, 'and unfortunately we'll have little time to consider them. With Otha camped in eastern Lamorkand, we don't have much time for extended contemplation.'

Dolmant adjourned the Hierocracy then and declared that they would reconvene within the hour.

At Ehlana's request, Sparhawk and Mirtai joined her in a small chamber in the Basilica for a light lunch. The young queen seemed a bit distracted and scarcely touched her food but sat instead scribbling rapidly on a scrap of paper.

'Ehlana,' Mirtai said sharply. 'Eat. You'll waste away if you don't eat.'

'Please, Mirtai,' the queen said, 'I'm trying to compose a speech. I have to address the Hierocracy this afternoon.'

'You don't have to say all that much, Ehlana,' Sparhawk

told her. 'Just tell them how honoured you are to be allowed to witness their deliberations, say a few unflattering things about Annias and invoke the blessings of God on the proceedings.'

'This is the first time they've ever been addressed by a queen, Sparhawk,' she said tartly.

'There have been queens before.'

'Yes, but none of them sat on a throne during an election. I looked it up. This is going to be an historic first, and I don't want to make a fool of myself.'

'You don't want to faint either,' Mirtai said, pointedly pushing the queen's plate back in front of her. Mirtai, Sparhawk noticed, had the soul of a bully.

There was a light rap at the door, and Talen entered, grinning impishly. He bowed to Ehlana. 'I just came by to tell you that King Soros won't be addressing the Hierocracy this afternoon,' he told Sparhawk, 'so you won't have to worry about being exposed as a scoundrel.'

'Oh?'

'His Majesty must have taken a chill, and it settled in his throat. He can't speak above a whisper.'

Ehlana frowned. 'How strange. It hasn't really been that cold lately. I don't want to wish the King of Pelosia any bad luck, but isn't this a lucky sort of thing to have happen just now?'

'Luck had very little to do with it, Your Majesty,' Talen grinned. 'Sephrenia almost dislocated her jaw and very nearly braided her fingers putting the spell together. Excuse me. I'm supposed to go and tell Dolmant and Emban. Then I have to report it to Wargun so that he doesn't bash in Soros's head to keep him quiet.'

After they had finished with their lunch, Sparhawk escorted the two ladies back to the audience chamber. 'Sparhawk?' Ehlana said just before they entered, 'do you like Dolmant, the Patriarch of Demos?'

'Very much,' he replied. 'He's one of my oldest friends – and that's not just because he used to be a Pandion.'

'I like him too,' she smiled. She said it as if something had just been settled.

Dolmant reconvened the Hierocracy and then asked each of the kings to address the assembled Patriarchs. As Sparhawk had suggested to Ehlana earlier, each monarch rose, thanked the Hierocracy for being permitted to be present, made a few references to Annias, Otha and Azash and then invoked the blessing of God upon the deliberations.

'And now, brothers and friends,' Dolmant said, 'we have a rare occasion here today. For the first time in history, a queen will address us.' He smiled ever so faintly. 'I would not for the world offend the mighty kings of western Eosia, but I must in all candour say that Ehlana, Queen of Elenia, is far lovelier than they are, and I think we may be surprised to discover that she's as wise as she is beautiful.'

Ehlana blushed charmingly. For the remainder of his life, Sparhawk was never able to discover how she could blush at will. She even tried to explain it to him a few times, but it was quite beyond his understanding.

The Queen of Elenia rose and stood with her face downcast for a moment as if in some confusion at Dolmant's prettily turned compliment. 'I thank you, Your Grace,' she said in a clear, ringing voice as she raised her head. All traces of the blush were now gone, and Ehlana had a very determined expression on her face.

Sparhawk's heart gave a sudden suspicious lurch. 'Get hold of something solid, gentlemen,' he warned his friends. 'I know that look on her face. I think she has a few surprises in store for us here.'

'I too must express my gratitude to the Hierocracy for allowing me to be present,' Ehlana began, 'and I will add my prayers to those of my brother monarchs, asking God to grant these nobles of the Church wisdom in their deliberations. Since I am the first woman to ever address the Hierocracy in such circumstances, however, might I ask that indulgence of the assembled Patriarchs that I might address a few additional remarks to them? If my words seem frivolous, I'm sure the learned Patriarchs will forgive me. I am but a woman and not very old. And we all know that young women are sometimes silly when they become excited.' She paused.

'Excited, did I say?' she continued, her voice like a silver trumpet. 'Nay, gentlemen, say instead that I am enraged! This monster, this cold bloodless beast, this – this Annias murdered my beloved father. He struck down the wisest and gentlest monarch in all Eosia!'

'*Aldreas?*' Kalten whispered in disbelief.

'And then,' Ehlana continued in that ringing voice, 'not content with breaking my heart, this ravening savage sought my life as well! Our Church is tainted now, gentlemen, besmirched because this villain ever professed holy orders. I would come here as a suppliant, a petitioner, to demand justice, but I will wring my *own* justice from the body of the man who murdered my father. I am but a weak woman, but I have a champion, gentlemen, a man who at my command will seek out and find this monstrous Annias even though the beast seeks to hide himself in the very bowels of Hell itself. Annias *will* face me. I swear this to you all, and generations yet unborn shall tremble at the memory of his fate. Our holy mother Church need not concern herself with dispensing justice to this wretch. The Church is gentle, compassionate, but *I*, gentlemen, am not.' So much for his queen's apparent submission to the dictates of the Church, Sparhawk thought.

Ehlana had paused again, her young face lifted in vengeful resolve. 'But what of this prize?' she asked, turning to look pointedly at the shrouded throne. 'Upon whom will you bestow this chair for which Annias was willing to drown the world in blood? To whom shall this piece of ornate furniture descend? For mistake me not, friends, that's all it is, a piece of furniture, heavy, ungainly and, I'm sure, not very comfortable. Whom will you sentence to bear the awful burdens of care and responsibility which go with this chair and which he will be forced to carry in this darkest hour of our holy mother's life? He must be wise, of course, that goes without saying, but all of the Patriarchs of the Church are wise. He must also be courageous, but are you not all as brave as lions? He must be shrewd, and make no mistake, there is a vast difference between wisdom and shrewdness. He must be clever, for he faces the master of deceit – not Annias, though Annias is deceitful enough; not Otha, sunk in his own foul debauchery; but Azash himself. Which of you will match strength and cunning and will with that spawn of Hell?'

'What is she *doing*?' Bevier whispered in a stunned voice.

'Isn't it obvious, Sir Knight?' Stragen murmured urbanely. 'She's selecting a new Archprelate.'

'That's absurd!' Bevier gasped. 'The Hierocracy chooses the Archprelate!'

'Right now, Sir Bevier, they'd elect *you* if she pointed that small pink finger at you. Look at them. She has the entire Hierocracy in the palm of her hand.'

'You have warriors among you, reverend Patriarchs,' Ehlana was saying, 'men of steel and valour, but could an armoured Archprelate match the guile of Azash? You have theologians among you, My Lords of the Church, men of such towering intellect that they can perceive the mind and intent of God Himself, but would such a man, attuned to the voice of Divine Truth, be prepared to counter the Master of Lies? There are those versed in Church Law and

353

those who are masters of Church politics. There are those who are strong, and those who are brave. There are those who are gentle, and those who are compassionate. If we could but choose the entire Hierocracy itself to lead us, we would be invincible, and the gates of Hell could not prevail against us!' Ehlana swayed, raising one trembling hand to her brow. 'Forgive me, gentlemen,' she said in a weak voice. 'The effects of the poison with which the serpent Annias sought to steal away my life do linger yet.'

Sparhawk half-started to his feet.

'Oh, *do* sit down, Sparhawk,' Stragen told him. 'You'll spoil her performance if you go clanking down there right now. Believe me, she's perfectly fine.'

'Our holy mother needs a champion, my Lords of the Church,' Ehlana continued in a weary voice, 'a man who is the distillation and essence of the Hierocracy itself, and I think that in your hearts you all know who that man is. May God give you the wisdom, the enlightenment, to turn to the one who even now is in your very midst, shrouded with true humility, but who extends his gentle hand to guide you, perhaps not even knowing that he does so, for this self-effacing Patriarch perhaps does not even know himself that he speaks with the Voice of God. Seek him in your hearts, My Lords of the Church, and lay this burden upon *him*, for only he can be our champion!' She swayed again, and her knees began to buckle. Then she wilted like a flower. King Wargun, his face awed and his eyes full of tears, leapt to his feet and caught her even as she fell.

'The perfect touch,' Stragen said admiringly. He grinned. 'Poor, poor Sparhawk,' he said. 'You haven't got a chance, you know.'

'Stragen, *will* you shut up?'

'What was that really all about?' Kalten asked in a baffled tone.

'She just appointed an Archprelate, Sir Kalten,' Stragen told him.

'Who? She didn't mention a single name.'

'Isn't it clear to you yet? She very carefully eliminated all the other contenders. There's only one possibility left. The other Patriarchs all know who he is, and they'll elect him – just as soon as one of them dares to mention his name. I'd tell you myself, but I don't want to spoil it for you.'

King Wargun had lifted the apparently unconscious Ehlana in his arms and was carrying her towards the bronze door at one side of the chamber.

'Go to her,' Sephrenia said to Mirtai. 'Try to keep her calm. She's very exhilarated right now – and *don't* let King Wargun come back in here. He might blurt something out and ruin everything.'

Mirtai nodded and rushed down to the floor.

The chamber was alive with excited conversation. Ehlana's fire and passion had ignited them all. Patriarch Emban sat with his eyes wide in stunned amazement. Then he grinned broadly, and then he covered his mouth with one hand and began to laugh.

'– obviously possessed by the Divine Hand of God himself,' one nearby monk was saying excitedly to another. 'But a *woman*? Why would God speak to us in the voice of a woman?'

'His ways are mysterious,' the other monk said in an awed voice, 'and unfathomable to man.'

It was with some difficulty that Patriarch Dolmant restored order. 'My brothers and friends,' he said. 'We must, of course, forgive the Queen of Elenia for her emotional outburst. I have known her since childhood, and I assure you that she is normally a completely self-possessed young woman. It is doubtless as she herself suggested. The last traces of the poison still linger and make her sometimes irrational.'

355

'Oh, this is *too* rare,' Stragen laughed to Sephrenia. '*He* doesn't even know.'

'Stragen,' she said crisply, 'hush.'

'Yes, little mother.'

Patriarch Bergsten, mail-shirted and dreadful in his ogre-horned helmet, rose and rapped the butt of his war-axe on the marble floor. 'Permission to speak?' He didn't actually ask.

'Of course, Bergsten,' Dolmant said.

'We are not here to discuss the vapourish indisposition of the Queen of Elenia,' the massive Patriarch of Emsat declared. 'We are here to select an Archprelate. I suggest that we move on with it. To that end, I place in nomination the name of Dolmant, Patriarch of Demos. Who will join his voice with mine in this nomination?'

'No!' Dolmant exclaimed in stunned dismay.

'The Patriarch of Demos is not in order,' Ortzel declared, rising to his feet. 'By custom and by law, as one who has been nominated, he may not speak further until this question has been decided. With the consent of my brothers, I would ask the esteemed Patriarch of Ucera to assume the chair.' He looked around. There appeared to be no dissent.

Emban, still grinning openly, waddled to the lectern and rather cavalierly dismissed Dolmant with a wave of one chubby hand. 'Has the Patriarch of Kadach concluded his remarks?' he asked.

'No,' Ortzel said, 'I have not.' Ortzel's face was still stern and bleak. Then, with no sign of the pain it must have caused him, he spoke firmly. 'I join my voice with that of my brother of Emsat. Patriarch Dolmant is the only possible choice for the Archprelacy.'

Then Makova rose. His face was dead white, and his jaws were clenched. 'God will punish you for this outrage!' he almost spat at his fellow Patriarchs. 'I will have no part in this absurdity!' He spun on his heel and stormed from the chamber.

'At least he's honest,' Talen observed.

'Honest?' Berit exclaimed. 'Makova?'

'Of course, revered teacher,' the boy grinned. 'Once somebody buys Makova, he stays bought – no matter how things turn out.'

The voting went swiftly after that as Patriarch after Patriarch rose to approve Dolmant's nomination. Emban's face grew sly as the last Patriarch, a feeble old man from Cammoria, was helped to his feet to murmur the name 'Dolmant' in a creaky voice.

'Well, Dolmant,' Emban said in mock surprise, 'it seems that only you and I are left. Is there someone you'd like to nominate, my friend?'

'I beg of you, my brothers,' Dolmant pleaded, 'don't do this.' He was openly weeping.

'The Patriarch of Demos is not in order,' Ortzel said gently. 'He must place a name in nomination or stand mute.'

'Sorry, Dolmant,' Emban grinned, 'but you heard what he said. Oh, incidentally, I'll join my voice with those of the others in nominating you. Are you *sure* you wouldn't like to nominate somebody?' He waited. 'Very well, then. I make it one hundred and twenty-six nominations for the Patriarch of Demos, one bolted and one abstention. Isn't that amazing? Shall we vote, my brothers, or shall we save some time and just declare Patriarch Dolmant the Archprelate by acclamation? I pause for your reply.'

It began with a single deep voice coming from somewhere down front. 'Dolmant!' the voice boomed. 'Dolmant!'

It was soon picked up. 'Dolmant!' they roared. 'Dolmant!' It went on for quite some time.

Then Emban raised his hand for silence. 'Awfully sorry

357

to be the one to tell you, old boy,' he drawled to Dolmant, 'but you don't seem to be a Patriarch any more. Why don't you and a couple of our brothers retire to the vestry for a few moments so they can help you try on your new robes?'

Chapter 18

The audience chamber was still filled with excited conversation, some of it in shouts. Patriarchs with looks of exaltation on their faces milled about on the marble floor, and Sparhawk heard the phrase 'inspired by God', repeated over and over in awed tones as he pushed his way through the crowd. Churchmen are traditionally very conservative, and they found that any hint that a mere woman might have actually guided the Hierocracy in its decision was unthinkable. The notion of Divine inspiration was a convenient way out. Obviously, it had not been Ehlana who had spoken, but God Himself. At the moment, Sparhawk was not concerned about theology. What he *was* concerned about was the condition of his queen. Stragen's explanation was plausible, of course, but Stragen had been talking about Sparhawk's queen – and his betrothed. Sparhawk wanted to see for himself that she was well.

She appeared to be not only well but in glowing health as he opened the door through which King Wargun had carried her. She even looked a little ridiculous as she stood half bent over with her ear pressed to the spot where the closed door had only recently been.

'You could hear much better from your seat out there in the chamber, My Queen,' Sparhawk said with some asperity.

'Oh, be still, Sparhawk,' she said tartly, 'and come in and shut the door.'

Sparhawk stepped through the doorway.

King Wargun stood with his back against the wall and

his eyes a little wild. Mirtai stood in front of him, poised. 'Get this she-dragon away from me, Sparhawk,' Wargun begged.

'Have you decided not to make an issue of my queen's theatrics, Your Majesty?' Sparhawk asked him politely.

'Admit that she made a fool of me? Don't be absurd, Sparhawk. I wasn't going to run out there and declare that I'd been a jackass in public. All I wanted to do was to tell everyone that your queen was all right, but I didn't even make it as far as the door when this huge woman came in here. She *threatened* me, Sparhawk! *Me*, of all people. Do you see that chair there?'

Sparhawk looked. The chair was upholstered, and large wads of horsehair were protruding out of a long gash in its back.

'It was merely a suggestion, Sparhawk,' Mirtai said mildly. 'I wanted Wargun to understand what might happen if he made any wrong decisions. It's all right now. Wargun and I are almost friends.' Mirtai, Sparhawk had noticed, never used titles.

'It's very improper to draw a knife on a king, Mirtai,' Sparhawk told her reprovingly.

'She didn't,' Wargun said. 'She did that with her knee.' He shuddered.

Sparhawk looked at the Tamul woman, puzzled.

Mirtai pulled aside her monk's robe, reached down and modestly lifted her kilt a few inches. As Talen had told him, she had curved knives strapped to her lower thighs so that the blades rode along the inside of her calves for about four inches. The knives appeared to be very sharp. He also noted in passing that both her knees were dimpled. 'It's a practical arrangement for a woman,' she explained. 'Men sometimes become playful at inconvenient times. The knives persuade them to go and play with someone else.'

360

'Isn't that illegal?' Wargun asked.

'Would you like to try to arrest her, Your Majesty?'

'*Will* you all stop that chattering?' Ehlana said sharply to them. 'You sound like a flock of magpies. This is what we're going to do. In a few moments, things will start to quieten down out there. Then Wargun will escort me back inside, and Mirtai and Sparhawk will follow. I'll lean on Wargun's arm and look properly weak and trembly. After all, I've either just fainted or had a Divine visitation – depending on which of the rumours I hear buzzing around out there you care to believe. We all want to be in our places before the Archprelate is escorted to his throne.'

'How are you going to explain that speech to them, Ehlana?' Wargun demanded.

'I'm not,' she replied. 'I'll have absolutely no memory of it whatsoever. They'll believe whatever they want to believe, and no one will dare to call me a liar, because either Sparhawk or Mirtai will challenge them if they do.' She smiled then. 'Was the man I chose more or less the one you had in mind, dear?' she asked Sparhawk.

'Yes, I think he is.'

'You may thank me properly then – when we're alone. Very well, then, let's go back inside.'

They all looked suitably grave as they re-entered the chamber. Ehlana leaned heavily on Wargun, her face looking wan and exhausted. There was a sudden, awed silence as the two monarchs resumed their places.

Patriarch Emban waddled forward, his face looking concerned. 'Is she all right?' he asked.

'She seems a bit better,' Sparhawk told him. It was not *exactly* a lie. 'She tells us that she has no memory of anything she said when she was addressing the Hierocracy. It might be better if we didn't press her on that point in her present condition, Your Grace.'

Emban gave Ehlana a shrewd look. 'I understand

perfectly, Sparhawk. I'll make a few suitable remarks to the Hierocracy.' He smiled at Ehlana. 'I'm so glad to see that you're feeling better, Your Majesty,' he said.

'Thank you, Your Grace,' she replied in a trembling little voice.

Emban returned to the lectern as Sparhawk and Mirtai went back up into the gallery to rejoin their friends. 'My brothers,' he said. 'I'm sure you'll all be happy to know that Queen Ehlana is recovering. She's asked me to apologize for anything she may have said during her remarks. The queen's health is still not good, I'm afraid, and she journeyed here to Chyrellos at great personal risk, so firm was her resolve to be present for our deliberations.'

They murmured their admiration for such devotion.

'It were best, I think,' Emban continued, 'if we were not to question Her Majesty too closely concerning the content of her remarks. It appears that she has no memory of her speech. This can be quite easily explained by her weakened condition. There is perhaps another explanation as well, but I think wisdom and consideration for Her Majesty dictates to us that we not pursue it.' Of such stuff legends are made.

And then there was a brassy fanfare of trumpets, and the door to the left side of the throne swung open. Dolmant, flanked by Ortzel and Bergsten, entered. The new Archprelate wore a plain white cassock, and his face was calm now. Sparhawk was struck by an odd notion. There were marked similarities between Dolmant's white cassock and Sephrenia's white robe. The thought led him to the brink of a speculation that might just have been mildly heretical.

The two Patriarchs, the one from Lamorkand and the other from Thalesia, escorted Dolmant to the throne, which had been unshrouded during their absence, and the Archprelate took his seat.

'And will Sarathi address us?' Emban said, stepping from behind the lectern and genuflecting.

'Sarathi?' Talen whispered to Berit.

'It's a very old name,' Berit explained quietly. 'When the Church was finally unified almost three thousand years ago, the very first Archprelate was named Sarathi. His name is remembered – and honoured – by addressing the Archprelate this way.'

Dolmant sat gravely on his gold throne. 'I have not sought this eminence, my brothers,' he told them, 'and I would be far happier had you not seen fit to thrust it upon me. We can only hope – all of us – that this is truly God's will.' He raised his face slightly. 'Now, we have much that needs to be done. I will call upon many of you to aid me, and, as is always the case, there will be changes here in the Basilica. I pray you, my brothers, do not be chagrined or downcast when Church offices are being reassigned, for it has ever been thus when a new Archprelate comes to this throne. Our holy mother faces her gravest challenge in half a millennium. My first act, therefore, must be to confirm the state of Crisis of the Faith, and I decree that this state shall continue until we have met the challenge and prevailed. And now, my brothers and dear friends, let us pray, and then shall we depart and go to our sundry duties.'

'Nice and short,' Ulath approved. 'Sarathi's getting off to a good start.'

'Was the queen *really* in hysterics when she made that speech?' Kalten curiously asked Sparhawk.

'Of course she wasn't,' Sparhawk snorted. 'She knew exactly what she was doing every second.'

'I sort of thought she might have been. I think your marriage is going to be filled with surprises, Sparhawk, but that's all right. The unexpected always keeps a man on his toes.'

363

As they were leaving the Basilica, Sparhawk fell back to have a word with Sephrenia. He found her a few feet back down a side passage deep in conversation with a man wearing a monk's robe. When the man turned, however, Sparhawk saw that he was not an Elene, but rather was a silvery-bearded Styric. The man bowed to the approaching knight. 'I will leave you now, dear sister,' he said to Sephrenia in Styric. His voice, deep and rich, belied his evident age.

'No, Zalasta, stay,' she said, laying one hand on his arm.

'I would not offend the Knights of the Church by my presence in their holy place, sister.'

'Sparhawk takes a bit more offending than the usual Church Knight, my dear friend,' she smiled.

'This is the legendary Sir Sparhawk?' the Styric said with some surprise. 'I am honoured, Sir Knight.' He spoke in heavily accented Elene.

'Sparhawk,' Sephrenia said, 'this is my oldest and dearest friend, Zalasta. We were children together in the same village.'

'I am honoured, Sioanda,' Sparhawk said in Styric, also bowing. Sioanda was a Styric word meaning 'friend of my friend'.

'Age has dimmed my eyes it seems,' Zalasta noted. 'Now that I look more closely at his face, I can indeed see that this is Sir Sparhawk. The light of his purpose shines all around him.'

'Zalasta has offered us his aid, Sparhawk,' Sephrenia said then. 'He is very wise and deeply schooled in the secrets.'

'We would be honoured, learned one,' Sparhawk said.

Zalasta smiled. 'I would be of small use on your quest, Sir Sparhawk,' he said in a slightly self-deprecating way. 'Were you to encase me in steel, I'm sure I would wither like a flower.'

Sparhawk tapped his breastplate. 'It's an Elene affectation, learned one,' he said, '– like pointed hats or brocade doublets. We can only hope that someday steel wardrobes will go out of fashion.'

'I had always thought Elenes to be a humourless race,' the Styric noted, 'but you are droll, Sir Sparhawk. I would be of little use to you in your trek, but at some future time, I may be able to assist you in some other matter of a certain importance.'

'Trek?' Sparhawk asked.

'I know not where you and my sister will go, Sir Knight, but I perceive many leagues hovering about you both. I have come to advise you both to steel your hearts and to be ever watchful. A danger avoided is sometimes preferable to a danger overcome.' Zalasta looked around. 'And my presence here is one of those avoidable dangers, I think. You are cosmopolitan, Sir Sparhawk, but I think that perhaps some of your comrades may be less sophisticated.' He bowed to Sparhawk, kissed Sephrenia's palms and then glided silently back up the shadowy side-passage.

'I haven't seen him in more than a century,' Sephrenia said. 'He's changed – just a little.'

'Most of us would change in that long a period, little mother,' Sparhawk smiled, '– except you, of course.'

'You're such a nice boy, Sparhawk.' She sighed. 'It all seems so long ago. Zalasta was always so serious when he was a child. Even then he was wise beyond belief. His grasp of the secrets is profound.'

'What's this trek he was talking about?'

'Do you mean to say you can't feel it? You can't feel the distance stretching in front of you?'

'Not noticeably, no.'

'Elenes,' she sighed. 'Sometimes I'm surprised that you can even feel the seasons turn.'

He ignored that. 'Where are we going?'

'I don't know. Not even Zalasta can perceive that. The future lying before us is dark, Sparhawk. I should have known that it would be, but I didn't think my way completely through it, I guess. We *are* going somewhere, though. Why aren't you with Ehlana?'

'The kings are all being solicitous. I can't get near her.' He paused. 'Sephrenia, she can see it too – the shadow, I mean. I think it's probably because she's wearing one of the rings.'

'That would stand to reason. Bhelliom's useless without the rings.'

'Does it put her in any kind of danger?'

'Of course it does, Sparhawk, but Ehlana's been in danger since the day she was born.'

'Isn't that just a little fatalistic?'

'Perhaps. I just wish *I* could see this shadow of yours. I might be able to identify it a little more precisely.'

'I can borrow Ehlana's ring and give them both to you,' he offered. 'Then *you* can take Bhelliom out of the pouch. I can almost guarantee that you'll see the shadow at that point.'

'Don't even suggest that, Sparhawk,' she shuddered. 'I wouldn't be much good to you if I were to suddenly vanish – permanently.'

'Sephrenia,' he said a bit critically, 'was I some sort of an experiment? You keep warning everybody not to touch Bhelliom, but you didn't even turn a hair when you were telling me to chase it down and take it away from Ghwerig. Wasn't *I* in a certain amount of danger too? Did you just wait to see if I'd explode when I put my hands on it?'

'Don't be silly, Sparhawk. Everyone *knows* that you were destined to wield Bhelliom.'

'*I* didn't.'

'Let's not pursue this, dear one. We have enough problems already. Just accept the fact that you and Bhelliom are linked. I think that shadow should be our concern right now. What is it, and what is it doing?'

'It seems to be following Bhelliom – and the rings. Can we discount the things Perraine was trying to do? Wasn't that Martel's idea – one that he came up with on his own?'

'I don't know that we'd be safe to assume that. Martel was controlling Perraine, but something else may have been controlling Martel – without his even knowing it.'

'I see that this is going to be another of the kind of discussions that give me headaches.'

'Just take precautions, dear one,' she told him. 'Don't relax your guard. Let's see if we can catch up with Ehlana. She'll be upset if you're not attentive.'

They were all somewhat subdued when they gathered together that evening. This time, however, they did not gather in the Pandion chapterhouse but rather in a large over-decorated chamber attached to the Archprelate's personal apartments. The room was normally the site of the meetings of the highest councils of the Church, and they had assembled there at Sarathi's personal request. Tynian, Sparhawk noticed, was conspicuously absent. The walls of the room were panelled, and it was adorned with blue drapes and carpeting. A very large religious fresco decorated the ceiling. Talen looked up and sniffed disdainfully. 'I could do a better job than that with my left hand,' he declared.

'There's a thought,' Kurik said. 'I think I'll ask Dolmant if he'd like to have the ceiling of the nave here in the Basilica decorated.'

'Kurik,' Talen said with some shock, 'that ceiling's bigger than a cow pasture. It'd take forty years to paint enough pictures to cover it.'

367

'You're young,' Kurik shrugged, 'and steady work might keep you out of trouble.'

The door opened, and Dolmant entered. They all rose from their seats and genuflected.

'Please,' Dolmant said wearily, 'spare me. People have been doing that ever since the overclever Queen of Elenia jammed me into a seat I didn't really want.'

'Why, Sarathi,' she protested, 'what a thing to say.'

'We have things to discuss, my friends,' Dolmant said, 'and decisions to make.' He took his seat at the head of the large conference table in the centre of the room. 'Please sit down, and let's get to work.'

'When would you like us to schedule your coronation, Sarathi?' Patriarch Emban asked.

'That can wait. Let's push Otha off our doorstep first. I don't think I'd care to have him attend. How do we proceed?'

King Wargun looked around. 'I'll throw out some ideas and see how the rest respond,' he said. 'The way I see it, we've got two options. We can march east until we run into the Zemochs and then fight them in open fields, or we can move out until we find suitable terrain and stop and wait for them. The first option would keep Otha farther away from Chyrellos, and the second would give us time to erect field fortifications. Both approaches have their advantages, and they both have their drawbacks as well.' He looked around again. 'What do you think?' he asked.

'I think we need to know what kind of a force we're facing,' King Dregos said.

'There are a lot of people in Zemoch,' old King Obler said.

'That's God's own truth,' Wargun scowled. 'They breed like rabbits.'

'We can expect to be outnumbered then,' Obler continued. 'If I remember my military strategy correctly, that would almost compel us to take up defensive positions. We'll have to erode Otha's forces before we can go on the offensive.'

'Another siege,' Komier groaned. 'I *hate* sieges.'

'We don't always get what we want, Komier,' Abriel told him. 'There's a third option, however, King Wargun. There are many fortified keeps and castles in Lamorkand. We can move out, occupy those strongholds in force and hold them. Otha won't be able to by-pass them, because if he does, the troops inside will be able to come out and decimate his reserves and destroy his supply trains.'

'Lord Abriel,' Wargun said, 'that strategy will spread us out all over central Lamorkand.'

'I'll admit that it has drawbacks,' Abriel conceded, 'but the last time Otha invaded, we met him head-on at Lake Randera. We virtually depopulated the continent in the process, and it took centuries for Eosia to recover. I'm not sure we want to repeat that.'

'We won, didn't we?' Wargun said bluntly.

'Do we really want to win that way again?'

'There may be another alternative,' Sparhawk said quietly.

'I'd certainly be glad to hear it,' Preceptor Darellon said. 'I'm not too happy with any of the options I've heard so far.'

'Sephrenia,' Sparhawk said, 'just how powerful *is* the Bhelliom really?'

'I've told you that it's the most powerful object in the world, dear one.'

'Now there's a thought,' Wargun said. 'Sparhawk could use Bhelliom to obliterate whole chunks of Otha's army. Incidentally, Sparhawk, you *are* going to return Bhelliom to the royal house of Thalesia when you're finished with it, aren't you?'

'We might discuss that, Your Majesty,' Sparhawk said.

'It wouldn't really do you all that much good, though. It won't do anything at all without the rings, and I don't feel much like surrendering *mine* yet. You can ask my queen how she feels about hers, if you wish.'

'My ring stays where it is,' Ehlana said flatly.

Sparhawk had been mulling over his earlier conversation with Sephrenia. He was growing increasingly certain that the impending confrontation was *not* going to be settled by vast armies clashing in central Lamorkand in the way that the one five hundred years earlier had been. He had no way to justify his certainty, since he had not reached it by logic but rather by some intuitive leap that was more Styric in nature than Elene. He somehow knew that it would be a mistake for him to immerse himself in an army. Not only would that delay him in something he must do, but it would also be dangerous. If the subversion of Sir Perraine had *not* been an independent act on Martel's part, then he would be exposing himself and his friends to thousands of potential enemies, all completely unidentifiable and all armed to the teeth. Once again he absolutely had to get clear of an Elene army. His idea grew more out of that necessity than out of any real conviction that it would work. 'Is there enough power in Bhelliom to destroy Azash?' he asked Sephrenia. He already knew the answer, of course, but he wanted her to confirm it for the others.

'What are you saying, Sparhawk?' she asked in a tone of profound shock. 'You're talking about destroying a God. The whole world trembles at such a suggestion.'

'I'm not raising the question to start a theological debate,' he said. 'Would Bhelliom be able to do it?'

'I don't know. No one's ever had the temerity to even suggest it before.'

'Where is Azash most vulnerable?' he asked.

'Only in His confinement. The Younger Gods of

Styricum chained Him within that clay idol Otha found centuries ago. That's one of the reasons He's been seeking Bhelliom so desperately. Only the Sapphire Rose can free Him.'

'And if the idol were to be destroyed?'

'Azash would be destroyed with it.'

'And what would happen if I went to the city of Zemoch, discovered that I couldn't destroy Azash with Bhelliom and smashed the jewel instead?'

'The city would be obliterated,' she said in a troubled tone, '– along with any mountain ranges in the vicinity.'

'I can't really lose then, can I? Either way, Azash ceases to exist. And, if what Krager told us is true, Otha's at Zemoch as well, along with Martel, Annias and various others. I could get them all. Once Azash and Otha are gone, the Zemoch invasion would disintegrate, wouldn't it?'

'You're talking about throwing your life away, Sparhawk,' Vanion said.

'Better one life than millions.'

'I absolutely forbid it!' Ehlana shouted.

'Forgive me, My Queen,' Sparhawk told her, 'but you ordered me to deal with Annias and the others. You can't really rescind that command – at least not to me, you can't.'

There was a polite rap on the door, and Tynian entered with the Domi, Kring. 'Sorry to be late,' the Deiran Knight apologized. 'The Domi and I have been busy with some maps. For some reason, the Zemochs have sent forces north from their main encampment on the Lamork border. There's an infestation of them in eastern Pelosia.'

Kring's eyes brightened when he saw King Soros. 'Ah, there you are, My King,' he said. 'I've been looking all over for you. I've got all sorts of Zemoch ears I'd like to sell you.'

King Soros whispered something. He still appeared to have a sore throat for some reason.

'It's starting to fit together,' Sparhawk told the council. 'Krager told us that Martel was taking Annias to the city of Zemoch to seek refuge with Otha.' He leaned back in his chair. 'I think the final solution to the problem we've been having for the last five centuries lies in the city of Zemoch and not on the plains of Lamorkand. *Azash* is our enemy, not Martel or Annias or Otha and his Zemochs, and we've got the means to destroy Azash once and for all in our hands now. Wouldn't we be foolish not to use it? I could wear the petals off Bhelliom destroying Zemoch infantry units with it, and we'd all grow old and grey on some fluid battlefield to the north of Lake Cammoria. Wouldn't it be better to go right to the heart of the problem – to Azash Himself? Let's have done with this so that it doesn't keep cropping up every half-eon or so.'

'It's strategically unsound, Sparhawk,' Vanion said flatly.

'Excuse me, my friend, but what's so strategically sound about a stalemate on a flat battlefield? It took more than a century to recover from the last battle between the Zemochs and the west. This way we at least have a chance to end it once and for all. If it appears not to be working, I'll destroy Bhelliom. Then Azash won't have any reason to come west again. He'll go and pester the Tamuls or something instead.'

'You'd never get through, Sparhawk,' Preceptor Abriel said. 'You heard what this Peloi said. There are Zemochs in eastern Pelosia as well as the ones down in eastern Lamorkand. Do you propose to wade through them all by yourself?'

'I think they'll stand aside for me, My Lord. Martel's going north – at least that's what he said. He may go as far north as Paler, or he may not. It doesn't really matter, because I'm going to follow him no matter *where* he goes. He *wants* me to follow him. He made that fairly clear down in that cellar, and he was very careful to make sure that I heard him because he wants to deliver me to Azash. I think I can trust him not to put anything in my way. I know it sounds a little peculiar, but I think we can actually trust Martel this time. If he really has to, he'll take his sword and clear a path for me.' He smiled bleakly. 'My brother's tender concern for my welfare touches my heart.' He looked at Sephrenia. 'You said that even suggesting the destruction of a God is unthinkable, didn't you? What would be the general reaction to the idea of destroying Bhelliom?'

'That's even more unthinkable, Sparhawk.'

'Then the notion that I might be considering it won't even occur to them, will it?'

She shook her head mutely, her eyes strangely frightened as she looked at him.

'That's our advantage then, My Lords,' Sparhawk declared. 'I can do the one thing that no one can bring himself to believe that I'll do. I can destroy the Bhelliom – or threaten to. Somehow I have the feeling that people – and Gods – are going to start getting out of my way if I do that.'

Preceptor Abriel was still stubbornly shaking his head. 'You'll be trying to bull your way through primitive Zemochs in eastern Pelosia and along the border, Sparhawk. Not even Otha has control over those savages.'

'Permission to speak, Sarathi?' Kring asked in a profoundly respectful tone.

'Of course, my son.' Dolmant looked a bit puzzled. He had no idea of who this fierce man was.

'I can get you through eastern Pelosia and well into Zemoch, friend Sparhawk,' Kring said. 'If the Zemochs are all spread out, my horsemen can ride right through

373

them. We'll leave a swath of bodies five miles wide from Paler to the Zemoch border – all minus their right ears of course.' Kring's broad grin was wolfish. He looked around in a self-congratulatory way. Then he saw Mirtai, who sat demurely beside Ehlana. His eyes went wide, and he first went pale and then bright red. Then he sighed lustily.

'I wouldn't, if I were you,' Sparhawk warned him.

'What?'

'I'll explain later.'

'I hate to admit it,' Bevier said, 'but this plan's looking better and better. We really shouldn't have much trouble at all getting to Otha's capital.'

'*We?*' Kalten asked.

'We *were* going to go along, weren't we, Kalten?'

'Has it got any chance at all of working, little mother?' Vanion asked.

'No, Lord Vanion, it hasn't!' Ehlana interrupted him. 'Sparhawk *can't* go to Zemoch and use Bhelliom to kill Azash because he doesn't have both rings. I've got one of them, and he'll have to kill me to get it away from me.'

That was something Sparhawk had not considered. 'My Queen –' he began.

'I have *not* given you leave to speak, Sir Sparhawk!' she told him. 'You will *not* pursue this vain and foolhardy scheme! You will *not* throw your life away! Your life is *mine*, Sparhawk! Mine! You do *not* have our permission to take it from us!'

'That's plain enough,' Wargun said, 'and it takes us right back to where we started from.'

'Perhaps not,' Dolmant said quietly. He rose to his feet. 'Queen Ehlana,' he said sternly, 'will you submit to the will of our holy mother, the Church?'

She looked at him defiantly.

'*Will* you?'

'I am a true daughter of the Church,' she said sullenly.

'I'm delighted to hear it, my child. It is the command of the Church that you surrender this trinket into her hands for some brief time that she may use it in furtherance of her work.'

'That's not fair, Dolmant,' she accused.

'Will you defy the Church, Ehlana?'

'I – I *can't*!' she wailed.

'Then give me the ring.' He held out his hand.

Ehlana burst into tears. She clutched his arms and buried her face in his robe.

'Give me the ring, Ehlana,' he repeated.

She looked up at him, dashing the tears from her eyes with one defiant hand.

'Only on one condition, Sarathi,' she countered.

'Will you try to bargain with our holy mother?'

'No, Sarathi, I am merely obeying one of her earlier commands. She instructs us to marry so that we may increase the congregation of the faithful. I will surrender the ring to you on the day you join me with Sir Sparhawk in marriage. I've worked too hard to get him to let him escape me now. Will our holy mother consent to this?'

'It seems fair to me,' Dolmant said, smiling benignly at Sparhawk, who was gaping at the two of them as he was traded off like a side of beef.

Ehlana had a very good memory. As Platime had instructed her, she spat in her hand. 'Done, then!' she said.

Dolmant had been around for a long time, so he recognized the gesture. He also spat on his palm. 'Done!' he said, and the two of them smacked their palms together, sealing Sparhawk's fate.

ZEMOCH

The TEMPLE

The PALACE

PART THREE

Zemoch

Chapter 19

The room was cool. The heat of the desert evaporated when the sun went down, and there was always an arid chill by morning. Sparhawk stood at the window as velvet night bled from the sky and the shadows in the street below shrank back into corners and doorways to be replaced by a pale greyness that was not so much light as it was an absence of dark.

Then the first of them emerged from a shadowy alley with a clay vessel balanced on her shoulder. She was robed and hooded in black, and a black veil covered the lower half of her face. She moved through the pale light with a grace so exquisite that it made Sparhawk's heart ache. Then there were others. One by one they emerged from doorways and alleys to join the silent procession, each with her clay vessel upon her shoulder, and each following a ritual so old that it had become instinctive. However it was that the men began their day, the women inevitably started theirs by going to the well.

Lillias stirred. 'Mahkra,' she said in a voice blurred with sleep, 'come back to bed.'

He could hear the bells in the distance even over the incessant bawling of the half-wild cows in the yards around him. The religion of this kingdom discouraged bells, so Sparhawk knew that the sound came from a place where members of his own faith were gathered. There was no other place to go, so he stumbled on towards the sound of the bells. The hilt of his sword was slippery with blood, and the weapon seemed very heavy now. He wanted to be free of its weight, and it would be so easy to let it slip from his fingers to lie lost in the dung-smelling darkness. A true knight, however, surrendered his sword only to death, and Sparhawk grimly clamped his fist about the sword-hilt and lurched on, following the bells. He was cold, and the blood flowing from his wounds seemed very warm, even comforting. He staggered on through the chill night with the blood flowing from his side warming him.

'Sparhawk.' It was Kurik's voice, and the hand shaking his shoulder was firm. 'Sparhawk, wake up. You're having a nightmare again.'

Sparhawk opened his eyes. He was sweating profusely.

'That same one?' Kurik asked.

Sparhawk nodded.

'Maybe you'll be able to put it to rest when you finally kill Martel.'

Sparhawk sat up in bed.

Kurik's face was creased with a broad grin. 'I thought it might have been a different one,' he said. 'This *is* your wedding day, after all. Bridegrooms always have bad dreams on the night before their weddings. It's sort of an old custom.'

'Was your sleep uneasy the night before you married Aslade?'

'Oh yes,' Kurik laughed. 'Something was chasing me, and I had to get to a seacoast so I could get on board a ship to escape. The only problem was that they kept moving the ocean. Do you want your breakfast now, or do you want to wait until after you've bathed and I shave you?'

'I can shave myself.'

'That wouldn't be a good idea today. Hold out your hand.'

Sparhawk extended his right hand. It was visibly trembling.

'You *definitely* shouldn't try to shave yourself today, My

Lord. Let's call it my wedding present to the queen. I won't let you go to her bed on her wedding night with your face in tatters.'

'What time is it?'

'A half-hour or so before dawn. Get up, Sparhawk. You've got a full day ahead of you. Oh, by the way, Ehlana sent you a present. It came last night after you fell asleep.'

'You should have got me up.'

'Why? You can't wear it in bed.'

'What is it?'

'Your crown, My Lord.'

'My *what?*'

'Crown. It's a sort of a hat. It won't keep off much in the way of weather, though.'

'What's she thinking about?'

'Propriety, My Lord. You're the Prince Consort – or you will be by tonight. It's not a bad crown – as crowns go. Gold, jewels, that sort of thing.'

'Where did she get it?'

'She had it made for you right after you left Cimmura to come here. She brought it along with her – sort of the way a fisherman always has a coil of line and a hook somewhere in his pocket. I gather that your bride didn't want to be unprepared in case an opportunity arose. She wants me to carry it on a velvet cushion during the ceremony tonight. As soon as the two of you are married, she's going to put it on your head.'

'Foolishness,' Sparhawk snorted, swinging his legs out of bed.

'Perhaps, but you'll learn in time that women look at the world differently from the way we do. It's one of the things that makes life interesting. Now, what's it to be? Your breakfast or your bath?'

They met that morning in the chapterhouse, since things

381

in the Basilica were in turmoil. The changes Dolmant was making were sweeping, and the clergy was scrambling about like ants rooted from a ripped-open anthill. The huge Patriarch Bergsten, still in his mail-shirt and wearing his ogre-horned helmet, was grinning as he entered Sir Nashan's study and stood his war-axe in the corner.

'Where's Emban?' King Wargun asked him, 'and Ortzel?'

'They're busy dismissing people. Sarathi's giving the Basilica a thorough house-cleaning. Emban's drawn up a list of the politically unreliable, and the populations of a number of monasteries are expanding sharply.'

'Makova?' Tynian asked.

'He was among the first to leave.'

'Who's first secretary?' King Dregos asked.

'Who else? Emban, of course, and Ortzel's the new head of the college of theologians. It's probably what he's best suited for anyway.'

'And you?' Wargun asked him.

'Sarathi's given me a rather specialized position,' Bergsten replied. 'We haven't come up with a name for it as yet.' He looked rather sternly at the Preceptors of the Church Knights. 'There's been some rather long-standing dissension among the militant orders,' he told them. 'Sarathi's asked me to put a stop to it.' His shaggy brows lowered ominously. 'I trust we understand each other, gentlemen.'

The Preceptors looked at each other a bit nervously.

'Now,' Bergsten continued, 'have we made any decisions here yet?'

'We're still arguing about that, Your Grace,' Vanion answered. Vanion's face was grey this morning for some reason, and he looked definitely unwell. Sparhawk sometimes forgot that Vanion was quite a bit older than he looked. 'Sparhawk's still bent on suicide, and we haven't been able to come up with any convincing alternatives. The rest of the Church Knights are going to move out tomorrow to occupy various fortresses and castles in Lamorkand, and the army will follow once they've been organized.'

Bergsten nodded. 'Exactly what are you going to do, Sparhawk?'

'I thought I'd go and destroy Azash, kill Martel, Otha and Annias and then come home, Your Grace.'

'Very funny,' Bergsten said dryly. 'Details, man. Give me details. I have to make a report to Sarathi, and he loves details.'

'Yes, Your Grace. We've all more or less agreed that we don't have much chance of catching up with Martel and his party before they get across into Zemoch. He's got a three-day start on us – counting today. Martel isn't very considerate of horses, and he has a lot of incentive to stay ahead of us.'

'Are you going to follow him, or just ride straight on to the Zemoch border?'

Sparhawk leaned back in his chair. 'We're a little tenuous on that, Your Grace,' he said thoughtfully. 'I'd like to catch Martel, certainly, but I'm not going to let that sidetrack me. My main goal is to get to the city of Zemoch before a general war breaks out in central Lamorkand. I had a talk with Krager, and he says that Martel plans to go north and then to try to cross over into Zemoch from somewhere up in Pelosia. I more or less want to do the same thing, so I'll follow him – but only up to a point. I'm not going to waste time chasing Martel all over northern Pelosia. If he starts wandering around up there, I'll break off the chase and go straight on to Zemoch. I've been playing Martel's game ever since I came back from Rendor. I don't think I want to play any more.'

'What are you going to do about all the Zemochs in eastern Pelosia?'

'That's where I come in, Your Grace,' Kring told him. 'There's a pass that leads into the interior. The Zemochs don't seem to know about it for some reason. My horsemen and I have been using it for years – any time ears get scarce along the border.' He stopped abruptly and looked with some consternation at King Soros. The King of Pelosia, however, was busy praying and appeared not to have heard the Domi's inadvertent revelation.

'That's about all there is to it, Your Grace,' Sparhawk concluded. 'Nobody really knows for sure what's going on in Zemoch, so we'll have to improvise once we get there.'

'How many of you are there?' Bergsten asked.

'The usual group. Five knights, Kurik, Berit and Sephrenia.'

'What about me?' Talen objected.

'*You* are going back to Cimmura, young man,' Sephrenia told him. 'Ehlana can keep an eye on you. You'll stay at the palace until we come back.'

'That's not fair!'

'Life is filled with injustice, Talen. Sparhawk and your father have plans for you, and they don't propose to let you get yourself killed before they have a chance to put them in motion.'

'Can I appeal to the Church for sanctuary, Your Grace?' Talen asked Bergsten quickly.

'No, I don't think so,' the armoured Patriarch replied.

'You have no idea how disappointed I am in our holy mother, Your Grace,' Talen sulked. 'Just for that, I don't think I'll join the Church after all.'

'Praise God,' Bergsten murmured.

'Amen,' Abriel sighed.

'May I be excused?' Talen asked in a huffy tone.

'No.' It was Berit, who sat by the door with his arms crossed and one leg thrust out to block the doorway.

Talen sat back down, looking injured.

The remainder of the discussion dealt with the deployment of troops at the various fortresses and castles in central Lamorkand. Sparhawk and his friends were not going to be involved in that, so the bridegroom's attention wandered. He did not actually think of anything very coherently, but sat instead staring wide-eyed at the floor.

The meeting broke up about noon, and they began to file out. There were many preparations to make, and they all had things to do.

'Friend Sparhawk,' Kring said as they left Nashan's study, 'might I have a word with you?'

'Of course, Domi.'

'It's sort of personal.'

Sparhawk nodded and led the scarred chief of the Peloi to a small chapel nearby. They both perfunctorily genuflected to the altar and then sat on a polished bench near the front of the chapel. 'What is it, Kring?' Sparhawk asked.

'I'm a plain man, friend Sparhawk,' Kring began, 'so I'll speak to the point. I'm mightily taken with that tall, beautiful woman who guards the Queen of Elenia.'

'I thought I detected something like that.'

'Do you think I might have any chance with her at all?' Kring's heart was in his eyes.

'I'm not really sure, my friend,' Sparhawk told him. 'I scarcely know Mirtai.'

'Is that her name? I never really had the chance to find out. Mirtai – it's got a nice sound to it, doesn't it? Everything about her is perfect. I have to ask this. Is she married?'

'I don't think so.'

'Good. It's always awkward to pay court to a woman if you have to kill her husband first. It seems to get things off to a bad start for some reason.'

'I think you should know that Mirtai's not an Elene, Kring. She's a Tamul, and her culture – and religion – are not the same as ours. Are your intentions honourable?'

'Of course. I think too much of her to insult her.'

'That's the first step anyway. If you approached her on any other footing, she'd probably kill you.'

'*Kill?*' Kring blinked in astonishment.

'She's a warrior, Kring. She's not like any other woman you've ever encountered.'

'Women can't be warriors.'

'Not Elene women, no. But as I said, Mirtai's an Atan Tamul. They don't look at the world the same way we do. As I understand it, she's already killed ten men.'

'Ten?' Kring gasped incredulously, swallowing hard. 'That's going to be a problem, Sparhawk.' Kring squared his shoulders. 'No matter, though. Perhaps after I marry her, I can train her to behave more properly.'

'I wouldn't make any wagers on that, my friend. If there's going to be any training, I think *you're* the one who'll be on the receiving end of it. I'd really advise you to drop the whole idea, Kring. I like you, and I'd hate to see you get yourself killed.'

'I'm going to have to think about this, Sparhawk,' Kring said in a disturbed tone of voice. 'This is a very unnatural situation we have here.'

'Yes.'

'Nonetheless, could I ask you to serve as my oma?'

'I don't understand the word.'

'It means friend. The one who goes to the woman – and to her father and brothers. You start by telling her how much I'm attracted to her and then tell her what a good man I am – the usual thing, you understand – what a great leader I am, how many horses I own, how many ears I've taken and what a great warrior I am.'

'That last should impress her.'

'It's just the simple truth, Sparhawk. I *am* the best, after all. I'll have all the time while we're riding to Zemoch to think it over. You might mention it to her before we leave, though – just to give her something to think about. Oh, I almost forgot. You can tell her that I'm a poet too. That always impresses women.'

'I'll do my best, Domi,' Sparhawk promised.

Mirtai's reaction was none too promising when Sparhawk broached the subject to her later that afternoon. 'That little bald one with the bandy legs?' she said incredulously. 'The one with all the scars on his face?' Then she collapsed in a chair, laughing uncontrollably.

'Well,' Sparhawk murmured philosophically as he left her, 'I tried.'

It was going to be an unconventional sort of wedding. There were no Elenian noblewomen in Chyrellos to attend Ehlana, for one thing. The only two ladies who were really close to her were Sephrenia and Mirtai. She insisted on their presence, and that raised some eyebrows. Even the worldly Dolmant choked on it. 'You *can't* bring two heathens into the nave of the Basilica during a religious ceremony, Ehlana.'

'It's my wedding, Dolmant. I can do anything I want to. I *will* have Sephrenia and Mirtai as attendants.'

'I forbid it.'

'Fine.' Her eyes grew flinty. 'No attendants, no wedding – and if there isn't a wedding, my ring stays right where it is.'

'That is an impossible young woman, Sparhawk,' the Archprelate fumed as he stormed out of the room where Ehlana was making her preparations.

'We prefer the term "spirited", Sarathi,' Sparhawk said mildly. Sparhawk was dressed in black velvet trimmed with silver. Ehlana had summarily rejected the idea of his being married in his armour. 'I don't want a blacksmith in our bed-chamber to help you get undressed, love,' she had told him. 'If you need help, I'll provide it – but I don't want to break all my fingernails in the process.'

There were noblemen by the score in the armies of western Eosia, and legions of clergy in the Basilica, and so that evening the vast, candlelit nave was almost as packed as it had been on the day of the funeral of the revered Cluvonus. The choir sang joyful anthems as the wedding guests filed in, and incense by the bale perfumed the air.

Sparhawk waited nervously in the vestry with those who were to attend him. His friends were all there, of course – Kalten, Tynian, Bevier, Ulath and the Domi, as well as Kurik, Berit and the Preceptors of the four orders. Ehlana's attendants, appropriately, were, in addition to Sephrenia and Mirtai, the kings of western Eosia and, oddly enough, Platime, Stragen and Talen. The queen had given no reason for these selections. It was altogether possible that there *were* no reasons.

'Don't do that, Sparhawk,' Kurik told his lord.

'Do what?'

'Don't keep pulling at the neck of your doublet like that. You'll rip it.'

'The tailor cut it too tight. It feels like a noose.'

Kurik did not answer that. He did, however, give Sparhawk an amused look.

The door opened, and Emban thrust his sweating face into the room. He was grinning broadly. 'Are we just about ready?' he asked.

'Let's get on with it,' Sparhawk said abruptly.

'Our bridegroom grows impatient, I see,' Emban said. 'Ah, to be young again. The choir's going to sing the traditional wedding hymn,' he told them. 'I'm sure that some of you are familiar with it. When they get to the final chord, I'll open the door, and then you gentlemen can escort our sacrificial lamb here to the altar. Please don't let him run away. That always disrupts the ceremony so much.' He chuckled wickedly and closed the door again.

'That's a very nasty little man,' Sparhawk grated.

'Oh, I don't know,' Kalten said. '*I* sort of like him.'

The wedding hymn was one of the oldest pieces of sacred music in the Elene faith. It was a song filled with joy. Brides traditionally paid very close attention to it. Grooms, on the other hand, usually scarcely heard it.

As the last notes died away, Patriarch Emban opened the door with a flourish, and Sparhawk's friends formed up around him to escort him into the nave. It would be perhaps inappropriate here to dwell upon the similarities of such a procession to the gathering of bailiffs escorting a condemned prisoner to the scaffold.

They proceeded directly across the front of the nave to the altar where Archprelate Dolmant, robed all in white trimmed with gold, awaited them. 'Ah, my son,' Dolmant said to Sparhawk with a faint smile, 'so good of you to join us.'

Sparhawk did not trust himself to answer that. He *did*, however, reflect rather bitterly on the fact that all his friends viewed the occasion as one filled with an enormous potential for humour.

Then, after a suitable pause, during which all the wedding guests rose to their feet, fell silent and craned their necks to gaze towards the back of the nave, the choir broke into the processional hymn, and the bridal party emerged from either side of the vestibule. First, one from either side, came Sephrenia and Mirtai. The disparity of the size of the two women was not immediately noted by the onlookers. What *was* noted and what raised a shocked gasp from the crowd was the obvious fact that both were clearly heathens. Sephrenia's white robe was almost defiantly Styric. A garland of flowers encircled her brow, and her face was calm. Mirtai's gown was of a

389

style unknown in Elenia. It was of a deep, royal blue and seemed to be unseamed. It was fastened at each shoulder with a jewelled clip, and a long gold chain caught it below the bust, crossed the Tamul woman's back, encircled her waist and then hugged her hips to the intricate knot low in the front with the tasselled ends nearly reaching the floor. Her golden arms were bare to the shoulders, flawlessly smooth, yet solidly muscled. She wore golden sandals, and her now-unbraided and glossy black hair flowed smoothly down her back, reaching to mid-thigh. A simple silver band encircled her head. About her wrists she wore not bracelets but rather burnished steel cuffs embossed with gold. As a concession to Elene sensibilities, she was not visibly armed.

The Domi Kring sighed lustily as she entered and with Sephrenia at her side, paced slowly down the aisle towards the altar.

Again there was the customary pause, and then the bride, her left hand resting lightly on the arm of old King Obler, emerged from the vestibule to stop so that all present might view her – not so much as a woman, but as a work of art. Her gown was of white satin, but brides are almost always gowned in white satin. This particular gown was lined with gold lamé, and the long sleeves were turned back to reveal that contrast. The sleeves themselves were cut long at the backs of the arms, reaching quite nearly to the floor. Ehlana wore a wide belt of beaten mesh gold inlaid with precious gems about her waist. A fabulous golden cape descended to the floor behind her to add its weight to her gleaming satin train. Her pale blonde hair was surmounted by a crown, not the traditional royal crown of Elenia, but rather a lacework of gold mesh highlighted with small, brightly-coloured gems interspersed with pearls. The crown held her veil in place, a veil which reached to her bodice in the front and overlaid her shoulders in the back and was so delicate and fine as to be scarcely more than mist. She carried a single white flower, and her pale young face was radiant.

'Where did they get the gowns on such short notice?' Berit whispered to Kurik.

'Sephrenia wriggled her fingers, I'd imagine.'

Dolmant gave the two of them a stern look, and they stopped whispering.

Following the Queen of Elenia there came the crowned kings, Wargun, Dregos, Soros and the Crown Prince of Lamorkand, who was standing in for his absent father, and by the ambassador of Cammoria, who was the representative of that kingdom. The Kingdom of Rendor was unrepresented, and no one had even thought to invite Otha of Zemoch.

The procession began slowly to move down the aisle towards the altar and the waiting bridegroom. Platime and Stragen brought up the rear, one of them on each side of Talen, who bore the white velvet cushion upon which rested that pair of ruby rings. It should be noted in passing that both Stragen and Platime were keeping a very close eye on the youthful thief.

Sparhawk considered his bride as, with glowing face, she approached. In those last few moments while he was still able to think coherently, he realized something at last which he had never fully admitted to himself. Ehlana had been a chore when she had been placed in his care years ago – not only a chore, but a humiliation as well. It is to his credit that he had felt no personal resentment towards her, for he had realized that she had been as much a victim of her father's caprice as he was himself. The first year and more had been trying. The girl-child who now so radiantly approached him had been timorous, and at first had spoken only to Rollo, a small, somewhat bedraggled stuffed toy animal which in those days was her

391

constant and probably only companion. In time, however, she had grown accustomed to Sparhawk's battered face and stern demeanour, and a somewhat tenuous friendship had been cemented on the day when an arrogant courtier had offered Princess Ehlana an impertinence and had been firmly rebuked by her knight-protector. It was undoubtedly the first time anyone had ever shed blood for her (the courtier's nose had bled profusely), and an entire new world had opened for the small, pale princess. From that moment, she had confided everything to her knight – even things he might have preferred she had not. She had no secrets from him, and he had come to know her as he had never known anyone else in the world. And that, of course, had ruined him for any other woman. The slight, as yet unformed princess had so intricately intertwined her very being with his that there was no possible way they could ever be separated, and that, finally, was why they were here in this place and at this time. If there had been only his own pain to consider, Sparhawk might have held firm in his rejection of the idea. He could not, however, endure *her* pain, and so –

The hymn concluded. Old King Obler delivered his kinswoman to her knight, and the bride and groom turned to face Archprelate Dolmant. 'I'm going to preach to you for a while,' Dolmant told them quietly. 'It's a sort of convention, and people expect me to do it. You don't really have to listen, but try not to yawn in my face if you can avoid it.'

'We wouldn't dream of it, Sarathi,' Ehlana assured him.

Dolmant spoke of the state of marriage – at some length. He then assured the bridal couple that once the ceremony had been completed, it would be perfectly all right for them to follow their natural inclinations – that it would not only be all right, but was in fact encouraged. He strongly suggested that they be faithful to each other and reminded them that any issue of their union must be raised in the Elene faith. Then he came to the 'wilt thou's', asking each of them in turn if they consented to be wed, bestowed all their worldly goods upon each other and promised to love, honour, obey, cherish and so forth. Then, since things were going so well, he moved right along into the exchanging of the rings, neither of which Talen had even managed to steal.

It was at that point that Sparhawk heard a soft, familiar sound that seemed to echo down from the dome itself. It was the faint trilling of pipes, a joyful sound filled with abiding love. Sparhawk glanced at Sephrenia. Her glowing smile said everything. For a moment he irrationally wondered what protocols had been involved when Aphrael had applied to the Elene God for permission to be present, and, it appeared, to add her blessing to His.

'What *is* that music?' Ehlana whispered, her lips not moving.

'I'll explain later,' Sparhawk murmured.

The song of Aphrael's pipes seemed to go unnoticed by the throng in the candlelit nave. Dolmant's eyes, however, widened slightly, and his face went a bit pale. He regained his composure and finally declared that Sparhawk and Ehlana were permanently, irrevocably, unalterably and definitively man and wife. He then invoked the blessings of God upon them in a nice little concluding prayer and finally gave Sparhawk permission to kiss his bride.

Sparhawk tenderly lifted Ehlana's veil and touched his lips to hers. No one actually kisses someone else very well in public, but the couple managed without looking too awkward about the whole business.

The wedding ceremony was followed immediately by Sparhawk's coronation as Prince Consort. He knelt to have the crown Kurik had carried into the nave on a purple velvet cushion placed upon his head by the young woman who had just promised – among other things – to obey him, but who now assumed the authority of his queen. Ehlana made a nice speech in a ringing voice with which she could probably have commanded rocks to move with some fair expectation of being obeyed. She said a number of things about him in her speech, mostly flattering, and concluded by firmly settling the crown on his head. Then, since he was on his knees anyway and his upturned face was convenient, she kissed him again. He noticed that she got much, much better at it with practice. 'You're *mine* now, Sparhawk,' she murmured with her lips still touching his. Then, though he was far from decrepit, she helped him to his feet. Mirtai and Kalten came forward with ermine-trimmed robes to place them on the shoulders of the royal pair, and then the two of them turned to receive the cheers of the throng within the nave.

There was a wedding supper following the ceremony. Sparhawk never remembered what was served at that supper nor even if he ate any of it. All he remembered was that it seemed to go on for centuries. Then at last he and his bride were escorted to the door of a lavish chamber high up in the east wing of one of the buildings that comprised the Church complex. He and Ehlana entered, and he closed and locked the door behind them.

There were furnishings in the room – chairs, tables, divans and the like – but all Sparhawk really saw was the stark reality of the bed. It was a high bed on a raised dais, and it had a substantial post at each corner.

'Finally,' Ehlana said with relief. 'I thought all of that was going to go on forever.'

'Yes,' Sparhawk agreed.

'Sparhawk?' she said then, and her tone was not the tone

of a queen, 'do you *really* love me? I know I forced you into this – first back in Cimmura and then here. Did you marry me because you really love me, or did you just defer to me because I'm the queen?' Her voice was trembling, and her eyes were very vulnerable.

'You're asking silly questions, Ehlana,' he told her gently. 'I'll admit that you startled me at first – probably because I had no idea that you felt this way. I'm not much of a catch, Ehlana, but I do love you. I've never loved anyone else, and never will. My heart's a little battered, but it's entirely yours.' Then he kissed her, and she seemed to melt against him.

The kiss lasted for quite some time, and after a few moments he felt one small hand slide caressingly up the back of his neck to remove his crown. He drew his face back and looked into her lustrous grey eyes. Then he gently removed *her* crown and let her veil slide to the floor. Gravely, they unfastened each other's ermine-trimmed robes and let them fall.

The window was open, and the night breeze billowed the gauze curtains and carried with it the night-time sounds of Chyrellos far below. Sparhawk and Ehlana did not feel the breeze, and the only sound they heard was the beating of each other's heart.

The candles no longer burned, but the room was not dark. The moon had risen by now, and it was a full moon that filled the night with a pale, silvery luminescence. The moonlight seemed caught in the filmy net of the curtains blowing softly at the window, and the glow of those curtains provided a subtler, more perfect light than that of any candle.

It was very late – or to be more precise, very early. Sparhawk had dozed off briefly, but his pale, moon-drenched wife shook him awake. 'None of that,' she told him. 'We only have this one night, and you're not going to waste it by sleeping.'

'Sorry,' he apologized. 'I've had a busy day.'

'Also a busy night,' she added with an arch little smile. 'Did you know that you snore like a thunderstorm?'

'It's the broken nose, I think.'

'That may cause problems in time, love. I'm a light sleeper.' Ehlana nestled down in his arms and sighed contentedly. 'Oh, this is very nice,' she said. 'We should have got married years ago.'

'I think your father might have objected – and if he hadn't, Rollo certainly would have. Whatever happened to Rollo, by the way?'

'His stuffing all came out after my father sent you into exile. I washed him and then folded him up and put him on the top shelf in my closet. I'll have him restuffed after our first baby is born. Poor Rollo. He saw some hard use after you were sent away. I cried all over him extensively. He was a very soggy little animal for several months.'

'Did you really miss me all that much?'

'Miss you? I thought I'd die. I wanted to die, actually.'

His arms tightened around her.

'Well now,' she said, 'why don't we talk about that?'

He laughed. 'Do you absolutely have to say everything that pops into your head?'

'When we're alone, yes. I have no secrets from you, my husband.' She remembered something. 'You said you were going to tell me about that music we heard during the ceremony.'

'That was Aphrael. I'll have to check with Sephrenia, but I rather strongly suspect that we've been married in more than one religion.'

'Good. That gives me another hold on you.'

'You don't really need any more, you know. You've had me in thrall since you were about six years old.'

396

'That's nice,' she said, snuggling even closer to him. 'God knows I was trying.' She paused. 'I must say, though, that I'm getting just a bit put out with your impertinent little Styric Goddess. She always seems to be around. For all we know, she's hovering unseen in some corner right now.' She stopped suddenly and sat up in bed. 'Do you suppose she might be?' she asked with some consternation.

'I wouldn't be surprised.' He was deliberately teasing her.

'*Sparhawk!*' The pale light of the moon made it impossible to be sure, but Sparhawk strongly suspected that his wife was blushing furiously.

'Don't concern yourself, love,' he laughed. 'Aphrael's exquisitely courteous. She'd never think of intruding.'

'But we can never really be sure, can we? I'm not sure I like her. I get the feeling that she's very much attracted to you, and I don't much care for the notion of immortal competition.'

'Don't be absurd. She's a child.'

'I was only about five years old the first time I saw you, Sparhawk, and I decided to marry you the minute you walked into the room.' She slid from the bed, crossed to the glowing window and parted the gauze curtains. The pale moonlight made her look very much like an alabaster statue.

'Shouldn't you put on a robe?' he suggested. 'You're exposing yourself to public scrutiny, you know.'

'Everybody in Chyrellos has been asleep for hours now. Besides, we're six floors above the street. I want to look at the moon. The moon and I are very close, and I want her to know how happy I am.'

'Pagan,' he smiled.

'I suppose I am at that,' she admitted, 'but all women feel a peculiar attachment to the moon. She touches us in ways a man could never understand.'

Sparhawk crawled out of bed and joined her at the window. The moon was very pale and very bright, but the fact that its pale light washed out all colour concealed to some degree the ruin Martel's siege had inflicted on the Holy City, although the smell of smoke was still very strong in the night air. The stars glittered in the sky. There was nothing really unusual about that, but they seemed especially brilliant on this night of all nights.

Ehlana pulled his arms about her and sighed. 'I wonder if Mirtai's sleeping outside my door,' she said. 'She does that, you know. Wasn't she ravishing tonight?'

'Oh yes. I didn't get the chance to tell you this, but Kring's completely overwhelmed by her. I've never seen a man so bowled over by love.'

'At least he's open and honest about it. I have to drag affectionate words out of you.'

'You know that I love you, Ehlana. I always have.'

'That's not precisely true. When I was still carrying Rollo around, you were only mildly fond of me.'

'It was more than that.'

'Oh, really? I saw the pained looks you used to give me when I was being childish and silly, my noble Prince Consort.' She frowned. 'That's a very cumbersome title. When I get back to Cimmura, I think I'll have a talk with Lenda. It seems to me there's an empty duchy somewhere – or if there isn't, I'll vacate one. I'm going to dispossess a few of Annias's henchmen anyway. How would you like to be a duke, Your Grace?'

'Thanks all the same, Your Majesty, but I think I can forgo the encumbrance of additional titles.'

'But I *want* to give you titles.'

'I'm sort of taken with "husband" personally.'

'Any man can be a husband.'

'But I'm the only one who's yours.'

'Oh, that's very nice. Practise a bit, Sparhawk, and you might even turn into a perfect gentleman.'

'Most of the perfect gentlemen I know are courtiers. They're not generally held in high regard.'

She shivered.

'You're cold,' he accused. 'I *told* you to put on a robe.'

'Why do I need a robe when I have this nice warm husband handy?'

He bent, picked her up in his arms and carried her back to the bed.

'I've dreamed of this,' she said as he gently put her on the bed, joined her and drew the covers over them. 'You know something, Sparhawk?' She snuggled down against him again. 'I used to worry about this night. I thought I'd be all nervous and shy, but I'm not at all – and do you know why?'

'No, I don't think so.'

'I think it's because we've really been married since the first moment I laid my eyes on you. All we were really doing was waiting for me to grow up so that we could formalize things.' She kissed him lingeringly. 'What time do you think it is?'

'A couple of hours until daylight.'

'Good. That gives us lots more time. You *are* going to be careful in Zemoch, aren't you?'

'I'm going to do my very best.'

'Please don't do heroic things just to impress me, Sparhawk. I'm already impressed.'

'I'll be careful,' he promised.

'Speaking of that – do you want my ring now?'

'Why don't you give it to me in public? Let Sarathi see us keep our part of the bargain.'

'Was I really too terrible to him?'

'You startled him a bit. Sarathi's not used to dealing with women like you. I think you unnerve him, my love.'

'Do I unnerve you too, Sparhawk?'

'Not really. I raised you, after all. I'm used to your little quirks.'

'You're really very fortunate, you know. Very few men have the opportunity to rear their own wives. That may give you something to think about on your way to Zemoch.' Her voice quavered then, and a sudden sob escaped her. 'I *swore* I wouldn't do this,' she wailed. 'I don't want you to remember me as being all weepy.'

'It's all right, Ehlana. I sort of feel the same way myself.'

'Why does the night have to run so fast? Could this Aphrael of yours stop the sun from coming up if we asked her to? Or maybe you could do it with the Bhelliom.'

'I don't think anything in the world has the power to do that, Ehlana.'

'What good are they all then?' She began to cry, and he took her into his arms and held her until the storm of her weeping had passed. Then he gently kissed her. One kiss became several, and the rest of the night passed without any further weeping.

Chapter 20

'But why does it have to be in public?' Sparhawk demanded, clanking around the room to settle his armour into place.

'It's expected, dear,' Ehlana replied calmly. 'You're a member of the royal family now, and you're obliged to appear in public on occasion. You get used to it after a while.' Ehlana, wearing a fur-trimmed blue velvet robe, sat at her dressing table.

'It's no worse than a tournament, My Lord,' Kurik told him. 'That's in public too. Now will you stop pacing around so I can get your sword-belt on straight?' Kurik, Sephrenia and Mirtai had arrived at the bridal chamber with the sun, Kurik carrying Sparhawk's armour, Sephrenia carrying flowers for the queen and Mirtai carrying breakfast. Emban came with them, and *he* carried the news that the formal farewell would take place on the steps of the Basilica.

'We haven't given the people or Wargun's troops much in the way of detail, Sparhawk,' the fat little Churchman cautioned, 'so you probably shouldn't get too specific if you start making speeches. We'll give you a rousing send-off and hint at the fact that you're going to save the world all by yourself. We're used to lying, so we'll even be able to sound convincing. It's all very silly, of course, but we'd appreciate your cooperation. The morale of the citizens and particularly of Wargun's troops is very important just now.' His round face took on a slightly disappointed cast. 'I suggested that we have you do something spectacular in the way

401

of magic to top things off, but Sarathi put his foot down.'

'Your tendency towards theatrics sometimes gets out of hand, Emban,' Sephrenia told him. The small Styric woman was toying with Ehlana's hair, experimenting with comb and brush.

'I'm a man of the people, Sephrenia,' Emban replied. 'My father was a tavern keeper, and I know how to please a crowd. The people love a good show, and that's what I wanted to give them.'

Sephrenia had lifted Ehlana's hair into a mass atop the queen's head. 'What do you think, Mirtai?' she asked.

'I liked it the way it was before,' the giantess replied.

'She's married now. The way she wore her hair before was the way a young girl would wear it. We have to do something with it to indicate that she's a married woman now.'

'Brand her,' Mirtai shrugged. 'That's what my people do.'

'Do *what*?' Ehlana exclaimed.

'Among my people, a woman is branded with her husband's mark when she marries – usually on the shoulder.'

'To indicate that she's his property?' the queen asked scornfully. 'What sort of mark does the *husband* wear?'

'He wears his wife's mark. Marriages are not undertaken lightly among my people.'

'I can see why,' Kurik said with a certain awe.

'Eat your breakfast before it gets cold, Ehlana,' Mirtai commanded.

'I don't really care all that much for fried liver, Mirtai.'

'It's not for you. My people lay some importance on the wedding night. Many brides become pregnant on that night – or so they say. That might be the result of practising before the ceremony, though.'

402

'*Mirtai!*' Ehlana gasped, flushing.

'You mean you didn't? I'm disappointed in you.'

'I didn't think of it,' Ehlana confessed. 'Why didn't you say something, Sparhawk?'

Emban for some reason was blushing furiously. 'Why don't I just run along?' he said. 'I have a million things to take care of.' And he bolted from the room.

'Was it something I said?' Mirtai asked innocently.

'Emban's a Churchman, dear,' Sephrenia told her, trying to stifle a laugh. 'Churchmen prefer not to know too much about such things.'

'Foolishness. Eat, Ehlana.'

The gathering on the steps of the Basilica was not *quite* a ceremony, but rather was one of those informally formal affairs customarily put on for public entertainment. Dolmant was there to lend solemnity to the affair. The kings, crowned and robed, were present to give things an official tone, and the Preceptors of the militant orders to add a martial note. Dolmant began things with a prayer. That was followed by brief remarks from the kings and then by slightly longer ones from the Preceptors. Sparhawk and his companions then knelt to receive the Archprelate's blessing, and the whole affair was concluded by the farewell between Ehlana and her Prince Consort. The Queen of Elenia, speaking once again in that oratorical tone, commanded her champion to go forth and conquer. She concluded by removing her ring and bestowing it upon him as a mark of her special favour. He responded by replacing it upon her hand with a ring surmounted with a heart-shaped diamond. Talen had been a bit evasive about how the ring had come into his possession when he had pressed it upon Sparhawk just prior to the gathering on the steps.

'And now, my champion,' Ehlana concluded, perhaps a bit dramatically, 'go forth with your brave companions, and know that our hopes, our prayers and all our faith ride with you. Take up the sword, my husband and champion, and defend me and our faith and our beloved homes against the vile hordes of heathen Zemoch!' And then she embraced him and bestowed a single brief kiss upon his lips.

'Nice speech, love,' he murmured his congratulations.

'Emban wrote it,' she confessed. 'He's got the soul of a meddler. Try to get word to me now and then, my husband, and in the name of God, be careful.'

He gently kissed her forehead, and then he and his friends strode purposefully to the foot of the marble stairs and their waiting horses as the bells of the Basilica rang out their own farewell. The Preceptors of the militant orders, who were to ride out with them a little way, followed. Kring and his mounted Peloi were already waiting in the street. Before they set out, Kring rode forward to where Mirtai stood, and his horse performed that ritual genuflection to her. Neither of them spoke, but Mirtai *did* look slightly impressed.

'All right, Faran,' Sparhawk said as he swung up into the saddle, 'it's all right for you to indulge yourself just a bit.'

The big, ugly roan's ears pricked forward eagerly, and he began to prance outrageously as the war-like party moved off in the direction of the east gate.

Once they had passed the gate, Vanion left Sephrenia's side and drew his horse in beside Faran. 'Stay alert, my friend,' he advised. 'Have you got Bhelliom where you can get your hands on it in a hurry if you have to?'

'It's inside my surcoat,' Sparhawk said. He looked closely at his friend. 'Don't take this wrong,' he said, 'but you're looking decidedly seedy this morning.'

'I'm tired more than anything, Sparhawk. Wargun kept us running pretty hard down there in Arcium. Take care of yourself, my friend. I want to go and talk with Sephrenia before we separate.'

Sparhawk sighed as Vanion rode back along the column to join the small, beautiful woman who had tutored generations of Pandions in the secrets of Styricum. Sephrenia and Vanion would never say anything overtly, even to each other, but Sparhawk knew how things stood between them, and he also knew how totally impossible their situation was.

Kalten pulled in beside him. 'Well, how did the wedding night go?' he asked, his eyes very bright.

Sparhawk gave him a long, flat look.

'You don't want to talk about it, I gather.'

'It's sort of private.'

'We've been friends since boyhood, Sparhawk. We've never had any secrets from each other.'

'We have now. It's about seventy leagues to Kadach, isn't it?'

'That's fairly close. If we push, we should be able to make it in five days. Did Martel sound at all concerned when he was talking with Annias down in that cellar? What I'm getting at is do you think he'll be worried enough about our following him to hurry right along?'

'He definitely wanted to leave Chyrellos.'

'He's probably pushing his horses hard then, wouldn't you say?'

'That's a safe bet.'

'His horses will tire if he runs them hard, so we still might have a chance to catch up with him after a few days. I don't know about how you feel about *him*, but *I'd* certainly like to catch Adus.'

'It's something to think about, all right. How's the country between Kadach and Motera?'

'Flat. Mostly farmland. Castles here and there. Farm villages. It's a great deal like eastern Elenia.' Kalten laughed. 'Have you taken a look at Berit this morning? He's having a little trouble adjusting to his armour. It doesn't fit him all that well.' Berit, the raw-boned young novice, had been promoted to a rank seldom used by the militant orders. He was now an apprentice knight rather than a novice. This legally enabled him to wear his own armour, but he did not as yet rate a 'sir'.

'He'll get used to it,' Sparhawk said. 'When we stop for the night, take him aside and show him how to pad the raw spots. We don't want him to start bleeding out of the joints of his armour. Be discreet about it, though. If I remember rightly, a young fellow's very proud and a little touchy when he first puts his armour on. That sort of passes after the first few blisters break.'

It was when they reached a hilltop several miles from Chyrellos that the Preceptors turned back. The advice and the cautions had all been given, and so there was little to do but clasp hands and to wish each other well. Sparhawk and his friends rather soberly watched as their leaders rode back to the Holy City.

'Well,' Tynian said, 'now that we're alone –'

'Let's talk for a few moments first,' Sparhawk said. He raised his voice. 'Domi,' he called, 'would you join us for a moment, please?'

Kring rode up the hill, an inquiring look on his face.

'Now then,' Sparhawk began, 'Martel seems to think that Azash will want us to get through without any difficulty, but Martel might be wrong. Azash has many servants, and He may very well loose them on us. He wants Bhelliom, not any satisfaction He might get from a personal confrontation. Kring, I think you'd better put out scouts. Let's not be taken by surprise.'

'I will, friend Sparhawk,' the Domi promised.

'If we *should* happen to encounter any of the servants of Azash, I want all of you to fall back and let me deal with them. I've got Bhelliom, and that should be all the advantage I'll need. Kalten raised the point that we might just overtake Martel. If we do, try to take Martel and Annias alive. The Church wants them to stand trial. I doubt that Arissa or Lycheas will offer much resistance, so take them as well.'

'And Adus?' Kalten asked eagerly.

'Adus can barely talk, so he wouldn't be of much value in any trial. You can have him – as a personal gift from me.'

They had gone perhaps another mile when they found Stragen sitting under a tree. 'I thought perhaps you'd got lost,' the slender thief drawled, rising to his feet.

'Do I sense a volunteer here?' Tynian suggested.

'Hardly, old boy,' Stragen said. 'I've never had occasion to visit Zemoch, and I think I want to keep it that way. Actually, I'm here as the queen's messenger, and her personal envoy. I'll ride along with you as far as the Zemoch border, if I may, and then I'll return to Cimmura to give her my report.'

'Aren't you spending a great deal of time away from your own business?' Kurik asked him.

'My business in Emsat sort of runs itself. Tel's looking out for my interests there. I need a vacation anyway.' He patted at his doublet in various places. 'Oh yes, here it is.' He drew out a folded sheet of parchment. 'A letter for you from your bride, Sparhawk,' he said, handing it over. 'It's the first of several I'm supposed to give you when the occasion dictates.'

Sparhawk moved Faran away from the others and broke the seal on Ehlana's note.

'Beloved,' it read. 'You've been gone for only a few hours, and I already miss you desperately. Stragen is carrying other messages for you – messages which I hope will inspire you when things aren't going well. They will also convey to you my unbending love and faith in you. I love you, my Sparhawk. Ehlana.'

'How did you get ahead of us?' Kalten was asking when Sparhawk rejoined them.

'You're wearing armour, Sir Kalten,' Stragen replied, 'and I'm not. You'd be amazed at how fast a horse can run when he's not burdened with all that excess iron.'

'Well?' Ulath asked Sparhawk, 'do we send him back to Chyrellos?'

Sparhawk shook his head. 'He's acting under orders from the queen. There's an implicit command to me involved in that as well. He comes along.'

'Remind me never to become a royal champion,' the Genidian Knight said. 'It seems to involve all sorts of politics and complications.'

The weather turned cloudy as they rode northeastwards along the Kadach road, although it did not rain as it had the last time they had been there. The southeastern border country of Lamorkand was more Pelosian in character than it was Lamork, and there were few castles atop the surrounding hills. Because of its proximity to Chyrellos, however, the landscape was dotted with monasteries and cloisters, and the sound of bells echoed mournfully across the fields.

'The clouds are moving in the wrong direction,' Kurik said as they were saddling their horses on the second morning out from Chyrellos. 'An east wind in mid-autumn is very bad news. I'm afraid we're in for a hard winter, and that's not going to be pleasant for the troops campaigning on the plains of central Lamorkand.'

They mounted and rode on towards the northeast. About mid-morning, Kring and Stragen rode forward to join Sparhawk at the head of the column. 'Friend Stragen here has been telling me some things about that Tamul woman, Mirtai,' Kring said. 'Did you ever get the chance to talk to her about me?'

'I sort of broke the ice on the subject,' Sparhawk said.

'I was afraid of that. Some of the things Stragen told me are giving me some second thoughts about the whole notion.'

'Oh?'

'Did you know that she has knives strapped to her knees and elbows?'

'Yes.'

'I understand that they stick out whenever she bends one of her arms or legs.'

'I think that's the idea, yes.'

'Stragen tells me that once when she was young, three ruffians set upon her. She bent an elbow and slashed one across the throat, drove her knee into the second one's crotch, knocked the third down with her fist and knifed him in the heart. I'm not entirely sure that I want a woman like that for a wife. What did she say? When you told her about me, I mean?'

'She laughed, I'm afraid.'

'*Laughed?*' Kring sounded shocked.

'I sort of gather that you're not exactly to her taste.'

'Laughed? At *me*?'

'I think your decision's wise, though, friend Kring,' Sparhawk said. 'I don't think you two would get along very well.'

Kring's eyes, however, were bulging. '*Laughed* at me, did she?' he said indignantly. 'Well, we'll just *see* about that!' And he whirled his horse and rode back to join his men.

'That might have worked out if you hadn't told him about the laughing,' Stragen observed. 'Now he'll go out of his way to pursue her. I sort of like him, and I hate to think of what Mirtai's likely to do to him if he gets too persistent.'

'Maybe we can talk him out of it,' Sparhawk said.

'I wouldn't really count on it.'

'What are you actually doing here, Stragen?' Sparhawk asked the blond man. 'In the southern kingdoms, I mean?'

Stragen looked off towards a nearby monastery, his eyes distant. 'Do you want the real truth, Sparhawk? Or would you like to give me a moment or two to fabricate a story for you?'

'Why don't we start out with the truth? If I don't like that, then you can make something up.'

Stragen flashed him a quick grin. 'All right,' he agreed. 'Up in Thalesia, I'm a counterfeit aristocrat. Down here, I'm the real thing – or very close to it. I associate with kings and queens, the nobility and the higher clergy on a more or less equal footing.' He raised one hand. 'I'm not deluding myself, my friend, so don't become concerned about my sanity. I know what I am – a bastard thief – and I know that my proximity to the gentry down here is only temporary and that it's based entirely on my usefulness. I'm tolerated, not really accepted. My ego, however, is sizeable.'

'I noticed that,' Sparhawk said with a gentle smile.

'Be nice, Sparhawk. Anyway, I'll accept this temporary and superficial equality – if only for the chance of some civilized conversation. Whores and thieves aren't really very stimulating companions, you understand, and about all they can really offer in the way of conversation is shop talk. Have you ever heard a group of whores sitting around talking shop?'

'I can't say that I have.'

Stragen shuddered. 'Absolutely awful. You learn things about men – and women – that you really don't want to know.'

'This won't last. You know that, don't you, Stragen? The time will come when things will return to normal, and people will start closing their doors to you again.'

'You're probably right, but it's fun to pretend for a little while. And when it's all over, I'll have that much more reason to despise you stinking aristocrats.' Stragen paused. 'I do sort of like *you* though, Sparhawk – for the time being, at least.'

As they rode northeastwards, they began to encounter groups of armed men. The Lamorks were never very far from full mobilization anyway, and they were able to respond to their king's call to arms quickly. In a melancholy repetition of the events of some five centuries earlier, men from all the kingdoms of western Eosia streamed towards a battlefield in Lamorkand. Sparhawk and Ulath passed the time conversing in Troll. Sparhawk was not certain when he might have occasion to talk to a Troll, but since he had learned the language, it seemed a shame to let it slip away. They reached Kadach at the end of a gloomy day when the sunset was staining the clouds to the west with an orange glow much like that of a distant forest fire. The wind from the east was stiff, and it carried with it the first faint chill of the oncoming winter. Kadach was a walled town, stiff and grey and rigidly unlovely. In what was to become a custom, Kring bade them goodnight and led his men on through the city and out of the east gate to set up camp in the fields beyond. The Peloi were uncomfortable when confined in cities with such urban frivolities as walls, rooms and roofs. Sparhawk and the rest of his friends found a comfortable inn near the centre of town, bathed, changed clothes and gathered in the common room for a supper of boiled ham and assorted vegetables. Sephrenia, as usual, declined the ham.

'I've never understood why people would want to boil a perfectly good ham,' Sir Bevier noted with some distaste.

'Lamorks over-salt their hams when they cure them,' Kalten explained. 'You have to boil a Lamork ham for quite a while before it's edible. They're a strange people. They try to make everything an act of courage – even eating.'

'Shall we go for a walk, Sparhawk?' Kurik suggested to his lord after they had eaten.

'I think I've had just about enough exercise for one day.'

'You *did* want to know which way Martel went, didn't you?'

'That's true, isn't it? All right, Kurik. Let's go nose around a bit.'

When they reached the street, Sparhawk looked around. 'This is likely to take us half the night,' he said.

'Hardly,' Kurik disagreed. 'We'll go to the east gate first, and if we don't find out anything there, we'll try the north one.'

'We just start asking people in the street?'

Kurik sighed. 'Use your head, Sparhawk. When people are on a journey, they usually start out first thing in the morning – about the same time that other people are going to work. A lot of workmen drink their breakfasts and so the taverns are usually open. When a tavern keeper's waiting for the first customer of the day, he watches the street fairly closely. Believe me, Sparhawk, if Martel left Kadach in the last three days, at least half a dozen tavern keepers saw him.'

'You're an extraordinarily clever fellow, Kurik.'

'Somebody in this party has to be, My Lord. As a group, knights don't spend a great deal of their time thinking.'

'Your class prejudices are showing, Kurik.'

'We all have these little flaws, I guess.'

The streets of Kadach were very nearly deserted, and the few citizens abroad hurried along with their cloaks

412

whipping around their ankles in the stiff wind. The torches set in the walls at intersections flared and streamed as the wind tore at them, casting wavering shadows that danced on the cobblestones of the streets.

The keeper of the first tavern they tried appeared to be his own best customer, and he had absolutely no idea of what time of day he normally opened his doors for business – or even what time of day it was now. The second tavern keeper was an unfriendly sort who spoke only in grunts. The third, however, proved to be a garrulous old fellow with a great fondness for conversation. 'Well, now,' he said, scratching at his head. 'Lessee iff'n I kin call it t' mind. The last three days, y' say?'

'About that, yes,' Kurik told him. 'Our friend said he'd meet us here, but we got delayed, and it looks as if he went on without us.'

'Kin ye describe him agin?'

'Fairly large man. He might have been wearing armour, but I couldn't swear to that. If his head was uncovered, you'd have noticed him. He's got white hair.'

'Can't seem t' recollect nobody like that. Might could be he went out one t' other gates.'

'That's possible, I suppose, but we're fairly sure he was going east. Maybe he left town before you opened for business.'

'Now that's hardly likely. I opens 'at door there when the watch opens the gate. Some of the fellers as works here in town lives on farms out yonder, an' I usually gets some fairly brisk trade of a mornin'. Would yer friend a-bin travellin' alone?'

'No,' Kurik replied. 'He had a Churchman with him, and a lady of aristocratic background. There'd also have been a slack-jawed young fellow who looks about as stupid as a stump, and a big, burly man with a face like a gorilla.'

'Oh, 'at bunch. You shoulda tole me 'bout ape-face right

413

off. They rode thoo here 'bout daylight yestiddy mornin'. 'At 'ere gorilla ye was talkin' about, he clumb down off'n his horse an' he come in here bellerin' fer ale. He don't talk none too good, does he?'

'It usually takes him about half a day to think up an answer when somebody says hello to him.'

The tavern keeper cackled shrilly. ''At's him, all right. He don't smell none too sweet neither, does he?'

Kurik grinned at him and spun a coin across the counter to him. 'Oh, I don't know,' he said. 'He isn't *too* much worse than an open cesspool. Thank you for the information, my friend.'

'Y' think ye'll be able t' ketch up with 'em?'

'Oh, we'll catch them all right,' Kurik replied fervently, 'sooner or later. Were there any others with them?'

'No. Jist 'em five. 'Ceptin' fer the gorilla, they all had ther cloaks pulled up 'round ther heads. 'At's probably how come I couldn't see the one with the white hair. They was movin' along at a purty good clip, though, so's iff'n ye wants t' ketch 'em, yer gonna have t' push yer horses some.'

'We can do that, my friend. Thanks again.' And Kurik and Sparhawk went back out into the street. 'Was that more or less what you needed to know, My Lord?' Kurik asked.

'That old fellow was a gold-mine, Kurik. We've gained a bit of time on Martel, we know that he doesn't have any troops with him, and we know that he's going towards Motera.'

'We know something else too, Sparhawk.'

'Oh? What's that?'

'Adus still needs a bath.'

Sparhawk laughed. 'Adus always needs a bath. We'll probably have to pour about a hogshead of water on him before we bury him. Otherwise, the ground might

414

just spit him back out again. Let's go on back to the inn.'

When Sparhawk and Kurik re-entered the low-beamed common room of the inn, however, they found that their party had expanded slightly. Talen sat all innocent-eyed at the table with a number of hard stares focused on him.

Chapter 21

'I'm a royal messenger,' the boy said quickly as Sparhawk and Kurik approached the table, 'so don't start reaching for your belts, either of you.'

'You're a royal *what*?' Sparhawk asked him.

'I'm carrying a message to you from the queen, Sparhawk.'

'Let's see the message.'

'I committed it to memory. We really wouldn't want messages like that falling into unfriendly hands, would we?'

'All right. Let's hear it then.'

'It's sort of private, Sparhawk.'

'That's all right. We're among friends.'

'I can't see why you're behaving this way. I'm just obeying the queen's command, that's all.'

'The message, Talen.'

'Well, she's getting ready to leave for Cimmura.'

'That's nice.' Sparhawk's tone was flat.

'And she's very worried about you.'

'I'm touched.'

'She's feeling well, though.' The additions Talen was tacking on were growing more and more lame.

'That's good to know.'

'She – um – she says that she loves you.'

'And?'

'Well – that's all, really.'

'It's a strangely garbled message, Talen. I think maybe you've left something out. Why don't you go over it again?'

'Well – um – she was talking to Mirtai and Platime – and me, of course – and she said that she wished there was some way she could get word to you to let you know what she was doing and exactly how she felt.'

'She said this to you?'

'Well – I was in the room when she said it.'

'Then we can't really say that she ordered you to come here, can we?'

'Well – not in so many words, I suppose, but aren't we supposed to sort of anticipate her wishes? She *is* the queen, after all.'

'May I?' Sephrenia asked.

'Of course,' Sparhawk replied. 'I've already found out what *I* want to know.'

'Maybe,' she said, 'maybe not.' She turned to the boy. 'Talen?'

'Yes, Sephrenia?'

'That's the weakest, most clumsy and obviously false story I've ever heard from you. It doesn't even make any sense, particularly in view of the fact that she's already sent Stragen to do more or less the same thing. Is that really the best you could come up with?'

He even managed to look embarrassed. 'It's not a lie,' he said. 'The queen said exactly what I told you she did.'

'I'm sure she did, but what was it that moved you to come galloping after us to repeat some idle comments?'

He looked a little confused.

'Oh, dear,' Sephrenia sighed. She began to scold Aphrael in Styric at some length.

'I think I missed something there.' Kalten sounded baffled.

'I'll explain in a moment, Kalten,' Sephrenia said. 'Talen, you have an enormous gift for spontaneous prevarication. What happened to it? Why didn't you just cook up a lie that was at least a little bit plausible?'

He squirmed a bit. 'It just wouldn't have seemed right,' he said sullenly.

'You felt that you shouldn't really lie to your friends, is that it?'

'Something like that, I guess.'

'Praise God!' Bevier said in stunned fervour.

'Don't be too quick to start offering up prayers of thanksgiving, Bevier,' she told him. 'Talen's apparent conversion isn't entirely what it seems to be. Aphrael's involved in it, and she's a terrible liar. Her convictions keep getting in the way.'

'Flute?' Kurik said. 'Again? Why would she send Talen here to join us?'

'Who knows?' Sephrenia laughed. 'Maybe she likes him. Maybe it's part of her obsession with symmetry. Maybe it's something else – something she wants him to do.'

'Then it wasn't really my fault, was it?' Talen said quickly.

'Probably not.' She smiled at him.

'That makes me feel better,' he said. 'I knew you wouldn't like it if I came after you, and I almost choked on all that truth. You should have spanked her when you had the chance, Sparhawk.'

'Do you have any idea at all of what they're talking about?' Stragen asked Tynian.

'Oh, yes,' Tynian replied. 'I'll explain it to you someday. You won't believe me, but I'll explain it anyway.'

'Did you find out anything about Martel?' Kalten asked Sparhawk.

'He rode out through the east gate early yesterday morning.'

'We've gained a day on him then. Did he have any troops with him?'

'Only Adus,' Kurik replied.

'I think it's time for you to tell them everything, Sparhawk,' Sephrenia said gravely.

'You're probably right,' he agreed. He drew in a deep breath. 'I'm afraid I haven't been entirely honest with you, my friends,' he admitted.

'What's new and different about that?' Kalten asked.

Sparhawk ignored him. 'I've been followed ever since I left Ghwerig's cave up in Thalesia.'

'That crossbowman?' Ulath suggested.

'He might have been involved, but we can't really be sure. The crossbowman – and the people he had working for him – was probably something Martel came up with. I can't be sure if it's still a problem or not. The one who was responsible is dead now.'

'Who was it?' Tynian asked intently.

'That's not particularly important.' Sparhawk had decided some time ago to keep Perraine's involvement an absolute secret. 'Martel has ways to force people to do what he tells them to do. That's one of the reasons we had to get away from the main body of the army. We wouldn't have been very effective if we'd had to spend most of our time trying to guard our backs from the attacks of people we could supposedly trust.'

'Who was following you if it wasn't the crossbowman?' Ulath persisted.

Sparhawk told them about the shadowy form that had haunted him for months now.

'And you think it's Azash?' Tynian asked him.

'It sort of fits together, wouldn't you say?'

'How would Azash have known where Ghwerig's cave was?' Sir Bevier asked. 'If that shadow's been following you since you left the cave, Azash would almost have to have known, wouldn't he?'

'Ghwerig was saying some fairly insulting things to Azash before Sparhawk killed him,' Sephrenia told them.

'There was a certain amount of evidence that Azash could hear him.'

'What sort of insults?' Ulath asked curiously.

'Ghwerig was threatening to cook Azash and eat him,' Kurik said shortly.

'That's a little daring – even for a Troll,' Stragen noted.

'I'm not so sure,' Ulath disagreed. 'I think Ghwerig was totally safe in that cave of his – at least safe from Azash. He didn't have too much to protect him from Sparhawk as it turned out, though.'

'Would one of you like to clarify that a bit?' Tynian asked him. 'You Thalesians are the experts on Trolls.'

'I'm not sure how much light we can throw on it,' Stragen said. 'We know a *little* bit more about Trolls than other Elenes, but not very much.' He laughed. 'When our ancestors first came to Thalesia, they couldn't tell Trolls from Ogres or bears. The Styrics told us most of what we know. It seems that when the Styrics first came to Thalesia, there were a few confrontations between the Younger Styric Gods and the Troll-Gods. The Troll-Gods realized fairly early on that they were badly overmatched, and they went into hiding. The legends say that Ghwerig and Bhelliom and the rings were sort of involved in hiding them. It's generally believed that they're somewhere in Ghwerig's cave and that Bhelliom's somehow protecting them from the Styric Gods.' He looked at Ulath. 'Wasn't that sort of what you were getting at?' he asked.

Ulath nodded. 'When you combine Bhelliom and the Troll-Gods, you're talking about enough power to make even Azash step around it a little carefully. That's probably why Ghwerig could make the kind of threats he did.'

'How many Troll-Gods are there?' Kalten asked.

'Five, aren't there, Ulath?' Stragen said.

Ulath nodded. 'The God of Eat,' he supplied, 'the God

420

of Kill, the God of –' He broke off and gave Sephrenia a slightly embarrassed look. 'Um – let's just call it the God of Fertility,' he continued lamely. 'Then there's the God of Ice – all kinds of weather, I suppose – and the God of Fire. Trolls have a fairly simple view of the world.'

'Then Azash *would* have known about it when Sparhawk came out of the cave with Bhelliom and the rings,' Tynian said, 'and He probably would have followed.'

'With unfriendly intentions,' Talen added.

'He's done it before,' Kurik shrugged. 'He sent the Damork to chase Sparhawk all over Rendor and the Seeker to try to run us down in Lamorkand. At least He's predictable.'

Bevier was frowning. 'I think we're overlooking something here,' he said.

'Such as?' Kalten asked.

'I can't quite put my finger on it,' Bevier admitted, 'but I get the feeling that it's fairly important.'

They left Kadach at dawn the following morning and rode eastward towards the city of Motera under skies that continued grey and cloudy. The murky sky, coupled with their conversation of the previous evening, made them all gloomy and downcast, and they rode mostly in silence. About noon, Sephrenia suggested a halt. 'Gentlemen,' she said quite firmly, 'this isn't a funeral procession, you know.'

'You could be wrong there, little mother,' Kalten said to her. 'I didn't find much to lift my spirits in last night's discussion.'

'I think we'd all better start looking for cheerful things to think about,' she told them. 'We're riding into some fairly serious danger. Let's not make it worse by piling gloom and depression on top of it. People who *think* they're going to lose usually do.'

'There's a lot of truth there,' Ulath agreed. 'One of my brother knights at Heid is absolutely convinced that every set of dice in the world hates him. I've never seen him win – not even once.'

'If he's been playing with *your* dice, I can see why,' Kalten accused.

'I'm hurt,' Ulath said plaintively.

'Enough to throw those dice away?'

'Well, no, not quite *that* much. We really ought to come up with something cheerful to talk about, though.'

'We could find some wayside tavern and get drunk, I suppose,' Kalten said hopefully.

'No,' Ulath shook his head. 'I've found that ale just makes a bad mood worse. After four or five hours of drinking, we'd probably all be crying into our tankards.'

'We could sing hymns,' Bevier suggested brightly.

Kalten and Tynian exchanged a long look, and then they both sighed.

'Did I ever tell you about the time when I was down in Cammoria and this lady of high station became enamoured of me?' Tynian began.

'Not that I recall,' Kalten replied rather quickly.

'Well, as I remember it –' Tynian began, and then told them a long, amusing and just slightly off-colour account of what was probably an entirely fictitious amorous adventure. Ulath followed by telling them the story of the unfortunate Genidian Knight who had aroused a passion in the heart of an Ogress. His description of the singing of the love-stricken female reduced them all to helpless laughter. The stories, richly embellished with detail and humour, lightened their mood, and they all felt much better by sunset when they halted for the day.

Even with frequent changes of horses, it took them twelve days to reach Motera, an unlovely town lying on a flat, marshy plain extending out from the west fork of the River Geros. They reached the city about midday. Sparhawk and Kurik once again sought out information while the rest of the party rested their horses in preparation for the ride northward towards Paler. Since they still had a number of hours of daylight left, they saw no reason to spend the night in Motera.

'Well?' Kalten asked Sparhawk as the big Pandion and his squire rejoined the group.

'Martel went north,' Sparhawk answered.

'We're still right behind him then,' Tynian said. 'Did we pick up any more time?'

'No,' Kurik replied. 'He's still two days ahead of us.'

'Well,' Tynian shrugged, 'since we're going that way anyhow –'

'How far is it to Paler?' Stragen asked.

'A hundred and fifty leagues,' Kalten told him. 'Fifteen days at least.'

'We're moving on in the season,' Kurik said. 'We're bound to run into snow in the mountains of Zemoch.'

'That's a cheery thought,' Kalten said.

'It's always good to know what to expect.'

The sky continued gloomy, though the air was cool and dry. About midway through their journey, they began to encounter the extensive diggings that had turned the ancient battlefield at Lake Randera into a wasteland. They saw a few of the treasure-hunters, but passed them without incident.

Perhaps something had changed it, or perhaps it was because he was out of doors instead of in some candlelit room, but *this* time when Sparhawk caught that faint glimmer of darkness and menacing shadow at the very corner of his vision, something was actually there. It was late in the afternoon of a depressing day which they had spent riding through a landscape denuded of all vegetation and littered with great mounds of raw, dug-over earth. When

Sparhawk caught that familiar flicker and its accompanying chill, he half-turned in his saddle and looked squarely at the shadow which had haunted him for so long. He reined Faran in. 'Sephrenia,' he said quite calmly.

'Yes?'

'You wanted to see it. I think that if you turn around rather slowly, you'll be able to look as much as you want. It's just beyond that large pond of muddy water.'

She turned to look.

'Can you see it?' he asked her.

'Quite clearly, dear one.'

'Gentlemen,' Sparhawk said to the others then, 'our shadowy friend seems to have come out of hiding. It's about a hundred and fifty yards behind us.'

They turned to look.

'It's almost like a cloud of some kind, isn't it?' Kalten noted.

'I've never seen a cloud like *that* before,' Talen shuddered. 'Dark, isn't it?'

'Why do you suppose it decided not to hide any more?' Ulath murmured.

They all turned, looking to Sephrenia for some kind of explanation.

'Don't ask *me*, gentlemen,' she said helplessly. 'Something has changed, though.'

'Well, at least we know that Sparhawk hasn't just been seeing things for all this time,' Kalten said. 'What do we do about it?'

'What *can* we do about it?' Ulath asked him. 'You don't have much luck fighting with clouds and shadows with axes or swords.'

'So? What do you suggest then?'

'Ignore it,' Ulath shrugged. 'It's the king's highway, so it's not breaking any laws if it wants to follow along, I guess.'

The next morning, however, the cloud was nowhere to be seen.

It was late in the autumn when they once again rode into the familiar city of Paler. As had become their custom, the Domi and his men camped outside the city walls, and Sparhawk and the others rode on to the same inn where they had stayed before.

'It's good to see you again, Sir Knight,' the innkeeper greeted Sparhawk as the black-armoured Pandion came back down the stairs.

'It's good to be back,' Sparhawk replied, not really meaning it. 'How far is it to the east gate from here?' he asked. It was time to start asking questions about Martel again.

'About three streets over, My Lord,' the innkeeper replied.

'It's closer than I thought.' Then something occurred to Sparhawk. 'I was just about to go out to ask around about a friend of mine who passed through Paler two days ago,' he said. 'You might be able to save me some time, neighbour.'

'I'll do what I can, Sir Knight.'

'He has white hair, and there's a fairly attractive lady with him, as well as a few others. It is possible that he stopped here in your inn?'

'Why, yes, My Lord. As a matter of fact, he did. They were asking questions about the road to Vileta – although I can't for the life of me think why anyone in his right mind would want to go into Zemoch at this particular time.'

'He has something he wants to take care of there, and he's always been a rash and foolhardy man. Was I right? Was it two days ago when he stopped?'

'Exactly two days, My Lord. He's riding hard, judging from the condition of his horses.'

'Do you happen to remember which room was his?'

425

'It's the one the lady with your party's staying in, My Lord.'

'Thank you, neighbour,' Sparhawk told him. 'We certainly wouldn't want our friend to get away from us.'

'Your friend was nice enough, but I certainly didn't care much for that big one who's with him. Does he improve at all once you get to know him?'

'Not noticeably, no. Thanks again, friend.' Sparhawk went back upstairs and rapped on Sephrenia's door.

'Come in, Sparhawk,' she replied.

'I wish you wouldn't do that,' he said as he entered.

'Do what?'

'Call me by name before you've even seen me. Couldn't you at least pretend that you don't know who's knocking at your door?'

She laughed.

'Martel went through here two days ago, Sephrenia. He stayed in this very room. Could that in any way be useful to us?'

She thought about it a moment. 'It may just be, Sparhawk. What sort of thing did you have in mind?'

'I'd sort of like to find out what his plans are. He knows we're right on his heels, and he's likely to try to delay us. I'd like to get a few specifics on any traps he may be laying for us. Can you arrange to let me see him? Or hear him at least?'

She shook her head. 'He's too far away.'

'Well, so much for that idea.'

'Perhaps not.' She thought for a moment. 'I think that perhaps it's time for you to get to know Bhelliom a little better, Sparhawk.'

'Would you like to clarify that?'

'There's some sort of connection between Bhelliom and the Troll-Gods and the rings. Let's investigate that.'

'Why involve the Troll-Gods at all, Sephrenia? If there's

a way to use Bhelliom, why not just do that and leave the Troll-Gods out of it altogether?'

'I'm not sure if Bhelliom would understand us, Sparhawk; and if it did, I'm not sure that *we'd* understand what it was doing to obey us.'

'It collapsed that cave, didn't it?'

'That was very simple. This is a little more complicated. The Troll-Gods would be much easier to talk with, I think, and I want to find out just how closely Bhelliom's linked to them if I can – and just how much you can control them by using Bhelliom.'

'You want to experiment, in other words.'

'You might put it that way, I suppose, but it might be safer to experiment now, when there's nothing crucial at stake, than later, when our lives might hinge on the outcome. Lock the door, Sparhawk. Let's not expose the others to this just yet.'

He crossed to the door and slid the iron bolt into place.

'You're not going to have time to think when you talk with the Troll-Gods, dear one, so get everything set in your mind before you start. You're going to issue commands and nothing else. Don't ask them questions, and don't seek out explanations. Just tell them to do things and don't worry about how they manage to obey. We want to see and hear the man who was in this room two sleeps ago. Just tell them to put his image –' she looked around the room, then pointed at the hearth, '– in that fire there. Tell Bhelliom that you *will* talk with one of the Troll-Gods – probably Khwaj, the Troll-God of fire. He's the most logical one to deal with flame and smoke.' Sephrenia obviously knew a great deal more about the Troll-Gods than she had told them.

'Khwaj,' Sparhawk repeated. Then he had a sudden

427

idea. 'What's the name of the Troll-God of eat?' he asked her.

'Ghnomb,' she replied. 'Why?'

'It's something I'm still working on. If I can put it together, I might try it and see if it works.'

'Don't extemporize, Sparhawk. You know how I feel about surprises. Take off your gauntlets, and remove Bhelliom from the pouch. Don't let it out of your grasp, and be sure that the rings are touching it at all times. Do you still remember the Troll language?'

'Yes. Ulath and I have been practising.'

'Good. You can speak to Bhelliom in Elene, but you'll have to speak to Khwaj in His own tongue. Tell me what you did today – in Troll.'

The words were halting at first, but after a few moments he became more fluent. The changeover from the Elene language to Troll involved a profound shift in his thinking. In their language itself lay some of the character of the Trolls. It was not a pleasant character, and it involved concepts entirely alien to the Elene mind – except at the deepest, most primitive level.

'All right,' she told him, 'come to the fire, and let's begin. Be like iron, Sparhawk. Don't hesitate or explain anything. Just give commands.'

He nodded and removed his gauntlets. The two blood-red rings, one on each of his hands, glowed in the firelight. He reached inside his surcoat and took out the pouch. Then he and his tutor stood before the hearth and looked into the crackling flames. 'Open the pouch,' Sephrenia instructed.

He worked the knots free.

'Now, take Bhelliom out. Order it to bring Khwaj to you. Then tell Khwaj what you want. You don't have to be too explicit. Khwaj will understand your thoughts. Pray that you never understand His.'

He drew in a deep breath and set the pouch down on the hearth. 'Here goes,' he said. He pulled the pouch open and took the Bhelliom out. The Sapphire Rose was icy cold as he touched it. He lifted it, trying to keep his sense of awe at the sight of it far away from his mind. 'Blue-Rose!' he snapped, holding the jewel in both hands. 'Bring the voice of Khwaj to me!'

He felt a strange shift in the jewel, and a single spot of bright red appeared deep within the azure petals. The Bhelliom suddenly grew hot in his hands.

'Khwaj!' Sparhawk barked in the language of Trolls, 'I am Sparhawk-from-Elenia. I have the rings. Khwaj must do as I command.'

Bhelliom shuddered in his hand.

'I seek Martel-from-Elenia,' Sparhawk continued. 'Martel-from-Elenia stayed in this place two sleeps ago. Khwaj *will* show Sparhawk-from-Elenia what he wishes to see in the fire. Khwaj *will* make it so Sparhawk-from-Elenia can hear what he wishes to hear. Khwaj *will* obey! *Now!*'

Faintly, as from very far away in some hollow place filled with echoes, there came a howl of rage, a howl overlaid with a crackling sound as of some huge fire. The flames dancing along the tops of the oak logs in the fireplace lowered until they were little more than a sickly glimmering. Then they rose, bright yellow and filling the entire opening with a sheet of nearly incandescent fire. Then they froze, no longer a flickering or a dancing but simply a flat, unwavering sheet of motionless yellow. The heat from the fireplace stopped at once as if a pane of thick glass had been set in front of it.

Sparhawk found himself looking into a tent. Martel, drawn and weary-looking, sat at a rough table across from Annias, who looked even worse.

'*Why* can't you find out where they are?' the Primate of Cimmura was demanding.

'I don't know, Annias,' Martel grated. 'I've called up every creature Otha gave me, and none of them has found anything.'

'Oh, mighty Pandion,' Annias sneered. 'Maybe you should have stayed in your order longer to give Sephrenia time to teach you more than parlour tricks for the amusement of children.'

'You're getting very close to the point of outliving your usefulness to me, Annias,' Martel said ominously. 'Otha and I can put *any* Churchman on the Archprelate's throne and achieve what we want. You're not really indispensable, you know.' And that answered the question of just *who* was taking orders from *whom* once and for all.

The tent-flap opened, and the ape-like Adus slouched in. His armour was a mismatched accumulation of bits and pieces of rust-splotched steel drawn from a half-dozen different cultures. Adus, Sparhawk noticed again, had no forehead. His hairline began at his shaggy eyebrows. 'It died,' he reported in a voice that was half-snarl.

'I should make you walk, you idiot,' Martel told him.

'It was a weak horse,' Adus shrugged.

'It was perfectly fine until you spurred it to death. Go and steal another one.'

Adus grinned. 'A farm horse?'

'Any kind of horse you can find. Don't take all night killing the farmer, though – or amusing yourself with his women. And don't burn the farmstead down. Let's not light up the sky and announce our location.'

Adus laughed – at least it *sounded* sort of like a laugh. Then he left the tent.

'How can you stand that brute?' Annias shuddered.

'Adus? He's not so bad. Think of him as a walking battle-axe. I use him for killing people; I don't sleep with him. Speaking of that, have you and Arissa resolved your differences yet?'

430

'That harlot!' Annias said with a certain contempt.

'You knew what she was when you took up with her, Annias,' Martel told him. 'I thought her depravity was part of what attracted you to her.' Martel leaned back. 'It must be Bhelliom,' he mused.

'What must?'

'It's probably the Bhelliom that's keeping my creatures from locating Sparhawk.'

'Wouldn't Azash Himself be able to find out?'

'I don't give orders to Azash, Annias. If He wants me to know something, He tells me. It could just be that Bhelliom's more powerful than He is. When we get to His temple, you can ask Him, if you're really curious about it. The question might offend Him, but it's entirely up to you.'

'How far have we come today?'

'No more than seven leagues. Our pace slowed notice-ably after Adus ripped out his horse's guts with his spurs.'

'How far to the Zemoch border?'

Martel unrolled a map and consulted it. 'I make it about fifty more leagues – five days or so. Sparhawk can't be more than three days behind us, so we'll have to keep up the pace.'

'I'm exhausted, Martel. I can't keep on going like this.'

'Every time you start brooding about how tired you are, just imagine how it would feel to have Sparhawk's sword sliding through your guts – or how exquisitely painful it's going to be when Ehlana beheads you with a pair of sewing scissors – or a bread-knife.'

'Sometimes I wish I'd never met you, Martel.'

'The feeling's entirely mutual, old boy. Once we cross the border into Zemoch, we should be able to slow Sparhawk down a bit. A few ambushes along the way ought to make him a bit more cautious.'

431

'We were ordered not to kill him,' Annias objected.

'Don't be an idiot. As long as he has Bhelliom, no human could possibly kill him. We were ordered not to kill *him* – even if we could – but Azash didn't say anything about the others. The loss of a few of his companions might upset our invincible enemy. He doesn't look very much like it, but Sparhawk's a sentimentalist at heart. You'd better go and get some sleep. We'll start out again just as soon as Adus gets back.'

'In the dark?' Annias sounded incredulous.

'What's the matter, Annias? Are you afraid of the dark? Think about swords in the belly or the sound of a bread-knife sawing on your neck bone. That should make you brave.'

'Khwaj!' Sparhawk said sharply. 'Enough! Go away now!'

The fire returned to normal.

'Blue-Rose!' Sparhawk said then. 'Bring the voice of Ghnomb to me!'

'What are you *doing*?' Sephrenia exclaimed, but Bhelliom had already started to respond. The pinpoint of light within the glowing blue petals was a sickly mixture of green and yellow, and Sparhawk suddenly had a foul taste in his mouth, a taste much like the smell of half-decayed meat.

'Ghnomb!' Sparhawk said in that harsh voice. 'I am Sparhawk-from-Elenia, and I have the rings. Ghnomb must do as I command. I hunt. Ghnomb will help me hunt. I am two sleeps behind the man-thing which is my prey. Ghnomb will make it so that my hunters and I can catch the man-thing we seek. Sparhawk-from-Elenia will tell Ghnomb when, and Ghnomb will aid our hunt. Ghnomb *will* obey!'

Again there was that hollow, echoing howl of rage, a howl filled this time with a slobbering gnawing sound and a horrid, wet smacking of lips.

432

'Ghnomb! Go away now!' Sparhawk commanded. 'Ghnomb *will* come again at Sparhawk-from-Elenia's command!'

The greenish-yellow spot vanished, and Sparhawk thrust the Bhelliom back into the pouch.

'Are you *mad*?' Sephrenia exclaimed.

'No, I don't think so. I want to be so close behind Martel that he won't have time to set up any ambushes.' He frowned. 'It's beginning to look as if the attempts to kill me really *were* Martel's own idea,' he said. 'He seems to have different orders now. That clarifies things a bit, but now I have to start worrying about how to protect you and the others.' He made a face. 'There's always *something*, isn't there?'

Chapter 22

'Sparhawk.' It was Kurik, and he was shaking his Lord into wakefulness. 'It's about an hour before dawn. You wanted me to wake you.'

'Don't you ever sleep?' Sparhawk sat up in his bed, yawning. Then he swung his legs out of bed and put his feet on the floor.

'I slept fine.' Kurik looked critically at his friend. 'You're not eating enough,' he accused. 'Your bones are sticking out. Get dressed. I'll go and wake the others, and then I'll come back and help you into your armour.'

Sparhawk rose and pulled on his quilted and rust-splotched undergarments.

'Very chic,' Stragen observed sardonically from the doorway. 'Is there some obscure part of the knightly code that prohibits laundering those garments?'

'They take a week to dry.'

'Are they really necessary?'

'Have you ever worn armour, Stragen?'

'God forbid.'

'Try it sometime. The padding keeps the armour from grinding off your skin in unusual places.'

'Ah, the things we endure in order to be stylish.'

'Are you really planning to turn back at the Zemoch border?'

'The queen's orders, old boy. Besides, I'd just be in your way. I'm profoundly unsuited to confront a God. Frankly, I think you're insane – no offence intended, of course.'

'Are you going back to Emsat from Cimmura?'

'If your wife gives me permission to leave. I really

should get back – if only to check over the books. Tel's fairly dependable, but he *is* a thief, after all.'

'And then?'

'Who knows?' Stragen shrugged. 'I'm at loose ends in the world, Sparhawk. I have a unique sort of freedom. I don't have to do anything I don't want to do. Oh, I almost forgot. I didn't really come by this morning to discuss the ins and outs of liberty with you.' He reached inside his doublet. 'A letter for you, My Lord,' he said with a mocking bow. 'From your wife, I believe.'

'How many of those do you have?' Sparhawk asked, taking the folded sheet. Stragen had delivered one of Ehlana's brief, impassioned notes to her husband in Kadach and yet another in Motera.

'That's a state secret, my friend.'

'Do you have some sort of agenda? Or are you distributing them when the spirit moves you?'

'A little of each, old boy. There *is* an agenda, of course, but I'm to use my own judgement in these matters. If I see that you're becoming downcast or moody, I'm supposed to brighten your day. I'll leave you to your reading now.' He stepped back out into the hallway and moved off down the corridor towards the stairs leading to the lower floor of the inn.

Sparhawk broke the seal and opened Ehlana's letter.

'Beloved,' it began. 'If all has gone well, you're in Paler by now – this is terribly awkward, you know. I'm trying to look into the future, and my eyes aren't strong enough for that. I'm talking to you from weeks and weeks in the past, and I haven't the faintest idea of what's been happening to you. I dare not tell you of my anguish or my desolation at this unnatural separation, for should I unburden my heart to you, I would weaken your resolve, and that could endanger you. I love you, my Sparhawk, and I am torn between wishing that I were a man so that I

435

could share your danger and, if need be, lay down my life for you, and glorying in the fact that I am a woman and can lose myself in your embrace.' From there Sparhawk's young queen launched into detailed reminiscence of their wedding night which was far too personal and private to bear repeating.

'How was the queen's letter?' Stragen asked as they were saddling their horses in the courtyard while the emerging dawn laid a dirty stain across the cloudy eastern horizon.

'Literate,' Sparhawk replied laconically.

'That's an unusual characterization.'

'Sometimes we lose sight of the real person lying behind the state robes, Stragen. Ehlana's a queen, right enough, but she's also an eighteen-year-old girl who seems to have read too many of the wrong books.'

'I'd hardly have expected such a clinical description from a new bridegroom.'

'I have a lot on my mind just now.' Sparhawk pulled the cinch of his saddle tighter. Faran grunted, filled his belly with air and deliberately stepped on his master's foot. Almost absently, the Pandion kneed his mount in the stomach. 'Keep your eyes open today, Stragen,' he advised. 'Some peculiar things are likely to happen.'

'Such as what?'

'I'm not really sure. If everything goes well, we'll cover a great deal more ground today than usual. Stay with the Domi and his Peloi. They're an emotional people, and out of the ordinary things sometimes upset them. Just keep assuring them that everything's under control.'

'Is it?'

'I haven't got the foggiest idea, old boy. I'm trying very hard to be optimistic about it, however.' Stragen, he felt, sort of had that coming.

The dawn came slowly that morning, since the cloud-cover rolling in from the east had thickened during the night. At the top of the long slope leading up from the northern end of the lead-grey sheet of Lake Randera, Kring and his Peloi joined them. 'It's good to be back in Pelosia again, friend Sparhawk,' Kring said, a good-humoured grin on his scarred face, 'even in this cluttered and over-ploughed part of the kingdom.'

'How many days to the Zemoch border, Domi?' Tynian asked.

'Five or six, friend Tynian,' the Domi replied.

'We'll start out in just a few moments,' Sparhawk told his friends. 'There's something Sephrenia and I have to do.' He motioned to his tutor and they rode some distance away from the group sitting their horses on the grassy hilltop. 'Well?' he said to her.

'Must you really do this, dear one?' she pleaded.

'I think so, yes. It's the only way I can think of to protect you and the others from ambushes when we reach the Zemoch border.' He reached inside his surcoat, removed the pouch and took off his gauntlets. Once again the Bhelliom felt very cold in his hands, a chill almost like the touch of ice. 'Blue-Rose!' he commanded, 'bring the voice of Ghnomb to me!'

The jewel sullenly warmed in his hands. Then the greenish-yellow spot appeared within its depths, accompanied by the rotten-meat taste in Sparhawk's mouth. 'Ghnomb!' he said, 'I am Sparhawk-from-Elenia, and I have the rings. I hunt now. Ghnomb *will* aid my hunting as I commanded. Ghnomb *will* do it! *Now!*'

He waited tensely, but nothing happened. He sighed. 'Ghnomb!' he said. 'Go away now!' He put the Sapphire Rose back into its pouch, knotted the strings and thrust the pouch back inside his surcoat. 'Well,' he said ruefully, 'so much for that. You said He'd let me know if He couldn't help. He just let me know, all right. It's a little awkward to find out about it at this stage of the proceedings, though.'

'Don't give up just yet, Sparhawk,' Sephrenia told him.

'Nothing happened, little mother.'

'Don't be too sure.'

'Well, let's go on back. It seems we're going to have to do this the hard way.'

The party rode out at a brisk trot, moving down the far side of the hill with the pale disc of the new-risen sun hanging behind the clouds on the eastern horizon. The farmland lying to the east of Paler was in the last stages of the harvest, and serfs were already in the fields, small figures in dun or blue looking like immobile toys far back from the road.

'Serfdom doesn't seem to encourage much enthusiasm for work,' Kurik observed critically. 'Those people out there don't seem to be moving at all.'

'If I were a serf, I don't think I'd be very interested in exerting myself either,' Kalten said.

They rode on at a canter, crossed a wide valley and climbed a low chain of hills. The clouds were a bit thinner here to the east, and the sun, just above the horizon, was more distinct. Kring sent out his patrols, and they rode on.

Something was wrong, but Sparhawk could not exactly put his finger on what it was. The air was very still, and the sound of the horses' hooves seemed quite loud and unnaturally crisp in the soft dirt of the road. Sparhawk looked around and saw that his friends' expressions seemed uneasy.

They were halfway across the next valley when Kurik reined in with a sudden oath. '*That* does it,' he said.

'What's the matter?' Sparhawk asked him.

'How long would you say we've been on the road?'

'An hour or so. Why?'

'Look at the sun, Sparhawk.'

Sparhawk looked at the eastern horizon where the almost obscured disc of the sun hung just over a gently rounded line of hills. 'It seems to be where it always is, Kurik,' he said. 'Nobody's moved it.'

'That's just the point, Sparhawk. It's *not* moving. It hasn't moved an inch since we started. It came up, and then it stopped.'

They all stared towards the east.

'It's fairly common, Kurik,' Tynian said. 'We've been riding up and down hills. That always seems to put the sun in a different position. Where it seems to be depends on how high up – or down – the hill you are.'

'I thought so myself, Sir Tynian – at first – but I'll swear to you that the sun hasn't moved since we left that hilltop to the east of Paler.'

'Be serious, Kurik,' Kalten scoffed. 'The sun *has* to move.'

'Not *this* morning apparently. What's going on here?'

'Sir Sparhawk!' Berit's voice was shrill, hovering just on the edge of hysteria. 'Look!'

Sparhawk turned his head in the direction the apprentice knight was pointing a shaking hand.

It was a bird – a completely ordinary-looking bird, a lark of some kind, Sparhawk judged. Nothing at all was unusual about it – if one were to overlook the fact that it hung absolutely motionless in mid-air, looking for all the world as if it had been stuck there with a pin.

They all looked around, their eyes a little wild. Then Sephrenia began to laugh.

'I don't really see anything funny about this, Sephrenia,' Kurik told her.

'Everything's fine, gentlemen,' she told them.

'*Fine?*' Tynian said. 'What's happened to the sun? – and that idiotic bird?'

'Sparhawk stopped the sun – and the bird.'

439

'*Stopped the sun!*' Bevier exclaimed. 'That's impossible!'

'Apparently not. Sparhawk talked with one of the Troll-Gods last night,' she told them. 'He said that we were hunting and that our prey was far ahead of us. He asked the Troll-God Ghnomb to help us catch up, and Ghnomb seems to be doing just that.'

'I don't follow you,' Kalten said. 'What's the sun got to do with hunting?'

'It's not all that complicated, Kalten,' she said calmly. 'Ghnomb stopped time, that's all.'

'*That's all?* How do you stop time?'

'I have no idea.' She frowned. 'Maybe "stopping time" isn't quite accurate. What's really happening is that we're moving outside time. We're in that winking of an eye between one second and the next.'

'What's keeping that bird up in the air, Lady Sephrenia?' Berit demanded.

'His last wing-beat, probably. The rest of the world is moving along quite normally. People out there aren't even aware of the fact that we're passing through. When the Gods do the things we ask them to do, they don't always do them in the way we expect. When Sparhawk told Ghnomb that he wanted to catch up to Martel, he was thinking about time more than the miles, so Ghnomb is moving us through time, not distance. He'll control time for as long as it takes us. Covering the distance is up to us.'

Then Stragen came forward at a gallop. 'Sparhawk!' he cried. 'What in God's name did you do?'

Sparhawk briefly explained. 'Just go back and calm the Peloi. Tell them that it's an enchantment. Explain that the world is frozen. Nothing will move until we get to where we want to go.'

'Is that the truth?'

'More or less, yes.'

440

'Do you actually think they'll believe me?'

'Invite them to come up with their own explanations if they don't like mine.'

'You *can* unfreeze things later, can't you?'

'Of course – at least I hope so.'

'Ah – Sephrenia?' Talen said tentatively. 'All the rest of the world is stopped dead, right?'

'Well, that's the way it appears to *us*. Nobody else perceives it that way, though.'

'Other people can't even see us then, right?'

'They won't even know we're here.'

A slow, almost reverent smile came to the boy's lips. 'Well, now,' he said. 'Well, well, well.'

Stragen's eyes also became very bright. 'Well now indeed, Your Grace,' he agreed.

'Never mind, you two,' Sephrenia said sharply.

'Stragen,' Sparhawk added as an afterthought, 'tell Kring that there's no real need to hurry. We might as well conserve the horses. Nobody out there is going to go anywhere or do anything until we get to where we want to go anyway.'

It was eerie to canter through that perpetual murky sunrise. It was neither cold nor warm nor damp nor dry. The world around them was silent, and unmoving birds dotted the air. Serfs stood like statues in the fields, and once they passed a tall white birch tree that had been brushed by a passing breeze just before the Troll-God Ghnomb had frozen time. A cloud of motionless golden leaves hung in the air to the leeward side of the tree.

'What time do you think it is?' Kalten asked after they had ridden for several leagues.

Ulath squinted at the sky. 'I make it about sunrise,' he replied.

'Oh, very, very funny, Ulath,' Kalten said sarcastically.

441

'I don't know about the rest of you, but I'm starting to get a little hungry.'

'You were born hungry,' Sparhawk told him.

They ate trail rations and moved on again. There was no real need to hurry, but the sense of urgency they had all felt since they had left Chyrellos nagged at them, and they were soon cantering. To have proceeded at a leisurely walk would have seemed unnatural.

An hour or so later – though it was really impossible to tell – Kring came up from the rear. 'I think there's something behind us, friend Sparhawk,' he said. Kring's tone had a respectful awe about it. It's not every day that one can talk with a man who stops the sun.

Sparhawk looked at him sharply. 'Are you sure?' he asked.

'Not really,' Kring admitted. 'It's a feeling more than anything. There's a very dark cloud low to the ground off to the south. It's a goodly way off, so it's hard to tell for sure, but it seems to be pacing us.'

Sparhawk looked towards the south. It was that same cloud again, larger, blacker and more ominous now. The shadow could follow him even *here*, it appeared. 'Have you seen it move at all?' he asked Kring.

'No, but we've come quite some distance since we stopped to eat, and it's still just over my right shoulder where it was when we set out.'

'Keep an eye on it,' Sparhawk said tersely. 'See if you can catch it actually moving.'

'Right,' the Domi agreed, wheeling his horse.

They set up camp for the 'night' after they had covered approximately the distance they would have gone in a normal day. The horses were confused, and Faran kept watching Sparhawk with a hard-eyed look of suspicion.

'It's not *my* fault, Faran,' Sparhawk said as he unsaddled the big roan.

'How can you lie to that poor beast like that, Sparhawk?' Kalten said from nearby. 'Have you no shame? It *is* your fault.'

Sparhawk slept poorly. The unchanging light was always there. He slept for as long as he could, and then rose. The others were also stirring.

'Good morning, Sparhawk,' Sephrenia said ironically. Her expression was a bit put out.

'What's the matter?'

'I miss my morning tea. I tried to heat some rocks in order to boil water, but it didn't work. Nothing works, Sparhawk – no spells, no magic – nothing. We're totally defenceless in this never-never land you and Ghnomb have created, you know.'

'What can attack us, little mother?' he asked gravely. 'We're outside time. We're somewhere where nothing can reach us.'

It was about 'noon' when they discovered just how wrong that particular assessment had been.

'It's moving, Sparhawk!' Talen shouted as they approached an immobile village. 'That cloud! It's moving!'

The cloud which Kring had noticed the day before was definitely moving now. It was inky-black. It rolled across the ground towards the small cluster of thatch-roofed serfs' huts huddled in a shallow dale, and a low rumble of sullen thunder, the first sound they had heard since Ghnomb had locked them in time, accompanied its inexorable march. Behind it, the trees and grasses were all dead and decaying, as if that momentary touch of darkness had blighted them in an instant. The cloud engulfed the village, and when it had passed, the village was gone as if it had never existed.

As the cloud drew nearer, Sparhawk heard a rhythmic sound, a kind of thudding as of dozens of bare heels striking the earth, and accompanying that, a brutish grunting as might come from a throng of beasts uttering low, guttural barks in evenly spaced unison.

'Sparhawk!' Sephrenia cried urgently. 'Use the Bhelliom! Break up that cloud! Call Khwaj!'

Sparhawk fumbled with the pouch, then threw his gauntlets to the ground and tore open the canvas sack with his bare hands. He lifted out the Sapphire Rose in both hands. 'Blue-Rose!' he half-shouted. 'Bring Khwaj!' The Bhelliom grew hot in his hands, and that single spark of red appeared in its petals.

'Khwaj,' Sparhawk half-shouted. 'I am Sparhawk-from-Elenia! Khwaj *will* burn away the dark which comes! Khwaj *will* make it so Sparhawk-from-Elenia can see what is inside the cloud! Do it, Khwaj! *Now!*'

Again there was that howl of frustration and rage as the Troll-God was compelled against His will to obey. Then, immediately in front of the rolling black cloud there rose a long, high sheet of roaring flame. Brighter and brighter the flame grew, and Sparhawk could feel the waves of intense heat blasting back at them from that wall of fire. The cloud advanced inexorably, seeming to ignore the wall.

'Blue-Rose!' Sparhawk snarled in the Troll tongue. 'Help Khwaj! Blue-Rose *will* send its power and the power of all the Troll-Gods to help Khwaj! Do it! *Now!*'

The answering blast of power nearly knocked Sparhawk from his saddle, and Faran reeled back, flattening his ears and baring his teeth.

Then the cloud stopped. Great rents and tears appeared in it, only to be almost instantly repaired. The flame undulated, rising then falling into sickly glimmerings, then flaring anew as the two forces contended with each other. At last the darkness of the cloud began to fade, even as night fades from the sky with the approach of dawn. The flames grew higher, more intensely bright. The cloud sickened yet more. It grew wispy and tattered.

'We're winning!' Kalten exclaimed.

'We?' Kurik said, picking up Sparhawk's gauntlets.

Then as if it had been ripped away by a gale, the cloud streamed away. Sparhawk and his friends saw what had made the grunting sound. They were immense and human-like, which is to say that they had arms and legs and heads. They were dressed in furs and carried weapons crafted of stone – axes and spears for the most part. Their humanity ended there. They had receding brows and protruding, muzzle-like mouths, and they were not so much hairy as they were furred. Although the cloud had dissipated, they continued their advance, a kind of shuffling trot. Their feet struck the ground in unison, and they barked that guttural grunt with each thudding step. They momentarily paused at regular intervals, and from somewhere in their midst there arose a high-pitched wail, a kind of shrill ululation. Then the rhythmic barking and stamping trot would begin again. They wore helmets of a sort, the skull-caps of unimaginable beasts decorated with horns, and their faces were smeared with coloured mud in intricate designs.

'Are they Trolls?' Kalten's voice was shrill.

'Not like any Trolls *I've* ever seen,' Ulath replied, reaching for his axe.

'All right, my children!' the Domi shouted to his men. 'Let us clear the beasts from our path!' He drew his sabre, held it aloft and shouted a great war-cry.

The Peloi charged.

'Kring!' Sparhawk yelled. 'Wait!'

But it was too late. Once unleashed, the savage tribesmen from the eastern marches of Pelosia could not again be reined in.

Sparhawk swore. He stuffed the Bhelliom inside his surcoat. 'Berit!' he commanded, 'take Sephrenia and Talen to the rear! The rest of you, let's lend a hand!'

It was not an organized fight in any sense of the word that civilized men would understand. After the first charge of Kring's tribesmen, everything disintegrated into a general mêlée of random savagery. The Church Knights discovered almost immediately that the grotesque creatures they faced did not seem to feel pain. It was impossible to determine if this was a natural characteristic of their species or if whatever had unleashed them had provided them with some additional defence. Beneath their shaggy fur lay a hide of unnatural toughness. This is not to say that swords bounced off them, but more often than not they did not cut cleanly. The best strokes opened only minimal wounds.

The Peloi, however, appeared to be having greater success with their sabres. The quick thrust of a sharp-pointed weapon was more effective than the massive overhand blows of heavy broadswords, and once their leathery hide had been penetrated, the savage brutes howled with pain. Stragen, his eyes alight, rode through the shaggy mass, the point of his slender rapier dancing, avoiding the clumsy strokes of stone axes, slipping the brutal thrusts of flint-tipped spears and then sinking effortlessly, almost delicately, deep into fur-covered bodies. 'Sparhawk!' he shouted. 'Their hearts are lower down in their bodies! Thrust at the belly, not the chest!'

It grew easier then. The Church Knights altered their tactics, thrusting with the points of their swords rather than chopping with the broad blades. Bevier regretfully hung his lochaber from his saddle horn and drew his sword. Kurik discarded his mace and drew his short blade. Ulath, however, stubbornly clung to his axe. His only concession to the exigencies of the situation was to use both hands to swing the weapon. His prodigious strength was sufficient to overcome such natural defences as horn-tough hide and inch-thick skulls.

446

The tide of the struggle turned then. The huge, uncomprehending beasts were unable to adjust to a changing situation, and more and more of them fell to the thrusting swords. One last small cluster continued to fight even after the majority of their pack-mates had been slain, but the lightning-like dashes of Kring's warriors whittled them away. The last one left standing was bleeding from a dozen sabre-thrusts. He raised his brutish face and shrieked that high-pitched ululation. The sound cut off abruptly as Ulath rode in, stood up in his stirrups to raise his axe high overhead and then split the wailing brute's head from crown to chin.

Sparhawk wheeled, his bloody sword in his fist, but all the creatures had fallen. He looked around more closely. Their victory had been costly. A dozen of Kring's men had been felled – not merely felled, but torn apart as well – and fully as many lay groaning on the bloody ground.

Kring sat crosslegged on the turf, cradling the head of one of his dying men. His face was filled with sorrow.

'I'm sorry, Domi,' Sparhawk said. 'Find out how many of your men are injured. We'll work out some way to have them cared for. How close would you say we are to the lands of your people?'

'A day and a half of hard riding, friend Sparhawk,' Kring replied, sadly closing the vacant eyes of the warrior who had just died. 'A bit less than twenty leagues.'

Sparhawk rode towards the rear where Berit sat on his horse with his axe in his hands guarding Talen and Sephrenia.

'Is it over?' Sephrenia asked, her eyes averted.

'Yes,' Sparhawk replied, dismounting. 'What were they, little mother? They looked like Trolls, but Ulath didn't think they really were.'

'They were dawn-men, Sparhawk. It's a very old and very difficult spell. The Gods – and a few of the most

447

powerful magicians of Styricum – can reach back into time and bring things – and creatures and men forward. The dawn-men haven't walked this earth for countless thousands of years. That's what we all were once – Elenes, Styrics, even Trolls.'

'Are you saying that humans and Trolls are related?' he asked her incredulously.

'Distantly. We've all changed over the eons. Trolls went one way, and we went another.'

'Ghnomb's frozen instant doesn't appear to be as safe as we thought it was.'

'No. Definitely not.'

'I think it's time to set the sun in motion again. We don't seem to be able to hide from whatever's chasing us by slipping through the cracks in time, and Styric magic doesn't work here. We'll be safer in ordinary time.'

'I think you're right, Sparhawk.'

Sparhawk took Bhelliom from its pouch once more and commanded Ghnomb to break the spell.

Kring's Peloi fashioned litters in which to carry their dead and wounded, and the party moved on, relieved to some degree that the birds actually flew now and that the sun was moving once again.

The next morning a roving Peloi patrol found them, and Kring rode forth to confer with his friends. His face was bleak when he returned. 'The Zemochs are setting fire to the grass,' he said angrily. 'I won't be able to help you much longer, friend Sparhawk. We have to protect our pastures, and that means we'll have to spread out all over our lands.'

Bevier looked at him speculatively. 'Wouldn't it be easier if the Zemochs all gathered in one place, Domi?' he asked.

'It would indeed, friend Bevier, but why would they do that?'

448

'To capture something of value, friend Kring.'

Kring looked interested. 'Such as what?'

'Gold,' Bevier shrugged, 'and women, and your herds.'

Kring looked shocked.

'It would be a trap, of course,' Bevier continued. 'You gather all your herds and your treasures and your womenfolk in one place with only a few of your Peloi to guard them. Then take the rest of your warriors and ride off, making sure that Zemoch scouts can see you leave. Then, once it gets dark, you slip back and take up positions nearby, keeping well out of sight. The Zemochs will all come running to steal your herds and treasures and women. Then you can fall on them all at once. That way you spare yourself all the trouble of hunting them down one by one. Besides, it would give your women a glorious opportunity to witness your bravery. I'm told that women melt with love when they have the chance to watch their menfolk destroy a hated enemy.' Bevier's grin was sly.

Kring's eyes narrowed as he thought it over. 'I like it!' he burst out after a moment. 'God strike me blind if I don't! We'll do it!' And he rode off to tell his people.

'Bevier,' Tynian said, 'sometimes you amaze me.'

'It's a fairly standard strategy for light cavalry, Tynian,' the young Cyrinic said modestly. 'I came across it in my study of military history. Lamork barons used that ploy a number of times before they started building castles.'

'I know, but you actually suggested using women for bait. I think you're just a little more worldly than you appear, my friend.'

Bevier blushed.

They followed after Kring at a somewhat slower pace, hindered by the wounded and the sorrowful line of horses carrying the dead. Kalten had a distant look on his face, and he seemed to be counting something up on his fingers.

449

'What's the trouble?' Sparhawk asked him.

'I'm trying to figure out just how much time we gained on Martel.'

'Not quite a day and a half,' Talen said promptly. 'A day and a third, actually. We're about six or seven hours behind him now. We average about a league an hour.'

'Twenty miles then,' Kalten said. 'You know, Sparhawk, if we rode all night tonight, we could be right inside his camp when the sun rises tomorrow.'

'We're not going to ride at night, Kalten. There's something very unfriendly out there, and I'd rather not have it surprise us in the dark.'

They made camp at sunset, and after they had eaten, Sparhawk and the others gathered in a large pavilion to consider their options.

'We more or less know what we're going to do,' Sparhawk began. 'Getting to the border shouldn't be any problem. Kring's going to lead his men away from his womenfolk anyway, so we'll have most of the Peloi warriors with us for at least part of the way. That's going to keep the Zemoch conventional forces at a distance, so we'll be safe from them until we reach the border. It's after we cross that line that we'll run into trouble, and the key to that is Martel. We're still going to have to push him to the point that he won't have time to gather up Zemochs to stand in our way.'

'Make up your mind, Sparhawk,' Kalten said. 'First you say we're not going to ride at night, and then you say you're going to push Martel.'

'We don't have to be actually on top of him to push him, Kalten. As long as he *thinks* we're close, he'll start running. I think I'll have a little talk with him while I've still got some daylight.' He looked around. 'I'll need about a dozen candles,' he said. 'Berit, would you mind?'

'Of course not, Sir Sparhawk.'

'Set them up on this table – close together and all in a row.' Sparhawk reached inside his surcoat and took out the Bhelliom again. He put it down on the table and laid a cloth over it to hide its seduction. When the lighted candles were in place, he uncovered the jewel and laid his ringed hands on it. 'Blue-Rose,' he commanded, 'bring Khwaj to me!'

The stone grew hot under his hands again, and the glowing red spot appeared deep within its petals. 'Khwaj!' Sparhawk said sharply. 'You know me. I will see the place where my enemy will sleep tonight. Make it appear in the fire, Khwaj! Now!'

The howl of anger was no longer a howl, but had diminished to a sullen whine. The candle flames lengthened, and their edges joined to form a solid sheet of bright yellow fire. The image appeared in the fire.

It was a small encampment, three tents only, and it lay in a grassy basin with a small lake at its centre. A grove of dark cedar trees stood across the lake from the camp, and a single camp-fire flickered in the lowering dusk at the centre of that half-circle of tents on the lake shore. Sparhawk carefully fixed the details in his mind. 'Take us closer to the fire, Khwaj!' he barked. 'Make it so that we can hear what is being said.'

The image changed as the apparent viewpoint drew nearer. Martel and the others sat around the fire, their faces gaunt with exhaustion. Sparhawk motioned to his friends, and they all leaned forward to listen.

'Where are they, Martel?' Arissa was asking acidly. 'Where are these brave Zemochs you counted on to protect us? Gathering wild flowers?'

'They're diverting the Peloi, Princess,' Martel replied. 'Do you really want those savages to catch up with us? Don't worry, Arissa. If your appetites are growing uncontrollable, I'll lend you Adus. He doesn't smell

451

very nice, but that's no great drawback where you're concerned, is it?'

Her eyes blazed with sudden hatred, but Martel ignored her. 'The Zemochs will hold off the Peloi,' he said to Annias, 'and unless Sparhawk's been riding horses to death – which he'd never do – he's still three days behind us. We don't really need any Zemochs until we cross the border. That's when I'll want to find some of them to start laying traps for my dear brother and his friends.'

'Khwaj!' Sparhawk said shortly, 'make it so that they can hear me! Now!'

The candle flames flickered, then steadied again.

'Awfully nice camp you have there, Martel,' Sparhawk said in an offhand manner. 'Are there any fish in the lake?'

'Sparhawk!' Martel gasped. 'How can you reach this far?'

'Far, old boy? It's not really all that far at all. I'm almost on top of you. If it'd been me, though, I'd have made camp in that cedar grove across the lake. There are whole races of people who want to kill you, brother mine, and it's hardly safe to make camp right out in the open the way you have.'

Martel sprang to his feet. 'Get the horses!' he shouted to Adus.

'Leaving so soon, Martel?' Sparhawk asked mildly. 'What a shame. I was so looking forward to meeting you face to face again. Ah well, no matter. I'll see you first thing in the morning. I think we can both stand to wait that long.' Sparhawk's grin was vicious as he watched the five of them saddling their horses. Their movements were panicky, and their eyes darted about wildly. They clambered onto their mounts and bolted off towards the east at a dead run, flogging their horses unmercifully.

'Come back, Martel,' Sparhawk called after them. 'You forgot your tents.'

452

Chapter 23

The land of the Peloi was a vast, unfenced grassland which had never known the touch of the plough. The winds of late autumn swept that eternal grassland under a lowering sky, sighing a mournful dirge for summer. They rode eastward towards a high, rocky pinnacle out in the centre of the plain with their cloaks drawn tightly about them to ward off the arid chill, and with their mood made sombre by the unending gloom.

They reached the rock pinnacle late that afternoon and found the land around it bustling with activity. Kring, who had gone on ahead to gather the Peloi, rode up to meet them, a rough bandage encircling his head.

'What happened to you, friend Kring?' Tynian asked him.

'There was some small dissatisfaction with Sir Bevier's plan, I'm afraid,' Kring replied ruefully. 'One of the dissidents slipped up behind me.'

'I would never have thought Peloi warriors would attack from the rear.'

'Of course they wouldn't, but my attacker wasn't a man. A Peloi woman of high rank sneaked around behind me and banged me on the head with a cooking pot.'

'I hope you had her suitably punished.'

'I couldn't really do that, friend Tynian. She's my own sister. Our mother would never have forgiven me if I'd had the little brat flogged. None of the women liked Bevier's idea at all, but my sister was the only one who dared to reprimand me about it.'

'Are your womenfolk concerned about their own safety?' Bevier asked him.

'Of course not. They're as brave as lionesses. What *does* concern them is the fact that one of them will be placed in charge of this women's camp. Peloi women are very sensitive about status. All the menfolk thought your plan was a splendid idea, but the women –' He spread his hands helplessly. 'What man can ever understand a woman?' He squared his shoulders then and got down to business. 'I've put my sub-chiefs to work on organizing the camp here. We'll leave a minimal force, and all the rest of us will make some show of riding towards the Zemoch border as if we planned to invade. From time to time at night we'll detach forces to sneak back here and take up positions in the surrounding hills to wait for the Zemochs. You'll all ride along and slip away when we get near the border.'

'A very sound plan, friend Kring,' Tynian approved.

'I sort of thought so myself,' Kring grinned. 'Come along, my friends. I'll take you to the tents of my clan. We're roasting a span of oxen for supper. We'll take salt together and talk of affairs.' He seemed to think of something. 'Friend Stragen,' he said, 'you know the Tamul woman Mirtai better than our other friends do. Is she at all gifted in the art of cooking?'

'I've never eaten anything she prepared, Domi,' Stragen admitted. 'She once told us of a journey she made on foot when she was a girl, though. As I understand it, she subsisted primarily on wolf.'

'*Wolf?* How do you cook a wolf?'

'I don't think she did. She was in a hurry, I guess, so she just ate the wolf as she went.'

Kring swallowed very hard. 'She ate him raw?' he asked in wonder. 'How did she manage to catch one?'

Stragen shrugged. 'Chased him down, more than likely,'

he replied. 'Then she tore off some of the choicer parts and ate him as she ran.'

'The poor wolf!' Kring exclaimed. Then he looked suspiciously at the Thalesian thief. 'Are you making this up, Stragen?' he demanded.

'Me?' Stragen's ice blue eyes were as innocent as those of a child.

They rode out at dawn the next morning, and Kring came back to ride beside Sparhawk. 'Stragen was only trying to fool me last night, wasn't he, Sparhawk?' he asked with a worried look.

'Probably,' Sparhawk replied. 'Thalesians are a strange people, and they have a peculiar sense of humour.'

'She *could* probably do it, though,' Kring said in admiration. ' – chase down a wolf and eat him raw, I mean.'

'I suppose she could if she wanted to,' Sparhawk admitted. 'I see that you're still thinking of her.'

'I think of very little else, Sparhawk. I've tried to push her from my mind, but it's of no use.' He sighed. 'My people will never accept her, I'm afraid. It might be all right if my rank were not such as it is, but if I marry her, she'll be Doma among the Peloi – the Domi's mate, and chief among the women. The other women would gnaw their livers in jealousy and would speak against her to their husbands. Then the men would speak against her in our councils, and I'd have to kill many of the friends I've had since boyhood. Her presence among us would tear my people asunder.' He sighed again. 'Perhaps I can arrange to get myself killed during the impending war. That way I can avoid making the choice between love and duty.' He straightened in his saddle. 'Enough of such womanly talk,' he said. 'After my people and I have annihilated the main force of the Zemochs, we'll harry the border country on both sides of the line. The Zemochs will have little time to concern themselves with you and your friends. Zemochs are easy to divert. We'll destroy their shrines and temples. That drives them insane for some reason.'

'You've thought this through rather carefully, haven't you, Kring?'

'It's always good to know where you're going, Sparhawk. When we march eastward, we'll stay on the road that leads northeastwards towards the Zemoch town of Vileta. Listen carefully, my friend. You're going to need directions if you want to find that pass I mentioned earlier.' He then spoke at some length to tell Sparhawk which way to go, stressing landmarks and distances as he went along.

'That's about it, friend Sparhawk,' he concluded. 'I wish I could do more. Are you sure you wouldn't like to have me bring a few thousand horsemen and come along with you?'

'I wouldn't mind the company, Kring,' Sparhawk replied, 'but that large a force would draw resistance, and that would delay us. We have friends on the plains of Lamorkand who are counting on us to reach the temple of Azash before the Zemochs overwhelm them.'

'I understand completely, friend Sparhawk.'

They rode east for two days, and then Kring told Sparhawk that he should turn south in the morning. 'I'd advise leaving about two hours before daylight, friend Sparhawk,' he said. 'If some Zemoch scout sees you and your friends ride out of the encampment in the daylight, he might get curious and follow you. The country to the south is fairly flat, so riding in the dark won't be all that dangerous. Good luck, my friend. There's a very great deal riding on your shoulders. We'll pray for you – when we're not busy killing Zemochs.'

The moon was rising above scattered clouds when Sparhawk came out of their pavilion for a breath of fresh air. Stragen followed him. 'Nice night,' the slender blond man said in his resonant voice.

'A bit chilly, though,' Sparhawk replied.

'Who'd want to live in a land of endless summer? I probably won't see you when you ride out, Sparhawk. I'm not what you'd call an early riser.' Stragen reached inside his doublet and drew out a packet of paper somewhat thicker than the previous ones. 'This is the last of them,' he said, handing over the packet. 'I've completed the task your queen laid upon me.'

'You did well, Stragen – I guess.'

'Give me a little more credit than *that*, Sparhawk. I did exactly as Ehlana commanded.'

'You could have saved yourself a long ride if you'd just given me all the letters at once, you know.'

'I didn't mind the ride all that much. I rather like you and your companions, you know – not enough to emulate your overwhelming nobility, of course, but I *do* like you.'

'I like you too, Stragen – not enough to trust you, of course – but well enough, I suppose.'

'Thank you, Sir Knight,' Stragen said with a mocking bow.

'Don't mention it, Milord,' Sparhawk grinned.

'Be careful in Zemoch, my friend,' Stragen said seriously. 'I'm very fond of your iron-willed young queen, and I'd rather you didn't break her heart by doing something stupid. Also, if Talen tells you something, pay attention to him. I know he's just a boy – and a thief to boot – but he has very good instincts and a rather astounding mind. It's altogether possible that he's the most intelligent person either of us will ever meet. Besides, he's lucky. Don't lose, Sparhawk. I don't much feature bowing down to Azash.' He made a face. 'Enough of that. I've got a maudlin streak in me sometimes. Let's go back inside and crack open a flagon or two for old times' sake – unless you want to read your mail.'

'I think I'll save it. I may get downhearted somewhere

in Zemoch, and I'll need something to lift my spirits at that point.'

The clouds had once again obscured the moon as they gathered early the next morning. Sparhawk sketched in their route, laying some stress on the landmarks Kring had mentioned. Then they mounted and rode out of the camp.

The darkness was so dense as to be virtually impenetrable. 'We could be riding around in circles out here, you know,' Kalten complained, his voice slightly sullen. Kalten had sat up late with the Peloi the previous evening, and his eyes had been bloodshot and his hands palsied when Sparhawk had awakened him.

'Just keep riding, Kalten,' Sephrenia told him.

'Of course,' he said sarcastically, 'but which way?'

'Southeast.'

'Fine, but which way is southeast?'

'That way.' She pointed off into the darkness.

'How do you know?'

She spoke rapidly to him in Styric for a moment. 'There,' she said. 'That should explain everything to you.'

'Little mother, I didn't understand one single word you said.'

'That's not my fault, dear one.'

The dawn came slowly that morning, since the cloudbanks lying to the east were particularly dense. As they rode south, they began to see the outlines of ragged peaks lying leagues off to the east – peaks which could only be in Zemoch.

It was late in the morning when Kurik reined in. 'There's that red peak you mentioned, Sparhawk,' he said, pointing.

'It looks as if it's bleeding, doesn't it?' Kalten observed. 'Or is that just my eyes?'

'A little of each perhaps, Kalten,' Sephrenia said. 'You shouldn't have drunk so much ale last night.'

'You should have told me about that last night, little mother,' he said mournfully.

'Very well then, gentlemen,' she said, 'it's time for you to change clothing, I think. Your armour might be a bit ostentatious in Zemoch. Put on your mail-shirts if you must, but I have Styric smocks for each of you. After you've changed, I'll do something about your faces.'

'I'm more or less used to mine,' Ulath told her.

'*You* may be, Ulath, but it might startle the Zemochs.'

The five knights and Berit removed their formal armour – the knights with a certain relief and Berit with obvious reluctance. Then they pulled on their only slightly less uncomfortable chain-mail and lastly the Styric smocks.

Sephrenia looked at them critically. 'Leave your sword-belts on over the smocks for now,' she said. 'I doubt that the Zemochs have any really set customs about how they wear their weapons. If we find out differently later, we can make adjustments. Now, stand still, all of you.' She went from man to man, touching their faces and repeating the same Styric incantation for each of them.

'It doesn't seem to have worked, Lady Sephrenia,' Bevier said, looking around at his companions. 'They all still look the same to me.'

'I'm not trying to disguise them from *you*, Bevier,' she smiled. She went to her saddlebag and took out a small hand-mirror. '*This* is how the Zemochs will see you.' She handed him the mirror.

Bevier took one look and then made the sign to ward off evil. 'Dear God!' he gasped, 'I look hideous!' He handed the mirror quickly to Sparhawk, and Sparhawk examined his strangely altered face carefully. His hair was still horse-tail black, but his weathered skin had become pale, a racial characteristic of all Styrics. His brows and

459

cheekbones had become prominent, almost rough-hewn. Sephrenia, he noted with a certain disappointment, had left his nose as it was. As much as he told himself that he really didn't mind the broken nose all that much, he nonetheless found that he had been curious to find out just how he might appear with a straight one for a change.

'I've made you resemble a pure Styric strain,' she told them. 'It's common enough in Zemoch, and I'm more comfortable with it. The sight of a mixed Elene and Styric nauseates me, for some reason.'

Then she extended her right arm, spoke at some length in Styric and then gestured. A dark spiral band that looked much like a tattoo encircled her forearm and wrist and culminated in an amazingly life-like representation of a snake's head on her palm.

'There's a reason for that, I suppose,' Tynian said, looking curiously at the marking.

'Of course. Shall we go then?'

The border between Pelosia and Zemoch was ill-defined, seeming to lie along a meandering line marked by the end of the tall grass. The soil to the east of that line was thin and rocky, and the vegetation stunted. The dark edge of a coniferous forest lay a mile or so up the steep slope. When they had covered perhaps half that distance, a dozen riders in dirty white smocks emerged from the trees and approached them.

'I'll handle this,' Sephrenia said. 'Just don't say anything, any of you, and try to look menacing.'

The approaching Zemochs reined in. Some of them had those unfinished-looking Styric features; some could easily pass for Elenes, and some appeared to be an unwholesome mixture of the two.

'All glory to the dread God of the Zemochs,' their leader intoned in bastardized Styric. The tongue he spoke was a mixture of that tongue and Elene, combining the worst features of both languages.

'You did not say his name, Kedjek,' Sephrenia said coldly.

'How did she know the fellow's name?' Kalten whispered to Sparhawk. Kalten obviously understood more Styric than he could pronounce.

'"Kedjek" isn't a name,' Sparhawk replied. 'It's an insult.'

The Zemoch's face went even more pale, and his black eyes narrowed with hate. 'Women and slaves do not speak so to members of the imperial guard!' he snapped.

'Imperial guard,' Sephrenia sneered. 'Neither you nor any of your men would make a wart on any part of an imperial guardsman. Say the name of our God so that I may know that you are of the true faith. Say it, Kedjek, lest ye die.'

'Azash,' the now-uncertain man muttered.

'His name is fouled by the tongue which speaks it,' she told him, 'but Azash sometimes enjoys defilement.'

The Zemoch straightened. 'I am commanded to gather the people,' he declared. 'The day is at hand when Blessed Otha will stretch forth his fist to crush and enslave the unbelievers of the west.'

'Obey then. Continue with your work. Be diligent, for Azash rewards lack of zeal with agonies.'

'I need no woman to instruct me,' he said coldly. 'Prepare to take your servants to the place of war.'

'Your authority does not extend to me.' She raised her right hand, her palm towards him. The markings about her forearm and wrist seemed to writhe and surge, and the image of the snake's head hissed, its forked tongue flickering. 'You have my permission to greet me,' she told him.

The Zemoch recoiled, his eyes wide with horror. Since

the ritual Styric greeting involved the kissing of the palms, Sephrenia's 'permission' was an open invitation to suicide. 'Forgive me, High Priestess,' he begged in a shaking voice.

'I don't think so,' she said flatly. She looked at the other Zemochs, who were goggle-eyed with fright. 'This piece of offal has offended me,' she told them. 'Do what is customary.'

The Zemochs leaped from their saddles, pulled their struggling leader from his horse and beheaded him on the spot. Sephrenia, who normally would have viewed such savagery with revulsion, looked on with no change of expression. 'Adequate,' she said flatly. 'Display what remains of him in the usual fashion and go on with your task.'

'Ah – um – Dread Priestess,' one of them faltered, 'we have no leader now.'

'*You* have spoken. Therefore *you* will lead. If you do well, you will be rewarded. If you do not do well, the punishment will be on your head. Now take this carrion out of my path.' She touched Ch'iel's flanks with her heels, and the slender white mare moved forward, delicately avoiding the puddles of blood on the ground.

'Leadership among the Zemochs appears to have certain hazards,' Ulath observed to Tynian.

'Truly,' Tynian agreed.

'Did you really have to do that to him, Lady Sephrenia?' Bevier asked in a choked voice.

'Yes. A Zemoch who offends the Priesthood is always punished, and in Zemoch, there is only one punishment.'

'How did you make the picture of the snake move?' Talen asked her, his eyes a little frightened.

'I didn't,' she replied. 'It only *seemed* to move.'

'Then it wouldn't really have bitten him, would it?'

'He'd have *thought* it had, and the results would have

462

been the same. How far did Kring tell you to go into this forest, Sparhawk?'

'About a day's ride,' he told her. 'We turn south at the eastern edge of the woods – just before we get to the mountains.'

'Let's ride on, then.'

They were all a bit awed by the apparent change in Sephrenia. The soulless arrogance she had displayed during the encounter with the Zemochs had been so radically different from her normal behaviour that she even frightened *them* to some degree. They rode on through the shadowy forest in a subdued silence, casting frequent looks in her direction. Finally, she reined in her palfrey. '*Will* you all stop that?' she said tartly. 'I haven't grown another head, you know. I'm posing as a Zemoch priestess, and I'm behaving in exactly the way a priestess of Azash would. When you imitate a monster, you sometimes have to do monstrous things. Now, let's ride on. Tell us a story, Tynian. Take our minds off the recent unpleasantness.'

'Yes, little mother,' the broad-faced Deiran agreed. Sparhawk had noticed that they had all, unconsciously perhaps, taken to addressing her in that form.

They camped in the forest that night and continued the following morning under still-cloudy skies. They were climbing steadily through the forest, and as they progressed, the air grew colder. It was about midday when they reached the eastern edge of the wood and turned south, staying perhaps a hundred yards back under the trees to take advantage of the concealment they offered.

As Kring had advised Sparhawk they would, they reached an extensive grove of blighted trees late in the day. The stark white band of dead trees spilled down from the mountainside like a leprous waterfall, foul-smelling, fungus-ridden and about a league wide. 'This place looks

'– and smells – like the outskirts of Hell,' Tynian said in a sombre tone.

'Maybe it's because of the cloudy weather,' Kalten told him.

'I don't think sunshine would help this place very much,' Ulath disagreed.

'What could have laid waste so vast a region?' Bevier asked with a shudder.

'The earth itself is diseased,' Sephrenia told him. 'Let's not linger too long in this accursed wood, dear ones. A man is not a tree, but the noxious miasma of this forest cannot be healthy.'

'We're losing daylight, Sephrenia,' Kurik said.

'That won't be a problem. There'll be light enough for us to press on after it grows dark.'

'What was it that diseased the earth, Lady Sephrenia?' Berit asked, looking around at the white trees thrusting upward from the contaminated soil like imploring skeletal hands.

'There's no way to know, Berit, but the reek of this place is the reek of death. Horrors beyond imagining may lie under the ground. Let's put this place behind us.'

The sky darkened with the approach of evening, but as night fell, the dead trees around them began to give off a sickly, greenish glow.

'Are you doing this, Sephrenia?' Kalten asked, 'making the light, I mean?'

'No,' she replied. 'The light isn't the result of magic.'

Kurik laughed a bit ruefully. 'I should have remembered that,' he said.

'Remembered what?' Talen asked him.

'Rotten logs and the like glow in the dark sometimes.'

'I didn't know that.'

'You've spent too much time in cities, Talen.'

464

'You have to go where your customers are,' the boy shrugged. 'You don't make much profit swindling frogs.'

They rode on through the first hours of night in that faint greenish glow, covering their noses and mouths with their cloaks. Not long before midnight they reached a steep, forested ridge. They rode on for some distance and then set up camp for the remainder of the night in a shallow, wooded basin where the night air seemed unusually sweet and pure after the endless hours in the fetid stink of the dead forest. The prospect they viewed the following morning as they crested the ridge was not a great deal more encouraging. What they had faced the previous day had been dead white. What lay in store for them today was just as dead, but it was black.

'What on earth is that?' Talen gasped, staring out over the bubbling expanse of sticky-looking black muck.

'The tar-bogs Kring mentioned,' Sparhawk replied.

'Can we go around them?'

'No. The tar seeps out of the face of a cliff, and the bogs run on for leagues out into the foothills.'

The tar-bogs appeared to be vast puddles of shiny black, glistening wet, bubbling and stretching to a rocky spur perhaps five miles to the south. Near the far side there rose a plume of bluish flame quite nearly as tall as the spire rising above the cathedral of Cimmura.

'How can we hope to cross that?' Bevier exclaimed.

'Carefully, I'd imagine,' Ulath replied. 'I've crossed a few quicksand bogs up in Thalesia. You spend a lot of time probing in front of you with a stick – a long one, preferably.'

'The Peloi have the trail marked,' Sparhawk assured them. 'They've poked sticks into solid ground.'

'Which side of the sticks are we supposed to stay on?' Kalten asked.

'Kring didn't say,' Sparhawk shrugged. 'I imagine we'll find out before we go very far, though.'

They rode down the ridge and moved at a careful walk out into the sticky black quagmire. The air hanging above the bogs was thick with the penetrating odour of naphtha, and Sparhawk began to feel somewhat light-headed after a short distance.

They plodded on, their pace slowed by the need for caution. Great viscous bubbles rose up from the depths of the naphtha sinks around them to pop with odd belching sounds. When they neared the southern end of the bog, they passed the burning pillar, a column of blue flame that roared endlessly as it shot up from the earth. Once they had passed that blazing shaft, the ground began to rise and they were soon out of the bogs. Perhaps it had been the heat from the burning gasses spurting from the earth that made the contrast so noticeable, but when they left the bogs behind, the air seemed much, much colder.

'We've got weather coming,' Kurik warned. 'Rain at first most likely, but I think there might be snow behind it.'

'No trip through the mountains is complete without snow,' Ulath observed.

'What are we supposed to look for now?' Tynian asked Sparhawk.

'That,' Sparhawk replied, pointing at a high cliff with broad yellow bands running diagonally across its face. 'Kring gives very good directions.' He peered on ahead and saw a tree with a patch of bark slashed away. 'Good,' he said. 'The trail to the pass is marked. Let's ride on before the rain starts.'

The pass was in fact an ancient stream-bed. The climate of Eosia had changed over the eons, and as Zemoch had grown more and more arid, the stream which had patiently carved the narrow ravine had dried up at its source, leaving a steep gully running back up into the towering cliff.

As Kurik had predicted, the rain began in the late afternoon. It was a steady drizzle that dampened everything.

'Sir Sparhawk,' Berit called from the rear. 'I think you should take a look at this.'

Sparhawk reined in and rode back. 'What is it, Berit?'

Berit pointed towards the west where the sunset was no more than a lighter shade of grey in the rainy sky. In the centre of that lighter spot hovered an amorphous cloud of inky black. 'It's moving the wrong way, Sir Sparhawk,' Berit said. 'All the other clouds are moving west. That one's coming east, right towards us. It looks sort of like the cloud those dawn-men were hiding in, doesn't it? The one that's been following us?'

Sparhawk's heart sank. 'It does indeed, Berit. Sephrenia!' he called.

She rode back to join them.

'It's there again,' Sparhawk told her, pointing.

'So I see. You didn't expect it to just go away, did you, Sparhawk?'

'I was hoping. Can we do anything?'

'No.'

He squared his shoulders. 'We keep going then,' he said.

The steep ravine wound up through the rock, and they followed it slowly as evening began to descend. Then they rounded a sharp bend in the ancient course and saw a rockslide, which was not a slide strictly speaking, but rather a collapsed wall – a place where the south face of the gap had broken free and fallen into the ravine to apparently block it entirely.

'That's fairly intimidating,' Bevier observed. 'I hope Kring gave you good directions, Sparhawk.'

'We're supposed to bear to the left here,' Sparhawk told them. 'We'll find a clump of limbs and logs and brush on the downhill side of the rockfall right up against the north wall of the ravine. When we pull those out of the way, we'll find a passageway leading under the slide. The Peloi use it when they ride back into Zemoch looking for ears.'

Kalten wiped his face. 'Let's go and look,' he said.

The pile of broken-off trees and tangled brush looked quite natural in the rapidly fading light, and it appeared to be no more than one of those random accumulations of driftwood and debris which wash down every ravine during the spring run-off. Talen dismounted, climbed up a steeply slanted log and peered into a dark gap in the tangle. 'Hello,' he shouted into the opening. The sound of his voice returned as a hollow echo.

'Let us know if someone answers,' Tynian called to him.

'This is it, Sparhawk,' the boy said. 'There's a large open space behind this pile.'

'We may as well get to work then,' Ulath suggested. He looked up at the rainy, darkening sky. 'We might want to give some thought to spending the night in there,' he added. 'It's out of the weather, and it's getting dark anyway.'

They fashioned yokes from pieces of driftwood and used the packhorses to pull aside the pile of logs and brush. The mouth of the passageway was triangular, since the outward side leaned against the north face of the ravine. The passage was narrow and smelled musty.

'It's dry,' Ulath noted, 'and it's out of sight. We could go back in there a little way and build a fire. If we don't dry our clothes off, these mail-shirts are going to be solid rust by morning.'

'Let's cover this opening first, though,' Kurik said. He didn't sound too hopeful about the notion of trying to hide behind a brush-pile from the shadowy cloud which had followed them since Thalesia, however.

After they had covered the opening, they took torches

from one of the packs, lit them and followed the narrow passageway a hundred yards or so to a place where it widened out.

'Good enough?' Kurik asked.

'At least it's dry,' Kalten said. He kicked at the sandy floor of the passage, turning up a chunk of bleached wood buried there. 'We might even be able to find enough wood for a fire.'

They set up their camp in the somewhat confined space, and they soon had a small fire going.

Talen came back from the passageway on ahead. 'It goes on for another few hundred yards,' he reported. 'The upper end's blocked with brush the same way the lower one was. Kring's very careful to keep this passage hidden.'

'What's the weather like on up ahead?' Kurik asked.

'There's some snow mixed with the rain now, father.'

'It looks as if I was right then. Oh, well, we've all been snowed on before, I guess.'

'Whose turn is it to do the cooking?' Kalten asked.

'Yours,' Ulath told him.

'It can't be mine again already.'

'Sorry, but it is.'

Grumbling, Kalten went to the packs and began to rummage around.

The meal consisted of Peloi trail rations, smoked mutton, dark bread and a thick soup made from dried peas. It was nourishing, but the flavour was hardly spectacular. After they had finished eating, Kalten began to clean up. He was gathering their plates when he suddenly stopped. 'Ulath?' he said suspiciously.

'Yes, Kalten?'

'In all the time we've been travelling together, I haven't seen you cook more than once or twice.'

'No, you probably haven't.'

'When does your turn come?'

'It doesn't. My job is to keep track of whose turn it is. You wouldn't really expect me to do that and cook too, would you? Fair is fair, after all.'

'Who appointed you?'

'I volunteered. Church Knights are supposed to do that when unpleasant tasks come up. That's one of the reasons people respect us so much.'

They sat around after that, staring moodily into the fire. 'It's days like today that make me wonder why I took up knighting for a career,' Tynian said. 'I had a chance to go into law when I was younger. I thought it would be boring, so I chose this instead. I wonder why.'

There was a general murmur of agreement.

'Gentlemen,' Sephrenia said, 'push this kind of thinking from your minds. I've told you before that if we grow melancholy or fall into despair, we'll be falling right into the hands of our enemies. One dark cloud hanging over our heads is enough. Let's not add clouds of our own making. When the light falters, the darkness wins.'

'If you're trying to cheer us up, you're going at it in a strange way, Sephrenia,' Talen told her.

She smiled faintly. 'Perhaps that *was* a bit dramatic, wasn't it? The point, my dear ones, is that we all have to be very alert. We must be wary of depression, dejection and above all, melancholy. Melancholy's a form of madness, you know.'

'What are we supposed to do?' Kalten asked her.

'It's really quite simple, Kalten,' Ulath said. 'You watch Tynian very closely. As soon as he begins behaving like a butterfly, tell Sparhawk about it. I'll watch *you* for signs of frogishness. Just as soon as you start trying to catch flies with your tongue, I'll know that you're starting to lose your grip on things.'

Chapter 24

There were snowflakes the size of half-crowns mixed with the drizzle that swirled down into the narrow pass. Sooty ravens hunched on tree-limbs, their feathers wet and their eyes angry. It was the kind of morning that cried out for stout walls, a sturdy roof and a cheery fire, but those amenities were not available, so Sparhawk and Kurik wormed their way deeper into the juniper thicket and waited.

'Are you sure?' Sparhawk whispered to his squire.

Kurik nodded. 'It was definitely smoke, Sparhawk,' he replied in a low voice, 'and somebody was doing a very bad job of frying bacon.'

'There isn't much we can do but wait,' Sparhawk said sourly. 'I don't want to blunder into anybody.' He tried to shift his position, but he was wedged in between the trunks of two scrubby trees.

'What's the matter?' Kurik whispered.

'There's water dripping off a limb just over me. It's running down the back of my neck.'

Kurik gave him a long, speculative look. 'How are you feeling, My Lord?' he asked.

'Wet. Thanks for asking, though.'

'You know what I mean. I'm supposed to keep an eye on you. You're the key to this whole business. It doesn't really matter if the rest of us start feeling sorry for ourselves, but if *you* start having doubts and fears, we're *all* in trouble.'

'Sephrenia's like a mother hen sometimes.'

'She loves you, Sparhawk. It's only natural for her to be concerned.'

'I'm a big boy now, Kurik. I'm even married.'

'Why, I do believe you're right. How strange that I missed that.'

'Very funny.'

They waited, straining their ears, but all they could hear was the sound of water dripping from tree-limbs.

'Sparhawk,' Kurik said finally.

'Yes?'

'If something happens to me, you'll look after Aslade, won't you? – and the boys?'

'Nothing's going to happen to you, Kurik.'

'Probably not, but I need to know anyway.'

'You've got a pension coming – quite a sizeable one, actually. I may have to sell off some acreage to cover it. Aslade will be well taken care of.'

'That's assuming *you* survive this trip as well,' Kurik said wryly.

'You don't have to worry about that, my friend. It's in my will. Vanion will see to it – or Ehlana.'

'You think of everything, don't you, Sparhawk?'

'I'm in a dangerous line of work. I'm sort of obliged to make provisions – just in case of accidents.' Sparhawk grinned at his friend. 'Is this particular subject designed to cheer me up in some obscure way?' he asked.

'I just wanted to know, that's all,' Kurik said. 'It's good to have your mind at rest about such things. Aslade should be able to set the boys up in trades of their own then.'

'Your boys already have a trade, Kurik.'

'Farming? Sometimes that's a little dubious.'

'I wasn't talking about farming. I've talked with Vanion about them. Your oldest boy's probably going to be entering his novitiate when this business is all over.'

'That's ridiculous, Sparhawk.'

'Not really. The Pandion order always needs good men, and if they're at all like their father, your sons are some

472

of the best. We'd have had *you* knighted years ago, but you wouldn't even let me talk about it. You're a stubborn man, Kurik.'

'Sparhawk, you –' Kurik broke off. 'Somebody's coming!' he hissed.

'This is pure idiocy,' a voice from the other side of the thicket said in the crude mixture of Elene and Styric that identified the speaker as a Zemoch.

'What did he say?' Kurik whispered. 'I can't follow that gibberish.'

'I'll tell you later.'

'Why don't you go back and tell Surkhel that he's an idiot, Houna?' the other voice suggested. 'I'm sure he'll be very interested in your opinion.'

'Surkhel *is* an idiot, Timak. He's from Korakach. They're all either insane or feeble-minded there.'

'Our orders come from Otha, not from Surkhel, Houna,' Timak said. 'Surkhel's just doing what he's told to do.'

'Otha,' Houna snorted. 'I don't believe there *is* an Otha. The priesthood just made him up. Who's ever seen him?'

'You're lucky I'm your friend, Houna. You could get yourself fed to the vultures for that kind of talk. Stop complaining so much. This isn't so bad. All we have to do is ride around looking for people in a countryside where there aren't any people. They've all been rounded up and sent off to Lamorkand already.'

'I'm tired of all the rain, that's all.'

'Be glad it's only raining water, Houna. When our friends encounter the Church Knights on the plains of Lamorkand, they'll probably run into cloudbursts of fire – or lightning – or poisonous snakes.'

'The Church Knights can't be *that* bad,' Houna scoffed. 'We've got Azash to protect us.'

'Some protection,' Timak sneered. 'Azash boils Zemoch babies down for soup-stock.'

'That's superstitious nonsense, Timak.'

'Have you ever known anybody who went to his temple and came back?'

A shrill whistle came from some distance off.

'That's Surkhel,' Timak said. 'It's time to move on, I guess. I wonder if he knows how irritating that whistling is?'

'He *has* to whistle, Timak. He hasn't learned how to talk yet. Let's go.'

'What did they say?' Kurik whispered. 'Who are they?'

'They seem to be a part of a patrol of some kind,' Sparhawk replied.

'Looking for us? Did Martel manage to send people out in spite of everything?'

'I don't think so. From what those two said, they're out to round up everybody who hasn't gone off to war. Let's gather up the others and move on.'

'What were they saying?' Kalten asked as they set out again.

'They were complaining,' Sparhawk said. 'They sounded like soldiers the whole world over. I think if we push aside all these horror-stories, we'll find that Zemochs aren't really all that much different from common people the world over.'

'They worship Azash,' Bevier said stubbornly. 'That makes them monsters by definition.'

'They *fear* Azash, Bevier,' Sparhawk corrected. 'There's a difference between fear and worship. I don't really think we need to embark on a war of total annihilation here in Zemoch. We need to clean out the fanatics and the élite troops – along with Azash and Otha, of course. After that, I think we can leave the common people alone to pick out their own theology, whether it's Elene or Styric.'

'They're a degenerate race, Sparhawk,' Bevier insisted

stubbornly. 'The intermarriage of Styric and Elene is an abomination in the eyes of God.'

Sparhawk sighed. Bevier was an arch-conservative, and nothing would be gained by arguing with him. 'We can sort all that out after the war, I think,' he said. 'It's safe enough to ride on now. Let's keep our eyes open, but I don't think we'll have to try to sneak through the countryside.'

They remounted and rode on up out of the pass onto a hilly plateau dotted here and there with groves of trees. The rain continued to fall, and the large, wet snowflakes mingled with it grew thicker as they continued eastward. They camped that night in a grove of spruce trees, and their fire, fed by damp twigs and branches, was small and sickly. They awoke the following morning to find the plateau covered with wet, slushy snow to a depth of perhaps three inches.

'It's time for a decision, Sparhawk,' Kurik said, looking out at the still-falling snow.

'Oh?'

'We can keep trying to follow this trail – which isn't very well marked to begin with and will probably disappear altogether in about an hour – or we can strike out to the north. We could be on the Vileta road by noon.'

'You have a certain preference, I gather?'

'You could say that, yes. I don't feature wandering around in strange country trying to find a trail that might not even lead to where we want to go.'

'All right then, Kurik,' Sparhawk said. 'Since you're so keen on this, we'll do it your way. All I was really concerned about was getting through the border country where Martel was planning to leave ambushes in our path anyway.'

'We'll lose half a day,' Ulath pointed out.

'We'll lose a lot more if we get turned around in these mountains,' Sparhawk replied. 'We don't have any specific appointment with Azash. He'll welcome us any time we get there.'

They rode north through the slushy snow with the thickly-falling flakes and the mist which accompanied them obscuring nearby hills. The wet snow plastered itself against them in sodden blankets, and their discomfort added to their gloom. Neither Ulath nor Tynian could lighten the mood with their few tentative efforts at humour, and after a while they rode in silence, each sunk in moody melancholy.

As Kurik had predicted, they reached the Vileta road about midday and turned east again. There was no evidence that the road had been travelled since the snow had begun to fall. Evening was undefined on that snow-clogged day, a gradual darkening of the pervading gloom. They took shelter for the night in an ancient, decrepit barn, and as they always did in hostile country, they took turns standing watch.

They bypassed Vileta late the following day. There was nothing in the town they wanted anyway, and there was no point in taking chances.

'Deserted,' Kurik said shortly as they rode past the town.

'How do you know that?' Kalten asked him.

'No smoke. The weather's chilly, and it's still snowing. They'd have fires going.'

'Oh.'

'I wonder if they forgot anything when they left,' Talen said, his eyes bright.

'Never mind,' Kurik told him flatly.

The snow abated somewhat the following day, and their mood noticeably brightened; but when they awoke the morning after that, it was snowing again, and their spirits plummeted once more.

'Why are we doing this, Sparhawk?' Kalten asked

morosely towards the end of the day. 'Why does it have to be us?'

'Because we're Church Knights.'

'There are other Church Knights, you know. Haven't we done enough already?'

'Do you want to go back? I didn't ask you – any of you – to come along, you know.'

Kalten shook his head. 'No, of course not. I don't know what came over me. Forget I said anything.'

Sparhawk, however, did not. That evening he drew Sephrenia to one side. 'I think we have a problem,' he said to her.

'Are you starting to have unusual feelings?' she asked quickly. 'Something that may be coming from somewhere outside yourself?'

'I didn't exactly follow that.'

'I think we've all noticed it a few times before. We've all been having these sudden bouts of doubt and depression.' She smiled slightly. 'That's not really in the character of Church Knights, you know. Most of the time you're optimistic to the point of insanity. These doubts and gloom are being imposed on us from the outside. Is that the sort of thing you're feeling? Is that the problem?'

'It's not me,' he assured her. 'I'm feeling a little low, but I think that's just the weather. It's the others I'm talking about. Kalten came up to me today, and he was asking me why *we* had to be the ones to do this. Kalten would never ask that kind of question. You usually have to hold him back, but now I think he just wants to pack it all up and go home. If my friends are all feeling this way, why don't I feel it too?'

She looked out into the still-falling snow. Once again he was struck by just how agelessly beautiful she was. 'I think He's afraid of you,' she said after a while.

'Kalten? That's nonsense.'

'That's not what I meant. It's Azash who's afraid of you, Sparhawk.'

'That's absurd.'

'I know, but I think it's true all the same. Somehow you have more control over Bhelliom than anyone else has ever had. Not even Ghwerig had such absolute power over the stone. That's what Azash is *really* afraid of. That's why He won't risk confronting you directly, and that's why He's trying to dishearten your friends. He's attacking Kalten and Bevier and the others because He's afraid to attack you.'

'You too?' he asked her. 'Are you in despair too?'

'Of course not.'

'Why of course?'

'It would take too long to explain. I'll take care of this, Sparhawk. Go to bed.'

They awoke the following morning to a familiar sound. It was clear and pure, and though the song of the pipes was in a minor key, it seemed filled with an ageless joy. A slow smile came to Sparhawk's lips, and he shook Kalten awake. 'We've got company,' he said.

Kalten sat up quickly, reaching for his sword, and then he heard the sound of the pipes. 'Well, now,' he grinned, 'it's about time. I'll be glad to see her again.'

They emerged from the tent and looked around. It was still snowing, and the stubborn mist hung back among the trees. Sephrenia and Kurik sat by the small fire in front of her tent.

'Where is she?' Kalten asked, looking out into the settling snow.

'She's here,' Sephrenia said calmly, sipping her tea.

'I can't see her.'

'You don't have to, Kalten. All you really need to know is that she's here.'

478

'It's not the same, Sephrenia.' His voice was just slightly disappointed.

'She finally went and did it, didn't she?' Kurik laughed.

'Did what?' Sephrenia asked him.

'She poached a group of Church Knights right out from under the nose of the Elene God.'

'Don't be silly. She wouldn't do that.'

'Oh, really? Take a look at Kalten there. That's the closest thing to adoration I've ever seen on his face. If I put together something that looked like an altar right now, he'd probably genuflect.'

'That's nonsense,' Kalten said, looking slightly embarrassed. 'I just like her, that's all. She makes me feel good when she's around.'

'Of course,' Kurik said sceptically.

'I don't know that we should pursue this line of thought when Bevier joins us,' Sephrenia cautioned. 'Let's not confuse him.'

The others also emerged from their tents smiling broadly. Ulath was actually laughing.

Their mood had lightened enormously, and the bleak morning seemed almost sunny. Even their horses seemed alert, almost frisky. Sparhawk and Berit went to where they were picketed to feed them their morning ration of grain. Faran normally greeted the morning with a flat look of dislike, but on this particular day the big, ugly roan seemed calm, even serene. He was looking intently at a large, spreading beech tree. Sparhawk glanced at the tree and then froze. The tree was half-concealed by mist, but he seemed quite clearly to see the familiar figure of the little girl who had just banished their despair with her joyful song. She appeared to be exactly the same as she had been the first time he had seen her. She sat upon a limb holding her shepherd's pipes to her lips. The headband of plaited grass encircled her glossy black hair. She still

479

wore the short, belted linen smock, and her grass-stained little feet were crossed at the ankles. Her large, dark eyes looked directly at him, and there was the hint of a dimple on each of her cheeks.

'Berit,' Sparhawk said quietly, 'look.'

The young apprentice turned, and then he suddenly stopped. 'Hello, Flute,' he greeted her, sounding strangely unsurprised.

Aphrael blew him a little trill of recognition and continued her song. Then the mist swirled about the tree, and when it cleared, she was no longer there. Her melody, however, continued.

'She looks well, doesn't she?' Berit said.

'How could she look otherwise?' Sparhawk laughed.

The days seemed to race by after that. What had been tedious plodding through gloom and snow now took on an almost holiday air. They laughed and joked and even ignored the weather, though it did not noticeably improve. It continued to snow each night and on into the morning, but at about noon each day, the snow gradually turned to rain, and the rain melted down each night's accumulation so that, although they rode through continual slush, the drifts did not pile up sufficiently to impede their progress. Intermittently as they rode, the sound of Aphrael's pipes hauntingly drifted out of the mist, urging them on.

It was several days later when they came over a hill to look down at the lead-grey expanse of the Gulf of Merjuk stretching before them, half-shrouded by mist and the chill drizzle, and huddled on the near shore was a sizeable cluster of low buildings.

'That would be Albak,' Kalten said. He wiped at his face and peered down at the town intently. 'I don't see any smoke,' he noted. 'No, wait. There's one live chimney – right near the centre of town.'

'We may as well go down there,' Kurik said. 'We're going to have to steal a boat.'

They rode down the hill and entered Albak. The streets were unpaved and clogged with slushy snow. The snow had not been churned into soupy muck, a clear indication that the town was uninhabited. The single column of smoke, thin and sickly-looking, rose from the chimney of a low, shed-like building facing what appeared to be a town square. Ulath sniffed at the air. 'A tavern, judging from the smell,' he said.

They dismounted and went inside. The room was long and low with smoke-stained beams and mouldy straw on the floor. It was cold and damp and smelled foul. There were no windows, and the only light came from a small fire flickering on a hearth at the far end. A hunchbacked man dressed in rags was kicking a bench to pieces to feed the fire. 'Who's there?' he cried out as they entered.

'Travellers,' Sephrenia replied in Styric, her tone strangely alien. 'We're looking for a place to spend the night.'

'Don't look here,' the hunchback growled. 'This is *my* place.' He threw several pieces of the bench into the fireplace, pulled a greasy blanket about his shoulders and sat back down, pulling an open beer-keg closer to him and then extending his hands towards the feeble flames.

'We'll gladly go somewhere else,' she said to him. 'We need a little information, though.'

'Go and ask somebody else.' He squinted at her. His eyes were oddly disconnected, looking off in different directions, and he looked to one side of her in that peculiar way of the nearly-blind.

Sephrenia crossed the straw-littered floor and faced the uncivil hunchback. 'You seem to be the only one here,' she told him.

'I am,' he said sullenly. 'All the rest went off to die in

Lamorkand. I'll die here. That way I don't have to walk so far. Now get out of here.'

She extended her arm and then turned it over in front of his stubbled face. The image of the serpent's head rose from her palm, its tongue flickering. The half-blind hunchback puckered his face, turning his head this way and that in an effort to see what she was holding. Then he cried out in fright, half-rose and stumbled back over his stool, spilling his beer-keg.

'You have my permission to offer your greeting,' Sephrenia said in an implacable tone.

'I didn't know who you were, Priestess,' he gibbered. 'Forgive me, please.'

'We'll see. Is there no one else in the town?'

'None, Priestess – only me. I'm too crippled to travel, and I can hardly see. They left me behind.'

'We seek another group of travellers – four men and a woman. One of the men has white hair. Another looks like an animal. Have you seen them?'

'Please don't kill me.'

'Then speak.'

'Some people passed through here yesterday. They may have been the ones you're looking for. I can't say for sure because they didn't come close enough to the fire for me to see their faces. I could hear them talking, though. They said they were going to Aka and from there to the capital. They stole Tassalk's boat.' The hunchback sat up on the floor, clasped his arms about him and began to rock back and forth rhythmically, moaning to himself.

'He's crazy,' Tynian said quietly to Sparhawk.

'Yes,' Sparhawk agreed sadly.

'All gone,' the hunchback crooned. 'All gone off to die for Azash. Kill the Elenes, then die. Azash loves death. All die. All die. All die for Azash.'

'We're going to take a boat,' Sephrenia cut through his ravings.

'Take. Take. Nobody will come back. All die, and Azash will eat them.'

Sephrenia turned her back on him and returned to where the others stood. 'We'll leave here now,' she said in a steely tone.

'What's going to happen to him?' Talen asked her, his voice subdued. 'He's all by himself here and nearly blind.'

'He'll die,' she replied in an abrupt tone of voice.

'All alone?' Talen's voice was half-sick.

'Everybody dies alone, Talen.' She resolutely led them from the stinking tavern.

Once she was outside, however, she broke down and wept.

Sparhawk went to his saddlebags and took out his map. He studied it with a frown. 'Why would Martel go to Aka?' he muttered to Tynian. 'It's leagues out of his way.'

'There's a road from Aka to Zemoch,' Tynian said, pointing at the map. 'We've been pushing him hard, and his horses are probably nearly exhausted.'

'Maybe that's it,' Sparhawk agreed. 'And Martel's never been very fond of going across country.'

'Will we follow the same route?'

'I don't think so. He doesn't know much about boats, so he'll wallow around out there in the gulf for several days. Kurik's a sailor though, so he can take us straight across. We should be able to make it from the east shore to the capital in about three days. We can still get there before he does. Kurik,' he called, 'let's go and find a boat.'

Sparhawk was leaning against the rail of the large, tar-smeared scow Kurik had selected. The surface winds had swung briefly around to the west, and their ship sped across the choppy waters of the gulf towards the east. Sparhawk reached inside his tunic and took out Ehlana's letter.

'Beloved,' it began. 'If all has gone well, you're very close to the Zemoch border by now – and I *must* believe that all has gone well or else I shall go mad. You and your companions *will* succeed, dearest Sparhawk. I know that as surely as if God himself had told it to me. Our lives are strangely controlled, my love. We were destined to love each other – and to marry. We had no real choice in this, I think – though I would certainly have chosen no other. Our meeting each other and our marriage were all a part of some grander design – even as was the gathering of your companions. Who in all the world could be more perfectly suited to aid you than the great men who ride with you? Kalten and Kurik, Tynian and Ulath, Bevier and dear Berit, so young and so very brave, all of them have joined with you in love and common purpose. You surely cannot fail, my beloved, not with such men at your side. Hasten, my champion and husband. Take your invincible companions to the lair of our ancient foe and confront him there. Let Azash tremble, for the Knight Sparhawk comes with Bhelliom in his fist, and not all the powers of Hell can prevail against him. Hasten, my beloved, and know that you are armed not merely with Bhelliom but with my love as well.

I love you,
Ehlana.'

Sparhawk read through the letter several times. His bride, he saw, had a very strong tendency towards oratory. Even her letters had the tone of a public address. Stirring though the message was, he might have preferred something a bit less polished, something more genuine. Although he knew that the emotions she expressed came from her heart, her fondness for the well-turned phrase somehow intruded itself between them. 'Oh well,' he sighed. 'She'll probably relax as we get to know each other better.'

Then Berit came up the deck, and Sparhawk remembered something. He read through the letter again and made a quick decision. 'Berit,' he called, 'do you suppose I could have a word with you?'

'Of course, Sir Sparhawk.'

'I thought you might like to see this.' Sparhawk handed him the letter.

Berit looked at it. 'But this is personal, Sir Sparhawk,' he objected.

'It concerns you, I think. It may help you to deal with a problem you've been having lately.'

Berit read through the letter, and a strange expression came over his face.

'Does that help at all?' Sparhawk asked him.

Berit flushed. 'Y-you knew?' he stammered.

Sparhawk smiled a bit wryly. 'I know it may be hard for you to believe, my friend, but I was young once myself. What's happened to you has probably happened to every young man who's ever lived. In my case, it was when I first went to court. She was a young noblewoman, and I was absolutely certain that the sun rose and set in her eyes. I still think of her on occasion – rather fondly, actually. She's older now, of course, but her eyes still make me weak when she looks at me.'

'But you're married, Sir Sparhawk.'

'That's fairly recent, and it has nothing whatsoever to do with what I felt for that young noblewoman. You'll waste a lot of dreams on Ehlana, I expect. We all do that in these cases, but maybe it makes better men of us.'

'Surely you won't tell the queen.' Berit seemed shocked.

'Probably not, no. It doesn't really concern her, so why

485

should I worry her about it? The point I'm trying to make here, Berit, is that what you're feeling is a part of growing up. Everybody goes through the same thing – if he's lucky.'

'You don't hate me then, Sir Sparhawk?'

'Hate you? God no, Berit. I'd be disappointed in you if you *didn't* feel this way about *some* young, pretty girl.'

Berit sighed. 'Thank you, Sir Sparhawk,' he said.

'Berit, before very long, you're going to be a full-fledged Pandion Knight, and then we'll be brothers. Do you suppose we could drop that "sir"? Just "Sparhawk" will do. I more or less recognize the name.'

'If you wish, Sparhawk,' Berit said. He offered his friend the letter.

'Why don't you keep it for me? I've got a lot of clutter in my saddlebags, and I wouldn't want to lose it.'

Then the two of them, their shoulders almost touching, went aft to see if Kurik needed any help with the ship.

They rigged a sea-anchor that evening, and when they awoke the following morning, they found that the rain and snow had passed, though the sky was still lead-grey.

'That cloud's there again, Sparhawk,' Berit reported, coming forward from the stern. 'It's a good long way behind us, but it's definitely there.'

Sparhawk looked aft. Now that he could actually see it, it did not seem quite so menacing. When it had been that vague shadow hovering always at the very edge of his vision, it had filled him with an unnamed dread. Now he had to be very careful not to think of it as little more than some minor annoyance. It *was* still dangerous, after all. A faint smile touched his lips. It appeared that even a God could blunder, could push something past the point of effectiveness.

'Why don't you just dissolve that thing with Bhelliom, Sparhawk?' Kalten asked irritably.

'Because it would just form up again. Why waste the effort?'

'You aren't going to do anything about it then?'

'Of course I am.'

'What?'

'I'm going to ignore it.'

About mid-morning they landed on a snowy beach, waded the horses ashore and set the boat adrift. Then they mounted and rode inland.

The eastern side of the gulf was far more arid than the mountains to the west had been, and the rocky hills were covered with a layer of fine black sand, thinly covered in sheltered spots with skiffs of powdery snow. The wind was bitingly cold, and it lifted clouds of dust and snow to engulf them as they pushed on. They rode through what seemed a perpetual twilight, their mouths and noses covered with scarves.

'Slow going,' Ulath observed laconically, carefully wiping dust from his eyes. 'Martel's decision to go by way of Aka might have been wise.'

'I'm sure it's just as cold and dusty on the road from Aka to Zemoch,' Sparhawk said. He smiled faintly. 'Martel's a fastidious sort. He absolutely abhors getting dirty. The notion of a couple of pounds of fine black sand mixed with snow sifting down the back of his neck sort of appeals to me for some reason.'

'That's very petty, Sparhawk,' Sephrenia chided.

'I know,' he replied. 'I'm like that sometimes.'

They took shelter that night in a cave, and when they emerged the following morning they found that the sky had cleared, although the wind had picked up and was stirring up clouds of the perpetual dust.

Berit was the sort of young man who took his responsibilities very seriously. He had taken it upon himself to scout around at first light, and he was just returning as the rest of them gathered at the cave mouth. They could clearly see his look of revulsion as he came nearer. 'There are some people out there, Sparhawk,' he said as he dismounted.

'Soldiers?'

'No. They have old people and women and children with them. They have a few weapons, but they don't seem to know how to handle them.'

'What are they doing?' Kalten asked.

Berit coughed nervously and looked around. 'I'd really rather not say, Sir Kalten, and I don't think we want Lady Sephrenia to see them. They've set up a sort of an altar with a clay idol on it, and they're doing things people shouldn't do in public. I think they're just a group of degenerate peasants.'

'We'd better tell Sephrenia,' Sparhawk decided.

'I couldn't do that, Sparhawk,' Berit said, blushing. 'I *couldn't* describe what they're doing in front of her.'

'Generalize, Berit. You don't have to be too specific.'

Sephrenia, however, proved to be curious. 'Exactly what are they doing, Berit?'

'I *knew* she was going to ask,' Berit muttered reproachfully to Sparhawk. 'They're – um – they're sacrificing animals, Lady Sephrenia, and they aren't wearing any clothes – even in this cold. They're smearing blood from the sacrifices on their bodies, and they're – um –'

'Yes,' she said. 'I'm familiar with the rite. Describe the people. Do they look Styric, or are they more Elene?'

'Many of them are fair-haired, Lady Sephrenia.'

'Ah,' she said, 'that's who they are then. They don't pose any particular danger. The idol is another matter, though. We can't leave it behind us. We have to smash it.'

'For the same reason we had to break the one in the cellar at Ghasek?' Kalten asked.

'Exactly.' She made a little face. 'I shouldn't really say

this, but the Younger Gods blundered when they confined Azash to that clay idol in the shrine near Ghanda. The idea was sound enough, but they overlooked something. The idol can be duplicated by men, and if certain rites are performed, the Spirit of Azash can enter the duplicates.'

'What do we do?' Bevier asked.

'We smash the idol before the rite's completed.'

The unclad Zemochs in the canyon were none too clean, and their hair was tangled and matted. Sparhawk had never truly realized before just how much of human ugliness is concealed by clothing. The naked worshippers appeared to be peasants and herdsmen, and they squealed with fright as the mail-shirted knights burst upon them. The fact that the attackers were disguised as Zemochs added to their confusion. They ran this way and that, bawling in terror.

Four of their number wore crude ecclesiastical robes, and they stood before the altar where they had just finished sacrificing a goat. Three of them gaped in stunned disbelief at the knights, but the fourth, a scraggly-bearded fellow with a narrow head, was weaving his fingers and speaking desperately in Styric. He released a series of apparitions which were so ineptly formed as to be laughable.

The knights rode directly through the apparitions and the milling crowd.

'Defend our God!' the priest shrieked, his lips flecked with foam. His parishioners, however, chose not to do that.

The mud idol on the crude altar seemed to be moving slightly, even as a distant hill seems to dance and waver in the shimmering heat of a summer afternoon. Wave upon wave of sheer malevolence emanated from it and the air was suddenly deathly cold. Sparhawk suddenly felt his strength draining away, and Faran faltered. Then the ground before the altar seemed to bulge. Something was stirring beneath the earth, something so dreadful that Sparhawk turned his eyes away in sick revulsion. The ground heaved, and Sparhawk felt cold fear grip his heart. The light began to fade from his eyes.

'No!' Sephrenia's voice rang out. 'Stand firm! It cannot hurt you!' She began to speak rapidly in Styric, then quickly held out her hand. What appeared there glowed brightly and seemed at first no larger than an apple, but as it rose into the air, it expanded and grew brighter and brighter until it was almost as if she had conjured up a small sun to hang in the air before the idol, and that sun brought with it a summer-like warmth that burned away the deathly chill. The ground ceased its restless heaving, and the idol froze, once again becoming motionless.

Kurik spurred his trembling gelding forward and swung his heavy chain-mace once. The grotesque idol shattered beneath the blow, and its shards flew out in all directions.

The naked Zemochs wailed in absolute despair.

Chapter 25

'Round them up, Sparhawk,' Sephrenia said, looking with a shudder at the naked Zemochs, 'and please make them put their clothes back on.' She looked at the altar. 'Talen,' she said, 'gather up the fragments of the idol. We won't want to leave them here.'

The boy didn't even argue with her.

The 'rounding up' did not take very long. Naked, unarmed people do not customarily resist when mailed men with sharp steel in their hands start giving orders. The priest with the narrow head continued to shriek at them, however, although he was very careful not to give them any other reason to chastise him. 'Apostates!' he howled. 'Defilers! I call upon Azash to –' His words trailed off into a kind of croak as Sephrenia extended her arm and the serpent head reared from her palm, its tongue flickering. He stared at the swaying image of the reptile, his eyes bulging. Then he collapsed and grovelled in the dirt before her.

Sephrenia looked around sternly, and the other Zemochs also sank to the ground with a horrified moan. 'Perverted ones!' she snarled at them in the corrupt Zemoch dialect. 'Your rite has been forbidden for centuries. Why have you chosen to disobey mighty Azash?'

'Our priests beguiled us, dread Priestess,' one shaggy-haired fellow gibbered. 'They told us that the prohibition of our rite was a Styric blasphemy. They said that it was the Styrics in our midst who were leading us away from the true God.' He seemed blind to the fact that Sephrenia herself was Styric. 'We are Elene,' he said proudly, 'and we know that we are the chosen ones.'

Sephrenia gave the Church Knights a look that conveyed volumes. Then she looked at the rag-tag band of unwashed 'Elenes' grovelling before her. She seemed about to speak once, her breath drawn in to deliver a shattering denunciation. Instead, however, she let out the breath, and when she spoke, her voice was clinically detached. 'You have strayed,' she told them, 'and that makes you unfit to join your countrymen in their holy war. You will return to your homes now. Go back to Merjuk and beyond, and venture no more to this place. Do not go near the temple of Azash, lest he destroy you.'

'Should we hang our priests?' the shaggy fellow asked her hopefully, 'or burn them perhaps?'

'No. Our God seeks worshippers, not corpses. Henceforth you will devote yourselves to the rites of purification and of reconciliation and the rites of the seasons only. You are as children, and as children shall you worship. Now go!' She straightened her arm, and the serpent-head emerging from her palm, reared up, swelling, growing and becoming not so much a serpent as a dragon. The dragon roared, and sooty flames shot from its mouth.

The Zemochs fled.

'You should have let them hang that one fellow at least,' Kalten said.

'No,' she replied. 'I just set them on the path of a different religion, and that religion forbids killing.'

'They're Elenes, Lady Sephrenia,' Bevier objected. 'You should have instructed them to follow the Elene faith.'

'With all its prejudices and inconsistencies, Bevier?' she asked. 'No, I don't think so. I pointed them in a gentler way. Talen, have you finished yet?'

'I've got all the pieces I could find, Sephrenia.'

492

'Bring them along.' She turned her white palfrey then and led them away from the rude altar.

They returned to the cave, gathered up their belongings and set out again.

'Where did they come from?' Sparhawk asked Sephrenia as they rode along in the biting cold.

'Northeastern Zemoch,' she replied, 'from the steppes north of Merjuk. They're primitive Elenes who haven't had the benefits of contact with civilized people the way the rest of you have.'

'Styrics, you mean?'

'Naturally. What other civilized people are there?'

'Be nice,' he chided her.

She smiled. 'The inclusion of orgies in the worship of Azash was a part of Otha's original strategy. It brought in the Elenes. Otha's an Elene himself, and he knows how strong those appetites are in your race. We Styrics have more exotic perversions. Azash really prefers those, but the primitives in the back country still hold to the old ways. They're relatively harmless.'

Talen drew in beside them. 'What do you want me to do with the pieces of that idol?' he asked.

'Throw them away,' she replied, '– one piece every mile or so. Scatter them thoroughly. The rite had already begun, and we don't want someone to gather up the pieces and put them back together again. The cloud's trouble enough. We don't want Azash Himself behind us as well.'

'Amen,' the boy said fervently. He rode off to one side, stood up in his stirrups and hurled a fragment of mud some distance away.

'We're safe then, aren't we?' Sparhawk said. 'Now that the idol's smashed, I mean? And as soon as Talen finishes scattering it?'

'Hardly, dear one. That cloud's still there.'

493

'But the cloud's never really hurt us, Sephrenia. It tried to make us melancholy and afraid, but that's about all – and Flute took care of that for us. If that's the best it can really do, it's not much of a threat.'

'Don't let yourself grow overconfident, Sparhawk,' she warned. 'The cloud – or shadow, whichever it is – is probably a creature of Azash, and that would make it at least as dangerous as the Damork or the Seeker.'

The countryside did not improve as they rode eastward, nor did the weather. It was bitterly cold, and the billowing clouds of black dust erased the sky. What little vegetation they saw was stunted and sickly. They were following something that sort of looked like a trail, though its drunken meanderings suggested wild cattle rather than men. The waterholes were infrequent, and the water in them was ice which had to be melted down to water the horses.

'Cursed dust!' Ulath suddenly bellowed at the sky, throwing aside the cloth which covered his mouth and nose.

'Steady,' Tynian said to him.

'What's the use of all this?' Ulath demanded, spitting out dust. 'We can't even tell which way we're going!' He pulled the cloth back across his face and rode on, muttering to himself.

The horses continued to plod on, their hooves kicking up little puffs of frozen dust.

The melancholy which had beset them in the mountains lying to the west of the Gulf of Merjuk was obviously returning, and Sparhawk rode on cautiously, watching with chagrin as the mood of his companions rapidly deteriorated even as he kept a wary eye on nearby ravines and rocky outcrops.

Bevier and Tynian were deep in a sombre conversation. 'It is a sin,' Bevier was saying stubbornly. 'To even suggest

494

it is a heresy and a blasphemy. The Fathers of the Church have reasoned it out, and reason, coming as it does *from* God, is *of* God. Thus God Himself tells us that He and He alone is Divine.'

'But –' Tynian began to object.

'Hear me out, my friend,' Bevier said to him. 'Since God tells us that there are no other Divinities, for us to believe otherwise is blackest sin. We are embarked upon a quest founded in childish superstition. The Zemochs are a danger, certainly, but they are a *worldly* danger, even as the Eshandists. They have no supernatural allies. We are throwing our lives away searching for a mythical foe who exists only in the diseased imaginations of our heathen enemies. I will reason with Sparhawk about this presently, and I have no doubt that he can be persuaded to abandon this vain quest.'

'That might be best,' Tynian agreed, albeit somewhat dubiously. The two of them seemed totally unaware that Sparhawk was clearly riding within earshot.

'You've got to talk with him, Kurik,' Kalten was saying to Sparhawk's squire. 'We haven't got a chance in the world.'

'*You* tell him,' Kurik growled. 'I'm a servant. It's not my place to tell my lord that he's a suicidal madman.'

'I honestly believe we should slip up behind him and tie him up. I'm not just trying to save my own life, you understand. I'm trying to save his too.'

'I feel the same way, Kalten.'

'They're coming!' Berit screamed, pointing at a nearby cloud of swirling dust. 'Arm yourselves!'

The war-like shouts of Sparhawk's friends were shrill, tinged with panic, and their charge had an air of desperation about it. They crashed into the dust-cloud, swinging their swords and axes at the unfeeling air.

'Help them, Sparhawk!' Talen cried, his voice shrill.

495

'Help them with what?'

'The monsters! They'll all be killed!'

'I rather doubt that, Talen,' Sparhawk replied coolly, watching his friends flailing at the dust-cloud with their weapons. 'They're more than a match for what they're facing.'

Talen glared at him for a moment, then rode several yards away, swearing to himself.

'I take it that you don't see anything in the dust either,' Sephrenia said calmly.

'That's all it is, little mother – just dust.'

'Let's deal with that right now.' She spoke briefly in Styric, then gestured.

The thickly billowing dust-cloud seemed to shudder and flinch in upon itself for a moment, and then it gave a long, audible sigh as it slithered to the ground.

'Where did they go?' Ulath roared, looking around and brandishing his axe.

The others looked equally baffled, and the looks they directed at Sparhawk were darkly suspicious.

They avoided him after that and rode with dark scowls, whispering to each other and frequently casting covert looks at him, looks filled with hostility. They made their night's encampment on the leeward side of a steep bluff where pale, sand-scoured rocks protruded from an unwholesome, diseased-looking bank of leprous clay. Sparhawk cooked their meal, and his friends chose not to linger with him at the fire after the meal as was customary. He shook his head in disgust and went to his blankets.

'Awaken, Sir Knight, an it please thee.' The voice was soft and gentle, and it seemed filled with love. Sparhawk opened his eyes. He found himself in a gaily-coloured pavilion, and beyond the open tent flap was a broad green meadow, all aswirl with wild flowers. There were trees, ancient and vast, their branches heavy with fragrant blossoms, and beyond the trees lay a sparkling sea of deep, deep blue, bejewelled with the gleams of reflected sunlight. The sky was as no other sky had ever been. It was a rainbow that covered the entire dome of the heavens, blessing all the world beneath.

The speaker who had awakened him stood nudging at him with her nose and pawing impatiently at the carpeted floor of the pavilion with one forehoof. She was small for a deer, and her coat was of such dazzling whiteness as to be almost incandescent. Her eyes were large and meltingly brown, and they reflected a docility, a trust and a sweet nature that tugged at the heart. Her manner, however, was insistent. She most definitely wanted him to get up.

'Have I slept overlong?' he asked, a bit concerned that he might have offended her.

'Thou wert a-weary, Sir Knight,' she replied, automatically, it seemed, coming to his defence even against self-criticism. 'Dress thyself with some care,' the gentle hind instructed, 'for I am bidden to bring thee into the presence of my mistress, who doth rule this realm and whom all her subjects adore.'

Sparhawk fondly stroked her snowy neck, and her great eyes melted with love. He rose and looked to his armour. It was as it should have been, jet black and embossed with silver. He was pleased to note as he drew it on that it had no more weight than gossamer silk. It was not steel, however. Though his great sword was imposing, it was, he knew, no more than ornamental in this fairy kingdom begirt by a jewelled sea and lying in happy contentment beneath its multi-coloured sky. Here were no dangers, no hate, no discord, and all was abiding peace and love.

'We must hasten,' the white deer told him. 'Our boat doth await us on yon strand where wavelets play in wanton

497

abandon in the ever-changing light of our enchanted sky.'
She led him with precise and delicate steps into the
flower-kissed meadow, a meadow so sweet-smelling as
to make the senses swoon.

They passed a white tigress lolling indolently upon
her back in the warm morning sunlight as her cubs,
large-footed and awkward, wrestled in the grass nearby
in mock ferocity. The white deer paused briefly to nuzzle
at the face of the tigress, and she was rewarded by a broad,
affectionate swipe of a huge pink tongue which dampened
one side of her snowy face from chin to ear-tip.

The flower-tipped grasses bowed before the warm
breeze as Sparhawk followed the white deer across the
meadow to the blue-tinged shade beneath the ancient
trees. Beyond the trees, an alabaster gravel strand sloped
gently down to an azure sea, and there awaited them a craft
more bird than ship. Slender was her prow, and graceful
as neck of swan. Two wings of snowy sail arose above her
oaken deck, and she tugged at her moorings as if eager
to be off.

Sparhawk considered the white doe, bent and, placing
one arm beneath her breast and the other behind her
haunch, he lifted her quite easily. She made no effort
to struggle, but a momentary alarm showed in her
huge eyes.

'Calm thyself,' he told her. 'I do but bear thee unto our
waiting ship that thou wilt encounter no sudden chill from
the waters which do stand between us and our craft.'

'Thou art kind, gentle knight,' she said, trustingly resting
her chin upon his shoulder as, with purposeful strides he
waded out into the playful wavelets.

Once they had boarded, their eager craft leapt forward,
bravely breasting the waves, and their destination soon
emerged before them. It was a small, verdant eyot
crowned with a sacred grove ancient beyond imagining,

and Sparhawk could clearly see the gleaming marble columns of a temple beneath those spreading limbs.

Other craft, no less graceful than his own and heedless of the vagaries of the wanton breeze, also made their way across that sapphire sea towards the eyot which beckoned to them. And as they stepped out upon a golden strand, Sir Sparhawk recognized the dearly-loved faces of his companions. Sir Kalten, steadfast and true, Sir Ulath, bull-strong and lion-brave, Sir –

Sparhawk half-woke, shaking his head to clear the cobwebs of cloying image and extravagant expression from his mind.

Somewhere a tiny foot stamped in exasperation. 'That *really* makes me cross, Sparhawk!' a familiar voice scolded him. 'Now go back to sleep at once!'

Slowly the valiant knights climbed the gentle slope leading to the eyot's grove-crested top, recounting to each other their morning's adventures. Sir Kalten was guided by a white badger, Sir Tynian by a white lion, Sir Ulath by a great white bear and Sir Bevier by a snowy dove. The young knight-to-be, Berit, was led by a white lamb, Kurik by a faithful white hound and Talen by a mink in ermine coat.

Sephrenia, clad in white and with her brow encircled by a garland of flowers, awaited them on the marble steps of the temple, and, seated quite calmly on the branch of an oak that predated every other living thing, was the queen of this fairy realm, the Child-Goddess Aphrael. She wore a gown instead of that rude smock, and her head was crowned with light. The playful subterfuge of the pipes was no longer necessary, and she raised her voice in a clear, pure song of greeting. Then she rose and walked down through the empty air as calmly as she might have descended a stair, and when she reached the cool, lush grass of the sacred grove, she danced, whirling and laughing among them, bestowing kisses by the score with her bow-like little mouth. Her tiny feet but lightly crushed the soft grass, but Sparhawk immediately saw the source of those greenish stains which had always perplexed him. She even kissed those snowy creatures which had guided the heroes into her exalted presence. The flowery descriptions came into Sparhawk's mind despite his best efforts to keep them out, and he groaned inwardly. Aphrael imperiously motioned for him to kneel, encircled his neck with her small arms and kissed him several times. 'If you don't stop making fun of me, Sparhawk,' she murmured for his ears alone, 'I'll strip you of your armour and turn you out to graze with the sheep.'

'Forgive mine error, Divine One,' he grinned at her.

She laughed and kissed him again. Sephrenia had once mentioned the fact that Aphrael enjoyed kisses. That did not appear to have changed very much.

They breakfasted on fruits unknown to man, then lounged at their ease on the soft grass as birds carolled to them from the limbs of the sacred grove. Then Aphrael rose to her feet and, after circling through the group once more for kisses, she spoke to them quite gravely. 'Though I have been desolate to have been absent from your midst for the past lonely months,' she began, 'I have not summoned ye here solely for this joyful reunion, glad though it makes my heart. Ye have gathered at my request and with my dear sister's aid –' she gave Sephrenia a smile of radiant love – 'so that I may impart unto ye certain truths. Forgive me that I must touch these truths but lightly, for they are the truths of the Gods, and are far beyond your grasp, I do fear; for much as I melt with love for each of ye, I must tell ye, not unkindly, that even as I have appeared as a child to ye, so ye now appear to me. Thus I will not assault the outer bounds of your understanding with matters beyond your reach.' She looked around at their uncomprehending expressions. 'What *is* the matter with you all?' she said in exasperation.

Sparhawk rose to his feet, crooked one finger at the little Goddess and led her off to one side.

'What?' she demanded crossly.

'Are you in the mood for some advice?' he asked her.

'I'll listen.' Her tone made no promises.

'You're stupefying them with eloquence, Aphrael. Kalten looks like a pole-axed ox at the moment. We're plain men, little Goddess. You'll have to speak to us plainly if you want us to understand.'

She pouted. 'I worked for weeks on that speech, Sparhawk.'

'It's a lovely speech, Aphrael. When you tell the other Gods about this – and I'm sure you will – recite it to them as if you had delivered it to us verbatim. They'll swoon with delight, I'm sure. For the sake of brevity – this night won't last forever, you know – *and* for the sake of clarity, give us the abbreviated version. You might consider suspending the thee's and thou's as well. They make you sound as if you're preaching a sermon, and sermons tend to put people to sleep.'

She pouted slightly. 'Oh, very well, Sparhawk,' she said, 'but you're taking all the fun out of this for me.'

'Can you ever forgive me?'

She stuck her tongue out at him and led him back to rejoin the others.

'This grouchy old bear suggests that I get to the point,' Aphrael said, giving Sparhawk a sly, sidelong glance. 'He's nice enough as a knight, I suppose, but he's a bit lacking in poetry. Very well, then, I've asked you to come here so that I can tell you a few things about Bhelliom – why it's so powerful – and so very dangerous.' She paused, knitting her raven-like brows. 'Bhelliom isn't substance,' she continued. 'It's spirit, and it predates the

501

stars. There are many such spirits, and each of them has many attributes. One of their more important attributes is colour. You see, what happens is –' She looked around at them. 'Maybe we can save that for some other day,' she decided. 'Anyway, these spirits were cast across the sky so that –' She broke off again. 'This is *very* difficult, Sephrenia,' she said in a plaintive little voice. '*Why* must these Elenes be so dense?'

'Because their God chooses not to explain things to them, Aphrael,' Sephrenia told her.

'He's such an old stick,' Aphrael said. 'He makes rules for no reason at all. That's all He ever does – make rules. He's so tiresome sometimes.'

'Why don't you go on with your story, Aphrael?'

'Very well.' The Child-Goddess looked at the knights. 'The spirits have colours, and they have a purpose,' she told them. 'I think you'll have to settle for that at the moment. One of the things they do is to make worlds. Bhelliom – which isn't its real name – made the blue ones. Seen from afar, this world is blue, because of its oceans. Other worlds are red, or green or yellow or any of countless other colours. These spirits make worlds by attracting the dust that blows forever through the emptiness, and the dust congeals around them like churned butter. But when Bhelliom made *this* world, it made a mistake. There was too much red dust. Bhelliom's essence is blue, and it can't bear red, but when you gather red dust together, you have –'

'Iron!' Tynian exclaimed.

'And you said they wouldn't understand,' Aphrael said reproachfully to Sparhawk. She rushed to Tynian and kissed him several times. 'Very well then,' she said happily. 'Tynian is exactly right. Bhelliom cannot bear iron because iron is red. To protect itself, it hardened its essence of blue into the sapphire – which Ghwerig

502

later carved into the shape of a rose. The iron – the red
– congealed around it, and Bhelliom was trapped within
the earth.'

They stared at her, still only vaguely comprehending.

'Just make it short,' Sparhawk advised.

'I *am*.'

'It's your story, Aphrael,' he shrugged.

'Bhelliom's been congealed even more because the
Troll-Gods are trapped inside it,' she continued.

'They're *what*?' Sparhawk gasped.

'Everybody knows *that*, Sparhawk. Where do you think
Ghwerig hid them from us when we were looking for
them?'

He uneasily remembered that Bhelliom and its unwilling
inhabitants lay no more than a few inches from his heart.

'The point of all this is that Sparhawk has threatened to destroy Bhelliom, and because he's an Elene
knight, he'll probably use his sword – or an axe – or
the spear of Aldreas, or something like that – something made of steel, which is to say iron. If he strikes
Bhelliom with something made of steel, he *will* destroy
it, and Bhelliom and the Troll-Gods are doing everything
in their power to keep him from ever coming near
enough to Azash for him to be tempted to raise his
sword against it. First they tried to attack *his* mind,
and when that didn't work, they began to attack *yours*.
It won't be long, dear ones, before one of you tries to
kill him.'

'Never!' Kalten half-shouted.

'If they continue to twist you, it *will* happen, Kalten.'

'We'll fall on our swords first,' Bevier declared.

'Why on earth would you want to do that?' she asked
him. 'All you have to do is confine the jewel in something
made of steel. That canvas pouch is marked with the
Styric symbols for iron, but Bhelliom and the Troll-Gods

503

are growing desperate, and symbols aren't enough now. You'll have to use the real thing.'

Sparhawk made a sour face, suddenly feeling just a little foolish.

'I've been thinking all along that the shadow – and now that cloud – had come from Azash,' he confessed.

Aphrael stared at him. 'You *what*?' she exclaimed.

'It seemed sort of logical,' he said lamely. 'Azash has been trying to kill me since this all started.'

'Why would Azash chase you around with clouds and shadows when He has much more substantial things at His command? Is that the very best all that logic could come up with?'

'I knew it!' Bevier exclaimed. 'I knew we were overlooking something when you first told us about that shadow, Sparhawk! It didn't really *have* to be Azash after all.'

Sparhawk suddenly felt very foolish.

'Why is it that I've got so much power over Bhelliom?' he asked her.

'Because of the rings.'

'Ghwerig had the rings before I did.'

'But they were clear stones then. Now they're red with the blood of your family and the blood of Ehlana's.'

'Just the colour is enough to make it obey me?'

Aphrael stared at him and then at Sephrenia. 'Do you mean they don't *know* why their blood is red?' she asked incredulously. 'What have you been *doing*, sister?'

'It's a difficult concept for them, Aphrael.'

The little Goddess stamped away, flinging her arms in the air and muttering Styric words she should not have known existed.

'Sparhawk,' Sephrenia said calmly, 'your blood is red because it has iron in it.'

'It *has*?' He was stunned. 'How's that possible?'

504

'Just believe what I say, Sparhawk. It's those blood-stained rings that give you so much power over the jewel.'

'What an amazing thing,' he said.

Aphrael returned then. 'Once Bhelliom is confined in steel, you'll have no further interference from the Troll-Gods,' she told them. 'The rest of you will stop plotting to kill Sparhawk, and you'll all be as one again.'

'Couldn't you have just told us what to do without all these explanations?' Kurik asked her. 'These are Church Knights, Flute. They're used to following orders they don't understand. They almost have to be.'

'I suppose I could have,' she admitted, laying one small hand caressingly on his bearded cheek, 'but I missed you – all of you – and I wanted you to see the place where I live.'

'Showing off?' he teased her.

'Well –' She blushed slightly. 'Is that so very, very improper?'

'It's a lovely island, Flute, and we're proud that you chose to show it to us.'

She threw her arms about his neck and smothered him with kisses. Her face, Sparhawk noticed, however, was wet with tears as she kissed the gruff squire.

'You must return now,' she told them, 'for the night is nearly over. First, however –'

The kissing went on for quite some time. When the dark-haired little Goddess came to Talen, she brushed her lips lightly against his and then started towards Tynian. She stopped, a speculative look on her face, and then returned to the young thief and did a more complete job on him. When she moved on, she was smiling mysteriously.

'And hath our gentle mistress resolved thy turmoil, Sir Knight?' the snowy hind asked as the swan-like boat returned the two of them to the alabaster strand where the gaily-coloured pavilion awaited them.

'I will know that with more certainty when mine eyes again open on the mundane world from which she summoned me, gentle creature,' he replied. He found that he could not help himself. The flowery speech came to his lips unbidden. He sighed ruefully.

The note of the pipes was slightly discordant, a scolding sort of note.

'An it please thee, dear Aphrael,' he surrendered.

'That's much better, Sparhawk.' The voice was no more than a whisper in his ears.

The small white deer led him back to the pavilion, and he laid him down again, a strange, bemused drowsiness coming over him.

'Remember me,' the hind said softly, nuzzling at his cheek.

'I will,' he promised, 'and gladly, for thy sweet presence doth ease my troubled soul and bids me rest.'

And then again he slept.

He awoke in an ugly world of black sand and chill, blowing dust reeking of things long dead. His hair was clogged with the dust, and it abraded his skin beneath his clothing. What had really awakened him, however, was a small, tinking sound, the sound of someone firmly tapping on ringing steel with a small hammer.

Despite the turmoil of the previous day, he felt enormously refreshed and at peace with the world.

The ringing sound of the hammer stopped, and Kurik crossed their dusty camp site with something in his hands. He held it out to Sparhawk. 'What do you think?' he asked. 'Will this lock it in?' What he was holding in his calloused hands was a chain-mail pouch. 'It's about the best I can do for now, My Lord. I don't have too much steel to work with.'

Sparhawk took the pouch and looked at his squire. 'You too?' he asked. 'You had a dream too?'

Kurik nodded. 'I talked with Sephrenia about it,' he said. 'We all had the same dream – it wasn't exactly a dream, though. She tried to explain it to me, but she lost me.' He paused. 'I'm sorry, Sparhawk. I doubted you. Everything seemed so futile and hopeless.'

'That was the Troll-Gods, Kurik. Let's get Bhelliom into the steel pouch so that it doesn't happen to you again.' He took up the canvas pouch and began to untie the strings.

'Wouldn't it be easier just to leave it inside the canvas sack?' Kurik asked.

'It might make it easier to put it into the steel one, but the time's coming when I might have to take it out in a hurry. I don't want any knots getting in my way when Azash is breathing down the back of my neck.'

'Sound thinking, My Lord.'

Sparhawk lifted the Sapphire Rose in both hands and held it directly in front of his face. 'Blue-Rose,' he said to it in Troll, 'I am Sparhawk-from-Elenia. Do you know me?'

The Rose flickered sullenly.

'Do you acknowledge my authority?'

The Rose grew dark, and he could feel its hatred.

He inched his right thumb up along his palm and turned the ring on his finger around. Then he held the ring against the flower-gem – not the band this time but the blood-stained stone itself. He pressed his hand firmly against the Sapphire Rose.

Bhelliom shrieked, and he could feel it writhing in his hand like a live snake. He relaxed the pressure slightly. 'I'm glad we understand each other,' he said. 'Hold open the pouch, Kurik.'

There was no resistance. The jewel seemed almost eager to enter its imprisonment.

'Neat,' Kurik said admiringly as Sparhawk wrapped a strand of soft iron wire around the top of the steel-link pouch.

'I thought it might be worth a try,' Sparhawk grinned. 'Are the others up yet?'

Kurik nodded. 'They're standing in line over by the fire. You might give some thought to issuing a general amnesty, Sparhawk. Otherwise, they'll fill up half the morning with apologies. Be particularly careful about Bevier. He's been praying since before daylight. It's likely to take him a long time to tell you just how guilty he feels.'

'He's a good boy, Kurik.'

'Of course he is. That's part of the problem.'

'Cynic.'

Kurik grinned at him.

As the two of them crossed the camp, Kurik looked up at the sky. 'The wind's died,' he observed, 'and the dust seems to be settling. Do you suppose –?' He left it tentative.

'Probably,' Sparhawk said. 'It sort of fits together, doesn't it? Well, here goes.' He cleared his throat as he approached his shamefaced friends. 'Interesting night, wasn't it?' he asked them conversationally. 'I was really getting attached to that little white deer. She had a cold, wet nose, though.'

They laughed, sounding a bit strained.

'All right,' he said then. 'Now we know where all the gloom was coming from, and there's not really much point in ploughing over it again and again, is there? It was nobody's fault, so why don't we forget about it? We've got more important things to think about right now.' He held up the steel-link pouch. 'Here's our blue friend,' he told them. 'I hope it's comfortable in its little iron sack, but

508

comfortable or not, that's where it's going to stay – at least until we need it. Whose turn is it to cook breakfast?'

'Yours,' Ulath told him.

'I cooked supper last night.'

'What's that got to do with it?'

'That's hardly fair, Ulath.'

'I just keep track of these things, Sparhawk. If you're interested in justice, go and talk with the Gods.'

The rest of them laughed, and everything was all right again.

While Sparhawk was preparing breakfast, Sephrenia joined him at the fire. 'I owe you an apology, dear one,' she confessed.

'Oh?'

'I didn't even suspect that the Troll-Gods might have been the source of that shadow.'

'I'd hardly call that your fault, Sephrenia. I was so convinced that it was Azash that I wasn't willing to admit any other possibility.'

'I'm supposed to know better, Sparhawk. I'm not supposed to rely on logic.'

'I think it might have been Perraine that led us in the wrong direction, little mother,' he said gravely. 'Those attacks of his came at Martel's direction, and Martel was simply following an earlier strategy laid down by Azash. Since it was just a continuation of what had been going on before, we had no reason to suspect that something new had entered the game. Even after we found out that Perraine had nothing to do with the shadow, the old idea still stuck. Don't blame yourself, Sephrenia, because I certainly don't blame you. What surprises me is that Aphrael didn't see that we were making a mistake and warn us about it.'

Sephrenia smiled a bit ruefully. 'I'm afraid it was because she couldn't believe that we didn't understand.

509

She has no real conception of just how limited we are, Sparhawk.'

'Shouldn't you tell her?'

'I'd sooner die.'

Kurik's speculation may or may not have been correct, but whether that constant wind which had choked them with dust for the past few days had been of natural origin or whether Bhelliom had roused it, it was gone now, and the air was clear and cold. The sky was bright, brittle blue, and the sun, cold and hard, hung above the eastern horizon. That, coupled with the vision of the preceding night, lifted their spirits enough to make it even possible for them to ignore the black cloud hovering on the horizon behind them.

'Sparhawk,' Tynian said, pulling his horse in beside Faran, 'I think I've finally figured it out.'

'Figured what out?'

'I think I know how Ulath decides whose turn it is to cook.'

'Oh? I'd like to hear that.'

'He just waits until somebody asks, that's all. As soon as somebody asks whose turn it is, Ulath appoints *him* to do the cooking.'

Sparhawk thought back. 'You could be right, you know,' he agreed, 'but what if nobody asks?'

'Then Ulath has to do the cooking himself. It happened once as I recall.'

Sparhawk thought it over. 'Why don't you tell the others?' he suggested. 'I think Ulath has a lot of turns coming, don't you?'

'He does indeed, my friend,' Tynian laughed.

It was about mid-afternoon when they reached a steep ridge of sharply-fractured black rock. There was a sort of a trail winding towards its top. When they were about half-way up, Talen called to Sparhawk from the rear. 'Why don't we stop here?' he suggested. 'I'll sneak on ahead and take a look.'

'It's too dangerous,' Sparhawk turned him down flatly.

'Grow up, Sparhawk. That's what I do. I'm a professional sneak. Nobody's going to see me. I can guarantee that.' The boy paused. 'Besides,' he added, 'if there's any kind of trouble, you're going to need grown men wearing steel to help you. I wouldn't be of much use in a fight, so I'm the only one you can really spare.' He made a face. 'I can't believe I just said that. I want you all to promise to keep Aphrael away from me. I think she's an unhealthy influence.'

'Forget it,' Sparhawk rejected the idea.

'No chance, Sparhawk,' the boy said impudently, rolling out of his saddle and hitting the ground running. 'None of you can catch me.'

'He's long overdue for a good thrashing,' Kurik growled as they watched the nimble boy scamper up the side of the ridge.

'He's right, though,' Kalten said. 'He's the only one we can really afford to lose. Somewhere along the way he's picked up a fairly wide streak of nobility. You should be proud of him, Kurik.'

'Pride wouldn't do me much good when it came time to try to explain to his mother why I let him get himself killed.'

Above them, Talen had disappeared almost as if the ground had opened and swallowed him. He emerged several minutes later from a fissure near the top of the ridge and ran back down the trail to rejoin them. 'There's a city out there,' he reported. 'It would almost have to be Zemoch, wouldn't it?'

Sparhawk took his map out of his saddlebag. 'How big is the city?'

'About the size of Cimmura.'

511

'It has to be Zemoch then. What does it look like?'

'I think it was sort of what they had in mind when they invented the word "ominous".'

'Was there any smoke?' Kurik asked him.

'Only coming from the chimneys of a couple of large buildings in the centre of the city. They seemed to be sort of connected. One of them has all kinds of spires, and the other one's got a big black dome.'

'The rest of the city must be deserted,' Kurik said. 'Have you ever been in Zemoch before, Sephrenia?'

'Once.'

'What's the place with all the spires?'

'Otha's palace.'

'And the one with the black dome?' Kurik did not really have to ask. They all knew the answer.

'The building with the black dome is the Temple of Azash. He's there – waiting for us.'

Chapter 26

Subterfuge had never really been an option, Sparhawk concluded as he and his companions put aside their minimal disguises to don their armour. Deceiving unsophisticated peasants and third-rate militiamen out in the countryside was one thing, but attempting to pass unchallenged through a deserted city patrolled by élite troops would have been futile. Ultimately they would be obliged to resort to force of arms, and under the circumstances, that meant full armour. Chain-mail was adequate for impromptu social get-togethers in rural surroundings, he thought wryly, but city life required greater formality. Country attire simply would not do.

'All right, what's the plan?' Kalten asked as the knights helped each other into their armour.

'I haven't exactly put one together yet,' Sparhawk admitted. 'To be perfectly honest with you, I didn't really think we'd get this far. I thought the best we could hope for was to get close enough to Otha's city to include it in the general destruction when I smashed the Bhelliom. As soon as we get settled into harness, we'll talk with Sephrenia.'

High, thin clouds had begun to drift in from the east during the afternoon, and as the day moved on towards sunset, those clouds began to thicken. The desiccated chill began to lessen, and it was replaced by a peculiar sultriness. There were occasional rumblings of thunder far beyond the eastern horizon when, as the sun was dying amidst bloody clouds, the knights gathered around Sephrenia.

'Our glorious leader here seems to have neglected a few strategic incidentals,' Kalten announced to sort of start things off.

'Be nice,' Sparhawk murmured to him.

'I am, Sparhawk. I haven't used the word "idiot" even once. The question that makes us all burn with curiosity is what do we do now?'

'Just offhand I'd say we could rule out a siege,' Ulath observed.

'Frontal assaults are always fun,' Tynian said.

'Do you mind?' Sparhawk said to them acidly. 'This is sort of how I see it, Sephrenia. We've got what appears to be a deserted city out there, but there are sure to be patrols of Otha's élite guards. We might possibly be able to avoid them, but it wouldn't be a good idea to pin too many hopes on that. I just wish I knew a little bit more about the city itself.'

'*And* about how good Otha's élite guards are,' Tynian added.

'They're adequate soldiers,' Bevier supplied.

'Would they be a match for Church Knights?' Tynian asked.

'No, but then who is?' Bevier said it with no trace of immodesty. 'They're probably about on a par with the soldiers in King Wargun's army.'

'You've been here before, Sephrenia,' Sparhawk said. 'Just exactly where are the palace and the temple located?'

'They're the same building actually,' she replied, 'and they're in the exact centre of the city.'

'Then it wouldn't really matter which gate we used, would it?'

She shook her head.

'Isn't it rather odd for a palace and a temple to be under the same roof?' Kurik asked.

'Zemochs are odd people,' she told him. 'Actually there

is some degree of separation, but you have to go *through* the palace to reach the temple. The temple itself doesn't have any outside entrances.'

'Then all we have to do is to ride to the palace and knock on the door,' Kalten said.

'No,' Kurik disagreed firmly. 'We *walk* to the palace, and we'll talk about knocking when we get there.'

'Walk?' Kalten sounded injured.

'Horses make too much noise on paved streets, and they're a little hard to hide when you need to take cover.'

'Walking any distance in full armour isn't much fun, Kurik.'

'You wanted to be a knight. As I remember it, you and Sparhawk even volunteered.'

'Could you sort of whistle up that invisibility spell Sparhawk told us about?' Kalten asked Sephrenia, '– the one Flute used to play on her pipes?'

She shook her head.

'Why not?'

She hummed a short musical phrase. 'Do you recognize that melody?' she asked him.

He frowned. 'I can't say that I do.'

'That was the traditional Pandion hymn. I'm sure you're familiar with it. Does that answer your question?'

'Oh. Music isn't one of your strong points, I see.'

'What would happen if you tried it and hit the wrong notes?' Talen asked curiously.

She shuddered. 'Please don't ask.'

'We skulk then,' Kalten said. 'So let's get to skulking.'

'Just as soon as it gets dark,' Sparhawk said.

It was a mile or more across a flat, dusty plain to the grim walls of Zemoch, and the armoured knights were all sweating profusely by the time they reached the west gate.

'Muggy,' Kalten said quietly, wiping his streaming face. 'Isn't there anything normal about Zemoch? It shouldn't be this sticky at this time of year.'

'There's definitely some unusual weather coming in,' Kurik agreed. The distant rumble of thunder and the pale flickers of lightning illuminating the cloudbanks lying to the east confirmed their observations.

'Maybe we could appeal to Otha for shelter from the storm,' Tynian said. 'What are the Zemoch views on hospitality?'

'Undependable,' Sephrenia replied.

'We'll want to be as quiet as we can once we're in the city,' Sparhawk cautioned.

Sephrenia lifted her head and looked off to the east, her pale face scarcely visible in the sultry darkness. 'Let's wait a bit,' she suggested. 'That storm's moving this way. Thunder would cover a great deal of incidental clinking.'

They waited, leaning against the basalt walls of the city as the crack and tearing roar of the thunder marched inexorably towards them.

'That should cover any noise we make,' Sparhawk said after about ten minutes. 'Let's get inside before the rain comes.'

The gate itself was made of crudely squared-off logs bound with iron, and it stood slightly ajar. Sparhawk and his companions drew their weapons and slipped through one by one.

There was a strange smell to the city, an odour that seemed to have no counterpart in any place Sparhawk had ever visited. It was an odour neither fair nor foul, but one which was more than anything peculiarly alien. There were no torches to provide illumination, of course, and they were forced to rely upon the intermittent flickers of lightning staining the purple cloudbanks rolling in from the east. The streets revealed by those flashes were narrow, and their paving-stones had been worn smooth by centuries of shuffling feet. The houses were tall and narrow, and their windows were small and for the most part barred. The perpetual dust storms which scoured the city had rubbed the stones of the houses quite smooth. The same gritty dust had gathered in corners and along the doorsills of the houses to give the city, which could not have been deserted for much more than a few months, the air of a ruin abandoned for eons.

Talen slipped up behind Sparhawk and rapped on his armour.

'Don't do that, Talen.'

'It got your attention, didn't it? I've got an idea. Are you going to argue with me about it?'

'I don't think so. What was it you wanted to argue about?'

'I have certain talents that are rather unique in this group, you know.'

'I doubt that you'll find very many purses to slit open, Talen. I don't see all that many people about.'

'Ha,' Talen said flatly. 'Ha. Ha. Ha. Now that you're past that, are you ready to listen?'

'I'm sorry. Go ahead.'

'None of the rest of you could really sneak through a graveyard without waking up half the occupants, right?'

'I wouldn't go quite *that* far.'

'I would. I'll go on ahead – not too far, but just far enough. I'll be able to come back and tell you about anybody coming – or hiding in ambush.'

Sparhawk didn't wait this time. He made a grab for the boy, but Talen slipped out of his reach quite easily. 'Don't do that, Sparhawk. You just make yourself look foolish.' He ran off a few feet, then stopped and slid his hand down into one boot. From its place of concealment he drew a

517

long needle-pointed dirk. Then he vanished up the dark, narrow street.

Sparhawk swore.

'What's the matter?' Kurik asked from not far behind him.

'Talen just ran off.'

'He did *what*?'

'He says he's going to scout on ahead. I tried to stop him, but I couldn't catch him.'

From somewhere off in the maze of twisting streets there came a deep, mindless kind of howling.

'What's that?' Bevier asked, taking a tighter grip on his long-handled lochaber axe.

'The wind maybe?' Tynian replied without much conviction.

'The wind isn't blowing.'

'I know, but I think I prefer to believe that's what's causing the noise anyway. I don't like the alternatives.'

They moved on, staying close to the sides of the houses and freezing involuntarily in their tracks with each flash of lightning and crack of thunder.

Talen came back, running on silent feet. 'There's a patrol coming,' he said, staying just back out of reach. 'Would you believe they're carrying torches? They're not trying to find anybody; they're trying to make sure they don't.'

'How many?' Ulath asked.

'A dozen or so.'

'Hardly enough to worry about then.'

'Why not just cut over to the next street through this alley? Then you won't even have to look at them, much less worry.' The boy darted into an alleyway and disappeared again.

'The next time we choose a leader, I think I'll vote for him,' Ulath murmured.

They moved on through the narrow, twisting streets. With Talen probing ahead of them, they were easily able to avoid the sporadic Zemoch patrols. As they worked their way nearer to the centre of the city, however, they reached a quarter where the houses were more imposing and the streets were wider. The next time Talen came back, a momentary flash of ghostly lightning revealed a disgusted expression on his face. 'There's another patrol just ahead,' he reported. 'The only trouble is that they're not patrolling. It looks as if they broke into a wine shop. They're sitting in the middle of the street drinking.'

Ulath shrugged. 'We'll just slip around them through the alleys again.'

'We can't,' Talen said. 'There aren't any alleys leading off this street. I haven't found any way to get around them, and we have to use this street. As nearly as I can tell, it's the only one in the district that leads to the palace. This town doesn't make any sense at all. None of the streets go where they're supposed to.'

'How many of these revellers do we have to contend with?' Bevier asked him.

'Five or six.'

'And they have torches?'

Talen nodded. 'They're just around this next turn in the street.'

'With the torches flaring right in their eyes, they won't be able to see in the dark very well.' Bevier flexed his arm, swinging his axe suggestively.

'What do you think?' Kalten asked Sparhawk.

'We might as well,' Sparhawk said. 'It doesn't sound as if they'll volunteer to get out of our way.'

It was more in the nature of simple murder than a fight. The carouse of the Zemoch patrol had advanced to the point where they were aggressively inattentive. The Church Knights simply walked up to them and cut them down. One of them cried out briefly, but his surprised shout was lost in a tearing crash of thunder.

Without a word the knights dragged the inert bodies to nearby doorways and concealed them. Then they gathered protectively around Sephrenia and continued along that wide, lightning-illuminated street towards the sea of smoky torches that appeared to be encircling Otha's palace.

Once again they heard that howling sound, a sound devoid of any semblance of humanity. Talen returned, making no effort to evade them this time. 'The palace isn't far ahead,' he said, speaking quietly despite the now almost continuous thunder. 'There are guards out front. They're wearing armour of some kind. It's got all kinds of steel points sticking out of it. They look like hedgehogs.'

'How many?' Kalten asked.

'More than I had time to count. Do you hear that wailing noise?'

'I've been trying not to.'

'I think you'd better get used to it. The guards are the ones making it.'

Otha's palace was larger than the Basilica in Chyrellos, but it had no architectural grace. Otha had begun his life as a goatherd, and the principle which seemed to guide his sense of taste could best be summed up in the single word, 'large'. So far as Otha was concerned, bigger was better. His palace had been constructed of fractured, rusty-black basalt rock. Because of its flat sides, basalt is easy for masons to work, but it offers little in the way of beauty. It lends itself to massive construction and not much else.

The palace reared like a mountain in the centre of Zemoch. There were towers, of course. Palaces always have towers, but the rough black spires clawing at the air above the main building had no grace, no balance and in most cases no evident purpose. Many of them had been started centuries before and then never finished. They jutted into the air, half-completed and surrounded by the rotting remains of crude scaffolding. The palace did not exude so much a sense of evil as it did of madness, of a kind of frenzied but purposeless effort.

Beyond the palace Sparhawk could see the swelling dome of the temple of Azash, a perfect rusty-black hemisphere constructed of huge, rigidly symmetrical hexagonal blocks of basalt which gave it the appearance of the nest of some enormous insect or some vast infected wound.

The area surrounding the palace and the adjoining temple was a kind of paved dead zone where there were no buildings nor trees nor monuments. It was simply a flat place extending out perhaps two hundred yards from the walls. It was lighted on this darkest of nights by thousands of torches thrust at random into the cracks between the flagstones to form what almost appeared to be a knee-high field of tossing fire.

The broad avenue which the knights were following appeared to continue directly across the fiery plaza to the main portal of the house of Otha, where it entered with undiminished breadth through the widest and highest pair of arched doors Sparhawk had ever seen. Those doors stood ominously open.

The guards stood in the space between the walls and that broad grain-field of torches. They were armoured, but their armour was more fantastic than any Sparhawk had ever seen. Their helmets had been wrought into the shape of skulls, and they were surmounted by branching steel antlers. The various joints – shoulder and elbow, hip and knee – were decorated with long spikes and flaring protrusions. Their forearms were studded with hooks, and the weapons they grasped were not so much weapons of death but of pain, with saw-tooth edges and razor-like barbs. Their shields were large and hideously painted.

Sir Tynian was Deiran, and Deirans from time immemorial have been the world's experts on armour. 'Now that's the most idiotic display of pure childishness I've ever seen in my life,' he said contemptuously to the others during a momentary lull in the thunder.

'Oh?' Kalten said.

'Their armour's almost useless. Good armour is supposed to protect the man wearing it but to give him a certain freedom of movement. There's not much point in turning yourself into a turtle.'

'It looks sort of intimidating, though.'

'That's all it really is – something worn for its appearance. All those spikes and hooks are useless, and worse yet, they'll just guide an opponent's weapon to vulnerable points. What were their armourers thinking of?'

'It's a legacy from the last war,' Sephrenia explained. 'The Zemochs were overwhelmed by the appearance of the Church Knights. They didn't understand the actual purpose of armour – only its frightening appearance, so their armourers concentrated on appearance rather than utility. Zemochs don't wear armour to protect themselves; they wear it to frighten their opponents.'

'I'm not the least bit frightened, little mother,' Tynian said gaily. 'This is going to be almost too easy.'

Then at some signal only Otha's hideously-garbed warriors could perceive, they all broke into that mindless wailing, a kind of gibbering howl devoid of any meaning.

'Is that supposed to be some kind of war-cry?' Berit asked nervously.

'It's about the best they can manage,' Sephrenia told him. 'Zemoch culture is basically Styric, and Styrics don't know anything about war. Elenes shout when they go to war. Those guards are just trying to imitate the sound.'

'Why don't you take out the Bhelliom and erase them, Sparhawk?' Talen suggested.

'No!' Sephrenia said sharply. 'The Troll-Gods are confined now. Let's not turn them loose again until we're in the presence of Azash. There's not too much point in unleashing Bhelliom on common soldiers and risking what we came here to do.'

'She has a point,' Tynian conceded.

'They aren't moving,' Ulath said, looking at the guards. 'I'm sure they can see us, but they aren't making any effort to form up and protect that doorway. If we can smash through to the door, go inside and close it behind us, we won't have to worry about them any more.'

'Now that may just be the most inept plan I've ever heard,' Kalten scoffed.

'Can you think of a better one?'

'No, as a matter of fact, I can't.'

'Well then?'

The knights formed up in their customary wedge formation and strode rapidly towards the gaping portal of Otha's palace. As they approached through that fiery field, an oddly familiar reek came momentarily to Sparhawk's nostrils.

As quickly as it had begun, the meaningless howling broke off, and the guards in their skull-faced armour stood motionless. They did not brandish their weapons or even attempt to gather more force before the portal. They simply stood.

Again there came that penetrating reek, but it was quickly swept away by a sudden wind. The lightning redoubled its fury and began to blast great chunks from nearby buildings with deafening crashes. The air about them seemed suddenly tinglingly alive.

'Down!' Kurik barked sharply. 'Everybody get down on the ground!'

They did not understand, but they all immediately

obeyed, diving for the ground with a great clattering of their armour.

The reason for Kurik's alarmed shout became immediately apparent. Two of the grotesquely armoured guards to the left of the massive doors were suddenly engulfed in a brilliant ball of bluish fire and were quite literally blasted to pieces. Their fellows did not move or even turn to look as scorched bits and pieces of armour showered upon them.

'It's the armour!' Kurik shouted over the crashing thunder. 'Steel attracts lightning! Stay down!'

The lightning continued to blast down into the metal-clad ranks of the skull-faced guardsmen, and the smell of burning flesh and hair gusted back across the broad plaza as the sudden wind swirled and rebounded from the high basalt walls of the palace.

'They're not even moving!' Kalten exclaimed. 'Nobody's *that* disciplined.'

Then as the storm continued its ponderous march, the sudden flurry of lightning moved on to shatter deserted houses instead of steel-clad men.

'Is it all right now?' Sparhawk demanded of his squire.

'I don't know for certain,' Kurik told him. 'If you start to feel any kind of tingling, get down immediately.'

They rose warily to their feet. 'Was that Azash?' Tynian asked Sephrenia.

'I don't think so. If Azash had thrown the lightning, I don't think he'd have missed us. It might have been Otha, though. Until we get to the temple, we're more likely to encounter Otha's work than anything conjured up by Azash.'

'Otha? Is he really that skilled?'

'Skilled probably isn't the right word,' she replied. 'Otha has great power, but he's clumsy. He's too lazy to practise.'

They continued their menacing advance, but the men

524

awaiting them in that grotesque armour still made no move either to attack or even to reinforce those of their number barring the door.

When Sparhawk reached the first of the guards, he raised his sword, and the previously motionless man howled at him and clumsily raised a broad-bladed axe embellished with useless spikes and barbs. Sparhawk slapped the axe aside and struck with his sword. The dreadful-looking armour was even less useful than Tynian had suggested. It was scarcely thicker than paper, and Sparhawk's sword-stroke slashed down into the guard's body as if it had met no resistance whatsoever. Even had he struck at a totally unprotected man, his sword should not have cut so deeply into the body.

Then the man he had just slaughtered collapsed, and his gashed armour gaped open. Sparhawk recoiled in sudden revulsion. The body inside the armour had not been the body of a living man. It appeared to be no more than blackened, slimy bones with a few shreds of rotting flesh clinging to them. A dreadful stink suddenly boiled out of the armour.

'They aren't alive!' Ulath roared. 'There's nothing in the armour but bones and rotting guts!'

Sickened, gagging with nausea, the knights fought on, hacking their way through their already dead enemies.

'Stop!' Sephrenia cried sharply.

'But –' Kalten started to object.

'Take one step backwards – all of you!'

They grudgingly stepped back a pace, and the outrageously armoured cadavers menacing them returned to immobility. Once again at that unseen and unheard signal they gave vent to that emotionless howl.

'What's going on?' Ulath demanded. 'Why aren't they attacking?'

'Because they're dead, Ulath,' Sephrenia said.

Ulath pointed at a crumpled form with his axe. 'Dead or not, this one still tried to stick his spear into me.'

'That's because you came to within reach of his weapon. Look at them. They're standing all around us, and they aren't making any move to assist their companions. Get me a torch, Talen.'

The boy wrested a torch from between two flagstones and handed it to her. She raised it and peered at the paving beneath their feet. 'That's frightening,' she said with a shudder.

'We will protect you, Lady Sephrenia,' Bevier assured her. 'You have nothing to fear.'

'There's nothing for any of us to fear, dear Bevier. What's truly frightening is the fact that Otha probably has more power at his command than any living human, but he's so stupid that he doesn't even know how to use it. We've spent centuries fearing an absolute imbecile.'

'Raising the dead *is* fairly impressive, Sephrenia,' Sparhawk suggested.

'Any Styric child can galvanize a corpse, but Otha doesn't even know what to do with them once he raises them. Each one of his dead guardians is standing on a flagstone, and that flagstone is all it's protecting.'

'Are you sure?'

'Test it and see for yourself.'

Sparhawk raised his shield and advanced on one of the stinking guards. As soon as his foot touched the flagstone, the skull-faced thing swung jerkily at him with a jagged-bladed axe. He easily deflected the stroke and stepped back. The guard returned to its former position and stood motionless as a statue.

The vast circle of guards ringing the palace and the temple howled their empty howl again.

Then to Sparhawk's horror, Sephrenia gathered her white robe about her and quite calmly began to thread her way through the ranks of the stinking dead. She stopped and glanced back at them. 'Oh *do* come along now. Let's get inside before the rain starts. Just don't step on any of their flagstones, that's all.'

It was eerie to step around those savagely threatening figures with their foul reek and their skull-like faces in the ghastly light of the dancing lightning, but no more dangerous in fact than avoiding nettles on a forest trail.

When they had passed the last of the dead sentries, Talen stopped and squinted along a diagonal rank of those guardians. 'Revered teacher,' he said quietly to Berit.

'Yes, Talen?'

'Why don't you push this one over?' Talen pointed at the back of one of the armoured figures, '– sort of off to the side?'

'Why?'

Talen grinned a wicked kind of grin. 'Just give it a shove, Berit. You'll see.'

Berit looked a bit puzzled, but he reached out with his axe and gave the rigid corpse a good shove. The armoured figure fell, crashing into another. The second corpse promptly beheaded the first, staggering back as it did so, and it was immediately chopped down by a third.

The chaos spread rapidly, and a sizeable number of the intimidating dead were dismembered by their fellows in a mindless display of unthinking savagery.

'That's a *very* good boy you have there, Kurik,' Ulath said.

'We have some hopes for him,' Kurik said modestly.

They turned towards the portal and then stopped. Hanging in mid-air in the very centre of the dark doorway was a misty face engraved upon the emptiness with sickly green flame. The face was grotesquely misshapen, a thing of towering, implacable evil – and it was familiar. Sparhawk had seen it before.

527

'*Azash!*' Sephrenia hissed. 'Stay back, all of you!'

They stared at the ghastly apparition.

'Is that really him?' Tynian asked in an awed voice.

'An image of him,' Sephrenia replied. 'It's more of Otha's work.'

'Is it dangerous?' Kalten asked her.

'To step into the doorway means death, and worse than death.'

'Are there any other ways to get in?' Kalten asked her, eyeing the glowing apparition fearfully.

'I'm sure there are, but I doubt if we'd ever be able to find them.'

Sparhawk sighed. He had decided a long time ago that he would do this when the time came. He regretted the argument it was going to cause more than the act itself. He detached Bhelliom's steel-mesh pouch from his belt. 'All right,' he said to his friends, 'you'd better get started. I can't give you any guarantees about how much time I'll be able to give you, but I'll hold off for as long as I can.'

'What are you talking about?' Kalten asked suspiciously.

'This is as close to Azash as we're going to get, I'm afraid. We all know what has to be done, and it's only going to take one of us to do it. If any of you ever makes it back to Cimmura, tell Ehlana that I wished that this had turned out differently. Sephrenia, is this close enough? Will Azash be destroyed?'

Her eyes were full of tears, but she nodded.

'Let's not get sentimental about this,' Sparhawk said brusquely. 'We don't have the time. I'm honoured to have known you – all of you. Now get out of here. That's an order.' He had to get them moving before they began making foolishly noble decisions. 'Go!' he roared at them. 'And watch how you step around those guards!'

They were moving now. Military men always respond

to commands – if the commands are shouted. They were moving, and that was all that was important. The whole gesture was probably futile anyway. If what Sephrenia had said was true, they would need at least a day to get beyond the area that would be totally destroyed when he smashed the Bhelliom, and there was little hope that he could remain undiscovered for that long. He had to at least try to give them that one slim chance, though. Perhaps no one would come out of the palace, and none of the patrols roving the streets would chance to see him. It was nice to think so, anyway.

He did not want to watch them go. It would be better that way. There were things to be done, things far more important than standing forlornly like a child who has misbehaved and is being left behind while the rest of the family goes off to the fair. He looked first to the right and then to the left. If Sephrenia had been right and if this was the only way into Otha's palace, it would be better to go off some distance from the gaping portal and its glowing apparition. That way, all he would need to concern himself about would be those patrols. Anyone – or anything – emerging from the palace wouldn't immediately see him. Left? or right? He shrugged. What difference did it make? Perhaps it might be better to slip around the outer perimeter of the palace and to wait against the wall of the temple itself. He'd be closer to Azash that way, and the Elder God would be closer to the centre of that absolute obliteration. He half-turned and saw them. They were standing beyond the ranks of the threatening dead. Their faces were resolute.

'What are you doing?' he called to them. 'I told you to get out of here.'

'We decided to wait for you,' Kalten called back.

Sparhawk took a threatening step towards them.

'Don't be foolish, Sparhawk,' Kurik said. 'You can't

afford to risk trying to sidestep your way through those dead men. If you make a single misstep, one of them will brain you from behind – and then Azash will get Bhelliom. Did we really come all this way just for that?'

Chapter 27

Sparhawk swore. Why couldn't they just do as they had been told? Then he sighed. He should have known they wouldn't obey. There was no help for it now, and no point in berating them about it.

He pulled off his gauntlet to take his water bottle from his belt, and his ring flashed blood-red in the torchlight. He worked the stopper out of the bottle and drank. The ring flashed in his eyes again. He lowered the bottle, looking thoughtfully at the ring. 'Sephrenia,' he said almost absently. 'I need you.'

She was at his side in a few moments.

'The Seeker was Azash, wasn't it?'

'That's an oversimplification, Sparhawk.'

'You know what I mean. When we were at King Sarak's grave in Pelosia, Azash spoke to you through the Seeker, but he ran away when I started after him with Aldreas's spear.'

'Yes.'

'And I used the spear to chase away that thing that came out of the mound in Lamorkand, and I killed Ghwerig with it.'

'Yes.'

'But it wasn't really the spear, was it? It isn't really all that much of a weapon, after all. It was the rings, wasn't it?'

'I don't see where you're going with this, Sparhawk.'

'Neither do I exactly.' He pulled off his other gauntlet and held his hands out, looking at the rings. 'They have a certain amount of power themselves, don't they? I think maybe I've been getting a little overwhelmed by the fact that they're the keys to Bhelliom. Bhelliom's got so much power that I've been overlooking things that can be done with just the rings alone. Aldreas's spear didn't really have anything to do with it – which is a good thing, actually, since it's standing in a corner in Ehlana's apartment back in Cimmura. Any weapon would have served just as well, wouldn't it?'

'As long as the rings were touching it, yes. Please, Sparhawk, just get to the point. Your Elene logic is tedious.'

'It helps me to think. I could clear that image out of the doorway with Bhelliom, but that would turn the Troll-Gods loose, and they'd be trying to stab me in the back every time I turned around. But the Troll-Gods have no connection with the rings. I can use the rings without waking Ghnomb and his friends. What would happen if I took my sword in both hands and touched it to that face hanging in the doorway?'

She stared at him.

'We aren't really talking about Azash here. We're dealing with Otha. I may not be the greatest magician in the world, but I really don't have to be as long as I have the rings. I think they may just be more than a match for Otha, wouldn't you say?'

'I can't tell you, Sparhawk.' Her tone was subdued. 'I don't know.'

'Why don't we try it and find out?' He turned and looked back across the ranks of the reeking dead. 'All right,' he called to his friends, 'come back here. We've got something to do.'

They slipped warily past the armoured cadavers and gathered around Sparhawk and his tutor. 'I'm going to try something that might not work,' he told them, 'and if it doesn't, you're going to have to deal with Bhelliom.'

He took the steel-mesh pouch from his belt. 'If what I try fails, spill Bhelliom out on the flagstones and smash it with a sword or an axe.' He gave the pouch to Kurik, handed Kalten his shield and drew his sword. He gripped its hilt in both hands and strode back to the vast doorway with the glowing apparition hanging in its centre. He lifted his sword. 'Wish me luck,' he said. Anything else would have smacked of bombast.

He straightened his arms, levelling his sword at the image etched in green fire before him. He steeled himself and deliberately stepped forward to bring his sword-point into contact with the burning enchantment.

The results were satisfyingly spectacular. The touch of the sword-point exploded the burning image, showering Sparhawk with a waterfall of multi-coloured sparks, and the detonation probably shattered every window for miles in any direction. Sparhawk and all of his friends were hurled to the ground, and the armoured corpses standing guard before the palace were felled like new-mown wheat. Sparhawk shook his head to clear away the ringing in his ears and struggled to get back on his feet again as he stared at the portal. One of the vast doors had been split down the middle, and the other hung precariously from a single hinge. The apparition was gone, and in its place hung a few tatters of wispy smoke. From deep inside the palace there came a prolonged, bat-like screech of agony.

'Is everybody all right?' Sparhawk shouted, looking at his friends.

They were struggling to their feet, their eyes slightly unfocused.

'Noisy,' was all Ulath said.

'Who's making all that noise inside?' Kalten asked.

'Otha, I'd imagine,' Sparhawk replied. 'Having one of your spells shattered gives you quite a turn.' He retrieved his gauntlets and the steel-mesh pouch.

'Talen!' Kurik shouted. 'No!'

But the boy had already walked directly into the open doorway. 'There doesn't seem to be anything here, father,' he reported, walking further inside and then back out again. 'Since I didn't vanish in a puff of smoke, I think we can say that it's safe.'

Kurik started to move towards the boy, his hands outstretched hungrily. Then he thought better of it and stopped, muttering curses.

'Let's go inside,' Sephrenia said. 'I'm sure every patrol in the city heard that blast. We can hope that they thought it was only thunder, but some of them are bound to come to investigate.'

Sparhawk picked up the pouch and tucked it back under his belt. 'We'll want to get out of sight once we're inside. Which way should we go?'

'Bear to the left once we're through the doorway. The passages on that side lead to the kitchens and the storerooms.'

'All right then. Let's go.'

That alien smell Sparhawk had noticed when they had first entered the city was stronger here in the dark corridors of the palace. The knights moved cautiously, listening to the echoes of the shouts of the élite guards. The palace was in turmoil, and even in a place as vast as this there were bound to be encounters. In most cases, Sparhawk and his friends evaded these by simply stepping into the dark chambers which lined the corridors. Sometimes, however, that was not possible, but the Knights of the Church were far more skilled at close combat than the Zemochs, and what noise the encounters produced was lost in the shouting that echoed through the corridors. They pressed on, their weapons at the ready.

It was nearly an hour later when they entered a large pastry kitchen where the banked fires provided a certain amount of light. They stopped there and closed and barred the doors.

'I'm all turned around,' Kalten confessed, stealing a small cake. 'Which way do we go?'

'Through that door, I think,' Sephrenia replied. 'The kitchens all open into a corridor that leads to the throne-room.'

'Otha eats in his throne-room?' Bevier asked in some surprise.

'Otha doesn't move around very much,' she answered. 'He can't walk any more.'

'What happened to him to cripple him?'

'His appetite. Otha eats almost constantly, and he's never been fond of exercise. His legs are too weak to carry him any more.'

'How many doors into the throne-room?' Ulath asked her.

She thought a moment, remembering. 'Four, I think. The one from the kitchens here; another coming in from the main palace; and the one leading to Otha's private quarters.'

'And the last?'

'The last entrance doesn't have a door. It's the opening that leads into the maze.'

'Our first move should be to block those then. We'll want some privacy when we talk with Otha.'

'And anybody else who happens to be there,' Kalten added. 'I wonder if Martel's managed to get here yet.' He took another cake.

'There's one way to find out,' Tynian said.

'In a moment,' Sparhawk said. 'What's this maze you mentioned, Sephrenia?'

'It's the route to the temple. There was a time when

535

people were fascinated by labyrinths. It's very complicated and very dangerous.'

'Is that the only way to get to the temple?'

She nodded.

'The worshippers walk *through* the throne-room to get to the temple?'

'Ordinary worshippers don't go into the temple, Sparhawk – only priests and sacrifices.'

'We should probably rush the throne-room then. We'll bar the doors, deal with whatever guards may be in there and then take Otha prisoner. If we put a knife to his throat, I don't think any of his soldiers will interfere with us.'

'Otha's a magician, Sparhawk,' Tynian reminded him. 'Taking him prisoner might not be as easy as it sounds.'

'Otha's no particular danger at the moment,' Sephrenia disagreed. 'We've all had spells come apart on us before. It takes a while to recover from that.'

'Are we ready then?' Sparhawk asked tensely.

They nodded, and he led them through the doorway.

The corridor leading from the kitchens to Otha's throne-room was narrow and not very long. Its far end was illuminated by ruddy torchlight. As they neared that light, Talen slipped on ahead, his soft-shod feet making no sound on the flagstone floor. He returned in a few moments. 'They're all there,' he whispered in a voice tight with excitement. '– Annias, Martel and the rest. It looks as if they just got here. They're still wearing travellers' cloaks.'

'How many guards in the room?' Kurik asked him.

'Not too many. Twenty or so at the most.'

'The rest of them are probably out in the halls looking for us.'

'Can you describe the room?' Tynian asked. 'And the places where the guards are standing?'

Talen nodded. 'This corridor opens out not far from

the throne itself. You'll be able to pick Otha out of the rest almost immediately. He looks a lot like a garden slug. Martel and the others are gathered around him. There are two guards at each of the doors – except for the archway right behind the throne. Nobody's guarding that one. The rest of the guards are scattered along the walls. They're wearing mail and swords, and each one of them is holding a long spear. There are a dozen or so burly fellows in loincloths squatting near the throne. They don't have any weapons.'

'Otha's bearers,' Sephrenia explained.

'You were right,' Talen told her. 'There are four doors – this one just ahead of us, another over on the far side of the room, the archway and a bigger one down at the end of the room.'

'The door that leads out into the rest of the palace,' Sephrenia said.

'*That's* the important one then,' Sparhawk decided. 'There's nobody in these kitchens but a few cooks, I'd imagine, and not very many people in Otha's bedroom, but there'll be soldiers on the other side of that main door. How far is it from this door to that one?'

'About two hundred feet,' the boy said.

'Who feels like running?' Sparhawk looked around at his friends.

'What do you say, Tynian?' Ulath asked. 'How fast can you cover two hundred feet?'

'As fast as *you* can, my friend.'

'We'll take care of it then, Sparhawk,' Ulath said.

'Don't forget that you promised to let me have Adus,' Kalten reminded his friend.

'I'll try to save him for you.'

They moved purposefully ahead towards the torchlit doorway. They paused just back from it, and then they rushed through. Ulath and Tynian sprinted towards the

537

main door. There were cries of shock and alarm as the knights burst into the throne-room. Otha's soldiers shouted conflicting orders to each other, but one officer overrode them all with the hoarse bellow, 'Protect the Emperor!'

The mailed guards lining the walls deserted their comrades at the doors and rushed to form a protective ring around the throne with their spears. Kalten and Bevier had almost negligently cut down the two guards at the entrance to the corridor leading back into the kitchens, and then Ulath and Tynian reached the main door where the two guards were desperately trying to open it to cry for help. Both men fell in the first flurry of strokes, and then Ulath set his massive back against the door and braced himself while Tynian pawed behind the nearby draperies looking for the bar to lock the door.

Berit dashed through the doorway beside Sparhawk, leaped over the still weakly moving guards on the floor and ran towards the door on the opposite side of the room with his axe raised. Even though he was encumbered by his armour, he ran like a deer across the polished floor of the throne-room and fell upon the two men guarding the door that led back to Otha's bed-chamber. He brushed aside their spears and disposed of them with two powerful axe-blows.

Sparhawk heard the solid metallic clank behind him as Kalten slammed the heavy iron bar into place.

There was a pounding on the outside of the door Ulath was holding closed and then Tynian found the iron bar and slid it into place. Berit barred his door as well.

'Very workmanlike,' Kurik approved. 'We still can't get to Otha, though.'

Sparhawk looked at the ring of spears around the throne and then at Otha himself. As Talen had said, the man who had terrified the west for the past five centuries looked much like the common slug. He was pallid white and totally hairless. His face was grossly bloated and so shiny with sweat as to look almost as if it were covered with slime. His paunch was enormous, and it protruded so far in front of him that it gave his arms the appearance of being stunted. He was incredibly dirty, and priceless rings decorated his greasy hands. He half lay on his throne as if something had hurled him back. His eyes were glazed, and his limbs and body were twitching convulsively. He had obviously still not recovered from the shock of the breaking of his spell.

Sparhawk drew in a deep breath to steady himself, looking around as he did so. The room itself was decorated with the ransom of kings. The walls were covered with hammered gold, and the columns were sheathed in mother-of-pearl. The floor was of polished black onyx and the draperies flanking each door were of blood-red velvet. Torches protruded from the walls at intervals, and very large iron braziers stood one on each side of Otha's throne.

And then at last, Sparhawk looked at Martel.

'Ah, Sparhawk,' the white-haired man drawled urbanely, 'so good of you to drop by. We've been expecting you.'

The words seemed almost casual, but there was the faintest hint of an edge to Martel's voice. He had *not* expected them to arrive so soon, and he had certainly not expected their sudden rush. He stood with Annias, Arissa and Lycheas within the safety of the ring of spears while Adus encouraged the spearmen with kicks and curses.

'We were in the neighbourhood anyway,' Sparhawk shrugged. 'How've you been, old boy? You look a bit travel-worn. Was it a difficult journey?'

'Nothing unbearable.' Martel inclined his head towards Sephrenia. 'Little mother,' he said, sounding once again oddly regretful.

539

Sephrenia sighed, but said nothing.

'I see we're all here,' Sparhawk continued. 'I do so enjoy these little get-togethers, don't you? They give us the chance to reminisce.' He looked at Annias, whose subordinate position to Martel was now clearly evident. 'You should have stayed in Chyrellos, Your Grace,' he said. 'You missed all the excitement of the election. Would you believe that the Hierocracy actually put Dolmant on the Archprelate's throne?'

A look of sudden anguish crossed the face of the Primate of Cimmura. 'Dolmant?' he choked in a stricken voice. In later years Sparhawk was to conclude that his revenge upon the Primate had been totally complete in that instant. The pain his simple statement had caused his enemy was beyond his ability to comprehend. The life of the Primate of Cimmura crumbled and turned to ashes in that single moment.

'Astonishing, isn't it?' Sparhawk continued relentlessly. 'Absolutely the last man anyone would have expected. Many in Chyrellos feel that the hand of God was involved. My wife, the Queen of Elenia – you remember her, don't you? Blonde girl, rather pretty, the one you poisoned – made a speech to the Patriarchs just as they were beginning their deliberations. It was *she* who suggested him. She was amazingly eloquent, but it's generally believed that her speech was inspired by God Himself – particularly in view of the fact that Dolmant was elected unanimously.'

'That's impossible!' Annias gasped. 'You're lying, Sparhawk!'

'You can verify it for yourself, Annias. When I take you back to Chyrellos, I'm sure you'll have plenty of time to examine the records of the meeting. There's quite a dispute in the works about who's going to have the pleasure of putting you on trial and executing you. It may drag on for years. Somehow you've managed to

540

offend just about everybody west of the Zemoch border. They all want to kill you for some reason.'

'You're being just a bit childish, Sparhawk,' Martel sneered.

'Of course I am. We all do that sometimes. It's really a shame the sunset was so uninspiring this evening, Martel, since it was the last one you're ever going to see.'

'That's true of one of us at any rate.'

'Sephrenia.' It was a rumbling, deep-toned gurgle more than a voice.

'Yes, Otha?' she replied calmly.

'Bid thy witless little Goddess farewell,' the slug-like man on the throne rumbled in antique Elene. His pig-like little eyes were focused now, though his hands still trembled. 'Thine unnatural kinship with the Younger Gods draws to its close. Azash awaits thee.'

'I rather doubt that, Otha, for I bring the unknown one with me. I found him long before he was born, and I have brought him here with Bhelliom in his fist. Azash fears him, Otha, and you would be wise to fear him too.'

Otha sank lower on his throne, his head seeming to retract turtle-like into the folds of his fat neck. His hand moved with surprising speed, and a beam of greenish light shot from it, a light levelled at the small Styric woman. Sparhawk, however, had been waiting for that. He had been holding his shield in both bare hands in a negligent-appearing posture. The blood-red stones of the rings were quite firmly pressed against the shield's steel rim. With practised speed he thrust the shield in front of his tutor. The beam of green light struck the shield and reflected back from its polished surface. One of the armoured guards was suddenly obliterated in a soundless blast that sprayed the throne-room with white-hot fragments of his chain-mail.

Sparhawk drew his sword. 'Have we just about finished with all this nonsense, Martel?' he asked bleakly.

'Wish I could oblige, old boy,' Martel replied, 'but Azash is waiting for us. You know how that goes.'

The hammering on the heavy door Tynian and Ulath were guarding grew louder.

'Is that someone knocking?' Martel said mildly. 'Be a good fellow, Sparhawk, and see who it is. All that banging sets my teeth on edge.'

Sparhawk started forward.

'Take the emperor to safety!' Annias barked to the barely-clad brutes squatting near the throne. With practised haste, the men inserted stout steel poles into recesses in the jewelled seat, set their shoulders under the poles and lifted the vast weight of their master from the pedestal-like base of the throne. Then they wheeled with the litter and trotted ponderously towards the arched opening behind the throne.

'Adus!' Martel commanded, 'keep them off me!' Then he too turned and herded Annias and his family along in Otha's wake as the brutish Adus pushed forward, flogging at Otha's spear-armed guards with the flat of his sword and bellowing unintelligible orders.

The hammering at the locked doors became a booming sound as the soldiers outside improvised battering rams.

'Sparhawk!' Tynian shouted. 'Those doors won't hold for long!'

'Leave them!' Sparhawk shouted back. 'Help us here! Otha and Martel are getting away!'

The soldiers Adus commanded had spread out to face Sparhawk, Kurik and Bevier not so much to engage them as to prevent their entering the arched doorway that led back into the labyrinth. Although he was in most respects, profoundly, even frighteningly stupid, Adus was a gifted warrior, and a fight of this nature, involving as it did a

542

simple situation and a manageable number of men, put him in his natural element. He directed Otha's guardsmen with grunts, kicks and blows, deploying them in pairs and trios to block individual opponents with their spears. The concept implicit in Martel's command was well within Adus's limited grasp. His purpose was to delay the knights long enough to enable Martel to escape, and perhaps no one was better suited for that than Adus.

As Kalten, Ulath, Tynian and Berit joined the fight, Adus gave ground. He had the advantage of numbers, but his Zemoch soldiers were no match for the steel-clad knights. He was, however, able to pull the bulk of his force back into the mouth of the maze where their spears could serve as an effective barrier.

And all the while the rhythmic booming of the battering-rams continued.

'We've got to get into that maze!' Tynian shouted. 'When those doors give way, we're going to be surrounded!'

It was Sir Bevier who took action. The young Cyrinic Knight was bravery personified, and on many occasions he had demonstrated a total disregard for his own personal safety. He strode forward, swinging his brutal, hook-pointed lochaber axe. He swung not at the soldiers, but at their spears, and a spear without a point is nothing more than a pole. Within moments he had effectively disarmed Adus's Zemochs – and had received a deep wound in his side, just above the hip. He fell back weakly with blood streaming from the rent in his armour.

'See to him!' Sparhawk barked to Berit and lunged forward to engage the Zemochs. Without their spears, the Zemochs were forced to fall back on their swords, and the advantage shifted to the Church Knights at that point. The armoured men chopped the Zemochs out of their path.

Adus assessed the situation quickly and stepped back into the archway.

'Adus!' Kalten bellowed, kicking a Zemoch out of his way.

'Kalten!' Adus roared. The brute took a step forward, his pig-like eyes hungry. Then he snarled and disembowelled one of his own soldiers to give vent to his frustration and disappeared back into the maze.

Sparhawk whirled about. 'How is he?' he demanded of Sephrenia, who knelt over the wounded Bevier.

'It's serious, Sparhawk.'

'Can you stop the bleeding?'

'Not entirely, no.'

Bevier lay, pale and sweating with the breastplate of his armour unbuckled and lying open like a clamshell. 'Go on, Sparhawk,' he said. 'I'll hold this doorway for as long as I can.'

'Don't be stupid,' Sparhawk snapped. 'Pad the wound as best you can, Sephrenia. Then buckle his armour back up. Berit, bring him along. Carry him if you have to.'

There was a splintering sound behind them in the throne-room as the booming continued.

'The doors are giving way, Sparhawk,' Kalten reported.

Sparhawk looked down the long arched corridor leading into the maze. Torches were set in iron rings at widely-spaced intervals. A sudden hope flared up in him. 'Ulath,' he said, 'you and Tynian bring up the rear. Shout if any of those soldiers breaking down the doors come up behind us.'

'I'll just hold you back, Sparhawk,' Bevier said weakly.

'No you won't,' Sparhawk replied. 'We're not going to run through this maze. We don't know what's in here, so we're not going to take any chances. All right, gentlemen, let's move out.'

They started down the long, straight corridor that led into the labyrinth, passing two or three unlighted entrances on either side as they went.

'Shouldn't we check those?' Kalten asked.

'It's probably not necessary,' Kurik said. 'Some of Adus's men were wounded, and there are blood-spatters on the floor. We know that Adus at least went this way.'

'That's no guarantee that *Martel* did,' Kalten said. 'Maybe he told Adus to lead us off in the wrong direction.'

'It's possible,' Sparhawk conceded, 'but this corridor is lighted, and none of the others are.'

'I'd hardly call it a maze if the way through it is marked with torches, Sparhawk,' Kurik pointed out.

'Maybe not, but as long as the torches and the blood-trail go the same way, we'll chance it.'

The echoing corridor made a sharp turn to the left at its far end. The vaulted walls and ceiling curving upward and inward gave the twisting passages that oppressive sense of being too low, and Sparhawk found himself instinctively ducking his head.

'They've broken through the doors in the throne-room, Sparhawk,' Ulath called from the rear. 'There are some torches bobbing around back in the entryway.'

'That more or less settles it,' Sparhawk said. 'We don't have time to start exploring side passages. Let's go on.'

The lighted corridor began to twist and turn at that point, and the spots of blood on the floor suggested that they were still on the same trail Adus had followed.

The corridor turned to the right.

'How are you bearing up?' Sparhawk asked Bevier, who was leaning heavily on Berit's shoulder.

'Fine, Sparhawk. As soon as I get my breath, I'll be able to make it without help.'

545

The corridor turned to the left again, then to the left again after only a few yards.

'We're going back the same way we came, Sparhawk,' Kurik declared.

'I know. Do we have any choice, though?'

'Not that I can think of, no.'

'Ulath,' Sparhawk called, 'are the men behind us gaining at all?'

'Not that I can see.'

'Maybe they don't know the way through the maze either,' Kalten suggested. 'I don't think anyone would visit Azash just for fun.'

The rush came out of a side corridor. Five spear-armed Zemoch soldiers dashed out of the dark entryway and bore down on Sparhawk, Kalten and Kurik. Their spears gave them some advantage – but not enough. After three of their number had been felled to lie writhing and bleeding on the flagstone floor, the other two fled back the way they had come.

Kurik seized a torch from one of the iron rings in the wall and led Sparhawk and Kalten into the dark, twisting corridor. After several minutes they saw the soldiers they were pursuing. The two men were fearfully edging their way through a stretch of the passage, each one of them hugging a wall.

'Now we've got them,' Kalten exulted, starting forward.

'Kalten!' Kurik's voice cracked. 'Stop!'

'What's wrong?'

'They're staying too close to the walls.'

'So?'

'What's wrong with the middle of the passageway?'

Kalten stared at the two frightened men clinging to the walls, his eyes narrowing. 'Let's find out,' he said. He prised up a small flagstone with his sword-point and hurled it at one of the soldiers, missing his mark by several feet.

'Let me do it,' Kurik told him. 'You can't throw anything with your armour binding up your shoulders the way it does.' He prised loose another stone. His aim was much more true. The rock he had thrown bounced off the soldier's helmet with a loud clang. The man cried out as he reeled back, trying desperately to grab some kind of hand-hold on the stone wall. He failed, however, and stepped onto the floor in the centre of the corridor.

The floor promptly fell open under him, and he dropped from sight with a despairing shriek. His companion, straining to see, also made a misstep and fell from the narrow ledge along the wall to follow his friend into the pit.

'Clever,' Kurik said. He advanced to the brink of the gaping pit and raised his torch. 'The bottom's studded with sharpened stakes,' he observed, looking down at the two men impaled below. 'Let's go back and tell the others. I think we'd better start watching where we put our feet.'

They returned to that torchlit main corridor as Ulath and Tynian joined them from the rear. Kurik tersely described the trap which had claimed the two Zemochs. He looked thoughtfully at the soldiers who had fallen here in the corridor and picked up one of their spears. 'These weren't Adus's men.'

'How do you know that?' Kalten asked him.

'Sir Bevier broke the spears of the ones who were with Adus. That means there are other soldiers here in the labyrinth – probably in small groups the same as this one. I'd guess that they're here to lead us into traps in the side corridors.'

'That's very obliging of them,' Ulath said.

'I don't follow your reasoning, Sir Ulath.'

'There are traps in the maze, but we have soldiers

547

around to spring them for us. All we have to do is catch them.'

'One of those silver linings people talk about?' Tynian asked.

'You could say that, yes. The Zemochs we catch might not look at it that way, though.'

'Are those soldiers behind us coming up very fast?' Kurik asked him.

'Not very.'

Kurik went back to the side corridor, holding his torch aloft. He was smiling grimly when he came back. 'There are torch rings in the side passages the same as there are in this one,' he told them. 'Why don't we move a few torches as we go along? We've been following the torches, and those soldiers have been following us. If the torches start leading them off into the side passages where the traps are, wouldn't they sort of slow down a bit?'

'I don't know about *them*,' Ulath said, 'but I know *I* would.'

Chapter 28

Zemoch soldiers periodically charged out of side corridors, their faces bearing the hopeless expressions of men who considered themselves already dead. The ultimatum, 'surrender or die', however, opened an option to them the existence of which they had not even been aware. Most of them leaped at the chance to seize it. Their effusive gratitude waned, however, when they found that they were expected to take the lead.

The traps designed to surprise the unwary were ingenious. In those passages where the floor did not drop open, the ceiling collapsed. The bottoms of most of the pits in the floor were studded with sharpened stakes, although several pits housed assorted reptiles – all venomous and all bad tempered. Once, when the designer of the labyrinth had evidently grown bored with pits and falling ceilings, the walls smashed forcefully together.

'There's something wrong here,' Kurik said, even as yet another despairing shriek echoed through the maze from behind them where the soldiers who had burst into the throne room were exploring side corridors.

'Things seem to be going rather well to me,' Kalten said.

'These soldiers live here, Kalten,' the squire said, 'and they don't seem to be any more familiar with this labyrinth than we are. We've just run out of prisoners again. I think it's time to consider a few things. Let's not make any blunders.'

They gathered in the centre of the corridor. 'This doesn't make any sense, you know,' Kurik told them.

'Coming to Zemoch?' Kalten said. 'I could have told you that back in Chyrellos.'

Kurik ignored that. 'We've been following a trail of blood spots on the floor, and that trail is still stretching on out in front of us – right down the middle of a torch-lit corridor.' He scraped one foot at a large blood-spot on the floor. 'If someone were really bleeding this hard, he would have been dead a long time ago.'

Talen bent, touched one finger to a glistening red spot on the floor and then touched the finger to his tongue. He spat. 'It isn't blood,' he said.

'What is it?' Kalten asked.

'I don't know, but it isn't blood.'

'We've been bamboozled then,' Ulath said sourly. 'I was beginning to wonder about that. What's worse, we're trapped in here. We can't even turn around and follow the torches back because we've been busily moving torches for the past half-hour or more.'

'This is what's known in logic as "defining the problem",' Bevier said with a weak smile. 'I think the next step is called "finding a solution".'

'I'm no expert at it,' Kalten admitted, 'but I don't think we're going to be able to logic our way out of this.'

'Why not use the rings?' Berit suggested. 'Couldn't Sparhawk just blow a hole straight through the maze?'

'The passages are mostly barrel-vaults, Berit,' Kurik said. 'If we start blowing holes in the walls, we'll have the ceiling down on our heads.'

'What a shame,' Kalten sighed. 'So many good ideas have to be discarded simply because they won't work.'

'Are we absolutely bent on solving the riddle of the maze?' Talen asked them. 'I mean, does finding the solution have some sort of religious significance?'

'None that I know of,' Tynian replied.

'Why stay inside the maze then?' the boy asked innocently.

'Because we're trapped here,' Sparhawk told him, trying to control his irritation.

'That's not exactly true, Sparhawk. We've never been really trapped. Kurik might be right about the danger involved in knocking down the walls, but he didn't say a thing about the ceiling.'

They stared at him. Then they all began to laugh a bit foolishly.

'We don't know what's up there, of course,' Ulath noted.

'We don't know what's around the next corner either, Sir Knight. And we'll never know what's above the ceiling until we have a look, will we?'

'It could just be open sky,' Kurik said.

'Is that any worse than what we have down here, father? Once we get outside, Sparhawk might be able to use the rings to break through the outer wall of the temple. Otha may find mazes entertaining, but I think I've more or less had enough amusement out of this one. One of the first rules Platime ever taught me was that if you don't like the game, don't play.'

Sparhawk looked questioningly at Sephrenia.

She was also smiling ruefully. 'I didn't even think of it myself,' she admitted.

'Can we do it?'

'I don't see any reason why not – as long as we stand back a way so that we don't get crushed by falling rubble. Let's have a look at this ceiling.'

They raised their torches to look up at the barrel-vaulted ceiling. 'Is that construction going to cause any kind of problem?' Sparhawk asked Kurik.

'Not really. The stones are laid in interlocking courses,

so they'll hold – eventually. There's going to be a lot of rubble, though.'

'That's all right, Kurik,' Talen said gaily. 'The rubble will give us something to climb up on.'

'It's going to take a great deal of force to knock loose any of those stone blocks, though,' Kurik said. 'The weight of the whole corridor is holding the vault together.'

'What would happen if a few of those blocks just weren't there any more?' Sephrenia asked him.

Kurik went to one of the upward-curving walls and probed at a crack between two stone blocks with his knife. 'They used mortar,' he said. 'It's fairly rotten, though. If you can dissolve a half-dozen of those blocks up there, a fairly sizeable piece of the ceiling will fall in.'

'But the whole corridor won't collapse?'

He shook his head. 'No. After a few yards of it tumble in, the structure will be sound again.'

'Can you really dissolve rocks?' Tynian asked Sephrenia curiously.

She smiled. 'No, dear one. But I *can* change them into sand – which amounts to the same thing, doesn't it?' She intently studied the ceiling for several moments. 'Ulath,' she said then, 'you're the tallest. Lift me up. I have to touch the stones.'

Ulath blushed a bright red, and they all knew why. Sephrenia was not the sort of person one put one's hands on.

'Oh, don't be such a goose, Ulath,' she told him. 'Lift me up.'

Ulath looked around menacingly. 'We aren't going to talk about this, are we?' he said to his friends. Then he bent and lifted her easily.

She clambered upward, looking not unlike someone climbing a tree. When she was high enough, she reached up and put the palms of her hands on several of the stones,

552

pausing briefly with each one. Her touch seemed almost caressing. 'That should do it,' she said. 'You can put me down again, Sir Knight.'

Ulath lowered her to the floor, and they retreated back down the corridor. 'Be ready to run,' she cautioned them. 'This is a little inexact.' She began to move her hands in front of her, speaking rapidly in Styric as she did so. Then she held out both hands, palms up, to release the spell.

Fine sand began to sift down from the ceiling, slithering out of the cracks between the roughly squared-off building blocks. At first it was only a trickle, but it steadily increased.

'Looks almost like water leaking out, doesn't it?' Kalten observed as the sand-flow increased.

The walls began to creak, and there were popping noises as the mortar between the stones started to crack.

'We can go back a bit further,' Sephrenia said, looking apprehensively at all the rock around them. 'The spell's working. We don't have to stand here to supervise it.' Sephrenia was a very complex little woman. She was sometimes timid about very ordinary things and at other times indifferent to horrendous ones. They walked further on back up the corridor as the building blocks near the place where the sand was now pouring down out of the ceiling creaked and groaned and grated together, settling in a fraction of an inch at a time to replace the sand.

When it came, it came all at once. A large section of the overhead vault collapsed with the grinding clatter of falling rock and a large cloud of eons-old dust that billowed down the corridor towards them, setting them all to coughing. As the dust gradually settled, they saw a large, jagged hole in the ceiling.

'Let's go and have a look,' Talen said. 'I'm curious to find out what's up there.'

'Could we wait just a bit longer?' Sephrenia asked fearfully. 'I'd really like to be sure that it's safe.'

They struggled up the pile of rubble from the fallen ceiling and boosted each other up through the hole. The area above the ceiling was a vast, domed emptiness, dusty and stale-smelling. The light from the torches they had brought with them from the corridor below seemed sickly and did not reach out as far as the walls – if walls to this dim place indeed existed. The floor resembled to a remarkable degree a field laced with the upward-bulging burrows of a colony of extraordinarily industrious moles, and they saw a number of structural peculiarities they had not perceived when down in the maze.

'Sliding walls,' Kurik said, pointing. 'They can change the maze any time they want to by closing off some passage and opening others. That's why those Zemoch soldiers didn't know where they were going.'

'There's a light,' Ulath told them, 'way over there to the left. It seems to be coming up from down below.'

'The temple maybe?' Kalten suggested.

'Or the throne-room again. Let's go and have a look.'

They threaded their way along the tops of the vaults for some distance and then came to a straight path that stretched in one direction towards the light Ulath had seen and off into the darkness in the other.

'No dust,' Ulath said, pointing at the stones of the path. 'This is used fairly often.'

The going was much faster on the straight pathway, and they soon reached the source of the flickering light. It was a flight of stone stairs leading down into a torchlit room – a room with four walls and no doors.

'That's ridiculous,' Kalten snorted.

'Not really,' Kurik disagreed, raising his torch to peer over the side of the path. 'That front wall slides on those tracks.' He pointed at a pair of metal tracks below that emerged from the room on the outside. He leaned forward to look more closely. 'There's no machinery out here, so there has to be a latch of some kind in that room. Sparhawk, let's go down and see if we can find it.'

The two of them went down the stairs into the room. 'What are we looking for?' Sparhawk asked his friend.

'How should I know? Something that looks ordinary but isn't.'

'That's not very specific, Kurik.'

'Just start pushing on rocks, Sparhawk. If you find one that can be depressed, it's probably the latch.'

They went along the walls pushing on rocks. After a few minutes, Kurik stopped, a slightly foolish look on his face. 'You can stop, Sparhawk,' he said. 'I found the latches.'

'Where?'

'There are torches on the side walls and on the back, right?'

'Yes. So what?'

'But there aren't any torches on the front wall – the one right in front of the foot of the stairs.'

'So?'

'There *are* a couple of torch rings, though.' Kurik went to the front wall and pulled on one of the rusty iron rings. There was a solid-sounding clank. 'Pull the other one, Sparhawk,' he suggested. 'Let's open this door and see what's behind it.'

'Sometimes you're so clever you make me sick, Kurik,' Sparhawk said sourly. Then he grinned. 'Let's get the others down here first,' he said. 'I'd rather not open that door and find half the Zemoch army behind it with only the two of us here to hold them off.' He went to the stairs and beckoned to his waiting friends, touching one finger to his lips as he did so to signal the need for silence.

They came down quietly to avoid clinking.

'Kurik found the latches,' Sparhawk whispered. 'We

don't know what's on the other side of the door, so we'd better be ready.'

Kurik motioned to them. 'The wall isn't too heavy,' he said quietly, 'and the track it slides on seems to be well greased. Berit and I should be able to move it. The rest of you should be ready for anything on the other side.'

Talen moved quickly to the corner on the left side and put his face close to the two intersecting walls. 'I'll be able to look through here just as soon as you get it open an inch or so,' he told his father. 'If I shout, slam it shut again.'

Kurik nodded. 'Are we ready?' he asked.

They all nodded, their weapons in their hands and their muscles tense.

Kurik and Berit pulled out on the torch rings and inched the wall aside slightly. 'Anything yet?' Kurik hissed to his son.

'Nobody's there,' Talen replied. 'It's a short corridor with just one torch. It seems to go back about twenty paces and then it turns to the left. There's quite a bit of light coming from beyond that turn.'

'All right, Berit,' Kurik said, 'let's open it all the way.'

The two of them slid the wall the rest of the way open.

'Now *that* is very, very clever,' Bevier said admiringly. 'The labyrinth down here doesn't go anywhere at all. The *real* route to the temple is up above it.'

'Let's find out where we are – in the temple or back at the throne-room,' Sparhawk said. 'And let's be as quiet as we can.'

Talen looked as if he were about to say something.

'Forget it,' Kurik told him. 'It's too dangerous. You just stay behind the rest of us with Sephrenia.'

They moved out into the short corridor where the single torch near the far end provided a dim, flickering light.

'I don't hear anything,' Kalten whispered to Sparhawk.

556

'People waiting in ambush don't usually make noise, Kalten.'

They paused just before the corridor turned sharply to the left. Ulath edged to the corner, pulled off his helmet and took a quick look, his head darting out and back once. 'Empty,' he said shortly. 'It seems to turn right about ten or fifteen paces further on.'

They moved on around the corner and crept along the short passage. Again they stopped at the corner, and Ulath popped his head out again. 'It's a kind of an alcove,' he whispered. 'There's an archway that opens out into a wider corridor. There's a lot of light out there.'

'Did you see anybody?' Kurik asked him.

'Not a soul.'

'That should be the main corridor out there,' Bevier murmured. 'The stairs that lead up out of the maze to the real route to the temple should be fairly close to the end of the labyrinth – either at the throne-room or at the temple.'

They rounded the corner into the alcove, and Ulath again took a quick look. 'It's the main corridor, all right,' he reported, 'and there's a turn a hundred paces off to the left.'

'Let's go up to that corner,' Sparhawk decided. 'If Bevier's right, the hallway beyond the corner should lead out of the maze. Sephrenia, you stay in here with Talen, Bevier and Berit. Kurik, you guard the door. The rest of us will go and have a look.' He leaned close to his squire and whispered. 'If things start to go wrong, get Sephrenia and the others back to the room at the foot of the stairs. Slide the wall shut and lock it.'

Kurik nodded. 'Be careful out there, Sparhawk,' he said quietly.

'You too, my friend.'

The four knights stepped out into the broad, vaulted

557

corridor and crept along towards the torchlit corner ahead. Kalten followed the rest of them, turning often to keep watch to the rear. At the corner, Ulath briefly poked out his head. Then he stepped back. 'We might have known,' he whispered disgustedly. 'It's the throne-room. We're right back where we started from.'

'Is there anybody in there?' Tynian asked.

'Probably, but why bother them? Let's just go on back to that staircase, slide the wall shut again and leave the people in the throne-room to take care of their own entertainment.'

It was as they were turning around that it happened. Adus, followed by a score of Zemoch soldiers, burst from a side passage not too far from the entrance to the alcove, and he was bellowing at the top of his lungs. Cries of alarm echoed into the corridor from the throne-room itself.

'Tynian! Ulath!' Sparhawk snapped, 'hold off the ones in the throne-room! Let's go, Kalten!' Then he and his blond friend dashed back towards the opening where Kurik stood guard.

Adus was far too limited to be anything but predictable. He savagely drove his soldiers on ahead of him and slouched forward, a brutal war-axe in his hand and an insane look in his pig-like eyes.

It was too far. Sparhawk saw that immediately. Adus was much closer to the arched entrance to the alcove than he and Kalten were, and there were already soldiers between him and his friend and the archway. He chopped a Zemoch out of his way. 'Kurik!' he shouted, 'fall back!'

But it was too late. Kurik had already engaged the ape-like Adus. His chain-mace whistled through the air, crunching into his opponent's armoured shoulders and chest, but Adus was in the grip of a killing frenzy, and he ignored those dreadful blows. Again and again he smashed at Kurik's shield with his war-axe.

Kurik was undoubtedly one of the most skilled men in the world when close fighting was involved, but Adus appeared totally mad. He hacked and kicked and bulled his way at Kurik, pushing and flailing with his battle-axe. Kurik was forced to retreat, giving ground grudgingly step by step.

Then Adus threw his shield aside, took his axe-handle in both hands and began to swing a rapid series of blows at Kurik's head. Forced finally into one last defence, Kurik grasped his shield with both hands and raised it to protect his head from those massive blows. Roaring in triumph, Adus swung – not at Kurik's head, but at his body. The brutal axe bit deep into the side of his chest, and blood gushed from his mouth and from the dreadful wound in his chest. 'Sparhawk!' he cried weakly, falling back against the side of the arch.

Adus raised his axe again.

'*Adus!*' Kalten roared, killing another Zemoch.

Adus checked the axe-blow he had aimed at Kurik's unprotected head and half-turned. '*Kalten!*' he bellowed back his challenge. He contemptuously kicked Sparhawk's friend out of his way and shambled towards the blond Pandion, his piggish eyes burning insanely beneath his shaggy brows.

Sparhawk and Kalten abandoned any semblance of swordsmanship and simply cut down anything in their paths, relying more on strength and fury than upon skill.

Adus, totally insane now, also chopped his way through his own soldiers to reach them.

Kurik stumbled out into the corridor, clutching at his bleeding chest and trying to shake out his chain-mace, but his legs faltered. He stumbled and fell. With enormous effort, he rose to his elbows and began to drag himself after the savage who had struck him down. Then his eyes went blank, and he fell onto his face.

'Kurik!' Sparhawk howled. The light seemed to fade from his eyes, and there was a deafening ringing in his ears. His sword suddenly appeared to have no weight. He cut down whatever appeared before him. At one point, he found himself chopping at the stones of the wall. It was the sparks somehow that returned him to his senses. Kurik would take him to task for damaging his sword-edge.

Somehow Talen had reached his father's side. He knelt, struggling to turn Kurik over. And then he wailed, a cry of unspeakable loss. 'He's dead, Sparhawk! My father's dead!'

The wrench of that cry nearly drove Sparhawk to his knees. He shook his head like some dumb animal. He hadn't heard that cry. He *could* not have heard it. He absently killed another Zemoch. Dimly, he heard the sound of fighting behind him and knew that Tynian and Ulath were engaging the soldiers from the throne-room.

Then Talen rose, sobbing and reaching down into his boot. His long, needle-pointed dirk came out gleaming in his fist, and he advanced on Adus from the rear, his soft-shod feet making no sound. Tears streamed down the boy's face, but his teeth were clenched with hate.

Sparhawk ran his sword through another Zemoch, even as Kalten sent another head rolling down the corridor.

Adus brained one of his own soldiers, roaring like an enraged bull.

The roar suddenly broke off. Adus gaped, his eyes bulging. His mismatched armour did not fit very well, and the back of his cuirass did not reach all the way to his hips. It was there, in that area covered only by chain-mail, that Talen had stabbed him. Chain-mail will ward off the blow of sword or axe, but it is no defence against a thrust. Talen's dirk drove smoothly into the half-witted brute's back just under the lower rim of the cuirass, seeking and finding Adus's kidney. Talen jerked his dirk free and stabbed again, on the other side this time.

Adus squealed like a stuck pig in a slaughter-house. He stumbled forward, one hand clutching at the small of his back and his face suddenly dead white with pain and shock.

Talen drove his dirk into the back of the animal's knee.

Adus stumbled a few more steps, dropping his axe and grabbing at his back with both hands. Then he fell writhing to the floor.

Sparhawk and Kalten cut down the remaining Zemoch soldiers, but Talen had already snatched up a fallen sword and, standing astride Adus's body, he was chopping at the brute's helmeted head. Then he reversed the sword and tried desperately to stab down through the breast-plate into Adus's writhing body, but he did not have enough strength to make his weapon penetrate. 'Help me!' he cried. 'Somebody help me!'

Sparhawk stepped to the weeping boy's side, his own eyes also streaming tears. He dropped his sword and reached out to take the hilt of the one which Talen was trying to drive into Adus. Then he took hold of the sword's cross-piece with his other hand. 'You do it like this, Talen,' he said almost clinically, as if he were merely giving instructions on the practice field.

Then, standing one on either side of the whimpering Adus, the boy and the man took hold of the sword, their hands touching on the hilt.

'We don't have to hurry, Sparhawk,' Talen grated from between clenched teeth.

'No,' Sparhawk agreed. 'Not really, if you don't want to.'

Adus shrieked as they slowly pushed the sword into him.

The shriek broke off as a great fountain of blood gushed from his mouth. 'Please!' he gurgled.

Sparhawk and Talen grimly twisted the sword.

Adus shrieked again, banging his head on the floor and beating a rapid tattoo on the flagstones with his heels. He arched his quivering body, belched forth another gusher of blood and collapsed in an inert heap.

Talen, weeping, sprawled across the body, clawing at the dead man's staring eyes. Then Sparhawk bent, gently picked the boy up and carried him back to where Kurik lay.

Chapter 29

There was still fighting in the torchlit corridor, the clash of steel on steel, cries, shouts, groans. Sparhawk knew that he must go to the aid of his friends, but the enormity of what had just happened left him stunned, unable to move. Talen knelt beside Kurik's lifeless body, weeping and pounding his fist on the flagstone floor.

'I have to go,' the big Pandion told the boy.

Talen did not answer.

'Berit,' Sparhawk called, 'come here.'

The young apprentice came cautiously out of the alcove, his axe in his hands.

'Help Talen,' Sparhawk said. 'Take Kurik back inside.'

Berit was staring in disbelief at Kurik.

'Move, boy!' Sparhawk said sharply, 'and take care of Sephrenia.'

'Sparhawk!' Kalten shouted. 'There are more of them coming!'

'On the way!' Sparhawk looked at Talen. 'I have to go,' he told the boy again.

'Go ahead,' Talen replied. Then he looked up, his tear-streaked face savage. 'Kill them all, Sparhawk,' he said fiercely. 'Kill them all.'

Sparhawk nodded. That would help Talen a bit, he thought as he returned to retrieve his sword. Anger was a good remedy for grief. He picked up his sword and turned, feeling his own rage burning in his throat. He also pitied the Zemoch soldiers as he went to rejoin Kalten. 'Fall back,' he told his friend in a coldly level tone. 'Get your breath.'

'Is there any hope?' Kalten asked, parrying a Zemoch spear-thrust.

'No.'

'I'm sorry, Sparhawk.'

It was a small group of soldiers, no doubt one of the detachments that had been trying to lure the knights into side passages. Sparhawk went towards them purposefully. It was good to be fighting. Fighting demanded every bit of a man's attention and pushed everything else from his mind. Sparhawk moved deftly against the half-dozen Zemochs. There was a certain obscure justice working now. Kurik had taught him every move, every technical nuance he was bringing to bear, and those skills were supplemented by a towering rage over his friend's death. In a very real sense, Kurik had made Sparhawk invincible. Even Kalten seemed shocked at his friend's sheer savagery. It was the work of no more than a few moments to kill five of the soldiers facing him. The last turned to flee, but Sparhawk passed his sword quickly to his shield-hand, bent and picked up a Zemoch spear. 'Take this with you,' he called after the fleeing man. Then he made a long, practised cast. The spear took the soldier squarely between the shoulder blades.

'Good throw,' Kalten said.

'Let's go and help Tynian and Ulath.' Sparhawk still felt a powerful need to kill people. He led his friend back towards the turn in the corridor where the Alcione Knight and his Genidian comrade were holding back the soldiers who had rushed into the maze from the throne-room in response to Adus's bellowed command.

'I'll take care of this,' Sparhawk said flatly.

'Kurik?' Ulath asked.

Sparhawk shook his head and began killing Zemochs again. He waded on, leaving the maimed behind him for his companions to dispatch.

'Sparhawk!' Ulath shouted. 'Stop! They're running!'

'Hurry!' Sparhawk yelled back. 'We can still catch them!'

'Let them go!'

'*No!*'

'You're keeping Martel waiting, Sparhawk,' Kalten said sharply. Kalten sometimes made a show of being stupid, but Sparhawk saw immediately just how smoothly his blond friend had brought him up short. Killing relatively innocent soldiers was no more than an idle pastime when compared to dealing once and for all with the white-haired renegade. He stopped. 'All right,' he panted, nearly exhausted from his exertions, 'let's go back. We've got to get past that sliding wall before the soldiers come back anyway.'

'Are you feeling any better?' Tynian asked as they started back towards the alcove.

'Not really,' Sparhawk said.

They passed Adus's body. 'Go on ahead,' Kalten told them. 'I'll be right along.'

Berit and Bevier awaited them at the entrance to the alcove.

'Did you chase them off?' Bevier asked.

'Sparhawk did,' Ulath grunted. 'He was very convincing.'

'Aren't they likely to gather reinforcements and come back?'

'Not unless their officers have very large whips, they won't.'

Sephrenia had arranged Kurik's body in a posture of repose. His cloak covered the dreadful wound which had spilled out his life. His eyes were closed and his face calm. Once again Sparhawk felt an unbearable grief. 'Is there any way –?' he began, even though he already knew the answer.

Sephrenia shook her head. 'No, dear one,' she replied. 'I'm sorry.' She sat beside the body holding the weeping Talen in her arms.

Sparhawk sighed. 'We're going to have to leave,' he told them. 'We have to get back to those stairs before anybody decides to follow us.' He looked back over his shoulder. Kalten was hurrying to join them, and he was carrying something wrapped in a Zemoch cloak.

'I'll do this,' Ulath said. He bent and picked Kurik up as if the powerful squire were no more than a child, and they retraced their steps to the foot of the stairs leading up into the dusty darkness above.

'Slide that wall back in place,' Sparhawk said, 'and see if you can find some way to wedge it shut.'

'We can do that from up above,' Ulath said. 'We'll block the track it slides on.'

Sparhawk grunted as he made some decisions. 'Bevier,' he said regretfully, 'we're going to have to leave you here, I'm afraid. You're badly wounded, and I've already lost enough friends today.'

Bevier started to object, but then changed his mind.

'Talen,' Sparhawk went on, 'you stay here with Bevier and your father.' He smiled a sad smile. 'We want to *kill* Azash; we don't want to steal Him.'

Talen nodded.

'And Berit –'

'Please, Sparhawk,' the young man said, his eyes filled with tears. '*Please* don't make me stay behind. Sir Bevier and Talen are safe here, and I might be able to help when we get to the temple.'

Sparhawk glanced at Sephrenia. She nodded. 'All right,' he said. He wanted to warn Berit to be careful, but that would have demeaned the apprentice, so he let it pass.

'Give me your war-axe and shield, Berit,' Bevier said,

his voice weak. 'Take these instead.' He handed Berit his lochaber and his burnished shield.

'I won't dishonour them, Sir Bevier,' Berit swore.

Kalten had stepped towards the rear of the chamber. 'There's a space back here under the stairs, Bevier. It might be a good idea for you and Kurik and Talen to wait for us under there. If the soldiers manage to break through the wall, the three of you won't be in plain sight.'

Bevier nodded as Ulath took up Kurik's body to conceal it behind the stairs.

'There's not much left to say, Bevier,' Sparhawk told the Cyrinic Knight, taking his hand. 'We'll try to come back as soon as we can.'

'I'll pray for you, Sparhawk,' Bevier said, 'for all of you.'

Sparhawk nodded, then knelt briefly at Kurik's side and took his squire's hand. 'Sleep well, my friend,' he murmured. Then he rose and started up the stairs without looking back.

The stairs at the far end of that broad, straight pathway that stretched across the mole-tunnel mounds of the labyrinth below were very wide and sheathed with marble. There was no sliding wall to conceal a chamber at the foot of those stairs, and no maze led away from the temple. No maze was needed.

'Wait here,' Sparhawk whispered to his friends, 'and put out those torches.' He crept forward, pulled off his helmet and lay down at the top of the stairs. 'Ulath,' he murmured, 'hold my ankles. I want to see what we're getting into.' With the huge Thalesian keeping him from tumbling in a steely clatter down the stairs, Sparhawk inched his way headfirst down the stairs until he could see out into the room beyond.

The temple of Azash was a place of nightmare. It was,

567

as the dome which roofed it implied, circular, and it was fully half a mile across. The curving, inwardly-sloping walls were of polished black onyx, as was the floor. It was much like looking into the very heart of night. The temple was not lighted by torches but by huge bonfires flaring and roaring in enormous iron basins set on girder-like legs. The vast chamber was encircled by tier upon tier of polished black terraces stepping down and down and down to a black floor far beneath.

At evenly-spaced intervals along the top terrace were twenty-foot marble statues of things which were for the most part not human. Then Sparhawk saw a Styric form among them and somewhat further along an Elene one. He realized that the statues were representations of the servants of Azash, and that humanity played a very small and insignificant part in that assemblage. The other servants dwelt in places at once very far away and at the same time very, very close.

Directly opposite the entrance through which he peered was the towering idol. Man's efforts to visualize and to represent his Gods are never wholly satisfactory. A lion-headed God is really the image of a human body with the head of a lion tacked on for the sake of contrast. Mankind perceives the face as the seat of the soul; the body is largely irrelevant. The icon of a God is not meant to be representational, and the face of the icon is intended to suggest the spirit of the God rather than to be an accurate recreation of His real features. The face of the idol rearing high above the polished black temple contained the sum of human depravity. Lust was there certainly and greed and gluttony; but there were other attributes in that face as well, attributes for which there were no names in any human tongue. Azash, to judge from His face, craved – required – things beyond human comprehension. There was a haggard, unsatisfied look about that face. It was the face of a Being with overpowering desires which would not – could not – be satisfied. The lips were twisted, the eyes brooding and cruel.

Sparhawk wrenched his eyes from that face. To look too long at it was to lose one's soul.

The body was not fully formed. It was as if the sculptor had been so overwhelmed by that face and all that it implied that he no more than sketched in the remainder of the figure. There was a spidery-like profusion of arms that extended in clusters of tentacles from vast shoulders. The body leaned back somewhat with its hips thrust forward obscenely, but what would have been the focus of that suggestive pose was not there. Instead there was a smooth, unwrinkled surface, shiny and looking very much like a burn scar. Sparhawk remembered the words Sephrenia had cast into the God's teeth during her confrontation with the Seeker at the north end of Lake Venne. Impotent, she had called Him, and emasculate. He preferred not to speculate on the means the Younger Gods may have used to mutilate their older relative. There was a pale greenish nimbus emanating from the idol, a glow much like that which had come from the face of the Seeker.

There was a ceremony of some sort taking place on the circular black floor far below in the sickly green glow coming from the altar. Sparhawk's mind recoiled from the notion of calling that ceremony a religious rite. The celebrants cavorted naked before the idol. Sparhawk was not some unworldly, cloistered monk. He was acquainted with the world, but the levels of perversion being demonstrated in that rite turned his stomach. The orgy which had so engrossed the primitive Elene Zemochs back in the mountains had been child-like, almost pure, by comparison. *These* celebrants appeared to be attempting to duplicate the perversions of non-humans, and their fixed stares and galvanic movements clearly showed that they would continue the ceremony until they died from sheer excess. The lower tiers of that huge, stair-stepped basin were packed with green-robed figures who raised a groaning discordant chant, an empty sound devoid of any thought or emotion.

Then a slight movement caught Sparhawk's eye, and he looked quickly towards his right. A group of people were gathered on the top terrace a hundred yards or more away beneath the leprous white statue of something that must have been dredged from the depths of madness. One of the figures had white hair.

Sparhawk twisted around and signalled to Ulath to pull him back up again.

'Well?' Kalten asked him.

'It's all one big room,' Sparhawk murmured. 'The idol is over on the far side, and there are wide terraces leading down to a floor in the middle.'

'What's that noise?' Tynian asked.

'They're holding some sort of rite. I think that chant's a part of it.'

'I'm not concerned about their religion,' Ulath rumbled. 'Are there any soldiers?'

Sparhawk shook his head.

'That's helpful. Anything else?'

'Yes. I need some magic, Sephrenia. Martel and the others are gathered on the top terrace. They're about a hundred paces off to the right. We need to know what they're saying. Are we close enough for your spell to work?'

She nodded. 'Let's move back away from the stairs,' she suggested. 'The spell makes a certain amount of light, and we don't want anyone to know that we're here just yet.'

They retreated back along the dusty pathway, and Sephrenia took Sir Bevier's polished shield from Berit. 'This should do it,' she said. She quickly cast the spell and released it. The knights gathered around the suddenly glowing shield, peering at the hazy figures appearing on its mirror-like surface. The voices coming from the image were tinny-sounding, but they were intelligible.

'Thine assurances to me that my gold would buy thee that throne from which thou couldst further our purposes were hollow, Annias,' Otha was saying in that gurgling rumble.

'It was Sparhawk again, Your Majesty,' Annias tried to excuse himself in an almost grovelling tone. 'He disrupted things – as we had feared he would.'

'Sparhawk!' Otha spat out a foul oath and slammed his fist down on the arm of his throne-like litter. 'The man's existence doth canker my soul. His very name doth cause me pain. Thou wert to keep him away from Chyrellos, Martel. Why didst thou fail me and my God?'

'I didn't really fail, Your Majesty,' Martel replied calmly, 'and neither did Annias for that matter. Putting His Grace on the Archprelate's throne was only a means to an end, and we've achieved that end. Bhelliom is under this very roof. The scheme to elevate Annias so that he could force the Elenes to surrender the jewel to us was filled with uncertainties. This has been much faster and much more direct. Results are what Azash wants, Your Majesty, not the success or failure of any of the interim steps.'

Otha grunted. 'Perhaps,' he conceded, 'but Bhelliom hath not been passively delivered into the possession of our God. It doth still lie in the hands of this Sparhawk. Ye have put armies in his path and he doth easily o'erwhelm them. Our Master hath sent servants more horrible than death itself to slay him, and he lives yet.'

'Sparhawk's only a man, after all,' Lycheas said in his whining voice. 'His luck can't last forever.'

Otha threw a look at Lycheas that quite plainly spoke of death. Arissa put her arm protectively around her son's

571

shoulders and looked as if she were about to come to his defence, but Annias shook his head warningly.

'Thou hast defiled thyself by acknowledging this bastard of thine, Annias,' Otha declared in a tone of towering contempt. He paused, looking at them. 'Can none of ye *understand*?' he suddenly roared. 'This Sparhawk is Anakha, the unknown. The destinies of all men are clearly visible – all men save Anakha. Anakha moves outside destiny. Even the Gods fear him. He and Bhelliom are linked in some way beyond the comprehension of the men or the Gods of this world, and the Goddess Aphrael serves them. We do not know their purpose. All that doth save us from them lies in the fact that Bhelliom's submission to Sparhawk is reluctant. Should it ever yield to him willingly, he will be a God.'

'But he's not a God yet, Your Majesty,' Martel smiled. 'He's trapped in that maze, and he'll never leave his companions behind to assault us alone. Sparhawk's predictable. That's why Azash accepted Annias and me. We know Sparhawk, and we know what he'll do.'

'And didst thou *know* that he would succeed as he hath?' Otha sneered. 'Didst thou *know* that his coming here would threaten our very existence – and the existence of our God?'

Martel looked at the obscenely cavorting figures on the floor below. 'How long will that continue?' he asked. 'We need some guidance from Azash at this point, and we can't get His attention while that's going on.'

'The rite is nearly complete,' Otha told him. 'The celebrants are beyond exhaustion. They will die soon.'

'Good. Then we'll be able to speak with our Master. He's *also* in danger.'

'Martel!' Otha said sharply, his voice filled with alarm. 'Sparhawk hath broken out of the maze! He hath reached the pathway to the temple!'

'Summon men to stop him!' Martel barked.

'I have, but they are far behind him. He will reach us before they can hinder him.'

'We must rouse Azash!' Annias cried in a shrill voice.

'To interrupt this rite is death,' Otha declared.

Martel straightened and took his ornate helmet out from under his arm. 'Then it's up to me, I guess,' he said bleakly.

Sparhawk raised his head. From far off in the direction of the palace he could hear the sound of battering rams pounding on a stone wall. 'That's enough,' he said to Sephrenia. 'We have to move. Otha's called soldiers to break down that wall that leads to the stairs near the palace.'

'I hope Bevier and Talen are out of sight,' Kalten said.

'They are,' Sparhawk told him. 'Bevier knows what he's doing. We're going to have to go down into the temple. This attic – or whatever you want to call it – is too open. If we try to fight here, we'll have soldiers coming at us from all sides.' He looked at Sephrenia. 'Is there some way we can block those stairs behind us?' he asked her.

Her eyes narrowed. 'I *think* so,' she replied.

'You sound a bit dubious.'

'No, not really. I can block the stairway easily enough, but I can't be sure whether Otha knows the counter-spell.'

'He won't know that you've blocked it until his soldiers arrive and can't come down the stairs, will he?' Tynian asked her.

'No. Actually he won't. Very good, Tynian.'

'Do we just run around that top terrace and confront the idol?' Kalten asked.

'We can't,' Sephrenia told him. 'Otha's a magician, you remember. He'd be hurling spells at our backs every step of the way. We'll have to confront him directly.'

'And Martel as well,' Sparhawk added. 'Now then, Otha doesn't dare to interrupt Azash while that rite's going on. We can take advantage of that. All we'll have to worry about is Otha himself. Can we deal with him, Sephrenia?'

She nodded. 'Otha's not brave,' she replied. 'If we threaten him, he'll use his power to shield himself from us. He'll count on the soldiers coming from the palace to deal with us.'

'We'll try it,' Sparhawk said. 'Are we all ready then?'

They nodded.

'Just be careful,' he told them, 'and I don't want any interference when I go after Martel. All right, let's go.'

They went to the head of the stairs, paused a moment, then drew in a collective deep breath and marched down with drawn weapons.

'Ah, there you are, old boy,' Sparhawk drawled to Martel, deliberately imitating the white-haired renegade's nonchalance, 'I've been looking all over for you.'

'I was right here, Sparhawk,' Martel replied, drawing his sword.

'So I see. I must have been turned around somehow. I hope I didn't keep you waiting.'

'Not at all.'

'Splendid. I hate being tardy.' He looked them over. 'Good. I see that we're all here.' He looked a bit more closely at the Primate of Cimmura. 'Really, Annias, you should try to get more sun. You're as white as a sheet.'

'Oh, before you two get started, Martel,' Kalten said, 'I brought you a present – a little memento of our visit. I'm sure you'll cherish it always.' He bent slightly and gave the cloak he was carrying a little flip, holding one edge firmly in his gauntleted fist. The cloak unfurled on the onyx floor. Adus's head rolled out and bounced across to stop at Martel's feet, where it lay staring up at him.

574

'How very kind of you, Sir Kalten,' Martel said from between clenched teeth. Seemingly indifferent, he kicked the head off to one side. 'I'm sure that obtaining this gift for me cost you a great deal.'

Sparhawk's fist tightened about his sword-hilt, and his brain seethed with hatred. 'It cost me Kurik, Martel,' he said in a flat voice, 'and now it's time to settle accounts.'

Martel's eyes widened briefly. 'Kurik?' he said in a stunned voice. 'I didn't expect that. I'm truly sorry, Sparhawk. I liked him. If you ever get back to Demos, give Aslade my sincerest apologies.'

'I don't think so, Martel. I won't insult Aslade by mentioning your name to her. Shall we get on with this?' Sparhawk began to move forward, his shield braced and his sword-point moving slowly back and forth like the head of a snake. Kalten and the others grounded their weapons and stood watching grimly.

'A gentleman to the end, I see,' Martel said, putting on his helmet and moving away from Otha's litter to give himself fighting room. 'Your good manners and your sense of fair play will be the death of you yet, Sparhawk. You had the advantage. You should have used it.'

'I'm not going to need it, Martel. You still have a moment or two for repentance. I'd advise you to use the time well.'

Martel smiled thinly. 'I don't think so, Sparhawk,' he said. 'I made my choice. I won't demean myself by changing it now.' He clapped down his visor.

They struck simultaneously, their swords ringing on each other's shields. They had trained together under Kurik's instruction as boys, so there was no possibility of some trick or feint giving either of them an opening. They were so evenly matched that there was no way to predict the outcome of this duel which had been a decade and more in the preparation.

Their first strokes were tentative as they carefully felt each other out, looking for alterations in technique or changes in their relative strength. To the untrained onlooker their hammering at each other might have seemed frenzied and without thought, but that was not the case. Neither of them was so enraged as to overextend himself and leave himself open. Great dents appeared in their shields, and showers of sparks cascaded down over them each time their sword-edges clashed against each other. Back and forth they struggled, moving slowly away from the spot where Otha's jewelled litter sat and where Annias, Arissa and Lycheas stood watching, wide-eyed and breathless. That too was a part of Sparhawk's strategy. He needed to draw Martel away from Otha so that Kalten and the others could menace the bloated emperor. To gain that end, he retreated a few paces now and then when it was not actually necessary, drawing Martel step by step away from his friends.

'You must be getting old, Sparhawk,' Martel panted, hammering at his former brother's shield.

'No more than you are, Martel.' Sparhawk delivered a massive blow that staggered his opponent.

Kalten, Ulath and Tynian, followed by Berit, who swung Sir Bevier's hideous lochaber, fanned out to advance on Otha and Annias. Slug-like Otha waved one arm, and a shimmering barrier appeared around his litter and Martel's companions.

Sparhawk felt the faintest of tingles along the back of his neck, and he knew that Sephrenia was weaving the spell which would block the stairs. He rushed at Martel, swinging his sword as rapidly as he could to so distract the white-haired man that he would not feel that faint familiar sensation which always accompanied the release of a friend's spell. Sephrenia had trained Martel, and he would know her touch.

The fight raged on. Sparhawk was panting and sweating now, and his sword-arm ached with weariness. He stepped back, lowering his sword slightly in the traditional wordless suggestion that they pause for long enough to get their breath. That suggestion was never considered a sign of weakness.

Martel also lowered his sword in agreement. 'Almost like old times, Sparhawk,' he panted, pushing open his visor.

'Close,' Sparhawk agreed. 'You've picked up some new tricks, I see.' He also opened his visor.

'I spent too much time in Lamorkand. Lamork swordsmanship is clumsy, though. Your technique seems to be a little Rendorish.'

'Ten years of exile there,' Sparhawk shrugged, breathing deeply as he tried to regain his wind.

'Vanion would skin both of us if he saw us flailing at each other this way.'

'He probably would. Vanion's a perfectionist.'

'That's God's own truth.'

They stood panting and staring intently into each other's eyes, watching for that minuscule narrowing that would preface a surprise blow. Sparhawk could feel the ache slowly draining from his right shoulder. 'Are you ready?' he asked finally.

'Any time you are.'

They clanged their visors shut again and resumed the fight.

Martel launched a complicated and extended series of sword-strokes. The series was familiar, since it was one of the oldest, and its conclusion was inevitable. Sparhawk moved his shield and his sword in the prescribed defence, but he had known as soon as Martel swung the first stroke that he was going to receive a near-stunning blow to the head. Kurik, however, had devised a modification to the

577

Pandion helmet not long after Martel's expulsion from the order, and when the renegade swung his heavy blow at Sparhawk's head, Sparhawk ducked his chin slightly to take the stroke full on the crest of his helmet – a crest which was now heavily reinforced. His ears rang nonetheless, and his knees buckled slightly. He was, however, able to parry the follow-up stroke which might well have disabled him.

Martel's reactions seemed somehow slower than Sparhawk remembered them as having been. His own blows, he conceded, probably no longer had the crisp snap of youth. They were both older, and an extended duel with a man of equal strength and skill ages one rapidly.

Then he suddenly understood, and the action came simultaneously with understanding. He unleashed a series of overhand strokes at Martel's head, and the renegade was forced to protect himself with both sword and shield. Then Sparhawk followed that flurry to the head with the traditional body-thrust. Martel knew it was coming, of course, but he simply could not move his shield rapidly enough to protect himself. The point of Sparhawk's sword crunched into his armour low on the right side of his chest and drove deeply into his body. Martel stiffened, and coughed a great spray of blood out through the slots of his visor. He tried weakly to keep his shield and sword up, but his hands were trembling violently. His legs began to shake. His sword fell from his hand, and his shield dropped to his side. He coughed again, a wet, tearing sound. Blood poured from his visor once more, and he slowly collapsed in a heap, face down. 'Finish it, Sparhawk,' he gasped.

Sparhawk pushed him over onto his back with one foot. He raised his sword, then lowered it again. He knelt beside the dying man. 'There's no need,' he said quietly, opening Martel's visor.

'How did you manage that?' Martel asked.

578

'It's that new armour of yours. It's too heavy. You got tired and started to slow down.'

'There's a certain justice there,' Martel said, trying to breathe shallowly so that the blood rapidly filling his lungs would not choke him again. 'Killed by my own vanity.'

'That's probably what kills us all – eventually.'

'It was a good fight, though.'

'Yes. It was.'

'And we finally found out which of us is the best. Perhaps it's the time for truth. I never had any real doubts, you know.'

'I did.'

Sparhawk knelt quietly, listening to Martel's breathing growing shallower and shallower. 'Lakus died, you know,' he said quietly, 'and Olven.'

'Lakus and Olven? I didn't know that. Was I in any way responsible?'

'No. It was something else.'

'That's some small comfort anyway. Could you call Sephrenia for me, Sparhawk? I'd like to say goodbye to her.'

Sparhawk raised his arm and motioned to the woman who had trained them both.

Her eyes were full of tears as she knelt across Martel's body from Sparhawk. 'Yes, dear one?' she said to the dying man.

'You always said I'd come to a bad end, little mother,' Martel said wryly, his voice no more than a whisper now, 'but you were wrong. This isn't so bad at all. It's almost like a formal deathbed. I get to depart in the presence of the only two people I've ever really loved. Will you bless me, little mother?'

She put her hands to his face and spoke gently in Styric. Then, weeping, she bent and kissed his pallid forehead.

When she raised her face again, he was dead.

Chapter 30

Sparhawk rose to his feet and helped Sephrenia to stand.

'Are you all right, dear one?' she whispered.

'I'm well enough.' Sparhawk stared hard at Otha.

'Congratulations, Sir Knight,' Otha rumbled ironically, his sweaty head gleaming in the light of the fires, 'and I thank thee. Long have I pondered the problem of Martel. He sought, methinks, to rise above himself, and his usefulness to me ended when thou and thy companions brought Bhelliom to me. I am well rid of him.'

'Call it a farewell gift, Otha.'

'Oh? Art thou leaving?'

'No, but you are.'

Otha laughed. It was a revolting sound.

'He's afraid, Sparhawk,' Sephrenia whispered. 'He's not sure that you can't break through his shield.'

'Can I?'

'I'm not sure either. He's very vulnerable now, though, because Azash is totally distracted by that rite.'

'That's a place to start then.' Sparhawk drew in a deep breath and started towards the bloated Emperor of Zemoch.

Otha flinched back and made a quick signal to the half-naked brutes around him. The bearers picked up the litter upon which he grossly sprawled and started towards the terraces leading down towards the onyx floor where the naked celebrants, twitching and blank-faced with exhaustion, continued their obscene rite. Annias, Arissa and Lycheas went with him, their eyes fearful as they stayed as close to his litter as possible to remain

580

within the questionable safety of the glowing nimbus of his protective shield. When the litter reached the onyx floor, Otha shouted to the green-robed priests, and they rushed forward, their faces alight with mindless devotion as they drew weapons from beneath their vestments.

From behind them, Sparhawk heard a sudden cry of frustrated chagrin. The soldiers rushing to the aid of their emperor had just encountered Sephrenia's barrier. 'Will it hold?' he asked her.

'It will unless one of those soldiers is stronger than I am.'

'Not too likely. That leaves only the priests then.' He looked at his friends. 'All right, gentlemen,' he said to them. 'Let's form up around Sephrenia and clear a path through here.'

The priests of Azash wore no armour, and the way they handled their weapons showed little evidence of skill. They were Styric for the most part, and the sudden appearance of hostile Church Knights in the holy centre of their religion had startled them and filled them with dismay. Sparhawk remembered something Sephrenia had once said. Styrics, she had told him, do not react well when they are surprised. The unexpected tends to confound them. He could feel a faint prickling sensation as he and his armoured friends started down the stair-stepped terraces, a prickling that told him that some few of the priests at least were attempting to put some form of spell together. He roared an Elene war cry, a harsh bellow filled with a lust for blood and violence. The prickling evaporated. 'Lots of noise, gentlemen!' he shouted to his friends. 'Keep them off-balance so they can't use magic!'

The Church Knights rushed down the black terraces bellowing war cries and brandishing their weapons. The priests recoiled, and then the knights were on them.

Berit pushed past Sparhawk, his eyes alight with enthusiasm and Sir Bevier's lochaber at the ready. 'Save your strength, Sparhawk,' he said gruffly, trying to make his voice deeper, more roughly masculine. He stepped purposefully in front of the startled Sparhawk and strode into the green-robed ranks facing them, swinging the lochaber like a scythe.

Sparhawk reached out to pull him back, but Sephrenia laid her hand on his wrist. 'No, Sparhawk,' she said. 'This is important to him, and he's in no particular danger.'

Otha had reached the polished altar in front of the idol and was staring at the carnage below in open-mouthed fright. Then he drew himself up. 'Approach then, Sparhawk!' he blustered. 'My God grows impatient!'

'I doubt that, Otha,' Sparhawk called back. 'Azash wants Bhelliom, but he doesn't want *me* to deliver it to him, because he doesn't know what I'm going to do with it.'

'Very good, Sparhawk,' Sephrenia murmured. 'Use your advantage. Azash will sense Otha's uncertainty, and He'll feel the same way.'

The temple echoed with the noise of blows, shrieks and groans as Sparhawk's friends systematically slaughtered the green-robed priests. They chopped their way through the tightly-packed ranks until they reached the foot of the first terrace below the altar.

In spite of everything, Sparhawk felt tightly exultant. He had not expected to make it this far, and his unexpected survival filled him with a sense of euphoric invincibility. 'Well, Otha,' he said, looking up those stair-stepped terraces at the bloated emperor, 'why don't you awaken Azash? Let's find out if the Elder Gods know how to die as well as men do.'

Otha gaped at him, then scrambled from his litter and crumpled to the floor as his puny legs refused to support him. 'Kneel!' he half-screamed at Annias. 'Kneel and pray to our God for deliverance!' The notion that his soldiers could not enter the temple obviously frightened Otha considerably.

'Kalten,' Sparhawk called to his friend, 'finish up with the priests, and then make sure that those soldiers don't break through and rush us from behind.'

'That's not necessary, Sparhawk,' Sephrenia said.

'I know, but it should keep them back out of harm's way.' He drew in a deep breath. 'Here we go, then.' He shook off his gauntlets, tucked his sword-blade under his arm and took the steel-mesh pouch from his belt. He unwrapped the wire which bound the pouch shut and shook Bhelliom out into his hand. The jewel seemed very hot, and light, wavering like heat-lightning on a summer's night, seethed among its petals. 'Blue-Rose!' he said sharply. 'You must do as I command!'

Otha, half-kneeling, half-squatting, was babbling a prayer to his God – a prayer made almost unintelligible by his fright. Annias, Lycheas and Arissa also knelt, and they stared up at the hideous face of the idol looming above them. Their eyes were filled with horror as they more closely beheld the reality of that God they had so willingly chosen to follow.

'Come, Azash!' Otha pleaded. 'Awaken! Hear the prayer of thy servants!'

The idol's deep-sunk eyes had been closed, but now they slowly opened, and that greenish fire blazed from them. Sparhawk felt wave upon wave of malevolence blazing at him from those baleful eyes, and he stood, stunned into near-insensibility by the titanic presence of a God.

The idol was moving! A kind of undulation rippled down its body and the tentacle-like arms sinuously reached forth – reaching towards the glowing stone in Sparhawk's hand, yearning towards the one thing in all the world which offered restoration and freedom.

'No!' Sparhawk's voice was a harsh rasp. He raised his sword above the Bhelliom. 'I'll destroy it!' he threatened, '– and you along with it!'

The idol seemed to recoil, and its eyes were suddenly filled with amazed shock. 'Why hast thou brought this ignorant savage into my presence, Sephrenia?' The voice was hollow, and it echoed throughout the temple and in Sparhawk's mind as well. Sparhawk knew that the mind of Azash could obliterate him in the space between two heartbeats, but for some reason Azash seemed afraid to bring his power to bear upon the rash man who stood menacing the Sapphire Rose with drawn sword.

'I do but obey my destiny, Azash,' Sephrenia replied calmly. 'I was born to bring Sparhawk to this place to face thee.'

'But what of the Destiny of this Sparhawk? Dost thou know what *he* is destined to do?' There was a kind of desperation in the voice of Azash.

'No man or God knoweth that, Azash,' she reminded him. 'Sparhawk is Anakha, and all the Gods have known and feared that one day Anakha would come and would move through this world committed to ends which none may perceive. I am the servant of his Destiny, whatever it may be, and I have brought him here that he may bring those ends to fruition.'

The idol seemed to tense itself, and then an irresistible command lashed out, overpowering and insistent, and the command was *not* directed at Sparhawk.

Sephrenia gasped and seemed almost to wilt like a flower before the first blast of winter. Sparhawk could actually feel her resolve fading. She wavered as the force of the mind of Azash peeled away her defences.

He tensed his arm and raised his sword higher. If

Sephrenia were to fall, they were lost, and he could not know if there would be time to deliver the last fatal stroke after her collapse. He drew the image of Ehlana's face in his mind and gripped his sword-hilt even more tightly.

The sound was not audible to anyone else. He knew that. It was in his mind only; only he could hear it. It was the insistent, commanding sound of shepherd's pipes, and there was a very strong overtone of irritation to it.

'*Aphrael!*' he called out in sudden relief.

A small firefly spark appeared in front of his face. 'Well, *finally*!' Flute's voice snapped angrily. 'What took you so *long*, Sparhawk? Don't you know that you have to *call* me?'

'No. I didn't know that. Help Sephrenia.'

There was no touch, no movement, no sound, but Sephrenia straightened, brushing at her brow with lightly-touching fingers as the idol's eyes burned and fixed themselves on that firefly spark.

'My daughter,' the voice of Azash said. 'Wilt thou cast thy lot with these mortals?'

'I am no daughter of thine, Azash.' Flute's voice was crisp. 'I willed *myself* into existence, as did my brothers and sisters when thou and thy kindred did tear at the fabric of reality with thy childish contention. I am thy daughter only through thy fault. Hadst thou and thy kindred turned ye aside from that reckless course which would have destroyed all, there would have been no need for me and mine.'

'I *will* have Bhelliom!' The hollow voice was the thunder and the earthquake, tearing at the very foundations of the earth.

'Thou shalt *not*!' Flute's voice was flatly contradictory. 'It was to deny thee and thy kind possession of Bhelliom that I and my kind came into existence. Bhelliom is not of this place, and it must not be held here in bondage to thee or to me or to the Troll-Gods or any other Gods of this world.'

'*I will have it!*' The voice of Azash rose to a scream.

'No. Anakha will destroy it first, and in its destruction shalt thou perish.'

The idol seemed to flinch. 'How *darest* thou!' it gasped. 'How darest thou even *speak* such horror? In the death of one of us lieth the seeds of the deaths of us all.'

'So be it then.' Aphrael's tone was indifferent. Then her light little voice took on a cruel note. 'Direct thy fury at *me*, Azash, and not at my children, for it was *I* who used the power of the rings to emasculate thee and to confine thee forever in that idol of mud.'

'It was *thou*?' The terrible voice seemed stunned.

'It was *I*. Thy power is so abated by thine emasculation that thou canst not escape thy confinement. Thou wilt *not* have Bhelliom, impotent Godling, and thus shalt thou be forever imprisoned. Thou shalt remain unmanned and confined until the farthest star burns down to ashes.' She paused, and when she spoke again it was in the tone of one slowly twisting a knife buried in the body of another. 'It was thine absurd and transparent proposal that all the Gods of Styricum unite to seize Bhelliom from the Troll-Gods – "for the good of all" – that gave me the opportunity to mutilate and confine thee, Azash. Thou hast none to blame but thyself for what hath befallen thee. And now Anakha hath brought Bhelliom and the rings – and even the Troll-Gods locked within the jewel – here to confront thee. I call upon thee to submit to the power of the Sapphire Rose – or to perish.'

There was a howl of inhuman frustration, but the idol made no move.

Otha, however, his eyes filled with panic, began to mutter a desperate spell. Then he hurled it forth, and the hideous statues encircling the interior of the vast temple began to shimmer, changing from marble-white to greens and blues and bloody reds, and the babble of their inhuman voices filled the dome. Sephrenia spoke two words in Styric, her voice calm. She gestured, and the statues froze again, congealing back into pallid marble.

Otha howled, and began to speak again, so frustrated and enraged that he did not even speak in Styric, but in his native Elene.

'Listen to me, Sparhawk,' Flute's musical voice was very soft.

'But Otha –'

'He's only babbling. My sister can deal with him. Pay attention. The time will come very soon when you'll have to act. I'll tell you when. Climb these stairs to the idol and keep your sword poised over Bhelliom. If Azash or Otha or anything else tries to keep you from reaching the idol, smash the Bhelliom. If all goes well and you reach the idol, touch Bhelliom to that place that looks burned and scarred.'

'Will that destroy Azash?'

'Of course not. The idol that's sitting there is only an encasement. The *real* idol is inside that big one. Bhelliom will shatter the big idol, and you'll be able to see Azash Himself. The real idol is quite small, and it's made of dried mud. As soon as you can see it, drop your sword and hold Bhelliom in both hands. Then use these exact words, "Blue-Rose, I am Sparhawk-from-Elenia. By the power of these rings I command Blue-Rose to return this image to the earth from which it came." Then touch Bhelliom to the idol.'

'What happens then?'

'I'm not sure.'

'*Aphrael!*' Sparhawk said it in a tone of startled protest.

'Bhelliom's Destiny is even more obscure than yours,

and I can't tell from one minute to the next what *you're* going to do.'

'Will it destroy Azash?'

'Oh yes – and quite possibly the rest of the world as well. Bhelliom wants to be free of this world, and this might just be the chance it's been waiting for.'

Sparhawk swallowed very hard.

'It's a gamble,' she conceded in an offhand way, 'but we never know which way the dice are going to turn up until we roll them, do we?'

The temple suddenly went totally dark as Sephrenia and Otha continued their struggle, and for a breathless moment it seemed as if that darkness might be eternal, so intense was it.

Then the light gradually returned. The fires in those great iron braziers renewed themselves, and gradually the flames rose again.

As the light returned, Sparhawk found that he was looking at Annias. The Primate of Cimmura's emaciated face was a ghastly white, and all thought had vanished from his eyes. Blinded by his obsessive ambition, Annias had never looked fully at the horror to which he had pledged his soul in his pursuit of the Archprelate's throne. Now at last he obviously perceived it, and now, just as obviously, it was too late. He stared at Sparhawk, his eyes pleading mutely for something – anything – which would save him from the pit which had opened before his feet.

Lycheas was blubbering, gibbering in terror, and Arissa held him in her arms, clinging to him actually, and her face was no less filled with horror than that of Annias.

The temple filled with noise and light, shattering sound and boiling smoke as Otha and Sephrenia continued to grapple.

'It's time, Sparhawk.' Flute's voice was very calm.

Sparhawk braced himself and started forward, his sword

held threateningly over the Sapphire Rose which seemed almost to cringe beneath that heavy steel blade.

'Sparhawk,' the little voice was almost wistful, 'I love you.'

The next sound he heard was not one of love, however. It was a snarling howl in the language of the Trolls. It was more than one voice, and it came from Bhelliom itself. Sparhawk reeled as the hatred of the Troll-Gods lashed at him. The pain was unendurable. He burned and froze at the same time, and his bones heaved and surged within his flesh. 'Blue-Rose!' he gasped, faltering, almost falling. 'Command the Troll-Gods to be silent. Blue-Rose will do it – *Now!*'

The agony continued, and the Trollish howling intensified.

'Then die, Blue-Rose!' Sparhawk raised his sword.

The howling broke off abruptly, and the pain stopped.

Sparhawk crossed the first onyx terrace and stepped up onto the next.

'Do not do this, Sparhawk.' The voice was in his mind. 'Aphrael is a spiteful child. She leads thee to thy doom.'

'I was wondering how long it was going to be, Azash,' Sparhawk said in a shaking voice as he crossed the second terrace. 'Why did you not speak to me before?'

The voice which had spoken in his mind was silent.

'Were you afraid, Azash?' he asked. 'Were you afraid that something you said might change that Destiny which you cannot see?' He stepped up onto the third terrace.

'Do not do this, Sparhawk.' The voice was pleading now. 'I can give thee the world.'

'No, thank you.'

'I can give thee immortality.'

'I'm not interested. Men are used to the idea of dying. It's only the Gods who find the thought so frightening.' He crossed the third terrace.

'I will destroy thy comrades if thou dost persist.'

'All men die sooner or later.' Sparhawk tried to sound convincingly indifferent. He stepped up onto the fourth terrace. He felt as if he were suddenly trying to wade through solid rock. Azash did not dare attack him directly, since that might trigger the fatal stroke which would destroy them all. Then Sparhawk saw his one absolute advantage. Not only could the Gods not see his Destiny; they could not see his thoughts either. Azash could not know when the decision to strike would come. Azash could not feel him make that decision and so He could not stop the sword-stroke. He decided to play on that advantage. Still locked in place, he sighed. 'Oh, well, if that's the way you want it.' He raised his sword again.

'*No!*' The cry came not only from Azash but from the snarling Troll-Gods as well.

Sparhawk crossed the fourth terrace. He was sweating profusely. He could hide his thoughts from the Gods, but not from himself. 'Now, Blue-Rose,' he said quietly to Bhelliom as he stepped up onto the fifth terrace, 'I *am* going to do this. You and Khwaj and Ghnomb and the others will aid me, or you will perish. A God must die here – one God or many. If you aid me, it will only be the one. If you do not, it will be the many.'

'*Sparhawk!*' Aphrael's voice was shocked.

'Don't interfere.'

There was a momentary hesitation. 'Can I help?' she whispered in a little-girl voice.

He thought for only an instant. 'All right, but this isn't the time for games – and don't startle me. My arm's set like a coiled spring.'

The firefly spark began to expand, softening from intensity to a glow, and Aphrael emerged from that glow, her shepherd's pipes held to her lips. As always her little feet were grass-stained. Her face was sombre as she lowered the pipes. 'Go ahead and smash it, Sparhawk,' she said sadly. 'They'll never listen to you.' She sighed. 'I grow weary of unending life anyway. Smash the stone and have done with it.'

The Bhelliom went absolutely dark, and Sparhawk felt it shudder violently in his hand. Then its blue glow returned, soft and submissive.

'They'll help now, Sparhawk,' Aphrael told him.

'You lied to them,' he accused.

'No, I lied to *you*. I wasn't talking to them.'

He could not help but laugh.

He crossed the fifth terrace. The idol was much closer now, and it loomed large in his sight. He could also see Otha, sweating and straining as he and Sephrenia engaged in that duel which Sparhawk knew, could he but see it, was far more titanic than the one he had fought with Martel. He could see more clearly now the stark terror in the face of Annias and the near-collapse of Arissa and her son.

Sparhawk could sense the gigantic presence of the Troll-Gods. They seemed so overpoweringly real that he could almost see their gigantic, hideous forms hovering protectively just behind him. He stepped up onto the sixth terrace. Three more to go. Idly he wondered if the number nine had some significance in the twisted minds of the worshippers of Azash. The God of the Zemochs threw everything to the winds at that point. He saw death inexorably climbing the stairs towards Him, and He began to unleash everything in His power in a desperate effort to ward off the black-armoured messenger carrying His glowing blue death to him.

Fire burst from beneath Sparhawk's feet, but before he even felt its heat, it was quenched in ice. A monstrous form lunged at him, springing from nothingness, but an even more intense fire than that which the ice had just vanquished consumed it. The Troll-Gods, unwilling certainly, but left without a choice through Sparhawk's adamantine ultimatum, were aiding him now, beating aside the defences of Azash to clear his path.

Azash began to shriek as Sparhawk stepped up onto the seventh terrace. A rush now was feasible, but Sparhawk decided against it. He did not want to be panting and shaking from exertion when the climactic moment arrived. He continued his steady, inexorable pace, crossing the seventh terrace as Azash unleashed horrors beyond imagining at him, horrors instantly quenched by the Troll-Gods or even by Bhelliom itself. He drew in a deep breath and stepped up onto the eighth terrace.

Then he was surrounded by gold – coins and ingots and lumps the size of a man's head. A cascade of bright jewels spilled out of nothing to run down over the gold like a river of blue and green and red, a rainbow-hued waterfall of wealth beyond imagining. Then the wealth began to diminish, great chunks of it vanishing to the gross sounds of eating. 'Thank you, Ghnomb,' Sparhawk murmured to the Troll-God of feeding.

An houri of heart-stopping loveliness beckoned to Sparhawk seductively, but was immediately assaulted by a lustful Troll. Sparhawk did not know the name of the Troll-God of mating, so he did not know whom to thank. He pushed on to step up onto the ninth and the last terrace.

'Thou *canst* not!' Azash shrieked. Sparhawk did not reply as he marched grimly towards the idol with Bhelliom still in one fist and his menacing sword in the other. Lightning flashed around him, but each bolt was absorbed by the growing sapphire aura with which Bhelliom protected him.

Otha had abandoned his fruitless duel with Sephrenia and crawled, sobbing in fright, towards the right side of the altar. Annias had collapsed on the left side of that same narrow onyx slab, and Arissa and Lycheas, clinging to each other, wailed.

Sparhawk reached the narrow altar. 'Wish me luck,' he whispered to the Child-Goddess.

'Of course, Father,' she replied.

Azash shrank back as Bhelliom's glow intensified, and the idol's burning eyes bulged with terror. Sparhawk saw that an immortal suddenly faced with the possibility of His own death is peculiarly defenceless. The idea alone erased all other thought, and Azash could only react at the simplest, most childish level. He lashed out, blindly hurling elemental fire at the black-armoured Pandion threatening His very existence. The shock was enormous as that incandescent green flame struck the equally brilliant blue flame of Bhelliom. The blue wavered, then solidified. The green shrank back, then pushed again at Sparhawk.

And there they locked, Bhelliom and Azash, each exerting irresistible force to protect its very existence. Neither of them would – or could – relent. Sparhawk had the unpleasant conviction that he might very well stand in this one place for all eternity with the jewel half-extended as Azash and Bhelliom remained locked in their struggle.

It came from behind him, spinning and whirring through the air with a sound almost like bird-wings. It passed over his head and clanged against the idol's stone chest, exploding forth a great shower of sparks. It was Bevier's hook-pointed lochaber axe. Berit, unthinking perhaps, had thrown the lochaber at the idol – a foolish gesture of puny defiance.

But it worked.

The idol flinched involuntarily from something which could not possibly hurt it, and its force, its fire, momentarily vanished. Sparhawk lunged forward with Bhelliom clutched in his left hand, thrusting it like a spear-point at the burn-scar low on the idol's belly. His hand went numb in the violent shock of contact.

The sound was deafening. Sparhawk was sure that it shook the entire world.

He bent his head and locked his muscles, pushing Bhelliom harder and harder against the shiny scar of Azash's emasculation. The God shrieked in agony. '*YE HAVE FAILED ME!*' He howled, and writhing, tentacle-like arms whipped out from either side of the idol's body to seize Otha – and Annias.

'Oh, my God!' the Primate of Cimmura shrieked, not to Azash, but to the God of his childhood. 'Save me! Protect me! Forgive –' His voice rose to an inarticulate screech as the tentacle tightened about him.

There was no finesse in the punishment inflicted upon the Emperor of Zemoch and the Primate of Cimmura. Maddened by pain and fear and a hunger to lash out at those He considered responsible, Azash reacted like an infuriated child. Other arms lashed out to seize the shrieking pair, and then, with cruel slowness, the undulating arms began to turn in opposite directions in that motion used by a washerwoman to wring out a dripping rag. Blood and worse spurted out from between the God's eel-like fingers as He inexorably wrung the lives of Otha and Annias from their writhing bodies.

Sickened, Sparhawk closed his eyes – but he could not close his ears. The shrieking grew worse, rising to strangled squeals at the very upper edge of hearing.

Then they fell silent, and there were two sodden thumps as Azash discarded what was left of His servants.

Arissa was retching violently over the unrecognizable remains of her lover and the father of her only child as the vast idol shuddered and cracked, raining chunks of carved rock as it disintegrated. Writhing arms solidified as they broke free and fell to smash into fragments on the floor. The grotesque face slid in pieces from the front of the head. A large piece of rock struck Sparhawk's armoured shoulder, and the impact quite nearly jarred Bhelliom from his hands. With a great cracking noise, the idol broke at the waist, and the vast upper trunk toppled backwards to smash into a million pieces on the polished black floor. A stump only remained, a kind of crumbling stone pedestal upon which sat that crude mud idol which Otha had first seen almost two thousand years before.

'*Thou canst not!*' The voice was the squeal of a small animal, a rabbit maybe, or perhaps a rat. '*I am a God! Thou art nothing! Thou art an insect! Thou art as dirt!*'

'Perhaps,' Sparhawk said, actually feeling pity for the pathetic little mud figurine. He dropped his sword and clasped Bhelliom firmly in both hands. 'Blue-Rose!' he said sharply. 'I am Sparhawk-from-Elenia! By the power of these rings I command Blue-Rose to return this image to the earth from which it came!' He thrust both hands and the Sapphire Rose forward. 'Thou hast hungered for Bhelliom, Azash,' he said. 'Have it then. Have it and all that it brings thee.' Then the Bhelliom touched the misshapen little idol. 'Blue-Rose will obey! *NOW!*' He clenched himself as he said it, expecting instant obliteration.

The entire temple shuddered, and Sparhawk felt a sudden oppressive sense of heaviness bearing down on him as if the air itself had the weight of tons. The flames of the huge fires sickened, lowering into fitful flickers as if some great weight pressed them down, smothering them.

And then the vast dome of the temple exploded upward and outward, hurling the hexagonal blocks of basalt miles away. With a sound that was beyond sound, the fires belched upward, becoming enormous pillars of intensely brilliant flame, columns that shot up through the gaping hole that had been the dome to illuminate the pregnant bellies of the clouds which had spawned the thunderstorm. Higher and higher those incandescent columns roared, searing the cloud mass above. And still they reared higher, wreathed with lightning as they burned the clouds away and ascended still into the darkness above, reaching towards the glittering stars.

Sparhawk, implacable and unrelenting, held the Sapphire Rose against the body of Azash, the skin of his wrist crawling as the God's tiny, impotent tentacles clutched at it as a mortally stricken warrior might clutch at the arm of a foe slowly twisting a sword-blade in his vitals. The voice of Azash, Elder God of Styricum, was a tiny squeal, a puny wail such as any small creature might make as it died. Then a change came over the little idol. Whatever had made it adhere together was gone, and with a slithering kind of sigh it came apart and settled into a heap of dust.

The great columns of flame slowly subsided, and the air which flooded into the ruined temple from the outside once again had the chill of winter.

Sparhawk felt no sense of triumph as he straightened. He looked at the Sapphire Rose glowing in his hand. He could feel its terror, and he could dimly hear the whimpering of the Troll-Gods locked in its azure heart.

Flute had somehow stumbled back down the terraces and wept in Sephrenia's arms.

'It's over, Blue-Rose,' Sparhawk said wearily to the Bhelliom. 'Rest now.' He slipped the jewel back into the pouch and absently twisted the wire to hold it shut.

There was the sound of running then, of frantic flight. Princess Arissa and her son fled down the onyx terraces towards the shiny floor below. So great was their fright that neither appeared to be even aware of the other as they stumbled down and down. Lycheas was younger than his mother, and his flight was swifter. He left her behind, leaping, falling, scrambling back to his feet again as he bolted.

Ulath, his face like stone, was waiting for him at the bottom – with his axe.

Lycheas shrieked once, and then his head flew out in a long, curving arc and landed on the onyx floor with a sickening sound such as a dropped melon might make.

'Lycheas!' Arissa shrieked in horror as her son's headless body fell limply at Ulath's feet. She stood frozen, gaping at the huge, blond-braided Thalesian who had begun to mount the onyx terraces towards her, his bloody axe half-raised. Ulath was not one to leave a job half-completed.

Arissa fumbled at the sash about her waist, pulled out a small glass vial and struggled to pull the stopper free.

Ulath did not slow his pace.

The vial was open now, and Arissa lifted her face and drank its contents. Her body instantly stiffened, and she gave a hoarse cry. Then she fell twitching to the floor of the terrace, her face black and her tongue protruding from her mouth.

'Ulath!' Sephrenia said to the still-advancing Thalesian. 'No. It isn't necessary.'

'Poison?' he asked her.

She nodded.

'I hate poison,' he said, stripping the blood off the edge of his axe with his thumb and forefinger. He flung the blood away and then ran a practised thumb along the edge. 'It's going to take a week to polish out all these nicks,' he said mournfully, turning and starting back down again, leaving the Princess Arissa sprawled on the terrace above him.

Sparhawk retrieved his sword and descended. He felt very, very tired now. He wearily picked up his gauntlets and crossed the littered floor to Berit, who stood staring at him in awe. 'That was a nice throw,' he said to the young man, putting his hand on Berit's armoured shoulder. 'Thank you, brother.'

Berit's smile was like the sun coming up.

'Oh, by the way,' Sparhawk added, 'you'd probably better go and find Bevier's axe. He's very fond of it.'

Berit grinned. 'Right away, Sparhawk.'

Sparhawk looked around at the corpse-littered temple, then up through the shattered dome at the stars twinkling overhead in the cold winter sky. 'Kurik,' he said without thinking, 'what time do you make it?' Then he broke off as a wave of unbearable grief overwhelmed him. He steeled himself. 'Is everybody all right?' he asked his friends, looking around. Then he grunted, not really trusting himself to speak. He drew in a deep breath. 'Let's get out of here,' he said gruffly.

They crossed the polished floor and went up the wide terraces to the top. Somehow in the vast upheaval of the encounter at the altar, all the statues encircling the wall had been shattered. Kalten stepped on ahead and looked up the marble stairs. 'The soldiers seem to have run off,' he reported.

Sephrenia countered the spell which had blocked the stairs and they started up.

'Sephrenia.' The voice was hardly more than a croak.

'She's still alive,' Ulath said almost accusingly.

'That happens once in a while,' Sephrenia said. 'Sometimes the poison takes a little longer.'

'Sephrenia, help me. Please help me.'

The small Styric woman turned and looked back across the temple at Princess Arissa, who had weakly raised her head to plead for her life.

Sephrenia's tone was as cold as death itself. 'No, Princess,' she replied. 'I don't think so.' Then she turned again and went on up the stairs with Sparhawk and the rest of them close behind her.

Chapter 31

The wind had changed at some time during the night, and it now blew steadily out of the west, bringing snow with it. The violent thunderstorm which had engulfed the city the previous night had unroofed many houses and exploded others. The streets were littered with debris and with a thin covering of wet snow. Berit had retrieved their horses, and Sparhawk and his friends rode slowly. There was no longer any need for haste. The cart Kalten had found in a side street trundled along behind them with Talen at the reins and Bevier resting in the back with Kurik's covered body. Kurik, Sephrenia assured them as they set out, would remain untouched by the corruption which is the final destiny of all men. 'I owe Aslade that much at least,' she murmured, nestling her cheek against Flute's glossy black hair. Sparhawk was a bit surprised to find that in spite of everything, he still thought of the Child-Goddess as Flute. She did not look all that much like a Goddess at the moment. She clung to Sephrenia, her face tear-streaked, and each time she opened her eyes, they were filled with horror and despair.

The Zemoch soldiers and the few remaining priests of Azash had fled the deserted city, and the slushy streets echoed with a kind of mournful emptiness. Something quite peculiar was happening to Otha's capital. The nearly total destruction of the temple had been completely understandable, of course. The only slightly less severe damage to the adjoining palace was probably to be expected. It was what was happening to the rest of the city that was inexplicable. The inhabitants had not really left the city that long ago, but their houses were collapsing – not all at once as might have been expected, given the explosive nature of what had taken place in the temple, but singly or in groups of two or three. It was somehow as if the decay which overcomes any abandoned city were taking place in the space of hours instead of centuries. The houses sagged, creaked mournfully and then slowly fell in on themselves. The city walls crumbled, and even the paving stones of the streets heaved up and then settled back, broken and scattered.

Their desperate plan had succeeded, but the cost had been beyond what any of them had been prepared to pay. There was no sense of triumph in their success, none of that exultation warriors normally feel in a victory. It was not merely the sorrowful burden of the cart which dampened their mood, however, but something deeper.

Bevier was pale from loss of blood, but his face was profoundly troubled. 'I still don't understand,' he confessed.

'Sparhawk is Anakha,' Sephrenia replied. 'It's a Styric word that means "without destiny". All men are subject to destiny, to fate – all men except Sparhawk. Somehow he moves outside destiny. We've known that he would come, but we didn't know when – or even who he would be. He's like no other man who's ever lived. He makes his *own* destiny, and his existence terrifies the Gods.'

They left the slowly collapsing city of Zemoch behind in the thickly swirling snow slanting in from the west, although they could hear the grinding rumble of falling buildings for quite some time as they rode southward along the road leading to the city of Korakach, some eighty leagues to the south. About mid-afternoon, as the snow was beginning to let up, they took shelter for the night in a deserted village. They were all very tired, and the thought of riding even one more mile was deeply repugnant to them. Ulath prepared their supper without even any attempt to resort to his usual subterfuge, and they sought their beds even before the light had begun to fade.

Sparhawk awoke suddenly, startled to find that he was in the saddle. They were riding along the brink of a wind-swept cliff with an angry sea ripping itself to tattered froth on the rocks far below. The sky overhead was threatening, and the wind coming in off the sea had a biting chill. Sephrenia rode in the lead, and she held Flute enfolded in her arms. The others trailed along behind Sparhawk, their cloaks drawn tightly around them and wooden-faced expressions of stoic endurance on their faces. They all seemed to be there, Kalten and Kurik, Tynian and Ulath, Berit and Talen and Bevier. Their horses plodded up the winding, weather-worn trail that followed the edge of the long, ascending cliff towards a jutting promontory that thrust a crooked, stony finger out into the sea. At the outermost tip of the rocky promontory stood a gnarled and twisted tree, its streaming branches flailing in the wind.

When she reached the tree, Sephrenia reined in her horse, and Kurik walked forward to lift Flute down. The squire's face was set, and he did not speak to Sparhawk as he passed. It seemed to Sparhawk that something was wrong – terribly wrong – but he could not exactly put his finger on it.

'Very well, then,' the little girl said to them. 'We're here to finish this, and we don't have all that much time.'

'Exactly what do you mean by "finish it"?' Bevier asked her.

'My family has agreed that we must put Bhelliom beyond the reach of men or Gods. No one must ever be able to find it or use it again. The others have given me one hour – and all of their power – to accomplish this. You may see some things that are impossible – you may even have noticed them already. Don't concern yourselves about them, and don't pester me with questions. We don't have that much time. We were ten when we set out, and we're the same ten now. It has to be that way.'

'We're going to throw it into the sea then?' Kalten asked her.

She nodded.

'Hasn't that been tried before?' Ulath asked her. 'The Earl of Heid threw King Sarak's crown into Lake Venne, as I recall, and Bhelliom still re-emerged.'

'The sea is much deeper than Lake Venne,' she told him, 'and the water out there is much deeper than it is anywhere else in the world, and no one knows where this particular shoreline is.'

'*We* do,' Ulath disagreed.

'Oh? Where is it? On which particular coast of which particular continent?' She pointed upward at the dense cloud racing overhead. 'And where's the sun? Which way is east and which is west? All you can really say for sure is that you're on a seacoast somewhere. You can tell anyone you like, and then every man who will ever live can start wading in the sea tomorrow, and they'll never find Bhelliom, because they'll never know exactly where to look.'

'Then you want me to throw it into the sea?' Sparhawk asked her as he dismounted.

'Not quite yet, Sparhawk,' she replied. 'There's something we have to do first. Would you get that sack I asked you to keep for me, Kurik?'

Kurik nodded, went back to his gelding and opened one of his saddlebags. Once again Sparhawk had that strong sense that something was wrong.

Kurik came back carrying a small canvas sack. He opened it and took out a small steel box with a hinged

602

lid and a stout hasp. He held it out to the little girl. She shook her head and held her hands behind her. 'I don't want to touch it,' she said. 'I just want to look at it to make sure it's right.' She bent forward and examined the box closely. When Kurik opened the lid, Sparhawk saw that the interior of the box was lined with gold. 'My brothers did well,' she approved. 'It's perfect.'

'Steel *will* rust in time, you know,' Tynian told her.

'No, dear one,' Sephrenia told him. 'That particular box will never rust.'

'What about the Troll-Gods, Sephrenia,' Bevier asked. 'They've shown us that they can reach out to the minds of men. Won't they be able to call someone and direct him to the place where the box lies hidden? I don't think they'll be happy lying at the bottom of the sea for all eternity.'

'The Troll-Gods can't reach out to men without the aid of Bhelliom,' she explained, 'and Bhelliom's powerless as long as it's locked in steel. It lay helpless in that iron deposit in Thalesia from the time this world was made until the day Ghwerig freed it. This may not be entirely foolproof, but it's the best we can do, I think.'

'Set the box down on the ground, Kurik,' Flute instructed, 'and open it. Sparhawk, take Bhelliom out of the pouch and tell it to sleep.'

'Forever?'

'I sort of doubt that. This world won't last that long, and once it's gone, Bhelliom will be free to continue its journey.'

Sparhawk took the pouch from his belt and untwisted the wire which held it closed. Then he upended the pouch and the Sapphire Rose fell out into his hand. He felt it shudder with a kind of relief as it was freed from its steel confinement. 'Blue-Rose,' he said calmly, 'I am Sparhawk-from-Elenia. Do you know me?'

It glowed a deep, hard blue, neither hostile nor particularly friendly. The muted snarls he seemed to hear deep in his mind, however, told him that the Troll-Gods did not share that neutrality.

'The time has come for you to sleep, Blue-Rose,' Sparhawk said to the jewel. 'There will be no pain, and when you awaken, you will be free.'

The jewel shuddered again, and its crystal glitter softened, almost as if in gratitude.

'Sleep now, Blue-Rose,' he said gently, holding the priceless thing in both hands. Then he placed it in the box and firmly closed the lid.

Wordlessly, Kurik handed him a small, cunningly-wrought lock. Sparhawk nodded and snapped the lock shut on the hasp, noting as he did that the lock had no keyhole. He looked questioningly at the Child-Goddess.

'Throw it into the sea,' she said, watching him intently.

A vast reluctance came over him. He knew that Bhelliom, confined as it was, could not be influencing him. The reluctance was his own. For a time, for a few short months, he had possessed something even more eternal than the stars, and he had somehow shared that just by touching it. It was that which made Bhelliom so infinitely precious. Its beauty, its perfection had never really had anything to do with it, though he yearned for just one last glimpse of it, one last touch of that soft blue glow on his hands. He knew that once he had cast it away, something very important would be gone from his life and that he would pass the remainder of his days with a vague sense of loss which might diminish with the passing of years, but would never wholly be gone.

He steeled himself, willing the pain of loss to come so that he might teach himself to endure it. Then he leaned back and threw the small steel object as far as he could out over the angry sea.

The hurtling steel box arched out over the crashing waves far below, and as it flew it began to glow, neither red nor blue nor any other colour, but rather sheer incandescent white. Far it went, further than any man could have thrown it, and then, like a shooting star, it fell in a long, graceful curve into the endlessly rolling sea.

'That's it then?' Kalten asked. 'That's all we have to do?'

Flute nodded, her eyes filled with tears. 'You can all go back now,' she told them. She sat down beneath the tree and sadly took her pipes out from under her tunic.

'Aren't you coming with us?' Talen asked her.

'No,' she sighed. 'I'll stay here for a while.' Then she lifted her pipes and began to play a sad song of regret and loss.

They had only ridden a short distance with the sound of the pipes sadly following them when Sparhawk turned to look back. The tree was still there, of course, but Flute was gone. 'She's left us again,' he told Sephrenia.

'Yes, dear one,' she sighed.

The wind picked up as they rode down from the promontory, and driven spray began to sting their faces. Sparhawk tried to pull the hood of his cloak forward to shield his face, but it was no use. No matter how hard he tried, the driving spray lashed at his cheeks and nose.

His face was still wet when he suddenly awoke and sat up. He mopped the salt brine away and reached inside his tunic.

Bhelliom was not there.

He knew that he would have to talk with Sephrenia, but there was something he wanted to find out first. He rose and went out of the house where they had set up their camp the previous day. Two doors down the street was the stable where they had put the cart in which Kurik lay.

Sparhawk gently turned back the blanket and touched his friend's cold face.

Kurik's face was wet, and when Sparhawk touched his fingertip to his tongue, he could taste the salt brine of the sea. He sat for a long time, his mind reeling back from the immensity of what the Child-Goddess had so casually dismissed as mere 'impossibilities'. The combined might of the Younger Gods of Styricum, it appeared, could accomplish *anything*. He decided at last not to even attempt a definition of what had happened. Dream or reality or something in between – what difference did it make? Bhelliom was safe now, and that was all that mattered.

They rode south to Korakach and on to Gaka Dorit, where they turned west towards Kadum on the Lamork border. Once they reached the lowlands, they began to encounter Zemoch soldiers fleeing to the east. There were no wounded with the soldiers, so there did not appear to have been a battle.

There was no sense of accomplishment or even of victory as they rode. The snow turned to rain as they came down out of the highlands, and the mournful dripping of the sky seemed to match their mood. There were no stories nor cheerful banter as they rode westward. They were all very tired, and all they really wanted to do was to go home.

King Wargun was at Kadum with a huge army. He was not moving, but sat firmly in place, waiting for the weather to break and for the ground to dry out. Sparhawk and the others were led to his headquarters, which, as might have been expected, were in a tavern.

'Now there's a real surprise,' the half-drunk monarch of Thalesia said to the Patriarch Bergsten as Sparhawk and his friends entered. 'I never thought I'd see *them* again. Ho, Sparhawk! come over by the fire. Have something to drink and tell us what you've been up to.'

Sparhawk removed his helmet and crossed the rush-covered tavern floor. 'We went to the city of Zemoch, Your Majesty,' he reported briefly. 'As long as we were there anyway, we killed Otha and Azash. Then we started back.'

Wargun blinked. 'That's right to the point,' he laughed. He looked around blearily. 'You there!' he bellowed at one of the guards at the door. 'Go and find Lord Vanion. Tell him that his men have arrived. Did you find somewhere to lock up your prisoners, Sparhawk?'

'We didn't take any prisoners, Your Majesty.'

'Now *that's* the way to make war. Sarathi's going to be cross with you, though. He really wanted Annias to stand trial.'

'We'd have brought him, Wargun,' Ulath told his king, 'but he wasn't very presentable.'

'Which one of you killed him?'

'Actually it was Azash, Your Majesty,' Tynian explained. 'The Zemoch God was very disappointed in Otha and Annias, so he did what seemed appropriate.'

'How about Martel – and Princess Arissa – and the bastard Lycheas?'

'Sparhawk killed Martel,' Kalten told him. 'Ulath chopped Lycheas's head off, and Arissa took poison.'

'Did she die?'

'We assume so. She was doing a fairly good job of it when we left her.'

Then Vanion came in and went immediately to Sephrenia. Their secret, which wasn't really a secret anyway, since everyone with eyes knew how they felt about each other, went out of the window as they embraced each other with a kind of fierceness uncharacteristic of either of them. Vanion kissed the cheek of the small woman he had loved

607

for decades. 'I thought I'd lost you,' he said in a voice thick with emotion.

'You know that I'll never leave you, dear one,' she said.

Sparhawk smiled faintly. That 'dear one' which she addressed to them all had rather neatly concealed the real 'dear ones' she directed to Vanion. There was a significant difference in the way she said it, he noticed.

Their recounting of what had taken place since they had left Zemoch was fairly complete. It was subdued, however, and it omitted a significant number of theological issues.

Then Wargun began a rambling and somewhat drink-slurred account of what had happened in Lamorkand and eastern Pelosia during the lengthy interval. The armies of the west, it appeared, had followed the strategy that had been worked out in Chyrellos before the campaign had begun, and the strategy seemed to have worked quite well.

'And then,' the tipsy monarch concluded, 'just when we were ready to get down to some serious fighting, the cowards all turned tail and ran. Why won't *anyone* stand and fight me?' Wargun's tone was plaintive. 'Now I'm going to have to chase them all over the mountains of Zemoch to catch them.'

'Why bother?' Sephrenia asked him.

'Why bother?' he exclaimed. 'To keep them from ever attacking us again, that's why.' Wargun was swaying in his seat, and he clumsily dipped another tankard of ale from the keg at his side.

'Why waste the lives of your men?' she asked. 'Azash is dead. Otha is dead. The Zemochs will never come again.'

Wargun glared at her. Then he pounded his fist on the table. 'I want to exterminate somebody!' he roared. 'You wouldn't let me wipe out the Rendors! You called me to

Chyrellos before I could finish up! But I'll be a cross-eyed Troll if I'll let you steal the Zemochs from me as well!' Then his eyes glazed, and he slid slowly under the table and began to snore.

'Your king has an amazing singleness of purpose, my friend,' Tynian said to Ulath.

'Wargun's a simple man,' Ulath shrugged. 'There isn't room in his head for more than one idea at a time.'

'I'll go with you to Chyrellos, Sparhawk,' Vanion said. 'I might be able to help you persuade Dolmant to pull Wargun up short.' That, of course, was not Vanion's real reason for accompanying them, but Sparhawk chose not to question his friend any more closely.

They left Kadum early the following morning. The knights had removed their armour and travelled in mail-shirts, tunics and heavy cloaks. That did not appreciably increase their speed, but it did make them more comfortable. The rain went on day after day, a dreary, foggy drizzle that seemed to wash out all signs of colour. They travelled through the sullen tag-end of winter, almost never really warm and certainly never wholly dry. They passed through Motera and rode on to Kadach, where they crossed the river and moved at a canter south towards Chyrellos. Finally, on a rainy afternoon they reached the top of a hill and looked down at the war-ravaged Holy City.

'I think our first step is to find Dolmant,' Vanion decided. 'It's going to take a while for a messenger to get back to Kadum to stop Wargun, and a break in the weather could start to dry out the fields in Zemoch.' Vanion began to cough, a tearing kind of cough.

'Aren't you feeling well?' Sparhawk asked him.

'I think I've picked up a cold, that's all.'

They did not enter Chyrellos as heroes. There were no parades, no fanfares, no cheering throngs throwing flowers. In point of fact, nobody even seemed to recognize them, and the only thing that was thrown was garbage from the windows of the upper floors of the houses they passed. Very little had been done in the way of repairs or reconstruction since Martel's armies had been driven out, and the citizens of Chyrellos existed in squalor among the ruins.

They entered the Basilica still muddy and travel-worn and went directly up to the administrative offices on the second floor. 'We have urgent news for the Archprelate,' Vanion said to the black-robed Churchman who sat at an ornate desk shuffling papers and trying to look important.

'I'm afraid that's absolutely out of the question,' the Churchman said, looking disdainfully at Vanion's muddy clothing. 'Sarathi's meeting with a deputation of Cammorian Primates at the moment. It's a very important conference, and it mustn't be interrupted by some unimportant military dispatch. Why don't you come back tomorrow?'

Vanion's nostrils went white, and he thrust back his cloak to free his sword-arm. Before things had the chance to turn ugly, however, Emban came along the hall. 'Vanion?' he exclaimed, 'and *Sparhawk*? When did you get back?'

'We only just arrived, Your Grace,' Vanion replied. 'There seems to be some question about our credentials here.'

'Not as far as I'm concerned. You'd better come inside.'

'But, Your Grace,' the Churchman objected, 'Sarathi's meeting with the Cammorian Patriarchs, and there are other deputations who have been waiting and are far more –' He broke off as Emban slowly turned on him.

'Who is this man?' Emban seemed to direct the question at the ceiling. Then he looked at the man behind the desk. 'Pack your things,' he instructed. 'You'll be leaving Chyrellos first thing in the morning. Take plenty of warm clothing. The monastery at Husdal is in northern Thalesia, and it's very cold there at this time of year.'

The Cammorian Primates were summarily dismissed, and Emban ushered Sparhawk and the others into the room where Dolmant and Ortzel waited.

'Why didn't you send word?' Dolmant demanded.

'We thought Wargun was going to take care of that, Sarathi,' Vanion told him.

'You trusted Wargun with a message *that* important? All right, what happened?'

Sparhawk, with occasional help from the others, recounted the story of the trip to Zemoch and told them of what had happened there.

'Kurik?' Dolmant said in a stricken voice at one point in the narrative.

Sparhawk nodded.

Dolmant sighed and bowed his head in sorrow. 'I imagine that one of you did something about that,' he said, his voice almost savage.

'His son did, Sarathi,' Sparhawk replied.

Dolmant was aware of Talen's irregular parentage. He looked at the boy with some surprise. 'How did you manage to kill a warrior in full armour, Talen?' he asked.

'I stabbed him in the back, Sarathi,' Talen replied in a flat tone of voice, '– right in the kidneys. Sparhawk had to help me drive the sword into him, though. I couldn't get through his armour with it all by myself.'

'And what will happen to you now, my boy?' Dolmant sadly asked him.

'We're going to give him a few more years, Sarathi,' Vanion said, 'and then we're going to enrol him as a novice in the Pandion order – along with Kurik's other sons. Sparhawk made Kurik a promise.'

'Isn't anybody going to ask *me* about this?' Talen demanded in an outraged tone.

'No,' Vanion told him, 'as a matter of fact, we're not.'

'A knight?' Talen protested. '*Me?* Have you people all taken leave of your senses?'

'It's not so bad, Talen,' Berit grinned, 'once you get used to it.'

Sparhawk continued with the story. A number of things had happened in Zemoch which Ortzel was theologically unprepared to accept, and as the story wound down, his eyes became glazed, and he sat in stupefied shock.

'And that's more or less what happened, Sarathi,' Sparhawk concluded. 'It's going to take me a while to get it all sorted out in my mind – the rest of my life, more than likely – and even then there are still going to be a lot of things I won't understand.'

Dolmant leaned thoughtfully back in his chair. 'I think that Bhelliom – and the rings – should be in Church custody,' he said.

'I'm sorry, Sarathi,' Sparhawk told him, 'but that's impossible.'

'You said *what?*'

'We don't have the Bhelliom any more.'

'What did you do with it?'

'We threw it into the sea, Sarathi,' Bevier replied.

Dolmant stared at him in dismay.

Patriarch Ortzel came to his feet with a look of outrage on his face. 'Without the permission of the Church?' he almost screamed. 'You did not even seek counsel from God?'

'We were acting on the instructions of another God, Your Grace,' Sparhawk told him. 'A Goddess, actually,' he corrected.

'*Heresy!*' Ortzel gasped.

'I don't really think so, Your Grace,' Sparhawk disagreed. 'Aphrael was the one who brought Bhelliom to me. She carried it up out of the chasm in Ghwerig's cave. After I'd done what we needed to do with it, it was only proper for me to return it to her. She didn't want it, though. She told me to throw it into the sea, so I did. We *are* instructed to be courteous, after all.'

'That does not apply in a situation such as this!' Ortzel stormed. 'The Bhelliom's too important to be treated as some mere trinket! Go back and find it at once and hand it over to the Church!'

'I think he's right, Sparhawk,' Dolmant said gravely. 'You're going to have to go and retrieve it.'

Sparhawk shrugged. 'As you wish, Sarathi,' he said. 'We'll start just as soon as you tell us which ocean to look in.'

'Surely you –' Dolmant looked at them helplessly.

'We have absolutely no idea, Sarathi,' Ulath assured him. 'Aphrael took us to a cliff somewhere on some coast, and we threw Bhelliom into the sea. It could have been any coast and any ocean. It may not even be on this world, for all I know. Do they have oceans on the moon? Bhelliom's gone for good, I'm afraid.'

The Churchmen stared at him in open dismay.

'I don't think your Elene God really wants Bhelliom, anyway, Dolmant,' Sephrenia told the Archprelate. 'I think your God – like all the others – is very relieved to know that it's lost for good. I think it frightens all of them. I know that it frightened Aphrael.' She paused. 'Have you noticed how long and dreary this winter's been?' she asked then. 'And how low your spirits are?'

'It's been a troubled time, Sephrenia,' Dolmant reminded her.

'Granted, but I didn't notice you dancing for joy when you heard that Azash and Otha are gone. Not even *that* could lift your spirits. Styrics believe that winter's a state of mind in the Gods. Something happened at Zemoch that's never happened before. We found out once and for all that the Gods can die too. I seriously doubt that any of us will feel spring in our souls until our Gods are able to come to grips with that. They're distracted and frightened now – and not really very interested in us – or our problems. They've left us to fend for ourselves for a while, I'm afraid. Our magic doesn't even seem to work any more for some reason. We're all alone now, Dolmant, and we'll have to endure this interminable winter until the Gods return.'

Dolmant leaned back in his chair again. 'You trouble me, little mother,' he said. He passed one hand wearily across his eyes. 'I'll be honest with you, though. I've felt this wintery despair myself for the last month and a half. I awoke in the middle of the night once weeping uncontrollably. I haven't smiled since, or felt any lightness of spirit. I thought it was only me, but perhaps not.' He paused. 'And that brings us face to face with our duty as representatives of the Church. We absolutely *must* find something to distract the minds of the faithful from this universal despair – something to give them purpose, if not joy. What could possibly do that?'

'The conversion of the Zemochs, Sarathi,' Bevier replied simply. 'They've followed an evil God for eons. Now they're Godless. What better task for the Church?'

'Bevier,' Emban said with a pained look. 'Are you by any chance striving for sainthood?' He looked at Dolmant. 'It's really a very good idea, though, Sarathi. It would keep the faithful busy. There's no question about that.'

'You'd better stop Wargun then, Your Grace,' Ulath advised. 'He's poised in Kadum. As soon as the ground gets dry enough to hold a horse, he's going to march into Zemoch and kill anything that moves.'

'I'll take care of that,' Emban promised, 'even if I

have to ride to Kadum myself and arm-wrestle him into submission.'

'Azash is – was – a Styric God,' Dolmant said, 'and Elene priests have never had much success trying to convert Styrics. Sephrenia, could you possibly help us? I'll even find some way to give you authority and official status.'

'No, Dolmant,' she said firmly.

'Why is everybody saying no to me today?' he asked plaintively. 'What's the problem, little mother?'

'I won't assist you in converting Styrics to a heathen religion, Dolmant.'

'*Heathen?*' Ortzel choked.

'It's a word that's used to describe someone who isn't of the true faith, Your Grace.'

'But the Elene faith *is* the true faith.'

'Not to me, it isn't. I find your religion repugnant. It's cruel, rigid, unforgiving and smugly self-righteous. It's totally without humanity, and I reject it. I'll have no part of this ecumenicism of yours, Dolmant. If I should aid you in converting the Zemochs, you'll turn next to western Styricum, and *that* is where you and I will fight.' She smiled then, a gentle, surprising smile that shone through the pervading gloom. 'As soon as she's feeling better, I think I'll have a little talk with Aphrael. She may just take an interest in the Zemochs herself.' The smile she directed at Dolmant at that point was almost radiant. 'That would put us on opposite sides of the fence, wouldn't it, Sarathi?' she suggested. 'I wish you all the best, though, old dear, but as they say, may the better man – or woman – win.'

The weather altered only slightly as they rode westward. The rain had ceased for the most part, but the sky remained cloudy, and the blustery wind still had the chill of winter in it. Their destination was Demos. They were taking Kurik home. Sparhawk was not really looking forward to telling Aslade that he had finally managed to get her husband killed. The gloom which had fallen over the earth following the death of Azash was heightened by the funereal nature of their journey. The armourers at the Pandion chapterhouse in Chyrellos had hammered the dents out of the armour of Sparhawk and his friends, and had even buffed off most of the rust. They rode now with a somewhat ornate black carriage that bore Kurik's body.

They made camp in a grove not far back from the road some five leagues from Demos, and Sparhawk and the other knights saw to their armour. They had decided by unspoken agreement that they would wear their formal garb the next day. When he was satisfied that his equipment was ready for tomorrow, Sparhawk started across the camp towards the black carriage which stood some distance from the fire. Talen rose from his place to join him. 'Sparhawk,' he said as they walked.

'Yes?'

'You're not really serious about this notion are you?'

'Which notion was that?'

'Putting me in training to become a Pandion.'

'Yes, as a matter of fact I am. I made some promises to your father.'

'I'll run away.'

'Then I'll catch you – or send Berit to do it.'

'That's not fair.'

'You didn't really expect life to throw honest dice, did you?'

'Sparhawk, I don't want to go to knight school.'

'We don't always get what we want, Talen. This is something your father wanted, and I'm not going to disappoint him.'

'What about me? What about what *I* want?'

'You're young. You'll adjust to it. After a while, you might even find that you like it.'

'Where are we going right now?' Talen's tone was sulky.

'I'm going to visit your father.'

'Oh. I'll go back to the fire then. I'd rather remember him the way he was.'

The carriage creaked as Sparhawk climbed up into it and sat down beside his squire's silent body. He did not say anything for quite some time. His grief had run itself out now and had been replaced with only a profound regret. 'We've come a long way together, haven't we, my old friend?' he said finally. 'Now you're going home to rest, and I have to go on alone.' He smiled faintly in the darkness. 'That was really very inconsiderate of you, Kurik. I was looking forward to growing old with you – older that is.'

He sat quietly for a time. 'I've taken care of your sons,' he added. 'You'll be very proud of them – even of Talen, although he may take a while to come around to the idea of respectability.'

He paused again. 'I'll break the news to Aslade as gently as I can,' he promised. Then he laid his hand on Kurik's. 'Goodbye, my friend,' he said.

The part he had dreaded the most, telling Aslade, turned out not to be necessary, since Aslade already knew. She wore a black country dress when she met them at the gate of the farm on which she and her husband had laboured for so many years. Her four sons, as tall as young trees, stood with her, also in their best clothes. Their sombre faces told Sparhawk that his carefully-prepared speech was unnecessary. 'See to your father,' Aslade told her sons.

They nodded and went to the black carriage.

'How did you find out?' Sparhawk asked her after she had embraced him.

617

'That little girl told us,' she replied simply. 'The one you brought with you when you were on your way to Chyrellos that time. She just appeared at the door one evening and told us. Then she went away.'

'You believed her?'

Aslade nodded. 'I knew that I must. She's not at all like other children.'

'No, she isn't. I'm very, very sorry, Aslade. When Kurik started getting older, I should have made him stay at home.'

'No, Sparhawk. That would have broken his heart. You're going to have to help me with something right now, though.'

'Anything at all, Aslade.'

'I need to talk with Talen.'

Sparhawk was not sure where this was leading. He motioned to the young thief, and Talen joined them.

'Talen,' Aslade said.

'Yes?'

'We're very proud of you, you know.'

'Me?'

'You avenged your father's death. Your brothers and I share that with you.'

He stared at her. 'Are you trying to say that you knew? About Kurik and me, I mean?'

'Of course I knew. I've known for a long time. This is what you're going to do – and if you don't, Sparhawk here will thrash you. You're going to Cimmura, and you're going to bring your mother back here.'

'*What?*'

'You heard me. I've met your mother a few times. I went to Cimmura to have a look at her just before you were born. I wanted to talk with her so that we could decide which of us would be best for your father. She's a nice girl – a little skinny, perhaps, but I can fatten her up once I get her here. She and I get along quite well, and we're all going to live here until you and your brothers enter your novitiates. After that, she and I can keep each other company.'

'You want *me* to live on a farm?' he asked incredulously.

'Your father would have wanted that, and I'm sure your mother wants it, and so do I. You're too good a boy to disappoint all three of us.'

'But –'

'Please don't argue with me, Talen. It's all settled. Now, let's go inside. I've cooked a dinner for us, and I don't want it to get cold.'

They buried Kurik beneath a tall elm tree on a hill overlooking his farm about noon the following day. The sky had been ominous all morning, but the sun broke through as Kurik's sons carried their father up the hill. Sparhawk was not as good as his squire had been at judging the weather, but the sudden appearance of a patch of blue sky and bright sunlight hovering just over the farm and touching no other part of the city of Demos made him more than a little suspicious.

The funeral was very simple and very moving. The local priest, an elderly, almost doddering man, had known Kurik since boyhood, and he spoke not so much of sorrow as of love. When it was over, Kurik's eldest son, Khalad, joined Sparhawk as they all walked back down the hill. 'I'm honoured that you thought I might be worthy to become a Pandion, Sir Sparhawk,' he said, 'but I'm afraid I'll have to decline.'

Sparhawk looked sharply at the husky, plain-faced young man whose black beard was only beginning to sprout.

'It's nothing personal, Sir Sparhawk,' Khalad assured him. 'It's just that my father had other plans for me. In a few weeks – after you've had the chance to get settled in, I'll be joining you in Cimmura.'

'You will?' Sparhawk was slightly taken aback by the lad's matter-of-fact manner.

'Of course, Sir Sparhawk. I'll be taking up my father's duties. It's a family tradition. My grandfather served yours – and your father, and my father served your father and you, so I'll be taking up where he left off.'

'That's not really necessary, Khalad. Don't you want to be a Pandion Knight?'

'What I want isn't important, Sir Sparhawk. I have other duties.'

They left the farmstead the next morning, and Kalten rode forward to join Sparhawk. 'Nice funeral,' he noted, '– if you happen to like funerals. I'd rather keep my friends around me, personally.'

'Do you want to help me with a problem?' Sparhawk asked him.

'I thought we'd already killed everybody who needs it.'

'Can you be serious?'

'That's a lot to ask, Sparhawk, but I'll try. What's this problem?'

'Khalad insists on being my squire.'

'So? It's the sort of thing country boys do – follow their fathers' trades.'

'I want him to become a Pandion Knight.'

'I still don't see any problem. Go ahead and get him knighted then.'

'He can't be a squire and a knight both, Kalten.'

'Why not? Take *you*, for example. You're a Pandion Knight, a member of the royal council, Queen's Champion *and* the Prince Consort. Khalad's got broad shoulders. He can handle both jobs.'

The more Sparhawk thought about that, the more he

liked it. 'Kalten,' he laughed, 'what would I ever do without you?'

'Flounder, most likely. You complicate things too much, Sparhawk. You really ought to try to keep them simple.'

'Thanks.'

'No charge.'

It was raining. A soft, silvery drizzle sifted down out of the late afternoon sky and wreathed around the blocky watchtowers of the city of Cimmura. A lone rider approached the city. He was wrapped in a dark, heavy traveller's cloak and rode a tall, shaggy roan horse with a long nose and flat, vicious eyes. 'We always seem to come back to Cimmura in the rain, don't we, Faran,' the rider said to his horse.

Faran flicked his ears.

Sparhawk had left his friends behind that morning and had ridden on ahead. They all knew why, and they had not argued with him about it.

'We can send word on ahead to the palace, if you'd like, Prince Sparhawk,' one of the guards at the east gate offered. Ehlana, it appeared, had made some issue of his new title. Sparhawk wished that she had not. It was going to take some getting used to.

'Thanks all the same, neighbour,' Sparhawk told the guard, 'but I'd sort of like to surprise my wife. She's young enough to still enjoy surprises.'

The guard grinned at him.

'Get back inside the guard-house, neighbour,' Sparhawk advised. 'You'll catch cold out here in the weather.'

He rode on into Cimmura. The rain was keeping almost everyone inside, and Faran's steel-shod hooves echoed on the cobblestones of the nearly empty streets.

Sparhawk dismounted in the palace courtyard and handed Faran's reins to a groom. 'Be a little careful of the horse, neighbour,' he cautioned the stableman. 'He's bad-tempered. Give him some hay and grain and rub him down, if you would please. He's had a hard trip.'

'I'll see to it, Prince Sparhawk.' There it was again. Sparhawk decided to have a word with his wife about it.

'Faran,' he said to his horse, 'behave yourself.'

The big roan gave him a flat, unfriendly look.

'It was a good ride,' Sparhawk said, laying one hand on Faran's powerfully muscled neck. 'Get some rest.' Then he turned and went up the stairs into the palace. 'Where's the queen?' he asked one of the soldiers at the door.

'In the council chamber, I believe, My Lord.'

'Thank you.' Sparhawk started down a long, candlelit corridor towards the council chamber.

The Tamul giantess Mirtai was emerging from the council chamber when he reached the door. 'What took you so long?' she asked, showing no particular sign of surprise.

'Some things came up,' he shrugged. 'Is she in there?'

Mirtai nodded. 'She's with Lenda and the thieves. They're talking about repairing streets.' She paused. 'Don't greet her *too* enthusiastically, Sparhawk,' she cautioned. 'She's with child.'

Sparhawk gave her a stunned look.

'Wasn't that sort of what you two had in mind on your wedding night?' She paused again. 'Whatever happened to that bandy-legged man who shaves his head?'

'Kring? The Domi?'

'What does "Domi" mean?'

'Chief – sort of. He's the leader of his people. He's still alive and well as far as I know. The last time I saw him, he was working on a plan to lure the Zemochs into a trap so that he could slaughter them.'

Her eyes suddenly glowed warmly.

'Why do you ask?' he wanted to know.

'No reason. Just curious.'

'Oh. I see.'

They went into the council chamber, and Sparhawk unfastened the neck of his dripping cloak. As chance had it, the Queen of Elenia had her back to the door when he entered. She and the Earl of Lenda, Platime and Stragen were bent over the large map spread out on the council table. 'I've been through that quarter of the city,' she was saying insistently, 'and I don't really think there's any help for it. The streets are so bad that patching just won't do. It's all going to have to be repaved.' Her rich, vibrant voice touched Sparhawk's heart, even when she was discussing so mundane a matter. He smiled and laid his wet cloak across a chair near the door.

'Of course we can't start until spring, Your Majesty,' Lenda pointed out, 'and even then we're going to be fearfully short of workers until the army returns from Lamorkand, and –' The old man broke off, staring at Sparhawk in astonishment.

The Prince Consort touched one finger to his lips as he approached the table to join them. 'I hate to disagree with Your Majesty,' he said in a clinical tone, 'but I think you should give more consideration to the condition of the highways rather than the streets here in Cimmura. Bad streets inconvenience the burghers, but if the farmers can't get their crops to market, it's more than just an inconvenience.'

'I *know* that, Sparhawk,' she said, still staring at the map, 'but –' She raised her flawless young face, her grey eyes stunned. 'Sparhawk?' Her voice was hardly more than a whisper.

'I really think Your Majesty should concentrate on the highways,' he continued seriously. 'The one between here and Demos is in really shocking –' That was about as far as he got with that particular subject.

'Gently,' Mirtai cautioned him as Ehlana hurled herself into his arms. 'Remember what I told you outside.'

'When did you get back?' Ehlana demanded.

'Just now. The others are a little behind. I rode on ahead – for several reasons.'

She smiled and kissed him again.

'Well, gentlemen,' Lenda said to Platime and Stragen, 'I think perhaps we can continue this discussion later.' He smiled. 'Somehow I don't really think we'll be able to command Her Majesty's full attention this evening.'

'Would you all mind too terribly much?' Ehlana asked them in a little-girl sort of voice.

'Of course not, baby sister,' Platime boomed. He grinned at Sparhawk. 'It's good to have you back, my friend. Maybe you can distract Ehlana enough so that she won't be poking her nose into the details of certain public works projects I have an interest in.'

'We won, I gather,' Stragen said.

'Sort of,' Sparhawk replied, remembering Kurik. 'Otha and Azash won't be bothering us any more at least.'

'That's the important thing,' the blond thief said. 'You can fill us in on the details later.' He looked at Ehlana's radiant face. '*Much* later, I'd imagine,' he added.

'Stragen,' Ehlana said firmly.

'Yes, Your Majesty?'

'Out.' She pointed imperiously at the door.

'Yes, ma'am.'

Sparhawk and his bride adjourned to the royal apartments shortly after that, accompanied only by Mirtai. Sparhawk was not really sure just how long the Tamul giantess intended to remain in attendance. He didn't want to offend her, but –

Mirtai, however, was very business-like. She gave a number of crisp commands to the queen's personal servants – commands having to do with hot baths,

suppers, privacy and the like, and then, after everything
in the royal apartment was to her satisfaction, she went to
the door, drawing a large key from under her sword-belt.
'Will that be all for tonight, Ehlana?' she asked.

'Yes, Mirtai,' the queen replied, 'and thank you so very
much.'

Mirtai shrugged. 'It's what I'm supposed to do. Don't
forget what I told you, Sparhawk.' She tapped the key
firmly against the door. 'I'll let you out in the morning,' she
said. Then she went out and closed the door behind her.
The sound of the key turning in the lock was very loud.

'She's such a bully,' Ehlana laughed a bit helplessly. 'She
absolutely ignores me when I give her any orders.'

'She's good for you, love,' Sparhawk smiled. 'She helps
you to keep your perspective.'

'Go and bathe, Sparhawk,' Ehlana commanded. 'You
smell all rusty. Then you can tell me about everything that
happened. Oh, by the way, I'll have my ring back now, if
you don't mind.'

He held out his hands. 'Which one is it?' he asked her.
'I can't for the life of me tell them apart.'

'It's this one, of course.' She pointed at the ring on his
left hand.

'How do you know?' he asked, removing the ring and
slipping it on her finger.

'Anyone can see that, Sparhawk.'

'If you say so,' he shrugged.

Sparhawk was really not accustomed to bathing in the
presence of young ladies, but Ehlana seemed unwilling to
let him out of her sight. Thus he began the story even as he
bathed and continued it while they ate. There were things
which Ehlana did not grasp and others she misunderstood,
but she was able to accept most of what had taken place.
She cried when he told her that Kurik had died, and her
expression grew fierce when he described the fates of

625

Annias and her aunt and cousin. There were a number of things he glossed over and others he did not mention at all. He found the evasive remark, 'You almost had to have been there' very useful a number of times. He made a rather special point of avoiding any mention of the nearly universal depression which seemed to have fallen over the world since the destruction of Azash. It did not seem to be a proper subject to be mentioned to a young woman in the initial months of her first pregnancy.

And then as they lay together in the close and friendly darkness, Ehlana told him of the events which had taken place here in the west during his absence.

Perhaps it was because they were in bed where such things normally happen, but for some reason the subject of dreams came up. 'It was so very strange, Sparhawk,' Ehlana said as she nestled down in the bed beside him. 'The entire sky was covered with a rainbow, and we were on an island, the most beautiful place I've ever seen. There were trees – very old – and a kind of marble temple with graceful white columns, and I was waiting there for you and our friends. And then you came, each of you led by a beautiful white animal. Sephrenia was waiting with me, and she looked very young, hardly more than a girl, and there was a child who played some shepherd's pipes and danced. She was almost like a little empress, and everybody obeyed her orders.' She giggled. 'She even called you a grouchy old bear. Then she started to talk about Bhelliom. It was all very deep, and I only could understand a little of it.'

None of them had grasped it all, Sparhawk remembered, and the dream had been more widespread than he had imagined. But why had Aphrael included Ehlana?

'That was sort of the end of that dream,' she continued, 'and you know all about the next one.'

'Oh?'

'You just described it to me,' she told him, 'right down to the last detail. For some reason, I dreamed every single thing that happened in the Temple of Azash in Zemoch. My blood kept running cold while you were telling me about it.'

'I wouldn't worry all that much about it,' he told her, trying to keep his voice casual. 'We're very close together, you know, and it's not really too strange that you'd know what I was thinking about.'

'Are you serious?'

'Of course. It happens all the time. Ask any married woman, and she'll tell you that she always knows what's on her husband's mind.'

'Well,' she said dubiously, 'maybe.' She snuggled closer to him. 'You're not being very attentive tonight, love,' she accused. 'Is it because I'm getting fat and ugly?'

'Of course not. You're in what's called a "delicate condition". Mirtai kept warning me to be careful. She'll carve out my liver if she thinks I've hurt you.'

'Mirtai isn't here, Sparhawk.'

'But she's still the only one with a key to that door.'

'Oh, no, she isn't, Sparhawk,' his queen said smugly, reaching under her pillow. 'The door locks from either side, and it won't open unless it's been unlocked from both sides.' She handed him a large key.

'A very cooperative door,' he smiled. 'Why don't I just slip on out to the other room and lock it from this side?'

'Why don't you do that? And don't get lost on your way back to bed. Mirtai told you to be careful, so you ought to practise that for a while.'

Later – quite a bit later actually – Sparhawk slipped out of bed and went to the window to look out at the rain-swept night. It was over now. He would no longer rise before the sun to watch the veiled women of Jiroch going to the well in the steely grey light of dawn, nor would he ride strange roads in distant lands with the Sapphire Rose nestled near his heart. He had returned at last, older certainly and sadder and infinitely less certain of things he had always before accepted without question. He had come home at last, his wars over, he hoped, and his travels complete. They called him Anakha, the man who makes his own destiny, and he grimly resolved that his entire destiny lay here in this unlovely city with the pale, beautiful young woman who slept only a few feet away.

It was good to have that settled once and for all, and it was with some sense of accomplishment that he turned back to the bed and to his wife.

Epilogue

Spring came grudgingly that year, and a sudden late freeze stripped all the fruit trees of their blossoms, obliterating any chance of a crop. The summer was wet and cloudy, and the harvest scanty.

The armies of western Eosia returned home from Lamorkand to immerse themselves in unrewarding toil in stubborn fields where only thistles grew in abundance. Civil war erupted in Lamorkand, but there was nothing unusual about that; there was a serf rebellion in Pelosia, and the number of beggars near the churches and at the gates of the cities of the west increased dramatically.

Sephrenia received the news of Ehlana's pregnancy with astonishment. The undeniable fact of that pregnancy seemed to baffle her, and that bafflement made her short-tempered, even waspish. In the usual course of time Ehlana gave birth to her first child, a daughter whom she and Sparhawk named Danae. Sephrenia gave the infant an extended examination, and it seemed somehow to Sparhawk that his tutor was almost offended by the fact that Princess Danae was totally normal and disgustingly healthy.

Mirtai calmly rearranged the queen's schedule to add the task of nursing to Ehlana's other royal duties. It should be noted in passing perhaps that Ehlana's ladies-in-waiting all jealously hated Mirtai, even though the giantess had never physically assaulted nor even spoken sharply to a single one of them.

The Church soon lost sight of her grand design in the east, turning instead to the south to seize an opportunity which presented itself there. Martel's enlistment of the most fervent Eshandists and his subsequent defeat at Chyrellos had decimated the ranks of that sect, leaving Rendor ripe for reassimilation into the congregation of the faithful. Although Dolmant sent his priests into Rendor in a spirit of love and reconciliation, that spirit lasted in most of his missionaries for only so long as the dome of the Basilica remained in view. The missions to Rendor were vengeful and punitive, and the Rendors responded in a fairly predictable fashion. After a number of the more strident and abrasive missionaries had been murdered, larger and larger detachments of Church Knights were sent into that southern kingdom to protect the unwelcome clergy and their meagre congregations of converts. Eshandist sentiments began to re-emerge, and there were once again rumours of caches of weapons out in the desert.

Civilized man believes that his cities are the crown of his culture and seems incapable of grasping the fact that the foundation of any kingdom is the land upon which it rests. When a nation's agriculture falters, its economy begins to collapse, and governments starved for revenue inevitably fall back on the most regressive of all forms of taxation, heaping additional burdens on an already suffering peasantry. Sparhawk and the Earl of Lenda had long and increasingly bitter arguments on that very issue, and they quite frequently stopped speaking to each other entirely.

Lord Vanion's health steadily deteriorated as the months wore on. Sephrenia tended his many infirmities as best she could, but finally on a blustery autumn morning some months following the birth of Princess Danae, the two of them were nowhere to be found, and when a white-robed Styric appeared at the Pandion Mother-house at Demos, announcing that he was assuming Sephrenia's duties, the worst of Sparhawk's suspicions were confirmed. Despite his pleading of prior commitments, he was pressed into assuming his friend's duties as interim Preceptor, an appointment Dolmant wished to make permanent, although Sparhawk resisted that notion strenuously.

Ulath, Tynian and Bevier stopped by the palace from time to time for visits, and their reports of what was happening in their homelands were no more cheerful than the news Sparhawk was receiving from the outlying districts of Elenia. Platime gravely reported that his far-flung informants had advised him that near-famine, epidemics and civil unrest were well-nigh universal. 'Hard times, Sparhawk,' the fat thief said with a philosophic shrug. 'No matter what we do to try to hold them off, hard times come along now and then.'

Sparhawk enrolled Kurik's four elder sons as Pandion novices, overriding Khalad's objections. Since Talen was still a bit young for military training, he was ordered to serve as a page in the palace where Sparhawk could keep an eye on him. Stragen, unpredictable as always, came often to Cimmura. Mirtai guarded Ehlana, bullied her when it was necessary and laughingly avoided the repeated marriage-proposals of Kring, who seemed to be able to find all manner of excuses to ride across the continent from eastern Pelosia to Cimmura.

The years ground on, and conditions did not improve. That first year of excessive rain was followed by three years of drought. Food was continually in short supply, and the governments of Eosia were starved for revenue. Ehlana's pale, beautiful face grew careworn, although Sparhawk did what he could to transfer as many burdens as possible from her shoulders to his own.

It was on a clear, chilly afternoon in late winter when something quite profound happened to the Prince Consort. He had spent the morning in a violent argument with the Earl of Lenda about a proposed new tax, and Lenda had become shrill, even abusive, accusing Sparhawk of systematically dismantling the government in his excessive concern for the well-being of the pampered, lazy peasantry. Sparhawk won the argument in the end, although he took no particular pleasure in that, since each victory drove the wedge between him and his old friend that much deeper.

He sat near the fire in the royal apartment in a kind of moody discontent, half-watching the activities of his four-year-old daughter, the Princess Danae. His wife, accompanied by Mirtai and Talen, was off on some errand in the city, and so Sparhawk and the tiny princess were alone.

Danae was a grave, serious child with glossy black hair, large eyes as dark as night and a mouth like a pink rosebud. Despite her serious demeanour, she was affectionate, frequently showering her parents with spontaneous kisses. At the moment, she was near the fireplace doing important things involving a ball.

It was the fireplace that brought everything to a head and changed Sparhawk's life forever. Danae miscalculated slightly, and her ball rolled directly into the grate. Without giving it any apparent thought, she quickly went to the fireplace, and before her father could stop her or even cry out, she reached into the flames and retrieved her toy. Sparhawk leaped to his feet with a strangled cry and rushed to her. He snatched her up and closely examined her hand.

'What is it, father?' she asked him quite calmly. Princess Danae was a precocious child. She had begun to speak early, and her speech by now was very nearly adult.

'Your hand! You burned it! You know better than to stick your hand into a fire.'

'It's not burnt,' she protested, holding it up and wiggling her fingers. 'See?'

'Don't go near the fire again,' he commanded.

'No, father.' She wriggled to be let down and then crossed the floor with her ball to continue her game in a safe corner.

Troubled, Sparhawk returned to his chair. One *can* thrust one's hand into a fire and snatch it back out again without being burned, but it had not seemed that Danae had moved her hand that quickly. Sparhawk began to look more closely at his child. He had been very busy for the past several months, so he had not really looked at her but had simply accepted the fact that she was there. Danae was at an age when certain changes occur quite rapidly, and those changes, it seemed, had taken place right under Sparhawk's inattentive gaze. As he looked at her now, however, a sudden chill gripped his heart. Unbelievingly, he saw something for the first time. He and his wife were Elenes. Their daughter was not.

He stared for a long time at his Styric daughter, then seized on the only possible explanation. '*Aphrael?*' he said in a stunned voice. Danae only looked a little bit like Flute, but Sparhawk could see no other possibility.

'Yes, Sparhawk?' Her voice betrayed no surprise.

'What have you done with my daughter?' he shouted, half-rising to his feet in agitation.

'Don't be absurd, Sparhawk,' she said quite calmly. 'I *am* your daughter.'

'That's impossible. How –?'

'You know I am, father. You were there when I was born. Did you think I was some kind of changeling? Some starling planted in your nest to supplant your own chick? That's a foolish Elene superstition, you know. We don't ever do that.'

He began to gain some control over his emotions. 'Do you plan to explain this?' he asked in as level a tone as he could manage, 'or am I supposed to guess?'

'Be nice, father. You wanted children, didn't you?'

'Well –'

'And mother's a queen. She has to give birth to a successor, doesn't she?'

'Of course, but –'

'She wouldn't have, you know.'

'*What?*'

'The poison Annias gave her made her barren. You have no idea how difficult it was for me to overcome that. Why do you think Sephrenia was so upset when she discovered that mother was pregnant? She knew about the effects of the poison, of course, and she was *very* put out with me for interfering – probably more because mother's an Elene than for any other reason. Sephrenia's very narrow-minded sometimes. Oh, *do* sit down, Sparhawk. You look ridiculous all stooped over like that. Either sit or stand. Don't hover in between.'

Sparhawk sank back into his chair, his mind reeling. 'But *why?*' he demanded.

'Because I love you and mother. She was destined to be childless, so I had to change her destiny just a bit.'

'And did you change mine as well?'

'How could I possibly do that? You're Anakha, remember? Nobody knows what your destiny is. You've always been a problem for us. Many felt that we shouldn't let you be born at all. I had to argue for centuries to persuade the others that we really needed you.' She looked down at herself. 'I'm going to have to pay attention to growing up, I suppose. I was Styric before, and Styrics can take these things in their stride. You Elenes are more excitable, and people might begin to talk if I were to remain a child for several centuries. I guess I'll have to do it the right way this time.'

'*This* time?'

'Of course. I've been born dozens of times.' She rolled

her eyes. 'It helps to keep me young.' Her small face grew very serious. 'Something terrible happened in the Temple of Azash, father, and I needed to hide from it for a while. Mother's womb was the perfect place to hide. It was so safe and secure there.'

'Then you *knew* what was going to happen in Zemoch,' he accused.

'I knew that *something* was going to happen, so I just covered all the possibilities.' She pursed her pink little mouth thoughtfully. 'This might be very interesting,' she said. 'I've never been a grown woman before – and certainly never a queen. I wish my sister were here. I'd like to talk with her about it.'

'Your sister?'

'Sephrenia.' She said it almost absently. 'She was the eldest daughter of my last parents. It's very nice having an older sister, you know. She's always been so very, very wise, and she always forgives me when I do something foolish.'

A thousand things suddenly clicked into place in Sparhawk's mind, things that had never really been explained before. 'How old *is* Sephrenia?' he asked.

She sighed. 'You *know* I'm not going to answer that, Sparhawk. Besides, I'm not really sure. The years don't mean as much to us as they do to you. In a general way, though, Sephrenia's hundreds of years old, maybe even a thousand – whatever that means.'

'Where is she now?'

'She and Vanion are off together. You knew how they felt about each other, didn't you?'

'Yes.'

'Astonishing. You *can* use your eyes after all.'

'What are they doing?'

'They're looking after things for me. I'm too busy to attend to business this time, and somebody has to mind the shop. Sephrenia can answer prayers as well as I can, and I don't have all that many worshippers.'

'Do you absolutely *have* to make all of this sound so commonplace?' His tone was plaintive.

'But it *is*, father. It's your Elene God who takes Himself so seriously. I've never once seen Him laugh. *My* worshippers are much more sensible. They love me, so they're tolerant of my mistakes.' She laughed suddenly, climbed up into his lap and kissed him. 'You're the best father I've ever had, Sparhawk. I can actually talk with you about these things without making your eyes pop out of their sockets.' She rested her head against his chest. 'What's really been going on, father? I know that things aren't going well, but Mirtai keeps putting me down for naps when people come to make reports to you, so I can't get very many details.'

'It hasn't been a good time for the world, Aphrael,' he said gravely. 'The weather's been very bad, and there have been famine and pestilence. Nothing seems to be going the way it should. If I were at all superstitious, I'd say that the whole world's been going through a long spell of very bad luck.'

'That's my family's fault, Sparhawk,' she admitted. 'We started feeling very sorry for ourselves after what happened to Azash, so we haven't been attending to business. I think that maybe it's time for *all* of us to grow up. I'll talk with the others and let you know what we decide.'

'I'd appreciate that.' Sparhawk could not actually believe this conversation was taking place.

'We have a bit of a problem, though,' she told him.

'Only one?'

'Stop that. I'm serious. What are we going to tell mother?'

'Oh, my God!' he said, his eyes suddenly going very wide. 'I hadn't thought of that.'

'We'll have to decide right now, you know, and I don't like to make up my mind in a hurry. She'd have a great deal of trouble believing this, wouldn't she? Particularly if it meant that she'd have to accept the fact that she's really barren and that I'm here as a result of my own choice instead of her personal appetites and fertility. Will it break her heart if we tell her who I really am?'

He thought about it. He knew his wife better than anyone else in the world possibly could. He remembered with an icy chill that momentary look of anguish which had filled her grey eyes when he had suggested that his gift of the ring had been a mistake. 'No,' he said finally, 'we can't tell her.'

'I didn't think so either, but I wanted to be sure.'

Something occurred to Sparhawk. 'Why did you include her in that dream? – the one about the island? And why did she dream about what happened in the temple? It was almost as if she'd been there.'

'She *was* there, father. She had to be. I was hardly in a position to leave her behind and go places by myself, was I? Let me down, please.'

He unwrapped his arms from about her, and she went to the window. 'Come here, Sparhawk,' she said after a moment.

He joined her at the window. 'What is it?' he asked her.

'Mother's coming back. She's down in the courtyard with Mirtai and Talen.'

Sparhawk looked out the window. 'Yes,' he agreed.

'I'm going to be a queen someday, aren't I?'

'Unless you decide to throw it all over and go and herd goats somewhere, yes.'

She let that pass. 'I'll need a champion then, won't I?'

'I suppose so. I could do it if you like.'

'When you're eighty years old? You're very imposing

637

right now, father, but I suspect you'll begin to get a little decrepit when you get older.'

'Don't rub it in.'

'Sorry. And I'll need a Prince Consort as well, won't I?'

'It's customary. Why are we talking about this now, though?'

'I want your advice, father, and your consent.'

'Isn't this a little premature? You're only four years old, you know.'

'A girl can't start thinking about these things too early.' She pointed down towards the courtyard. 'I think that one right down there will do very nicely, don't you?' She sounded almost as if she were choosing a new ribbon for her hair.

'*Talen?*'

'Why not? I like him. He's going to be a knight – *Sir* Talen, if you can believe that. He's funny and really much nicer than he seems – besides, I can beat him at draughts, and we can't spend *all* our time in bed, the way you and mother do.'

'*Danae!*'

'What?' She looked up at him. 'Why are you blushing, father?'

'Never mind. You just watch what you say, young lady, or I *will* tell your mother who you really are.'

'Fine,' she said serenely, 'and then I'll tell her about Lillias. How would you like that?'

They looked at each other, and then they laughed.

It was about a week later. Sparhawk was hunched over a desk in the room he used as an office glaring at the Earl of Lenda's latest proposal, an absurd idea which would quite nearly double the government payroll. He scribbled an angry note at the bottom. 'Why not just make everyone in the whole kingdom a government employee, Lenda? Then we can all starve together.'

The door opened, and his daughter entered, carrying a rather disreputable-looking stuffed toy animal by one leg.

'I'm busy, Danae,' he said shortly.

She closed the door firmly. 'You're a grouch, Sparhawk,' she said crisply.

He looked around quickly, went to the door to the adjoining room and carefully closed it. 'Sorry, Aphrael,' he apologized. 'I'm a little out of sorts.'

'I noticed that. Everybody in the palace has noticed that.' She held out her toy. 'Would you like to kick Rollo across the room? He won't mind, and it might make you feel better.'

He laughed, feeling just a little silly. 'That *is* Rollo, isn't it? Your mother used to carry him in exactly the same way – before his stuffing fell out.'

'She had him restuffed and gave him to me,' Aphrael said. 'I guess I'm supposed to carry him around, though I can't for the life of me think why. I'd really much rather have a baby goat.'

'This is something important, I take it?'

'Yes. I had a long talk with the others.'

His mind shied away from the implications contained in that simple statement. 'What did they say?'

'They weren't really very nice, father. They're all blaming *me* for what happened in Zemoch. They wouldn't even listen to me when I tried to tell them that it was all *your* fault.'

'*My* fault? Thanks.'

'They're not going to help at all,' she continued, 'so it's going to be up to you and me, I'm afraid.'

'We're going to go fix the world? All by ourselves?'

'It's not really all *that* difficult, father. I've made some

639

arrangements. Our friends will begin arriving very soon. Act as if you're surprised to see them, and then don't let them leave.'

'Are they going to help us?'

'They're going to help *me*, father. I'll need them around me when I do this. I'm going to need a great deal of love to make it work. Hello, mother.' She said it without even turning towards the door.

'Danae,' Ehlana chided her daughter, 'you know you're not supposed to disturb your father when he's working.'

'Rollo wanted to see him, mother,' Danae lied glibly. 'I told him that we weren't supposed to bother father when he's busy, but you know how Rollo is.' She said it so seriously that it almost sounded plausible. Then she lifted the disreputable-looking toy animal and shook her finger in his face. 'Bad, bad Rollo,' she scolded.

Ehlana laughed and rushed to her daughter. 'Isn't she adorable?' she said happily to Sparhawk as she knelt to embrace the little girl.

'Oh, yes,' he smiled. 'She's that, all right. She's even better at that than you were.' He made a rueful face. 'I think it's my destiny to be wrapped around the fingers of a pair of very devious little girls.'

The Princess Danae and her mother put their cheeks together and gave him an almost identical look of artfully-contrived innocence.

Their friends began to arrive the next day, and each of them had a perfectly legitimate reason for being in Cimmura. For the most part, those reasons involved the bringing of bad news. Ulath had come south from Emsat to report that the years of hard drinking had finally begun to take their toll on King Wargun's liver. 'He's the colour of an apricot,' the big Thalesian told them. Tynian told them that the ancient King Obler appeared to be slipping into his dotage, and Bevier advised that word coming out of Rendor hinted at the strong possibility of another Eshandist uprising. In marked contrast, Stragen reported that *his* business had taken a marked turn for the better, and that particular news was probably even worse than all the rest.

Despite all the bad news, the old friends took advantage of what appeared to be a chance meeting to stage something in the nature of a reunion.

It was good to have them all around him again, Sparhawk decided one morning as he slipped out of bed quietly to avoid awakening his sleeping wife, but sitting up talking with them for half the night and then rising early to attend to his other duties was leaving him more than a little short of sleep.

'Close the door, father,' Danae said quietly as he came out of the bedroom. She sat curled up in a large chair near the fire. She was wearing her nightdress, and her bare feet had those tell-tale grass-stains on them.

Sparhawk nodded, closed the door and joined her by the fire.

'They're all here now, Sparhawk,' Danae told him, 'so let's get started with this.'

'Exactly what are we going to do?' he asked her.

'*You're* going to suggest a ride in the country.'

'I'll need a reason for that, Danae. The weather's not really suitable for pleasure trips.'

'Any sort of reason will do, father. Think something up and suggest it. They'll all think it's a wonderful idea – I can guarantee that. Take them towards Demos. Sephrenia, Vanion and I will join you a little way out of town.'

'Would you like to clarify that a little bit? You're already here.'

'I'll be there too, Sparhawk.'

'You're going to be in two places at the same time?'

641

'It's not really all *that* difficult, Sparhawk. We do it all the time.'

'Maybe, but that's not really a good way to keep your identity a secret, you know.'

'No one will guess. I'll look like Flute to them.'

'There's not really all that much difference between you and Flute, you know.'

'Not to you, perhaps, but the others see me a little differently.' She rose from her chair. 'Take care of it, Sparhawk,' she told him with an airy wave of her hand. Then she went towards the door, negligently dragging Rollo behind her.

'I give up,' Sparhawk muttered.

'I heard that, father,' she said without even turning.

When they all gathered for breakfast later that morning, it was Kalten who provided the opening Sparhawk needed. 'I wish there were some way we could all get out of Cimmura for a few days,' the blond Pandion said critically. He looked at Ehlana. 'I'm not trying to be offensive, Your Majesty, but the palace isn't really a very good place to have a reunion. Every time things get off to a good start, some courtier comes in with something that absolutely *has* to have Sparhawk's immediate attention.'

'He's got a point there,' Ulath agreed. 'A good reunion's a lot like a good tavern-brawl. It's not nearly as much fun if it's interrupted every time it gets going.'

Sparhawk suddenly remembered something. 'Were you serious the other day, love?' he asked his wife.

'I'm always serious, Sparhawk. Which day were we talking about?'

'The day when you were talking about bestowing a duchy on me?'

'I've been trying to do that for four years now. I don't know why I bother any more. You always find some reason to decline them.'

'I shouldn't really do that, I suppose – at least not until I've had a chance to look them over.'

'Where are you going with this, Sparhawk?' she asked.

'We need a place for uninterrupted celebration, Ehlana.'

'Brawling,' Ulath corrected.

Sparhawk grinned at him. 'Anyway,' he continued, 'I really should go and have a look at this duchy. It's off towards Demos, as I recall. We might want to have a rather close look at the manor-house.'

'We?' she asked him.

'A little advice never hurts a man when he's trying to make a decision. I think we *all* ought to go and take a look at this duchy. What do the rest of you think?'

'The strength of a good leader lies in his ability to make the obvious appear innovative,' Stragen drawled.

'We really ought to get out more often anyway, dear,' Sparhawk told his wife. 'We can take a little holiday, and all we'll really have to worry about is whether or not Lenda puts two dozen of his relatives on the public payroll while we're gone.'

'I wish you all the enjoyment in the world, my friends,' Platime said, 'but I'm a kindly sort of fellow, and it distresses me to see a full-grown horse break down and cry every time I go to mount him. I'll stay here and keep an eye on Lenda.'

'You can ride in the carriage,' Mirtai told him.

'Which carriage was that, Mirtai?' Ehlana asked her.

'The one you're going to ride in to keep the weather off you.'

'I don't need a carriage.'

Mirtai's eyes flashed. 'Ehlana! she snapped. 'Don't argue!'

'But –'

'Hush, Ehlana!'

'Yes, Mirtai,' the queen sighed submissively.

They approached the outing with an almost holiday air. Even Faran felt it, and as *his* contribution to the festivities, he managed to step on both of Sparhawk's feet at the same time while his master was trying to mount.

The weather seemed to be almost in abeyance as they set out. The sky was overcast rather than cloudy, and the biting chill which had characterized the winter moderated, becoming, if not warm, at least bearable. There was not even a hint of a breeze, and Sparhawk was uneasily reminded of the endless now of that moment the Troll-God Ghnomb had frozen for them on the road leading eastward from Paler.

They left Cimmura behind and followed the road leading towards the cities of Lenda and Demos. Sparhawk had been spared the unsettling possibility of actually seeing his daughter in two places at the same time by Mirtai's decision that the weather was not suitable for the little princess to be making journeys and that she should remain in the palace in the care of her nurse. Sparhawk foresaw a titanic clash of wills looming in the future. The time was bound to come when Mirtai and Danae would run into each other head on. He was rather looking forward to it, actually.

It was not far from the place on the road where they had encountered the Seeker that they found Sephrenia and Vanion seated by a small fire with Flute characteristically seated on the limb of a nearby oak. Vanion, looking younger and more fit than he had in years, rose to greet his friends. As Sparhawk had more or less expected, Vanion wore a white Styric robe and no sword. 'You've been well, I trust,' the big Pandion asked as he dismounted.

'Tolerable, Sparhawk. And you?'

'No complaints, My Lord.'

And then they abandoned that particular pose and

embraced each other roughly as the others all gathered around them.

'Who's been chosen to replace me as Preceptor?' Vanion asked.

'We've been urging the Hierocracy to appoint Kalten, My Lord,' Sparhawk told him blandly.

'You *what*?' Vanion's face was filled with chagrin.

'Sparhawk,' Ehlana reproached her husband, 'that's cruel.'

'He's just trying to be funny, Vanion,' Kalten said sourly. 'Sometimes his humour's as twisted as his nose. Actually *he's* the one who's in charge.'

'Thank God!' Vanion said fervently.

'Dolmant's been trying to persuade him to accept a permanent appointment, but our friend here keeps begging off – some nonsense about having too many jobs already.'

'If you people spread me any thinner, you'll be able to see daylight through me,' Sparhawk complained.

Ehlana had been looking with a certain awe at Flute, who, as she usually did, sat on the tree limb with her grass-stained feet crossed at the ankles and her pipes to her lips. 'She looks exactly the way she did in that dream,' she murmured to Sparhawk.

'She never changes,' Sparhawk replied. 'Well, not *too* much, anyway.'

'Are we permitted to talk to her?' The young queen's eyes were actually a little frightened.

'Why are you standing over there whispering, Ehlana?' Flute asked.

'How do I address her?' the queen nervously asked her husband.

He shrugged. 'We call her Flute. Her other name's a little formal.'

'Help me down, Ulath,' the little girl commanded.

'Yes, Flute,' the big Thalesian replied automatically. He went to the tree and lifted the small divinity down and set her feet on the winter-browned grass.

Flute took outrageous advantage of the fact that as Danae she already knew Stragen, Platime and Mirtai in addition to her mother. She spoke with them all quite familiarly, which noticeably added to their sense of awe. Mirtai in particular seemed quite shaken. 'Well, Ehlana,' the little girl said finally, 'are we going to just stand here and stare at each other? Aren't you even going to thank me for the splendid husband I provided for you?'

'You're cheating, Aphrael,' Sephrenia scolded her.

'I know, dear sister, but it's so much fun.'

Ehlana laughed helplessly and held out her arms. Flute crowed with delight and ran to her.

Flute and Sephrenia joined Ehlana, Mirtai and Platime in the carriage. Just before they set out, however, the little Goddess thrust her head out of the window. 'Talen,' she called sweetly.

'What?' Talen's tone was wary. Sparhawk rather suspected that Talen might just have had one of those chilling premonitions which beset young men and deer in almost the same way when they sense that they are being hunted.

'Why don't you join us here in the carriage?' Aphrael suggested in honeyed tones.

Talen looked a bit apprehensively at Sparhawk.

'Go ahead,' Sparhawk told him. Talen was his friend, certainly – but Danae *was* his daughter, after all.

They rode on then. After several miles, Sparhawk began to have a vague sense of unease. Although he had been travelling the road between Demos and Cimmura since he had been a young man, it suddenly began to look strange to him. There were hills in places where there should not have been hills, and they passed a large, prosperous-looking farmstead Sparhawk had never seen before. He began to check his map.

'What's the matter?' Kalten asked him.

'Is there any way we could have made a wrong turn? I've been travelling this road back and forth for over twenty years now, and suddenly the usual landmarks aren't there any more.'

'Oh, that's fine, Sparhawk,' Kalten said sarcastically. He turned and looked back over his shoulder at the others. 'Our glorious leader here has managed to get us lost,' he announced. 'We blindly followed him half-way across the world, and now he manages to lose his way not five leagues from home. I don't know about the rest of you, but I'm beginning to experience a severe erosion of confidence here.'

'Do *you* want to do this?' Sparhawk asked him flatly.

'And lose this opportunity to sit back and carp and criticize? Don't be silly.'

They were obviously not going to reach any recognizable destination before dark, and they had not come prepared for camping out in the open. Sparhawk began to grow alarmed.

Flute thrust her head out of one of the windows of the carriage. 'What's the matter, Sparhawk?' she asked.

'We're going to have to find some place to stay the night,' he told her, 'and we haven't passed any kind of house for the last ten miles.'

'Just keep going, Sparhawk,' she instructed.

'It's going to start getting dark before long, Flute.'

'Then we'd better hurry, hadn't we?' She disappeared back inside the carriage.

They reached a hilltop just at dusk and looked out over a valley that absolutely *could* not have been where it was. The land below was grassy and gently rolling, dotted here and there with copses of white-trunked birch trees. About half-way down the hill was a low, sprawling, thatch-roofed house with golden candlelight streaming from its windows.

'Maybe they'll put us up for the night,' Stragen suggested.

'Hurry right along now, gentlemen,' Flute instructed from the carriage. 'Supper's waiting, and we don't want it to get cold.'

'She enjoys doing that to people, doesn't she?' Stragen said.

'Oh, yes,' Sparhawk agreed, 'probably more than anything else she gets to do.'

Had it been somewhat smaller, the house might have been called a cottage. The rooms, however, were large and there were many of them. The furnishings were rustic but well made, there were candles everywhere, and each scrupulously-clean fireplace had a cheery fire dancing on the grate. There was a long table in the central room and it was set with what could only be called a banquet. There was not a single soul in the house, however.

'Do you like it?' Flute asked them with an anxious expression.

'It's lovely,' Ehlana exclaimed, impulsively embracing the little girl.

'I'm awfully sorry,' Flute apologized, 'but I just couldn't bring myself to offer you ham. I know you Elenes all love it, but –' She shuddered.

'I think we can make do with what's here, Flute,' Kalten said, surveying the table with his eyes alight, 'don't you, Platime?'

The fat thief was looking almost reverently at all the food. 'Oh, my goodness yes, Kalten,' he agreed enthusiastically. 'This'll be just fine.'

They all ate more than was really good for them, and sat afterwards, sighing with that most pleasant of discomforts.

Berit came around the table and leaned over Sparhawk's shoulder. 'She's doing it again, Sparhawk,' the young knight murmured.

'Doing what?'

'The fires have been burning ever since we got here, and they still don't need any more wood, and the candles aren't even melting down.'

'It's her house, I suppose,' Sparhawk shrugged.

'I know, but –' Berit looked uncomfortable. 'It's unnatural,' he said finally.

'Berit,' Sparhawk pointed out with a gentle smile, 'we just rode through an impossible landscape to reach a house that isn't really here to eat a banquet that nobody prepared, and you're going to worry about a few little things like perpetually burning candles and fireplaces that don't need wood?'

Berit laughed and went back to his chair.

The Child-Goddess took her duties as hostess very seriously. She even seemed anxious as she escorted them to their rooms and carefully explained a number of things that did not really need to be explained.

'She's such a dear little thing, isn't she?' Ehlana said to Sparhawk when they were alone. 'She seems so desperately concerned about the comfort and well-being of her guests.'

'Styrics are a bit more casual about these things,' Sparhawk explained. 'Flute's not really used to Elenes, and we make her nervous.' He smiled. 'She's trying very, very hard to make a good impression.'

'But she's a Goddess.'

'She still gets nervous.'

'Is it my imagination, or is she a great deal like our own Danae?'

'All little girls are similar, I suppose,' he replied carefully, 'just like all little boys.'

649

'Perhaps,' Ehlana conceded, 'but she even seems to *smell* like Danae, and they both seem to be very fond of kisses.' She paused, and then her face brightened. 'We really should introduce them to each other, Sparhawk. They'd love each other, and they'd be wonderful play-mates.'

Sparhawk nearly choked on *that* idea.

The rhythm of the hoof-beats was familiar, and it was that more than anything which awakened Sparhawk early the next morning. He muttered an oath and swung his legs out of the bed.

'What is it, dear?' Ehlana asked in a sleepy voice.

'Faran got loose,' he said in an irritated tone. 'He managed to pull his picket-line free somehow.'

'He won't run away, will he?'

'And miss all the entertainment staying just out of my reach all morning will give him? Of course not.' Sparhawk pulled on a robe and went to the window. It was only then that he heard the sound of Flute's pipes.

The sky over this mysterious valley was overcast, as it had been all winter. Dirty-looking clouds, chill and unpromising, stretched from horizon to horizon, hurried along by a blustery wind.

There was a broad meadow not far from the house, and Faran was cantering easily in a wide circular course around the meadow. He wore no saddle nor bridle, and there was something almost joyful in his stride. Flute lay face up on his back with her pipes to her lips. Her head was nestled comfortably on his surging front shoulders, her knees were crossed, and she was beating time on the big roan's rump with one little foot. The scene was so familiar that all Sparhawk could do was stare.

'Ehlana,' he said finally, 'I think you might want to see this.'

She came to the window. 'What on *earth* is she doing?' she exclaimed. 'Go and stop her, Sparhawk. She'll fall off and get hurt.'

'No, actually she won't. She and Faran have played together like this before. He won't let her fall off – even if she could.'

'What are they doing?'

'I have no idea,' he admitted, although that was not entirely true. 'I think it's significant, though,' he added. He leaned out of the window and looked first to the left and then to the right. The others were all at the windows, their faces filled with surprise as they watched their little hostess.

The blustery wind faltered, then died as Flute continued her song, and the winter-brown grass in the dooryard ceased its dead rattling.

The trilling song of the Child-Goddess rose into the sky as Faran continued to tirelessly circle the meadow, and as she played, the dirty-looking murk overhead opened and rolled back almost as a bolster is turned back on a bed, and a deep blue sky dotted with fluffy, sunrise-touched clouds appeared.

Sparhawk and the others stared up in wonder at that suddenly-revealed sky, and, as children sometimes will, they saw pink dragons and rosy griffins caught somehow in the wonder of the clouds that streamed and coalesced, piling higher and higher only to come apart again as all the spirits of air and earth and sky joined to welcome that spring which the world had feared might never come.

The Child-Goddess Aphrael rose to her feet and stood on the big roan's surging back. Her glossy black hair streamed out behind her, and the sound of her pipes soared up to meet the sunrise. Then, even as she played, she began to dance, whirling and swaying, her grass-stained little feet flickering as she danced and joyously lifted her song.

Earth and sky and Faran's broad back were all one to Aphrael as she danced, and she whirled as easily on insubstantial air as upon the now-verdant turf or that surging roan back.

Awe-struck, they watched from the house that wasn't really there, and their sombre melancholy dropped away. Their hearts grew full as the Child-Goddess played for them that joyous, forever new song of redemption and renewal, for now at last the dread winter had passed, and spring had once again returned.

David Eddings

The Hidden City

Book Three of the Tamuli

THE ULTIMATE BATTLE

Sparhawk, the greatest of Pandion Knights, has offered freedom to the Troll-Gods trapped in the Blue Rose in exchange for their aid in fighting Cyrgon, the sinister god of the Cyrgai. But Cyrgon has turned to the unspeakable arts of Zemoch magic in his war against the Tamul Empire. He has brought back to the world the very essence of evil which was cast out at the beginning of time by Azash and the other Elder Gods. Klæl! As ancient as the Blue Rose, and as powerful.

The ultimate battle between Blue Rose and Klæl must be fought – though Ehlana is is held prisoner by the enemy in the Hidden City, defended by Klæl. The time for strategy, and hope, is past.

The final, breathtaking volume of the Tamuli, full of battles, astonishing magic and awesome gods, reveals David Eddings at his triumphant best.

ISBN 0 586 21317 1

David Eddings

The Shining Ones

Book two of
The Tamuli

HAVOC AND WAR

Prince Sparhawk is pledged to fight the enemies of the
Tamul Emperor Sarabian with all the skill and cunning of a
Pandion Knight. Meanwhile his Queen, Ehlana, educates
Sarabian in the art of ruthless statesmanship. Sarabian is
transformed from a mere puppet ruler into a formidable
politician. But still Trolls, vampires, werewolves, zombies,
ghouls and Ogres form a vast conspiracy to take over the
Empire. Most disturbing of all are reported sightings of the
Shining Ones amongst the hordes. These luminous beings
inspire more fear than the rest combined. And Sparhawk
and his companions must resurrect the sacred jewel of the
Troll-Gods to combat them.

The enemies of the Empire know that possession of the
jewel makes Sparhawk as dangerous as any god. But gods
are among his foes. And while Sparhawk defends the far-
flung Tamul Empire, he cannot also protect his beautiful
Queen.

David Eddings, the greatest of modern fantasy writers,
unveils the hidden powers at work in the story of Sparhawk
and the Tamul Empire, an epic for our times.

ISBN 0 586 21316 3

David Eddings

Domes of Fire

Book one of
The Tamuli

PRINCE SPARHAWK AND
THE TROLL-GODS

Queen Ehlana and the Pandion Knight Sir Sparhawk are
married, their kingdom peaceful at last, their union
blessed with a very special daughter named Danae. But
soon trouble sweeps westward from the Tamul Empire to
disrupt not only the living of Eosia but the dead: horrific
armies are being raised from the dust of the long-past Age
of Heroes, threatening the peace won at such cost in
Zemoch.

Prince Sparhawk is called upon to help the Tamuli nations
defeat these ancient horrors. Perhaps the Troll-Gods are
once more loose in the world! With Ehlana and a retinue
of Pandion Knights, Sparhawk will make the hazardous
journey to the Tamul Empire . . . only to discover in fire-
domed Matherion, the incandescent Tamul capital, that
the enemy is already within its gates.

Full of marvels and humour, romance and shrewdness,
above all full of magic, the resources of the epic form are
mined deep by the greatest of modern fantasy writers.

ISBN 0 586 21313 9